EVERYMAN'S LIBRARY

EVERYMAN,
I WILL GO WITH THEE,
AND BE THY GUIDE,
IN THY MOST NEED
TO GO BY THY SIDE

DASHIELL HAMMETT

THE DAIN CURSE
THE GLASS KEY
AND
SELECTED STORIES

WITH AN INTRODUCTION
BY JAMES ELLROY

EVERYMAN'S LIBRARY
Alfred A. Knopf New York London Toronto
307

THIS IS A BORZOI BOOK
PUBLISHED BY ALFRED A. KNOPF

First included in Everyman's Library, 2007

Typography by Peter B. Willberg

The Dain Curse was originally serialized in *Black Mask*, November 1928–February 1929, and first published by Alfred A. Knopf, Inc. in 1929 (New York) and 1930 (London).
The Glass Key was originally serialized in *Black Mask*, March–June 1930 and first published by Alfred A. Knopf, Inc. in 1931 (New York and London).
The four short stories were originally published in *Black Mask*, 'The House in Turk Street' in April 1924, 'The Girl with the Silver Eyes' in June 1924, 'The Big Knockover' in February 1927 and '$106,000 Blood Money' in May 1927.
 Published in the United States by Alfred A. Knopf, a division of Random House, Inc., New York, and in Canada by Random House of Canada Limited, Toronto. Distributed by Random House, Inc., New York. Published in the United Kingdom by Everyman's Library, Northburgh House, 10 Northburgh Street, London EC1V 0AT, and distributed by Random House (UK) Ltd.

US website: www.randomhouse.com/everymans

ISBN: 978-0-307-26669-9 (US)
1-84159-307-9 & 978-1-84159-307-4 (UK)

A CIP catalogue reference for this book is available from the British Library

Book design by Barbara de Wilde and Carol Devine Carson

Typeset in the UK by AccComputing, North Barrow, Somerset

Printed and bound in Germany by GGP Media GmbH, Pössneck

DASHIELL HAMMETT

CONTENTS

INTRODUCTION

Dashiell Hammett was allegedly offered five G's to perform a contract hit. It is a highly extrapolatable – most likely mythic – premise. He was a Pinkerton operative at the time. A stooge for Anaconda Copper made the offer. The intended victim was a union organizer. The stooge had every reason to believe that Hammett would take the job – post-World War I Pinkertons were a goon squad paranoically fearful of all perceived Reds. Hammett's mythic refusal is a primer on situational ethics. He knew it was wrong and didn't do it. He stayed with an organization that in part suppressed dissent and entertained murderous offers on occasion. He stayed because he loved the work and figured he could chart a moral course through it. He was right and wrong. That disjuncture is the great theme of his work.

It explains why Hammett's vision is exponentially more complex than that of his near-contemporary Raymond Chandler. Chandler wrote the man he wanted to be – gallant and suffused with a lively satirist's wit. Hammett wrote the man he feared he might be – tenuous and skeptical in all human dealings, corruptible and addicted to violent intrigue. He stayed on the job. The job defined him. His job description was in some part "Oppression." That made him in large part a fascist tool. He knew it. He later embraced Marxist thought as a right-wing toady and used leftist dialectic for ironic definition. Detective work both fueled and countermanded his chaotic moral state and gave him something consistently engaging to do.

The jurist-critic David T. Bazelon wrote this on Hammett: "The core of his art is the masculine figure in American society. He is primarily a job holder. He goes at his job with a bloodthirsty determination that proceeds from an unwillingness to go beyond it. This relationship to the job is perhaps typically American. The idea of doing or not doing a job competently has replaced the whole larger issue of good and evil."

The job-holder Hammett lived and wrote in the agitated condition this epigram implies. Detective work was a job. Writing was a job. The craft within both was The Maneuver. The workday Hammett stealth-walked through a world of laudanum-guzzling grifters and bent cops susceptible to night sweats and visions. It was the Boom. The mechanized horror of the Great War roiled in recent memory. The Maneuver was steeped in drudgework punctuated by brief bursts of action. Read files, tail, surveil. Write reports, proffer bribes, track down suspects and on occasion risk danger. Speak the language of duplicity and male one-upmanship. Solve cases in a rigorously circumscribed fashion and wonder how they ramify beyond final-report status. Observe how crime seamlessly pervades the body politic and defines a whole culture. Take The Maneuver and exalt its language and turn it into popular fiction.

This presented Hammett with a second – and wildly challenging – disjuncture. Detective work was by nature prosaic. File prowls, blown tails, attenuated stakeouts. Crime stories demanded near continuous action. File prowls must yield revelation. Blown tails must provide climax. Stakeouts must further plot at all costs. Hammett knew this going in: crime fiction was preposterous melodrama with a gnat-sized reality base. Never in the worldwide annals of crime had there been a single case rife with multiple shootouts, homicidal seductresses, and wall-to-wall mayhem succinctly resolved at tale's end. Hammett had to fit social realism into a suffocatingly contrived form. He did it with language – densely spare exposition and multilayered dialogue. He gave us a spellbinding male discourse – The Maneuver as moral crusade, the job holders' aria and torch song.

Ridiculous coincidence and buffoonish contrivance cohere behind its force. Hammett's male-speak is the gab of the grift, the scam, the dime hustle. It's the poke, the probe, the veiled query, the grab for advantage. It's the threat, the dim sanction, the offer of friendship cloaked in betrayal. Plot holes pop through Hammett's stories like speed bumps. The body count accretes with no more horror than pratfalls in farce. It doesn't matter. The language is always there. The talk is richly textured and more than richly male, and the counterbalance renders it all real.

It's the language of suspicion, alienation, and the big grasp for survival. It's a constant jolt of physical movement and conversation. Hammett's heroes move and talk, move and talk, move and talk. They are professional followers, entrappers, and interlocutors. They flourish in a context of continuous mendacity. They pride themselves on their lie-detection prowess. They go at professional liars with great zeal and find their own dissembling skills in no way disconcerting. It is a harrowing workday context. They have placed themselves in it consciously. It's an antidote to the squarejohn life and a daily gauntlet of stimulation. Hammett's workday men risk peril for trifling remuneration and never question the choice. They are lab rats in perpetual reaction to stimuli. They are ascetics tamping down emotional turbulence and willing it flatlined in the name of the job. The great satisfactions of the job are the mastery of danger and the culling of facts to form a concluding physical truth. These facts comprise the closing of the case and thus the story. Hammett's men stand hollowly proud in their constant case conclusions. They are in no way affirmed or redeemed. *They have survived.* They are hopped-up versions of the schmuck clerk who got through one more shift at Wal-Mart. Their mundane world swirls around them and ignores them. Hammett's invasively corrupt world swirls around his workmen and belittles them with its sheer size.

The Continental Op is Hammett's ultimate workday drone. He's famously unnamed and famously unattractive. He caroms through Hammett's first two novels, subsumed by lunatic events. He tails and talks, lies and lie-detects, plays off factions. He ties up cases and stands dead still, fat and implacable. The next case will show up soon. He'll find the language for it. He'll probably survive it. He'll stand dead still, fat and implacable again. He'll be a bit more ground down and frayed at the soul. He'll go on from there. He'll personify Ross Macdonald's assessment of Hammett's work as "Deadpan Tragedy."

The Op speaks the first words of *Red Harvest*: "I first heard Personville called Poisonville by a red-haired mucker named Hickey Dewey in the Big Ship in Butte." That line stands as the tonal chord for the entire hardboiled canon. It's as exemplifyingly forceful as the two hammer blows that begin Beethoven's Third Symphony. Hammett equates human beings with toxic substances and goes south from there.

Red Harvest was published in 1929. It's a coda to the Boom and a prophecy of the Depression. The Op witnesses and largely precipitates a hallucinogenic bloodbath in a Montana mining town. He pits labor against management and cops against crooks. He waddles and bluffs his way through uncountable interrogations and acclimates himself to fatalities in war-zone numbers. He drinks laudanum and wakes up with a woman shivved to death. His actions create a momentary peace in Poisonville. That peace will soon shatter. It doesn't matter. He's moved on already – to the labyrinthine and largely incomprehensible events of *The Dain Curse.*

The Dain Curse exemplifies the sophomore curse novel. *Red Harvest* was tight and cohesive and rooted in the recent shock of the Anaconda Copper wars. Its sequel is a hodgepodge of religious cult antics and baroque family lore. The story is divided equally and unconvincingly between San Francisco and a small coastal town. Hammett wrote the book for magazine serialization. That publication gambit reveals itself in the narrative flow. The story runs in fits and starts and loopy plot turns. Hammett's imperiously strong suit of moment-to-moment language cannot surmount basic inconsistency. The story slogs and jerks to a foreshortened and abrupt conclusion. *Red Harvest* was all dark power. *The Dain Curse* is all grotesquerie. It lacks context. The colorful geography and a few pithy characters fail to eclipse the what's-going-on-here?/ was-this-book-written-on-booze? issue. *The Dain Curse* is recognizably Hammettian in this manner: it's a little jazz-age relic and his final ode to the Boom. Throughout, there are blasts of anything-goes America that only he could have written. *The Dain Curse* is a pure mystery novel written on contract. *Red Harvest* was a steeped-in-history novel written on spec. It displayed the advantage of personal history linked to politics.

Hammett views politics as crime most cancerous and genteel. It's crime buttressed by unspoken sanction. It's crime facilitated by a callous legal system. It's crime enforced by vicious cops in hobnailed boots stomping the downtrodden. Hammett treats politics-as-crime in deadpan fashion. He assumes that the reader knows this: politics is The Maneuver as public spectacle and reverential shuck. That means America was a land grab. That means all political discourse is disingenuous. That means his workmen heroes refuse to soliloquize or indict – they know the game is rigged and they're feeding off scraps of trickle-down graft.

Hammett saw himself as actively complicit. The realization may have fueled his self-destructive path with alcohol and women. He was a Pinkerton. He was a workman. He worked on a case-by-case basis and stepped back from judging the continued ramification of his work. He signed on to work for an enforcement agency that squashed workers flat. He knew it was wrong. He knew *he* was wrong. He did the job on an ad hoc basis and couched his maneuverings within The Maneuver in a personal moral code. The monstrous force of systemic corruption cast his code and his own job holder's life in extreme miniature and rendered everything about him small – except his guilt.

Something other than guilt drives Ned Beaumont in *The Glass Key*. Beaumont acts and reacts, but never ponders. He never thinks. He never tells us why he's doing what he's doing. His lack of explanation couched in constant action obscures motive and tells us that the absence of introspection is essential to the successful maneuver. The plot of *The Glass Key* is one long maneuver speedballing toward a futile resolution. It's Hammett's flat-affect tale of grasping men who want things and don't know what to do with them when they get them. It's a short novel with epic sweep and a treatise on The Maneuver as one long grab for power.

Ned Beaumont is a political fixer. He's a functioning drunk and a compulsive gambler on a losing streak. He works for a ward boss named Paul Madvig. Madvig runs a mid-size burg near New York City. Beaumont and Madvig have a tentative friendship based on interlocking needs within The Maneuver. Beaumont lives alone in a hotel suite. Madvig lives with his elderly mother and a twenty-year-old daughter from some gone bust and never explained marriage. He wants to marry a senator's daughter. It's a two-front maneuver: personal/political. The senator's son is murdered. Madvig's the key suspect. It's an election year. Factions want him voted out, factions want him re-elected. He wants the woman to solidify his political base and to sate an odd and gnawing tenderness within him. A gambler stiffed Ned Beaumont for three grand and change. They're both sleeping with the same woman. Ned wants his gelt. The gambler may have killed the senator's son. Ned sets out to grab his money and exonerate or doom Paul Madvig in the process.

It's a near-breathless errand of deadly import. It's a cavalcade of Depression-era fiends in extremis. Hammett gives us dollar-driven D.A.'s, psychopathic hoodlums, women poised with murderous intent. The story is all dialogue and movement. Horrible and heedless self-interest defines every character. The movement within movement exceeds breathlessness. People drink and light cigarettes continually. It's fuel for The Maneuver. Politicians blithely consider homicide as a political option. Mentions of kickbacks, bribes, payoffs, bagmen, feral goons, strumpets, pimps, building contracts and quashed indictments abound. *The Glass Key* is a conversational epic. Casual talk dismissively embraces issues of great moral weight. The who-killed-the-senator's-son? quest pales behind the theme of expediency. The who-gets-the-senator's-daughter? quest ends on a bleak footnote. The survivors retain their survival skills in a somewhat diminished fashion. Their journey has stained them in ways they cannot comprehend and has impeded their shots at successful future maneuvers. They'll go on anyway. The game is fixed and that's what they do.

The Glass Key is Hammett's last great work of fiction. It's a brand-new and unique world cut from whole literary cloth. It's a model of economical storytelling and thematic compression. It's somber and invigorating in equal measure. It's a predator's vision of the American jungle, and a book with a deep and troubled love for America – this huckster's paradise – itself.

The two novels and four stories in this volume give us Hammett with a sure precision. He was the great poet of the great American collision – personal honor and corruption, opportunity and fatality.

James Ellroy

SELECT BIBLIOGRAPHY

For biographical information about Dashiell Hammett and for quotations from his letters, articles and interviews, the following books are invaluable:

JOHNSON, DIANE, *Dashiell Hammett: A Life* (New York: Random House, 1983).

LAYMAN, RICHARD, *Shadow Man: The Life of Dashiell Hammett* (New York: Harcourt Brace Jovanovich, 1981).

MELLEN, JOAN, *Hellman and Hammett* (New York: HarperCollins, 1996).

STEIN, GERTRUDE, *Everybody's Autobiography* (New York: Random House, 1937).

VAN VECHTEN, CARL, ed., *Selected Writings of Gertrude Stein* (New York: Vintage Books, 1972).

Books by Dashiell Hammett

Red Harvest (New York: Alfred A. Knopf, 1929).

The Dain Curse (New York: Alfred A. Knopf, 1929).

The Maltese Falcon (New York: Alfred A. Knopf, 1930).

The Glass Key (New York: Alfred A. Knopf, 1931).

The Thin Man (New York: Alfred A. Knopf, 1934).

The Big Knockover: Selected Short Stories and Short Novels (New York: Random House, 1966).

The Continental Op (New York: Random House, 1974).

Woman in the Dark (New York: Alfred A. Knopf, 1988).

Nightmare Town: Stories, edited by Kirby McCauley, Martin H. Greenberg, and Ed Gorman (New York: Alfred A. Knopf, 1999).

Selected Letters of Dashiell Hammett, edited by Richard Layman, with Julie M. Rivett, Foreword by Josephine Hammett Marshall (Washington, D.C.: Counterpoint Press, February 2001).

CHRONOLOGY

DATE	AUTHOR'S LIFE	LITERARY CONTEXT
1894	Samuel Dashiell Hammett born 27 May in St Mary's County, Maryland to Richard Thomas Hammett and Annie Bond Dashiell.	Conan Doyle: *The Memoirs of Sherlock Holmes.* Conan Doyle visits US for lecture tour. Twain: *Pudd'nhead Wilson.*
1896		Fitzgerald born.
1898		
1899		Hemingway and Nabokov born. James: *The Awkward Age.* Chopin: *The Awakening.* Hornung: *Raffles: The Amateur Cracksman.*
1900		Dreiser: *Sister Carrie.* Conrad: *Lord Jim.* Freud: *The Interpretation of Dreams.*
1901	Family moves to Baltimore.	Kipling: *Kim.* Mann: *Buddenbrooks.*
1902		Steinbeck born. Conan Doyle: *The Hound of the Baskervilles.*
1904		James: *The Golden Bowl.*
1905		Wharton: *The House of Mirth.* Conan Doyle: *The Return of Sherlock Holmes.*
1906		
1907		Conrad: *The Secret Agent.*
1908	Attends Baltimore Polytechnic Institute. Leaves after less than a year to work at various jobs.	
1909		Stein: *Three Lives.* W. C. Williams: *Poems.*
1912		Dreiser: *The Financier.*
1913		Frost: *A Boy's Will.* Cather: *O Pioneers!* Lawrence: *Sons and Lovers.*

HISTORICAL EVENTS

The US becomes the leading manufacturing nation in the world. Beginning of Freudian psychoanalysis. Nicholas II becomes Tsar of Russia.

William McKinley elected US president. Klondike Gold Rush.

Invention of the cash register. Rockefeller 'retires' worth *c.* $200 million.

Spanish-American War.

Outbreak of Boer War. Alfred Hitchcock born.

US population 76 million. US railroad network just under 200,000 miles. First International Socialist Congress in Paris. Planck's quantum theory.

President McKinley assassinated. Succeeded by Theodore Roosevelt, ushering in a progressive era in American politics. Marconi transmits messages across the Atlantic. Death of Queen Victoria and accession of Edward VII in Britain.

War breaks out between Japan and Russia.

Einstein's theory of relativity. First Russian Revolution.

San Francisco earthquake.

Cubist exhibition in Paris.

First Ford Model T car.

Woodrow Wilson elected US president. Sinking of *Titanic*. Charlie Chaplin's first film.

Completion of new, even grander Grand Central Station building in New York. Post-Impressionist exhibition in New York.

DATE	AUTHOR'S LIFE	LITERARY CONTEXT
1914		E. Burroughs: *Tarzan of the Apes.* Joyce: *Dubliners.*
1915	Detective for Pinkerton's National Detective Service.	Ford: *The Good Soldier.* Kafka: *Metamorphosis.*
1917		Eliot: *Prufrock and Other Observations.* Conan Doyle: *His Last Bow.*
1918	Enlists in army.	Cather: *My Ántonia.* Adams: *The Education of Henry Adams.*
1919	Discharged from army with disability pension following bouts of 'flu, pneumonia and tuberculosis. Returns to work at Pinkerton's.	*Black Mask*, pulp magazine, set up. Anderson: *Winesburg, Ohio.* Reed: *Ten Days that Shook the World.* Mencken: *The American Language.*
1920	Works as Pinkerton's operative in Spokane, Washington, Idaho and Montana. Is hospitalized, where he meets nurse Josephine ('Jose') Dolan.	Wharton: *The Age of Innocence.* Fitzgerald: *This Side of Paradise.* Lewis: *Main Street.* Christie: *The Mysterious Affair at Styles* (first novel). Pound: *Hugh Selwyn Mauberly.*
1921	Marries Jose Dolan on 7 July in San Francisco. Daughter Mary Jane born 15 October.	Dos Passos: *Three Soldiers.* Lawrence: *Women in Love.* Pirandello: *Six Characters in Search of an Author.*
1922	First short stories published in *Smart Set* and *Black Mask.*	Eliot: *The Wasteland.* Joyce: *Ulysses.* Lewis: *Babbitt.* Carroll John Daly creates the first hard-boiled detective in 'The False Burton Combs.'
1923	Introduces the Continental Op in *Black Mask* short story 'Arson Plus.'	
1925	'The Scorched Face' (novelette) published in *Black Mask.*	Dreiser: *An American Tragedy.* Fitzgerald: *The Great Gatsby.* Dos Passos: *Manhattan Transfer.* Lewis: *Arrowsmith.* Loos: *Gentlemen Prefer Blondes.* Stein: *The Making of Americans.* Woolf: *Mrs Dalloway.* Kafka: *The Trial.*

CHRONOLOGY

HISTORICAL EVENTS

Outbreak of World War I. President Wilson proclaims US neutrality. Ludlow Massacre: striking miners killed in Colorado. Panama Canal opens.

US joins war in Europe. Industrial Workers of the World lead a strike in the copper mines of Arizona. Russian October Revolution.

Wilson proposes 'Fourteen Points' for world peace. World War I ends 11 November. Worldwide 'flu epidemic kills millions. Civil war in Russia (to 1921).

Versailles Peace Treaty (which the US later refuses to ratify). 'Red scare.' Seattle General Strike shuts down city and leads to arrests among socialists (February). Race riots throughout US during the summer. Communist Party founded in Chicago (September). Steel strike in the Midwest (September–January): more than 350,000 workers demand higher wages, an 8-hour day and recognition of unions. Troops are brought in and strikers routed. The Eighteenth Amendment, prohibiting the manufacture and sale of intoxicating liquors, is ratified. The Nineteenth Amendment – Female Suffrage – is passed.

Post-war slump (to 1921). League of Nations formed (following an isolationist foreign policy, the US declines to join.) Republican Warren G. Harding elected president. The 'jazz age.'

Quota laws restrict immigration to the US (further restrictions made in 1924). Wage cuts and massive unemployment cause unrest and increase in violence: Hoover Commission suggests price cuts and shorter hours rather than wage increases. Battle of Blair Mountain – culmination of West Virginia Mine War.

Ku Klux Klan attracting widespread support in the South and beyond. Herrin Massacre: bloody clashes between strikers and strike-breakers in Illinois. Following a protectionist economic policy, the government increases tariffs across the board. Radio broadcasting boom begins. Mussolini gains power in Italy. Russia becomes USSR: Stalin becomes General Secretary of the Communist Party.

Economic boom in US (to 1929). Calvin Coolidge becomes preisdent after Harding's death. US Steel implements the 8-hour day.

Al Capone a powerful force in Chicago. 'Monkey Trial' in Dayton, Tennessee finds against John Scopes for teaching Darwin's theory of evolution in a state school. First public demonstration of television in the US.

DATE	AUTHOR'S LIFE	LITERARY CONTEXT
1926	Advertising manager for jeweller Albert Samuels. Daughter Josephine Rebecca born 24 May.	Fitzgerald: *All the Sad Young Men.* Faulkner: *Soldier's Pay.* Hemingway: *The Sun Also Rises.* O'Neill: *The Great God Brown.* Hughes: *The Weary Blues.* Christie: *The Murder of Roger Ackroyd.*
1927	First part of *Red Harvest* (originally called 'Poisonville') published in *Black Mask.*	Proust: *Remembrance of Things Past* (posthumous). Woolf: *To the Lighthouse.* Cather: *Death Comes for the Archbishop.* Wilder: *The Bridge of San Luis Rey.* Conan Doyle: *The Case Book of Sherlock Holmes.*
1928		O'Neill: *Strange Interlude.* Waugh: *Decline and Fall.* Bulgakov: *The Master and Margarita* (to 1940).
1929	*Red Harvest* and *The Dain Curse* published by Knopf. Moves to New York. First part of *The Maltese Falcon* and 'Fly Paper' (a novelette) published in *Black Mask.*	Hemingway: *A Farewell to Arms.* Faulkner: *The Sound and the Fury.* Wolfe: *Look Homeward, Angel.* Remarque: *All Quiet on the Western Front.*
1930	*The Maltese Falcon* published by Knopf. *Roadhouse Nights,* a movie based on *Red Harvest,* released by Paramount. Moves to Hollywood; meets Lillian Hellman.	Faulkner: *As I Lay Dying.* Crane: *The Bridge.* Frost: *Collected Poems.* O'Neill: *Mourning Becomes Electra.* Freud: *Civilization and its Discontents.*
1931	*The Glass Key* published. Moves back to New York. First film version of *The Maltese Falcon,* starring Ricardo Cortez and Bebe Daniels, released by Warner Brothers. Hammett co-writes screenplay.	
1932		Crane dies. Huxley: *Brave New World.* Faulkner: *Light in August.* Caldwell: *Tobacco Road.* Erle Stanley Gardner: *The Case of the Velvet Claws* (first Perry Mason novel).

HISTORICAL EVENTS

First liquid fuel rocket. General strike in UK.

Execution of Sacco and Vanzetti. First 'talkie' – *The Jazz Singer.* Lindbergh's solo Atlantic flight. Trotsky expelled from Communist Party in USSR.

Republican Herbert Hoover elected US president. 26 million cars and 13 million radios in use in US. First 'Mickey Mouse' cartoon. Gershwin: *An American in Paris.* Amelia Earhart becomes the first woman to fly the Atlantic solo.

Wall Street Crash, 24 October; mass unemployment. US establishes Federal Loans. Beginning of world depression. Al Capone arrested. Museum of Modern Art in New York founded. Land speed record set at 231 mph.

Unemployment rises to 13 million. US tariffs raised by 50–100%. Empire State Building opened. Gandhi begins civil disobedience campaign in India.

Al Capone found guilty of tax evasion and sent to prison (the first time a charge was made to stick). Britain abandons Gold Standard. Invention of the electric razor.

Lindbergh's son kidnapped. Franklin Roosevelt, Democrat, elected US president and announces New Deal. Stock prices in the US fall to 20% of their 1929 value.

DATE	AUTHOR'S LIFE	LITERARY CONTEXT
1933	Novella 'Woman in the Dark' published in *Liberty*. Condensed version of *The Thin Man* published in *Redbook*.	Book burnings in Nazi Germany. West: *Miss Lonelyhearts*.
1934	*The Thin Man* published. Film version starring William Powell and Myrna Loy released by MGM (five other *Thin Man* movies would follow between 1934 and 1947.)	Cain: *The Postman Always Rings Twice* (banned in Boston.) Fitzgerald: *Tender is the Night*. Miller: *Tropic of Cancer*. Waugh: *A Handful of Dust*. Christie: *Murder on the Orient Express*.
1935	Meets Gertrude Stein.	Wolfe: *Of Time and the River*. Lewis: *It Can't Happen Here*.
1936	Secretly joins Communist Party. *Satan Met a Lady*, a second film version of *The Maltese Falcon*, is released by Warner Brothers. *After the Thin Man* released by MGM.	Faulkner: *Absalom, Absalom!* Dos Passos: *The Big Money*. Cain: *Double Indemnity*. Mitchell: *Gone with the Wind*. Eliot: *Collected Poems*. Lorca killed by Fascist militia in Spain.
1937		Hemingway: *To Have and Have Not*. Steinbeck: *Of Mice and Men*. Dos Passos: *U.S.A*. Stevens: *The Man with the Blue Guitar*.
1938		Cummings: *Collected Poems*. Waugh: *Scoop*. Sartre: *Nausea*. Beckett: *Murphy*.
1939		Chandler: *The Big Sleep*. Steinbeck: *The Grapes of Wrath*. Joyce: *Finnegans Wake*.
1940		Fitzgerald dies. Hemingway: *For Whom the Bell Tolls*. Chandler: *Farewell, My Lovely*. Greene: *The Power and the Glory*.
1941	Elected president of League of American Writers. John Huston's film version of *The Maltese Falcon*, starring Humphrey Bogart and Mary Astor, released by Warner Brothers.	Fitzgerald: *The Last Tycoon* (posthumous.) Brecht: *Mother Courage*. Woolf and Joyce die.

HISTORICAL EVENTS

The Twenty-First Amendment, repealing prohibition, ratified. Hitler appointed Chancellor of Germany. USSR recognized by US. By this year 11,000 of the 25,000 banks in the US have failed.

Depth of the Great Depression. Stalin institutes purges of the Communist Party in Russia. Al Capone sent to Alcatraz.

National Labour Relations Act gives workers right to form or join unions. Transcontinental air service begins in US. Mussolini invades Abyssinia. Gershwin: *Porgy and Bess.*

Roosevelt re-elected by a landslide. Spanish Civil War begins. Abdication of King Edward VIII who wishes to marry the American divorcee Wallis Simpson. Hitler and Mussolini form Rome–Berlin axis.

Japan invades China. First jet engine and nylon stockings. In the US approximately 75 million visit movies every week. Moscow show trials of Communist Party opponents of Stalin. Strike against Republic Steel in Chicago: four strikers killed, 44 injured.

Germany annexes Austria; Munich crisis. Pogroms against Jews in Germany. Hitchcock: *The Lady Vanishes.*

World War II begins. First commercial transatlantic flights. Vivien Leigh and Clark Gable star in *Gone with the Wind.*

Churchill prime minister in UK. Fall of Paris. Battle of Britain. Assassination of Trotsky in Mexico. Extraction of plutonium from uranium. Penicillin developed.

Japanese attack on Pearl Harbor. US enters war 11 December. Hitler invades Russia. US introduces 'lease-lend' system of aid to Britain. Orson Welles: *Citizen Kane.* Beginnings of 'bebop.'

DATE	AUTHOR'S LIFE	LITERARY CONTEXT
1942	Hammett rejoins army as a private.	Chandler: *The High Window.* Paul: *A Narrow Street.* Camus: *The Stranger.*
1943	Sent to Fort Randall, Alaska. Co-writes screenplay *Watch on the Rhine* with Lillian Hellman.	Chandler: *The Lady in the Lake.*
1944		Williams: *The Glass Menagerie.* Eliot: *Four Quartets.*
1945	Honourably discharged as a master sergeant. Returns to New York.	Orwell: *Animal Farm.* Waugh: *Brideshead Revisited.* Thurber: *The Thurber Carnival.* Borges: *Fictions.* Dreiser dies.
1946	Elected president of Communist-sponsored Civil Rights Congress of New York. Begins teaching courses in mystery writing at Jefferson School of Social Science.	Chandler wins Mystery Writers of America's Edgar Allan Poe Award (also in 1954). Goodis: *Dark Passage.* O'Neill: *The Iceman Cometh.*
1947		*The Diary of Anne Frank.* Williams: *A Streetcar Named Desire.*
1948		Eliot wins Nobel Prize. Mailer: *The Naked and the Dead.*
1949		Chandler: *The Little Sister.* Faulkner wins Nobel Prize. Orwell: *Nineteen Eighty-four.* Greene: *The Third Man.* Miller: *Death of a Salesman.*
1950		Chandler: 'The Simple Art of Murder,' 'Goldfish.' Eliot: *The Cocktail Party.*
1951	Questioned before US District Court about Civil Rights Congress bail fund. Found guilty of contempt of court and sentenced to six months in prison, where his health deteriorates.	Jones: *From Here to Eternity.* Salinger: *The Catcher in the Rye.* Frost: *Complete Poems.*
1952	Moves to Katonah, New York. Begins work on a novel; fragment is later published as *Tulip* in *The Big Knockover*, a collection of his stories published in 1966.	Beckett: *Waiting for Godot.* Ellison: *The Invisible Man.* O'Connor: *Wise Blood.* Steinbeck: *East of Eden.*

HISTORICAL EVENTS

Rommel defeated at El Alamein. Build-up of American air force in Free China. World's first nuclear reactor constructed at Chicago University. Irving Berlin: 'White Christmas.'

Russians defeat Germans at Stalingrad. Allied armies victorious in North Africa. Allied invasion of Italy.

Allied landings in Normandy; German retreat; liberation of Paris. Roosevelt elected for fourth term in US. *Double Indemnity* released (screenplay part-written by Raymond Chandler).

Unconditional surrender of Germany. Suicide of Hitler. World War II ends after bombing of Hiroshima and Nagasaki. Foundation of United Nations. Truman president of US; Attlee prime minister in UK. Strike wave across America (to 1946).

Churchill gives 'Iron Curtain' speech. Cold War begins. Film of *The Big Sleep* with Humphrey Bogart and Lauren Bacall.

Al Capone dies. Film of *Dark Passage* starring Bogart and Bacall. India proclaimed independent.

Jewish state of Israel comes into existence. Month-long coal miners' strike in America. Hitchcock: *Rope.*

Chinese revolution. Northern Atlantic Treaty signed at Washington. Russian Blockade lifted. Orson Welles stars in *The Third Man.*

Senator Joseph McCarthy accuses State Department of being riddled with Communists, and begins the worst of the American blacklist period. Korean War (to 1953.)

President Truman dismisses General MacArthur as commander of the UN forces in Korea. Rogers and Hammerstein: *South Pacific.* Hitchcock: *Strangers on a Train* (screenplay part-written by Chandler). Churchill re-elected prime minister in UK.

Eisenhower elected US president. Gary Cooper stars in *High Noon.* China accuses US of waging germ warfare in Korea. Batista overthrows Cuban government. Accession of Elizabeth II. First contraceptive pill.

DATE	AUTHOR'S LIFE	LITERARY CONTEXT
1953	Subpoenaed by Senator Joseph McCarthy to testify before his Senate subcommittee.	Chandler: *The Long Goodbye.* Faulkner: *Requiem for a Nun.* Williams: *Camino Real.*
1954		Hemingway wins Nobel Prize. Stevens: *Collected Poems.* Amis: *Lucky Jim.*
1955	Suffers heart attack at Lillian Hellman's house on Martha's Vineyard.	Nabokov: *Lolita.* Williams: *Cat on a Hot Tin Roof.* Miller: *A View from the Bridge.*
1956		O'Neill: *Long Day's Journey into Night.* Goodis: *Shoot the Piano Player.* Osborne: *Look Back in Anger.*
1957		Kerouac: *On the Road.*
1958		Pasternak's *Doctor Zhivago* published throughout world (except USSR). Capote: *Breakfast at Tiffany's.*
1959		W. S. Burroughs: *Naked Lunch.* Grass: *The Tin Drum.*
1960		Updike: *Rabbit, Run.* O'Connor: *The Violent Bear It Away.*
1961	Dies of lung cancer on 10 January 1961 in New York City. Buried at Arlington National Cemetery.	Hemingway dies. Heller: *Catch-22.* Williams: *Night of the Iguana.*

HISTORICAL EVENTS

Experiments in colour television in the US. Stalin dies.

Communist Party outlawed in US. Marlon Brando stars in *On the Waterfront*. Hitchcock: *Dial M for Murder* and *Rear Window*. Vietnamese Communists defeat French at Dien Bien Phu.

Soviets invade Hungary. Suez Crisis. Eisenhower re-elected as US president. Transatlantic telephone service linking Britain and the US.

Civil Rights Act in US; race riots in southern US.
Alaska becomes 49th state of US. Bernstein: *West Side Story*. Hitchcock: *Vertigo*. Beginning of space exploration.

Batista flees Cuba; Castro seizes power.

John F. Kennedy elected US president. Brezhnev becomes president of USSR. John Wayne stars in *The Alamo*.

First US troops sent to Vietnam. Berlin Wall constructed. Yuri Gagarin becomes first man in space.

THE HOUSE IN TURK STREET

I HAD BEEN told that the man for whom I was hunting lived in a certain Turk Street block, but my informant hadn't been able to give me his house number. Thus it came about that late one rainy afternoon I was canvassing this certain block, ringing each bell, and reciting a myth that went like this:

"I'm from the law office of Wellington and Berkeley. One of our clients – an elderly lady – was thrown from the rear platform of a street car last week and severely injured. Among those who witnessed the accident was a young man whose name we don't know. But we have been told that he lives in this neighborhood." Then I would describe the man I wanted, and wind up: "Do you know of anyone who looks like that?"

All down one side of the block the answers were: "No," "No," "No."

I crossed the street and started on the other side. The first house: "No." The second: "No." The third. The fourth. The fifth –

No one came to the door in answer to my first ring. After a while, I rang again. I had just decided that no one was at home, when the knob turned slowly and a little old woman opened the door. She was a very fragile little old woman, with a piece of gray knitting in one hand, and faded eyes that twinkled pleasantly behind goldrimmed spectacles. She wore a stiffly starched apron over a black dress.

"Good evening," she said in a thin friendly voice. "I hope you didn't mind waiting. I always have to peep out to see who's there before I open the door – an old woman's timidity."

"Sorry to disturb you," I apologized. "But –"

"Won't you come in, please?"

"No; I just want a little information. I won't take much time."

"I wish you would come in," she said, and then added with mock severity, "I'm sure my tea is getting cold."

She took my damp hat and coat, and I followed her down a narrow hall to a dim room, where a man got up as we entered. He was old too, and stout, with a thin white beard that fell upon a white vest that was as stiffly starched as the woman's apron.

"Thomas," the little fragile woman told him; "this is Mr. –"

"Tracy," I said, because that was the name I had given the other residents of the block; but I came as near blushing when I said it as I have in fifteen years. These folks weren't made to be lied to.

Their name, I learned, was Quarre; and they were an affectionate old couple. She called him "Thomas" every time she spoke to him, rolling the name around in her mouth as if she liked the taste of it. He called her "my dear" just as frequently, and twice he got up to adjust a cushion more comfortably to her frail back.

I had to drink a cup of tea with them and eat some little spiced cookies before I could get them to listen to a question. Then Mrs. Quarre made little sympathetic clicking sounds with her tongue and teeth, while I told about the elderly lady who had fallen off a street car. The old man rumbled in his beard that it was "a damn shame," and gave me a fat cigar.

Finally I got away from the accident, and described the man I wanted.

"Thomas," Mrs. Quarre said, "isn't that the young man who lives in the house with the railing – the one who always looks so worried?"

The old man stroked his snowy beard and pondered for a moment.

"But, my dear," he rumbled at last, "hasn't he got dark hair?"

She beamed upon her husband. "Thomas is *so* observant," she said with pride. "I had forgotten; but the young man I spoke of does have dark hair, so he couldn't be the one."

The old man then suggested that one who lived in the block below might be my man. They discussed this one at some length before they decided that he was too tall and too old. Mrs. Quarre suggested another. They discussed that one, and voted against him. Thomas offered a candidate; he was weighed and discarded. They chattered on.

Darkness settled. The old man turned on a light in a tall lamp that threw a soft yellow circle upon us, and left the rest of the room dim. The room was a large one, and heavy with the thick hangings and bulky horsehair furniture of a generation ago. I didn't expect to get any information here; but I was comfortable, and the cigar was a good one. Time enough to go out into the drizzle when I had finished my smoke.

Something cold touched the nape of my neck.

"Stand up!"

I didn't stand up: I couldn't. I was paralyzed. I sat and blinked at the Quarres.

And looking at them, I knew that something cold *couldn't* be against the back of my neck; a harsh voice *couldn't* have ordered me to stand up. It wasn't possible!

Mrs. Quarre still sat primly upright against the cushions her husband had adjusted to her back; her eyes still twinkled with friendliness behind her glasses. The old man still stroked his white beard, and let cigar smoke drift unhurriedly from his nostrils.

They would go on talking about the young men in the neighborhood who might be the man I wanted. Nothing had happened. I had dozed.

"Get up!" The cold thing against my neck jabbed deep into the flesh.

I stood up. "Frisk him," the harsh voice came from behind.

The old man carefully laid his cigar down, came to me, and ran his hands over my body. Satisfied that I was unarmed, he emptied my pockets, dropping the contents upon the chair that I had just left.

"That's all," he told the man behind me, and returned to his chair.

"Turn around, you!" the harsh voice ordered.

I turned and faced a tall, gaunt, raw-boned man of about my own age, which is thirty-five. He had an ugly face – hollow-cheeked, bony, and spattered with big pale freckles. His eyes were of a watery blue, and his nose and chin stuck out abruptly. "Know me?" he asked.

"No."

"You're a liar!"

I didn't argue the point; he was holding a gun in one big freckled hand.

"You're going to know me pretty well before you're through with me," this big ugly man threatened. "You're going to –"

"Hook!" a voice came from a portièred doorway – the doorway through which the ugly man had no doubt crept up behind me. "Hook, come here!" The voice was feminine – young, clear, and musical.

"What do you want?" the ugly man called over his shoulder.

"*He's* here."

"All right!" He turned to Thomas Quarre. "Keep this joker safe."

From somewhere among his whiskers, his coat, and his stiff white vest, the old man brought out a big black revolver, which he handled with no signs of unfamiliarity.

The ugly man swept up the things that had been taken

from my pockets, and carried them through the portières with him.

Mrs. Quarre smiled up at me. "Do sit down, Mr. Tracy," she said.

I sat.

Through the portières a new voice came from the next room; a drawling baritone voice whose accent was unmistakably British; cultured British. "What's up, Hook?" this voice was asking.

The harsh voice of the ugly man:

"Plenty's up, I'm telling you! They're on to us! I started out a while ago; and as soon as I got to the street, I seen a man I knowed on the other side. He was pointed out to me in Philly five–six years ago. I don't know his name, but I remember his mug – he's a Continental Detective Agency man. I came back in right away, and me and Elvira watched him out of the window. He went to every house on the other side of the street, asking questions or something. Then he came over and started to give this side a whirl, and after a while he rings the bell. I tell the old woman and her husband to get him in, stall him along, and see what he says for himself. He's got a song and dance about looking for a guy what seen an old woman bumped by a street car – but that's the bunk! He's gunning for us. I went in and stuck him up just now. I meant to wait till you come, but I was scared he'd get nervous and beat it."

The British voice: "You shouldn't have shown yourself to him. The others could have taken care of him."

Hook: "What's the diff? Chances is he knows us all anyway. But supposing he didn't, what diff does it make?"

The drawling British voice: "It may make a deal of difference. It was stupid."

Hook, blustering: "Stupid, huh? You're always bellyaching about other people being stupid. To hell with you, I say! Who does all the work? Who's the guy that swings all the jobs? Huh? Where –"

The young feminine voice: "Now, Hook, for God's sake don't make that speech again. I've listened to it until I know it by heart!"

A rustle of papers, and the British voice: "I say, Hook, you're correct about his being a detective. Here is an identification card."

The feminine voice from the next room: "Well, what's to be done? What's our play?"

Hook: "That's easy to answer. We're going to knock this sleuth off!"

The feminine voice: "And put our necks in the noose?"

Hook, scornfully: "As if they ain't there if we don't! You don't think this guy ain't after us for the L.A. job, do you?"

The British voice: "You're an ass, Hook, and a quite hopeless one. Suppose this chap is interested in the Los Angeles affair, as is probable; what then? He is a Continental operative. Is it likely that his organization doesn't know where he is? Don't you think they know he was coming up here? And don't they know as much about us – chances are – as he does? There's no use killing him. That would only make matters worse. The thing to do is to tie him up and leave him here. His associates will hardly come looking for him until tomorrow."

My gratitude went out to the British voice! Somebody was in my favor, at least to the extent of letting me live. I hadn't been feeling very cheerful these last few minutes. Somehow, the fact that I couldn't see these people who were deciding whether I was to live or die, made my plight seem all the more desperate. I felt better now, though far from gay; I had confidence in the drawling British voice; it was the voice of a man who habitually carries his point.

Hook, bellowing: "Let me tell you something, brother: that guy's going to be knocked off! That's flat! I'm taking no chances. You can jaw all you want to about it, but I'm looking out for my own neck and it'll be a lot safer with that guy where he can't talk. That's flat."

The feminine voice, disgustedly: "Aw, Hook, be reasonable!"

The British voice, still drawling, but dead cold: "There's no use reasoning with you, Hook, you've the instincts and the intellect of a troglodyte. There is only one sort of language that you understand; and I'm going to talk that language to you, my son. If you are tempted to do anything silly between now and the time of our departure, just say this to yourself two or three times: 'If he dies, I die.' Say it as if it were out of the Bible – because it's that true."

There followed a long space of silence, with a tenseness that made my not particularly sensitive scalp tingle.

When, at last, a voice cut the silence, I jumped as if a gun had been fired; though the voice was low and smooth enough.

It was the British voice, confidently victorious, and I breathed again.

"We'll get the old people away first," the voice was saying. "You take charge of our guest, Hook. Tie him up while I get the bonds, and we'll be gone in less than half an hour."

The portières parted and Hook came into the room – a scowling Hook whose freckles had a greenish tinge against the sallowness of his face. He pointed a revolver at me, and spoke to the Quarres, short and harsh: "He wants you." They got up and went into the next room.

Hook, meanwhile, had stepped back to the doorway, still menacing me with his revolver; and pulled loose the plush ropes that were around the heavy curtains. Then he came around behind me, and tied me securely to the highbacked chair; my arms to the chair's arms, my legs to the chair's legs, my body to the chair's back and seat; and he wound up by gagging me with the corner of a cushion that was too well-stuffed.

As he finished lashing me into place, and stepped back to scowl at me, I heard the street door close softly, and then light footsteps ran back and forth overhead.

Hook looked in the direction of those footsteps, and his little watery blue eyes grew cunning. "Elvira!" he called softly.

The portières bulged as if someone had touched them, and the musical feminine voice came through. "What?"

"Come here."

"I'd better not. He wouldn't –"

"Damn him!" Hook flared up. "Come here!"

She came into the room and into the circle of light from the tall lamp; a girl in her early twenties, slender and lithe, and dressed for the street, except that she carried her hat in one hand. A white face beneath a bobbed mass of flame-colored hair. Smoke-gray eyes that were set too far apart for trustworthiness – though not for beauty – laughed at me; and her red mouth laughed at me, exposing the edges of little sharp animal-teeth. She was as beautiful as the devil, and twice as dangerous.

She laughed at me – a fat man, all trussed up with red plush rope, and with the corner of a green cushion in my mouth – and she turned to the ugly man. "What do you want?"

He spoke in an undertone, with a furtive glance at the ceiling, above which soft steps still padded back and forth.

"What say we shake him?"

Her smoke-gray eyes lost their merriment and became calculating.

"There's a hundred thousand he's holding – a third of it's mine. You don't think I'm going to take a Mickey Finn on that, do you?"

"Course not! Supposing we get the hundred-grand?"

"How?"

"Leave it to me, kid; leave it to me! If I swing it, will you go with me? You know I'll be good to you."

She smiled contemptuously, I thought – but he seemed to like it.

"You're whooping right you'll be good to me," she said. "But listen, Hook: we couldn't get away with it – not unless you *get him*. I know him! I'm not running away with anything that belongs to him unless he is fixed so that he can't come after it."

Hook moistened his lips and looked around the room at nothing. Apparently he didn't like the thought of tangling with the owner of the British drawl. But his desire for the girl was too strong for his fear.

"I'll do it!" he blurted. "I'll get him! Do you mean it, kid? If I get him, you'll go with me?"

She held out her hand. "It's a bet," she said and he believed her.

His ugly face grew warm and red and utterly happy, and he took a deep breath and straightened his shoulders. In his place, I might have believed her myself – all of us have fallen for that sort of thing at one time or another – but sitting tied up on the side-lines, I knew that he'd have been better off playing with a gallon of nitro than with this baby. She was dangerous! There was a rough time ahead for Hook!

"This is the lay –" Hook began, and stopped, tongue-tied.

A step had sounded in the next room.

Immediately the British voice came through the portières, and there was exasperation to the drawl now: "This is really too much! I can't" – he said *reahly* and *cawnt* – "leave for a moment without having things done all wrong. Now just what got into you, Elvira, that you must go in and exhibit yourself to our detective?"

Fear flashed into her smoke-gray eyes, and out again, and she spoke airily. "Don't be altogether yellow," she said. "Your precious neck can get along all right without so much guarding."

The portières parted, and I twisted my head around as far as I could get it for my first look at this man who was responsible for my still being alive. I saw a short fat man, hatted and coated for the street, and carrying a tan traveling bag in one hand.

Then his face came into the yellow circle of light, and I saw that it was a Chinese face. A short fat Chinese, immaculately clothed in garments that were as British as his accent.

"It isn't a matter of color," he told the girl – and I understood now the full sting of her jibe; "it's simply a matter of ordinary wisdom."

His face was a round yellow mask, and his voice was the same emotionless drawl that I had heard before; but I knew that he was as surely under the girl's sway as the ugly man – or he wouldn't have let her taunt bring him into the room. But I doubted that she'd find this Anglicized Oriental as easily handled as Hook.

"There was no particular need," the Chinese was still talking, "for this chap to have seen any of us." He looked at me now for the first time, with little opaque eyes that were like two black seeds. "It's quite possible that he didn't know any of us, even by description. This showing ourselves to him is the most arrant sort of nonsense."

"Aw, hell, Tai!" Hook blustered. "Quit your belly-aching, will you? What's the diff? I'll knock him off, and that takes care of that!"

The Chinese set down his tan bag and shook his head.

"There will be no killing," he drawled, "or there will be quite a bit of killing. You don't mistake my meaning, do you, Hook?"

Hook didn't. His Adam's apple ran up and down with the effort of his swallowing and behind the cushion that was choking me, I thanked the yellow man again.

Then this red-haired she-devil put her spoon in the dish.

"Hook's always offering to do things that he has no intention of doing," she told the Chinese.

Hook's ugly face blazed red at this reminder of his promise to *get* the Chinese, and he swallowed again, and his eyes looked as if nothing would have suited him better than an opportunity to crawl under something. But the girl had him; her influence was stronger than his cowardice.

He suddenly stepped close to the Chinese, and from his advantage of a full head in height scowled down into the round yellow face.

"Tai," the ugly man snarled; "you're done. I'm sick and tired of all this dog you put on – acting like you was a king or something. I'm going to –"

He faltered, and his words faded away into silence. Tai looked up at him with eyes that were as hard and black and inhuman as two pieces of coal. Hook's lips twitched and he flinched away a little.

I stopped sweating. The yellow man had won again. But I had forgotten the red-haired she-devil. She laughed now – a mocking laugh that must have been like a knife to the ugly man.

A bellow came from deep in his chest, and he hurled one big fist into the round blank face of the yellow man.

The force of the punch carried Tai all the way across the room, and threw him on his side in one corner.

But he had twisted his body around to face the ugly man even as he went hurtling across the room – a gun was in his hand before he went down – and he was speaking before his legs had settled upon the floor – and his voice was a cultured British drawl.

"Later," he was saying, "we will settle this thing that is between us. Just now you will drop your pistol and stand very still while I get up."

Hook's revolver – only half out of his pocket when the Oriental had covered him – thudded to the rug. He stood rigidly still while Tai got to his feet, and Hook's breath came out noisily, and each freckle stood ghastlily out against the dirty scared white of his face.

I looked at the girl. There was contempt in the eyes with which she looked at Hook, but no disappointment.

Then I made a discovery: *something had changed in the room near her!*

I shut my eyes and tried to picture that part of the room as it had been before the two men had clashed. Opening my eyes suddenly, I had the answer.

On the table beside the girl had been a book and some magazines. They were gone now. Not two feet from the girl was the tan bag that Tai had brought into the room. Suppose the bag had held the bonds from the Los Angeles job that they had mentioned. It probably had. What then? It probably now held the book and magazines that had been on the table. The girl had stirred up the trouble between the two men to distract their attention while she made a switch. Where would the loot be, then? I didn't know, but I suspected that it was too bulky to be on the girl's slender person.

Just beyond the table was a couch, with a wide red cover that went all the way down to the floor. I looked from the couch to the girl. She was watching me, and her eyes twinkled with a flash of mirth as they met mine coming from the couch. The couch it was!

By now the Chinese had pocketed Hook's revolver, and was talking to him: "If I hadn't a dislike for murder, and didn't think that you will perhaps be of some value to Elvira and me in effecting our departure, I should certainly relieve us of the handicap of your stupidity now. But I'll give you one more chance. I would suggest, however, that you think carefully before you give way to any more of your violent impulses." He turned to the girl. "Have you been putting foolish ideas in our Hook's head?"

She laughed. "Nobody could put any kind in it."

"Perhaps you're right," he said, and then came over to test the lashings about my arms and body.

Finding them satisfactory, he picked up the tan bag, and held out the gun he had taken from the ugly man a few minutes before.

"Here's your revolver, Hook, now try to be sensible. We may as well go now. The old man and his wife will do as they were told. They are on their way to a city that we needn't mention by name in front of our friend here, to wait for us and their share of the bonds. Needless to say, they will wait a long while – they are out of it now. But between ourselves there must be no more treachery. If we're to get clear, we must help each other."

According to the best dramatic rules, these folks should have made sarcastic speeches to me before they left, but they didn't. They passed me without even a farewell look, and went out of sight into the darkness of the hall.

Suddenly the Chinese was in the room again, running tiptoe – an open knife in one hand, a gun in the other. This was the man I had been thanking for saving my life! He bent over me.

The knife moved on my right side, and the rope that held that arm slackened its grip. I breathed again, and my heart went back to beating.

"Hook will be back," Tai whispered, and was gone.

On the carpet, three feet in front of me, lay a revolver.

The street door closed, and I was alone in the house for a while.

You may believe that I spent that while struggling with the red plush ropes that bound me. Tai had cut one length, loosening my right arm somewhat and giving my body more play, but I was far from free. And his whispered "Hook will be back" was all the spur I needed to throw my strength against my bonds.

I understood now why the Chinese had insisted so strongly upon my life being spared. *I was the weapon with which Hook was to be removed!* The Chinese figured that Hook would make some excuse as soon as they reached the street, slip back into the house, knock me off, and rejoin his confederates. If he didn't do it on his own initiative, I suppose the Chinese would suggest it.

So he had put a gun within reach and had loosened my

ropes as much as he could, not to have me free before he himself got away.

This thinking was a side-issue. I didn't let it slow up my efforts to get loose. The *why* wasn't important to me just now – the important thing was to have that revolver in my hand when the ugly man came back.

Just as the front door opened, I got my right arm completely free, and plucked the strangling cushion from my mouth. The rest of my body was still held by the ropes – held loosely – but held.

I threw myself, chair and all, forward, breaking the fall with my free arm. The carpet was thick. I went down on my face, with the heavy chair atop me, all doubled up, but my right arm was free of the tangle, and my right hand grasped the gun. The dim light hit upon a man hurrying into the room – a glint of metal in his hand.

I fired.

He caught both hands to his belly, bent double, and slid out across the carpet.

That was over. But that was far from being all. I wrenched at the plush ropes that held me, while my mind tried to sketch what lay ahead.

The girl had switched the bonds, hiding them under the couch – there was no question of that. She had intended coming back for them before I had time to get free. But Hook had come back first, and she would have to change her plan. What more likely than that she would now tell the Chinese that Hook had made the switch? What then? There was only one answer: Tai would come back for the bonds – both of them would come. Tai knew that I was armed now, but they had said that the bonds represented a hundred thousand dollars. That would be enough to bring them back!

I kicked the last rope loose and scrambled to the couch. The bonds were beneath it: four thick bundles, done up with heavy rubber bands. I tucked them under one arm, and went over to the man who was dying near the door. His gun was under one of his legs. I pulled it out, stepped over him, and went into the dark hall. Then I stopped to consider.

The girl and the Chinese would split to tackle me. One would come in the front door and the other in the rear. That would be the safest way for them to handle me. My play, obviously, was to wait just inside one of those doors for them. It would be foolish for me to leave the house. That's exactly what they would be expecting at first – and they would be lying in ambush.

Decidedly, my play was to lie low within sight of this front door and wait until one of them came through it – as one of them surely would, when they had tired of waiting for me to come out.

Toward the street door, the hall was lighted with the glow that filtered through the glass from the street lights. The stairway leading to the second-story threw a triangular shadow across part of the hall – a shadow that was black enough for any purpose. I crouched low in this three-cornered slice of night, and waited.

I had two guns: the one the Chinese had given me, and the one I had taken from Hook. I had fired one shot; that would leave me eleven still to use – unless one of the weapons had been used since it was loaded. I broke the gun Tai had given me, and in the dark ran my fingers across the back of the cylinder. My fingers touched *one* shell – under the hammer. Tai had taken no chances; he had given me one bullet – the bullet with which I had dropped Hook.

I put that gun down on the floor, and examined the one I had taken from Hook. It was *empty*. The Chinese had taken no chances at all! He had emptied Hook's gun before returning it to him after their quarrel.

I was in a hole! Alone, unarmed, in a strange house that

would presently hold two who were hunting me – and that one of them was a woman didn't soothe me any – she was none the less deadly on that account.

For a moment I was tempted to make a dash for it; the thought of being out in the street again was pleasant; but I put the idea away. That would be foolishness, and plenty of it. Then I remembered the bonds under my arm. They would have to be my weapon; and if they were to serve me, they would have to be concealed.

I slipped out of my triangular shadow and went up the stairs. Thanks to the street lights, the upstairs rooms were not too dark for me to move around. Around and around I went through the rooms, hunting for a place to hide the bonds. But when suddenly a window rattled, as if from the draught created by the opening of an outside door somewhere, I still had the loot in my hands.

There was nothing to do now but to chuck them out of a window and trust to luck. I grabbed a pillow from a bed, stripped off the white case, and dumped the bonds into it. Then I leaned out of an already open window and looked down into the night, searching for a desirable dumping place: I didn't want the bonds to land on anything that would make a racket.

And, looking out of the window, I found a better hiding place. The window opened into a narrow court, on the other side of which was a house of the same sort as the one I was in. That house was of the same height as this one, with a flat tin roof that sloped down the other way. The roof wasn't far from me – not too far to chuck the pillow case. I chucked it. It disappeared over the edge of the roof and crackled softly on the tin.

Then I turned on all the lights in the room, lighted a cigarette (we all like to pose a little now and then), and sat down on the bed to await my capture. I might have stalked my enemies through the dark house, and possibly have nabbed them; but most likely I would simply have succeeded in getting myself shot. And I don't like to be shot.

The girl found me.

She came creeping up the hall, an automatic in each hand, hesitated for an instant outside the door, and then came in on the jump. And when she saw me sitting peacefully on the side of the bed, her eyes snapped scornfully at me, as if I had done something mean. I suppose she thought I should have given her an opportunity to shoot.

"I got him, Tai," she called, and the Chinese joined us.

"What did Hook do with the bonds?" he asked point blank.

I grinned into his round yellow face and led my ace.

"Why don't you ask the girl?"

His face showed nothing, but I imagined that his fat body stiffened a little within its fashionable British clothing. That encouraged me, and I went on with my little lie that was meant to stir things up.

"Haven't you rapped to it," I asked, "that they were fixing up to ditch you?"

"You dirty liar!" the girl screamed, and took a step toward me.

Tai halted her with an imperative gesture. He stared through her with his opaque black eyes, and as he stared the blood slid out of his face. She had this fat yellow man on her string, right enough, but he wasn't exactly a harmless toy.

"So that's how it is?" he said slowly, to no one in particular. Then to me: "Where did they put the bonds?"

The girl went close to him and her words came tumbling over each other: "Here's the truth of it, Tai, so help me God! I switched the stuff myself. Hook wasn't in it. I was going to run out on both of you. I stuck them under the couch downstairs, but they're not there now. That's the God's truth!"

He was eager to believe her, and her words had the ring of truth to them. And I knew that – in love with her as he was

– he'd more readily forgive her treachery with the bonds than he would forgive her for planning to run off with Hook; so I made haste to stir things up again.

"Part of that is right enough," I said. "She did stick the bonds under the couch – but Hook was in on it. They fixed it up between them while you were upstairs. He was to pick a fight with you, and during the argument she was to make the switch, and that is exactly what they did."

I had him! As she wheeled savagely toward me, he stuck the muzzle of an automatic in her side – a smart jab that checked the angry words she was hurling at me.

"I'll take your guns, Elvira," he said, and took them.

"Where are the bonds now?" he asked me.

I grinned. "I'm not with you, Tai. I'm against you."

"I don't like violence," he said slowly, "and I believe you are a sensible person. Let us traffic, my friend."

"You name it," I suggested.

"Gladly! As a basis for our bargaining, we will stipulate that you have hidden the bonds where they cannot be found by anyone else; and that I have you completely in my power, as the shilling shockers used to have it."

"Reasonable enough," I said; "go on."

"The situation, then, is what gamblers call a stand-off. Neither of us has the advantage. As a detective, you want us; but we have you. As thieves, we want the bonds; but you have them. I offer you the girl in exchange for the bonds, and that seems to me an equitable offer. It will give me the bonds and a chance to get away. It will give you no small degree of success in your task as a detective. Hook is dead. You will have the girl. All that will remain is to find me and the bonds again – by no means a hopeless task. You will have turned a defeat into half a victory, with an excellent chance to make it a complete one."

"How do I know that you'll give me the girl?"

He shrugged. "Naturally, there can be no guarantee. But,

knowing that she planned to desert me for the swine who lies dead below, you can't imagine that my feelings for her are the most friendly. Too, if I take her with me, she will want a share in the loot."

I turned the lay-out over in my mind.

"This is the way it looks to me," I told him at last. "You aren't a killer. I'll come through alive no matter what happens. All right, why should I swap? You and the girl will be easier to find again than the bonds, and they are the most important part of the job anyway. I'll hold on to them, and take my chances on finding you folks again. Yes, I'm playing it safe."

"No, I'm not a killer," he said, very softly; and he smiled the first smile I had seen on his face. It wasn't a pleasant smile: and there was something in it that made you want to shudder. "But I am other things, perhaps, of which you haven't thought. But this talking is to no purpose. Elvira!"

The girl came obediently forward.

"You will find sheets in one of the bureau drawers," he told her. "Tear one or two of them into strips strong enough to tie up our friend securely."

The girl went to the bureau. I wrinkled my head, trying to find a not too disagreeable answer to the question in my mind. The answer that came first wasn't nice: *torture*.

Then a faint sound brought us all into tense motionlessness.

The room we were in had two doors: one leading into the hall, the other into another bedroom. It was through the hall door that the faint sound had come – the sound of creeping feet.

Swiftly, silently, Tai moved backward to a position from which he could watch the hall door without losing sight of the girl and me – and the gun poised like a live thing in his fat hand was all the warning we needed to make no noise.

The faint sound again, just outside the door.

The gun in Tai's hand seemed to quiver with eagerness.

Through the other door – the door that gave to the next

room – popped Mrs. Quarre, an enormous cocked revolver in her thin hand.

"Let go it, you nasty heathen," she screeched.

Tai dropped his pistol before he turned to face her, and he held his hands up high – all of which was very wise.

Thomas Quarre came through the hall door then; he also held a cocked revolver – the mate of his wife's – though, in front of his bulk, his didn't look so enormously large.

I looked at the old woman again, and found little of the friendly fragile one who had poured tea and chatted about the neighbors. This was a witch if there ever was one – a witch of the blackest, most malignant sort. Her little faded eyes were sharp with ferocity, her withered lips were taut in a wolfish snarl, and her thin body fairly quivered with hate.

"I knew it," she was shrilling. "I told Tom as soon as we got far enough away to think things over. I knew it was a frame-up! I knew this supposed detective was a pal of yours! I knew it was just a scheme to beat Thomas and me out of our shares! Well, I'll show you, you yellow monkey! Where are them bonds? Where are they?"

The Chinese had recovered his poise, if he had ever lost it.

"Our stout friend can tell you perhaps," he said. "I was about to extract the information from him when you so – ah – dramatically arrived."

"Thomas, for goodness sakes don't stand there dreaming," she snapped at her husband, who to all appearances was still the same mild old man who had given me an excellent cigar. "Tie up this Chinaman! I don't trust him an inch, and I won't feel easy until he's tied up."

I got up from my seat on the side of the bed, and moved cautiously to a spot that I thought would be out of the line of fire if the thing I expected happened.

Tai had dropped the gun that had been in his hand, but he hadn't been searched. The Chinese are a thorough people; if one of them carries a gun at all, he usually carries two or three or more. One gun had been taken from Tai, and if they tried to truss him up without frisking him, there was likely to be fireworks. So I moved to one side.

Fat Thomas Quarre went phlegmatically up to the Chinese to carry out his wife's orders – and bungled the job perfectly.

He put his bulk between Tai and the old woman's gun.

Tai's hands moved. An automatic was in each.

Once more Tai ran true to racial form. When a Chinese shoots he keeps on until his gun is empty.

When I yanked Tai over backward by his fat throat, and slammed him to the floor, his guns were still barking metal; and they clicked empty as I got a knee on one of his arms. I didn't take any chances. I worked on his throat until his eyes and tongue told me that he was out of things for a while. Then I looked around.

Thomas Quarre was against the bed, plainly dead, with three round holes in his starched white vest.

Across the room, Mrs. Quarre lay on her back. Her clothes had somehow settled in place around her fragile body, and death had given her once more the gentle friendly look she had worn when I first saw her.

The red-haired girl Elvira was gone.

Presently Tai stirred, and after taking another gun from his clothes, I helped him sit up. He stroked his bruised throat with one fat hand and looked coolly around the room.

"Where's Elvira?" he asked.

"Got away – for the time being."

He shrugged. "Well, you can call it a decidedly successful operation. The Quarres and Hook dead; the bonds and I in your hands."

"Not so bad," I admitted, "but will you do me a favor?"

"If I may."

"Tell me what the hell this is all about!"

"All about?" he asked.

"Exactly! From what you people have let me overhear,

I gather that you pulled some sort of job in Los Angeles that netted you a hundred-thousand-dollars' worth of bonds; but I can't remember any recent job of that size down there."

"Why, that's preposterous!" he said with what, for him, was almost wild-eyed amazement. "Preposterous! Of course you know all about it!"

"I do not! I was trying to find a young fellow named Fisher who left his Tacoma home in anger a week or two ago. His father wants him found on the quiet, so that he can come down and try to talk him into going home again. I was told that I might find Fisher in this block of Turk Street, and that's what brought me here."

He didn't believe me. He never believed me. He went to the gallows thinking me a liar.

When I got out into the street again (and Turk Street was a lovely place when I came free into it after my evening in that house!) I bought a newspaper that told me most of what I wanted to know.

A boy of twenty – a messenger in the employ of a Los Angeles stock and bond house – had disappeared two days before, while on his way to a bank with a wad of bonds. That same night this boy and a slender girl with bobbed red hair had registered at a hotel in Fresno as *J. M. Riordan and wife.* The next morning the boy had been found in his room – murdered. The girl was gone. The bonds were gone.

That much the paper told me. During the next few days, digging up a little here and a little there, I succeeded in piecing together most of the story.

The Chinese – whose full name was Tai Choon Tau – had been the brains of the mob. Their game had been a variation of the always-reliable badger game. Tai would pick out some youth who was messenger or runner for a banker or broker – one who carried either cash or negotiable securities in large quantities.

The girl Elvira would then *make* this lad, get him all fussed up over her – which shouldn't have been very hard for her – and then lead him gently around to running away with her and whatever he could grab in the way of his employer's bonds or currency.

Wherever they spent the first night of their flight, there Hook would appear – foaming at the mouth and loaded for bear. The girl would plead and tear her hair and so forth, trying to keep Hook – in his rôle of irate husband – from butchering the youth. Finally she would succeed, and in the end the youth would find himself without either girl or the fruits of his thievery.

Sometimes he had surrendered to the police. Two we found had committed suicide. The Los Angeles lad had been built of tougher stuff than the others. He had put up a fight, and Hook had had to kill him. You can measure the girl's skill in her end of the game by the fact that not one of the half dozen youths who had been trimmed had said the least thing to implicate her; and some of them had gone to great trouble to keep her out of it.

The house in Turk Street had been the mob's retreat, and, that it might be always a safe one, they had not worked their game in San Francisco. Hook and the girl were supposed by the neighbors to be the Quarres' son and daughter – and Tai was the Chinese cook. The Quarres' benign and respectable appearances had also come in handy when the mob had securities to be disposed of.

The Chinese went to the gallows. We threw out the widest and finest-meshed of dragnets for the red-haired girl; and we turned up girls with bobbed red hair by the scores. But the girl Elvira was not among them.

I promised myself that some day . . .

THE GIRL WITH THE SILVER EYES

A BELL JANGLED me into wakefulness. I rolled to the edge of my bed and reached for the telephone. The neat voice of the Old Man – the Continental Detective Agency's San Francisco manager – came to my ears:

"Sorry to disturb you, but you'll have to go up to the Glenton Apartments on Leavenworth Street. A man named Burke Pangburn, who lives there, phoned me a few minutes ago asking to have someone sent up to see him at once. He seemed rather excited. Will you take care of it? See what he wants." I said I would and, yawning, stretching and cursing Pangburn – whoever he was – got my fat body out of pajamas and into street clothes.

The man who had disturbed my Sunday morning sleep – I found when I reached the Glenton – was a slim, white-faced person of about twenty-five, with big brown eyes that were red-rimmed just now from either sleeplessness or crying, or both. His long brown hair was rumpled when he opened the door to admit me; and he wore a mauve dressing-robe spotted with big jade parrots over wine-colored silk pajamas.

The room into which he led me resembled an auctioneer's establishment just before the sale – or maybe one of these alley tea rooms. Fat blue vases, crooked red vases, lanky yellow vases, vases of various shapes and colors; marble statuettes, ebony statuettes, statuettes of any material; lanterns, lamps and candlesticks; draperies, hangings and rugs of all sorts; odds and ends of furniture that were all somehow queerly designed; peculiar pictures hung here and there in unexpected places. A hard room to feel comfortable in.

"My fiancée," he began immediately in a high-pitched voice that was within a notch of hysteria, "has disappeared! Something has happened to her! Foul play of some horrible sort! I want you to find her – to save her from this terrible thing that . . ."

I followed him this far and then gave it up. A jumble of words came out of his mouth – "spirited away . . . mysterious something . . . lured into a trap" – but they were too disconnected for me to make anything out of them. So I stopped trying to understand him, and waited for him to babble himself empty of words.

I have heard ordinarily reasonable men, under stress of excitement, run on even more crazily than this wild-eyed youth; but his dress – the parroted robe and gay pajamas – and his surroundings – this deliriously furnished room – gave him too theatrical a setting; made his words sound utterly unreal.

He himself, when normal, should have been a rather nice-looking lad: his features were well spaced and, though his mouth and chin were a little uncertain, his broad forehead was good. But standing there listening to the occasional melodramatic phrase that I could pick out of the jumbled noises he was throwing at me, I thought that instead of parrots on his robe he should have had cuckoos.

Presently he ran out of language and was holding his long, thin hands out to me in an appealing gesture, saying:

"Will you?" over and over. "Will you? Will you?"

I nodded soothingly, and noticed that tears were on his thin cheeks.

"Suppose we begin at the beginning," I suggested, sitting down carefully on a carved bench affair that didn't look any too strong.

"Yes! Yes!" He was standing legs apart in front of me, running his fingers through his hair. "The beginning. I had a letter from her every day until –"

"That's not the beginning," I objected. "Who is she? What is she?"

"She's Jeanne Delano!" he exclaimed in surprise at my ignorance. "And she is my fiancée. And now she is gone, and I know that –"

The phrases "*victim of foul play,*" "*into a trap*" and so on began to flow hysterically out again.

Finally I got him quieted down and, sandwiched in between occasional emotional outbursts, got a story out of him that amounted to this:

This Burke Pangburn was a poet. About two months before, he had received a note from a Jeanne Delano – forwarded from his publishers – praising his latest book of rhymes. Jeanne Delano happened to live in San Francisco, too, though she hadn't known that he did. He had answered her note, and had received another. After a little of this they met. If she really was as beautiful as he claimed, then he wasn't to be blamed for falling in love with her. But whether or not she was really beautiful, he thought she was, and he had fallen hard.

This Delano girl had been living in San Francisco for only a little while, and when the poet met her she was living alone in an Ashbury Avenue apartment. He did not know where she came from or anything about her former life. He suspected – from certain indefinite suggestions and peculiarities of conduct which he couldn't put in words – that there was a cloud of some sort hanging over the girl; that neither her past nor her present were free from difficulties. But he hadn't the least idea what those difficulties might be. He hadn't cared. He knew absolutely nothing about her, except that she was beautiful, and he loved her, and she had promised to marry him. Then, on the third of the month – exactly twenty-one days before this Sunday morning – the girl had suddenly left San Francisco. He had received a note from her, by messenger.

This note, which he showed me after I had insisted point blank on seeing it, read:

> Burkelove:
>
> Have just received a wire, and must go East on next train. Tried to get you on the phone, but couldn't. Will write you as soon as I know what my address will be. If anything. [These two words were erased and could be read only with great difficulty.] Love me until I'm back with you forever.
>
> Your JEANNE

Nine days later he had received another letter from her, from Baltimore, Maryland. This one, which I had a still harder time getting a look at, read:

> Dearest Poet:
>
> It seems like two years since I have seen you, and I have a fear that it's going to be between one and two months before I see you again.
>
> I can't tell you now, beloved, about what brought me here. There are things that can't be written. But as soon as I'm back with you, I shall tell you the whole wretched story.
>
> If anything should happen – I mean to me – you'll go on loving me forever, won't you, beloved? But that's foolish. Nothing is going to happen. I'm just off the train, and tired from traveling.
>
> Tomorrow I shall write you a long, long letter to make up for this.
>
> My address here is 215 N. Stricker St. Please, Mister, at least one letter a day!
>
> Your own JEANNE

For nine days he had had a letter from her each day – with two on Monday to make up for the none on Sunday. And then her letters had stopped. And the daily letters he had sent to the address she gave – 215 N. Stricker Street – had begun to come back to him, marked "Not known." He had sent a telegram, and the telegraph company had informed him that its Baltimore office had been unable to find a Jeanne Delano at the North Stricker Street address.

For three days he had waited, expecting hourly to hear from the girl, and no word had come. Then he had bought a ticket for Baltimore.

"But," he wound up, "I was afraid to go. I know she's in some sort of trouble – I can feel that – but I'm a silly poet. I can't deal with mysteries. Either I would find nothing at all or, if by luck I did stumble on the right track, the probabilities are that I would only muddle things; add fresh complications, perhaps endanger her life still further. I can't go blundering at it in that fashion, without knowing whether I am helping or harming her. It's a task for an expert in that sort of thing. So I thought of your agency. You'll be careful, won't you? It may be – I don't know – that she won't want assistance. It may be that you can help her without her knowing anything about it. You are accustomed to that sort of thing; you can do it, can't you?"

I turned the job over and over in my mind before answering him. The two great bugaboos of a reputable detective agency are the persons who bring in a crooked plan or a piece of divorce work all dressed up in the garb of a legitimate operation, and the irresponsible person who is laboring under wild and fanciful delusions – who wants a dream run out.

This poet – sitting opposite me now twining his long, white fingers nervously – was, I thought, sincere; but I wasn't so sure of his sanity.

"Mr. Pangburn," I said after a while, "I'd like to handle this thing for you, but I'm not sure that I can. The Continental is rather strict, and, while I believe this thing is on the level, still I am only a hired man and have to go by the rules. Now if you could give us the endorsement of some firm or person of standing – a reputable lawyer, for instance, or any legally responsible party – we'd be glad to go ahead with the work. Otherwise, I am afraid –"

"But I know she's in danger!" he broke out. "I know that – And I can't be advertising her plight – airing her affairs – to everyone."

"I'm sorry, but I can't touch it unless you can give me some such endorsement." I stood up. "But you can find plenty of detective agencies that aren't so particular."

His mouth worked like a small boy's, and he caught his lower lip between his teeth. For a moment I thought he was going to burst into tears. But instead he said slowly: "I dare say you are right. Suppose I refer you to my brother-in-law, Roy Axford. Will his word be sufficient?"

"Yes."

Roy Axford – R. F. Axford – was a mining man who had a finger in at least half of the big business enterprises of the Pacific Coast; and his word on anything was commonly considered good enough for anybody.

"If you can get in touch with him now," I said, "and arrange for me to see him today, I can get started without much delay."

Pangburn crossed the room and dug a telephone out from among a heap of his ornaments. Within a minute or two he was talking to someone whom he called "Rita."

"Is Roy home? . . . Will he be home this afternoon? . . . No, you can give him a message for me, though. . . . Tell him I'm sending a gentleman up to see him this afternoon on a personal matter – personal from me – and that I'll be very grateful if he'll do what I want. . . . Yes. . . . You'll find out, Rita. . . . It isn't a thing to talk about over the phone. . . . Yes, thanks!"

He pushed the telephone back into its hiding place and turned to me.

"He'll be at home until two o'clock. Tell him what I told you and if he seems doubtful, have him call me up. You'll have to tell him the whole thing; he doesn't know anything at all about Miss Delano."

"All right. Before I go, I want a description of her."

"She's beautiful! The most beautiful woman in the world!"

That would look nice on a reward circular.

"That isn't exactly what I want," I told him. "How old is she?"

"Twenty-two."

"Height?"

"About five feet eight inches, or possibly nine."

"Slender, medium or plump?"

"She's inclined toward slenderness, but she –"

There was a note of enthusiasm in his voice that made me fear he was about to make a speech, so I cut him off with another question.

"What color hair?"

"Brown – so dark it's almost black – and it's soft and thick and –"

"Yes, yes. Long or bobbed?"

"Long and thick and –"

"What color eyes?"

"You've seen shadows on polished silver when –"

I wrote down *gray eyes* and hurried on with the interrogation.

"Complexion?"

"Perfect!"

"Uh-huh. But is it light, or dark, or florid, or sallow, or what?"

"Fair."

"Face oval, or square, or long and thin, or what shape?"

"Oval."

"What shaped nose? Large, small, turned-up –"

"Small and regular!" There was a touch of indignation in his voice.

"How did she dress? Fashionably? Did she favor bright or quiet colors?"

"Beaut –" And then as I opened my mouth to head him

off he came down to earth with: "Very quietly – usually dark blues and browns."

"What jewelry did she wear?"

"I've never seen her wear any."

"Any scars, or moles?" The horrified look on his white face urged me on to give him a full shot. "Or warts, or deformities that you know?"

He was speechless, but he managed to shake his head.

"Have you a photograph of her?"

"Yes, I'll show you."

He bounded to his feet, wound his way through the room's excessive furnishings and out through a curtained doorway. Immediately he was back with a large photograph in a carved ivory frame. It was one of these artistic photographs – a thing of shadows and hazy outlines – not much good for identification purposes. She was beautiful – right enough – but that meant nothing; that's the purpose of an artistic photograph.

"This the only one you have?"

"Yes."

"I'll have to borrow it, but I'll get it back to you as soon as I have my copies made."

"No! No!" he protested against having his lady love's face given to a lot of gumshoes. "That would be terrible!"

I finally got it, but it cost me more words than I like to waste on an incidental.

"I want to borrow a couple of her letters, or something in her writing, too," I said.

"For what?"

"To have photostatic copies made. Handwriting specimens come in handy – give you something to go over hotel registers with. Then, even if going under fictitious names, people now and then write notes and make memorandums."

We had another battle, out of which I came with three envelopes and two meaningless sheets of paper, all bearing the girl's angular writing.

"She have much money?" I asked, when the disputed photograph and handwriting specimens were safely tucked away in my pocket.

"I don't know. It's not the sort of thing that one would pry into. She wasn't poor; that is, she didn't have to practice any petty economies; but I haven't the faintest idea either as to the amount of her income or its source. She had an account at the Golden Gate Trust Company, but naturally I don't know anything about its size."

"Many friends here?"

"That's another thing I don't know. I think she knew a few people here, but I don't know who they were. You see, when we were together we never talked about anything but ourselves. There was nothing we were interested in but each other. We were simply –"

"Can't you even make a guess at where she came from, who she was?"

"No. Those things didn't matter to me. She was Jeanne Delano, and that was enough for me."

"Did you and she ever have any financial interests in common? I mean, was there ever any transaction in money or other valuables in which both of you were interested?"

What I meant, of course, was had she got into him for a loan, or had she sold him something, or got money out of him in any other way.

He jumped to his feet, and his face went fog-gray. Then he sat down – slumped down – and blushed scarlet.

"Pardon me," he said thickly. "You didn't know her, and of course you must look at the thing from all angles. No, there was nothing like that. I'm afraid you are going to waste time if you are going to work on the theory that she was an adventuress. There was nothing like that! She was a girl with something terrible hanging over her; something that called her to Baltimore suddenly; something that has taken her away from me. Money? What could money have to do with it? I love her!"

*

R. F. Axford received me in an office-like room in his Russian Hill residence: a big blond man, whose forty-eight or -nine years had not blurred the outlines of an athlete's body. A big, full-blooded man with the manner of one whose self-confidence is complete and not altogether unjustified. "What's our Burke been up to now?" he asked amusedly when I told him who I was. His voice was a pleasant vibrant bass.

I didn't give him all the details.

"He was engaged to marry a Jeanne Delano, who went East about three weeks ago and then suddenly disappeared. He knows very little about her; thinks something has happened to her; and wants her found."

"Again?" His shrewd blue eyes twinkled. "And to a Jeanne this time! She's the fifth within a year, to my knowledge, and no doubt I missed one or two while I was in Hawaii. But where do I come in?"

"I asked him for responsible endorsement. I think he's all right, but he isn't, in the strictest sense, a responsible person. He referred me to you."

"You're right about his not being, in the strictest sense, a responsible person." The big man screwed up his eyes and mouth in thought for a moment. Then: "Do you think that something has really happened to the girl? Or is Burke imagining things?"

"I don't know. I thought it was a dream at first. But in a couple of her letters there are hints that something was wrong."

"You might go ahead and find her then," Axford said. "I don't suppose any harm will come from letting him have his Jeanne back. It will at least give him something to think about for a while."

"I have your word for it then, Mr. Axford, that there will be no scandal or anything of the sort connected with the affair?"

"Assuredly! Burke is all right, you know. It's simply that he is spoiled. He has been in rather delicate health all his life; and then he has an income that suffices to keep him modestly, with a little over to bring out books of verse and buy doodaws for his rooms. He takes himself a little too solemnly – is too much the poet – but he's sound at bottom."

"I'll go ahead with it, then," I said, getting up. "By the way, the girl has an account at the Golden Gate Trust Company, and I'd like to find out as much about it as possible, especially where her money came from. Clement, the cashier, is a model of caution when it comes to giving out information about depositors. If you could put in a word for me it would make my way smoother."

"Be glad to."

He wrote a couple of lines across the back of a card and gave it to me; and, promising to call on him if I needed further assistance, I left.

I telephoned Pangburn that his brother-in-law had given the job his approval. I sent a wire to the agency's Baltimore branch, giving what information I had. Then I went up to Ashbury Avenue, to the apartment house in which the girl had lived.

The manager – an immense Mrs. Clute in rustling black – knew little, if any, more about the girl than Pangburn. The girl had lived there for two and a half months; she had had occasional callers, but Pangburn was the only one that the manager could describe to me. The girl had given up the apartment on the third of the month, saying that she had been called East, and she had asked the manager to hold her mail until she sent her new address. Ten days later Mrs. Clute had received a card from the girl instructing her to forward her mail to 215 N. Stricker Street, Baltimore, Maryland. There had been no mail to forward.

The single thing of importance that I learned at the apartment house was that the girl's two trunks had been taken away by a green transfer truck. Green was the color used by one of the city's largest transfer companies.

I went then to the office of this transfer company, and found a friendly clerk on duty. (A detective, if he is wise, takes pains to make and keep as many friends as possible among transfer company, express company and railroad employees.) I left the office with a memorandum of the transfer company's check numbers and the Ferry baggageroom to which the two trunks had been taken.

At the Ferry Building, with this information, it didn't take me many minutes to learn that the trunks had been checked to Baltimore. I sent another wire to the Baltimore branch, giving the railroad check numbers.

Sunday was well into night by now, so I knocked off and went home.

Half an hour before the Golden Gate Trust Company opened for business the next morning I was inside, talking to Clement, the cashier. All the traditional caution and conservatism of bankers rolled together would but be one-two-three to the amount usually displayed by this plump, white-haired old man. But one look at Axford's card, with "*Please give the bearer all possible assistance*" inked across the back of it, made Clement even eager to help me.

"You have, or have had, an account here in the name of Jeanne Delano," I said. "I'd like to know as much as possible about it: to whom she drew checks, and to what amounts; but especially all you can tell me about where her money came from."

He stabbed one of the pearl buttons on his desk with a pink finger, and a lad with polished yellow hair oozed silently into the room. The cashier scribbled with a pencil on a piece of paper and gave it to the noiseless youth, who disappeared. Presently he was back, laying a handful of papers on the cashier's desk.

Clement looked through the papers and then up at me.

"Miss Delano was introduced here by Mr. Burke Pangburn on the sixth of last month, and opened an account with eight hundred and fifty dollars in cash. She made the following deposits after that: four hundred dollars on the tenth; two hundred and fifty on the twenty-first; three hundred on the twenty-sixth; two hundred on the thirtieth; and twenty thousand dollars on the second of this month. All of these deposits except the last were made with cash. The last one was a check."

He handed it to me: a Golden Gate Trust Company check.

Pay to the order of Jeanne Delano, twenty thousand dollars.
(Signed) BURKE PANGBURN

It was dated the second of the month.

"Burke Pangburn!" I exclaimed, a little stupidly. "Was it usual for him to draw checks to that amount?"

"I think not. But we shall see."

He stabbed the pearl button again, ran his pencil across another slip of paper, and the youth with the polished yellow hair made a noiseless entrance, exit, entrance, and exit. The cashier looked through the fresh batch of papers that had been brought to him.

"On the first of the month, Mr. Pangburn deposited twenty thousand dollars – a check against Mr. Axford's account here."

"Now how about Miss Delano's withdrawals?" I asked.

He picked up the papers that had to do with her account again.

"Her statement and canceled checks for last month haven't been delivered to her yet. Everything is here. A check for eighty-five dollars to the order of H. K. Clute on the fifteenth of last month; one 'to cash' for three hundred dollars on the twentieth, and another of the same kind for one hundred dollars on the twenty-fifth. Both of these checks were apparently cashed here by her. On the third of this month she closed out her account, with a check to her own order for twenty-one thousand, five hundred and fifteen dollars."

"And that check?"

"Was cashed here by her."

I lighted a cigarette, and let these figures drift around in my head. None of them – except those that were fixed to Pangburn's and Axford's signatures – seemed to be of any value to me. The Clute check – the only one the girl had drawn in anyone else's favor – had almost certainly been for rent.

"This is the way of it," I summed up aloud. "On the first of the month, Pangburn deposited Axford's check for twenty thousand dollars. The next day he gave a check to that amount to Miss Delano, which she deposited. On the following day she closed her account, taking between twenty-one and twenty-two thousand dollars in currency."

"Exactly," the cashier said.

Before going up to the Glenton Apartments to find out why Pangburn hadn't come clean with me about the twenty thousand dollars, I dropped in at the agency, to see if any word had come from Baltimore. One of the clerks had just finished decoding a telegram. It read:

> Baggage arrived Mt. Royal Station on eighth. Taken away same day. Unable to trace. 215 North Stricker Street is Baltimore Orphan Asylum. Girl not known there. Continuing our efforts to find her.

The Old Man came in from luncheon as I was leaving. I went back into his office with him for a couple of minutes.

"Did you see Pangburn?" he asked.

"Yes. I'm working on his job now – but I think it's a bust."

"What is it?"

"Pangburn is R. F. Axford's brother-in-law. He met a girl a couple of months ago, and fell for her. She sizes up as a worker. He doesn't know anything about her. The first of the month he got twenty thousand dollars from his brother-in-law and passed it over to the girl. She blew, telling him she had been called to Baltimore, and giving him a phony address that turns out to be an orphan asylum. She sent her trunks to Baltimore, and sent him some letters from there – but a friend could have taken care of the baggage and could have remailed her letters for her. Of course, she would have needed a ticket to check the trunks on, but in a twenty-thousand-dollar game that would be a small expense. Pangburn held out on me; he didn't tell me a word about the money. Ashamed of being easy pickings, I reckon. I'm going to the bat with him on it now."

The Old Man smiled his mild smile that might mean anything, and I left.

Ten minutes of ringing Pangburn's bell brought no answer. The elevator boy told me he thought Pangburn hadn't been in all night. I put a note in his box and went down to the railroad company's offices, where I arranged to be notified if an unused Baltimore–San Francisco ticket was turned in for redemption.

That done, I went up to the *Chronicle* office and searched the files for weather conditions during the past month, making a memorandum of four dates upon which it had rained steadily day and night. I carried my memorandum to the offices of the three largest taxicab companies.

That was a trick that had worked well for me before. The girl's apartment was some distance from the street car line, and I was counting upon her having gone out – or having had a caller – on one of those rainy dates. In either case, it was very likely that she – or her caller – had left in a taxi in preference to walking through the rain to the car line. The taxicab companies' daily records would show any calls from her address, and the fares' destinations.

The ideal trick, of course, would have been to have the records searched for the full extent of the girl's occupancy of the apartment; but no taxicab company would stand for having that amount of work thrust upon them, unless it was a matter of life and death. It was difficult enough for me to persuade them to turn clerks loose on the four days I had selected.

I called up Pangburn again after I left that last taxicab office, but he was not at home. I called up Axford's residence, thinking that the poet might have spent the night there, but was told that he had not.

Late that afternoon I got my copies of the girl's photograph and handwriting, and put one of each in the mail for Baltimore. Then I went around to the three taxicab companies' offices and got my reports. Two of them had nothing for me. The third's records showed two calls from the girl's apartment.

On one rainy afternoon a taxi had been called, and one passenger had been taken to the Glenton Apartments. That passenger, obviously, was either the girl or Pangburn. At half-past twelve one night another call had come in, and this passenger had been taken to the Marquis Hotel.

The driver who had answered this second call remembered it indistinctly when I questioned him, but he thought that his fare had been a man. I let the matter rest there for the time; the Marquis isn't a large hotel as San Francisco hotels go, but it is too large to make canvassing its guests for the one I wanted practicable.

I spent the evening trying to reach Pangburn, with no success. At eleven o'clock I called up Axford, and asked him if he had any idea where I might find his brother-in-law.

"Haven't seen him for several days," the millionaire said. "He was supposed to come up for dinner last night, but didn't. My wife tried to reach him by phone a couple times today, but couldn't."

The next morning I called Pangburn's apartment before I got out of bed, and got no answer.

Then I telephoned Axford and made an appointment for ten o'clock at his office.

"I don't know what he's up to now," Axford said good-naturedly when I told him that Pangburn had apparently been away from his apartment since Sunday, "and I suppose there's small chance of guessing. Our Burke is nothing if not erratic. How are you progressing with your search for the damsel in distress?"

"Far enough to convince me that she isn't in a whole lot of distress. She got twenty thousand dollars from your brother-in-law the day before she vanished."

"Twenty thousand dollars from Burke? She must be a wonderful girl! But wherever did he get that much money?"

"From you."

Axford's muscular body straightened in his chair. "From me?"

"Yes – your check."

"He did not."

There was nothing argumentative in his voice; it simply stated a fact.

"You didn't give him a check for twenty thousand dollars on the first of the month?"

"No."

"Then," I suggested, "perhaps we'd better take a run over to the Golden Gate Trust Company."

Ten minutes later we were in Clement's office.

"I'd like to see my canceled checks," Axford told the cashier.

The youth with the polished yellow hair brought them in presently – a thick wad of them – and Axford ran rapidly through them until he found the one he wanted. He studied that one for a long while, and when he looked up at me he shook his head slowly but with finality.

"I've never seen it before."

Clement mopped his head with a white handkerchief, and

tried to pretend that he wasn't burning up with curiosity and fears that his bank had been gypped.

The millionaire turned the check over and looked at the endorsement.

"Deposited by Burke," he said in the voice of one who talks while he thinks of something entirely different, "on the first."

"Could we talk to the teller who took in the twenty-thousand-dollar check that Miss Delano deposited?" I asked Clement.

He pressed one of his desk's pearl buttons with a fumbling pink finger, and in a minute or two a little sallow man with a hairless head came in.

"Do you remember taking a check for twenty thousand from Miss Jeanne Delano a few weeks ago?" I asked him.

"Yes, sir! Yes, sir! Perfectly."

"Just what do you remember about it?"

"Well, sir, Miss Delano came to my window with Mr. Burke Pangburn. It was his check. I thought it was a large check for him to be drawing, but the book-keepers said he had enough money in his account to cover it. They stood there – Miss Delano and Mr. Pangburn – talking and laughing while I entered the deposit in her book, and then they left, and that was all."

"This check," Axford said slowly, after the teller had gone back to his cage, "is a forgery. But I shall make it good, of course. That ends the matter, Mr. Clement, and there must be no more to-do about it."

"Certainly, Mr. Axford. Certainly."

Clement was all enormously relieved smiles and head-noddings, with this twenty-thousand-dollar load lifted from his bank's shoulders.

Axford and I left the bank then and got into his coupé, in which we had come from his office. But he did not immediately start the engine. He sat for a while staring at the traffic of Montgomery Street with unseeing eyes.

"I want you to find Burke," he said presently, and there was no emotion of any sort in his bass voice. "I want you to find him without risking the least whisper of scandal. If my wife knew of all this – She mustn't know. She thinks her brother is a choice morsel. I want you to find him for me. The girl doesn't matter any more, but I suppose that where you find one you will find the other. I'm not interested in the money, and I don't want you to make any special attempt to recover that; it could hardly be done, I'm afraid, without publicity. I want you to find Burke before he does something else."

"If you want to avoid the wrong kind of publicity," I said, "your best bet is to spread the right kind first. Let's advertise him as missing, fill the papers up with his pictures and so forth. They'll play him up strong. He's your brother-in-law and he's a poet. We can say that he has been ill – you told me that he had been in delicate health all his life – and that we fear he has dropped dead somewhere or is suffering under some mental derangement. There will be no necessity of mentioning the girl or the money, and our explanation may keep people – especially your wife – from guessing the truth when the fact that he is missing leaks out. It's bound to leak out somehow."

He didn't like my idea at first, but I finally won him over.

We went up to Pangburn's apartment then, easily securing admittance on Axford's explanation that we had an engagement with him and would wait there for him. I went through the rooms inch by inch, prying into each hole and hollow and crack; reading everything that was written anywhere, even down to his manuscripts; and I found nothing that threw any light on his disappearance.

I helped myself to his photographs – pocketing five of the dozen or more that were there. Axford did not think that any of the poet's bags or trunks were missing from the pack-room. I did not find his Golden Gate Trust Company deposit book.

I spent the rest of the day loading the newspapers up with

what we wished them to have; and they gave my ex-client one grand spread: first-page stuff with photographs and all possible trimmings. Anyone in San Francisco who didn't know that Burke Pangburn – brother-in-law of R. F. Axford and author of *Sandpatches and Other Verse* – was missing, either couldn't read or wouldn't.

This advertising brought results. By the following morning, reports were rolling in from all directions, from dozens of people who had seen the missing poet in dozens of places. A few of these reports looked promising – or at least possible – but the majority were ridiculous on their faces.

I came back to the agency from running out one that had – until run out – looked good, to find a note asking me to call up Axford.

"Can you come down to my office now?" he asked when I got him on the wire.

There was a lad of twenty-one or -two with Axford when I was ushered into his office: a narrow-chested, dandified lad of the sporting clerk type.

"This is Mr. Fall, one of my employees," Axford told me. "He says he saw Burke Sunday night."

"Where?" I asked Fall.

"Going into a roadhouse near Halfmoon Bay."

"Sure it was him?"

"Absolutely! I've seen him come in here to Mr. Axford's office often enough to know him. It was him all right."

"How'd you come to see him?"

"I was coming up from further down the shore with some friends, and we stopped in at the roadhouse to get something to eat. As we were leaving, a car drove up and Mr. Pangburn and a girl or woman – I didn't notice her particularly – got out and went inside. I didn't think anything of it until I saw in the paper last night that he hadn't been seen since Sunday. So then I thought to myself that –"

"What roadhouse was this?" I cut in.

"The White Shack."

"About what time?"

"Somewhere between eleven-thirty and midnight, I guess."

"He see you?"

"No. I was already in our car when he drove up."

"What did the woman look like?"

"I don't know. I didn't see her face, and I can't remember how she was dressed or even if she was short or tall."

That was all Fall could tell me. We shooed him out of the office, and I used Axford's telephone to call up "Wop" Healey's dive in North Beach and leave word that when "Porky" Grout came in he was to call up "Jack." That was a standing arrangement by which I got word to Porky whenever I wanted to see him, without giving anybody a chance to tumble to the connection between us.

"Know the White Shack?" I asked Axford, when I was through.

"I know where it is, but I don't know anything about it."

"Well, it's a tough hole. Run by 'Tin-Star' Joplin, an ex-yegg who invested his winnings in the place when Prohibition made the roadhouse game good. He makes more money now than he ever heard of in his piking safe-ripping days. Retailing liquor is a side-line with him; his real profit comes from acting as a relay station for the booze that comes through Halfmoon Bay for points beyond; and the dope is that half the booze put ashore by the Pacific rum fleet is put ashore in Halfmoon Bay.

"The White Shack is a tough hole, and it's no place for your brother-in-law to be hanging around. I can't go down there myself without stirring things up; Joplin and I are old friends. But I've got a man I can put in there for a few nights. Pangburn may be a regular visitor, or he may even be staying there. He wouldn't be the first one Joplin had ever let hide out there. I'll put this man of mine in the place for a week, anyway, and see what he can find."

"It's all in your hands," Axford said.

From Axford's office I went straight to my rooms, left the outer door unlocked, and sat down to wait for Porky Grout. I had waited an hour and a half when he pushed the door open and came in. " 'Lo! How's tricks?" He swaggered to a chair, leaned back in it, put his feet on the table and reached for a pack of cigarettes that lay there.

That was Porky Grout. A pasty-faced man in his thirties, neither large nor small, always dressed flashily – even if sometimes dirtily – and trying to hide an enormous cowardice behind a swaggering carriage, a blustering habit of speech, and an exaggerated pretense of self-assurance.

But I had known him for three years; so now I crossed the room and pushed his feet roughly off the table, almost sending him over backward.

"What's the idea?" He came to his feet, crouching and snarling. "Where do you get that stuff? Do you want a smack in the –"

I took a step toward him. He sprang away, across the room. "Aw, I didn't mean nothin'. I was only kiddin'!"

"Shut up and sit down," I advised him.

I had known this Porky Grout for three years, and had been using him for nearly that long, and I didn't know a single thing that could be said in his favor. He was a coward. He was a liar. He was a thief, and a hop-head. He was a traitor to his kind and, if not watched, to his employers. A nice bird to deal with! But detecting is a hard business, and you use whatever tools come to hand. This Porky was an effective tool if handled right, which meant keeping your hand on his throat all the time and checking up every piece of information he brought in.

His cowardice was – for my purpose – his greatest asset. It was notorious throughout the criminal Coast; and though nobody – crook or not – could possibly think him a man to be trusted, nevertheless he was not actually distrusted. Most of his fellows thought him too much the coward to be dangerous; they thought he would be afraid to betray them; afraid of the summary vengeance that crookdom visits upon the squealer. But they didn't take into account Porky's gift for convincing himself that he was a lion-hearted fellow, when no danger was near. So he went freely where he desired and where I sent him, and brought me otherwise unobtainable bits of information.

For nearly three years I had used him with considerable success, paying him well, and keeping him under my heel. *Informant* was the polite word that designated him in my reports; the underworld has even less lovely names than the common *stool-pigeon* to denote his kind.

"I have a job for you," I told him, now that he was seated again, with his feet on the floor. His loose mouth twitched up at the left corner, pushing that eye into a knowing squint. "I thought so." He always says something like that.

"I want you to go down to Halfmoon Bay and stick around Tin-Star Joplin's joint for a few nights. Here are two photos" – sliding one of Pangburn and one of the girl across the table. "Their names and descriptions are written on the backs. I want to know if either of them shows up down there, what they're doing, and where they're hanging out. It may be that Tin-Star is covering them up."

Porky was looking knowingly from one picture to the other. "I think I know this guy," he said out of the corner of his mouth that twitches. That's another thing about Porky. You can't mention a name or give a description that won't bring that same remark, even though you make them up.

"Here's some money." I slid some bills across the table. "If you're down there more than a couple of nights, I'll get some more to you. Keep in touch with me, either over this phone or the under-cover one at the office. And – remember this – lay off the stuff! If I come down there and find you all snowed up, I promise that I'll tip Joplin off to you."

He had finished counting the money by now – there wasn't

a whole lot to count – and he threw it contemptuously back on the table.

"Save that for newspapers," he sneered. "How am I goin' to get anywheres if I can't spend no money in the joint?"

"That's plenty for a couple of days' expenses; you'll probably knock back half of it. If you stay longer than a couple of days, I'll get more to you. And you get your pay when the job is done, and not before."

He shook his head and got up. "I'm tired of pikin' along with you. You can turn your own jobs. I'm through!"

"If you don't get down to Halfmoon Bay tonight, you *are* through," I assured him, letting him get out of the threat whatever he liked.

After a little while, of course, he took the money and left. The dispute over expense money was simply a preliminary that went with every job I sent him out on.

After Porky had cleared out, I leaned back in my chair and burned half a dozen Fatimas over the job. The girl had gone first with the twenty thousand dollars, and then the poet had gone; and both had gone, whether permanently or not, to the White Shack. On its face, the job was an obvious affair. The girl had given Pangburn the *work* to the extent of having him forge a check against his brother-in-law's account; and then, after various moves whose value I couldn't determine at the time, they had gone into hiding together.

There were two loose ends to be taken care of. One of them – the finding of the confederate who had mailed the letters to Pangburn and who had taken care of the girl's baggage – was in the Baltimore branch's hands. The other was: Who had ridden in the taxicab that I had traced from the girl's apartment to the Marquis Hotel?

That might not have any bearing upon the job, or it might. Suppose I could find a connection between the Marquis Hotel and the White Shack. That would make a completed chain of some sort. I searched the back of the telephone directory and found the roadhouse number. Then I went up to the Marquis Hotel. The girl on duty at the hotel switchboard, when I got there, was one with whom I had done business before. "Who's been calling Halfmoon Bay numbers?" I asked her.

"My God!" She leaned back in her chair and ran a pink hand gently over the front of her rigidly waved red hair. "I got enough to do without remembering every call that goes through. This ain't a boarding-house. We have more'n one call a week."

"You don't have many Halfmoon Bay calls," I insisted, leaning an elbow on the counter and letting a folded five-spot peep out between the fingers of one hand. "You ought to remember any you've had lately."

"I'll see," she sighed, as if willing to do her best on a hopeless task.

She ran through her tickets.

"Here's one – from room 522, a couple weeks ago."

"What number was called?"

"Halfmoon Bay 51."

That was the roadhouse number. I passed over the five-spot.

"Is 522 a permanent guest?"

"Yes. Mr. Kilcourse. He's been here three or four months."

"What is he?"

"I don't know. A perfect gentleman, if you ask me."

"That's nice. What does he look like?"

"He's a young man, but his hair is turning gray. He's dark and handsome. Looks like a movie actor."

"Bull Montana?" I asked, as I moved off toward the desk.

The key to 522 was in its place in the rack. I sat down where I could keep an eye on it. Perhaps an hour later a clerk took it out and gave it to a man who did look somewhat like an actor. He was a man of thirty or so, with dark skin, and dark hair that showed gray around the ears. He stood a good six feet of fashionably dressed slenderness.

Carrying the key, he disappeared into an elevator.

I called up the agency then and asked the Old Man to send Dick Foley over. Ten minutes later Dick arrived. He's a little shrimp of a Canadian – there isn't a hundred and ten pounds of him – who is the smoothest shadow I've ever seen, and I've seen most of them.

"I have a bird in here I want tailed," I told Dick. "His name is Kilcourse and he's in room 522. Stick around outside, and I'll give you the spot on him." I went back to the lobby and waited some more.

At eight o'clock Kilcourse came down and left the hotel. I went after him for half a block – far enough to turn him over to Dick – and then went home, so that I would be within reach of a telephone if Porky Grout tried to get in touch with me. No call came from him that night.

When I arrived at the agency the next morning, Dick was waiting for me. "What luck?" I asked.

"Damnedest!" The little Canadian talks like a telegram when his peace of mind is disturbed, and just now he was decidedly peevish. "Took me two blocks. Shook me. Only taxi in sight."

"Think he made you?"

"No. Wise head. Playing safe."

"Try him again, then. Better have a car handy, in case he tries the same trick again."

My telephone jingled as Dick was going out. It was Porky Grout, talking over the agency's unlisted line. "Turn up anything?" I asked.

"Plenty," he bragged.

"Good! Are you in town?"

"Yes."

"I'll meet you in my rooms in twenty minutes," I said.

The pasty-faced informant was fairly bloated with pride in himself when he came through the door I had left unlocked for him. His swagger was almost a cakewalk; and the side of his mouth that twitches was twisted into a knowing leer that would have fit a Solomon.

"I knocked it over for you, kid," he boasted. "Nothin' to it – for me! I went down there and talked to ever'body that knowed anything, seen ever'thing there was to see, and put the X-rays on the whole dump. I made a –"

"Uh-huh," I interrupted. "Congratulations and so forth. But just what did you turn up?"

"Now le'me tell you." He raised a dirty hand in a traffic-cop sort of gesture. "Don't crowd me. I'll give you all the dope."

"Sure," I said. "I know. You're great, and I'm lucky to have you to knock off my jobs for me, and all that! But is Pangburn down there?"

"I'm gettin' around to that. I went down there and –"

"Did you see Pangburn?"

"As I was sayin', I went down there and –"

"Porky," I said, "I don't give a damn what you did! Did you see Pangburn?"

"Yes. I seen him."

"Fine! Now what did you see?"

"He's camping down there with Tin-Star. Him and the broad that you give me a picture of are both there. She's been there a month. I didn't see her, but one of the waiters told me about her. I seen Pangburn myself. They don't show themselves much – stick back in Tin-Star's part of the joint – where he lives – most of the time. Pangburn's been there since Sunday. I went down there and –"

"Learn who the girl is? Or anything about what they're up to?"

"No. I went down there and –"

"All right! *Went down there* again tonight. Call me up as soon as you know positively Pangburn is there – that he hasn't gone out. Don't make any mistakes. I don't want to come down there and scare them up on a false alarm. Use the agency's under-cover line, and just tell whoever answers that you won't be in town until late. That'll mean that Pangburn is there; and it'll let you call up from Joplin's without giving the play away."

"I got to have more dough," he said, as he got up. "It costs –"

"I'll file your application," I promised. "Now beat it, and let me hear from you tonight, the minute you're sure Pangburn is there."

Then I went up to Axford's office. "I think I have a line on him," I told the millionaire. "I hope to have him where you can talk to him tonight. My man says he was at the White Shack last night, and is probably living there. If he's there tonight, I'll take you down, if you want."

"Why can't we go now?"

"No. The place is too dead in the daytime for my man to hang around without making himself conspicuous, and I don't want to take any chances on either you or me showing ourselves there until we're sure we're coming face to face with Pangburn."

"What do you want me to do then?"

"Have a fast car ready tonight, and be ready to start as soon as I get word to you."

"Righto. I'll be at home after five-thirty. Phone me as soon as you're ready to go, and I'll pick you up."

At nine-thirty that evening I was sitting beside Axford on the front seat of a powerfully engined foreign car, and we were roaring down a road that led to Halfmoon Bay. Porky's telephone call had come.

Neither of us talked much during that ride, and the imported monster under us made it a short ride. Axford sat comfortable and relaxed at the wheel, but I noticed for the first time that he had a rather heavy jaw.

The White Shack is a large building, square-built of imitation stone. It is set away back from the road, and is approached by two curving driveways, which, together, make a semi-circle whose diameter is the public road. The center of this semi-circle is occupied by sheds under which Joplin's patrons stow their cars, and here and there around the sheds are flower-beds and clumps of shrubbery. We were still going at a fair clip when we turned into one end of this semi-circular driveway, and –

Axford slammed on his brakes, and the big machine threw us into the windsheld as it jolted into an abrupt stop – barely in time to avoid smashing into a cluster of people who had suddenly loomed up.

In the glow from our headlights faces stood sharply out; white, horrified faces, furtive faces, faces that were callously curious. Below the faces, white arms and shoulders showed, and bright gowns and jewelry, against the duller background of masculine clothing.

This was the first impression I got, and then, by the time I had removed my face from the windshield, I realized that this cluster of people had a core, a thing about which it centered. I stood up, trying to look over the crowd's heads, but I could see nothing.

Jumping down to the driveway, I pushed through the crowd.

Face down on the white gravel a man sprawled – a thin man in dark clothes – and just above his collar, where the head and neck join, was a hole. I knelt to peer into his face. Then I pushed through the crowd again, back to where Axford was just getting out of the car, the engine of which was still running, "Pangburn is dead – shot!"

Methodically, Axford took off his gloves, folded them and put them in a pocket. Then he nodded his understanding of what I had told him, and walked toward where the crowd stood around the dead poet. I looked after him until he had vanished in the throng. Then I went winding through the outskirts of the crowd, hunting for Porky Grout.

I found him standing on the porch, leaning against a pillar. I passed where he could see me, and went on around to the side of the roadhouse that afforded most shadow.

In the shadows Porky joined me. The night wasn't cool, but his teeth were chattering. "Who got him?" I demanded.

"I don't know," he whined, and that was the first thing of which I had ever known him to confess complete ignorance. "I was inside, keepin' an eye on the others."

"What others?"

"Tin-Star, and some guy I never seen before, and the broad. I didn't think the kid was going out. He didn't have no hat."

"What *do* you know about it?"

"A little while after I phoned you, the girl and Pangburn came out from Joplin's part of the joint and sat down at a table around on the other side of the porch, where it's fairly dark. They eat for a while and then this other guy comes over and sits down with 'em. I don't know his name, but I think I've saw him around town. He's a tall guy, in fancy rags."

That would be Kilcourse.

"They talk for a while and then Joplin joins 'em. They sit around the table laughin' and talkin' for maybe a quarter of a hour. Then Pangburn gets up and goes indoors. I got a table that I can watch 'em from, and the place is crowded, and I'm afraid I'll lose my table if I leave it, so I don't follow the kid. He ain't got no hat; I figure he ain't goin' nowhere. But he must of gone through the house and out front, because pretty soon there's a noise that I thought was a auto backfire, and then the sound of a car gettin' away quick. And then some guy squawks that there's a dead man outside. Ever'body runs out here, and it's Pangburn."

"You dead sure that Joplin, Kilcourse and the girl were all at the table when Pangburn was killed?"

"Absolutely," Porky said, "if this dark guy's name is Kilcourse."

"Where are they now?"

"Back in Joplin's hang-out. They went up there as soon as they seen Pangburn had been croaked."

I had no illusions about Porky. I knew he was capable of selling me out and furnishing the poet's murderer with an alibi. But there was this about it: if Joplin, Kilcourse or the girl had fixed him, and had fixed my informant, then it was hopeless for me to try to prove that they weren't on the rear porch when the shot was fired. Joplin had a crowd of hangers-on who would swear to anything he told them without batting an eye. There would be a dozen supposed witnesses to their presence on the rear porch.

Thus the only thing for me to do was to take it for granted that Porky was coming clean with me. "Have you seen Dick Foley?" I asked, since Dick had been shadowing Kilcourse.

"No."

"Hunt around and see if you can find him. Tell him I've gone up to talk to Joplin, and tell him to come on up. Then you can stick around where I can get hold of you if I want you."

I went in through a French window, crossed an empty dance-floor and went up the stairs that led to Tin-Star Joplin's living quarters in the rear second story. I knew the way, having been up there before. Joplin and I were old friends.

I was going up now to give him and his friends a shake-down on the off-chance that some good might come of it, though I knew that I had nothing on any of them. I could have tied something on the girl, of course, but not without advertising the fact that the dead poet had forged his brother-in-law's signature to a check. And that was no go.

"Come in," a heavy, familiar voice called when I rapped on Joplin's living-room door. I pushed the door open and went in.

Tin-Star Joplin was standing in the middle of the floor: a big-bodied ex-yegg with inordinately thick shoulders and an expressionless horse face. Beyond him Kilcourse sat dangling one leg from the corner of a table, alertness hiding behind an amused half-smile on his handsome dark face. On the other side of the room a girl whom I knew for Jeanne Delano sat on the arm of a big leather chair. And the poet hadn't exaggerated when he told me she was beautiful.

"You!" Joplin grunted disgustedly as soon as he recognized me. "What the hell do *you* want?"

"What've you got?"

My mind wasn't on this sort of repartee, however; I was studying the girl. There was something vaguely familiar about her – but I couldn't place her. Perhaps I hadn't seen her before; perhaps much looking at the picture Pangburn had given me was responsible for my feeling of recognition. Pictures will do that.

Meanwhile, Joplin had said: "Time to waste is one thing I ain't got."

And I had said: "If you'd saved up all the time different judges have given you, you'd have plenty."

I had seen the girl somewhere before. She was a slender girl in a glistening blue gown that exhibited a generous spread of front, back and arms that were worth showing. She had a mass of dark brown hair above an oval face of the color that pink ought to be. Her eyes were wide-set and a gray shade that wasn't altogether unlike the shadows on polished silver that the poet had compared them to. I studied the girl, and she looked back at me with level eyes, and still I couldn't place her. Kilcourse still sat dangling a leg from the table corner.

Joplin grew impatient. "Will you stop gandering at the girl, and tell me what you want of me?" he growled.

The girl smiled then, a mocking smile that bared the edges of razor-sharp little animal-teeth. And with the smile I knew her!

Her hair and skin had fooled me. The last time I had seen her – the only time I had seen her before – her face had been marble-white, and her hair had been short and the color of fire. She and an older woman and three men and I had played hide-and-seek one evening in a house in Turk Street over a matter of the murder of a bank messenger and the theft of a hundred thousand dollars' worth of Liberty Bonds. Through her intriguing three of her accomplices had died that evening, and the fourth – the Chinese – had eventually gone to the gallows at Folsom Prison. Her name had been Elvira then, and since her escape from the house that night we had been fruitlessly hunting her from border to border, and beyond.

Recognition must have shown in my eyes in spite of the effort I made to keep them blank, for, swift as a snake, she had left the arm of the chair and was coming forward, her eyes more steel than silver.

I put my gun in sight.

Joplin took a half-step toward me. "What's the idea?" he barked.

Kilcourse slid off the table, and one of his thin dark hands hovered over his necktie.

"This is the idea," I told them. "I want the girl for a murder a couple months back, and maybe – I'm not sure – for tonight's. Anyway, I'm –"

The snapping of a light-switch behind me, and the room went black.

I moved, not caring where I went so long as I got away from where I had been when the lights went out.

My back touched a wall and I stopped, crouching low.

"Quick, kid!" A hoarse whisper that came from where I thought the door should be.

But both of the room's doors, I thought, were closed, and could hardly be opened without showing gray rectangles. People moved in the blackness, but none got between me and the lighter square of windows.

Something clicked softly in front of me – too thin a click for the cocking of a gun – but it could have been the opening of a spring-knife, and I remembered that Tin-Star Joplin had a fondness for that weapon.

"Let's go!" A harsh whisper that cut through the dark like a blow.

Sounds of motion, muffled, indistinguishable . . . one sound not far away . . .

Abruptly a strong hand clamped one of my shoulders, a hard-muscled body strained against me. I stabbed out with my gun, and heard a grunt.

The hand moved up my shoulder toward my throat.

I snapped up a knee, and heard another grunt.

A burning point ran down my side.

I stabbed again with my gun – pulled it back until the muzzle was free of the soft obstacle that had stopped it, and squeezed the trigger. The crash of the shot. Joplin's voice in my ear, a curiously matter-of-fact voice: "God damn! That got me."

I spun away from him then, toward where I saw the dim yellow of an open door. I had heard no sounds of departure. I had been too busy. But I knew that Joplin had tied into me while the others made their get-away.

Nobody was in sight as I jumped, slid, tumbled down the steps – any number at a time. A waiter got in my path as I plunged toward the dance-floor. I don't know whether his interference was intentional or not. I didn't ask. I slammed the flat of my gun in his face and went on. Once I jumped a leg that came out to trip me; and at the outer door I had to smear another face.

Then I was out in the semi-circular driveway, from one end of which a red tail-light was turning east into the country road.

While I sprinted for Axford's car I noticed that Pangburn's body had been removed. A few people still stood around the spot where he had lain, and they gaped at me now with open mouths.

The car was as Axford had left it, with idling engine. I swung it through a flower-bed and pointed it east on the public road. Five minutes later I picked up the red point of a tail-light again.

The car under me had more power than I would ever need, more than I would have known how to handle. I don't know how fast the one ahead was going, but I closed in as if it had been standing still.

A mile and a half, or perhaps two –

Suddenly a man was in the road ahead – a little beyond the reach of my lights. The lights caught him, and I saw that it was Porky Grout!

Porky Grout standing facing me in the middle of the road, the dull metal of an automatic in each hand.

The guns in his hands seemed to glow dimly red and then go dark in the glare of my headlights – glow and then go dark, like two bulbs in an automatic electric sign.

The windshield fell apart around me.

Porky Grout – the informant whose name was a synonym for cowardice the full length of the Pacific Coast – stood in the center of the road shooting at a metal comet that rushed down upon him. . . .

I didn't see the end.

I confess frankly that I shut my eyes when his set white face showed close over my radiator. The metal monster under me trembled – not very much – and the road ahead was empty except for the fleeing red light. My windshield was gone. The wind tore at my uncovered hair and brought tears to my squinted-up eyes.

Presently I found that I was talking to myself, saying, "That was Porky. That was Porky." It was an amazing fact. It was no surprise that he had double-crossed me. That was to be expected. And for him to have crept up the stairs behind me and turned off the lights wasn't astonishing. But for him to have stood straight up and died –

An orange streak from the car ahead cut off my wonderment. The bullet didn't come near me – it isn't easy to shoot accurately from one moving car into another – but at the pace I was going it wouldn't be long before I was close enough for good shooting.

I turned on the searchlight above the dashboard. It didn't quite reach the car ahead, but it enabled me to see that the girl was driving. While Kilcourse sat screwed around beside her, facing me. The car was a yellow roadster.

I eased up a little. In a duel with Kilcourse here I would have been at a disadvantage, since I would have had to drive as well as shoot. My best play seemed to be to hold my distance until we reached a town, as we inevitably must. It wasn't midnight yet. There would be people on the streets of any town, and policemen. Then I could close in with a better chance of coming off on top.

A few miles of this and my prey tumbled to my plan. The yellow roadster slowed down, wavered, and came to rest with its length across the road. Kilcourse and the girl were out immediately and crouching in the road on the far side of their barricade.

I was tempted to dive pell-mell into them, but it was a weak temptation, and when its short life had passed I put on the brakes and stopped. Then I fiddled with my searchlight until it bore full upon the roadster.

A flash came from somewhere near the roadster's wheels, and the searchlight shook violently, but the glass wasn't touched. It would be their first target, of course, and . . .

Crouching in my car, waiting for the bullet that would smash the lens, I took off my shoes and overcoat.

The third bullet ruined the light.

I switched off the other lights, jumped to the road, and when I stopped running I was squatting down against the near side of the yellow roadster. As easy and safe a trick as can be imagined.

The girl and Kilcourse had been looking into the glare of a powerful light. When that light suddenly died, and the weaker ones around it went, too, they were left in pitch unseeing blackness, which must last for the minute or longer that their eyes would need to readjust themselves to the gray-black of the night. My stockinged feet had made no sound on the macadam road, and now there was only a roadster between us; and I knew it and they didn't.

From near the radiator Kilcourse spoke softly:

"I'm going to try to knock him off from the ditch. Take a shot at him now and then to keep him busy."

"I can't see him," the girl protested.

"Your eyes'll be all right in a second. Take a shot at the car anyway."

I moved toward the radiator as the girl's pistol barked at the empty touring car.

Kilcourse, on hands and knees, was working his way toward the ditch that ran along the south side of the road. I gathered my legs under me, intent upon a spring and a blow with my gun upon the back of his head. I didn't want to kill him, but I wanted to put him out of the way quick. I'd have the girl to take care of, and she was at least as dangerous as he.

As I tensed for the spring, Kilcourse, guided perhaps by some instinct of the hunted, turned his head and saw me – saw a threatening shadow.

Instead of jumping I fired.

I didn't look to see whether I had hit him or not. At that range there was little likelihood of missing. I bent double and slipped back to the rear of the roadster, keeping on my side of it. Then I waited.

The girl did what I would perhaps have done in her place. She didn't shoot or move toward the place the shot had come from. She thought I had forestalled Kilcourse in using the ditch and that my next play would be to circle around behind her. To offset this, she moved around the rear of the roadster, so that she could ambush me from the side nearest Axford's car.

Thus it was that she came creeping around the corner and poked her delicately chiseled nose plunk into the muzzle of the gun that I held ready for her.

She gave a little scream.

Women aren't always reasonable: they are prone to disregard trifles like guns held upon them. So I grabbed her gun hand, which was fortunate for me. As my hand closed around the weapon, she pulled the trigger, catching a chunk of my forefinger between hammer and frame. I twisted the gun out of her hand; released my finger.

But she wasn't done yet. With me standing there holding a gun not four inches from her body, she turned and bolted off toward where a clump of trees made a jet-black blot to the north.

When I recovered from my surprise at this amateurish procedure, I stuck both her gun and mine in my pockets, and set out after her, tearing the soles of my feet at every step.

She was trying to get over a wire fence when I caught her.

"Stop playing, will you?" I said crossly, as I set the fingers of my left hand around her wrist and started to lead her back to the roadster. "This is a serious business. Don't be so childish!"

"You are hurting my arm."

I knew I wasn't hurting her arm, and I knew this girl for the direct cause of four, or perhaps five, deaths; yet I loosened my grip on her wrist until it wasn't much more than a friendly clasp. She went back willingly enough to the roadster, where, still holding her wrist, I switched on the lights. Kilcourse lay just beneath the headlight's glare, huddled on his face, with one knee drawn up under him.

I put the girl squarely in the line of light.

"Now stand there," I said, "and behave. The first break you make, I'm going to shoot a leg out from under you," and I meant it.

I found Kilcourse's gun, pocketed it, and knelt beside him. He was dead, with a bullet-hole above his collar-bone.

"Is he –" her mouth trembled.

"Yes."

She looked down at him, and shivered a little.

"Poor Fag," she whispered.

I've gone on record as saying that this girl was beautiful, and, standing there in the dazzling white of the headlights, she was more than that. She was a thing to start crazy thoughts even in the head of an unimaginative middle-aged thief-catcher. She was –

Anyhow, I suppose that is why I scowled at her and said:

"Yes, poor Fag, and poor Hook, and poor Tai, and poor kid of a Los Angeles bank messenger, and poor Burke," calling the roll, so far as I knew it, of men who had died loving her.

She didn't flare up. Her big gray eyes lifted, and she looked at me with a gaze that I couldn't fathom, and her lovely oval face under the mass of brown hair – which I knew was phony – was sad.

"I suppose you do think –" she began.

But I had had enough of this; I was uncomfortable along the spine.

"Come on," I said. "We'll leave Kilcourse and the roadster here for now."

She said nothing, but went with me to Axford's big machine, and sat in silence while I laced my shoes. I found a robe on the back seat for her.

"Better wrap this around your shoulders. The windshield is gone. It'll be cool."

She followed my suggestion without a word, but when I had edged our vehicle around the rear of the roadster, and had straightened out in the road again, going east, she laid a hand on my arm.

"Aren't we going back to the White Shack?"

"No. Redwood City – the county jail."

A mile perhaps, during which, without looking at her, I knew she was studying my rather lumpy profile. Then her hand was on my forearm again and she was leaning toward me so that her breath was warm against my cheek. "Will you stop for a minute? There's something – some things I want to tell you."

I brought the car to a halt in a cleared space of hard soil off to one side of the road, and screwed myself a little around in the seat to face her more directly.

"Before you start," I told her, "I want you to understand that we stay here for just so long as you talk about the Pangburn affair. When you get off on any other line – then we finish our trip to Redwood City."

"Aren't you even interested in the Los Angeles affair?"

"No. That's closed. You and Hook Riordan and Tai Choon Tau and the Quarres were equally responsible for the messenger's death, even if Hook did the actual killing. Hook and the Quarres passed out the night we had our party in Turk Street. Tai was hanged last month. Now I've got you. We had enough evidence to swing the Chinese, and we've even more against you. That is done – finished – completed. If you want to tell me anything about Pangburn's death, I'll listen. Otherwise –"

I reached for the self-starter.

A pressure of her fingers on my arm stopped me.

"I do want to tell you about it," she said earnestly. "I want you to know the truth about it. You'll take me to Redwood City, I know. Don't think that I expect – that I have any foolish hopes. But I'd like you to know the truth about this thing. I don't know why I should care especially what you think, but –"

Her voice dwindled off to nothing.

Then she began to talk very rapidly – as people talk when they fear interruptions before their stories are told – and she sat leaning slightly forward, so that her beautiful oval face was very close to mine.

"After I ran out of the Turk Street house that night – while you were struggling with Tai – my intention was to get away from San Francisco. I had a couple of thousand dollars, enough to carry me any place. Then I thought that going away would be what you people would expect me to do, and that the safest thing for me to do would be to stay right here. It isn't hard for a woman to change her appearance. I had bobbed red hair, white skin, and wore gay clothes. I simply dyed my hair, bought these transformations to make it look long, put color on my face, and bought some dark clothes. Then I took an apartment on Ashbury Avenue under the name of Jeanne Delano, and I was an altogether different person.

"But, while I knew I was perfectly safe from recognition anywhere, I felt more comfortable staying indoors for a while, and, to pass the time, I read a good deal. That's how I happened to run across Burke's book. Do you read poetry?"

I shook my head. An automobile going toward Halfmoon Bay came into sight just then – the first one we'd seen since we left the White Shack. She waited until it had passed before she went on, still talking rapidly.

"Burke wasn't a genius, of course, but there was something about some of his things that – something that got inside me. I wrote him a little note, telling him how much I had enjoyed these things, and sent it to his publishers. A few days later I had a note from Burke, and I learned that he lived in San Francisco. I hadn't known that.

"We exchanged several notes, and then he asked if he could call, and we met. I don't know whether I was in love with him or not, even at first. I did like him, and, between the ardor of his love for me and the flattery of having a fairly well-known poet for a suitor, I really thought that I loved him. I promised to marry him.

"I hadn't told him anything about myself, though now I know that it wouldn't have made any difference to him. But I was afraid to tell him the truth, and I wouldn't lie to him, so I told him nothing.

"Then Fag Kilcourse saw me one day on the street, and

knew me in spite of my new hair, complexion and clothes. Fag hadn't much brains, but he had eyes that could see through anything. I don't blame Fag. He acted according to his code. He came up to my apartment, having followed me home; and I told him that I was going to marry Burke and be a respectable housewife. That was dumb of me. Fag was square. If I had told him that I was ribbing Burke up for a trimming, Fag would have let me alone, would have kept his hands off. But when I told him that I was through with the graft, had 'gone queer,' that made me his meat. You know how crooks are: everyone in the world is either a fellow crook or a prospective victim. So if I was no longer a crook, then Fag considered me fair game.

"He learned about Burke's family connections, and then he put it up to me – twenty thousand dollars, or he'd turn me up. He knew about the Los Angeles job, and he knew how badly I was wanted. I was up against it then. I knew I couldn't hide from Fag or run away from him. I told Burke I had to have twenty thousand dollars. I didn't think he had that much, but I thought he could get it. Three days later he gave me a check for it. I didn't know at the time how he had raised it, but it wouldn't have mattered if I had known. I had to have it.

"But that night he told me where he got the money; that he had forged his brother-in-law's signature. He told me because, after thinking it over, he was afraid that when the forgery was discovered I would be caught with him and considered equally guilty. I'm rotten in spots, but I wasn't rotten enough to let him put himself in the pen for me, without knowing what it was all about. I told him the whole story. He didn't bat an eye. He insisted that the money be paid Kilcourse, so that I would be safe, and began to plan for my further safety.

"Burke was confident that his brother-in-law wouldn't send him over for forgery, but, to be on the safe side, he insisted that I move and change my name again and lay low until we knew how Axford was going to take it. But that night, after he had gone, I made some plans of my own. I did like Burke – I liked him too much to let him be the goat without trying to save him, and I didn't have a great deal of faith in Axford's kindness. This was the second of the month. Barring accidents, Axford wouldn't discover the forgery until he got his canceled checks early the following month. That gave me practically a month to work in.

"The next day I drew all my money out of the bank, and sent Burke a letter, saying that I had been called to Baltimore, and I laid a clear trail to Baltimore, with baggage and letters and all, which a pal there took care of for me. Then I went down to Joplin's and got him to put me up. I let Fag know I was there, and when he came down I told him I expected to have the money for him in a day or two.

"He came down nearly every day after that, and I stalled him from day to day, and each time it got easier. But my time was getting short. Pretty soon Burke's letters would be coming back from the phony address I had given him, and I wanted to be on hand to keep him from doing anything foolish. And I didn't want to get in touch with him until I could give him the twenty thousand, so he could square the forgery before Axford learned of it from his canceled checks.

"Fag was getting easier and easier to handle, but I still didn't have him where I wanted him. He wasn't willing to give up the twenty thousand dollars – which I was, of course, holding all this time – unless I'd promise to stick with him for good. And I still thought I was in love with Burke, and I didn't want to tie myself up with Fag, even for a little while.

"Then Burke saw me on the street one Sunday night. I was careless, and drove into the city in Joplin's roadster – the one back there. And, as luck would have it, Burke saw me. I told him the truth, the whole truth. And he told me that he had just hired a private detective to find me. He was like a child in some ways: it hadn't occurred to him that the sleuth would dig up anything about the money. But I knew the forged check would be found in a day or two at the most. I knew it!

"When I told Burke that he went to pieces. All his faith in his brother-in-law's forgiveness went. I couldn't leave him the way he was. He'd have babbled the whole thing to the first person he met. So I brought him back to Joplin's with me. My idea was to hold him there for a few days, until we could see how things were going. If nothing appeared in the papers about the check, then we could take it for granted that Axford had hushed the matter up, and Burke could go home and try to square himself. On the other hand, if the papers got the whole story, then Burke would have to look for a permanent hiding-place, and so would I.

"Tuesday evening's and Wednesday morning's papers were full of the news of his disappearance, but nothing was said about the check. That looked good, but we waited another day for good measure. Fag Kilcourse was in on the game by this time, of course, and I had had to pass over the twenty thousand dollars, but I still had hopes of getting it – or most of it – back, so I continued to string him along. I had a hard time keeping off Burke, though, because he had begun to think he had some sort of right to me, and jealousy made him wicked. But I got Tin-Star to throw a scare into him, and I thought Burke was safe.

"Tonight one of Tin-Star's men came up and told us that a man named Porky Grout, who had been hanging around the place for a couple of nights, had made a couple of cracks that might mean he was interested in us. Grout was pointed out to me, and I took a chance on showing myself in the public part of the place, and sat at a table close to his. He was plain rat – as I guess you know – and in less than five minutes I had him at my table, and half an hour later I knew that he had tipped you off that Burke and I were in the White Shack. He didn't tell me all this right out, but he told me more than enough for me to guess the rest.

"I went up and told the others. Fag was for killing both Grout and Burke right away. But I talked him out of it. That wouldn't help us any, and I had Grout where he would jump in the ocean for me. I thought I had Fag convinced, but – We finally decided that Burke and I would take the roadster and leave, and that when you got here Porky Grout was to pretend he was hopped up, and point out a man and a woman – any who happened to be handy – as the ones he had taken for us. I stopped to get a cloak and gloves, and Burke went on out to the car alone – and Fag shot him. I didn't know he was going to! I wouldn't have let him! Please believe that! I wasn't as much in love with Burke as I had thought, but please believe that after all he had done for me I wouldn't have let them hurt him!

"After that it was a case of stick with the others whether I liked it or not, and I stuck. We ribbed Grout to tell you that all three of us were on the back porch when Burke was killed, and we had any number of others primed with the same story. Then you came up and recognized me. Just my luck that it had to be you – the only detective in San Francisco who knew me!

"You know the rest: how Porky Grout came up behind you and turned off the lights, and Joplin held you while we ran for the car; and then, when you closed in on us, Grout offered to stand you off while we got clear, and now. . . ."

Her voice died, and she shivered a little. The robe I had given her had fallen away from her white shoulders. Whether or not it was because she was so close against my shoulder, I shivered, too. And my fingers, fumbling in my pocket for a cigarette, brought it out twisted and mashed.

"That's all there is to the part you promised to listen to," she said softly, her face turned half away. "I wanted you to know. You're a hard man, but somehow I –"

I cleared my throat, and the hand that held the mangled cigarette was suddenly steady.

"Now don't be crude, sister," I said. "Your work has been too smooth so far to be spoiled by rough stuff now."

She laughed – a brief laugh that was bitter and reckless and just a little weary, and she thrust her face still closer to mine, and the gray eyes were soft and placid.

"Little fat detective whose name I don't know" – her voice had a tired huskiness in it, and a tired mockery – "you think I am playing a part, don't you? You think I am playing for liberty. Perhaps I am. I certainly would take it if it were offered me. But – Men have thought me beautiful, and I have played with them. Women are like that. Men have loved me and, doing what I liked with them, I have found men contemptible. And then comes this little fat detective whose name I don't know, and he acts as if I were a hag – an old squaw. Can I help then being piqued into some sort of feeling for him? Women are like that. Am I so homely that any man has a right to look at me without even interest? Am I ugly?"

I shook my head. "You're quite pretty," I said, struggling to keep my voice as casual as the words.

"You beast!" she spat, and then her smile grew gentle again. "And yet it is because of that attitude that I sit here and turn myself inside out for you. If you were to take me in your arms and hold me close to the chest that I am already leaning against, and if you were to tell me that there is no jail ahead for me just now, I would be glad, of course. But, though for a while you might hold me, you would then be only one of the men with which I am familiar: men who love and are used and are succeeded by other men. But because you do none of these things, because you are a wooden block of a man, I find myself wanting you. Would I tell you this, little fat detective, if I were playing a game?"

I grunted non-committally, and forcibly restrained my tongue from running out to moisten my dry lips.

"I'm going to this jail tonight if you are the same hard man who has goaded me into whining love into his uncaring ears, but before that, can't I have one whole hearted assurance that you think me a little more than 'quite pretty'? Or at least a hint that if I were not a prisoner your pulse might beat a little faster when I touch you? I'm going to this jail for a long while – perhaps to the gallows. Can't I take my vanity there not quite in tatters to keep me company? Can't you do some slight thing to keep me from the afterthought of having bleated all this out to a man who was simply bored?"

Her lids had come down half over the silver-gray eyes, her head had tilted back so far that a little pulse showed throbbing in her white throat; her lips were motionless over slightly parted teeth, as the last word had left them. My fingers went deep into the soft white flesh of her shoulders. Her head went further back, her eyes closed, one hand came up to my shoulder.

"You're beautiful as all hell!" I shouted crazily into her face, and flung her against the door.

It seemed an hour that I fumbled with starter and gears before I had the car back in the road and thundering toward the San Mateo County jail. The girl had straightened herself up in the seat again, and sat huddled within the robe I had given her. I squinted straight ahead into the wind that tore at my hair and face, and the absence of the windshield took my thoughts back to Porky Grout.

Porky Grout, whose yellowness was notorious from Seattle to San Diego, standing rigidly in the path of a charging metal monster, with an inadequate pistol in each hand. She had done that to Porky Grout – this woman beside me! She had done that to Porky Grout, and he hadn't even been human! A slimy reptile whose highest thought had been a skinful of dope had gone grimly to death that she might get away – she – this woman whose shoulders I had gripped, whose mouth had been close under mine!

I let the car out another notch, holding the road somehow.

We went through a town: a scurrying of pedestrians for

safety, surprised faces staring at us, street lights glistening on the moisture the wind had whipped from my eyes. I passed blindly by the road I wanted, circled back to it, and we were out in the country again.

At the foot of a long, shallow hill I applied the brakes and we snapped to motionless.

I thrust my face close to the girl's.

"Furthermore, you are a liar!" I knew I was shouting foolishly, but I was powerless to lower my voice. "Pangburn never put Axford's name on that check. He never knew anything about it. You got in with him because you knew his brother-in-law was a millionaire. You pumped him, finding out everything he knew about his brother-in-law's account at the Golden Gate Trust. You stole Pangburn's bank book – it wasn't in his room when I searched it – and deposited the forged Axford check to his credit, knowing that under those circumstances the check wouldn't be questioned. The next day you took Pangburn into the bank, saying you were going to make a deposit. You took him in because with him standing beside you the check to which *his* signature had been forged wouldn't be questioned. You knew that, being a gentleman, he'd take pains not to see what you were depositing.

"Then you framed the Baltimore trip. He told the truth to me – the truth so far as he knew it. Then you met him Sunday night – maybe accidentally, maybe not. Anyway, you took him down to Joplin's, giving him some wild yarn that he would swallow and that would persuade him to stay there for a few days. That wasn't hard, since he didn't know anything about either of the twenty-thousand-dollar checks. You and your pal Kilcourse knew that if Pangburn disappeared nobody would ever know that he hadn't forged the Axford check, and nobody would ever suspect that the second check was phony. You'd have killed him quietly, but when Porky tipped you off that I was on my way down you had to move quick – so you shot him down. That's the truth of it!" I yelled.

All this while she watched me with wide gray eyes that were calm and tender, but now they clouded a little and a pucker of pain drew her brows together.

I yanked my head away and got the car in motion.

Just before we swept into Redwood City one of her hands came up to my forearm, rested there for a second, patted the arm twice, and withdrew.

I didn't look at her, nor, I think, did she look at me, while she was being booked. She gave her name as Jeanne Delano, and refused to make any statement until she had seen an attorney. It all took a very few minutes.

As she was being led away, she stopped and asked if she might speak privately with me.

We went together to a far corner of the room.

She put her mouth close to my ear so that her breath was warm again on my cheek, as it had been in the car, and whispered the vilest epithet of which the English language is capable.

Then she walked out to her cell.

THE BIG KNOCKOVER

I FOUND PADDY the Mex in Jean Larrouy's dive.

Paddy – an amiable con man who looked like the King of Spain – showed me his big white teeth in a smile, pushed a chair out for me with one foot, and told the girl who shared his table, "Nellie, meet the biggest-hearted dick in San Francisco. This little fat guy will do anything for anybody, if only he can send 'em over for life in the end." He turned to me, waving his cigar at the girl: "Nellie Wade, and you can't get anything on her. She don't have to work – her old man's a bootlegger."

She was a slim girl in blue – white skin, long green eyes, short chestnut hair. Her sullen face livened into beauty when she put a hand across the table to me, and we both laughed at Paddy.

"Five years?" she asked.

"Six," I corrected.

"Damn!" said Paddy, grinning and hailing a waiter. "Some day I'm going to fool a sleuth."

So far he had fooled all of them – he had never slept in a hoosegow.

I looked at the girl again. Six years before, this Angel Grace Cardigan had buncoed half a dozen Philadelphia boys out of plenty. Dan Morey and I had nailed her, but none of her victims would go to bat against her, so she had been turned loose. She was a kid of nineteen then, but already a smooth grifter.

In the middle of the floor one of Larrouy's girls began to sing "Tell Me What You Want and I'll Tell You What You Get." Paddy the Mex tipped a gin bottle over the glasses of ginger ale the waiter had brought. We drank and I gave Paddy a piece of paper with a name and address penciled on it.

"Itchy Maker asked me to slip you that," I explained. "I saw him in the Folsom big house yesterday. It's his mother, he says, and he wants you to look her up and see if she wants anything. What he means, I suppose, is that you're to give her his cut from the last trick you and he turned."

"You hurt my feelings," Paddy said, pocketing the paper and bringing out the gin again.

I downed the second gin-ginger ale and gathered in my feet, preparing to rise and trot along home. At that moment four of Larrouy's clients came in from the street. Recognition of one of them kept me in my chair. He was tall and slender and all dolled up in what the well-dressed man should wear. Sharp-eyed, sharp-faced, with lips thin as knife-edges under a small pointed mustache – Bluepoint Vance. I wondered what he was doing three thousand miles away from his New York hunting-grounds.

While I wondered I put the back of my head to him, pretending interest in the singer, who was now giving the customers "I Want to Be a Bum." Beyond her, back in a corner, I spotted another familiar face that belonged in another city – Happy Jim Hacker, round and rosy Detroit gunman twice sentenced to death and twice pardoned.

When I faced front again, Bluepoint Vance and his three companions had come to rest two tables away. His back was to us. I sized up his playmates.

Facing Vance sat a wide-shouldered young giant with red hair, blue eyes and a ruddy face that was good-looking in a tough, savage way. On his left was a shifty-eyed dark girl in a floppy hat. She was talking to Vance. The red-haired giant's attention was all taken by the fourth member of the party, on his right. She deserved it.

She was neither tall nor short, thin nor plump. She wore a black Russian tunic affair, green-trimmed and hung with silver dinguses. A black fur coat was spread over the chair behind her. She was probably twenty. Her eyes were blue, her mouth red, her teeth white, the hair-ends showing under her black-green-and-silver turban were brown, and she had a nose. Without getting steamed up over the details, she was nice. I said so. Paddy the Mex agreed with a "That's what," and Angel Grace suggested that I go over and tell Red O'Leary I thought her nice.

"Red O'Leary the big bird?" I asked, sliding down in my seat so I could stretch a foot under the table between Paddy and Angel Grace. "Who's his nice girl friend?"

"Nancy Regan, and the other one's Sylvia Yount."

"And the slicker with his back to us?" I probed.

Paddy's foot, hunting the girl's under the table, bumped mine.

"Don't kick me, Paddy," I pleaded. "I'll be good. Anyway, I'm not going to stay here to be bruised. I'm going home."

I swapped so-longs with them and moved toward the street, keeping my back to Bluepoint Vance.

At the door I had to step aside to let two men come in. Both knew me, but neither gave me a tumble – Sheeny Holmes (not the old-timer who staged the Moose Jaw looting back in the buggy-riding days) and Denny Burke, Baltimore's King of Frog Island. A good pair – neither of them would think of taking a life unless assured of profit and political protection.

Outside, I turned down toward Kearny Street, strolling along, thinking that Larrouy's joint had been full of crooks this one night, and that there seemed to be more than a sprinkling of prominent visitors in our midst. A shadow in a doorway interrupted my brainwork.

The shadow said, "Ps-s-s-s!"

Stopping, I examined the shadow until I saw it was Beno, a hophead newsie who had given me a tip now and then in the past – some good, some phony.

"I'm sleepy," I growled as I joined Beno and his armload

of newspapers in the doorway, "and I've heard the story about the Mormon who stuttered, so if that's what's on your mind, say so, and I'll keep going."

"I don't know nothin' about no Mormons," he protested, "but I know somethin' else."

"Well?"

" 'S all right for you to say 'Well,' but what I want to know is, what am I gonna get out of it?"

"Flop in the nice doorway and go shut-eye," I advised him, moving toward the street again. "You'll be all right when you wake up."

"Hey! Listen, I got somethin' for you. Hones' to Gawd!"

"Well?"

"Listen!" He came closer, whispering. "There's a caper rigged for the Seaman's National. I don't know what's the racket, but it's real . . . Hones' to Gawd! I ain't stringin' you. I can't give you no monickers. You know I would if I knowed 'em. Hones' to Gawd. Gimme ten bucks. It's worth that to you, ain't it? This is straight dope – hones' to Gawd!"

"Yeah, straight from the nose-candy!"

"No! Hones' to Gawd! I –"

"What *is* the caper, then?"

"I don't know. All I got was that the Seaman's is gonna be nicked. Hones' to –"

"Where'd you get it?"

Beno shook his head. I put a silver dollar in his hand.

"Get another shot and think up the rest of it," I told him, "and if it's amusing enough I'll give you the other nine bucks."

I walked on down to the corner, screwing up my forehead over Beno's tale. By itself, it sounded like what it probably was – a yarn designed to get a dollar out of a trusting gumshoe. But it wasn't altogether by itself. Larrouy's – just one drum in a city that had a number – had been heavy with grifters who were threats against life and property. It was worth a look-see, especially since the insurance company covering the Seaman's National Bank was a Continental Detective Agency client.

Around the corner, twenty feet or so along Kearny Street, I stopped.

From the street I had just quit came two bangs – the reports of a heavy pistol. I went back the way I had come. As I rounded the corner I saw men gathering in a group up the street. A young Armenian – a dapper boy of nineteen or twenty – passed me, going the other way, sauntering along, hands in pockets, softly whistling "Brokenhearted Sue."

I joined the group – now becoming a crowd – around Beno. Beno was dead, blood from two holes in his chest staining the crumpled newspapers under him.

I went up to Larrouy's and looked in. Red O'Leary, Bluepoint Vance, Nancy Regan, Sylvia Yount, Paddy the Mex, Angel Grace, Denny Burke, Sheeny Holmes, Happy Jim Hacker – not one of them was there.

Returning to Beno's vicinity, I loitered with my back to a wall while the police arrived, asked questions, learned nothing, found no witnesses, and departed, taking what was left of the newsie with them.

I went home and to bed.

In the morning I spent one hour in the Agency file room, digging through the gallery and records. We didn't have anything on Red O'Leary, Denny Burke, Nancy Regan, Sylvia Yount, and only some guesses on Paddy the Mex. Nor were there any open jobs definitely chalked against Angel Grace, Bluepoint Vance, Sheeny Holmes and Happy Jim Hacker, but their photos were there. At ten o'clock – bank opening time – I set out for the Seaman's National, carrying these photos and Beno's tip.

The Continental Detective Agency's San Francisco office is located in a Market Street office building. The Seaman's

National Bank occupies the ground floor of a tall gray building in Montgomery Street, San Francisco's financial center. Ordinarily, since I don't like even seven blocks of unnecessary walking, I would have taken a streetcar. But there was some sort of traffic jam on Market Street, so I set out afoot, turning off along Grand Avenue.

A few blocks of walking, and I began to see that something was wrong with the part of town I was heading for. Noises for one thing – roaring, rattling, explosive noises. At Sutter Street a man passed me, holding his face with both hands and groaning as he tried to push a dislocated jaw back in place. His cheek was scraped red.

I went down Sutter Street. Traffic was in a tangle that reached to Montgomery Street. Excited, bare-headed men were running around. The explosive noises were clearer. An automobile full of policemen went down past me, going as fast as traffic would let it. An ambulance came up the street, clanging its gong, taking to the sidewalks where the traffic was worst.

I crossed Kearny Street on the trot. Down the other side of the street two patrolmen were running. One had his gun out. The explosive noises were a drumming chorus ahead.

Rounding into Montgomery Street, I found few sightseers ahead of me. The middle of the street was filled with trucks, touring cars, taxis – deserted there. Up in the next block – between Bush and Pine Streets – hell was on a holiday.

The holiday spirit was gayest in the middle of the block, where the Seaman's National Bank and the Golden Gate Trust Company faced each other across the street.

For the next six hours I was busier than a flea on a fat woman.

Late that afternoon I took a recess from bloodhounding and went up to the office for a powwow with the Old Man. He was leaning back in his chair, staring out the window, tapping on his desk with the customary long yellow pencil.

A tall, plump man in his seventies, this boss of mine, with

a white-mustached, baby-pink, grandfatherly face, mild blue eyes behind rimless spectacles, and no more warmth in him than a hangman's rope. Fifty years of crook-hunting for the Continental had emptied him of everything except brains and a soft-spoken, gently smiling shell of politeness that was the same whether things went good or bad – and meant as little at one time as another. We who worked under him were proud of his cold-bloodedness. We used to boast that he could spit icicles in July, and we called him Pontius Pilate among ourselves, because he smiled politely when he sent us out to be crucified on suicidal jobs.

He turned from the window as I came in, nodded me to a chair, and smoothed his mustache with the pencil. On his desk the afternoon papers screamed the news of the Seaman's National Bank and Golden Gate Trust Company double-looting in five colors.

"What is the situation?" he asked, as one would ask about the weather.

"The situation is a pip," I told him. "There were a hundred and fifty crooks in the push if there was one. I saw a hundred myself – or think I did – and there were slews of them that I didn't see – planted where they could jump out and bite when fresh teeth were needed. They bit, too. They bushwacked the police and made a merry wreck out of 'em – going and coming. They hit the two banks at ten sharp – took over the whole block – chased away the reasonable people – dropped the others. The actual looting was duck soup to a mob of that size. Twenty or thirty of 'em to each of the banks while the others held the street. Nothing to it but wrap up the spoils and take 'em home.

"There's a highly indignant businessmen's meeting down there now – wild-eyed stockholders up on their hind legs yelling for the chief of police's heart's blood. The police didn't do any miracles, that's a cinch, but no police department is equipped to handle a trick of that size – no matter how well they think they are. The whole thing lasted less than twenty minutes. There were, say, a hundred and fifty thugs in on it, loaded for bear, every play mapped to the inch. How are you going to get enough coppers down there, size up the racket, plan your battle, and put it over in that little time? It's easy enough to say the police should look ahead – should have a dose for every emergency – but these same birds who are yelling, 'Rotten,' down there now would be the first to squawk, 'Robbery,' if their taxes were boosted a couple of cents to buy more policemen and equipment.

"But the police fell down – there's no question about that – and there will be a lot of beefy necks that feel the ax. The armored cars were no good, the grenading was about fifty-fifty, since the bandits knew how to play that game, too. But the real disgrace of the party was the police machine guns. The bankers and brokers are saying they were fixed. Whether they were deliberately tampered with or were only carelessly taken care of, is anybody's guess, but only one of the damned things would shoot, and it not very well.

"The getaway was north on Montgomery to Columbus. Along Columbus the parade melted, a few cars at a time, into side streets. The police ran into an ambush between Washington and Jackson, and by the time they had shot their way through it the bandit cars had scattered all over the city. A lot of 'em have been picked up since then – empty.

"All the returns aren't in yet, but right now the score stands something like this: The haul will run God only knows how far into the millions – easily the richest pickings ever got with civilian guns. Sixteen coppers were knocked off, and three times that many wounded. Twelve innocent spectators, bank clerks and the like, were killed and about as many banged around. There are two bandits and five shot-ups who might be either thugs or spectators that got too close. The bandits lost seven dead that we know of and thirty-one prisoners, most of them bleeding somewhere.

"One of the dead was Fat Boy Clarke. Remember him? He shot his way out of a Des Moines courtroom three or four years ago. Well, in his pocket we found a piece of paper, a map of Montgomery Street between Pine and Bush, the block of the looting. On the back of the map were typed instructions, telling him exactly what to do and when to do it. An X on the map showed him where he was to park the car in which he arrived with his seven men, and there was a circle where he was to stand with them, keeping an eye on things in general and on the windows and roofs of the buildings across the street in particular. Figures 1, 2, 3, 4, 5, 6, 7, 8 on the map marked doorways, steps, a deep window, and so on, that were to be used for shelter if shots had to be traded with those windows and roofs. Clarke was to pay no attention to the Bush Street end of the block, but if the police charged the Pine Street end he was to move his men up there, distributing them among points marked a, b, c, d, e, f, g, and h. (His body was found on the spot marked a.) Every five minutes during the looting he was to send a man to an automobile standing in the street at a point marked on the map with a star, to see if there were any new instructions. He was to tell his men that if he were shot down one of them must report to the car, and a new leader would be given them. When the signal for the getaway was given, he was to send one of his men to the car in which he had come. If it was still in commission, this man was to drive it, not passing the car ahead of him. If it was out of whack, the man was to report to the star-marked car for instructions how to get a new one. I suppose they counted on finding enough parked cars to take care of this end. While Clarke waited for his car he and his men were to throw as much lead as possible at every target in their district, and none of them was to board the car until it came abreast of them. Then they were to drive out Montgomery to Columbus to – blank.

"Get that?" I asked. "Here are a hundred and fifty gunmen,

split into groups under group-leaders, with maps and schedules showing what each man is to do, showing the fire-plug he's to kneel behind, the brick he's to stand on, where he's to spit – everything but the name and address of the policeman he's to shoot! It's just as well Beno couldn't give me the details – I'd have written it off as a hophead's dream!"

"Very interesting," the Old Man said, smiling blandly.

"The Fat Boy's was the only timetable we found," I went on with my history. "I saw a few friends among the killed and caught, and the police are still identifying others. Some are local talent, but most of 'em seem to be imported stock. Detroit, Chicago, New York, St. Louis, Denver, Portland, L.A., Philly, Baltimore – all seem to have sent delegates. As soon as the police get through identifying them I'll make out a list.

"Of those who weren't caught, Bluepoint Vance seems to be the main squeeze. He was in the car that directed operations. I don't know who else was there with him. The Shivering Kid was in on the festivities, and I think Alphabet Shorty McCoy, though I didn't get a good look at him. Sergeant Bender told me he spotted Toots Salda and Darby M'Laughlin in the push, and Morgan saw the Dis-and-Dat Kid. That's a good cross section of the lay-out – gunmen, swindlers, hijackers from all over Rand-McNally.

"The Hall of Justice has been a slaughterhouse all afternoon. The police haven't killed any of their guests – none that I know of – but they're sure-God making believers out of them. Newspaper writers who like to sob over what they call the third degree should be down there now. After being knocked around a bit, some of the guests have talked. But the hell of it is they don't know a whole lot. They know some names – Denny Burke, Toby the Lugs, Old Pete Best, Fat Boy Clarke and Paddy the Mex were named – and that helps some, but all the smacking power in the police force arm can't bring out anything else.

"The racket seems to have been organized like this: Denny Burke, for instance, is known as a shifty worker in Baltimore. Well, Denny talks to eight or ten likely boys, one at a time. 'How'd you like to pick up a piece of change out on the Coast?' he asks them. 'Doing what?' the candidate wants to know. 'Doing what you're told,' the King of Frog Island says. 'You know me. I'm telling you this is the fastest picking ever rigged, a kick in the pants to go through – airtight. Everybody in on it will come home lousy with cash – and they'll all come home if they don't dog it. That's all I'm spilling. If you don't like it – forget it.'

"And these birds did know Denny, and if he said the job was good that was enough for them. So they put in with him. He told them nothing. He saw that they had guns, gave 'em each a ticket to San Francisco and twenty bucks, and told them where to meet him here. Last night he collected them and told them they went to work this morning. By that time they had moved around the town enough to see that it was bubbling over with visiting talent, including such moguls as Toots Salda, Bluepoint Vance and the Shivering Kid. So this morning they went forth with the King of Frog Island at their head to do their stuff.

"The other talkers tell varieties of the same tale. The police found room in their crowded jail to stick in a few stool-pigeons. Since few of the bandits knew very many of the others, the stools had an easy time of it, but the only thing they could add to what we've got is that the prisoners are looking for a wholesale delivery tonight. They seem to think their mob will crash the prison and turn 'em loose. That's probably a lot of chewing gum, but anyway this time the police will be ready.

"That's the situation as it stands now. The police are sweeping the streets, picking up everybody who needs a shave or can't show a certificate of attendance signed by his parson, with special attention to outward-bound trains, boats and automobiles. I sent Jack Counihan and Dick Foley down North Beach way to play the joints and see if they can pick up anything."

"Do you think Bluepoint Vance was the actual directing intelligence in this robbery?" the Old Man asked.

"I hope so – we know him."

The Old Man turned his chair so his mild eyes could stare out the window again, and he tapped his desk reflectively with the pencil.

"I'm afraid not," he said in a gently apologetic tone. "Vance is a shrewd, resourceful and determined criminal, but his weakness is one common to his type. His abilities are all for present action and not for planning ahead. He has executed some large operations, but I've always thought I saw in them some other mind at work behind him."

I couldn't quarrel with that. If the Old Man said something was so, then it probably was, because he was one of these cautious babies who'll look out of the window at a cloudburst and say, "It seems to be raining," on the off-chance that somebody's pouring water off the roof.

"And who is this arch-*gonif*?" I asked.

"You'll probably know that before I do," he said, smiling benignantly.

I went back to the Hall and helped boil more prisoners in oil until around eight o'clock, when my appetite reminded me I hadn't eaten since breakfast. I attended to that, and then turned down toward Larrouy's, ambling along leisurely, so the exercise wouldn't interfere with my digestion. I spent three-quarters of an hour in Larrouy's, and didn't see anybody who interested me especially. A few gents I know were present, but they weren't anxious to associate with me – it's not always healthy in criminal circles to be seen wagging your chin with a sleuth right after a job has been turned.

Not getting anything there, I moved up the street to Wop

Healy's – another hole. My reception was the same here – I was given a table and let alone. Healy's orchestra was giving "Don't You Cheat" all they had while those customers who felt athletic were roughing it out on the dance floor. One of the dancers was Jack Counihan, his arms full of a big olive-skinned girl with a pleasant, thick-featured stupid face.

Jack was a tall, slender lad of twenty-three or -four who had drifted into the Continental's employ a few months before. It was the first job he'd ever had and he wouldn't have had it if his father hadn't insisted that if sonny wanted to keep his fingers in the family till, he'd have to get over the notion that squeezing through a college graduation was enough work for one lifetime. So Jack came to the Agency. He thought gumshoeing would be fun. In spite of the fact that he'd rather catch the wrong man than wear the wrong necktie, he was a promising young thief-catcher. A likable youngster, well-muscled for all his slimness, smooth-haired, with a gentleman's face and a gentleman's manner, nervy, quick with head and hands, full of the don't-give-a-damn gaiety that belonged to his youthfulness. He was jingle-brained, of course, and needed holding, but I would rather work with him than with a lot of old-timers I knew.

Half an hour passed with nothing to interest me.

Then a boy came into Healy's from the street – a small kid, gaudily dressed, very pressed in the pants-legs, very shiny in the shoes, with an impudent sallow face of pronounced cast. This was the boy I had seen sauntering down Broadway a moment after Beno had been rubbed out.

Leaning back in my chair so that a woman's wide-hatted head was between us, I watched the young Armenian wind between tables to one in a far corner, where three men sat. He spoke to them – offhand perhaps a dozen words – and moved away to another table where a snub-nosed, black-haired man sat alone. The boy dropped into the chair facing snub-nose, spoke a few words, sneered at snub-nose's questions, and ordered a drink. When his glass was empty he crossed the room to speak to a lean buzzard-faced man, and then went out of Healy's.

I followed him out, passing the table where Jack sat with the girl, catching his eye. Outside, I saw the young Armenian half a block away. Jack Counihan caught up with me, passed me. With a Fatima in my mouth I called to him, "Got a match, brother?"

While I lighted my cigarette with a match from the box he gave me I spoke to him behind my hands, "The goose in the glad rags – tail him. I'll string behind you. I don't know him, but if he blipped Beno off for talking to me last night, he knows me. On his heels!"

Jack pocketed his matches and went after the boy. I gave Jack a lead and then followed him. And then an interesting thing happened.

The street was fairly well filled with people, mostly men, some walking, some loafing on corners and in front of soft-drink parlors. As the young Armenian reached the corner of an alley where there was a light, two men came up and spoke to him, moving a little apart so that he was between them. The boy would have kept walking, apparently paying no attention to them, but one checked him by stretching an arm out in front of him. The other man took his right hand out of his pocket and flourished it in the boy's face so that the nickel-plated knuckles on it twinkled in the light. The boy ducked swiftly under the threatening hand and outstretched arm, and went on across the alley, walking, and not even looking over his shoulder at the two men who were now closing on his back.

Just before they reached him another reached them – a broad-backed, long-armed, ape-built man I had not seen before. Each arm caught a man. By the napes of their necks he yanked them away from the boy's back, shook them till their hats fell off, smacked their skulls together with a crack that was like a broom-handle breaking, and dragged their rag limp bodies out of sight up the alley. While this was happening the boy walked jauntily down the street, without a backward glance.

When the skull-cracker came out of the alley I saw his face in the light – a dark-skinned heavily lined face, broad and flat, with jaw-muscles bulging like abscesses under his ears. He spit, hitched his pants, and swaggered down the street after the boy.

The boy went into Larrouy's. The skull-cracker followed him in. The boy came out, and in his rear – perhaps twenty feet behind – the skull-cracker rolled. Jack had tailed them into Larrouy's while I had held up the outside.

"Still carrying messages?" I asked.

"Yes. He spoke to five men in there. He's got plenty of bodyguard, hasn't he?"

"Yeah," I agreed. "And you be damned careful you don't get between them. If they split, I'll shadow the skull-cracker, you keep the goose."

We separated and moved after our game. They took us to all the hangouts in San Francisco, to cabarets, grease-joints, pool-rooms, saloons, flophouses, hockshops, gambling joints and what have you. Everywhere the kid found men to speak his dozen words to, and between calls, he found them on street corners.

I would have liked to get behind some of these birds, but I didn't want to leave Jack alone with the boy and his body-guard – they seemed to mean too much. And I couldn't stick Jack on one of the others, because it wasn't safe for me to hang too close to the Armenian boy. So we played the game as we had started it, shadowing our pair from hole to hole, while night got on toward morning.

It was a few minutes past midnight when they came out of a small hotel up on Kearny Street, and for the first time since we had seen them they walked together, side by side, up to

Green Street, where they turned east along the side of Telegraph Hill. Half a block of this, and they climbed the front steps of a ramshackle furnished-room house and disappeared inside. I joined Jack Counihan on the corner where he had stopped.

"The greetings have all been delivered," I guessed, "or he wouldn't have called in his bodyguard. If there's nothing stirring within the next half hour I'm going to beat it. You'll have to take a plant on the joint till morning."

Twenty minutes later the skull-cracker came out of the house and walked down the street.

"I'll take him," I said. "You stick to the other baby."

The skull-cracker took ten or twelve steps from the house and stopped. He looked back at the house, raising his face to look at the upper stories. Then Jack and I could hear what had stopped him. Up in the house a man was screaming. It wasn't much of a scream in volume. Even now, when it had increased in strength, it barely reached our ears. But in it – in that one wailing voice – everything that fears death seemed to cry out its fear. I heard Jack's teeth click. I've got horny skin all over what's left of my soul, but just the same my forehead twitched. The scream was so damned weak for what it said.

The skull-cracker moved. Five gliding strides carried him back to the house. He didn't touch one of the six or seven front steps. He went from pavement to vestibule in a spring no monkey could have beaten for swiftness, ease or silence. One minute, two minutes, three minutes, and the screaming stopped. Three more minutes and the skull-cracker was leaving the house again. He paused on the sidewalk to spit and hitch his pants. Then he swaggered off down the street.

"He's your meat, Jack," I said. "I'm going to call on the boy. He won't recognize me now."

The street door of the rooming-house was not only unlocked but wide open. I went through it into a hallway, where a dim light burning upstairs outlined a flight of steps. I climbed them and turned toward the front of the house. The scream had come from the front – either this floor or the third. There was a fair likelihood of the skull-cracker having left the room door unlocked, just as he had not paused to close the street door.

I had no luck on the second floor, but the third knob I cautiously tried on the third floor turned in my hand and let its door edge back from the frame. In front of this crack I waited a moment, listening to nothing but a throbbing snore somewhere far down the hallway. I put a palm against the door and eased it open another foot. No sound. The room was black as an honest politician's prospects. I slid my hand across the frame, across a few inches of wallpaper, found a light button, pressed it. Two globes in the center of the room threw their weak yellow light on the shabby room and on the young Armenian who lay dead across the bed.

I went into the room, closed the door and stepped over to the bed. The boy's eyes were wide and bulging. One of his temples was bruised. His throat gaped with a red slit that ran actually from ear to ear. Around the slit, in the few spots not washed red, his thin neck showed dark bruises. The skull-cracker had dropped the boy with a poke in the temple and had choked him until he thought him dead. But the kid had revived enough to scream – not enough to keep from screaming. The skull-cracker had returned to finish the job with a knife. Three streaks on the bed-clothes showed where the knife had been cleaned.

The lining of the boy's pockets stuck out. The skull-cracker had turned them out. I went through his clothes, but with no better luck than I expected – the killer had taken everything. The room gave me nothing – a few clothes, but not a thing out of which information could be squeezed.

My prying done, I stood in the center of the floor scratching my chin and considering. In the hall a floorboard creaked.

Three backward steps on my rubber heels put me in the musty closet, dragging the door all but half an inch shut behind me.

Knuckles rattled on the room door as I slid my gun off my hip. The knuckles rattled again and a feminine voice said, "Kid, oh, Kid!" Neither knuckles nor voice was loud. The lock clicked as the knob turned. The door opened and framed the shifty-eyed girl who had been called Sylvia Yount by Angel Grace.

Her eyes lost their shiftiness for surprise when they settled on the boy.

"Holy hell!" she gasped, and was gone.

I was half out of the closet when I heard her tiptoeing back. In my hole again, I waited, my eye to the crack. She came in swiftly, closed the door silently, and went to lean over the dead boy. Her hands moved over him, exploring the pockets whose linings I had put back in place.

"Damn such luck!" she said aloud when the unprofitable frisking was over, and went out of the house.

I gave her time to reach the sidewalk. She was headed toward Kearny Street when I left the house. I shadowed her down Kearny to Broadway, up Broadway to Larrouy's. Larrouy's was busy, especially near the door, with customers going and coming. I was within five feet of the girl when she stopped a waiter and asked, in a whisper that was excited enough to carry, "Is Red here?"

The waiter shook his head. "Ain't been in tonight."

The girl went out of the dive, hurrying along on clicking heels to a hotel in Stockton Street.

While I looked through the glass front, she went to the desk and spoke to the clerk. He shook his head. She spoke again and he gave her paper and envelope, on which she scribbled with the pen beside the register. Before I had to leave for a safer position from which to cover her exit, I saw which pigeonhole the note went into.

From the hotel the girl went by streetcar to Market and Powell Streets, and then walked up Powell to O'Farrell, where a fat-faced young man in gray overcoat and gray hat left the curb to link arms with her and lead her to a taxi stand up O'Farrell Street. I let them go, making a note of the taxi number – the fat-faced man looked more like a customer than a pal.

It was a little shy of two in the morning when I turned back into Market Street and went up to the office. Fiske, who holds down the Agency at night, said Jack Counihan had not reported; nothing else had come in. I told him to rouse me an operative, and in ten or fifteen minutes he succeeded in getting Mickey Linehan out of bed and on the wire.

"Listen, Mickey," I said, "I've got the nicest corner picked out for you to stand on the rest of the night. So pin on your diapers and toddle down there, will you?"

In between his grumbling and cursing I gave him the name and number of the Stockton Street hotel, described Red O'Leary, and told him which pigeonhole the note had been put in.

"It mightn't be Red's home, but the chance is worth covering," I wound up. "If you pick him up, try not to lose him before I can get somebody down there to take him off your hands." I hung up during the outburst of profanity this insult brought.

The Hall of Justice was busy when I reached it, though nobody had tried to shake the upstairs prison loose yet. Fresh lots of suspicious characters were being brought in every few minutes. Policemen in and out of uniform were everywhere. The detective bureau was a beehive.

Trading information with the police detectives, I told them about the Armenian boy. We were making up a party to visit the remains when the captain's door opened and Lieutenant Duff came into the assembly room.

"*Allez! Oop!*" he said, pointing a thick finger at O'Gar,

Tully, Reecher, Hunt and me. "There's a thing worth looking at in Fillmore."

We followed him out to an automobile.

A gray frame house in Fillmore Street was our destination. A lot of people stood in the street looking at the house. A police-wagon stood in front of it, and police uniforms were indoors and out.

A red-mustached corporal saluted Duff and led us into the house, explaining as we went, " 'Twas the neighbors give us a rumble, complaining of the fighting, and when we got here, faith, there weren't no fight left in nobody."

All the house held was fourteen dead men.

Eleven of them had been poisoned – overdoses of knockout drops in their booze, the doctor said. The other three had been shot, at intervals along the hall. From the looks of the remains, they had drunk a toast – a loaded one – and those who hadn't drunk, whether because of temperance or suspicious natures, had been gunned as they tried to get away.

The identity of the bodies gave us an idea of what their toast had been. They were all thieves – they had drunk their poison to the day's looting.

We didn't know all the dead men then, but all of us knew some of them, and the records told us who the others were later. The completed list read like *Who's Who in Crookdom.*

There was the Dis-and-Dat Kid, who had crushed out of Leavenworth only two months before; Sheeny Holmes; Snohomish Shitey, supposed to have died a hero in France in 1919; L. A. Slim, from Denver, sockless and underwearless as usual, with a thousand-dollar bill sewed in each shoulder of his coat; Spider Girrucci wearing a steel-mesh vest under his shirt and a scar from crown to chin where his brother had carved him years ago; Old Pete Best, once a congressman; Nigger Vohan, who once won $175,000 in a Chicago crap game – *Abracadabra* tattooed on him in three places; Alphabet Shorty McCoy; Tom Brooks, Alphabet Shorty's brother-in-law, who invented the Richmond razzle-dazzle and bought three hotels with the profits; Red Cudahy, who stuck up a Union Pacific train in 1924; Denny Burke; Bull McGonickle, still pale from fifteen years in Joliet; Toby the Lugs, Bull's running-mate, who used to brag about picking President Wilson's pocket in a Washington vaudeville theatre; and Paddy the Mex.

Duff looked them over and whistled.

"A few more tricks like this," he said, "and we'll all be out of jobs. There won't be any grifters left to protect the tax-payers from."

"I'm glad you like it," I told him. "Me – I'd hate like hell to be a San Francisco copper the next few days."

"Why especially?"

"Look at this – one grand piece of double-crossing. This village of ours is full of mean lads who are waiting right now for these stiffs to bring 'em their cut of the stick-up. What do you think's going to happen when the word gets out that there's not going to be any gravy for the mob? There are going to be a hundred and more stranded thugs busy raising getaway dough. There'll be three burglaries to a block and a stick-up to every corner until the carfare's raised. God bless you, my son, you're going to sweat for your wages!"

Duff shrugged his thick shoulders and stepped over bodies to get to the telephone. When he was through I called the Agency.

"Jack Counihan called a couple of minutes ago," Fiske told me, and gave me an Army Street address. "He says he put his men in there, with company."

I phoned for a taxi, and then told Duff, "I'm going to run out for a while. I'll give you a ring here if there's anything to the angle, or if there isn't. You'll wait?"

"If you're not too long."

I got rid of my taxicab two blocks from the address Fiske had given me, and walked down Army Street to find Jack Counihan planted on a dark corner.

"I got a bad break," was what he welcomed me with. "While I was phoning from the lunchroom up the street some of my people ran out on me."

"Yeah? What's the dope?"

"Well, after that apey chap left the Green Street house he trolleyed to a house in Fillmore Street, and –"

"What number?"

The number Jack gave was that of the death-house I had just left.

"In the next ten or fifteen minutes just about that many other chaps went into the same house. Most of them came afoot, singly or in pairs. Then two cars came up together, with nine men in them – I counted them. They went into the house, leaving their machines in front. A taxi came past a little later, and I stopped it, in case my chap should motor away.

"Nothing happened for at least half an hour after the nine chaps went in. Then everybody in the house seemed to become demonstrative – there was a quantity of yelling and shooting. It lasted long enough to awaken the whole neighborhood. When it stopped, ten men – I counted them – ran out of the house, got into the two cars and drove away. My man was one of them.

"My faithful taxi and I cried *Yoicks* after them, and they brought us here, going into that house down the street in front of which one of their motors still stands. After half an hour or so I thought I'd better report, so, leaving my taxi around the corner – where it's still running up expenses – I went up to Fiske. And when I came back, one of the cars was gone – and I, woe is me! – don't know who went with it. Am I rotten?"

"Sure! You should have taken their cars along to the phone

with you. Watch the one that's left while I collect a strong-arm squad."

I went up to the lunchroom and phoned Duff, telling him where I was, and, "If you bring your gang along maybe there'll be profit in it. A couple of carloads of folks who were in Fillmore Street and didn't stay there came here, and part of 'em may still be here, if you make it sudden."

Duff brought his four detectives and a dozen uniformed men with him. We hit the house front and back. No time was wasted ringing the bell. We simply tore down the doors and went in. Everything inside was black until flashlights lit it up. There was no resistance. Ordinarily the six men we found in there would have damned near ruined us in spite of our outnumbering them. But they were too dead for that.

We looked at one another sort of open-mouthed.

"This is getting monotonous," Duff complained, biting off a hunk of tobacco. "Everybody's work is pretty much the same thing over and over, but I'm tired of walking into roomfuls of butchered crooks."

The catalogue here had fewer names than the other, but they were bigger names. The Shivering Kid was here – nobody would collect all the reward money piled up on him now; Darby M'Laughlin, his horn-rimmed glasses crooked on his nose, ten thousand dollars' worth of diamonds on fingers and tie; Happy Jim Hacker; Donkey Marr, the last of the bowlegged Marrs, killers all, father and five sons; Toots Salda, the strongest man in crookdom, who had once picked up and run away with two Savannah coppers to whom he was handcuffed; and Rumdum Smith, who killed Lefty Read in Chi in 1916 – a rosary wrapped around his left wrist.

No gentlemanly poisoning here – these boys had been mowed down with a .30-.30 rifle fitted with a clumsy but effective homemade silencer. The rifle lay on the kitchen table. A door connected the kitchen with the dining room.

Directly opposite the door, double doors – wide open – opened into the room in which the dead thieves lay. They were all close to the front wall, lying as if they had been lined up against the wall to be knocked off.

The gray-papered wall was spattered with blood, punctured with holes where a couple of bullets had gone all the way through. Jack Counihan's young eyes picked out a stain on the paper that wasn't accidental. It was close to the floor, beside the Shivering Kid, and the Kid's right hand was stained with blood. He had written on the wall before he died – with fingers dipped in his own and Toots Salda's blood. The letters in the words showed breaks and gaps where his fingers had run dry, and the letters were crooked and straggly, because he must have written them in the dark.

By filling in the gaps, allowing for the kinks, and guessing where there weren't any indications to guide us, we got two words: *Big Flora*.

"They don't mean anything to me," Duff said, "but it's a name and most of the names we have belong to dead men now, so it's time we were adding to our list."

"What do you make of it?" asked bullet-headed O'Gar, detective-sergeant in the Homicide Detail, looking at the bodies. "Their pals got the drop on them, lined them against the wall, and the sharp-shooter in the kitchen shot 'em down – bing-bing-bing-bing-bing-bing?"

"It reads that way," the rest of us agreed.

"Ten of 'em came here from Fillmore Street," I said. "Six stayed here. Four went to another house – where part of 'em are now cutting down the other part. All that's necessary is to trail the corpses from house to house until there's only one man left – and he's bound to play it through by croaking himself, leaving the loot to be recovered in the original packages. I hope you folks don't have to stay up all night to find the remains of that last thug. Come on, Jack, let's go home for some sleep."

*

It was exactly 5 a.m. when I separated the sheets and crawled into my bed. I was asleep before the last draw of smoke from my goodnight Fatima was out of my lungs. The telephone woke me at 5:15.

Fiske was talking, "Mickey Linehan just phoned that your Red O'Leary came home to roost half an hour ago."

"Have him booked," I said, and was asleep again by 5:17.

With the help of the alarm clock I rolled out of bed at nine, breakfasted, and went down to the detective bureau to see how the police had made out with the redhead. Not so good.

"He's got us stopped," the captain told me. "He's got alibis for the time of the looting and for last night's doings. And we can't even vag the son-of-a-gun. He's got means of support. He's salesman for Humperdickel's Universal Encyclopaediac Dictionary of Useful and Valuable Knowledge, or something like it. He started peddling these pamphlets the day before the knockover, and at the time it was happening he was ringing doorbells and asking folks to buy his durned books. Anyway, he's got three witnesses that say so. Last night he was in a hotel from eleven to four-thirty this morning, playing cards, and he's got witnesses. We didn't find a durned thing on him or in his room."

I borrowed the captain's phone to call Jack Counihan's house.

"Could you identify any of the men you saw in the cars last night?" I asked when he had been stirred out of bed.

"No. It was dark and they moved too fast. I could barely make sure of my chap."

"Can't, huh?" the captain said. "Well, I can hold him twenty-four hours without laying charges, and I'll do that, but I'll have to spring him unless you can dig up something."

"Suppose you turn him loose now," I suggested after thinking through my cigarette for a few minutes. "He's got himself all alibied up, so there's no reason why he should hide out on us. We'll let him alone all day – give him time to make sure he isn't being tailed – and then we'll get behind him tonight and stay behind him. Any dope on Big Flora?"

"No. That kid that was killed in Green Street was Bernie Bernheimer, alias the Motsa Kid. I guess he was a dip – he ran with dips – but he wasn't very –"

The buzz of the phone interrupted him. He said, "Hello, yes," and "Just a minute," into the instrument, and slid it across the desk to me.

A feminine voice: "This is Grace Cardigan. I called your agency and they told me where to get you. I've got to see you. Can you meet me now?"

"Where are you?"

"In the telephone station on Powell Street."

"I'll be there in fifteen minutes," I said.

Calling the Agency, I got hold of Dick Foley and asked him to meet me at Ellis and Market right away. Then I gave the captain back his phone, said "See you later," and went uptown to keep my dates.

Dick Foley was on his corner when I got there. He was a swarthy little Canadian who stood nearly five feet in his high-heeled shoes, weighed a hundred pounds minus, talked like a Scotchman's telegram, and could have shadowed a drop of salt water from Golden Gate to Hong Kong without ever losing sight of it.

"You know Angel Grace Cardigan?" I asked him.

He saved a word by shaking his head, no.

"I'm going to meet her in the telephone station. When I'm through, stay behind her. She's smart, and she'll be looking for you, so it won't be duck soup, but do what you can."

Dick's mouth went down at the corners and one of his rare long-winded streaks hit him. "Harder they look, easier they are," he said.

He trailed along behind me while I went up to the station. Angel Grace was standing in the doorway. Her face was more sullen than I had ever seen it, and therefore less beautiful – except her green eyes, which held too much fire for sullenness. A rolled newspaper was in one of her hands. She neither spoke, smiled nor nodded.

"We'll go to Charley's, where we can talk," I said, guiding her down past Dick Foley.

Not a murmur did I get out of her until we were seated cross-table in the restaurant booth, and the waiter had gone off with our orders. Then she spread the newspaper out on the table with shaking hands.

"Is this on the level?" she demanded.

I looked at the story her shaking finger tapped – an account of the Fillmore and Army Street findings, but a cagey account. A glance showed that no names had been given, that the police had censored the story quite a bit. While I pretended to read I wondered whether it would be to my advantage to tell the girl the story was a fake. But I couldn't see any clear profit in that, so I saved my soul a lie.

"Practically straight," I admitted.

"You were there?" She had pushed the paper aside to the floor and was leaning over the table.

"With the police."

"Was –" Her voice broke huskily. Her white fingers wadded the tablecloth in two little bunches halfway between us. She cleared her throat. "Who was – ?" was as far as she got this time.

A pause. I waited. Her eyes went down, but not before I had seen water dulling the fire in them. During the pause the waiter came in, put our food down, went away.

"You know what I want to ask?" she said presently, her voice low, choked. "Was he? Was he? For God's sake tell me!"

I weighed them – truth against lie, lie against truth. Once more truth triumphed.

"Paddy the Mex was shot – killed – in the Fillmore Street house," I said.

The pupils of her eyes shrank to pinpoints – spread again until they almost covered the green irises. She made no sound. Her face was empty. She picked up a fork and lifted a forkful of salad to her mouth – another. Reaching across the table, I took the fork out of her hand.

"You're only spilling it on your clothes," I growled. "You can't eat without opening your mouth to put the food in."

She put her hands across the table, reaching for mine, trembling, holding my hand with fingers that twitched so that the nails scratched me.

"You're not lying to me?" she half sobbed, half chattered. "You're on the square! You were white to me that time in Philly! Paddy always said you were one white dick! You're not tricking me?"

"Straight up," I assured her. "Paddy meant a lot to you?"

She nodded dully, pulling herself together, sinking back in a sort of stupor.

"The way's open to even up for him," I suggested.

"You mean –?"

"Talk."

She stared at me blankly for a long while, as if she was trying to get some meaning out of what I had said. I read the answer in her eyes before she put it in words.

"I wish to God I could! But I'm Paperbox-John Cardigan's daughter. It isn't in me to turn anybody up. You're on the wrong side. I can't go over. I wish I could. But there's too much Cardigan in me. I'll be hoping every minute that you nail them, and nail them dead right, but –"

"Your sentiments are noble, or words to that effect," I sneered at her. "Who do you think you are – Joan of Arc? Would your brother Frank be in stir now if his partner, Johnny the Plumber, hadn't put the finger on him for the Great Falls bulls? Come to life, dearie! You're a thief among thieves, and those who don't double-cross get crossed. Who rubbed your

Paddy the Mex out? Pals! But you mustn't slap back at 'em because it wouldn't be clubby. My God!"

My speech only thickened the sullenness in her face.

"I'm going to slap back," she said, "but I can't, can't split. I can't tell you. If you were a gun, I'd – anyway, what help I get will be on my side of the game. Let it go at that, won't you? I know how you feel about it, but – will you tell me who besides – who else was – was found in those houses?"

"Oh, sure!" I snarled. "I'll tell you everything. I'll let you pump me dry. But you mustn't give me any hints, because it might not be in keeping with the ethics of your highly honorable profession!"

Being a woman, she ignored all this, repeating, "Who else?"

"Nothing stirring. But I will do this – I'll tell you a couple who weren't there – Big Flora and Red O'Leary."

Her dopiness was gone. She studied my face with green eyes that were dark and savage.

"Was Bluepoint Vance?" she demanded.

"What do you guess?" I replied.

She studied my face for a moment longer and then stood up.

"Thanks for what you've told me," she said, "and for meeting me like this. I do hope you win."

She went out to be shadowed by Dick Foley. I ate my lunch.

At four o'clock that afternoon Jack Counihan and I brought our hired automobile to rest within sight of the front door of the Stockton hotel.

"He cleared himself with the police, so there's no reason why he should have moved, maybe," I told Jack, "and I'd rather not monkey with the hotel people, not knowing them. If he doesn't show by late we'll have to go up against them then."

We settled down to cigarettes, guesses on who'd be the next heavyweight champion and where to get good gin and what to do with it, the injustice of the new Agency ruling that for purposes of expense accounts Oakland was not to be considered out of town, and similar exciting topics, which carried us from four o'clock to ten minutes past nine.

At 9:10 Red O'Leary came out of the hotel.

"God is good," said Jack as he jumped out of the machine to do the footwork while I stirred the motor.

The fire-topped giant didn't take us far. Larrouy's front door gobbled him. By the time I had parked the car and gone into the dive, both O'Leary and Jack had found seats. Jack's table was on the edge of the dance floor. O'Leary's was on the other side of the establishment against the wall, near a corner. A fat blond couple were leaving the table back in that corner when I came in, so I persuaded the waiter who was guiding me to a table to make it that one.

O'Leary's face was three-quarters turned away from me. He was watching the front door, watching it with an earnestness that turned suddenly to happiness when a girl appeared there. She was the girl Angel Grace had called Nancy Regan. I have already said she was nice. Well, she was. And the cocky little blue hat that hid all her hair didn't handicap her niceness any tonight.

The redhead scrambled to his feet and pushed a waiter and a couple of customers out of his way as he went to meet her. As reward for his eagerness he got some profanity that he didn't seem to hear and a blue-eyed, white-toothed smile that was – well – nice. He brought her back to his table and put her in a chair facing me, while he sat very much facing her.

His voice was a baritone rumble out of which my snooping ears could pick no words. He seemed to be telling her a lot, and she listened as if she liked it.

"But, Reddy, dear, you shouldn't," she said once. Her voice – I know other words, but we'll stick to this one – was nice. Outside of the musk in it, it had quality. Whoever this gunman's moll was, she either had had a good start in life or had learned her stuff well. Now and then, when the orchestra came up for air, I would catch a few words, but they didn't tell me anything except that neither she nor her rowdy playmate had anything against the other.

The joint had been nearly empty when she came in. By ten o'clock it was fairly crowded, and ten o'clock is early for Larrouy's customers. I began to pay less attention to Red's girl – even if she was nice – and more to my other neighbors. It struck me that there weren't many women in sight. Checking up on that, I found damned few women in proportion to the men. Men – rat-faced men, hatchet-faced men, square-jawed men, slack-chinned men, pale men, scrawny men, funny-looking men, tough-looking men, ordinary men – sitting two to a table, four to a table, more coming in – and damned few women.

These men talked to one another as if they weren't much interested in what they were saying. They looked casually around the joint with eyes that were blankest when they came to O'Leary. And always those casual, bored glances did rest on O'Leary for a second or two.

I returned my attention to O'Leary and Nancy Regan. He was sitting a little more erect in his chair than he had been, but it was an easy, supple erectness and though his shoulders had hunched a bit, there was no stiffness in them. She said something to him. He laughed, turning his face toward the center of the room, so that he seemed to be laughing not only at what she said, but also at these men who sat around him, waiting. It was a hearty laugh, young and careless.

The girl looked surprised for a moment, as if something in the laugh puzzled her; then she went on with whatever she was telling him. She didn't know she was sitting on dynamite, I decided. O'Leary knew. Every inch of him, every gesture, said, "I'm big, strong, young, tough and red-headed. When you boys want to do your stuff I'll be here."

Time slid by. Few couples danced. Jean Larrouy went

around with dark worry in his round face. His joint was full of customers, but he would rather have had it empty.

By eleven o'clock I stood up and beckoned to Jack Counihan. He came over, we shook hands, exchanged *How's everything* and *Getting muches*, and he sat at my table.

"What is happening?" he asked under cover of the orchestra's din. "I can't see anything, but there is something in the air. Or am I being hysterical?"

"You will be presently. The wolves are gathering, and Red O'Leary's the lamb. You could pick a tenderer one if you had a free hand, maybe. But these bimbos once helped pluck a bank, and when payday came there wasn't anything in their envelopes, not even any envelopes. The word got out that maybe Red knew how come. Hence this. They're waiting now – maybe for somebody – maybe till they get enough hooch in them."

"And we sit here because it's the nearest table to the target for all these fellows' bullets when the blooming lid blows off?" Jack inquired. "Let's move over to Red's table. It's still nearer, and I rather like the appearance of the girl with him."

"Don't be impatient, you'll have your fun," I promised him. "There's no sense in having this O'Leary killed. If they bargain with him in a gentlemanly way, we'll lay off. But if they start heaving things at him, you and I are going to pry him and his girl friend loose."

"Well spoken, my hearty!" He grinned, whitening around the mouth. "Are there any details, or do we just simply and unostentatiously pry 'em loose?"

"See the door behind me, to the right? When the pop-off comes, I'm going back there and open it up. You hold the line midway between. When I yelp, you give Red whatever help he needs to get back there."

"Aye, aye!" He looked around the room at the assembled plug-uglies, moistened his lips, and looked at the hand holding his cigarette, a quivering hand. "I hope you won't think I'm in a funk," he said. "But I'm not an antique murderer like you. I get a reaction out of this prospective slaughtering."

"Reaction, my eye," I said. "You're scared stiff. But no nonsense, mind! If you try to make a vaudeville act out of it I'll ruin whatever those gorillas leave of you. You do what you're told, and nothing else. If you get any bright ideas, save 'em to tell me about afterward."

"Oh, my conduct will be most exemplary!" he assured me.

It was nearly midnight when what the wolves waited for came. The last pretense of indifference went out of faces that had been gradually taking on tenseness. Chairs and feet scraped as men pushed themselves back a little from their tables. Muscles flexed bodies into readiness for action. Tongues licked lips and eyes looked eagerly at the front door.

Bluepoint Vance was coming into the room. He came alone, nodding to acquaintances on this side and that, carrying his tall body gracefully, easily, in its well-cut clothing. His sharp-featured face was smilingly self-confident. He came without haste and without delay to Red O'Leary's table. I couldn't see Red's face, but muscles thickened the back of his neck. The girl smiled cordially at Vance and gave him her hand. It was naturally done. She didn't know anything.

Vance turned his smile from Nancy Regan to the red-haired giant – a smile that was a trifle cat-to-mousey.

"How's everything, Red?" he asked.

"Everything suits me," bluntly.

The orchestra had stopped playing. Larrouy, standing by the street door, was mopping his forehead with a handkerchief. At the table to my right, a barrel-chested, broken-nosed bruiser in a widely striped suit was breathing heavily between his gold teeth, his watery gray eyes bulging at O'Leary, Vance and Nancy. He was in no way conspicuous – there were too many others holding the same pose.

Bluepoint Vance turned his head, called to a waiter, "Bring me a chair."

The chair was brought and put at the unoccupied side of the table, facing the wall. Vance sat down, slumping back in the chair, leaning indolently toward Red, his left arm hooked over the chairback, his right hand holding a cigarette.

"Well, Red," he said when he was thus installed, "have you got any news for me?"

His voice was suave, but loud enough for those at nearby tables to hear.

"Not a word." O'Leary's voice made no pretense of friendliness, nor of caution.

"What, no spinach?" Vance's thin-lipped smile spread, and his dark eyes had a mirthful but not pleasant glitter. "Nobody gave you anything to give me?"

"No," said O'Leary, emphatically.

"My goodness!" said Vance, the smile in his eyes and mouth deepening, and getting still less pleasant. "That's ingratitude! Will you help me collect, Red?"

"No."

I was disgusted with this redhead – half-minded to let him go under when the storm broke. Why couldn't he have stalled his way out – fixed up a fancy tale that Bluepoint would have had to halfway accept? But no – this O'Leary boy was so damned childishly proud of his toughness that he had to make a show of it when he should have been using his bean. If it had been only his own carcass that was due for a beating, it would have been all right. But it wasn't all right that Jack and I should have to suffer. This big chump was too valuable to lose. We'd have to get ourselves all battered up saving him from the rewards of his own pig-headedness. There was no justice in it.

"I've a lot of money coming to me, Red," Vance spoke hazily, tauntingly. "And I need that money." He drew on his cigarette, casually blew the smoke into the redhead's face, and drawled, "Why, do you know the laundry charges twenty-six cents just for doing a pair of pajamas? I need money."

"Sleep in your underclothes," said O'Leary.

Vance laughed. Nancy Regan smiled, but in a bewildered way. She didn't seem to know what it was all about, but she couldn't help knowing that it was about something.

O'Leary leaned forward and spoke deliberately, loud enough for any to hear, "Bluepoint, I've got nothing to give you – now or ever. And that goes for anybody else that's interested. If you or them think I owe you something – try and get it. To hell with you, Bluepoint Vance! If you don't like it – you've got friends here. Call 'em on!"

What a prime young idiot! Nothing would suit him but an ambulance – and I must be dragged along with him.

Vance grinned evilly, his eyes glittering into O'Leary's face. "You'd like that, Red?"

O'Leary hunched his big shoulders and let them drop.

"I don't mind a fight," he said. "But I'd like to get Nancy out of it." He turned to her. "Better run along, honey, I'm going to be busy."

She started to say something, but Vance was talking to her. His words were lightly spoken, and he made no objection to her going. The substance of what he told her was that she was going to be lonely without Red. But he went intimately into the details of that loneliness.

Red O'Leary's right hand rested on the table. It went up to Vance's mouth. The hand was a fist when it got there. A wallop of that sort is awkward to deliver. The body can't give it much. It had to depend on the arm muscles, and not on the best of those. Yet Bluepoint Vance was driven out of his chair and across to the next table.

Larrouy's chairs went empty. The shindig was on.

"On your toes," I growled at Jack Counihan, and, doing my best to look like the nervous little fat man I was, I ran toward the back door, passing men who were moving not yet swiftly toward O'Leary. I must have looked the part of a scared trouble-dodger, because nobody stopped me, and I reached the door before the pack had closed on Red. The door was closed, but not locked. I wheeled with my back to it, blackjack in right hand, gun in left. Men were in front of me, but their backs were to me.

O'Leary was towering in front of his table, his tough red face full of bring-on-your-hell, his big body balanced on the balls of his feet. Between us, Jack Counihan stood, his face turned to me, his mouth twitching in a nervous grin, his eyes dancing with delight. Bluepoint Vance was on his feet again. Blood trickled from his thin lips, down his chin. His eyes were cool. They looked at Red O'Leary with the businesslike look of a logger sizing up the tree he's going to bring down. Vance's mob watched Vance.

"Red!" I bawled into the silence. "This way, Red!"

Faces spun to me – every face in the joint – millions of them.

"Come on, Red!" Jack Counihan yelped, taking a step forward, his gun out.

Bluepoint Vance's hand flashed to the V of his coat. Jack's gun snapped at him. Bluepoint had thrown himself down before the boy's trigger was yanked. The bullet went wide, but Vance's draw was gummed.

Red scooped the girl up with his left arm. A big automatic blossomed in his right fist. I didn't pay much attention to him after that. I was busy.

Larrouy's home was pregnant with weapons – guns, knives, saps, knucks, club-swung chairs and bottles, miscellaneous implements of destruction. Men brought their weapons over to mingle with me. The game was to nudge me away from my door. O'Leary would have liked it. But I was no fire-haired young rowdy. I was pushing forty, and I was twenty pounds overweight. I had the liking for ease that goes with that age and weight. Little ease I got.

A squint-eyed Portuguese slashed at my neck with a knife that spoiled my necktie. I caught him over the ear with the side of my gun before he could get away, saw the ear tear loose. A grinning kid of twenty went down for my legs – football stuff. I felt his teeth in the knee I pumped up, and felt them break. A pock-marked mulatto pushed a gun-barrel over the shoulder of the man in front of him. My blackjack crunched the arm of the man in front. He winced sidewise as the mulatto pulled the trigger – and had the side of his face blown away.

I fired twice – once when a gun was leveled within a foot of my middle, once when I discovered a man standing on a table not far off taking careful aim at my head. For the rest I trusted to my arms and legs, and saved bullets. The night was young and I had only a dozen pills – six in the gun, six in my pocket.

It was a swell bag of nails. Swing right, swing left, kick, swing right, swing left, kick. Don't hesitate, don't look for targets. God will see that there's always a mug there for your gun or blackjack to sock, a belly for your foot.

A bottle came through and found my forehead. My hat saved me some, but the crack didn't do me any good. I swayed and broke a nose where I should have smashed a skull. The room seemed stuffy, poorly ventilated. Somebody ought to tell Larrouy about it. How do you like that lead-and-leather pat on the temple, blondy? This rat on my left is getting too close. I'll draw him in by bending to the right to poke the mulatto, and then I'll lean back into him and let him have it. Not bad! But I can't keep this up all night. Where are Red and Jack? Standing off watching me?

Somebody socked me in the shoulder with something – a piano from the feel of it. I couldn't miss it. Another thrown bottle took my hat and part of my scalp. Red O'Leary and Jack Counihan smashed through, dragging the girl between them.

*

While Jack put the girl through the door, Red and I cleared a little space in front of us. He was good at that. I didn't dog it on him, but I did let him get all the exercise he wanted.

"All right!" Jack called.

Red and I went through the door, slammed it shut. It wouldn't hold even if locked. O'Leary sent three slugs through it to give the boys something to think about, and our retreat got under way.

We were in a narrow passageway lighted by a fairly bright light. At the other end was a closed door. Halfway down, to the right, steps led up.

"Straight ahead?" asked Jack, who was in front.

O'Leary said, "Yes," and I said, "No. Vance will have that blocked by now if the bulls haven't. Upstairs – the roof."

We reached the stairs. The door behind us burst open. The light went out. The door at the other end of the passage slammed open. No light came through either door. Vance would want light. Larrouy must have pulled the switch, trying to keep his dump from being torn to toothpicks.

Tumult boiled in the dark passage as we climbed the stairs by the touch system. Whoever had come through the back door was mixing it with those who had followed us – mixing it with blows, curses and an occasional shot. More power to them! We climbed, Jack leading, the girl next, then me, and last of all, O'Leary.

Jack was gallantly reading road signs to the girl, "Careful of the landing, half a turn to the left now, put your right hand on the wall and –"

"Shut up!" I growled at him. "It's better to have her falling down than to have everybody in the drum fall on us."

We reached the second floor. It was black as black. There were three stories to the building.

"I've mislaid the blooming stairs," Jack complained.

We poked around in the dark, hunting for the flight that should lead up toward the roof. We didn't find it. The riot downstairs was quieting. Vance's voice was telling his push that they were mixing it with each other, asking where we had gone. Nobody seemed to know. We didn't know, either.

"Come on," I grumbled, leading the way down the dark hall toward the back of the building. "We've got to go somewhere."

There was still noise downstairs, but no more fighting. Men were talking about getting lights. I stumbled into a door at the end of the hall, pushed it open. A room with two windows through which came a pale glow from the street lights. It seemed brilliant after the hall. My little flock followed me in and we closed the door.

Red O'Leary was across the room, his noodle to an open window.

"Back street," he whispered. "No way down unless we drop."

"Anybody in sight?" I asked.

"Don't see any."

I looked around the room – bed, couple of chairs, chest of drawers, and a table.

"The table will go through the window," I said. "We'll chuck it as far as we can and hope the racket will lead 'em out there before they decide to look up here."

Red and the girl were assuring each other that each was still all in one piece. He broke away from her to help me with the table. We balanced it, swung it, let it go. It did nicely, crashing into the wall of the building opposite, dropping down into a backyard to clang and clatter on a pile of tin, or a collection of garbage cans, or something beautifully noisy. You couldn't have heard it more than a block and a half away.

We got away from the window as men bubbled out of Larrouy's back door.

The girl, unable to find any wounds on O'Leary, had turned to Jack Counihan. He had a cut cheek. She was monkeying with it and a handkerchief.

"When you finish that," Jack was telling her, "I'm going out and get one on the other side."

"I'll never finish if you keep talking – you jiggle your cheek."

"That's a swell idea," he exclaimed. "San Francisco is the second largest city in California. Sacramento is the State capital. Do you like geography? Shall I tell you about Java? I've never been there, but I drink their coffee. If –"

"Silly!" she said, laughing. "If you don't hold still I'll stop now."

"Not so good," he said. "I'll be still."

She wasn't doing anything except wiping blood off his cheek, blood that had better been let dry there. When she finished this perfectly useless surgery, she took her hand away slowly, surveying the hardly noticeable results with pride. As her hand came on a level with his mouth, Jack jerked his head forward to kiss the tip of one passing finger.

"Silly!" she said again, snatching her hand away.

"Lay off that," said Red O'Leary, "or I'll knock you off."

"Pull in your neck," said Jack Counihan.

"Reddy!" the girl cried too late.

The O'Leary right looped out. Jack took the punch on the button, and went to sleep on the floor. The big redhead spun on the balls of his feet to loom over me.

"Got anything to say?" he asked.

I grinned down at Jack, up at Red.

"I'm ashamed of him," I said. "Letting himself be stopped by a palooka who leads with his right."

"You want to try it?"

"Reddy! Reddy!" the girl pleaded, but nobody was listening to her.

"If you'll lead with your right," I said.

"I will," he promised, and did.

I grandstanded, slipping my head out of the way, laying a forefinger on his chin.

"That could have been a knuckle," I said.

"Yes? This one is."

I managed to get under his left, taking the forearm across the back of my neck. But that about played out the acrobatics. It looked as if I would have to see what I could do to him, if anything. The girl grabbed his arm and hung on.

"Reddy, darling, haven't you had enough fighting for one night? Can't you be sensible, even if you are Irish?"

I was tempted to paste the big chew while his playmate had him tied up.

He laughed down at her, ducked his head to kiss her mouth, and grinned at me.

"There's always some other time," he said good-naturedly.

"We'd better get out of here if we can," I said. "You've made too much rumpus for it to be safe."

"Don't get it up in your neck, little man," he told me. "Hold on to my coattails and I'll pull you out."

The big tramp. If it hadn't been for Jack and me he wouldn't have had any coattail by now.

We moved to the door, listened there, heard nothing.

"The stairs to the third floor must be up front," I whispered. "We'll try for them now."

We opened the door carefully. Enough light went past us into the hall to show a promise of emptiness. We crept down the hall, Red and I each holding one of the girl's hands. I hoped Jack would come out all right, but he had put himself to sleep, and I had troubles of my own.

I hadn't known that Larrouy's was large enough to have two miles of hallway. It did. It was an even mile in the darkness to the head of the stairs we had come up. We didn't pause there to listen to the voices below. At the end of the next mile O'Leary's foot found the bottom step of the flight leading up.

Just then a yell broke out at the head of the other flight. "All up – they're up here!"

A white light beamed up on the yeller, and a brogue addressed him from below, "Come on down, ye windbag."

"The police," Nancy Regan whispered, and we hustled up our newfound steps to the third floor.

More darkness, just like that we'd left. We stood still at the top of the stairs. We didn't seem to have any company.

"The roof," I said. "We'll risk matches."

Back in a corner our feeble match-light found us a ladder nailed to the wall, leading to a trap in the ceiling. As little later as possible we were on Larrouy's roof, the trap closed behind us.

"All silk so far," said O'Leary, "and if Vance's rats and the bulls will play a couple of seconds longer – bingavast."

I led the way across the roofs. We dropped ten feet to the next building, climbed a bit to the next, and found on the other side of it a fire-escape that ran down to a narrow court with an opening into the back street.

"This ought to do it," I said, and went down.

The girl came behind me, and then Red. The court into which we dropped was empty – a narrow cement passage between buildings. The bottom of the fire-escape creaked as it hinged down under my weight, but the noise didn't stir anything. It was dark in the court, but not black.

"When we hit the street, we split," O'Leary told me, without a word of gratitude for my help – the help he didn't seem to know he had needed. "You roll your hoop, we'll roll ours."

"Uh-huh," I agreed, chasing my brains around in my skull. "I'll scout the alley first."

Carefully I picked my way down to the end of the court and risked the top of my hatless head to peep into the back street. It was quiet, but at the corner, a quarter of a block above, two loafers seemed to be loafing attentively. They weren't coppers. I stepped out into the back street and beckoned them. They couldn't recognize me at that distance, in that light, and there was no reason why they shouldn't think me one of Vance's crew, if they belonged to him.

As they came toward me I stepped back into the court and hissed for Red. He wasn't a boy you had to call twice to a row. He got to me just as they arrived. I took one. He took the other.

Because I wanted a disturbance, I had to work like a mule to get it. These bimbos were a couple of lollipops for fair. There wouldn't have been an ounce of fight in a ton of them. The one I had didn't know what to make of my roughing him around. He had a gun, but he managed to drop it first thing, and in the wrestling it got kicked out of reach. He hung on while I sweated ink jockeying him around into position. The darkness helped, but even at that it was no cinch to pretend he was putting up a battle while I worked him around behind O'Leary, who wasn't having any trouble at all with his man.

Finally I made it. I was behind O'Leary, who had his man pinned against the wall with one hand, preparing to sock him again with the other. I clamped my left hand on my playmate's wrist, twisted him to his knees, got my gun out, and shot O'Leary in the back, just below the right shoulder.

Red swayed, jamming his man into the wall. I beaned mine with the gun butt.

"Did he get you, Red?" I asked, steadying him with an arm, knocking his prisoner across the noodle.

"Yeah."

"Nancy," I called.

She ran to us.

"Take his other side," I told her. "Keep on your feet, Red, and we'll make the sneak O.K."

The bullet was too freshly in him to slow him up yet, though his right arm was out of commission. We ran down the back street to the corner. We had pursuers before we made it. Curious faces looked at us in the street. A policeman a block away began to move our way. The girl helping O'Leary on one side, me on the other, we ran half a block away from the copper, to where I had left the automobile Jack and I had used. The street was active by the time I got the machinery grinding and the girl had Red stowed safely in the back seat. The copper sent a yell and a high bullet after us. We left the neighborhood.

I didn't have any special destination yet, so after the necessary first burst of speed I slowed up a little, went around lots of corners, and brought the bus to rest in a dark street beyond Van Ness Avenue.

Red was drooping in one corner of the back, the girl holding him up, when I screwed around in my seat to look at them.

"Where to?" I asked.

"A hospital, a doctor, something!" the girl cried. "He's dying!"

I didn't believe that. If he was, it was his own fault. If he had had enough gratitude to take me along with him as a friend I wouldn't have had to shoot him so I could go along as nurse. "Where to, Red?" I asked him, prodding his knee with a finger.

He spoke thickly, giving me the address of the Stockton Street hotel.

"That's no good," I objected. "Everybody in town knows you bunk there, and if you go back, it's lights out for yours. Where to?"

"Hotel," he repeated.

I got up, knelt on the seat, and leaned back to work on him. He was weak. He couldn't have much resistance left. Bulldozing a man who might after all be dying wasn't gentlemanly, but I had invested a lot of trouble in this egg, trying to get him to lead me to his friends, and I wasn't going to quit in the stretch. For a while it looked as if he wasn't weak enough yet, as if I'd have to shoot him again. But the girl sided with me, and between us we finally convinced him that his only safe bet was to go somewhere where he could hide while he got the right kind of care. We didn't actually convince him – we wore him out and he gave in because he was too weak to argue longer. He gave me an address out by Holly Park.

Hoping for the best, I pointed the machine thither.

The house was a small one in a row of small houses. We took the big boy out of the car and between us to the door. He could just about make it with our help. The street was dark. No light showed from the house. I rang the bell.

Nothing happened. I rang again, and then once more.

"Who is it?" a harsh voice demanded from the inside.

"Red's been hurt," I said.

Silence for a while. Then the door opened half a foot. Through the opening a light came from the interior, enough light to show the flat face and bulging jaw-muscles of the skull-cracker who had been the Motsa Kid's guardian and executioner.

"What the hell?" he asked.

"Red was jumped. They got him," I explained, pushing the limp giant forward.

We didn't crash the gate that way. The skull-cracker held the door as it was.

"You'll wait," he said, and shut the door in our faces. His voice sounded from within, "Flora." That was all right – Red had brought us to the right place.

When he opened the door again he opened it all the way, and Nancy Regan and I took our burden into the hall. Beside the skull-cracker stood a woman in a low-cut black silk gown – Big Flora, I supposed.

She stood at least five feet ten in her high-heeled slippers. They were small slippers, and I noticed that her ringless hands were small. The rest of her wasn't. She was broad-shouldered, deep-bosomed, thick-armed, with a pink throat which for all its smoothness was muscled like a wrestler's. She was about my age – close to forty – with very curly and very yellow bobbed hair, very pink skin, and a handsome, brutal face. Her deep-set eyes were gray, her thick lips were well-shaped, her nose was just broad enough and curved enough to give her a look of strength, and she had chin enough to support it. From forehead to throat her pink skin was underlaid with smooth, thick, strong muscles.

This Big Flora was no toy. She had the look and the poise of a woman who could have managed the looting and the double-crossing afterward. Unless her face and body lied, she had all the strength of physique, mind and will that would be needed, and some to spare. She was made of stronger stuff than either the ape-built bruiser at her side or the red-haired giant I was holding.

"Well?" she asked, when the door had been closed behind us. Her voice was deep but not masculine – a voice that went well with her looks.

"Vance ganged him in Larrouy's. He took one in the back," I said.

"Who are you?"

"Get him to bed," I stalled. "We've got all night to talk."

She turned, snapping her fingers. A shabby little old man darted out of a door toward the rear. His brown eyes were very scary. "Get to hell upstairs," she ordered. "Fix the bed, get hot water and towels."

The little old man scrambled up the stairs like a rheumatic rabbit.

The skull-cracker took the girl's side of Red, and he and I carried the giant up to a room where the little man was scurrying around with basins and cloth. Flora and Nancy Regan followed us. We spread the wounded man facedown on the bed and stripped him. Blood still ran from the bullet hole. He was unconscious.

Nancy Regan went to pieces.

"He's dying! Get a doctor! Oh, Reddy, dearest –"

"Shut up!" said Big Flora. "The damned fool ought to croak – going to Larrouy's tonight!" She caught the little man by the shoulder and threw him at the door. "Zonite and more water," she called after him. "Give me your knife, Pogy."

The ape-built man took from his pocket a springknife with a long blade that had been sharpened until it was narrow and thin. This is the knife, I thought, that cut the Motsa Kid's throat.

With it, Big Flora cut the bullet out of Red O'Leary's back.

The ape-built Pogy kept Nancy Regan over in a corner of the room while the operating was done. The little scared man knelt beside the bed, handing the woman what she asked for, mopping up Red's blood as it ran from the wound.

I stood beside Flora, smoking cigarettes from the pack she had given me. When she raised her head, I would transfer the cigarette from my mouth to hers. She would fill her lungs with a draw that ate half the cigarette and nod. I would take the cigarette from her mouth. She would blow out the smoke and bend to her work again. I would light another cigarette from what was left of that one, and be ready for her next smoke.

Her bare arms were blood to the elbows. Her face was damp with sweat. It was a gory mess, and it took time. But when she straightened up for the last smoke, the bullet was out of Red, the bleeding had stopped, and he was bandaged.

"Thank God that's over," I said, lighting one of my own cigarettes. "Those pills you smoke are terrible."

The little scared man was cleaning up. Nancy Regan had fainted in a chair across the room, and nobody was paying any attention to her.

"Keep your eye on this gent, Pogy," Big Flora told the skull-cracker, nodding at me, "while I wash up."

I went over to the girl, rubbed her hands, put some water on her face, and got her awake.

"The bullet's out. Red's sleeping. He'll be picking fights again within a week," I told her.

She jumped up and ran over to the bed.

Flora came in. She had washed and changed her blood-stained black gown for a green kimono affair, which gaped here and there to show a lot of orchid-colored underthings.

"Talk," she commanded, standing in front of me. "Who, what and why?"

"I'm Percy Maguire," I said, as if this name, which I had just thought up, explained everything.

"That's the who," she said, as if my phony alias explained nothing. "Now what's the what and why?"

The ape-built Pogy, standing on one side, looked me up and down. I'm short and lumpy. My face doesn't scare children, but it's a more or less truthful witness to a life that hasn't been over-burdened with refinement and gentility. The evening's entertainment had decorated me with bruises and scratches, and had done things to what was left of my clothes.

"Percy," he echoed, showing wide-spaced yellow teeth in a grin. "My Gawd, brother, your folks must of been color-blind!"

"That's the what and why," I insisted to the woman, paying no attention to the wheeze from the zoo. "I'm Percy Maguire, and I want my hundred and fifty thousand dollars."

The muscles in her brows came down over her eyes.

"You've got a hundred and fifty thousand dollars, have you?"

I nodded up into her handsome brutal face.

"Yeah," I said. "That's what I came for."

"Oh, you haven't got them? You want them?"

"Listen, sister, I want my dough." I had to get tough if this play was to go over. "This swapping *Oh-have-yous* and *Yes-I-haves* don't get me anything but a thirst. We were in the big knockover, see? And after that, when we find the payoff's a bust, I said to the kid I was training with, 'Never mind, Kid, we'll get our whack. Just follow Percy.' And then Bluepoint comes to me to throw in with him, and I said, 'Sure' and me and the kid throw in with him until we all come across Red in the dump tonight. Then I told the kid, 'These coffee-and-doughnut guns are going to rub Red out, and that won't get us anything. We'll take him away from 'em and make him steer us to where Big Flora's sitting on the jack. We ought to be good for a hundred and fifty grand apiece, now that there's damned few in on it. After we get that, if we want to bump Red off, all right. But business before pleasure, and a hundred and fifty thou is business.' So we did. We opened an out for the big boy when he didn't have any. The kid got mushy with the broad along the road and got knocked for a loop. That was all right with me. If she was worth a hundred and fifty grand to him – fair enough. I came on with Red. I pulled the big tramp out after he stopped the slug. By rights I ought to collect the kid's dib, too – making three hundred thou for me – but give me the hundred and fifty I started out for and we'll call it even-steven."

I thought this hocus ought to stick. Of course I wasn't counting on her ever giving me any money, but if the rank and file of the mob hadn't known these people, why should these people know everybody in the mob?

Flora spoke to Pogy, "Get that damned heap away from the front door."

I felt better when he went out. She wouldn't have sent him out to move the car if she had meant to do anything to me right away.

"Got any food in the joint?" I asked, making myself at home.

She went to the head of the steps and yelled down, "Get something for us to eat."

Red was still unconscious. Nancy Regan sat beside him, holding one of his hands. Her face was drained white. Big Flora came into the room again, looked at the invalid, put a hand on his forehead, felt his pulse.

"Come on downstairs," she said.

"I – I'd rather stay here, if I may," Nancy Regan said. Voice and eyes showed utter terror of Flora.

The big woman, saying nothing, went downstairs. I followed her to the kitchen, where the little man was working on ham and eggs at the range. The window and back door, I saw, were reinforced with heavy planking and braced with timbers nailed to the floor. The clock over the sink said 2:50 a.m.

Flora brought out a quart of liquor and poured drinks for herself and me. We sat at the table and while we waited for our food she cursed Red O'Leary and Nancy Regan, because he had got himself disabled keeping a date with her at a time when Flora needed his strength most. She cursed them individually, as a pair, and was making it a racial matter by cursing all the Irish when the little man gave us our ham and eggs.

We had finished the solids and were stirring hooch in our second cups of coffee when Pogy came back. He had news.

"There's a couple of mugs hanging around the corner that I don't much like."

"Bulls or – ?" Flora asked.

"Or," he said.

Flora began to curse Red and Nancy again. But she had pretty well played that line out already. She turned to me.

"What the hell did you bring them here for?" she demanded. "Leaving a mile-wide trail behind you! Why didn't you let the lousy bum die where he got his dose?"

"I brought him here for my hundred and fifty grand. Slip it to me and I'll be on my way. You don't owe me anything else. I don't owe you anything. Give me my rhino instead of lip and I'll pull my freight."

"Like hell you will," said Pogy.

The woman looked at me under lowered brows and drank her coffee.

*

Fifteen minutes later the shabby little old man came running into the kitchen, saying he had heard feet on the roof. His faded brown eyes were dull as an ox's with fright, and his withered lips writhed under his straggly yellow-white mustache.

Flora profanely called him a this-and-that kind of old one-thing-and-another and chased him upstairs again. She got up from the table and pulled the green kimono tight around her big body.

"You're here," she told me, "and you'll put in with us. There's no other way. Got a rod?"

I admitted I had a gun but shook my head at the rest of it.

"This is not my wake – yet," I said. "It'll take one hundred and fifty thousand berries, spot cash, paid in the hand, to buy Percy in on it."

I wanted to know if the loot was on the premises.

Nancy Regan's tearful voice came from the stairs, "No, no, darling! Please, please, go back to bed! You'll kill yourself, Reddy, dear!"

Red O'Leary strode into the kitchen. He was naked except for a pair of gray pants and his bandage. His eyes were feverish and happy. His dry lips were stretched in a grin. He had a gun in his left hand. His right arm hung useless. Behind him trotted Nancy. She stopped pleading and shrank behind him when she saw Big Flora.

"Ring the gong, and let's go," the half-naked redhead laughed. "Vance is in our street."

Flora went over to him, put her fingers on his wrist, held them there a couple of seconds, and nodded.

"You crazy son-of-a-gun," she said in a tone that was more like maternal pride than anything else. "You're good for a fight right now. And a damned good thing, too, because you're going to get it."

Red laughed – a triumphant laugh that boasted of his toughness – then his eyes turned to me. Laughter went out of them and a puzzled look drew them narrow.

"Hello," he said. "I dreamed about you, but I can't remember what it was. It was – Wait. I'll get it in a minute. It was – By God! I dreamed it was you that plugged me!"

Flora smiled at me, the first time I had seen her smile, and she spoke quickly, "Take him, Pogy!"

I twisted obliquely out of my chair.

Pogy's fist took me in the temple. Staggering across the room, struggling to keep my feet, I thought of the bruise on the dead Motsa Kid's temple.

Pogy was on me when the wall bumped me upright.

I put a fist – spat! – in his flat nose. Blood squirted, but his hairy paws gripped me. I tucked my chin in, ground the top of my head into his face. The scent Big Flora used came strong to me. Her silk clothes brushed against me. With both hands full of my hair she pulled my head back, stretching my neck for Pogy. He took hold of it with his paws. I quit. He didn't throttle me any more than was necessary, but it was bad enough.

Flora frisked me for a gun and blackjack.

".38 Special," she named the caliber of the gun. "I dug a .38 special bullet out of you, Red." The words came faintly to me through the roaring in my ears.

The little old man's voice was chattering in the kitchen. I couldn't make out anything he said. Pogy's hands went away from me. I put my own hands to my throat. It was hell not to have any pressure at all there. The blackness went slowly away from my eyes, leaving a lot of little purple clouds that floated around and around. Presently I could sit up on the floor. I knew by that I had been lying down on it.

The purple clouds shrank until I could see past them enough to know there were only three of us in the room now. Cringing in a chair, back in a corner, was Nancy Regan. On another chair, beside the door, a black pistol in his hand, sat the scared little old man. His eyes were desperately frightened. Gun and hand shook at me. I tried to ask him to either stop shaking or move his gun away from me, but I couldn't get any words out yet.

Upstairs, guns boomed, their reports exaggerated by the smallness of the house.

The little man winced.

"Let me get out," he whispered with unexpected abruptness, "and I will give you everything. I will! Everything – if you will let me get out of this house!"

This feeble ray of light where there hadn't been a dot gave me back the use of my vocal apparatus. "Talk turkey," I managed to say.

"I will give you those upstairs – that she-devil. I will give you the money, I will give you all – if you will let me go out. I am old. I am sick. I cannot live in prison. What have I to do with robberies? Nothing. Is it my fault that she-devil – ? You have seen it here. I am a slave – I who am near the end of my life. Abuse, cursings, beatings – and those are not enough. Now I must go to prison because that she-devil is a she-devil. I am an old man who cannot live in prisons. You let me go out. You do me that kindness. I will give you that she-devil – those other devils – the money they stole. That I will do!" Thus this panic-stricken little old man squirming and fidgeting on his chair.

"How can I get you out?" I asked, getting up from the floor, my eye on his gun. If I could get to him while we talked.

"How not? You are a friend of the police – that I know. The police are here now – waiting for daylight before they come into this house. I myself with my old eyes saw them take Bluepoint Vance. You can take me out past your friends, the police. You do what I ask, and I will give you those devils and their moneys."

"Sounds good," I said, taking a careless step toward him. "But can I just stroll out of here when I want to?"

"No! No!" he said, paying no attention to the second step I took toward him. "But first I will give you those three devils. I will give them to you alive but without power. And their money. That I will do, and then you will take me out – and this girl here." He nodded suddenly at Nancy, whose white face, still nice in spite of its terror, was mostly wide eyes just now. "She, too, has nothing to do with those devils' crimes. She must go with me."

I wondered what this old rabbit thought he could do. I frowned exceedingly thoughtful while I took still another step toward him.

"Make no mistake," he whispered earnestly. "When that she-devil comes back into this room you will die – she will kill you certainly."

Three more steps and I would be close enough to take hold of him and his gun.

Footsteps were in the hall. Too late for a jump.

"Yes?" he hissed desperately.

I nodded a split-second before Big Flora came through the door.

She was dressed for action in a pair of blue pants that were probably Pogy's, beaded moccasins, a silk waist. A ribbon held her curly hair back from her face. She had a gun in one hand, one in each hip pocket.

The one in her hand swung up.

"You're done," she told me, quite matter-of-fact.

My newly acquired confederate whined, "Wait, wait, Flora! Not here like this, please! Let me take him into the cellar."

She scowled at him, shrugging her silken shoulders.

"Make it quick," she said. "It'll be light in another half-hour."

I felt too much like crying to laugh at them. Was I supposed to think this woman would let the rabbit change her plans? I suppose I must have put some value on the old gink's help, or I wouldn't have been so disappointed when this little comedy told me it was a frame-up. But any hold they worked me into couldn't be any worse than the one I was in.

So I went ahead of the old man into the hall, opened the door he indicated, switched on the basement light, and went down the rough steps.

Behind me he was whispering, "I'll first show you the moneys, and then I will give you those devils. And you will not forget your promise? I and that girl shall go out through the police?"

"Oh, yes," I assured the old joker.

He came up beside me, sticking a gun butt in my hand.

"Hide it," he hissed, and, when I had pocketed that one, gave me another, producing them with his free hand from under his coat.

Then he actually showed me the loot. It was still in the boxes and bags in which it had been carried from the banks. He insisted on opening some of them to show me the money – green bundles belted with the bank's yellow wrappers. The boxes and bags were stacked in a small brick cell that was fitted with a padlocked door, to which he had the key.

He closed the door when we were through looking, but he did not lock it, and he led me back part of the way we had come.

"That, as you see, is the money," he said. "Now for those. You will stand here, hiding behind these boxes."

A partition divided the cellar in half. It was pierced by a doorway that had no door. The place the old man told me to hide was close beside this doorway, between the partition and four packing cases. Hiding there, I would be to the right of, and a little behind, anyone who came downstairs and walked through the cellar toward the cell that held the money. That is, I would be in that position when they went to go through the doorway in the partition.

The old man was fumbling beneath one of the boxes. He brought out an eighteen-inch length of lead pipe stuffed in a similar length of black garden hose. He gave this to me as he explained everything.

"They will come down here one at a time. When they are about to go through this door, you will know what to do with this. And then you will have them, and I will have your promise. Is it not so?"

"Oh, yes," I said, all up in the air. He went upstairs. I crouched behind the boxes, examining the guns he had given me – and I'm damned if I could find anything wrong with them. They were loaded and they seemed to be in working order. That finishing touch completely balled me up. I didn't know whether I was in a cellar or a balloon.

When Red O'Leary, still naked except for pants and bandage, came into the cellar, I had to shake my head violently to clear it in time to bat him across the back of the noodle as his first bare foot stepped through the doorway. He sprawled down on his face.

The old man scurried down the steps, full of grins.

"Hurry! Hurry!" he panted, helping me drag the redhead back into the money cell. Then he produced two pieces of cord and tied the giant hand and foot.

"Hurry!" he panted again as he left me to run upstairs, while I went back to my hiding place and hefted the lead pipe, wondering if Flora had shot me and I was now enjoying the rewards of my virtue – in a heaven where I could enjoy myself forever and ever socking folks who had been rough with me down below.

The ape-built skull-cracker came down, reached the door. I cracked his skull. The little man came scurrying. We dragged Pogy to the cell, tied him up.

"Hurry!" panted the old gink, dancing up and down in his excitement. "That she-devil next – and strike hard!" He scrambled upstairs and I could hear his feet pattering overhead.

I got rid of some of my bewilderment, making room for a little intelligence in my skull. This foolishness we were up to wasn't so. It couldn't be happening. Nothing ever worked out just that way. You didn't stand in corners and knock down people one after the other like a machine, while a scrawny little bozo up at the other end fed them to you. It was too damned silly! I had enough!

I passed up my hiding place, put down the pipe and found another spot to crouch in, under some shelves, near the steps. I hunkered down here with a gun in each fist. This game I was playing in was – it had to be – gummy around the edges. I wasn't going to stay put any longer.

Flora came down the steps. Behind her trotted the little man.

Flora had a gun in each hand. Her gray eyes were everywhere. Her head was down like an animal's coming to a fight. Her nostrils quivered. Her body, coming down neither slowly nor swiftly, was balanced like a dancer's. If I live to a million I'll never forget the picture this handsome brutal woman made coming down those unplaned cellar stairs. She was a beautiful fight-bred animal going to a fight.

She saw me as I straightened.

"Drop 'em!" I said, but I knew she wouldn't.

The little man flicked a limp brown blackjack out of his sleeve and knocked her behind the ear just as she swung her left gun on me. I jumped over and caught her before she hit the cement.

"Now, you see!" the old man said gleefully. "You have the money and you have them. And now you will get me and that girl out."

"First we'll stow this with the others," I said.

After he had helped me do that I told him to lock the cell door. He did, and I took the key with one hand, his neck with the other. He squirmed like a snake while I ran my other hand over his clothes removing the blackjack and a gun, and finding a money-belt around his waist.

"Take it off," I ordered. "You don't carry anything out with you."

His fingers worked with the buckle, dragged the belt from under his clothes, let it fall on the floor. It was padded fat.

Still holding his neck, I took him upstairs, while the girl still sat frozen on the kitchen chair. It took a stiff hooker of whiskey and a lot of words to thaw her into understanding that she was going out with the old man and that she wasn't to say a word to anybody, especially not to the police.

"Where's Reddy?" she asked when color had come back into her face – which had even at the worst never lost its niceness – and thoughts to her head.

I told her he was all right, and promised her he would be in a hospital before the morning was over. She didn't ask anything else. I shooed her upstairs for her hat and coat, went with the old man while he got his hat, and then put the pair of them in the front ground-floor room.

"Stay here till I come for you," I said, and I locked the door and pocketed the key when I went out.

The front door and the front window on the ground floor had been planked and braced like the rear ones. I didn't like to risk opening them, even though it was fairly light by now. So I went upstairs, fashioned a flag of truce out of a pillow-slip and a bed-slat, hung it out a window, waited until a heavy voice said, "All right, speak your piece," and then I showed myself and told the police I'd let them in.

It took five minutes' work with a hatchet to pry the front door loose. The chief of police, the captain of detectives, and half the force were waiting on the front steps and pavement when I got the door open. I took them to the cellar and turned Big Flora, Pogy and Red O'Leary over to them, with the money. Flora and Pogy were awake, but not talking.

While the dignitaries were crowded around the spoils I went upstairs. The house was full of police sleuths. I swapped greetings with them as I went through to the room where I had left Nancy Regan and the old gink. Lieutenant Duff was trying the locked door, while O'Gar and Hunt stood behind him.

I grinned at Duff and gave him the key.

He opened the door, looked at the old man and the girl – mostly at her – and then at me. They were standing in the center of the room. The old man's faded eyes were miserably worried, the girl's blue ones were darkly anxious. Anxiety didn't ruin her looks a bit.

"If that's yours I don't blame you for locking it up," O'Gar muttered in my ear.

"You can run along now," I told the two in the room. "Get all the sleep you need before you report for duty again."

They nodded and went out of the house.

"That's how your Agency evens up?" Duff said. "The she-employees make up in looks for the ugliness of the he's."

Dick Foley came into the hall.

"How's your end?" I asked.

"Finis. The Angel led me to Vance. He led here. I led the bulls here. They got him – got her."

Two shots crashed in the street.

We went to the door and saw excitement in a police car down the street. We went down there. Bluepoint Vance, handcuffs on his wrists, was writhing half on the seat, half on the floor.

"We were holding him here in the car, Houston and me," a hard-mouthed plain-clothes man explained to Duff. "He made a break, grabbed Houston's gat with both hands. I had to drill him – twice. The cap'll raise hell! He specially wanted him kept here to put up against the others. But God knows I wouldn't of shot him if it hadn't been him or Houston!"

Duff called the plain-clothes man a damned clumsy mick as they lifted Vance up on the seat. Bluepoint's tortured eyes focused on me.

"I – know – you?" he asked painfully. "Continental – New – York?"

"Yes," I said.

"Couldn't – place – you – Larrouy's – with – Red?"

"Yeah," I told him. "Got Red, Flora, Pogy and the cush."

"But – not – Papa – dop – oul – os."

"Papa does what?" I asked impatiently, a shiver along my spine.

He pulled himself up on the seat.

"Papadopoulos," he repeated, with an agonizing summoning of the little strength left in him. "I tried – shoot him – saw him – walk 'way – with girl – bull – too damn quick – wish . . ."

His words ran out. He shuddered. Death wasn't a sixteenth of an inch behind his eyes. A white-coated intern tried to get past me into the car. I pushed him out of the way and leaned in taking Vance by the shoulders. The back of my neck was ice. My stomach was empty.

"Listen, Bluepoint," I yelled in his face. "Papadopoulos? Little old man? Brains of the push?"

"Yes," Vance said, and the last live blood in him came out with the word.

I let him drop back on the seat and walked away.

Of course! How had I missed it? The little scoundrel – if he hadn't, for all his scaredness, been the works, how could he have so neatly turned the others over to me one at a time? They had been absolutely cornered. It was be killed fighting, or surrender and be hanged. They had no other way out. The police had Vance, who could and would tell them that the little buzzard was the headman – there wasn't even a chance for him beating the courts with his age, his weakness and his mask of being driven around by the others.

And there I had been – with no choice but to accept his offer. Otherwise lights out for me. I had been putty in his hands, his accomplices had been putty. He had slipped the cross-over on them as they had helped him slip it over on the others – and I had sent him safely away.

Now I could turn the city upside down for him – my promise had been only to get him out of the house – but . . .

What a life!

$106,000 BLOOD MONEY

"I'M TOM-TOM CAREY," he said, drawling the words.

I nodded at the chair beside my desk and weighed him in while he moved to it. Tall, wide-shouldered, thick-chested, thin-bellied, he would add up to say a hundred and ninety pounds. His swarthy face was hard as a fist, but there was nothing ill-humored in it. It was the face of a man of forty-something who lived life raw and thrived on it. His blue clothes were good and he wore them well.

In the chair he twisted brown paper around a charge of Bull Durham and finished introducing himself, "I'm Paddy the Mex's brother."

I thought maybe he was telling the truth. Paddy had been like this fellow in coloring and manner.

"That would make your real name Carrera," I suggested.

"Yes." He was lighting a cigarette. "Alfredo Estanislao Cristobal Carrera, if you want all the details."

I asked him how to spell Estanislao, wrote the name down on a slip of paper, adding *alias Tom-Tom Carey*, rang for Tommy Howd, and told him to have the file clerk see if we had anything on it.

"While your people are opening graves I'll tell you why I'm here," the swarthy man drawled through smoke when Tommy had gone away with the paper.

"Tough, Paddy being knocked off like that," I said.

"He was too damned trusting to live long," his brother explained. "This is the kind of hombre he was – the last time I saw him was four years ago, here in San Francisco. I'd come in from an expedition down to – never mind where. Anyway

I was flat. Instead of pearls all I'd got out of the trip was a bullet-crease over my hip. Paddy was dirty with fifteen thousand or so he'd just nicked somebody for. The afternoon I saw him he had a date that he was leery of toting so much money. So he gives me the fifteen thousand to hold for him till that night."

Tom-Tom Carey blew out smoke and smiled softly past me at a memory.

"That's the kind of hombre he was," he went on. "He'd trust even his own brother. I went to Sacramento that afternoon and caught a train east. A girl in Pittsburgh helped me spend the fifteen thousand. Her name was Laurel. She liked rye whiskey with milk for a chaser. I used to drink it with her till I was all curdled inside, and I've never had any appetite for *schmierkäse* since. So there's a hundred thousand dollars reward on this Papadopoulos, is there?"

"And six. The insurance companies put up a hundred thousand, the bankers' association five, and the city a thousand."

Tom-Tom Carey chucked the remains of his cigarette in the cuspidor and began to assemble another one.

"Suppose I hand him to you?" he asked. "How many ways will the money have to go?"

"None of it will stop here," I assured him. "The Continental Detective Agency doesn't touch reward money – and won't let its hired men. If any of the police are in on the pinch, they'll want a share."

"But if they aren't, it's all mine?"

"If you turn him in without help, or without any help except ours."

"I'll do that." The words were casual. "So much for the arrest. Now for the conviction part. If you get him, are you sure you can nail him to the cross?"

"I ought to be, but he'll have to go up against a jury – and that means anything can happen."

The muscular brown hand holding the brown cigarette made a careless gesture.

"Then maybe I'd better get a confession out of him before I drag him in," he said offhand.

"It would be safer that way," I agreed. "You ought to let that holster down an inch or two. It brings the gun butt too high. The bulge shows when you sit down."

"Uh-huh. You mean the one on the left shoulder. I took it away from a fellow after I lost mine. Strap's too short. I'll get another one this afternoon."

Tommy came in with a folder labeled, Carey, Tom-Tom, 1361-C. It held some newspaper clippings, the oldest dated ten years back, the youngest eight months. I read them through, passing each one to the swarthy man as I finished it. Tom-Tom Carey was written down in them as soldier of fortune, gun-runner, seal poacher, smuggler, and pirate. But it was all alleged, supposed and suspected. He had been captured variously but never convicted of anything.

"They don't treat me right," he complained placidly when we were through reading. "For instance stealing that Chinese gunboat wasn't my fault. I was forced to do it – I was the one that was double-crossed. After they'd got the stuff aboard they wouldn't pay for it. I couldn't unload it. I couldn't do anything but take gunboat and all. The insurance companies must want this Papadopoulos plenty to hang a hundred thousand on him."

"Cheap enough if it lands him," I said. "Maybe he's not all the newspapers picture him as, but he's more than a handful. He gathered a whole damned army of strong-arm men here, took over a block in the center of the financial district, looted the two biggest banks in the city, fought off the whole police department, made his getaway, ditched the army, used some of his lieutenants to bump off some more of them – that's where your brother Paddy got his – then with the help of Pogy Reeve, Big Flora Brace and Red O'Leary, wiped out the rest of his lieutenants. And remember, these lieutenants weren't schoolboys – they were slick grifters like Bluepoint

Vance and the Shivering Kid and Darby M'Laughlin – birds who knew their what's what."

"Uh-huh." Carey was unimpressed. "But it was a bust just the same. You got all the loot back, and he just managed to get away himself."

"A bad break for him," I explained. "Red O'Leary broke out with a complication of love and vanity. You can't chalk that against Papadopoulos. Don't get the idea he's half-smart. He's dangerous, and I don't blame the insurance companies for thinking they'll sleep better if they're sure he's not out where he can frame some more tricks against their policy-holding banks."

"Don't know much about this Papadopoulos, do you?"

"No." I told the truth. "And nobody does. The hundred-thousand offer made rats out of half the crooks in the country. They're as hot after him as we – not only because of the reward but because of his wholesale double-crossing. And they know just as little about him as we do – that he's had his fingers in a dozen or more jobs, that he was the brains behind Bluepoint Vance's bond tricks, and that his enemies have a habit of dying young. But nobody knows where he came from, or where he lives when he's home. Don't think I'm touting him as a Napoleon or a Sunday supplement mastermind – but he's a shifty, tricky old boy. As you say, I don't know much about him – but there are lots of people I don't know much about."

Tom-Tom Carey nodded to show me he understood the last part and began making his third cigarette.

"I was in Nogales when Angel Grace Cardigan got word to me that Paddy had been done in," he said. "That was nearly a month ago. She seemed to think I'd romp up here pronto – but it was no skin off my face. I let it sleep. But last week I read in a newspaper about all this reward money being posted on the hombre she blamed for Paddy's rub-out. That made it different – a hundred-thousand dollars different. So I shipped up here, talked to her, and then came in to make sure there'll be nothing between me and the blood money when I put the loop on this Papadoodle."

"Angel Grace sent you to me?" I inquired.

"Uh-huh – only she don't know it. She dragged you into the story – said you were a friend of Paddy's, a good guy for a sleuth and hungry as hell for this Papadoodle. So I thought you'd be the gent for me to see."

"When did you leave Nogales?"

"Tuesday – last week."

"That," I said, prodding my memory, "was the day after Newhall was killed across the border."

The swarthy man nodded. Nothing changed in his face.

"How far from Nogales was that?" I asked.

"He was gunned down near Oquitoa – that's somewhere around sixty miles southwest of Nogales. You interested?"

"No – except I was wondering about your leaving the place where he was killed the day after he was killed, and coming up where he had lived. Did you know him?"

"He was pointed out to me in Nogales as a San Francisco millionaire going with a party to look at some mining property in Mexico. I was figuring on maybe selling him something later, but the Mexican patriots got him before I did."

"And so you came north?"

"Uh-huh. The hubbub kind of spoiled things for me. I had a nice little business in – call it supplies – to and fro across the line. This Newhall killing turned the spotlight on that part of the country. So I thought I'd come up and collect that hundred thousand and give things a chance to settle down there. Honest, brother, I haven't killed a millionaire in weeks, if that's what's worrying you."

"That's good. Now as I get it, you're counting on landing Papadopoulos. Angel Grace sent for you, thinking you'd run him down just to even up for Paddy's killing, but it's the money you want, so you figure on playing with me as well as the Angel. That right?"

"Check."

"You know what'll happen if she learns you're stringing along with me?"

"Uh-huh. She'll chuck a convulsion – kind of balmy on the subject of keeping clear of the police, isn't she?"

"She is – somebody told her something about honor among thieves once and she's never got over it. Her brother's doing a hitch up north now – Johnny the Plumber sold him out. Her man Paddy was mowed down by his pals. Did either of those things wake her up? Not a chance. She'd rather have Papadopoulos go free than join forces with us."

"That's all right," Tom-Tom Carey assured me. "She thinks I'm the loyal brother – Paddy couldn't have told her much about me – and I'll handle her. You having her shadowed?"

I said, "Yes – ever since she was turned loose. She was picked up the same day Flora and Pogy and Red were grabbed, but we hadn't anything on her except that she had been Paddy's ladylove, so I had her sprung. How much dope did you get out of her?"

"Descriptions of Papadoodle and Nancy Regan, and that's all. She don't know any more about them than I do. Where does this Regan girl fit in?"

"Hardly any, except that she might lead us to Papadopoulos. She was Red's girl. It was keeping a date with her that upset the game. When Papadopoulos wriggled out he took the girl with him. I don't know why. She wasn't in on the stick-ups."

Tom-Tom Carey finished making and lighting his fourth cigarette and stood up.

"Are we teamed?" he asked as he picked up his hat.

"If you turn in Papadopoulos I'll see that you get every nickel you're entitled to," I replied. "And I'll give you a clear field – I won't handicap you with too much of an attempt to keep my eyes on your actions."

He said that was fair enough, told me he was stopping at a hotel in Ellis Street, and went away.

Calling the late Taylor Newhall's office on the phone, I was told that if I wanted any information about his affairs I should try his country residence, some miles south of San Francisco. I tried it. A ministerial voice that said it belonged to the butler told me that Newhall's attorney, Franklin Ellert, was the person I should see. I went over to Ellert's office.

He was a nervous, irritable old man with a lisp and eyes that stuck out with blood pressure.

"Is there any reason," I asked point-blank, "for supposing that Newhall's murder was anything more than a Mexican bandit outburst? Is it likely that he was killed purposely, and not resisting capture?"

Lawyers don't like to be questioned. This one sputtered and made faces at me and let his eyes stick out still further and, of course, didn't give me an answer.

"How? How?" he snapped disagreeably. "Exthplain your meaning, thir!"

He glared at me and then at the desk, pushing papers around with excited hands, as if he were hunting for a police whistle. I told my story – told him about Tom-Tom Carey.

Ellert sputtered some more, demanded, "What the devil do you mean?" and made a complete jumble of the papers on his desk.

"I don't mean anything," I growled back. "I'm just telling you what was said."

"Yeth! Yeth! I know!" He stopped glaring at me and his voice was less peevish. "But there ith abtholutely no reathon for thuthpecting anything of the thort. None at all, thir, none at all!"

"Maybe you're right." I turned to the door. "But I'll poke into it a little anyway."

"Wait! Wait!" He scrambled out of his chair and ran around

the desk to me. "I think you are mithtaken, but if you are going to invethtigate it I would like to know what you dithcover. Perhapth you'd better charge me with your regular fee for whatever ith done, and keep me informed of your progreth. Thatisthfactory?"

I said it was, came back to his desk and began to question him. There was, as the lawyer had said, nothing in Newhall's affairs to stir us up. The dead man was several times a millionaire, with most of his money in mines. He had inherited nearly half his money. There was no shady practice, no claim-jumping, no trickery in his past, no enemies. He was a widower with one daughter. She had everything she wanted while he lived, and she and her father had been very fond of one another. He had gone to Mexico with a party of mining men from New York who expected to sell him some property there. They had been attacked by bandits, had driven them off, but Newhall and a geologist named Parker had been killed during the fight.

Back in the office I wrote a telegram to our Los Angeles branch, asking that an operative be sent to Nogales to pry into Newhall's killing and Tom-Tom Carey's affairs. The clerk to whom I gave it to be coded and sent told me the Old Man wanted to see me. I went into his office and was introduced to a short, roly-poly man named Hook.

"Mr. Hook," the Old Man said, "is the proprietor of a restaurant in Sausalito. Last Monday he employed a waitress named Nelly Riley. She told him she had come from Los Angeles. Her description, as Mr. Hook gives it, is quite similar to the description you and Counihan have given of Nancy Regan. Isn't it?" he asked the fat man.

"Absolutely. It's exactly what I read in the papers. She's five feet five inches tall, about, and medium in size, and she's got blue eyes and brown hair, and she's around twenty-one or -two, and she's got looks, and the thing that counts most is she's high-hat as the devil – she don't think nothin's good enough for her. Why, when I tried to be a little sociable she told me to keep my 'dirty paws' to myself. And then I found out she didn't know hardly nothing about Los Angeles, though she claimed to have lived there two or three years. I bet you she's the girl, all right," and he went on talking about how much reward money he ought to get.

"Are you going back there now?" I asked him.

"Pretty soon. I got to stop and see about some dishes. Then I'm going back."

"This girl will be working?"

"Yes."

"Then, we'll send a man over with you – one who knows Nancy Regan."

I called Jack Counihan in from the operatives' room and introduced him to Hook. They arranged to meet in half an hour at the ferry and Hook waddled out.

"This Nelly Riley won't be Nancy Regan," I said. "But we can't afford to pass up even a hundred-to-one chance."

I told Jack and the Old Man about Tom-Tom Carey and my visit to Ellert's office. The Old Man listened with his usual polite attentiveness. Young Counihan – only four months in the man-hunting business – listened with wide eyes.

"You'd better run along now and meet Hook," I said when I had finished, leaving the Old Man's office with Jack. "And if she should be Nancy Regan – grab her and hang on." We were out of the Old Man's hearing, so I added, "And for God's sake don't let your youthful gallantry lead you to a poke in the jaw this time. Pretend you're grown up."

The boy blushed, said, "Go to hell!" adjusted his necktie, and set off to meet Hook.

I had some reports to write. After I had finished them I put my feet on my desk, made cavities in a package of Fatimas and thought about Tom-Tom Carey until six o'clock. Then

I went down to the States for my abalone chowder and minute steak and home to change clothes before going out Sea Cliff way to sit in a poker game.

The telephone interrupted my dressing. Jack Counihan was on the other end.

"I'm in Sausalito. The girl wasn't Nancy, but I've got hold of something else. I'm not sure how to handle it. Can you come over?"

"Is it important enough to cut a poker game for?"

"Yes, it's – I think it's big." He was excited. "I wish you would come over. I really think it's a lead."

"Where are you?"

"At the ferry there. Not the Golden Gate, the other."

"All right. I'll catch the first boat."

An hour later I walked off the boat in Sausalito. Jack Counihan pushed through the crowd and began talking, "Coming down here on my way back –"

"Hold it till we get out of the mob," I advised him. "It must be tremendous – the eastern point of your collar is bent."

He mechanically repaired this defect in his otherwise immaculate costuming while we walked to the street, but he was too intent on whatever was on his mind to smile.

"Up this way," he said, guiding me around a corner. "Hook's lunchroom is on the corner. You can take a look at the girl if you like. She's of the same size and complexion as Nancy Regan, but that is all. She's a tough little job who probably was fired for dropping her chewing gum in the soup the last place she worked."

"All right. That lets her out. Now what's on your mind?"

"After I saw her I started back to the ferry. A boat came in while I was still a couple of blocks away. Two men who must have come in on it came up the street. They were Greeks, rather young, tough, though ordinarily I shouldn't have paid much attention to them. But, since Papadopoulos is a Greek, we have been interested in them, of course, so I looked at these chaps. They were arguing about something as they walked, not talking loud, but scowling at one another. As they passed me the chap on the gutter side said to the other, 'I tell him it's been twenty-nine days.'

"Twenty-nine days. I counted back and it's just twenty-nine days since we started hunting for Papadopoulos. He is a Greek and these chaps were Greeks. When I finished counting I turned around and began to follow them. They took me all the way through the town and up a hill on the fringe. They went to a little cottage – it couldn't have more than three rooms – set back in a clearing in the woods by itself. There was a 'For Sale' sign on it, and no curtains in the windows, no sign of occupancy – but on the ground behind the back door there was a wet place, as if a bucket or pan of water had been thrown out.

"I stayed in the bushes until it got a little darker. Then I went closer. I could hear people inside, but I couldn't see anything through the windows. They're boarded up. After a while the two chaps I had followed came out, saying something in a language I couldn't understand to whoever was in the cottage. The cottage door stayed open until the two men had gone out of sight down the path – so I couldn't have followed them without being seen by whoever was at the door.

"Then the door was closed and I could hear people moving around inside – or perhaps only one person – and could smell cooking, and some smoke came out of the chimney. I waited and waited and nothing more happened and I thought I had better get in touch with you."

"Sounds interesting," I agreed.

We were passing under a street light. Jack stopped me with a hand on my arm and fished something out of his overcoat pocket.

"Look!" He held it out to me. A charred piece of blue cloth. It could have been the remains of a woman's hat that had been three-quarters burned. I looked at it under the street light and then used my flashlight to examine it more closely.

"I picked it up behind the cottage while I was nosing around," Jack said, "and –"

"And Nancy Regan wore a hat of that shade the night she and Papadopoulos vanished," I finished for him. "On to the cottage."

We left the street lights behind, climbed the hill, dipped down into a little valley, turned into a winding sandy path, left that to cut across sod between trees to a dirt road, trod half a mile of that, and then Jack led the way along a narrow path that wound through a black tangle of bushes and small trees. I hoped he knew where he was going.

"Almost there," he whispered to me.

A man jumped out of the bushes and took me by the neck.

My hands were in my overcoat pocket – one holding the flashlight, the other my gun.

I pushed the muzzle of the pocketed gun toward the man – pulled the trigger.

The shot ruined seventy-five dollars' worth of overcoat for me. But it took the man away from my neck.

That was lucky. Another man was on my back.

I tried to twist away from him – didn't altogether make it – felt the edge of a knife along my spine.

That wasn't so lucky – but it was better than getting the point.

I butted back at his face – missed – kept twisting and squirming while I brought my hands out of my pockets and clawed at him.

The blade of his knife came flat against my cheek. I caught the hand that held it and let myself go down backward – him under.

He said, "Uh!"

I rolled over, got hands and knees on the ground, was grazed by a fist, scrambled up.

Fingers dragged at my ankle.

My behavior was ungentlemanly. I kicked the fingers away – found the man's body – kicked it twice – hard.

Jack's voice whispered my name. I couldn't see him in the blackness, nor could I see the man I had shot.

"All right here," I told Jack. "How did you come out?"

"Top-hole. Is that all of it?"

"Don't know, but I'm going to risk a peek at what I've got."

Tilting my flashlight down at the man under my foot, I snapped it on. A thin blond man, his face bloodsmeared, his pink-rimmed eyes jerking as he tried to play 'possum in the glare.

"Come out of it!" I ordered.

A heavy gun went off back in the bush – another, lighter one. The bullets ripped through the foliage.

I switched off the light, bent to the man on the ground, knocked him on the top of the head with my gun.

"Crouch down low," I whispered to Jack.

The smaller gun snapped again, twice. It was ahead, to the left.

I put my mouth to Jack's ear. "We're going to that damned cottage whether anybody likes it or no. Keep low and don't do any shooting unless you see what you're shooting at. Go ahead."

Bending as close to the ground as I could, I followed Jack up the path. The position stretched the slash in my back – a scalding pain from between my shoulders almost to my waist. I could feel blood trickling down over my hips – or thought I could.

The going was too dark for stealthiness. Things crackled under our feet, rustled against our shoulders. Our friends in the bush used their guns. Luckily the sound of twigs breaking and leaves rustling in pitch blackness isn't the best of targets. Bullets zipped here and there, but we didn't stop any of them.

Neither did we shoot back. We halted where the end of the bush left the night a weaker gray.

"That's it," Jack said about a square shape ahead.

"On the jump," I grunted and lit out for the dark cottage.

Jack's long slim legs kept him easily at my side as we raced across the clearing.

A man-shape oozed from behind the blot of the building and his gun began to blink at us. The shots came so close together that they sounded like one long stuttering bang.

Pulling the youngster with me I flopped, flat to the ground except where a ragged-edged empty tin-can held my face up.

From the other side of the building another gun coughed. From a tree-stem to the right, a third. Jack and I began to burn powder back at them.

A bullet kicked my mouth full of dirt and pebbles. I spit mud and cautioned Jack, "You're shooting too high. Hold it low and pull easy."

A hump showed in the house's dark profile. I sent a bullet at it.

A man's voice yelled, "Ow-ooh!" and then, lower but very bitter, "Oh, damn you – damn you!"

For a warm couple of seconds bullets spattered all around us. Then there was not a sound to spoil the night's quietness.

When the silence had lasted five minutes, I got myself up on hands and knees and began to move forward, Jack following. The ground wasn't made for that sort of work. Ten feet of it was enough. We stood up and walked the rest of the way to the building.

"Wait," I whispered, and leaving Jack at one corner of the building, I circled it, seeing nobody, hearing nothing but the sounds I made.

We tried the front door. It was locked but rickety. Bumping it open with my shoulder, I went indoors – flashlight and gun in my fists.

The shack was empty.

Nobody – no furnishings – no traces of either in the two bare rooms – nothing but bare wooden walls, bare floor, bare ceiling with a stovepipe connected to nothing through it.

Jack and I stood in the middle of the floor, looked at the emptiness, and cursed the dump from back door to front for being empty. We hadn't quite finished when feet sounded outside, a white light beamed on the open doorway, and a cracked voice said, "Hey! You can come out one at a time – kind of easy-like!"

"Who says so?" I asked, snapping off the flashlight, moving over close to a side wall.

"A whole goldurned flock of deputy sheriffs," the voice answered.

"Couldn't you push one of 'em in and let us get a look at him?" I asked. "I've been choked and carved and shot at tonight until I haven't got much faith left in anybody's word."

A lanky knock-kneed man with a thin leathery face appeared in the doorway. He showed me a buzzer, I fished out my credentials, and the other deputies came in. There were three of them in all.

"We were driving down the road bound for a little job near the point when we heard the shooting," the lanky one explained. "What's up?"

I told him.

"This shack's been empty a long while," he said when I had finished. "Anybody could have camped in it easy enough. Think it was that Papadopoulos, huh? We'll kind of look around for him and his friends – especially since there's that nice reward money."

We searched the woods and found nobody. The man I had knocked down and the man I shot were both gone.

Jack and I rode back to Sausalito with the deputies. I hunted up a doctor there and had my back bandaged. He said the cut was long but shallow. Then we returned to San Francisco and separated in the direction of our homes.

And thus ended the day's doings.

Here is something that happened next morning. I didn't see it. I heard about it a little before noon and read about it in the papers that afternoon. I didn't know then that I had personal interest in it, but later I did – so I'll put it in here where it happened.

At ten o'clock that morning, into busy Market Street staggered a man who was naked from the top of his battered head to the soles of his bloodstained feet. From his bare chest and sides and back, little ribbons of flesh hung down, dripping blood. His left arm was broken in two places. The left side of his bald head was smashed in. An hour later he died in the emergency hospital – without having said a word to anyone, with the same vacant, distant look in his eyes.

The police easily ran back the trail of blood drops. They ended with a red smear in an alley beside a small hotel just off Market Street. In the hotel the police found the room from which the man had jumped, fallen or been thrown. The bed was soggy with blood. On it were torn and twisted sheets that had been knotted and used for rope. There was also a towel that had been used as a gag.

The evidence read that the naked man had been gagged, trussed up and worked on with a knife. The doctors said the ribbons of flesh had been cut loose, not torn or clawed. After the knife-user had gone away, the naked man had worked free of his bonds and, probably crazed by pain, had either jumped or fallen out of the window. The fall had crushed his skull and broken his arm, but he had managed to walk a block and a half.

The hotel management said the man had been there two days. He was registered as H. F. Barrows, City. He had a black Gladstone bag in which, besides clothes, shaving implements and so on, the police found a box of .38 cartridges, a black handkerchief with eyeholes cut in it, four skeleton keys, a small jimmy and a quantity of morphine, with a needle and the rest of the kit. Elsewhere in the room they found the rest of his clothes, a .38 revolver and two quarts of liquor. They didn't find a cent.

The supposition was that Barrows had been a burglar, and that he had been tied up, tortured and robbed, probably by pals, between eight and nine that morning. Nobody knew anything about him. Nobody had seen his visitor or visitors. The room next to his on the left was unoccupied. The occupant of the room on the other side had left for his work in a furniture factory before seven o'clock.

While this was happening I was at the office, sitting forward in my chair to spare my back, reading reports, all of which told how operatives attached to various Continental Detective Agency branches had continued to fail to turn up any indications of the past, present or future whereabouts of Papadopoulos and Nancy Regan. There was nothing novel about these reports – I had been reading similar ones for three weeks.

The Old Man and I went out to luncheon together, and I told him about the previous night's adventures in Sausalito while we ate. His grandfatherly face was as attentive as always, and his smile as politely interested, but when I was half through my story he turned his mild blue eyes from my face to his salad, and he stared at his salad until I had finished talking. Then, still not looking up, he said he was sorry I had been cut. I thanked him and we ate a while.

Finally he looked at me. The mildness and courtesy he habitually wore over his cold-bloodedness were in his face and eyes and voice as he said, "This first indication that Papadopoulos is still alive came immediately after Tom-Tom Carey's arrival."

It was my turn to shift my eyes.

I looked at the roll I was breaking while I said, "Yes."

That afternoon a phone call came in from a woman out

in the Mission who had seen some highly mysterious happenings and was sure they had something to do with the well-advertised bank robberies. So I went out to see her and spent most of the afternoon learning that half of her happenings were imaginary and the other half were the efforts of a jealous wife to get the low-down on her husband.

It was nearly six o'clock when I returned to the Agency. A few minutes later Dick Foley called me on the phone. His teeth were chattering so I could hardly get the words. C-c-anyoug-g-get-t-townt-t-tooth-ar-r-rbr-r-spittle?"

"What?" I asked, and he said the same thing again, or worse. But by this time I had guessed that he was asking me if I could get down to the Harbor Hospital.

I told him I could in ten minutes, and with the help of a taxi I did.

The little Canadian operative met me at the hospital door. His clothes and hair were dripping wet, but he had had a shot of whiskey and his teeth had stopped chattering.

"Damned fool jumped in bay!" he barked as if it were my fault.

"Angel Grace?"

"Who else was I shadowing? Got on Oakland ferry. Moved off by self by rail. Thought she was going to throw something over. Kept eye on her. Bingo! She jumps." Dick sneezed. "I was goofy enough to jump after her. Held her up. Were fished out. In there," nodding his wet head toward the interior of the hospital.

"What happened before she took the ferry?"

'Nothing. Been in joint all day. Straight out to ferry."

"How about yesterday?"

"Apartment all day. Out at night with man. Roadhouse. Home at four. Bad break. Couldn't tail him off."

"What did he look like?"

The man Dick described was Tom-Tom Carey.

"Good," I said. "You'd better beat it home for a hot bath and some dry rags." I went in to see the near-suicide.

She was lying on her back on a cot, staring at the ceiling. Her face was pale, but it always was, and her green eyes were no more sullen than usual. Except that her short hair was dark with dampness she didn't look as if anything out of the ordinary had happened.

"You think of the funniest things to do," I said when I was beside the bed.

She jumped and her face jerked around to me, startled. Then she recognized me and smiled – a smile that brought into her face the attractiveness that habitual sullenness kept out. "You have to keep in practice – sneaking up on people?" she asked. "Who told you I was here?"

"Everybody knows it. Your pictures are all over the front pages of the newspapers, with your life history and what you said to the Prince of Wales."

She stopped smiling and looked steadily at me. "I got it!" she exclaimed after a few seconds. "That runt who came in after me was one of your ops – tailing me. Wasn't he?"

"I didn't know anybody had to go in after you," I answered. "I thought you came ashore after you had finished your swim. Didn't you want to land?"

She wouldn't smile. Her eyes began to look at something horrible. "Oh! Why didn't they let me alone?" she wailed, shuddering. "It's a rotten thing, living."

I sat down on a small chair beside the white bed and patted the lump her shoulder made in the sheets. "What was it?" I was surprised at the fatherly tone I achieved. "What did you want to die for, Angel?"

Words that wanted to be said were shiny in her eyes, tugged at muscles in her face, shaped her lips – but that was all. The words she said came out listlessly, but with a reluctant sort of finality. They were, "No. You're law, I'm thief. I'm staying on my side of the fence. Nobody can say –"

"All right! All right!" I surrendered. "But for God's sake don't make me listen to another of those ethical arguments. Is there anything I can do for you?"

"Thanks, no."

"There's nothing you want to tell me?"

She shook her head.

"You're all right now?"

"Yes. I was being shadowed, wasn't I? Or you wouldn't have known about it so soon."

"I'm a detective – I know everything. Be a good girl."

From the hospital I went up to the Hall of Justice, to the police detective bureau. Lieutenant Duff was holding down the captain's desk. I told him about the Angel's dive.

"Got any idea what she was up to?" he wanted to know when I had finished.

"She's too far off center to figure. I want her vagged."

"Yeah? I thought you wanted her loose so you could catch her."

"That's about played out now. I'd like to try throwing her in the can for thirty days. Big Flora is in waiting trial. The Angel knows Flora was one of the troupe that rubbed out her Paddy. Maybe Flora don't know the Angel. Let's see what will come of mixing the two babies for a month."

"Can do," Duff agreed. "This Angel's got no visible means of support and it's a cinch she's got no business running around jumping in people's bays. I'll put the word through."

From the Hall of Justice I went up to the Ellis Street hotel at which Tom-Tom Carey had told me he was registered. He was out. I left word that I would be back in an hour and used that hour to eat. When I returned to the hotel the tall swarthy man was sitting in the lobby. He took me up to his room and set out gin, orange juice and cigars.

"Seen Angel Grace?" I asked.

"Yes, last night. We did the dumps."

"Seen her today?"

"No."

"She jumped in the bay this afternoon."

"The hell she did." He seemed moderately surprised.

"She was fished out. She's O.K."

The shadow in his eyes could have been some slight disappointment.

"She's a funny sort of kid," he remarked. "I wouldn't say Paddy didn't show good taste when he picked her, but she's a queer one!"

"How's the Papadopoulos hunt progressing?"

"It is. But you oughtn't have split on your word. You half-way promised you wouldn't have me shadowed."

"I'm not the big boss," I apologized. "Sometimes what I want don't fit in with what the headman wants. This shouldn't bother you much – you can shake him, can't you?"

"Uh-huh. That's what I've been doing. But it's a damned nuisance jumping in and out of taxis and back doors."

We talked and drank a few minutes longer, and then I left Carey's room and hotel, and went to a drugstore telephone booth, where I called Dick Foley's home, and gave Dick the swarthy man's description and address. "I don't want you to tail Carey, Dick. I want you to find out who is trying to tail him – and that shadower is the bird you're to stick to. The morning will be time enough to start – get yourself dried out."

And that was the end of that day.

I woke to a disagreeable rainy morning. Maybe it was the weather; maybe I'd been too frisky the day before; anyway the slit in my back was like a foot-long boil. I phoned Dr. Canova, who lived on the floor below me, and had him look at the cut before he left for his downtown office. He re-bandaged it and told me to take life easy for a couple of days. It felt better after he had fooled with it, but I phoned the Agency and told the Old Man that unless something exciting broke I was going to stay on sick-call all day.

I spent the day propped up in front of the gas-log, reading and smoking cigarettes that wouldn't burn right on account of the weather. That night I used the phone to organize a poker game, in which I got very little action one way or the other. In the end I was fifteen dollars ahead, which was just about five dollars less than enough to pay for the booze my guests had drunk on me.

My back was better the following day, and so was the day. I went down to the Agency. There was a memorandum on my desk saying Duff had phoned that Angel Grace Cardigan had been vagged – thirty days in the city prison. There was a familiar pile of reports from various branches on their operatives' inability to pick up anything on Papadopoulos and Nancy Regan. I was running through these when Dick Foley came in.

"Made him," he reported. "Thirty or thirty-two. Five, six. Hundred, thirty. Sandy hair, complexion. Blue eyes. Thin face, some skin off. Rat. Lives dump in Seventh Street."

"What did he do?"

"Tailed Carey one block. Carey shook him. Hunted for Carey till two in morning. Didn't find him. Went home. Take him again?"

"Go up to his flophouse and find out who he is."

The little Canadian was gone half an hour.

"Sam Arlie," he said when he returned. "Been there six months. Supposed to be barber – when he's working – if ever."

"I've got two guesses about this Arlie," I told Dick. "The first is that he's the gink who carved me in Sausalito the other night. The second is that something's going to happen to him."

It was against Dick's rules to waste words, so he said nothing. I called Tom-Tom Carey's hotel and got the swarthy man on the wire. "Come over," I invited him. "I've got some news for you."

"As soon as I'm dressed and breakfasted," he promised.

"When Carey leaves here you're to go along behind him," I told Dick after I had hung up. "If Arlie connects with him now, maybe there'll be something doing. Try to see it."

Then I phoned the detective bureau and made a date with Sergeant Hunt to visit Angel Grace Cardigan's apartment. After that I busied myself with paper work until Tommy came in to announce the swarthy man from Nogales.

"The jobbie who's tailing you," I informed him when he had sat down and begun work on a cigarette, "is a barber named Arlie," and I told him where Arlie lived.

"Yes. A slim-faced, sandy lad?"

I gave him the description Dick had given me.

"That's the hombre," Tom-Tom Carey said. "Know anything else about him?"

"No."

"You had Angel Grace vagged."

It was neither an accusation nor a question, so I didn't answer it.

"It's just as well," the tall man went on. "I'd have had to send her away. She was bound to gum things with her foolishness when I got ready to swing the loop."

"That'll be soon?"

"That all depends on how it happens." He stood up, yawned and shook his wide shoulders. "But nobody would starve to death if they decided not to eat any more till I'd got him. I oughtn't have accused you of having me shadowed."

"It didn't spoil my day."

Tom-Tom Carey said, "So long," and sauntered out.

I rode down to the Hall of Justice, picked up Hunt, and we went to the Bush Street apartment house in which Angel Grace Cardigan had lived. The manager – a highly scented fat woman with a hard mouth and soft eyes – already knew her tenant was in the cooler. She willingly took us up to the girl's room.

The Angel wasn't a good housekeeper. Things were clean

enough, but upset. The kitchen sink was full of dirty dishes. The folding bed was worse than loosely made up. Clothes and odds and ends of feminine equipment hung over everything from bathroom to kitchen.

We got rid of the landlady and raked the place over thoroughly. We came away knowing all there was to know about the girl's wardrobe, and a lot about her personal habits. But we didn't find anything pointing Papadopoulos-ward.

No report came in on the Carey–Arlie combination that afternoon or evening, though I expected to hear from Dick every minute.

At three o'clock in the morning my bedside phone took my ear out of the pillows. The voice that came over the wire was the Canadian op's.

"Exit Arlie," he said.

"R.I.P.?"

"Yep."

"How?"

"Lead."

"Our lad's?"

"Yep."

"Keep till morning?"

"Yep."

"See you at the office," and I went back to sleep.

When I arrived at the Agency at nine o'clock, one of the clerks had just finished decoding a night letter from the Los Angeles operative who had been sent over to Nogales. It was a long telegram, and meaty.

It said that Tom-Tom Carey was well known along the border. For some six months he had been engaged in over-the-line traffic – guns going south, booze and probably dope and immigrants coming north. Just before leaving there the previous week he had made inquiries concerning one Hank Barrows. This Hank Barrows' description fit the H. F. Barrows who had been cut into ribbons, who had fallen out of the hotel window and died.

The Los Angeles operative hadn't been able to get much of a line on Barrows, except that he hailed from San Francisco, had been on the border only a few days and had apparently returned to San Francisco. The operative had turned up nothing new on the Newhall killing – the signs still read that he had been killed resisting capture by Mexican patriots.

Dick Foley came into my office while I was reading the news. When I had finished he gave me his contribution to the history of Tom-Tom Carey.

"Tailed him out of here. To hotel. Arlie on corner. Eight o'clock, Carey out. Garage. Hire car without driver. Back hotel. Checked out. Two bags. Out through park. Arlie after him in flivver. My boat after Arlie. Down boulevard. Off crossroad. Dark. Lonely. Arlie steps on gas. Closed in. Bang! Carey stops. Two guns going. Exit Arlie. Carey back to city. Hotel Marquis. Registers George F. Danby, San Diego. Room 622."

"Did Tom-Tom frisk Arlie after he dropped him?"

"No. Didn't touch him."

"So? Take Mickey Linehan with you. Don't let Carey get out of your sight. I'll get somebody up to relieve you and Mickey late tonight, if I can, but he's got to be shadowed twenty-four hours a day until –" I didn't know what came after that so I stopped talking.

I took Dick's story into the Old Man's office and told it to him, winding up, "Arlie shot first, according to Foley, so Carey gets a self-defence on it, but we're getting action at last and I don't want to do anything to slow it up. So I'd like to keep what we know about this shooting quiet for a couple of days. It won't increase our friendship any with the county sheriff if he finds out what we're doing, but I think it's worth it."

"If you wish," the Old Man agreed, reaching for his ringing phone.

He spoke into the instrument and passed it on to me. Detective-sergeant Hunt was talking, "Flora Brace and Grace Cardigan crushed out just before daylight. The chances are they –"

I wasn't in a humor for details. "A clean sneak?" I asked.

"Not a lead on 'em so far, but –"

"I'll get the details when I see you. Thanks," and I hung up. "Angel Grace and Big Flora have escaped from the city prison," I passed the news on to the Old Man.

He smiled courteously, as if at something that didn't especially concern him. "You were congratulating yourself on getting action," he murmured.

I turned my scowl to a grin, mumbled, "Well, maybe," went back to my office and telephoned Franklin Ellert. The lisping attorney said he would be glad to see me, so I went over to his office.

"And now, what progreth have you made?" he asked eagerly when I was seated beside his desk.

"Some. A man named Barrows was also in Nogales when Newhall was killed, and also came to San Francisco right after. Carey followed Barrows up here. Did you read about the man found walking the streets naked, all cut up?"

"Yeth."

"That was Barrows. Then another man comes into the game – a barber named Arlie. He was spying on Carey. Last night, in a lonely road south of here, Arlie shot at Carey. Carey killed him."

The old lawyer's eyes came out another inch. "What road?" he gasped.

"You want the exact location?"

"Yeth!"

I pulled his phone over, called the Agency, had Dick's report read to me, gave the attorney the information he wanted.

It had an effect on him. He hopped out of his chair. Sweat

was shining along the ridges wrinkles made in his face. "Mith Newhall ith down there alone! That path ith only half a mile from her houth!"

I frowned and beat my brains together, but I couldn't make anything out of it. "Suppose I put a man down there to look after her?" I suggested.

"Exthellent!" His worried face cleared until there weren't more than fifty or sixty wrinkles in it. "She would prefer to thtay there during her firth grief over her fatherth death. You will thend a capable man?"

"The Rock of Gibraltar is a leaf in the breeze beside him. Give me a note for him to take down. Andrew MacElroy is his name."

While the lawyer scribbled the note I used his phone again to call the Agency, to tell the operator to get hold of Andy and tell him I wanted him. I ate lunch before I returned to the Agency. Andy was waiting when I got there.

Andy MacElroy was a big boulder of a man – not very tall, but thick and hard of head and body. A glum, grim man with no more imagination than an adding machine. I'm not even sure he could read. But I was sure that when Andy was told to do something, he did it and nothing else. He didn't know enough not to.

I gave him the lawyer's note to Miss Newhall, told him where to go and what to do, and Miss Newhall's troubles were off my mind.

Three times that afternoon I heard from Dick Foley and Mickey Linehan. Tom-Tom Carey wasn't doing anything very exciting, though he had bought two boxes of .44 cartridges in a Market Street sporting goods establishment.

The afternoon papers carried photographs of Big Flora Brace and Angel Grace Cardigan, with a story of their escape. The story was as far from the probable facts as newspaper stories generally are. On another page was an account of the discovery of the dead barber in the lonely road. He had been shot in the head and in the chest, four times in all. The county officials' opinion was that he had been killed resisting a stick-up and that the bandits had fled without robbing him.

At five o'clock Tommy Howd came to my door. "That guy Carey wants to see you again," the freckle-faced boy said.

"Shoot him in."

The swarthy man sauntered in, said "Howdy," sat down, and made a brown cigarette. "Got anything special on for tonight?" he asked when he was smoking.

"Nothing I can't put aside for something better. Giving a party?"

"Uh-huh. I had thought of it. A kind of surprise party for Papadoodle. Want to go along?"

It was my turn to say, "Uh-huh."

"I'll pick you up at eleven – Van Ness and Geary," he drawled. "But this has got to be a kind of tight party – just you and me – and him."

"No. There's one more who'll have to be in on it. I'll bring him along."

"I don't like that." Tom-Tom Carey shook his head slowly, frowning amiably over his cigarette. "You sleuths oughtn't outnumber me. It ought to be one and one."

"You won't be outnumbered," I explained. "This jobbie I'm bringing won't be on my side more than yours. And it'll pay you to keep as sharp an eye on him as I do – and to see he don't get behind either of us if we can help it."

"Then what do you want to lug him along for?"

"Wheels within wheels," I grinned.

The swarthy man frowned again, less amiably now. "The hundred and six thousand reward money – I'm not figuring on sharing that with anybody."

"Right enough," I agreed. "Nobody I bring along will declare themselves in on it."

"I'll take your word for it." He stood up. "And we've got to watch this hombre, huh?"

"If we want everything to go all right."

"Suppose he gets in the way – cuts up on us. Can we put it to him, or do we just say, 'Naughty! Naughty!' "

"He'll have to take his own chances."

"Fair enough." His hard face was good-natured again as he moved toward the door. "Eleven o'clock at Van Ness and Geary."

I went back into the operatives' room, where Jack Counihan was slumped down in a chair reading a magazine.

"I hope you've thought up something for me to do," he greeted me. "I'm getting bedsores from sitting around."

"Patience son, patience – that's what you've got to learn if you're ever going to be a detective. Why, when I was a child your age, just starting in with the Agency, I was lucky –"

"Don't start that," he begged. Then his good-looking young face got earnest. "I don't see why you keep me cooped up here. I'm the only one besides you who really got a good look at Nancy Regan. I should think you would have me out hunting for her."

"I told the Old Man the same thing," I sympathized. "But he is afraid to risk something happening to you. He says in all his fifty years of gumshoeing he's never seen such a handsome op, besides being a fashion plate and a social butterfly and the heir to millions. His idea is we ought to keep you as sort of showpiece and not let you –"

"Go to hell!" Jack said, all red in the face.

"But I persuaded him to let me take the cotton packing off you tonight," I continued. "So meet me at Van Ness and Geary before eleven o'clock."

"Action?" He was all eagerness.

"Maybe."

"What are we going to do?"

"Bring your little pop-gun along." An idea came into my

head and I worded it. "You'd better be all dressed up – evening duds."

"Dinner coat?"

"No – the limit – everything but the high hat. Now for your behavior: you're not supposed to be an op. I'm not sure just what you're supposed to be, but it doesn't make any difference. Tom-Tom Carey will be along. You act as if you were neither my friend nor his – as if you didn't trust either of us. We'll be cagey with you. If anything is asked that you don't know the answer to you fall back on hostility. But don't crowd Carey too far. Got it?"

"I – I think so." He spoke slowly, screwing up his forehead. "I'm to act as if I was going along on the same business as you, but that outside of that we weren't friends. As if I wasn't willing to trust you. That it?"

"Very much. Watch yourself. You'll be swimming in nitroglycerine all the way."

"What is up? Be a good chap and give me some idea."

I grinned up at him. He was a lot taller than I.

"I could," I admitted, "but I'm afraid it would scare you off. So I'd better tell you nothing. Be happy while you can. Eat a good dinner. Lots of condemned folks seem to eat hearty breakfasts of ham and eggs just before they parade out to the rope. Maybe you wouldn't want 'em for dinner, but –"

At five minutes to eleven that night, Tom-Tom Carey brought a black touring car to the corner where Jack and I stood waiting in a fog that was like a damp fur coat.

"Climb in," he ordered as we came to the curb.

I opened the front door and motioned Jack in. He rang up the curtain on his little act, looking coldly at me and opening the rear door.

"I'm going to sit back here," he said bluntly.

"Not a bad idea," and I climbed in beside him.

Carey twisted around in his seat and he and Jack stared at each other for a while. I said nothing, did not introduce them.

When the swarthy man had finished sizing the youngster up, he looked from the boy's collar and tie – all of his evening clothes not hidden by his overcoat – to me, grinned, and drawled, "Your friend's a waiter, huh?"

I laughed, because the indignation that darkened the boy's face and popped his mouth open was natural, not part of his acting. I pushed my foot against his. He closed his mouth, said nothing, looked at Tom-Tom Carey and me as if we were specimens of some lower form of animal life.

I grinned back at Carey and asked, "Are we waiting for anything?"

He said we weren't, left off staring at Jack, and put the machine in motion. He drove us out through the park, down the boulevard. Traffic going our way and the other loomed out of and faded into the fog-thick night. Presently we left the city behind and ran out of the fog into clear moonlight. I didn't look at any of the machines running behind us, but I knew that in one of them Dick Foley and Mickey Linehan should be riding.

Tom-Tom Carey swung our car off the boulevard into a road that was smooth and well made, but not much traveled.

"Wasn't a man killed down along here somewhere last night?" I asked.

Carey nodded his head without turning it and, when we had gone another quarter-mile, said, "Right here."

We rode a little slower now, and Carey turned off his lights. In the road that was half moon-silver, half shadow-gray, the machine barely crept along for perhaps a mile. We stopped in the shade of tall shrubs that darkened a spot of the road.

"All ashore that's going ashore," Tom-Tom Carey said, and got out of the car.

Jack and I followed him. Carey took off his overcoat and threw it into the machine.

"The place is just around the bend, back from the road," he told us. "Damn this moon! I was counting on fog."

I said nothing, nor did Jack. The boy's face was white and excited.

"We'll beeline it," Carey said, leading the way across the road to a high wire fence.

He went over the fence first, then Jack, then – the sound of someone coming along the road from ahead stopped me. Signaling silence to the two men on the other side of the fence, I made myself small beside a bush. The coming steps were light, quick, feminine.

A girl came into the moonlight just ahead. She was a girl of twenty-something, neither tall nor short, thin nor plump. She was short-skirted, bare-haired, sweatered. Terror was in her white face, in the carriage of her hurrying figure – but something else was there too – more beauty than a middle-aged sleuth was used to seeing.

When she saw Carey's automobile bulking in the shadow, she stopped abruptly, with a gasp that was almost a cry.

I walked forward, saying, "Hello, Nancy Regan."

This time the gasp was a cry. "Oh! Oh!" Then, unless the moonlight was playing tricks, she recognized me and terror began to go away from her. She put both hands out to me, with relief in the gesture.

"Well?" A bearish grumble came from the big boulder of a man who had appeared out of the darkness behind her. "What's all this?"

"Hello, Andy," I greeted the boulder.

"Hullo," MacElroy echoed and stood still.

Andy always did what he was told to do. He had been told to take care of Miss Newhall. I looked at the girl and then at him again.

"Is this Miss Newhall?" I asked.

"Yeah," he rumbled. "I came down like you said, but she told me she didn't want me – wouldn't let me in the house. But you hadn't said anything about coming back. So I just camped outside, moseying around, keeping my eyes on things. And when I seen her shinnying out a window a little while ago, I just went on along behind her to take care of her, like you said I was to do."

Tom-Tom Carey and Jack Counihan came back into the road, crossed it to us. The swarthy man had an automatic in one hand. The girl's eyes were glued on mine. She paid no attention to the others.

"What is it all about?" I asked her.

"I don't know," she babbled, her hands holding on to mine, her face close to mine. "Yes, I'm Ann Newhall. I didn't know. I thought it was fun. And then when I found out it wasn't, I couldn't get out of it."

Tom-Tom Carey grunted and stirred impatiently. Jack Counihan was staring down the road. Andy MacElroy stood stolid in the road, waiting to be told what to do next. The girl never once looked from me to any of these others.

"How did you get in with them?" I demanded. "Talk fast."

I had told the girl to talk fast. She did. For twenty minutes she stood there and turned out words in a chattering stream that had no breaks except where I cut in to keep her from straying from the path I wanted her to follow. It was jumbled, almost incoherent in spots, and not always plausible, but the notion stayed with me throughout that she was trying to tell the truth – most of the time.

And not for a fraction of a second did she turn her gaze from my eyes. It was as if she was afraid to look anywhere else.

This millionaire's daughter had, two months before, been one of a party of four young people returning late at night from some sort of social affair down the coast. Somebody suggested that they stop at a roadhouse along their way – a particularly tough joint. Its toughness was its attraction, of course – toughness was more or less of a novelty to them. They got a firsthand view of it that night, for, nobody knew just how, they found themselves taking part in a row before they had been ten minutes in the dump.

The girl's escort had shamed her by showing an unreasonable amount of cowardice. He had let Red O'Leary turn him over his knee and spank him – and had done nothing about it afterward. The other youth in the party had been not much braver. The girl, insulted by this meekness, had walked across to the red-haired giant who had wrecked her escort, and she had spoken to him loud enough for everybody to hear, "Will you please take me home?"

Red O'Leary was glad to do it. She left him a block or two from her city house. She told him her name was Nancy Regan. He probably doubted it, but he never asked her any questions, pried into her affairs. In spite of the difference in their worlds, a genuine companionship had grown up between them. She liked him. He was so gloriously a roughneck that she saw him as a romantic figure. He was in love with her, knew she was miles above him, and so she had no trouble making him behave so far as she was concerned.

They met often. He took her to all the rowdy holes in the bay district, introduced her to yeggs, gunmen, swindlers, told her wild tales of criminal adventuring. She knew he was a crook, knew he was tied up in the Seamen's National and Golden Gate Trust jobs when they broke. But she saw it all as a sort of theatrical spectacle. She didn't see it as it was.

She woke up the night they were in Larrouy's and were jumped by the crooks that Red had helped Papadopoulos and the others double-cross. But it was too late then for her to wriggle clear. She was blown along with Red to Papadopoulos' hangout after I had shot the big lad. She saw then what her romantic figures really were – what she had mixed herself with.

When Papadopoulos escaped, taking her with him, she was wide awake, cured, through forever with her dangerous trifling with outlaws. So she thought. She thought Papadopoulos was the little, scary old man he seemed to be – Flora's slave, a harmless old duffer too near the grave to have any evil in him. He had been whining and terrified. He begged her not to forsake him, pleaded with her while tears ran down his withered cheeks, begging her to hide him from Flora. She took him to her country house and let him fool around in the garden, safe from prying eyes. She had no idea that he had known who she was all along, had guided her into suggesting this arrangement.

Even when the newspapers said he had been the commander-in-chief of the thug army, when the hundred-and-six-thousand-dollar reward was offered for his arrest, she believed in his innocence. He convinced her that Flora and Red had simply put the blame for the whole thing on him so they could get off with lighter sentences. He was such a frightened old gink – who wouldn't have believed him?

Then her father's death in Mexico had come and grief had occupied her mind to the exclusion of most other things until this day, when Big Flora and another girl – probably Angel Grace Cardigan – had come to the house. She had been deathly afraid of Big Flora when she had seen her before. She was more afraid now. And she soon learned that Papadopoulos was not Flora's slave but her master. She saw the old buzzard as he really was. But that wasn't the end of her awakening.

Angel Grace had suddenly tried to kill Papadopoulos. Flora had overpowered her. Grace, defiant, had told them she was Paddy's girl. Then she had screamed at Ann Newhall, "And you, you damned fool, don't you know they killed your father? Don't you know – ?"

Big Flora's fingers, around Angel Grace's throat, stopped her words. Flora tied up the Angel and turned to the Newhall girl.

"You're in it," she said brusquely. "You're in it up to your neck. You'll play along with us, or else. Here's how it stands, dearie. The old man and I are both due to step off if we're caught. And you'll do the dance with us. I'll see to that. Do what you're told and we'll all come through all right. Get funny and I'll beat holy hell out of you."

The girl didn't remember much after that. She had a dim recollection of going to the door and telling Andy she didn't want his services. She did this mechanically, not even needing to be prompted by the big blonde woman who stood close behind her. Later, in the same fearful daze, she had gone out her bedroom window, down the vine-covered side of the porch, and away from the house, running along the road, not going anywhere, just escaping.

That was what I learned from the girl. She didn't tell me all of it. She told me very little of it in those words. But that is the story I got by combining her words, her manner of telling them, her facial expressions, with what I already knew and what I could guess.

And not once while she talked had her eyes turned from mine. Not once had she shown that she knew there were other men standing in the road with us. She stared into my face with a desperate fixity, as if she was afraid not to, and her hands held mine as if she might sink through the ground if she let go.

"How about your servants?" I asked.

"There aren't any there now."

"Papadopoulos persuaded you to get rid of them?"

"Yes – several days ago."

"Then Papadopoulos, Flora and Angel Grace are alone in the house now?"

"Yes."

"They know you ducked?"

"I don't know. I don't think they do. I had been in my room some time. I don't think they suspected I'd dare do anything but what they told me."

It annoyed me to find I was staring into the girl's eyes as fixedly as she into mine, and that when I wanted to take my gaze away it wasn't easily done. I jerked my eyes away from her, took my hands away.

"The rest of it you can tell me later," I growled, and turned to give Andy MacElroy his orders. "You stay here with Miss Newhall until we get back from the house. Make yourselves comfortable in the car."

The girl put a hand on my arm. "Am I – ? Are you – ?"

"We're going to turn you over to the police, yes," I assured her.

"No! No!"

"Don't be childish," I begged. "You can't run around with a mob of cutthroats, get yourself tied up in a flock of crimes, and then when you're tripped say, 'Excuse it, please,' and go free. If you tell the whole story in court – including the parts you haven't told me – the chances are you'll get off. But there's no way in God's world for you to escape arrest. Come on," I told Jack and Tom-Tom Carey. "We've got to shake it up if we want to find our folks at home."

Looking back as I climbed the fence, I saw that Andy had put the girl in the car and was getting in himself. "Just a moment," I called to Jack and Carey, who were already starting across the field.

"Thought of something else to kill time," the swarthy man complained.

I went back across the road to the car and spoke quickly and softly to Andy, "Dick Foley and Mickey Linehan should be hanging around the neighborhood. As soon as we're out of sight, hunt 'em up. Turn Miss Newhall over to Dick. Tell him to take her with him and beat it for a phone – rouse the sheriff. Tell Dick he's to turn the girl over to the sheriff, to hold for the San Francisco police. Tell him he's not to give her up to anybody else – not even to me. Got it?"

"Got it."

"All right. After you've told him that and have given him

the girl, then you bring Mickey Linehan to the Newhall house as fast as you can make it. We'll likely need all the help we can get as soon as we can get it."

"Got you," Andy said.

"What are you up to?" Tom-Tom Carey asked suspiciously when I rejoined Jack and him.

"Detective business."

"I ought to have come down and turned the trick all by myself," he grumbled. "You haven't done a damned thing but waste time since we started."

"I'm not the one that's wasting it now."

He snorted and set out across the field again, Jack and I following him. At the end of the field there was another fence to be climbed. Then we came over a little wooded ridge and the Newhall house lay before us – a large white house, glistening in the moonlight, with yellow rectangles where blinds were down over the windows of lighted rooms. The lighted rooms were on the ground floor. The upper floor was dark. Everything was quiet.

"Damn the moonlight!" Tom-Tom Carey repeated, bringing another automatic out of his clothes so that he now had one in each hand.

Jack started to take his gun out, looked at me, saw I was letting mine rest, let his slide back in his pocket.

Tom-Tom Carey's face was a dark stone mask – slits for eyes, slit for mouth – the grim mask of a manhunter, a mankiller. He was breathing softly, his big chest moving gently. Beside him Jack Counihan looked like an excited schoolboy. His face was ghastly, his eyes all stretched out of shape, and he was breathing like a tire pump. But his grin was genuine, for all the nervousness in it.

"We'll cross to the house on this side," I whispered. "Then one of us can take the front, one the back, and the other can wait till he sees where he's needed most. Right?"

"Right," the swarthy one agreed.

"Wait!" Jack exclaimed. "The girl came down the vines from an upper window. What's the matter with my going up that way? I'm lighter than either of you. If they haven't missed her, the window would still be open. Give me ten minutes to find the window, get through it, and get myself placed. Then when you attack I'll be there behind them. How's that?" he demanded applause.

"And what if they grab you as soon as you light?" I objected.

"Suppose they do. I can make enough racket for you to hear. You can gallop to the attack while they're busy with me. That'll be just as good."

"Blue hell!" Tom-Tom Carey barked. "What good's all that? The other way's best. One of us at the front door, one at the back, kick 'em in and go in shooting."

"If this new one works, it'll be better," I gave my opinion. "If you want to jump in the furnace, Jack, I won't stop you. I won't cheat you out of your heroics."

"No!" the swarthy man snarled. "Nothing doing!"

"Yes," I contradicted him. "We'll try it. Better take twenty minutes, Jack. That won't give you any time to waste."

He looked at his watch and I at mine, and he turned toward the house.

Tom-Tom Carey, scowling darkly, stood in his way. I cursed and got between the swarthy man and the boy. Jack went around my back and hurried away across the too-bright space between us and the house.

"Keep your feet on the ground," I told Carey. "There are a lot of things to this game you don't know anything about."

"Too damned many!" he snarled, but he let the boy go.

There was no open second-story window on our side of the building. Jack rounded the rear of the house and went out of sight.

A faint rustling sounded behind us. Carey and I spun

together. His guns went up. I stretched out an arm across them, pushing them down.

"Don't have a hemorrhage," I cautioned him. "This is just another of the things you don't know about."

The rustling had stopped.

"All right," I called softly.

Mickey Linehan and Andy MacElroy came out of the tree-shadows.

Tom-Tom Carey stuck his face so close to mine that I'd have been scratched if he had forgotten to shave that day.

"You double-crossing –"

"Behave! Behave! A man of your age!" I admonished him. "None of these boys want any of your blood money."

"I don't like this gang stuff," he snarled. "We –"

"We're going to need all the help we can get," I interrupted, looking at my watch. I told the two operatives: "We're going to close in on the house now. Four of us ought to be able to wrap it up snug. You know Papadopoulos, Big Flora and Angel Grace by description. They're in there. Don't take any chances with them – Flora and Papadopoulos are dynamite. Jack Counihan is trying to ease inside now. You two look after the back of the joint. Carey and I will take the front. We'll make the play. You see that nobody leaks out on us. Forward march!"

The swarthy man and I headed for the front porch – a wide porch, grown over with vines on the side, yellowly illuminated now by the light that came through four curtained French windows.

We hadn't taken our first steps across the porch when one of these tall windows moved – opened.

The first thing I saw was Jack Counihan's back.

He was pushing the casement open with a hand and foot, not turning his head.

Beyond the boy – facing him across the brightly lighted room – stood a man and woman. The man was old, small, scrawny, wrinkled, pitifully frightened – Papadopoulos. I saw he had shaved off his straggly white mustache. The woman was tall, full-bodied, pink-fleshed and yellow-haired – a she-athlete of forty with clear gray eyes set deep in a handsome brutal face – Big Flora Brace. They stood very still, side by side, watching the muzzle of Jack Counihan's gun.

While I stood in front of the window looking at this scene, Tom-Tom Carey, his two guns up, stepped past me, going through the tall window to the boy's side. I did not follow him into the room.

Papadopoulos' scary brown eyes darted to the swarthy man's face. Flora's gray ones moved there deliberately, and then looked past him to me.

"Hold it, everybody!" I ordered, and moved away from the window, to the side of the porch where the vines were thinnest.

Leaning out between the vines, so my face was clear in the moonlight, I looked down the side of the building. A shadow in the shadow of the garage could have been a man. I put an arm out in the moonlight and beckoned. The shadow came toward me – Mickey Linehan. Andy MacElroy's head peeped around the back of the house. I beckoned again and he followed Mickey.

I returned to the open window.

Papadopoulos and Flora – a rabbit and a lioness – stood looking at the guns of Carey and Jack. They looked again at me when I appeared, and a smile began to curve the woman's full lips.

Mickey and Andy came up and stood beside me. The woman's smile died grimly.

"Carey," I said, "you and Jack stay as is. Mickey, Andy, go in and take hold of our gifts from God."

When the two operatives stepped through the window – things happened.

Papadopoulos screamed.

Big Flora lunged against him, knocking him at the back door. "Go! Go!" she roared.

Stumbling, staggering, he scrambled across the room.

Flora had a pair of guns – sprung suddenly in her hands. Her big body seemed to fill the room, as if by willpower she had become a giantess. She charged – straight at the guns Jack and Carey held – blotting the back door and the fleeing man from their fire.

A blur to one side was Andy MacElroy moving.

I had a hand on Jack's gun arm.

"Don't shoot," I muttered in his ear.

Flora's guns thundered together. But she was tumbling. Andy had crashed into her. Had thrown himself at her legs as a man would throw a boulder.

When Flora tumbled, Tom-Tom Carey stopped waiting.

His first bullet was sent so close past her that it clipped her curled yellow hair. But it went past – caught Papadopoulos just as he went through the door. The bullet took him low in the back – smeared him out on the floor.

Carey fired again – again – again – into the prone body.

"It's no use," I growled. "You can't make him any deader."

He chuckled and lowered his guns.

"Four into a hundred and six." All his ill-humor, his grimness was gone. "That's twenty-six thousand, five hundred dollars each of those slugs was worth to me."

Andy and Mickey had wrestled Flora into submission and were hauling her up off the floor.

I looked from them back to the swarthy man, muttering, "It's not all over yet."

"No?" He seemed surprised. "What next?"

"Stay awake and let your conscience guide you," I replied, and turned to the Counihan youngster. "Come along, Jack."

I led the way out through the window and across the porch, where I leaned against the railing. Jack followed and stood in front of me, his gun still in his hand, his face white and tired from nervous tension. Looking over his shoulder, I could see the room we had just quit. Andy and Mickey and Flora sitting between them on a sofa. Carey stood a little to one side, looking curiously at Jack and me. We were in the middle of the band of light that came through the open window. We could see inside – except that Jack's back was that way – and could be seen from there, but our talk couldn't be overheard unless we made it loud.

All that was as I wanted it.

"Now tell me about it," I ordered Jack.

"Well, I found the open window," the boy began.

"I know all that part," I cut in. "You came in and told your friends – Papadopoulos and Flora – about the girl's escape, and that Carey and I were coming. You advised them to make out you had captured them single-handed. That would draw Carey and me in. With you unsuspected behind us, it would be easy for the three of you to grab the two of us. After that you could stroll down the road and tell Andy I had sent you for the girl. That was a good scheme – except that you didn't know I had Dick and Mickey up my sleeve, didn't know I wouldn't let you get behind me. But all that isn't what I want to know. I want to know why you sold us out – and what you think you're going to do now."

"Are you crazy?" His young face was bewildered, his young eyes horrified. "Or is this some – ?"

"Sure, I'm crazy," I confessed. "Wasn't I crazy enough to let you lead me into that trap in Sausalito? But I wasn't too crazy to figure it out afterward. I wasn't too crazy to see that Ann Newhall was afraid to look at you. I'm not crazy enough to think you could have captured Papadopoulos and Flora unless they wanted you to. I'm crazy – but in moderation."

Jack laughed – a reckless young laugh, but too shrill. His eyes didn't laugh with mouth and voice. While he was laughing his eyes looked from me to the gun in his hand and back to me.

"Talk, Jack," I pleaded huskily, putting a hand on his shoulder. "For God's sake why did you do it?"

The boy shut his eyes, gulped, and his shoulders twitched. When his eyes opened they were hard and glittering and full of merry hell. "The worst part of it," he said harshly, moving his shoulder from under my hand, "is that I wasn't a very good crook, was I? I didn't succeed in deluding you."

I said nothing.

"I suppose you've earned your right to the story," he went on after a little pause. His voice was consciously monotonous, as if he was deliberately keeping out of it every tone or accent that might seem to express emotion. He was too young to talk naturally. "I met Ann Newhall three weeks ago, in my own home. She had gone to school with my sisters, though I had never met her before. We knew each other at once, of course – I knew she was Nancy Regan, she knew I was a Continental operative.

"So we went off by ourselves and talked things over. Then she took me to see Papadopoulos. I liked the old boy and he liked me. He showed me how we together could accumulate unheard-of piles of wealth. So there you are. The prospect of all that money completely devastated my morals. I told him about Carey as soon as I had heard from you, and I led you into that trap, as you say. He thought it would be better if you stopped bothering us before you found the connection between Newhall and Papadopoulos.

"After that failure, he wanted me to try again, but I refused to have a hand in any more fiascos. There's nothing sillier than a murder that doesn't come off. Ann Newhall is quite innocent of everything except folly. I don't think she has the slightest suspicion that I have had any part in the dirty work beyond refraining from having everybody arrested. That, my dear Sherlock, about concludes the confession."

I had listened to the boy's story with a great show of sympathetic attentiveness. Now I scowled at him and spoke accusingly, but still not without friendliness.

"Stop spoofing! The money Papadopoulos showed you didn't buy you. You met the girl and were too soft to turn her in. But your vanity – your pride in looking at yourself as a pretty cold proposition – wouldn't let you admit it even to yourself. You had to have a hard-boiled front. So you were meat to Papadopoulos' grinder. He gave you a part you could play to yourself – a super-gentleman-crook, a mastermind, a desperate suave villain, and all that kind of romantic garbage. That's the way you went, my son. You went as far as possible beyond what was needed to save the girl from the hoosegow – just to show the world, but chiefly yourself, that you were not acting through sentimentality, but according to your own reckless desires. There you are. Look at yourself."

Whatever he saw in himself – what I had seen or something else – his face slowly reddened, and he wouldn't look at me. He looked past me at the distant road.

I looked into the lighted room beyond him. Tom-Tom Carey had advanced to the center of the floor, where he stood watching us. I jerked a corner of my mouth at him – a warning.

"Well," the boy began again, but he didn't know what to say after that. He shuffled his feet and kept his eyes from my face.

I stood up straight and got rid of the last trace of my hypocritical sympathy.

"Give me your gun, you lousy rat!" I snarled at him.

He jumped back as if I had hit him. Craziness writhed in his face. He jerked his gun chest-high.

Tom-Tom Carey saw the gun go up. The swarthy man fired twice. Jack Counihan was dead at my feet.

Mickey Linehan fired once. Carey was down on the floor, bleeding from the temple.

I stepped over Jack's body, went into the room, knelt beside the swarthy man. He squirmed, tried to say something, died before he could get it out. I waited until my face was straight before I stood up.

Big Flora was studying me with narrowed gray eyes. I stared back at her.

"I don't get it all yet," she said slowly, "but if you –"

"Where's Angel Grace?" I interrupted.

"Tied to the kitchen table," she informed me, and went on with her thinking aloud. "You've dealt a hand that –"

"Yeah," I said sourly, "I'm another Papadopoulos."

Her big body suddenly quivered. Pain clouded her handsome brutal face. Two tears came out of her lower eyelids.

I'm damned if she hadn't loved the old scoundrel!

It was after eight in the morning when I got back to the city. I ate breakfast and then went up to the Agency, where I found the Old Man going through his morning mail.

"It's all over," I told him. "Papadopoulos knew Nancy Regan was Taylor Newhall's heiress. When he needed a hiding place after the bank jobs flopped, he got her to take him down to the Newhall country place. He had two holds on her. She pitied him as a misused old duffer, and she was – even if innocently – an accomplice after the fact in the stick-ups.

"Pretty soon Papa Newhall had to go to Mexico on business. Papadopoulos saw a chance to make something. If Newhall was knocked off, the girl would have millions – and the old thief knew he could take them away from her. He sent Barrows down to the border to buy the murder from some Mexican bandits. Barrows put it over, but talked too much. He told a girl in Nogales that he had to go back 'to Frisco to collect plenty from an old Greek,' and then he'd return and buy her the world. The girl passed the news on to Tom-Tom Carey. Carey put a lot of twos together and got at least a dozen for an answer. He followed Barrows up here.

"Angel Grace was with him the morning he called on

Barrows here – to find out if his 'old Greek' really was Papadopoulos, and where he could be found. Barrows was too full of morphine to listen to reason. He was so dope-deadened that even after the dark man began to reason with a knife-blade he had to whittle Barrows all up before he began to feel hurt. The carving sickened Angel Grace. She left, after vainly trying to stop Carey. And when she read in the afternoon papers what a finished job he had made of it, she tried to commit suicide, to stop the images from crawling around in her head.

"Carey got all the information Barrows had, but Barrows didn't know where Papadopoulos was hiding. Papadopoulos learned of Carey's arrival – you know how he learned. He sent Arlie to stop Carey. Carey wouldn't give the barber a chance – until the swarthy man began to suspect Papadopoulos might be at the Newhall place. He drove down there, letting Arlie follow. As soon as Arlie discovered his destination, Arlie closed in, hell-bent on stopping Carey at any cost. That was what Carey wanted. He gunned Arlie, came back to town, got hold of me, and took me down to help wind things up.

"Meanwhile, Angel Grace, in the cooler, had made friends with Big Flora. She knew Flora but Flora didn't know her. Papadopoulos had arranged a crush-out for Flora. It's always easier for two to escape than one. Flora took the Angel along, took her to Papadopoulos. The Angel went for him, but Flora knocked her for a loop.

"Flora, Angel Grace and Ann Newhall, alias Nancy Regan, are in the county jail," I wound up. "Papadopoulos, Tom-Tom Carey and Jack Counihan are dead."

I stopped talking and lighted a cigarette, taking my time, watching cigarette and match carefully throughout the operation. The Old Man picked up a letter, put it down without reading it, picked up another.

"They were killed in the course of making arrests?" His mild voice held nothing but its usual unfathomable politeness.

"Yes. Carey killed Papadopoulos. A little later he shot Jack. Mickey – not knowing – not knowing anything except that the dark man was shooting at Jack and me – we were standing apart talking – shot and killed Carey." The words twisted around my tongue, wouldn't come out straight. "Neither Mickey nor Andy know that Jack – Nobody but you and I know exactly what the thing – exactly what Jack was doing. Flora Brace and Ann Newhall did know, but if we say he was acting on orders all the time, nobody can deny it."

The Old Man nodded his grandfatherly face and smiled, but for the first time in the years I had known him I knew what he was thinking. He was thinking that if Jack had come through alive we would have had the nasty choice between letting him go free or giving the Agency a black eye by advertising the fact that one of our operatives was a crook.

I threw away my cigarette and stood up. The Old Man stood also, and held out a hand to me.

"Thank you," he said.

I took his hand, and I understood him, but I didn't have anything I wanted to confess – even by silence.

"It happened that way," I said deliberately. "I played the cards so we would get the benefit of the breaks – but it just happened that way."

He nodded, smiling benignantly.

"I'm going to take a couple of weeks off," I said from the door. I felt tired, washed out.

THE DAIN CURSE

To Albert S. Samuels

PART 1

THE DAINS

1 EIGHT DIAMONDS

IT WAS A DIAMOND all right, shining in the grass half a dozen feet from the blue brick wall. It was small, not more than a quarter of a carat in weight, and unmounted. I put it in my pocket and began searching the lawn as closely as I could without going at it on all fours.

I had covered a couple of square yards of sod when the Leggetts' front door opened.

A woman came out on the broad stone top step and looked down at me with good-humored curiosity.

She was a woman of about my age, forty, with darkish blond hair, a pleasant plump face, and dimpled pink cheeks. She had on a lavender-flowered white housedress.

I stopped poking in the grass and went up to her, asking: "Is Mr. Leggett in?"

"Yes." Her voice was placid as her face. "You wish to see him?"

I said I did.

She smiled at me and at the lawn.

"You're another detective, aren't you?"

I admitted that.

She took me up to a green, orange, and chocolate room on the second floor, put me in a brocaded chair, and went to call her husband from his laboratory. While I waited, I looked around the room, deciding that the dull orange rug under my feet was probably both genuinely oriental and genuinely ancient, that the walnut furniture hadn't been ground out by machinery, and that the Japanese pictures on the wall hadn't been selected by a prude.

Edgar Leggett came in saying: "I'm sorry to have kept you waiting, but I couldn't break off till now. Have you learned something?"

His voice was unexpectedly harsh, rasping, though his manner was friendly enough. He was a dark-skinned erect man in his middle forties, muscularly slender and of medium height. He would have been handsome if his brown face hadn't been so deeply marked with sharp, hard lines across the forehead and from nostrils down across mouth-corners. Dark hair, worn rather long, curled above and around the broad, grooved forehead. Red-brown eyes were abnormally bright behind horn-rimmed spectacles. His nose was long, thin, and high-bridged. His lips were thin, sharp, nimble, over a small, bony chin. His black and white clothes were well made and cared for.

"Not yet," I said to his question. "I'm not a police detective – Continental Agency – for the insurance company – and I'm just starting."

"Insurance company?" He seemed surprised, raising dark eyebrows above the dark tops of his spectacles.

"Yeah. Didn't – ?"

"Surely," he said, smiling, stopping my words with a small flourish of one hand. It was a long, narrow hand with over-developed finger-tips, ugly as most trained hands are. "Surely. They would have been insured. I hadn't thought of that. They weren't my diamonds, you know; they were Halstead's."

"Halstead and Beauchamp? I didn't get any details from the insurance company. You had the diamonds on approval?"

"No. I was using them experimentally. Halstead knew of my work with glass – coloring it, staining or dyeing it, after its manufacture – and he became interested in the possibility of the process being adapted to diamonds, particularly in improving off-color stones, removing yellowish and brownish tinges, emphasizing blues. He asked me to try it and five weeks ago gave me those diamonds to work on. There were eight of them, none especially valuable. The largest weighed only a trifle more than half a carat, some of the others only a quarter, and except for two they were all of poor color. They're the stones the burglar got."

"Then you hadn't succeeded?" I asked.

"Frankly," he said, "I hadn't made the slightest progress. This was a more delicate matter, and on more obdurate material."

"Where'd you keep them?"

"Usually they were left lying around in the open – always in the laboratory, of course – but for several days now they had been locked in the cabinet – since my last unsuccessful experiment."

"Who knew about the experiments?"

"Anyone, everyone – there was no occasion for secrecy."

"They were stolen from the cabinet?"

"Yes. This morning we found our front door open, the cabinet drawer forced, and the diamonds gone. The police found marks on the kitchen door. They say the burglar came in that way and left by the front door. We heard nothing last night. And nothing else was taken."

"The front door was ajar when I came downstairs this morning," Mrs. Leggett said from the doorway. "I went upstairs and awakened Edgar, and we searched the house and found the diamonds gone. The police think the man I saw must have been the burglar."

I asked about the man she had seen.

"It was last night, around midnight, when I opened the bedroom windows before going to bed. I saw a man standing upon the corner. I can't say, even now, that there was anything very suspicious-looking about him. He was standing there as if waiting for somebody. He was looking down this way, but not in a way to make me think he was watching this house. He was a man past forty, I should say, rather short and broad – somewhat of your build – but he had a bristly brown mustache and was pale. He wore a soft hat and overcoat – dark – I think they were brown. The police think that's the same man Gabrielle saw."

"Who?"

"My daughter Gabrielle," she said. "Coming home late one night – Saturday night, I think it was – she saw a man and thought he had come from our steps; but she wasn't sure and didn't think anything more of it until after the burglary."

"I'd like to talk to her. Is she home?"

Mrs. Leggett went out to get her.

I asked Leggett: "Were the diamonds loose?"

"They were unset, of course, and in small manila envelopes – Halstead and Beauchamp's – each in a separate envelope, with a number and the weight of the stone written in pencil. The envelopes are missing too."

Mrs. Leggett returned with her daughter, a girl of twenty or less in a sleeveless white silk dress. Of medium height, she looked more slender than she actually was. She had hair as curly as her father's, and no longer, but of a much lighter brown. She had a pointed chin and extremely white, smooth skin, and of her features only the green-brown eyes were large: forehead, mouth, and teeth were remarkably small. I stood up to be introduced to her, and asked about the man she had seen.

"I'm not positive that he came from the house," she said, "or even from the lawn." She was sullen, as if she didn't like being questioned. "I thought he might have, but I only saw him walking up the street."

"What sort of looking man was he?"

"I don't know. It was dark. I was in the car, he was walking up the street. I didn't examine him closely. He was about your size. It might have been you, for all I know."

"It wasn't. That was Saturday night?"

"Yes – that is, Sunday morning."

"What time?"

"Oh, three o'clock or after," she said impatiently.

"Were you alone?"

"Hardly."

I asked her who was with her and finally got a name: Eric Collinson had driven her home. I asked where I could find Eric Collinson. She frowned, hesitated, and said he was employed by Spear, Camp and Duffy, stockbrokers. She also said she had a putrid headache and she hoped I would excuse her now, as she knew I couldn't have any more questions to ask her. Then, without waiting for any reply I might have made to that, she turned and went out of the room. Her ears, I noticed when she turned, had no lobes, and were queerly pointed at the top.

"How about your servants?" I asked Mrs. Leggett.

"We've only one – Minnie Hershey, a Negress. She doesn't sleep here, and I'm sure she had nothing to do with it. She's been with us for nearly two years and I can vouch for her honesty."

I said I'd like to talk to Minnie, and Mrs. Leggett called her in. The servant was a small, wiry mulatto girl with the straight black hair and brown features of an Indian. She was very polite and very insistent that she had nothing to do with the theft of the diamonds and had known nothing about the burglary until she arrived at the house that morning. She gave me her home address, in San Francisco's darktown.

Leggett and his wife took me up to the laboratory, a large room that covered all but a small fifth of the third story. Charts hung between the windows on the white-washed wall. The wooden floor was uncovered. An X-ray machine – or something similar – four or five smaller machines, a forge, a wide sink, a large zinc table, some smaller porcelain ones, stands, racks of glassware, siphon-shaped metal tanks – that sort of stuff filled most of the room.

The cabinet the diamonds had been taken from was a green-painted steel affair with six drawers all locking together. The second drawer from the top – the one the diamonds had been in – was open. Its edge was dented where a jimmy or chisel had been forced between it and the frame. The other drawers were still locked. Leggett said the forcing of the diamond drawer had jammed the locking mechanism so that he would have to get a mechanic to open the others.

We went downstairs, through a room where the mulatto was walking around behind a vacuum cleaner, and into the kitchen. The back door and its frame were marked much as the cabinet was, apparently by the same tool.

When I had finished looking at the door, I took the diamond out of my pocket and showed it to the Leggetts, asking: "Is this one of them?"

Leggett picked it out of my palm with forefinger and thumb, held it up to the light, turned it from side to side, and said: "Yes. It has that cloudy spot down at the culet. Where did you get it?"

"Out front, in the grass."

"Ah, our burglar dropped some of his spoils in his haste."

I said I doubted it.

Leggett pulled his brows together behind his glasses, looked at me with smaller eyes, and asked sharply: "What do you think?"

"I think it was planted there. Your burglar knew too much. He knew which drawer to go to. He didn't waste time on anything else. Detectives always say: 'Inside job,' because it saves work if they can find a victim right on the scene; but I can't see anything else here."

Minnie came to the door, still holding the vacuum cleaner, and began to cry that she was an honest girl, and nobody had any right to accuse her of anything, and they could search her and her home if they wanted to, and just because she was a colored girl was no reason, and so on and so on; and not all of it could be made out, because the vacuum cleaner was still humming in her hand and she sobbed while she talked. Tears ran down her cheeks.

Mrs. Leggett went to her, patted her shoulder, and said: "There, there. Don't cry, Minnie. I know you hadn't anything to do with it, and so does everybody else. There, there." Presently she got the girl's tears turned off and sent her upstairs.

Leggett sat on a corner of the kitchen table and asked: "You suspect someone in this house?"

"Somebody who's been in it, yeah."

"Whom?"

"Nobody yet."

"That" – he smiled, showing white teeth almost as small as his daughter's – "means everybody – all of us?"

"Let's take a look at the lawn," I suggested. "If we find any more diamonds I'll say maybe I'm mistaken about the inside angle."

Half-way through the house, as we went towards the front door, we met Minnie Hershey in a tan coat and violet hat, coming to say good-bye to her mistress. She wouldn't, she said tearfully, work anywhere where anybody thought she had stolen anything. She was just as honest as anybody else, and more than some, and just as much entitled to respect, and if she couldn't get it one place she could another, because she knew places where people wouldn't accuse her of stealing things after she had worked for them for two long years without ever taking so much as a slice of bread.

Mrs. Leggett pleaded with her, reasoned with her, scolded her, and commanded her, but none of it was any good. The brown girl's mind was made up, and away she went.

Mrs. Leggett looked at me, making her pleasant face as severe as she could, and said reprovingly: "Now see what you've done."

I said I was sorry, and her husband and I went out to examine the lawn. We didn't find any more diamonds.

2 LONG-NOSE

I PUT IN A couple of hours canvassing the neighborhood, trying to place the man Mrs. and Miss Leggett had seen. I didn't have any luck with that one, but I picked up news of another. A Mrs. Priestly – a pale semi-invalid who lived three doors below the Leggetts – gave me the first line on him.

Mrs. Priestly often sat at a front window at night when she couldn't sleep. On two of these nights she had seen the man. She said he was a tall man, and young, she thought, and he walked with his head thrust forward. The street was too poorly lighted for her to describe his coloring and clothes.

She had first seen him a week before. He had passed up and down on the other side of the street five or six times, at intervals of fifteen or twenty minutes, with his face turned as if watching something – or looking for something – on Mrs. Priestly's – and the Leggetts' – side of the street. She thought it was between eleven and twelve o'clock that she had seen him the first time that night, and around one o'clock the last. Several nights later – Saturday – she had seen him again, not walking this time, but standing on the corner below, looking up the street, at about midnight. He went away after half an hour, and she had not seen him again.

Mrs. Priestly knew the Leggetts by sight, but knew very little about them, except that the daughter was said to be a bit wild. They seemed to be nice people, but kept to themselves. He had moved into the house in 1921, alone except for the housekeeper – a Mrs. Begg, who, Mrs. Priestly understood, was now with a family named Freemander in Berkeley. Mrs.

Leggett and Gabrielle had not come to live with Leggett until 1923.

Mrs. Priestly said she had not been at her window the previous night and therefore had not seen the man Mrs. Leggett had seen on the corner.

A man named Warren Daley, who lived on the opposite side of the street, down near the corner where Mrs. Priestly had seen her man, had, when locking up the house Sunday night, surprised a man – apparently the same man – in the vestibule. Daley was not at home when I called, but, after telling me this much, Mrs. Daley got him on the phone for me.

Daley said the man had been standing in the vestibule, either hiding from or watching someone up the street. As soon as Daley opened the door, the man ran away, down the street, paying no attention to Daley's "What are you doing there?" Daley said he was a man of thirty-two or -three, fairly well dressed in dark clothes, and had a long, thin, and sharp nose.

That was all I could shake the neighborhood down for. I went to the Montgomery Street offices of Spear, Camp and Duffy and asked for Eric Collinson.

He was young, blond, tall, broad, sunburned, and dressy, with the good-looking unintelligent face of one who would know everything about polo, or shooting, or flying, or something of that sort – maybe even two things of that sort – but not much about anything else. We sat on a fatted leather seat in the customers' room, now, after market hours, empty except for a weedy boy juggling numbers on the board. I told Collinson about the burglary and asked him about the man he and Miss Leggett had seen Saturday night.

"He was an ordinary-looking chap, as far as I could see. It was dark. Short and chunky. You think he took them?"

"Did he come from the Leggett house?" I asked.

"From the lawn, at least. He seemed jumpy – that's why I thought perhaps he'd been nosing around where he shouldn't. I suggested I go after him and ask him what he was up to, but

Gaby wouldn't have it. Might have been a friend of her father's. Did you ask him? He goes in for odd eggs."

"Wasn't that late for a visitor to be leaving?"

He looked away from me, so I asked: "What time was it?"

"Midnight, I dare say."

"Midnight?"

"That's the word. The time when the graves give up their dead, and ghosts walk."

"Miss Leggett said it was after three o'clock."

"You see how it is!" he exclaimed, blandly triumphant, as if he had demonstrated something we had been arguing about. "She's half blind and won't wear glasses for fear of losing beauty. She's always making mistakes like that. Plays abominable bridge – takes deuces for aces. It was probably a quarter after twelve, and she looked at the clock and got the hands mixed."

I said: "That's too bad," and "Thanks," and went up to Halstead and Beauchamp's store in Geary Street.

Watt Halstead was a suave, pale, bald, fat man, with tired eyes and a too tight collar. I told him what I was doing and asked him how well he knew Leggett.

"I know him as a desirable customer and by reputation as a scientist. Why do you ask?"

"His burglary's sour – in spots anyway."

"Oh, you're mistaken. That is, you're mistaken if you think a man of his caliber would be mixed up in anything like that. A servant, of course; yes, that's possible: it often happens, doesn't it? But not Leggett. He is a scientist of some standing – he has done some remarkable work with color – and, unless our credit department has been misinformed, a man of more than moderate means. I don't mean that he is wealthy in the modern sense of the word, but too wealthy for a thing of that sort. And, confidentially, I happen to know that his present balance in the Seaman's National Bank is in excess of ten thousand dollars. Well – the eight diamonds were worth no more than a thousand or twelve or thirteen hundred dollars."

"At retail? Then they cost you five or six hundred?"

"Well," smiling, "seven fifty would be nearer."

"How'd you come to give him the diamonds?"

"He's a customer of ours, as I've told you, and when I learned what he had done with glass, I thought what a wonderful thing it would be if the same method could be applied to diamonds. Fitzstephan – it was largely through him that I learned of Leggett's work with glass – was skeptical, but I thought it worth trying – still think so – and persuaded Leggett to try."

Fitzstephan was a familiar name. I asked: "Which Fitzstephan was that?"

"Owen, the writer. You know him?"

"Yeah, but I didn't know he was on the coast. We used to drink out of the same bottle. Do you know his address?"

Halstead found it in the telephone book for me, a Nob Hill apartment.

From the jeweler's I went to the vicinity of Minnie Hershey's home. It was a Negro neighborhood, which made the getting of reasonably accurate information twice as unlikely as it always is.

What I managed to get added up to this: The girl had come to San Francisco from Winchester, Virginia, four or five years ago, and for the last half-year had been living with a Negro called Rhino Tingley. One told me Rhino's first name was Ed, another Bill, but they agreed that he was young, big, and black and could easily be recognized by the scar on his chin. I was also told that he depended for his living on Minnie and pool; that he was not bad except when he got mad – then he was supposed to be a holy terror; and that I could get a look at him the early part of almost any evening in either Bunny Mack's barber-shop or Big-foot Gerber's cigar-store.

I learned where these joints were and then went downtown again, to the police detective bureau in the Hall of Justice. Nobody was in the pawnshop detail office. I crossed the corridor and asked Lieutenant Duff whether anybody had been put on the Leggett job.

He said: "See O'Gar."

I went into the assembly room, looking for O'Gar and wondering what he – a homicide detail detective-sergeant – had to do with my job. Neither O'Gar nor Pat Reddy, his partner, was in. I smoked a cigarette, tried to guess who had been killed, and decided to phone Leggett.

"Any police detective been in since I left?" I asked when his harsh voice was in my ear.

"No, but the police called up a little while ago and asked my wife and daughter to come to a place in Golden Gate Avenue to see if they could identify a man there. They left a few minutes ago. I didn't accompany them, not having seen the supposed burglar."

"Whereabouts in Golden Gate Avenue?"

He didn't remember the number, but he knew the block – above Van Ness Avenue. I thanked him and went out there.

In the designated block I found a uniformed copper standing in the doorway of a small apartment house. I asked him if O'Gar was there.

"Up in three ten," he said.

I rode up in a rickety elevator. When I got out on the third floor, I came face to face with Mrs. Leggett and her daughter, leaving.

"Now I hope you're satisfied that Minnie had nothing to do with it," Mrs. Leggett said chidingly.

"The police found your man?"

"Yes."

I said to Gabrielle Leggett: "Eric Collinson says it was only midnight, or a few minutes later, that you got home Saturday night."

"Eric," she said irritably, passing me to enter the elevator, "is an ass."

Her mother, following her into the elevator, reprimanded her amiably: "Now, dear."

I walked down the hall to a doorway where Pat Reddy stood talking to a couple of reporters, said hello, squeezed past them into a short passage-way, and went through that to a shabbily furnished room where a dead man lay on a wall bed.

Phels, of the police identification bureau, looked up from his magnifying glass to nod at me and then went on with his examination of a mission table's edge.

O'Gar pulled his head and shoulders in the open window and growled: "So we got to put up with you again?"

O'Gar was a burly, stolid man of fifty, who wore wide-brimmed black hats of the movie-sheriff sort. There was a lot of sense in his hard bullet-head, and he was comfortable to work with.

I looked at the corpse – a man of forty or so, with a heavy, pale face, short hair touched with gray, a scrubby, dark mustache, and stocky arms and legs. There was a bullet hole just over his navel, and another high on the left side of his chest.

"It's a man," O'Gar said as I put the blankets over him again. "He's dead."

"What else did somebody tell you?" I asked.

"Looks like him and another guy glaumed the ice, and then the other guy decided to take a one-way split. The envelopes are here" – O'Gar took them out of his pocket and ruffled them with a thumb – "but the diamonds ain't. They went down the fire-escape with the other guy a little while back. People spotted him making the sneak, but lost him when he cut through the alley. Tall man with a long nose. This one" – he pointed the envelopes at the bed – "has been here a week. Name of Louis Upton, with New York labels. We don't know him. Nobody in the dump'll say they ever saw him with anybody else. Nobody'll say they know Long-nose."

Pat Reddy came in. He was a big, jovial youngster, with almost brains enough to make up for his lack of experience. I told him and O'Gar what I had turned up on the job so far.

"Long-nose and this bird taking turns watching Leggett's?" Reddy suggested.

"Maybe," I said, "but there's an inside angle. How many envelopes have you got there, O'Gar?"

"Seven."

"Then the one for the planted diamond is missing."

"How about the yellow girl?" Reddy asked.

"I'm going out for a look at her man tonight," I said. "You people trying New York on this Upton?"

"Uh-huh," O'Gar said.

3 SOMETHING BLACK

AT THE NOB HILL address Halstead had given me, I told my name to the boy at the switchboard and asked him to pass it on to Fitzstephan. I remembered Fitzstephan as a long, lean, sorrel-haired man of thirty-two, with sleepy gray eyes, a wide, humorous mouth, and carelessly worn clothes; a man who pretended to be lazier than he was, would rather talk than do anything else, and had a lot of what seemed to be accurate information and original ideas on any subject that happened to come up, as long as it was a little out of the ordinary.

I had met him five years before, in New York, where I was digging dirt on a chain of fake mediums who had taken a coal-and-ice dealer's widow for a hundred thousand dollars. Fitzstephan was plowing the same field for literary material. We became acquainted and pooled forces. I got more out of the combination than he did, since he knew the spook racket inside and out; and, with his help, I cleaned up my job in a couple of weeks. We were fairly chummy for a month or two after that, until I left New York.

"Mr. Fitzstephan says to come right up," the switchboard boy said.

His apartment was on the sixth floor. He was standing at its door when I got out of the elevator.

"By God," he said, holding out a lean hand, "it *is* you!"

"None other."

He hadn't changed any. We went into a room where half a dozen bookcases and four tables left little room for anything else. Magazines and books in various languages, papers, clippings, proof sheets, were scattered everywhere – all just as it used to be in his New York rooms.

We sat down, found places for our feet between table legs, and accounted roughly for our lives since we had last seen one another. He had been in San Francisco for a little more than a year – except, he said, for week-ends, and two months hermiting in the country, finishing a novel. I had been there nearly five years. He liked San Francisco, he said, but wouldn't oppose any movement to give the West back to the Indians.

"How's the literary grift go?" I asked.

He looked at me sharply, demanding: "You haven't been reading me?"

"No. Where'd you get that funny idea?"

"There was something in your tone, something proprietary, as in the voice of one who has bought an author for a couple of dollars. I haven't met it often enough to be used to it. Good God! Remember once I offered you a set of my books as a present?" He had always liked to talk that way.

"Yeah. But I never blamed you. You were drunk."

"On sherry – Elsa Donne's sherry. Remember Elsa? She showed us a picture she had just finished, and you said it was pretty. Sweet God, wasn't she furious! You said it so vapidly and sincerely and as if you were so sure that she would like your saying it. Remember? She put us out, but we'd both already got plastered on her sherry. But you weren't tight enough to take the books."

"I was afraid I'd read them and understand them," I explained, "and then you'd have felt insulted."

A Chinese boy brought us cold white wine.

Fitzstephan said: "I suppose you're still hounding the unfortunate evil-doer?"

"Yeah. That's how I happened to locate you. Halstead tells me you know Edgar Leggett."

A gleam pushed through the sleepiness in his gray eyes, and

he sat up a little in his chair, asking: "Leggett's been up to something?"

"Why do you say that?"

"I didn't say it. I asked it." He made himself limp in the chair again, but the gleam didn't go out of his eyes. "Come on, out with it. Don't try to be subtle with me, my son; that's not your style at all. Try it and you're sunk. Out with it: what's Leggett been up to?"

"We don't do it that way," I said. "You're a storywriter. I can't trust you not to build up on what I tell you. I'll save mine till after you've spoken your piece, so yours won't be twisted to fit mine. How long have you known him?"

"Since shortly after I came here. He's always interested me. There's something obscure in him, something dark and inviting. He is, for instance, physically ascetic – neither smoking or drinking, eating meagerly, sleeping, I'm told, only three or four hours a night – but mentally, or spiritually, sensual – does that mean anything to you? – to the point of decadence. You used to think I had an abnormal appetite for the fantastic. You should know him. His friends – no, he hasn't any – his choice companions are those who have the most outlandish ideas to offer: Marquard and his insane figures that aren't figures, but the boundaries of areas in space that are the figures; Denbar Curt and his algebraism; the Haldorns and their Holy Grail sect; crazy Laura Joines; Farnham –"

"And you," I put in, "with explanations and descriptions that explain and describe nothing. I hope you don't think any of what you've said means anything to me."

"I remember you now: you were always like that." He grinned at me, running thin fingers through his sorrel hair. "Tell me what's up while I try to find one-syllable words for you."

I asked him if he knew Eric Collinson. He said he did; there was nothing to know about him except that he was engaged to Gabrielle Leggett, that his father was the lumber

Collinson, and that Eric was Princeton, stocks and bonds, and hand-ball, a nice boy.

"Maybe," I said, "but he lied to me."

"Isn't that like a sleuth?" Fitzstephan shook his head, grinning. "You must have had the wrong fellow – somebody impersonating him. The Chevalier Bayard doesn't lie, and, besides, lying requires imagination. You've – or wait! Was a woman involved in your question?"

I nodded.

"You're correct, then," Fitzstephan assured me. "I apologize. The Chevalier Bayard always lies when a woman is involved, even if it's unnecessary and puts her to a lot of trouble. It's one of the conventions of Bayardism, something to do with guarding her honor or the like. Who was the woman?"

"Gabrielle Leggett," I said, and told him all I knew about the Leggetts, the diamonds, and the dead man in Golden Gate Avenue. Disappointment deepened in his face while I talked.

"That's trivial, dull," he complained when I had finished. "I've been thinking of Leggett in terms of Dumas, and you bring me a piece of gimcrackery out of O. Henry. You've let me down, you and your shabby diamonds. But" – his eyes brightened again – "this may lead to something. Leggett may or may not be criminal, but there's more to him than a two-penny insurance swindle."

"You mean," I asked, "that he's one of these master minds? So you read newspapers? What do you think he is? King of the bootleggers? Chief of an international crime syndicate? A white-slave magnate? Head of a dope ring? Or queen of the counterfeiters in disguise?"

"Don't be an idiot," he said. "But he's got brains, and there's something black in him. There's something he doesn't want to think about, but must not forget. I've told you that he's thirsty for all that's dizziest in thought, yet he's cold as a fish, but with a bitter-dry coldness. He's a neurotic who keeps his body fit and sensitive and ready – for what? – while he drugs his mind with lunacies. Yet he's cold and sane. If a man has a past that he wants to forget, he can easiest drug his mind against memory through his body, with sensuality if not with narcotics. But suppose the past is not dead, and this man must keep himself fit to cope with it should it come into the present. Well, then he would be wisest to anæsthetize his mind directly, letting his body stay strong and ready."

"And this past?"

Fitzstephan shook his head, saying: "If I don't know – and I don't – it isn't my fault. Before you're through, you'll know how difficult it is to get information out of that family."

"Did you try?"

"Certainly. I'm a novelist. My business is with souls and what goes on in them. He's got one that attracts me, and I've always considered myself unjustly treated by his not turning himself inside out for me. You know, I doubt if Leggett's his name. He's French. He told me once he came from Atlanta, but he's French in outlook, in quality of mind, in everything except admission."

"What of the rest of the family?" I asked. "Gabrielle's cuckoo, isn't she?"

"I wonder." Fitzstephan looked curiously at me. "Are you saying that carelessly, or do you really think she's off?"

"I don't know. She's odd, an uncomfortable sort of person. And, then, she's got animal ears, hardly any forehead; and her eyes shift from green to brown and back without ever settling on one color. How much of her affairs have you turned up in your snooping around?"

"Are you – who make your living snooping – sneering at my curiosity about people and my attempts to satisfy it?"

"We're different," I said. "I do mine with the object of putting people in jail, and I get paid for it, though not as much as I should."

"That's not different," he said. "I do mine with the object

of putting people in books, and I get paid for it, though not as much as I should."

"Yeah, but what good does that do?"

"God knows. What good does putting them in jail do?"

"Relieves congestion," I said. "Put enough people in jail, and cities wouldn't have traffic problems. What do you know about this Gabrielle?"

"She hates her father. He worships her."

"How come the hate?"

"I don't know; perhaps because he worships her."

"There's no sense to that," I complained. "You're just being literary. What about Mrs. Leggett?"

"You've never eaten one of her meals, I suppose? You'd have no doubts if you had. None but a serene, sane soul ever achieved such cooking. I've often wondered what she thinks of the weird creatures who are her husband and daughter, though I imagine she simply accepts them as they are without even being conscious of their weirdness."

"All this is well enough in its way," I said, "but you still haven't told me anything definite."

"No, I haven't," he replied, "and that, my boy, is it. I've told you what I know and what I imagine, and none of it is definite. That's the point – in a year of trying I've learned nothing definite about Leggett. Isn't that – remembering my curiosity and my usual skill in satisfying it – enough to convince you that the man is hiding something and knows how to hide it?"

"Is it? I don't know. But I know I've wasted enough time learning nothing that anybody can be jailed for. Dinner tomorrow night? Or the next?"

"The next. About seven o'clock?"

I said I would stop for him, and went out. It was then after five o'clock. Not having had any luncheon, I went up to Blanco's for food, and then to darktown for a look at Rhino Tingley.

I found him in Big-foot Gerber's cigar-store, rolling a fat cigar around in his mouth, telling something to the other Negroes – four of them – in the place.

". . . says to him: 'Nigger, you talking yourself out of skin,' and I reaches out my hand for him, and, 'fore God, there weren't none of him there excepting his footprints in the ce-ment pavement, eight feet apart and heading home."

Buying a package of cigarettes, I weighed him in while he talked. He was a chocolate man of less than thirty years, close to six feet tall and weighing two hundred pounds plus, with big yellow-balled pop eyes, a broad nose, a big blue-lipped and blue-gummed mouth, and a ragged black scar running from his lower lip down behind his blue and white striped collar. His clothes were new enough to look new, and he wore them sportily. His voice was a heavy bass that shook the glass of the showcases when he laughed with his audience.

I went out of the store while they were laughing, heard the laughter stop short behind me, resisted the temptation to look back, and moved down the street toward the building where he and Minnie lived. He came abreast of me when I was half a block from the flat.

I said nothing while we took seven steps side by side.

Then he said: "You the man that been inquirying around about me?"

The sour odor of Italian wine was thick enough to be seen.

I considered, and said: "Yeah."

"What you got to do with me?" he asked, not disagreeably, but as if he wanted to know.

Across the street Gabrielle Leggett, in brown coat and brown and yellow hat, came out of Minnie's building and walked south, not turning her face towards us. She walked swiftly and her lower lip was between her teeth.

I looked at the Negro. He was looking at me. There was nothing in his face to show that he had seen Gabrielle Leggett, or that the sight of her meant anything to him.

I said: "You've got nothing to hide, have you? What do you care who asks about you?"

"All the same, I'm the party to come to if you wants to know about me. You the man that got Minnie fired?"

"She wasn't fired. She quit."

"Minnie don't have to take nobody's lip. She –"

"Let's go over and talk to her," I suggested, leading the way across the street. At the front door he went ahead, up a flight of stairs, down a dark hall to a door which he opened with one of the twenty or more keys on his ring.

Minnie Hershey, in a pink kimono trimmed with yellow ostrich feathers that looked like little dead ferns, came out of the bedroom to meet us in the living-room. Her eyes got big when she saw me.

Rhino said: "You know this gentleman, Minnie."

Minnie said: "Y-yes."

I said: "You shouldn't have left the Leggetts' that way. Nobody thinks you had anything to do with the diamonds. What did Miss Leggett want here?"

"There been no Miss Leggetts here," she told me. "I don't know what you talking about."

"She came out as we were coming in."

"Oh! *Miss* Leggett. I thought you said *Mrs*. Leggett. I beg your pardon. Yes, sir. Miss Gabrielle was sure enough here. She wanted to know if I wouldn't come back there. She thinks a powerful lot of me, Miss Gabrielle does."

"That," I said, "is what you ought to do. It was foolish, leaving like that."

Rhino took the cigar out of his mouth and pointed the red end at the girl.

"You away from them," he boomed, "and you stay away from them. You don't have to take nothing from nobody." He put a hand in his pants pocket, lugged out a thick bundle of paper money, thumped it down on the table, and rumbled: "What for you have to work for folks?"

He was talking to the girl, but looking at me, grinning, gold teeth shining against purplish mouth. The girl looked at him scornfully, said: "Lead him around, *vino*," and turned to me again, her brown face tense, anxious to be believed, saying earnestly: "Rhino got that money in a crap game, mister. Hope to die if he didn't."

Rhino said: "Ain't nobody's business where I got my money. I got it. I got –" He put his cigar on the edge of the table, picked up the money, wet a thumb as big as a heel on a tongue like a bathmat, and counted his roll bill by bill down on the table. "Twenty – thirty – eighty – hundred – hundred and ten – two hundred and ten – three hundred and ten – three hundred and thirty – three hundred and thirty-five – four hundred and thirty-five – five hundred and thirty-five – five hundred and eighty-five – six hundred and five – six hundred and ten – six hundred and twenty – seven hundred and twenty – seven hundred and seventy – eight hundred and twenty – eight hundred and thirty – eight hundred and forty – nine hundred and forty – nine hundred and sixty – nine hundred and seventy – nine hundred and seventy-five – nine hundred and ninety-five – ten hundred and fifteen – ten hundred and twenty – eleven hundred and twenty – eleven hundred and seventy. Anybody want to know what I got, that's what I got – eleven hundred and seventy dollars. Anybody want to know where I get it, maybe I tell them, maybe I don't. Just depend on how I feel about it."

Minnie said: "He won it in a crap game, mister, up the Happy Day Social Club. Hope to die if he didn't."

"Maybe I did," Rhino said, still grinning widely at me. "But supposing I didn't?"

"I'm no good at riddles," I said, and, after again advising Minnie to return to the Leggetts, left the flat. Minnie closed the door behind me. As I went down the hall I could hear her voice scolding and Rhino's chesty bass laughter.

In a downtown Owl drug-store I turned to the Berkeley

section of the telephone directory, found only one Freemander listed, and called the number. Mrs. Begg was there and consented to see me if I came over on the next ferry.

The Freemander house was set off a road that wound uphill towards the University of California.

Mrs. Begg was a scrawny, big-boned woman, with not much gray hair packed close around a bony skull, hard gray eyes, and hard, capable hands. She was sour and severe, but plain-spoken enough to let us talk turkey without a lot of preliminary hemming and hawing.

I told her about the burglary and my belief that the thief had been helped, at least with information, by somebody who knew the Leggett household, winding up: "Mrs. Priestly told me you had been Leggett's housekeeper, and she thought you could help me."

Mrs. Begg said she doubted whether she could tell me anything that would pay me for my trip from the city, but she was willing to do what she could, being an honest woman and having nothing to conceal from anybody. Once started, she told me a great deal, damned near talking me earless. Throwing out the stuff that didn't interest me, I came away with this information:

Mrs. Begg had been hired by Leggett, through an employment agency, as housekeeper in the spring of 1921. At first she had a girl to help her, but there wasn't enough work for two, so, at Mrs. Begg's suggestion, they let the girl go. Leggett was a man of simple tastes and spent nearly all his time on the top floor, where he had his laboratory and a cubbyhole bedroom. He seldom used the rest of the house except when he had friends in for an evening. Mrs. Begg didn't like his friends, though she could say nothing against them except that the way they talked was a shame and a disgrace. Edgar Leggett was as nice a man as a person could want to know, she said, only so secretive that it made a person nervous. She was never allowed to go up on the third floor, and the door of the laboratory was always kept locked. Once a month a Jap would come in to clean it up under Leggett's supervision. Well, she supposed he had a lot of scientific secrets, and maybe dangerous chemicals, that he didn't want people poking into, but just the same it made a person uneasy. She didn't know anything about her employer's personal or family affairs and knew her place too well to ask him any questions.

In August 1923 – it was a rainy morning, she remembered – a woman and a girl of fifteen, with a lot of suitcases, had come to the house. She let them in and the woman asked for Mr. Leggett. Mrs. Begg went up to the laboratory door and told him, and he came down. Never in all her born days had she seen such a surprised man as he was when he saw them. He turned absolutely white, and she thought he was going to fall down, he shook that bad. She didn't know what Leggett and the woman and the girl said to one another that morning, because they jabbered away in some foreign language, though the lot of them could talk English as good as anybody else, and better than most, especially that Gabrielle when she got to cursing. Mrs. Begg had left them and gone on about her business. Pretty soon Leggett came out to the kitchen and told her his visitors were a Mrs. Dain, his sister-in-law, and her daughter, neither of whom he had seen for ten years; and that they were going to stay there with him. Mrs. Dain later told Mrs. Begg that they were English, but had been living in New York for several years. Mrs. Begg said she liked Mrs. Dain, who was a sensible woman and a first-rate housewife, but that Gabrielle was a tartar. Mrs. Begg always spoke of the girl as "that Gabrielle."

With the Dains there, and with Mrs. Dain's ability as a housekeeper, there was no longer any place for Mrs. Begg. They had been very liberal, she said, helping her find a new place and giving her a generous bonus when she left. She hadn't seen any of them since, but, thanks to the careful watch she habitually kept on the marriage, death, and birth notices in the morning papers, she had learned, a week after she left, that a marriage license had been issued to Edgar Leggett and Alice Dain.

4 THE VAGUE HARPERS

WHEN I ARRIVED at the agency at nine the next morning, Eric Collinson was sitting in the reception room. His sunburned face was dingy without pinkness, and he had forgotten to put stickum on his hair.

"Do you know anything about Miss Leggett?" he asked, jumping up and meeting me at the door. "She wasn't home last night, and she's not home yet. Her father wouldn't say he didn't know where she was, but I'm sure he didn't. He told me not to worry, but how can I help worrying? Do you know anything about it?"

I said I didn't and told him about seeing her leave Minnie Hershey's the previous evening. I gave him the mulatto's address and suggested that he ask her. He jammed his hat on his head and hurried off.

Getting O'Gar on the phone, I asked him if he had heard from New York yet.

"Uh-huh," he said. "Upton – that's his right name – was once one of you private dicks – had a agency of his own – till '23, when him and a guy named Harry Ruppert were sent over for trying to fix a jury. How'd you make out with the shine?"

"I don't know. This Rhino Tingley's carrying an eleven-hundred-case roll. Minnie says he got it with the rats and mice. Maybe he did: it's twice what he could have peddled Leggett's stuff for. Can you try to have it checked? He's supposed to have got it at the Happy Day Social Club."

O'Gar promised to do what he could and hung up.

I sent a wire to our New York branch, asking for more

dope on Upton and Ruppert, and then went up to the county clerk's office in the municipal building, where I dug into the August and September 1923 marriage-license file. The application I wanted was dated August 26 and bore Edgar Leggett's statement that he was born in Atlanta, Georgia, on March 6, 1883, and that this was his second marriage; and Alice Dain's statement that she was born in London, England, on October 22, 1888, and that she had not been married before.

When I returned to the agency, Eric Collinson, his yellow hair still further disarranged, was again lying in wait for me.

"I saw Minnie," he said excitedly, "and she couldn't tell me anything. She said Gaby was there last night to ask her to come back to work, but that's all she knew about her. But she – she's wearing an emerald ring that I'm positive is Gaby's."

"Did you ask her about it?"

"Who? Minnie? No. How could I? It would have been – you know."

"That's right," I agreed, thinking of Fitzstephan's Chevalier Bayard, "we must always be polite. Why did you lie to me about the time you and Miss Leggett got home the other night?"

Embarrassment made his face more attractive-looking and less intelligent.

"That was silly of me," he stammered, "but I didn't – you know – I thought you – I was afraid –"

He wasn't getting anywhere. I suggested: "You thought that was a late hour and didn't want me to get wrong notions about her?"

"Yes, that's it."

I shooed him out and went into the operatives' room, where Mickey Linehan – big, loose-hung, red-faced – and Al Mason – slim, dark, sleek – were swapping lies about the times they had been shot at, each trying to pretend he had been more frightened than the other. I told them who was who and what was what on the Leggett job – as far as my knowledge went, and it didn't go far when I came to putting it in words – and sent Al out to keep an eye on the Leggetts' house, Mickey to see how Minnie and Rhino behaved.

Mrs. Leggett, her pleasant face shadowed, opened the door when I rang the bell an hour later. We went into the green, orange, and chocolate room, where we were joined by her husband. I passed on to them the information about Upton that O'Gar had received from New York and told them I had wired for more dope on Ruppert.

"Some of your neighbors saw a man who was not Upton loitering around," I said, "and a man who fits the same description ran down the fire-escape from the room Upton was killed in. We'll see what Ruppert looks like."

I was watching Leggett's face. Nothing changed in it. His too bright red-brown eyes held interest and nothing else.

I asked: "Is Miss Leggett in?"

He said: "No."

"When will she be in?"

"Probably not for several days. She's gone out of town."

"Where can I find her?" I asked, turning to Mrs. Leggett. "I've some questions to ask her."

Mrs. Leggett avoided my gaze, looking at her husband.

His metallic voice answered my question: "We don't know, exactly. Friends of hers, a Mr. and Mrs. Harper, drove up from Los Angeles and asked her to go along on a trip up in the mountains. I don't know which route they intended taking, and doubt if they had any definite destination."

I asked questions about the Harpers. Leggett admitted knowing very little about them. Mrs. Harper's first name was Carmel, he said, and everybody called the man Bud, but Leggett wasn't sure whether his name was Frank or Walter. Nor did he know the Harpers' Los Angeles address. He thought they had a house somewhere in Pasadena, but wasn't sure, having, in fact, heard something about their selling the house, or perhaps only intending to. While he told me this nonsense, his wife sat staring at the floor, lifting her blue eyes twice to look swiftly, pleadingly, at her husband.

I asked her: "Don't you know anything more about them than that?"

"No," she said weakly, darting another glance at her husband's face, while he, paying no attention to her, stared levelly at me.

"When did they leave?" I asked.

"Early this morning," Leggett said. "They were staying at one of the hotels – I don't know which – and Gabrielle spent the night with them so they could start early."

I had enough of the Harpers. I asked: "Did either of you – any of you – know anything about Upton – have any dealings with him of any sort – before this affair?"

Leggett said: "No."

I had other questions, but the kind of replies I was drawing didn't mean anything, so I stood up to go. I was tempted to tell him what I thought of him, but there was no profit in that.

He got up too, smiling politely, and said: "I'm sorry to have caused the insurance company all this trouble through what was, after all, probably my carelessness. I should like to ask your opinion: do you really think I should accept responsibility for the loss of the diamonds and make it good?"

"The way it stands," I said, "I think you should; but that wouldn't stop the investigation."

Mrs. Leggett put her handkerchief to her mouth quickly.

Leggett said: "Thanks." His voice was casually polite. "I'll have to think it over."

On my way back to the agency I dropped in on Fitzstephan for half an hour. He was writing, he told me, an article for the *Psychopathological Review* – that's probably wrong, but it was something on that order – condemning the hypothesis of an unconscious or subconscious mind as a snare and a delusion, a pitfall for the unwary and a set of false whiskers for the charlatan, a gap in psychology's roof that made it impossible, or nearly, for the sound scholar to smoke out such faddists as, for example, the psychoanalyst and the behaviorist, or words to that effect. He went on like that for ten minutes or more, finally coming back to the United States with: "but how are you getting along with the problem of the elusive diamonds?"

"This way and that way," I said, and told him what I had learned and done so far.

"You've certainly," he congratulated me when I finished, "got it all as tangled and confused as possible."

"It'll be worse before it's better," I predicted. "I'd like to have ten minutes alone with Mrs. Leggett. Away from her husband, I imagine things could be done with her. Could you get anything out of her? I'd like to know why Gabrielle has gone, even if I can't learn where."

"I'll try," Fitzstephan said willingly. "Suppose I go out there tomorrow afternoon – to borrow a book. Waite's *Rosy Cross* will do it. They know I'm interested in that sort of stuff. He'll be working in the laboratory, and I'll refuse to disturb him. I'll have to go at it in an offhand way, but maybe I can get something out of her."

"Thanks," I said. "See you tomorrow night."

I spent most of the afternoon putting my findings and guesses on paper and trying to fit them together in some sort of order. Eric Collinson phoned twice to ask if I had any news of his Gabrielle. Neither Mickey Linehan nor Al Mason reported anything. At six o'clock I called it a day.

5 GABRIELLE

THE NEXT DAY brought happenings.

Early in the morning there was a telegram from our New York office. Decoded, it read:

> LOUIS UPTON FORMER PROPRIETOR DETECTIVE AGENCY HERE STOP ARRESTED SEPTEMBER FIRST ONE NINE TWO THREE FOR BRIBING TWO JURORS IN SEXTON MURDER TRIAL STOP TRIED TO SAVE HIMSELF BY IMPLICATING HARRY RUPPERT OPERATIVE IN HIS EMPLOY STOP BOTH MEN CONVICTED STOP BOTH RELEASED FROM SING SING FEBRUARY SIX THIS YEAR STOP RUPPERT SAID TO HAVE THREATENED TO KILL UPTON STOP RUPPERT THIRTY TWO YEARS FIVE FEET ELEVEN INCHES HUNDRED FIFTY POUNDS BROWN HAIR AND EYES SALLOW COMPLEXION THIN FACE LONG THIN NOSE WALKS WITH STOOP AND CHIN OUT STOP MAILING PHOTOGRAPHS

That placed Ruppert definitely enough as the man Mrs. Priestly and Daley had seen and the man who had probably killed Upton.

O'Gar called me on the phone to tell me: "That dinge of yours – Rhino Tingley – was picked up in a hock shop last night trying to unload some jewelry. None of it was loose diamonds. We haven't been able to crack him yet, just got him identified. I sent a man out to Leggett's with some of the stuff, thinking it might be theirs, but they said no."

That didn't fit in anywhere. I suggested: "Try Halstead and Beauchamp. Tell them you think the stuff is Leggett's. Don't tell them he said it wasn't."

Half an hour later the detective-sergeant phoned me again, from the jewelers', to tell me that Halstead had positively identified two pieces – a string of pearls and a topaz brooch – as articles Leggett had purchased there for his daughter.

"That's swell," I said. "Now will you do this? Go out to Rhino's flat and put the screws on his woman, Minnie Hershey. Frisk the joint, rough her up; the more you scare her, the better. She may be wearing an emerald ring. If she is, or if it – or any other jewelry that might be the Leggetts' – is there, you can take it away with you; but don't stay too long and don't bother her afterwards. I've got her covered. Just stir her up and beat it."

"I'll turn her white," O'Gar promised.

Dick Foley was in the operatives' room, writing his report on a warehouse robbery that had kept him up all night. I chased him out to help Mickey with the mulatto.

"Both of you tail her if she leaves her joint after the police are through," I said, "and as soon as you put her in anywhere, one of you get to a phone and let me know."

I went back to my office and burned cigarettes. I was ruining the third one when Eric Collinson phoned to ask if I had found his Gabrielle yet.

"Not quite, but I've got prospects. If you aren't busy, you might come over and go along with me – if it so happens that there turns out to be some place to go."

He said, very eagerly, that he would do that.

A few minutes later Mickey Linehan phoned: "The high yellow's gone visiting," and gave me a Pacific Avenue address.

The phone rang again before I got it out of my hand.

"This is Watt Halstead," a voice said. "Can you come down to see me for a minute or two?"

"Not now. What is it?"

"It's about Edgar Leggett, and it's quite puzzling. The police brought some jewelry in this morning, asking whether we knew whose it was. I recognized a string of pearls and a brooch that Edgar Leggett bought from us for his daughter last year – the brooch in the spring, the pearls at Christmas.

After the police had gone, I, quite naturally, phoned Leggett; and he took the most peculiar attitude. He waited until I had told him about it, then said: 'I thank you very much for your interference in my affairs,' and hung up. What do you suppose is the matter with him?"

"God knows. Thanks. I've got to run now, but I'll stop in when I get a chance."

I hunted up Owen Fitzstephan's number, called it, and heard his drawled: "Hello."

"You'd better get busy on your book-borrowing if any good's to come of it," I said.

"Why? Are things taking place?"

"Things are."

"Such as?" he asked.

"This and that, but it's no time for anybody who wants to poke his nose into the Leggett mysteries to be dilly-dallying with pieces about unconscious minds."

"Right," he said: "I'm off to the front now."

Eric Collinson had come in while I was talking to the novelist.

"Come on," I said, leading the way out towards the elevators. "This might not be a false alarm."

"Where are we going?" he asked impatiently. "Have you found her? Is she all right?"

I replied to the only one of his questions that I had the answer to by giving him the Pacific Avenue address Mickey had given me. It meant something to Collinson. He said: "That's Joseph's place."

We were in the elevator with half a dozen other people. I held my response down to a "Yeah?"

He had a Chrysler roadster parked around the corner. We got into it and began bucking traffic and traffic signals toward Pacific Avenue.

I asked: "Who is Joseph?"

"Another cult. He's the head of it. He calls his place the

Temple of the Holy Grail. It's the fashionable one just now. You know how they come and go in California. I don't like having Gabrielle there, if that's where she is – though – I don't know – they may be all right. He's one of Mr. Leggett's queer friends. Do you know that she's there?"

"Maybe. Is she a member of the cult?"

"She goes there, yes. I've been there with her."

"What sort of a layout is it?"

"Oh, it seems to be all right," he said somewhat reluctantly. "The right sort of people: Mrs. Payson Laurence, and the Ralph Colemans, and Mrs. Livingston Rodman, people like that. And the Haldorns – that's Joseph and his wife Aaronia – seem to be quite all right, but – but I don't like the idea of Gabrielle going there like this." He missed the end of a cable car with the Chrysler's right wheel. "I don't think it's good for her to come too much under their influence."

"You've been there; what is their brand of hocus-pocus?" I asked.

"It isn't hocus-pocus, really," he replied, wrinkling his forehead. "I don't know very much about their creed, or anything like that, but I've been to their services with Gabrielle, and they're quite as dignified, as beautiful even, as either Episcopalian or Catholic services. You mustn't think that this is the Holy Roller or House of David sort of thing. It isn't at all. Whatever it is, it is quite first-rate. The Haldorns are people of – of – well, more culture than I."

"Then what's the matter with them?"

He shook his head gloomily. "I honestly don't know that anything is. I don't like it. I don't like having Gabrielle go off like this without letting anybody know where she's gone. Do you think her parents knew where she had gone?"

"No."

"I don't think so either," he said.

From the street the Temple of the Holy Grail looked like what it had originally been, a six-story yellow brick apartment building. There was nothing about its exterior to show that it wasn't still that. I made Collinson drive past it to the corner where Mickey Linehan was leaning his lopsided bulk against a stone wall. He came to the car as it stopped at the curb.

"The dark meat left ten minutes ago," he reported, "with Dick behind her. Nobody else that looks like anybody you listed has been out."

"Camp here in the car and watch the door," I told him. "We're going in," I said to Collinson. "Let me do most of the talking."

When we reached the Temple door I had to caution him: "Try not breathing so hard. Everything will probably be oke."

I rang the bell. The door was opened immediately by a broad-shouldered, meaty woman of some year close to fifty. She was a good three inches taller than my five feet six. Flesh hung in little bags on her face, but there was neither softness nor looseness in her eyes and mouth. Her long upper lip had been shaved. She was dressed in black, black clothes that covered her from chin and ear-lobes to within less than an inch of the floor.

"We want to see Miss Leggett," I said.

She pretended she hadn't understood me.

"We want to see Miss Leggett," I repeated, "Miss Gabrielle Leggett."

"I don't know." Her voice was bass. "But come in."

She took us not very cheerfully into a small, dimly lighted reception room to one side of the foyer, told us to wait there, and went away.

"Who's the village blacksmith?" I asked Collinson.

He said he didn't know her. He fidgeted around the room. I sat down. Drawn blinds let in too little light for me to make out much of the room, but the rug was soft and thick, and what I could see of the furniture leaned towards luxury rather than severity.

Except for Collinson's fidgeting, no sound came from

anywhere in the building. I looked at the open door and saw that we were being examined. A small boy of twelve or thirteen stood there staring at us with big dark eyes that seemed to have lights of their own in the semi-darkness.

I said: "Hello, son."

Collinson jumped around at the sound of my voice.

The boy said nothing. He stared at me for at least another minute with the blank, unblinking, embarrassing stare that only children can manage completely, then turned his back on me and walked away, making no more noise going than he had made coming.

"Who's that?" I asked Collinson.

"It must be the Haldorns' son Manuel. I've never seen him before."

Collinson walked up and down. I sat and watched the door. Presently a woman, walking silently on the thick carpet, appeared there and came into the reception room. She was tall, graceful; and her dark eyes seemed to have lights of their own, like the boy's. That was all I could see clearly then.

I stood up.

She addressed Collinson: "How do you do? This is Mr. Collinson, isn't it?" Her voice was the most musical I had ever heard.

Collinson mumbled something or other and introduced me to the woman, calling her Mrs. Haldorn. She gave me a warm, firm hand and then crossed the room to raise a blind, letting in a fat rectangle of afternoon sun. While I blinked at her in the sudden brightness, she sat down and motioned us into chairs.

I saw her eyes first. They were enormous, almost black, warm, and heavily fringed with almost black lashes. They were the only live, human, real things in her face. There was warmth and there was beauty in her oval, olive-skinned face, but, except for the eyes, it was warmth and beauty that didn't seem to have anything to do with reality. It was as if her face were not a face, but a mask that she had worn until it had almost become a face. Even her mouth, which was a mouth to talk about, looked not so much like flesh as like a too perfect imitation of flesh, softer and redder and maybe warmer than genuine flesh, but not genuine flesh. Above this face, or mask, uncut black hair was tied close to her head, parted in the middle, and drawn across temples and upper ears to end in a knot on the nape of her neck. Her neck was long, strong, slender; her body tall, fully fleshed, supple; her clothes dark and silky, part of her body.

I said: "We want to see Miss Leggett, Mrs. Haldorn."

She asked curiously: "Why do you think she is here?"

"That doesn't make any difference, does it?" I replied quickly, before Collinson could say something wrong. "She is. We'd like to see her."

"I don't think you can," she said slowly. "She isn't well, and she came here to rest, particularly to get away from people for a while."

"Sorry," I said, "but it's a case of have to. We wouldn't have come like this if it hadn't been important."

"It is important?"

"Yeah."

She hesitated, said: "Well, I'll see," excused herself, and left us.

"I wouldn't mind moving in here myself," I told Collinson.

He didn't know what I was talking about. His face was flushed and excited.

"Gabrielle may not like our coming here like this," he said.

I said that would be too bad.

Aaronia Haldorn returned to us.

"I'm really very sorry," she said, standing in the doorway, smiling politely, "but Miss Leggett doesn't wish to see you."

"I'm sorry she doesn't," I said, "but we'll have to see her."

She drew herself up straight and her smile went away.

"I beg your pardon?" she said.

"We'll have to see her," I repeated, keeping my voice amiable. "It's important, as I told you."

"I am sorry." Even the iciness she got into her voice didn't keep it from being beautiful. "You cannot see her."

I said: "Miss Leggett's an important witness, as you probably know, in a robbery and murder job. Well, we've got to see her. If it suits you better, I'm willing to wait half an hour till we can get a policeman up here with whatever authority you make necessary. We're going to see her."

Collinson said something unintelligible, though it sounded apologetic.

Aaronia Haldorn made the slightest of bows.

"You may do as you see fit," she said coldly. "I do not approve of your disturbing Miss Leggett against her wishes, and so far as my permission is concerned, I do not give it. If you insist, I cannot prevent you."

"Thanks. Where is she?"

"Her room is on the fifth floor, just beyond the stairs, to the left."

She bent her head a little once more and went away.

Collinson put a hand on my arm, mumbling: "I don't know whether I – whether we ought to do this. Gabrielle's not going to like it. She won't –"

"Suit yourself," I growled, "but I'm going up. Maybe she won't like it, but neither do I like having people running away and hiding when I want to ask them about stolen diamonds."

He frowned, chewed his lips, and made uncomfortable faces, but he went along with me. We found an automatic elevator, rode to the fifth floor, and went down a purple-carpeted corridor to the door just beyond the stairs on the left-hand side.

I tapped the door with the back of my hand. There was no answer from inside. I tapped again, louder.

A voice sounded inside the room. It might have been anybody's voice, though probably a woman's. It was too faint for us to know what it said and too smothered for us to know who was saying it.

I poked Collinson with my elbow and ordered: "Call her."

He pulled at his collar with a forefinger and called hoarsely: "Gaby, it's Eric."

That didn't bring an answer.

I thumped the wood again, calling: "Open the door."

The voice inside said something that was nothing to me. I repeated my thumping and calling. Down the corridor a door opened and a sallow thin-haired old man's head stuck out and asked: "What's the matter?" I said: "None of your damned business," and pounded the door again.

The inside voice came strong enough now to let us know that it was complaining, though no words could be made out yet. I rattled the knob and found that the door was unlocked. Rattling the knob some more, I worked the door open an inch or so. Then the voice was clearer. I heard soft feet on the floor. I heard a choking sob. I pushed the door open.

Eric Collinson made a noise in his throat that was like somebody very far away yelling horribly.

Gabrielle Leggett stood beside the bed, swaying a little, holding the white foot-rail of the bed with one hand. Her face was white as lime. Her eyes were all brown, dull, focused on nothing, and her small forehead was wrinkled. She looked as if she knew there was something in front of her and was wondering what it was. She had on one yellow stocking, a brown velvet skirt that had been slept in, and a yellow chemise. Scattered around the room were a pair of brown slippers, the other stocking, a brown and gold blouse, a brown coat, and a brown and yellow hat.

Everything else in the room was white: white-papered walls and white-painted ceiling; white-enameled chairs, bed, table, fixtures – even to the telephone – and woodwork; white felt on the floor. None of the furniture was hospital furniture, but solid whiteness gave it that appearance. There were two windows, and two doors besides the one I had opened. The door on the left opened into a bathroom, the one on the right into a small dressing-room.

I pushed Collinson into the room, followed him, and closed the door. There was no key in it, and no place for a key, no lock of any fixable sort. Collinson stood gaping at the girl, his jaw sagging, his eyes as vacant as hers; but there was more horror in his face. She leaned against the foot of the bed and stared at nothing with dark, blank eyes in a ghastly, puzzled face.

I put an arm around her and sat her on the side of the bed, telling Collinson: "Gather up her clothes." I had to tell him twice before he came out of his trance.

He brought me her things and I began dressing her. He dug his fingers into my shoulder and protested in a voice that would have been appropriate if I had been robbing a poor-box:

"No! You can't –"

"What the hell?" I asked, pushing his hand away. "You can have the job if you want it."

He was sweating. He gulped and stuttered: "No, no! I couldn't – it –" He broke off and walked to the window.

"She told me you were an ass," I said to his back, and discovered I was putting the brown and gold blouse on her backwards. She might as well have been a wax figure, for all the help she gave me, but at least she didn't struggle when I wrestled her around, and she stayed where I shoved her.

By the time I had got her into coat and hat, Collinson had come away from the window and was spluttering questions at me. What was the matter with her? Oughtn't we to get a doctor? Was it safe to take her out? And when I stood up, he took her away from me, supporting her with his long, thick arms, babbling: "It's Eric, Gaby. Don't you know me? Speak to me. What is the matter, dear?"

"There's nothing the matter except that she's got a skinful of dope," I said. "Don't try to bring her out of it. Wait till we get her home. You take this arm and I'll take that. She can walk all right. If we run into anybody, just keep going and let me handle them. Let's go."

We didn't meet anybody. We went out to the elevator, down in it to the ground floor, across the foyer, and into the street without seeing a single person.

We went down to the corner where we had left Mickey in the Chrysler.

"That's all for you," I told him.

He said: "Right, so long," and went away.

Collinson and I wedged the girl between us in the roadster, and he put it in motion.

We rode three blocks. Then he asked: "Are you sure home's the best place for her?"

I said I was. He didn't say anything for five more blocks and then repeated his question, adding something about a hospital.

"Why not a newspaper office?" I sneered.

Three blocks of silence, and he started again: "I know a doctor who –"

"I've got work to do," I said; "and Miss Leggett home now, in the shape she's in now, will help me get it done. So she goes home."

He scowled, accusing me angrily: "You'd humiliate her, disgrace her, endanger her life, for the sake of –"

"Her life's in no more danger than yours or mine. She's simply got a little more of the junk in her than she can stand up under. And she took it. I didn't give it to her."

The girl we were talking about was alive and breathing between us – even sitting up with her eyes open – but knowing no more of what was going on than if she had been in Finland.

We should have turned to the right at the next corner. Collinson held the car straight and stepped it up to forty-five miles an hour, staring ahead, his face hard and lumpy.

"Take the next turn," I commanded.

"No," he said, and didn't. The speedometer showed a 50, and people on the sidewalks began looking after us as we whizzed by.

"Well?" I asked, wriggling an arm loose from the girl's side.

"We're going down the peninsula," he said firmly. "She's not going home in her condition."

I grunted: "Yeah?" and flashed my free hand at the controls. He knocked it aside, holding the wheel with one hand, stretching the other out to block me if I tried again.

"Don't do that," he cautioned me, increasing our speed another half-dozen miles. "You know what will happen to all of us if you –"

I cursed him, bitterly, fairly thoroughly, and from the heart. His face jerked around to me, full of righteous indignation because, I suppose, my language wasn't the kind one should use in a lady's company.

And that brought it about.

A blue sedan came out of a cross-street a split second before we got there. Collinson's eyes and attention got back to his driving in time to twist the roadster away from the sedan, but not in time to make a neat job of it. We missed the sedan by a couple of inches, but as we passed behind it our rear wheels started sliding out of line. Collinson did what he could, giving the roadster its head, going with the skid, but the corner curb wouldn't co-operate. It stood stiff and hard where it was. We hit it sidewise and rolled over on the lamp-post behind it. The lamp-post snapped, crashed down on the sidewalk. The roadster, over on its side, spilled us out around the lamp-post. Gas from the broken post roared up at our feet.

Collinson, most of the skin scraped from one side of his face, crawled back on hands and knees to turn off the roadster's engine. I sat up, raising the girl, who was on my chest, with me. My right shoulder and arm were out of whack, dead. The girl was making whimpering noises in her chest, but

I couldn't see any marks on her except a shallow scratch on one cheek. I had been her cushion, had taken the jolt for her. The soreness of my chest, belly, and back, the lameness of my shoulder and arm, told me how much I had saved her.

People helped us up. Collinson stood with his arms around the girl, begging her to say she wasn't dead, and so on. The smash had jarred her into semi-consciousness, but she still didn't know whether there had been an accident or what. I went over and helped Collinson hold her up – though neither needed help – saying earnestly to the gathering crowd: "We've got to get her home. Who can – ?"

A pudgy man in plus fours offered his services. Collinson and I got in the back of his car with the girl, and I gave the pudgy man her address. He said something about a hospital, but I insisted that home was the place for her. Collinson was too upset to say anything. Twenty minutes later we took the girl out of the car in front of her house. I thanked the pudgy man profusely, giving him no opportunity to follow us indoors.

6 THE MAN FROM DEVIL'S ISLAND

AFTER SOME DELAY – I had to ring twice – the Leggetts' door was opened by Owen Fitzstephan. There was no sleepiness in his eyes: they were hot and bright, as they were when he found life interesting. Knowing the sort of things that interested him, I wondered what had happened.

"What have you been doing?" he asked, looking at our clothes, at Collinson's bloody face, at the girl's scratched cheek.

"Automobile accident," I said. "Nothing serious. Where's everybody?"

"Everybody," he said, with peculiar emphasis on the word, "is up in the laboratory;" and then to me: "Come here."

I followed him across the reception hall to the foot of the stairs, leaving Collinson and the girl standing just inside the street door. Fitzstephan put his mouth close to my ear and whispered:

"Leggett's committed suicide."

I was more annoyed than surprised. I asked: "Where is he?"

"In the laboratory. Mrs. Leggett and the police are up there. It happened only half an hour ago."

"We'll all go up," I said.

"Isn't it rather unnecessary," he asked, "taking Gabrielle up there?"

"Might be tough on her," I said irritably, "but it's necessary enough. Anyway, she's coked-up and better able to stand the shock than she will be later, when the stuff's dying out in her." I turned to Collinson. "Come on, we'll go up to the laboratory."

I went ahead, letting Fitzstephan help Collinson with the girl. There were six people in the laboratory: a uniformed copper – a big man with a red mustache – standing beside the door; Mrs. Leggett, sitting on a wooden chair in the far end of the room, her body bent forward, her hands holding a handkerchief to her face, sobbing quietly; O'Gar and Reddy, standing by one of the windows, close together, their heads rubbing over a sheaf of papers that the detective-sergeant held in his thick fists; a gray-faced, dandified man in dark clothes, standing beside the zinc table, twiddling eye-glasses on a black ribbon in his hand; and Edgar Leggett, seated on a chair at the table, his head and upper body resting on the table, his arms sprawled out. O'Gar and Reddy looked up from their reading as I came in. Passing the table on my way to join them at the window, I saw blood, a small black automatic pistol lying close to one of Leggett's hands, and seven unset diamonds grouped by his head.

O'Gar said, "Take a look," and handed me part of his sheaf of paper – four stiff white sheets covered with very small, precise, and regular handwriting in black ink. I was getting interested in what was written there when Fitzstephan and Collinson came in with Gabrielle Leggett.

Collinson looked at the dead man at the table. Collinson's face went white. He put his big body between the girl and her father.

"Come in," I said.

"This is no place for Miss Leggett now," he said hotly, turning to take her away.

"We ought to have everybody in here," I told O'Gar. He nodded his bullet head at the policeman. The policeman put a hand on Collinson's shoulder and said: "You'll have to come in, the both of you."

Fitzstephan placed a chair by one of the end windows for the girl. She sat down and looked around the room – at the dead man, at Mrs. Leggett, at all of us – with eyes that were dull but no longer completely blank. Collinson stood beside her, glaring at me. Mrs. Leggett hadn't looked up from her handkerchief.

I spoke to O'Gar, clearly enough for the others to hear: "Let's read the letter out loud."

He screwed up his eyes, hesitated, then thrust the rest of his sheaf at me, saying: "Fair enough. You read it."

I read:

"To the police: –

"My name is Maurice Pierre de Mayenne. I was born in Fécamp, department of Seine-Inférieure, France, on March 6, 1883, but was chiefly educated in England. In 1903 I went to Paris to study painting, and there, four years later, I made the acquaintance of Alice and Lily Dain, orphan daughters of a British naval officer. I married Lily the following year, and in 1909 our daughter Gabrielle was born.

"Shortly after my marriage I had discovered that I had made a most horrible mistake, that it was Alice, and not my wife Lily, whom I really loved. I kept this discovery to myself until the child was past the most difficult baby years; that is, until she was nearly five, and then told my wife, asking that she divorce me so I could marry Alice. She refused.

"On June 6, 1913, I murdered Lily and fled with Alice and Gabrielle to London, where I was soon arrested and returned to Paris, to be tried, found guilty, and sentenced to life imprisonment on the Iles du Salut. Alice, who had had no part in the murder, no knowledge of it until after it was done, and who had accompanied us to London only because of her love for Gabrielle, was also tried, but justly acquitted. All this is a matter of record in Paris.

"In 1918 I escaped from the islands with a fellow convict named Jacques Labaud, on a flimsy raft. I do not know – we never knew – how long we were adrift on the ocean, nor, toward the last, how long we went without food and water. Then Labaud could stand no more, and died. He died of starvation and exposure. I did not kill him. No living creature could have been feeble enough for me to have killed it, no matter what my desire. But when Labaud was dead there was enough food for one, and I lived to be washed ashore in the Golfo Triste.

"Calling myself Walter Martin, I secured employment with a British copper mining company at Aroa, and within a few months had become private secretary to Philip Howart, the resident manager. Shortly after this promotion I was approached by a cockney named John Edge, who outlined to me a plan by which we could defraud the company of a hundred-odd pounds monthly. When I refused to take part in the fraud, Edge revealed his knowledge of my identity, and threatened exposure unless I assisted him. That Venezuela had no extradition treaty with France might save me from being returned to the islands, Edge said; but that was not my chief danger: Labaud's body had been cast ashore, undecomposed enough to show what had happened to him, and I, an escaped murderer, would be under the necessity of proving to a Venezuelan court that I had not killed Labaud in Venezuelan waters to keep from starving.

"I still refused to join Edge in his fraud, and prepared to go away. But while I was making my preparations he killed Howart and looted the company safe. He urged me to flee with him, arguing that I could not face the police investigation even if he did not expose me. That was true enough: I went with him. Two months later, in Mexico City, I learned why Edge had been so desirous of my company. He had a firm hold on me, through his knowledge of my identity, and a great – an unjustified – opinion of my ability; and he intended using me to commit crimes that were beyond his grasp. I was determined, no matter what happened, no matter what became necessary, never to return to the Iles du Salut; but neither did I intend becoming a professional criminal. I attempted to desert Edge in Mexico City; he found me, we fought; and I killed him. I killed him in self-defense: he struck me first.

"In 1920 I came to the United States, to San Francisco, changed my name once more – to Edgar Leggett – and began making a new place for myself in the world, developing experiments with color that I had attempted as a young artist in Paris. In 1923, believing that Edgar Leggett could never now be connected with Maurice de Mayenne, I sent for Alice and Gabrielle, who were then living in New York, and Alice and I were married. But the past was not dead, and there was no unbridgeable chasm between Leggett and Mayenne. Alice, not hearing from me after my escape, not knowing what had happened to me, employed a private detective to find me, a Louis Upton. Upton sent a man named Ruppert to South America, and Ruppert succeeded in tracing me step by step from my landing in the Golfo Triste up to, but no farther than, my departure from Mexico City after Edge's death. In doing this, Ruppert of course learned of the deaths of Labaud, Howart and Edge; three deaths of which I was guiltless, but of which – or at least of one or more of which – I most certainly, my record being what it is, would be convicted if tried.

"I do not know how Upton found me in San Francisco. Possibly he traced Alice and Gabrielle to me. Late last Saturday night he called upon me and demanded money as the price of silence. Having no money available at the time, I put him off until Tuesday, when I gave him the diamonds as part payment. But I was desperate. I knew what being at Upton's mercy would mean, having experienced the same thing with Edge. I determined to kill him. I decided to pretend the diamonds had been stolen, and to so inform you, the police. Upton, I was confident, would thereupon immediately communicate with me. I would make an appointment with him and shoot him down in cold blood, confident that I would have no difficulty in arranging a story that would make me seem justified in having killed this known burglar, in whose possession, doubtless, the stolen diamonds would be found.

"I think the plan would have been successful. However, Ruppert – pursuing Upton with a grudge of his own to settle – saved me from killing Upton by himself killing him. Ruppert, the man who had traced my course from Devil's Island to Mexico City, had also, either from Upton or by spying on Upton, learned that Mayenne was Leggett, and, with the police after him for Upton's murder, he came here, demanding that I shelter him, returning the diamonds, claiming money in their stead.

"I killed him. His body is in the cellar. Out front, a detective is watching my house. Other detectives are busy elsewhere inquiring into my affairs. I have not been able satisfactorily to explain certain of my actions, nor to avoid contradictions, and, now that I am actually suspect, there is little chance of the past's being kept secret. I have always known – have known it most surely when I would not admit it to myself – that this would one day happen. I am not going back to Devil's Island. My wife and daughter had neither knowledge of nor part in Ruppert's death.

"Maurice de Mayenne."

7 THE CURSE

NOBODY SAID anything for some minutes after I had finished reading. Mrs. Leggett had taken her handkerchief from her face to listen, sobbing softly now and then. Gabrielle was looking jerkily around the room, light fighting cloudiness in her eyes, her lips twitching as if she was trying to get words out but couldn't.

I went to the table, bent over the dead man, and ran my hand over his pockets. The inside coat pocket bulged. I reached under his arm, unbuttoned and pulled open his coat, taking a brown wallet from the pocket. The wallet was thick with paper money – fifteen thousand dollars when we counted it later.

Showing the others the wallet's contents, I asked:

"Did he leave any message besides the one I read?"

"None that's been found," O'Gar said. "Why?"

"Any that you know of, Mrs. Leggett?" I asked.

She shook her head.

"Why?" O'Gar asked again.

"He didn't commit suicide," I said. "He was murdered."

Gabrielle Leggett screamed shrilly and sprang out of her chair, pointing a sharp-nailed white finger at Mrs. Leggett.

"She killed him," the girl shrieked. "She said, 'Come back here,' and held the kitchen door open with one hand, and picked up the knife from the drain-board with the other, and when he went past her she pushed it in his back. I saw her do it. She killed him. I wasn't dressed, and when I heard them coming I hid in the pantry, and I saw her do it."

Mrs. Leggett got to her feet. She staggered, and would have

fallen if Fitzstephan hadn't gone over to steady her. Amazement washed her swollen face empty of grief.

The gray-faced dandified man by the table – Doctor Riese, I learned later – said, in a cold, crisp voice:

"There is no stab wound. He was shot through the temple by a bullet from this pistol, held close, slanting up. Clearly suicide, I should say."

Collinson forced Gabrielle down to her chair again, trying to calm her. She was working her hands together and moaning.

I disagreed with the doctor's last statement, and said so while turning something else over in my mind.

"Murder. He had this money in his pocket. He was going away. He wrote that letter to the police to clear his wife and daughter, so they wouldn't be punished for complicity in his crimes. Did it," I asked O'Gar, "sound to you like the dying statement of a man who was leaving a wife and daughter he loved? No message, no word, to them – all to the police."

"Maybe you're right," the bullet-headed man said; "but supposing he was going away, he still didn't leave them any –"

"He would have told them – either on paper or talking – something before he went, if he had lived long enough. He was winding up his affairs, preparing to go away, and – Maybe he *was* going to commit suicide, though the money and the tone of the letter make me doubt it; but even in that case my guess is that he didn't, that he was killed before he had finished his preparations – maybe because he was taking too long a time. How was he found?"

"I heard," Mrs. Leggett sobbed; "I heard the shot, and ran up here, and he – he was like that. And I went down to the telephone, and the bell – the doorbell – rang, and it was Mr. Fitzstephan, and I told him. It couldn't – there was nobody else in the house to – to kill him."

"You killed him," I said to her. "He was going away. He wrote this statement, shouldering your crimes. You killed

Ruppert down in the kitchen. That's what the girl was talking about. Your husband's letter sounded enough like a suicide letter to pass for one, you thought; so you murdered him – murdered him because you thought his confession and death would hush up the whole business, keep us from poking into it any further."

Her face didn't tell me anything. It was distorted, but in a way that might have meant almost anything. I filled my lungs and went on, not exactly bellowing, but getting plenty of noise out:

"There are half a dozen lies in your husband's statement – half a dozen that I can peg now. He didn't send for you and his daughter. You traced him here. Mrs. Begg said he was the most surprised man she had ever seen when you arrived from New York. He didn't give Upton the diamonds. His account of why he gave them to Upton and of what he intended doing afterwards is ridiculous: it's simply the best story he could think of on short notice to cover you up. Leggett would have given him money or he would have given him nothing; he wouldn't have been foolish enough to give him somebody else's diamonds and have all this stink raised.

"Upton traced you here and he came to you with his demand – not to your husband. You had hired Upton to find Leggett; you were the one he knew; he and Ruppert had traced Leggett for you, not only to Mexico City, but all the way here. They'd have squeezed you before this if they hadn't been sent to Sing Sing for another trick. When they got out, Upton came here and made his play. You framed the burglary; you gave Upton the diamonds; and you didn't tell your husband anything about it. Your husband thought the burglary was on the level. Otherwise, would he – a man with his record – have risked reporting it to the police?

"Why didn't you tell him about Upton? Didn't you want him to know that you had had him traced step by step from Devil's Island to San Francisco? Why? His southern record was a good additional hold on him, if you needed one? You didn't want him to know you knew about Labaud and Howart and Edge?"

I didn't give her a chance to answer any of these questions, but sailed ahead, turning my voice loose:

"Maybe Ruppert, following Upton here, got in touch with you, and you had him kill Upton, a job he was willing to do on his own hook. Probably, because he did kill him and he did come to you afterwards, and you thought it necessary to put the knife into him down in the kitchen. You didn't know the girl, hiding in the pantry, saw you; but you did know that you were getting out of your depth. You knew that your chances of getting away with Ruppert's murder were slim. Your house was too much in the spotlight. So you played your only out. You went to your husband with the whole story – or as much of it as could be arranged to persuade him – and got him to shoulder it for you. And then you handed him this – here at the table.

"He shielded you. He had always shielded you. *You*," I thundered, my voice in fine form by now, "killed your sister Lily, his first wife, and let him take the fall for you. *You* went to London with him after that. Would you have gone with your sister's murderer if you had been innocent? *You* had him traced here, and you came here after him, and *you* married him. *You* were the one who decided he had married the wrong sister, and *you* killed her."

"She did! She did!" cried Gabrielle Leggett, trying to get up from the chair in which Collinson was holding her. "She –"

Mrs. Leggett drew herself up straight, and smiled, showing strong yellowish teeth set edge to edge. She took two steps toward the center of the room. One hand was on her hip, the other hanging loosely at her side. The housewife – Fitzstephan's serene sane soul – was suddenly gone. This was a blonde woman whose body was rounded, not with the plumpness of contented, well-cared-for early middle age, but with the cushioned, soft-sheathed muscles of the hunting cats, whether in jungle or alley.

I picked up the pistol from the table and put it in my pocket.

"You wish to know who killed my sister?" Mrs. Leggett asked softly, speaking to me, her teeth clicking together between words, her mouth smiling, her eyes burning. "She, the dope fiend, Gabrielle – she killed her mother. She is the one he shielded."

The girl cried out something unintelligible.

"Nonsense," I said. "She was a baby."

"Oh, but it is not nonsense," the woman said. "She was nearly five, a child of five playing with a pistol that she had taken from a drawer while her mother slept. The pistol went off and Lily died. An accident, of course, but Maurice was too sensitive a soul to bear the thought of her growing up knowing that she had killed her mother. Besides, it was likely that Maurice would have been convicted in any event. It was known that he and I were intimate, that he wanted his freedom from Lily; and he was at the door of Lily's bedroom when the shot was fired. But that was a slight matter to him: his one desire was to save the child from memory of what she had done, so her life might not be blackened by the knowledge that she had, however accidentally, killed her mother."

What made this especially nasty was the niceness with which the woman smiled as she talked, and the care – almost fastidious – with which she selected her words, mouthing them daintily. She went on:

"Gabrielle was always, even before she became addicted to drugs, a child of, one might say, limited mentality; and so, by the time the London police had found us, we had succeeded in quite emptying her mind of the last trace of memory, that is, of this particular memory. This is, I assure you, the entire truth. She killed her mother; and her father, to use your expression, took the fall for her."

"Fairly plausible," I conceded, "but it doesn't hang together right. There's a chance that you made Leggett believe that, but I doubt it. I think you're trying to hurt your step-daughter because she's told us of seeing you knife Ruppert downstairs."

She pulled her lips back from her teeth and took a quick step toward me, her eyes wide and white-ringed; then she checked herself, laughed sharply, and the glare went from her eyes – or maybe went back through them, to smolder behind them. She put her hands on her hips and smiled playfully, airily, at me and spoke playfully to me, while mad hatred glowed behind eyes, smile, and voice.

"Am I? Then I must tell you this, which I should not tell you unless it was true. I taught her to kill her mother. Do you understand? I taught her, trained her, drilled her, rehearsed her. Do you understand that? Lily and I were true sisters, inseparable, hating one another poisonously. Maurice, he wished to marry neither of us – why should he? – though he was intimate enough with both. You are to try to understand that literally. But we were poverty-ridden and he was not, and, because we were and he wasn't, Lily wished to marry him. And I, I wished to marry him because she did. We were true sisters, like that in all things. But Lily got him, first – trapped him – that is crude but exact – into matrimony.

"Gabrielle was born six or seven months later. What a happy little family we were. I lived with them – weren't Lily and I inseparable? – and from the first Gabrielle had more love for me than for her mother. I saw to that: there was nothing her Aunt Alice wouldn't do for her dear niece; because her preferring me infuriated Lily, not that Lily herself loved the child so much, but that we were sisters; and whatever one wanted the other wanted, not to share, but exclusively.

"Gabrielle had hardly been born before I began planning what I should some day do; and when she was nearly five I did it. Maurice's pistol, a small one, was kept in a locked drawer high in a chiffonier. I unlocked the drawer, unloaded the pistol, and taught Gabrielle an amusing little game. I would lie on Lily's bed, pretending to sleep. The child would push a chair to the chiffonier, climb up on it, take the pistol from the drawer, creep over to the bed, put the muzzle of the pistol to my head, and press the trigger. When she did it well, making little or no noise, holding the pistol correctly in her tiny hands, I would reward her with candy, cautioning her against saying anything about the game to her mother or to anyone else, as we were going to surprise her mother with it.

"We did. We surprised her completely one afternoon when, having taken aspirin for a headache, Lily was sleeping in her bed. That time I unlocked the drawer but did not unload the pistol. Then I told the child she might play the game with her mother; and I went to visit friends on the floor below, so no one would think I had had any part in my dear sister's demise. I thought Maurice would be away all afternoon. I intended, when I heard the shot, to rush upstairs with my friends and find with them that the child playing with the pistol had killed her mother.

"I had little fear of the child's talking afterwards. Of, as I have said, limited mentality, loving and trusting me as she did, and in my hands both before and during any official inquiry that might be made, I knew I could very easily control her, make sure that she said nothing to reveal my part in the – ah – enterprise. But Maurice very nearly spoiled the whole thing. Coming home unexpectedly, he reached the bedroom door just as Gabrielle pressed the trigger. The tiniest fraction of a second earlier, and he would have been in time to save his wife's life.

"Well, that was unfortunate in that it led to his being convicted; but it certainly prevented his ever suspecting me; and his subsequent desire to wipe from the child's mind all remembrance of the deed relieved me of any further anxiety or effort. I did follow him to this country after his escape from Devil's Island, and I did follow him to San Francisco when Upton had found him for me; and I used Gabrielle's love for me and her hatred of him – I had carefully cultivated that with skilfully clumsy attempts to persuade her to forgive him for murdering her mother – and the necessity of keeping her in ignorance of the truth, and my record of faithfulness to him and her, to make him marry me, to make him think that marrying me would in some sense salvage our ruined lives. The day he married Lily I swore I would take him away from her. And I did. And I hope my dear sister in hell knows it."

The smile was gone. Mad hatred was no longer *behind* eyes and voice: it was *in* them, and in the set of her features, the pose of her body. This mad hatred – and she as part of it – seemed the only live thing in the room. The eight of us who looked at and listened to her didn't, for the moment, count: we were alive to her, but not to each other, nor to anything but her.

She turned from me to fling an arm out at the girl on the other side of the room; and now her voice was throaty, vibrant, with savage triumph in it; and her words were separated into groups by brief pauses, so that she seemed to be chanting them.

"You're her daughter," she cried; "and you're cursed with the same black soul and rotten blood that she and I and all the Dains have had; and you're cursed with your mother's blood on your hands in babyhood; and with the twisted mind and the need for drugs that are my gifts to you; and your life will be black as your mother's and mine were black; and the lives of those you touch will be black as Maurice's was black; and your –"

"Stop!" Eric Collinson gasped. "Make her stop."

Gabrielle Leggett, both hands to her ears, her face twisted with terror, screamed once – horribly – and fell forward out of her chair.

Pat Reddy was young at manhunting, but O'Gar and I should have known better than to stop watching Mrs. Leggett even for a half-second, no matter how urgently the girl's scream and fall pulled at our attention. But we did look at the girl – if for less than half a second – and that was long enough. When we looked at Mrs. Leggett again, she had a gun in her hand, and she had taken her first step towards the door.

Nobody was between her and the door: the uniformed copper had gone to help Collinson with Gabrielle Leggett. Nobody was behind her: her back was to the door and by turning she had brought Fitzstephan into her field of vision. She glared over the black gun, burning eyes darting from one to another of us, taking another step backward, snarling: "Don't you move."

Pat Reddy shifted his weight to the balls of his feet. I frowned at him, shaking my head. The hall and stairs were better places in which to catch her: in here somebody would die.

She backed over the sill, blew breath between her teeth with a hissing, spitting sound, and was gone down the hall.

Owen Fitzstephan was first through the door after her. The policeman got in my way, but I was second out. The woman had reached the head of the stairs, at the other end of the dim hall, with Fitzstephan, not far behind, rapidly overtaking her.

He caught her on the between-floors landing, just as I reached the top of the stairs. He pinned one of her arms to her body, but the other, with the gun, was free. He grabbed at it and missed. She twisted the muzzle in to his body as I – with my head bent to miss the edge of the floor – leaped down at them.

I landed on them just in time, crashing into them, smashing them into the corner of the wall, sending her bullet, meant for the sorrel-haired man, into a step.

We weren't standing up. I caught with both hands at the flash of her gun, missed, and had her by the waist. Close to my chin Fitzstephan's lean fingers closed on her gun-hand wrist.

She twisted her body against my right arm. My right arm was still lame from our spill out of the Chrysler. It wouldn't hold. Her thick body went up, turning over on me.

Gunfire roared in my ear, burnt my cheek.

The woman's body went limp.

When O'Gar and Reddy pulled us apart she lay still. The second bullet had gone through her throat.

I went up to the laboratory. Gabrielle Leggett, with the doctor and Collinson kneeling beside her, was lying on the floor.

I told the doctor: "Better take a look at Mrs. Leggett. She's on the stairs. Dead, I think, but you'd better take a look."

The doctor went out. Collinson, chafing the unconscious girl's hands, looked at me as if I were something there ought to be a law against, and said:

"I hope you're satisfied with the way your work got done."

"It got done," I said.

8 BUT AND IF

FITZSTEPHAN AND I ate one of Mrs. Schindler's good dinners that evening in her low-ceilinged basement, and drank her husband's good beer. The novelist in Fitzstephan was busy trying to find what he called Mrs. Leggett's psychological basis.

"The killing of her sister is plain enough, knowing her character as we now do," he said, "and so are the killing of her husband, her attempt to ruin her niece's life when she was exposed, and even her determination to kill herself on the stairs rather than be caught. But the quiet years in between – where do they fit in?"

"It's Leggett's murder that doesn't fit in," I argued. "The rest is all one piece. She wanted him. She killed her sister – or had her killed – in a way to tie him to her; but the law pulled them apart. There was nothing she could do about that, except wait and hope for the chance that always existed, that he would be freed some day. We don't know of anything else she wanted then. Why shouldn't she be quiet, holding Gabrielle as her hostage against the chance she hoped for, living comfortably enough, no doubt, on his money? When she heard of his escape, she came to America and set about finding him. When her detective located him here she came to him. He was willing to marry her. She had what she wanted. Why should she be anything but quiet? She wasn't a trouble-maker for the fun of it – one of these people who act out of pure mischief. She was simply a woman who wanted what she wanted and was willing to go to any length to get it. Look how patiently, and for how many years, she hid her hatred from the girl. And her wants weren't even very extravagant. You won't find the key to her in any complicated derangements. She was simple as an animal, with an animal's simple ignorance of right and wrong, dislike for being thwarted, and spitefulness when trapped."

Fitzstephan drank beer and asked:

"You'd reduce the Dain curse, then, to a primitive strain in the blood?"

"To less than that, to words in an angry woman's mouth."

"It's fellows like you that take all the color out of life." He sighed behind cigarette smoke. "Doesn't Gabrielle's being made the tool of her mother's murder convince you of the necessity – at least the poetic necessity – of the curse?"

"Not even if she *was* the tool, and that's something I wouldn't bet on. Apparently Leggett didn't doubt it. He stuffed his letter with those ancient details to keep her covered up. But we've only got Mrs. Leggett's word that he actually saw the child kill her mother. On the other hand, Mrs. Leggett said, in front of Gabrielle, that Gabrielle had been brought up to believe her father the murderer – so we can believe that. And it isn't likely – though it's possible – that he would have gone that far except to save her from knowledge of her own guilt. But, from that point on, one guess at the truth is about as good as another. Mrs. Leggett wanted him and she got him. Then why in hell did she kill him?"

"You jump around so," Fitzstephan complained. "You answered that back in the laboratory. Why don't you stick to your answer? You said she killed him because the letter sounded enough like a pre-suicide statement to pass, and she thought it and his death would ensure her safety."

"That was good enough to say then," I admitted; "but not now, in cold blood, with more facts to fit in. She had worked and waited for years to get him. He must have had some value to her."

"But she didn't love him, or there is no reason to suppose she did. He hadn't that value to her. He was to her no more than a trophy of the hunt; and that's a value not affected by death – one has the head embalmed and nailed on the wall."

"Then why did she keep Upton away from him? Why did she kill Ruppert? Why should she have carried the load for him there? It was his danger. Why did she make it hers if he had no value to her? Why did she risk all that to keep him from learning that the past had come to life again?"

"I think I see what you're getting at," Fitzstephan said slowly. "You think –"

"Wait – here's another thing. I talked to Leggett and his wife together a couple of times. Neither of them addressed a word to the other either time, though the woman did a lot of acting to make me think she would have told me something about her daughter's disappearance if it had not been for him."

"Where did you find Gabrielle?"

"After seeing Ruppert murdered, she beat it to the Haldorns' with what money she had and her jewelry, turning the jewelry over to Minnie Hershey to raise money on. Minnie bought a couple of pieces for herself – her man had picked himself up a lot of dough in a crap game a night or two before: the police checked that – and sent the man out to peddle the rest. He was picked up in a hock-shop, just on general suspicion."

"Gabrielle was leaving home for good?" he asked.

"You can't blame her – thinking her father a murderer, and now catching her step-mother in the act. Who'd want to live in a home like that?"

"And you think Leggett and his wife were on bad terms? That may be: I hadn't seen much of them lately, and wasn't intimate enough with them to have been let in on a condition of that sort if it had existed. Do you think he had perhaps learned something – some of the truth about her?"

"Maybe, but not enough to keep him from taking the fall for her on Ruppert's murder; and what he had learned wasn't connected with this recent affair, because the first time I saw him he really believed in the burglary. But then –"

"Aw, shut up! You're never satisfied until you've got two buts and an if attached to everything. I don't see any reason for doubting Mrs. Leggett's story. She told us the whole thing quite gratuitously. Why should we suppose that she'd lie to implicate herself?"

"You mean in her sister's murder? She'd been acquitted of that, and I suppose the French system's like ours in that she couldn't be tried again for it, no matter what she confessed. She didn't give anything away, brother."

"Always belittling," he said. "You need more beer to expand your soul."

At the Leggett–Ruppert inquests I saw Gabrielle Leggett again, but was not sure that she even recognized me. She was with Madison Andrews, who had been Leggett's attorney and was now his estate's executor. Eric Collinson was there, but, peculiarly, apparently not with Gabrielle. He gave me nods and nothing else.

The newspapers got hold of what Mrs. Leggett had said happened in Paris in 1913, and made a couple-day fuss over it. The recovery of Halstead and Beauchamp's diamonds let the Continental Detective Agency out: we wrote *Discontinued* at the bottom of the Leggett record. I went up in the mountains to snoop around for a gold-mine-owner who thought his employees were gypping him.

I expected to be in the mountains for at least a month: inside jobs of that sort take time. On the evening of my tenth day there I had a long-distance call from the Old Man, my boss.

"I'm sending Foley up to relieve you," he said. "Don't wait for him. Catch tonight's train back. The Leggett matter is active again."

PART 2
THE TEMPLE

9 TAD'S BLIND MAN

MADISON ANDREWS was a tall gaunt man of sixty with ragged white hair, eyebrows, and mustache that exaggerated the ruddiness of his bony hard-muscled face. He wore his clothes loose, chewed tobacco, and had twice in the past ten years been publicly named co-respondent in divorce suits.

"I dare say young Collinson has babbled all sorts of nonsense to you," he said. "He seems to think I'm in my second childhood, as good as told me so."

"I haven't seen him," I said. "I've only been back in town a couple of hours, long enough to go to the office and then come here."

"Well," he said, "he is her fiancé, but I am responsible for her, and I preferred following Doctor Riese's counsel. He is her physician. He said that letting her go to the Temple for a short stay would do more to restore her to mental health than anything else we could do. I couldn't disregard his advice. The Haldorns may be, probably are, charlatans, but Joseph Haldorn is certainly the only person to whom Gabrielle has willingly talked, and in whose company she has seemed at peace, since her parents' deaths. Doctor Riese said that to cross her in her desire to go to the Temple would be to send her mind deeper into its illness. Could I snap my fingers at his opinion because young Collinson didn't like it?"

I said: "No."

"I have no illusions concerning the cult," he went on defending himself. "It is probably as full of quackery as any other. But we are not concerned with its religious aspect. We're interested in it as therapeutics, as a cure for Gabrielle's mind. Even if the character of its membership were not such that I could count with certainty on Gabrielle's safety, I should still have been tempted to let her go. Her recovery is, as I see it, the thing with which we should be most concerned, and nothing else should be allowed to interfere with that."

He was worried. I nodded and kept quiet, waiting to learn what was worrying him. I got it little by little as he went on talking around in circles.

On Doctor Riese's advice and over Collinson's protests he had let Gabrielle Leggett go to the Temple of the Holy Grail to stay awhile. She had wanted to go, no less prominently respectable a person than Mrs. Livingston Rodman was staying there at the time, the Haldorns had been Edgar Leggett's friends: Andrews let her go. That had been six days ago. She had taken the mulatto, Minnie Hershey, with her as maid. Doctor Riese had gone to see her each day. On four days he had found her improved. On the fifth day her condition had alarmed him. Her mind was more completely dazed than it had ever been, and she had the symptoms of one who had been subjected to some sort of shock. He couldn't get anything out of her. He couldn't get anything out of Minnie. He couldn't get anything out of the Haldorns. He had no way of learning what had happened, or if anything had happened.

Eric Collinson had held Riese up for daily reports on Gabrielle. Riese told him the truth about his last visit. Collinson hit the ceiling. He wanted the girl taken away from the Temple immediately: the Haldorns were preparing to murder her, according to his notion. He and Andrews had a swell row. Andrews thought that the girl had simply suffered a relapse from which she would most speedily recover if left where she wished to stay. Riese was inclined to agree with Andrews. Collinson didn't. He threatened to create a stink if they didn't yank her away *pronto*.

That worried Andrews. It wouldn't look so good for him, the hard-headed lawyer, letting his ward go to such a place, if anything happened to her. On the other hand, he said he really believed it was for her benefit to stay there. And he didn't want anything to happen to her. He finally reached a compromise with Collinson. Gabrielle should be allowed to remain in the Temple for a few more days at least, but somebody should be put in there to keep an eye on her, and to see that the Haldorns weren't playing any tricks on her.

Riese had suggested me: my luck in hitting on the manner of Leggett's death had impressed him. Collinson had objected that my brutality was largely responsible for Gabrielle's present condition, but he had finally given in. I already knew Gabrielle and her history, and I hadn't made such a total mess of that first job: my efficiency offset my brutality, or words to that effect. So Andrews had phoned the Old Man, offered him a high enough rate to justify pulling me off another job, and there I was.

"The Haldorns know you are coming," Andrews wound up. "It doesn't matter what they think about it. I simply told them that Doctor Riese and I had decided that, until Gabrielle's mind became more settled, it would be best to have a competent man on hand in case of emergency, as much perhaps to safeguard others as her. There is no need of my giving you instructions. It is simply a matter of taking every precaution."

"Does Miss Leggett know I'm coming?"

"No, and I don't think we need say anything to her about it. You'll make your watch over her as unobtrusive as possible, of course, and I doubt that she will, in her present state of mind, pay enough attention to your presence to resent it. If she does – well, we'll see."

Andrews gave me a note to Aaronia Haldorn.

An hour and a half later I was sitting opposite her in the Temple reception room while she read it. She put it aside and offered me long Russian cigarettes in a white jade box. I apologized for sticking to my Fatimas, and worked the lighter on the smoking stand she pushed out between us. When our cigarettes were burning, she said:

"We shall try to make you as comfortable as possible. We are neither barbarians nor fanatics. I explain this because so many people are surprised to find us neither. This is a temple, but none of us supposes that happiness, comfort, or any of the ordinary matters of civilized living, will desecrate it. You are not one of us. Perhaps – I hope – you will become one of us. However – do not squirm – you won't, I assure you, be annoyed. You may attend our services or not, as you choose, and you may come and go as you wish. You will show us, I am sure, the same consideration we show you, and I am equally sure that you will not interfere in any way with anything you may see – no matter how peculiar you may think it – so long as it does not promise to affect your – patient."

"Of course not," I promised.

She smiled, as if to thank me, rubbed her cigarette's end in the ash tray, and stood up, saying: "I'll show you your room."

Not a word had been said by either of us about my previous visit.

Carrying my hat and gladstone bag, I followed her to the elevator. We got out at the fifth floor.

"That is Miss Leggett's room," Aaronia Haldorn said, indicating the door that Collinson and I had taken turns knocking a couple of weeks before. "And this is yours." She opened the door that faced Gabrielle's across the corridor.

My room was a duplicate of hers, except that it was without a dressing-room. My door, like hers, had no lock.

"Where does her maid sleep?" I asked.

"In one of the servants' rooms on the top floor. Doctor Riese is with Miss Leggett now, I think. I'll tell him you have arrived."

I thanked her. She went out of my room, closing the door.

Fifteen minutes later Doctor Riese knocked and came in.

"I am glad you are here," he said, shaking hands. He had a

crisp, precise way of turning out his words, sometimes emphasizing them by gesturing with the black-ribboned glasses in his hand. I never saw the glasses on his nose. "We shan't need your professional skill, I trust, but I am glad you are here."

"What's wrong?" I asked in what was meant for a tone that invited confidences.

He looked sharply at me, tapped his glasses on his left thumb-nail, and said:

"What is wrong is, so far as I know, altogether in my sphere. I know of nothing else wrong." He shook my hand again. "You'll find your part quite boring, I hope."

"But yours isn't?" I suggested.

He stopped turning away towards the door, frowned, tapped his glasses with his thumb-nail again, and said:

"No, it is not." He hesitated, as if deciding whether to say something more, decided not to, and moved to the door.

"I've a right to know what you honestly think about it," I said.

He looked sharply at me again. "I don't know what I honestly think about it." A pause. "I am not satisfied." He didn't look satisfied. "I'll be in again this evening."

He went out and shut the door. Half a minute later he opened the door, said, "Miss Leggett is extremely ill," shut the door again and went away.

I grumbled, "This is going to be a lot of fun," to myself, sat down at a window and smoked a cigarette.

A maid in black and white knocked on the door and asked me what I wanted for luncheon. She was a hearty pink and plump blonde somewhere in the middle twenties, with blue eyes that looked curiously at me and had jokes in them. I took a shot of Scotch from the bottle in my bag, ate the luncheon the maid presently returned with, and spent the afternoon in my room.

By keeping my ears open I managed to catch Minnie as she came out of her mistress's room at a little after four. The mulatto's eyes jerked wide when she saw me standing in my doorway.

"Come in," I said. "Didn't Doctor Riese tell you I was here?"

"No, sir. Are – are you –? You're not wanting anything with Miss Gabrielle?"

"Just looking out for her, seeing that nothing happens to her. And if you'll keep me wised up, let me know what she says and does, and what others say and do, you'll be helping me, and helping her; because then I won't have to bother her."

The mulatto said, "Yes, yes," readily enough, but, as far as I could learn from her brown face, my co-operative idea wasn't getting across any too well.

"How is she this afternoon?" I asked.

"She's right cheerful this afternoon, sir. She like this place."

"How'd she spend the afternoon?"

"She – I don't know, sir. She just kind of spent it – quiet like."

Not much news there. I said:

"Doctor Riese thinks she'll be better off not knowing I'm here, so you needn't say anything to her about me."

"No, sir, I sure won't," she promised, but it sounded more polite than sincere.

In the early evening Aaronia Haldorn came in and invited me down to dinner. The dining-room was paneled and furnished in dark walnut. There were ten of us at the table.

Joseph Haldorn was tall, built like a statue, and wore a black silk robe. His hair was thick, long, white, and glossy. His thick beard, trimmed round, was white and glossy. Aaronia Haldorn introduced me to him, calling him "Joseph," as if he had no last name. All the others addressed him in the same way. He gave me a white even-toothed smile and a warm strong hand. His face, healthily pink, was without line or wrinkle. It was a tranquil face, especially the clear brown eyes, somehow making you feel at peace with the world. The same soothing quality was in his baritone voice.

He said: "We are happy to have you here."

The words were merely polite, meaningless, yet, as he said them, I actually believed that for some reason he was happy. Now I understood Gabrielle Leggett's desire to come to this place. I said that I, too, was happy to be there, and while I was saying it I actually thought I was.

Besides Joseph and his wife and their son at the table there was Mrs. Rodman, a tall frail woman with transparent skin, faded eyes, and a voice that never rose above a murmur; a man named Fleming, who was young, dark, very thin, and wore a dark mustache and the detached air of one busy with his own thoughts; Major Jeffries, a well-tailored, carefully mannered man, stout and bald and sallow; his wife, a pleasant sort of person in spite of a kittenishness thirty years too young for her; a Miss Hillen, sharp of chin and voice, with an intensely eager manner; and Mrs. Pavlov, who was quite young, had a high-cheek-boned dark face, and avoided everybody's eyes.

The food, served by two Filipino boys, was good. There was not much conversation and none of it was religious. It wasn't so bad.

After dinner I returned to my room. I listened at Gabrielle Leggett's door for a few minutes, but heard nothing. In my room I fidgeted and smoked and waited for Doctor Riese to show up as he had promised. He didn't show up. I supposed that one of the emergencies that are regular parts of doctors' lives had kept him elsewhere, but his not coming made me irritable. Nobody went in or out of Gabrielle's room. I tiptoed over to listen at her door a couple of times. Once I heard nothing. Once I heard faint meaningless rustling sounds.

At a little after ten o'clock I heard some of the inmates going past my door, probably on their way to their rooms for the night.

At five minutes past eleven I heard Gabrielle's door open. I opened mine. Minnie Hershey was going down the corridor toward the rear of the building. I was tempted to call her, but didn't. My last attempt to get anything out of her had been a flop, and I wasn't feeling tactful enough now to stand much chance of having better luck.

By this time I had given up hopes of seeing Riese before the following day.

I switched off my lights, left my door open, and sat there in the dark, looking at the girl's door and cursing the world. I thought of Tad's blind man in a dark room hunting for a black hat that wasn't there, and knew how he felt.

At a little before midnight Minnie Hershey, in hat and coat as if she had just come in from the street, returned to Gabrielle's room. She didn't seem to see me. I stood up silently and tried to peep past her when she opened the door, but didn't have any luck.

Minnie remained there until nearly one o'clock, and when she came out she closed the door very softly, walking tiptoe. That was an unnecessary precaution on the thick carpet. Because it was unnecessary it made me nervous. I went to my door and called in a low voice:

"Minnie."

Maybe she didn't hear me. She went on tiptoeing down the corridor. That increased my jumpiness. I went after her quickly and stopped her by catching one of her wiry wrists.

Her Indian face was expressionless.

"How is she?" I asked.

"Miss Gabrielle's all right, sir. You just leave her alone," she mumbled.

"She's not all right. What's she doing now?"

"She's sleeping."

"Coked?"

She raised angry maroon eyes and let them drop again, saying nothing.

"She sent you out to get dope?" I demanded, tightening my grip on her wrist.

"She sent me out to get some – some medicine – yes, sir."

"And took some and went to sleep?"

"Y-yes, sir."

"We'll go back and take a look at her," I said.

The mulatto tried to jerk her wrist free. I held it. She said: "You leave me alone, Mister, or else I'll yell."

"I'll leave you alone after we've had our look, maybe," I said, turning her around with my other hand on her shoulder. "So if you're going to yell you can get started right now."

She wasn't willing to go back to her mistress's room, but she didn't make me drag her. Gabrielle Leggett was lying on her side in bed, sleeping quietly, the bedclothes stirring gently with her breathing. Her small white face, at rest, with brown curls falling over it, looked like a sick child's.

I turned Minnie loose and went back to my room. Sitting there in the dark I understood why people bit their fingernails. I sat there for an hour or more, and then, Goddamning myself for an old woman, I took off my shoes, picked the most comfortable chair, put my feet on another, hung a blanket over me, and went to sleep facing Gabrielle Leggett's door through my open doorway.

10 DEAD FLOWERS

I OPENED MY eyes drowsily, decided that I had dozed off for only a moment, closed my eyes, drifted back into slumber, and then roused myself sluggishly again. Something wasn't right.

I forced my eyes open, then closed them, and opened them again. Whatever wasn't right had to do with that. Blackness was there when they were open and when they were closed. That should have been reasonable enough: the night was dark, and my windows were out of the street lights' range. That should have been reasonable enough, but it wasn't: I remembered that I had left my door open, and the corridor lights had been on. Facing me was no pale rectangle of light framed by my doorway, with Gabrielle's door showing through.

I was too awake by now to jump up suddenly. I held my breath and listened, hearing nothing but the tick of my wristwatch. Cautiously moving my hand, I looked at the luminous dial – 3:17. I had been asleep longer than I had supposed, and the corridor light had been put out.

My head was numb, my body stiff and heavy, and there was a bad taste in my mouth. I got out from under the blanket, and out of my chairs, moving awkwardly, my muscles stubborn. I crept on stockinged feet to the door, and bumped into the door. It had been closed. When I opened it the corridor light was burning as before. The air that came in from the corridor seemed surprisingly fresh, sharp, pure.

I turned my face back into the room, sniffing. There was an odor of flowers, faint, stuffy, more the odor of a closed place in which flowers had died than of flowers themselves.

Lilies of the valley, moonflowers, perhaps another one or two. I spent time trying to divide the odor into its parts, seriously trying to determine whether a trace of honeysuckle was actually present. Then I vaguely remembered having dreamed of a funeral. Trying to recall exactly what I had dreamed, I leaned against the doorframe and let sleep come into me again.

The jerking up of my neck muscles when my head sunk too low aroused me. I wrestled my eyes open, standing there on legs that weren't part of me, stupidly wondering why I didn't go to bed. While I drowsed over the idea that there might be some reason why I shouldn't sleep, if I could only think of it, I put a hand against the wall to steady myself. The hand touched the light button. I had sense enough to push it.

Light scorched my eyes. Squinting, I could see a world that was real to me, and could remember that I had work to do. I made for the bathroom, where cold water on head and face left me still stupid and muddled, but at least partly conscious.

I turned off my lights, crossed to Gabrielle's door, listened, and heard nothing. I opened the door, stepped inside, and closed the door. My flashlight showed me an empty bed with covers thrown down across the foot. I put a hand in the hollow her body had made in the bed – cold. There was nobody in bathroom or dressing-alcove. Under the edge of the bed lay a pair of green mules, and a green dressing-gown, or something of the sort, was hanging over the back of a chair.

I went to my room for my shoes, and then walked down the front stairs, intending to go through the house from bottom to top. I would go silently first, and then, if, as was likely enough, I ran across nothing, I could start kicking in doors, turning people out of bed, and raising hell till I turned up the girl. I wanted to find her as soon as possible, but she had too long a start for a few minutes to make much difference now; so if I didn't waste any time, neither did I run.

I was half-way between the second and first floors when I saw something move below – or, rather, saw the movement of something without actually seeing it. It moved from the direction of the street-door towards the interior of the house. I was looking towards the elevator at the time as I walked down the stairs. The banister shut off my view of the street-door. What I saw was a flash of movement across half a dozen of the spaces between the banister's uprights. By the time I had brought my eyes into focus there, there was nothing to see. I thought I had seen a face, but that's what anybody would have thought in my position, and all I had actually seen was the movement of something pale.

The lobby, and what I could see of the corridors, were vacant when I reached the ground-floor. I started towards the rear of the building, and stopped. I heard, for the first time since I had awakened, a noise that I hadn't made. A shoe-sole had scuffed on the stone steps the other side of the street-door.

I walked to the front door, got one hand on the bolt, the other hand on the latch, snapped them back together, and yanked the door open with my left hand, letting my right hang within a twist of my gun.

Eric Collinson stood on the top step.

"What the hell are you doing here?" I asked sourly.

It was a long story, and he was too excited to make it a clear one. As nearly as I could untangle it from his words, he had been in the habit of phoning Doctor Riese daily for reports on Gabrielle's progress. Today – or rather yesterday – and last night, he had failed to get the doctor on the wire. He had called up as late as two o'clock this morning. Doctor Riese was not at home, he had been told, and none of the household knew where he was or why he was not at home. Collinson had then, after the two-o'clock call, come to the neighborhood of the Temple, on the chance that he might see me and get some word of the girl. He hadn't intended, he said, coming to the door until he saw me looking out.

"Until you did what?" I asked.

"Saw you."

"When?"

"A minute ago, when you looked out."

"You didn't see me," I said. "What did you see?"

"Somebody looking out, peeping out. I thought it was you, and came up from the corner where I was sitting in the car. Is Gabrielle all right?"

'Sure," I said. There was no use telling him I was hunting for her, and have him blow up on me. "Don't talk so loud. Riese's people don't know where he is?"

"No – they seem worried. But that's all right if Gabrielle's all right." He put a hand on my upper arm. "Could – could I see her? Just for a second? I won't say anything. She needn't even know I've seen her. I don't mean now – but can't you arrange it?"

This bird was young, tall, strong, and perfectly willing to have himself broken into pieces for Gabrielle Leggett. I knew something was wrong. I didn't know what. I didn't know what I would have to do to make it right, and how much help I would need. I couldn't afford to turn him away. On the other hand, I couldn't give him the low-down on the racket – that would have turned him into a wild man. I said:

"Come in. I'm on an inspection trip. You can go along if you keep quiet, and afterwards we'll see what we can do."

He came in, looking and acting as if I were St. Peter letting him into Heaven. I closed the door and led him through the lobby, down the main corridor. So far as we could see we had the joint to ourselves. And then we didn't.

Gabrielle Leggett came around a corner just ahead of us. She was barefooted. Her only clothing was a yellow silk nightgown that was splashed with dark stains. In both hands, held out in front of her as she walked, she carried a large dagger, almost a sword. It was red and wet. Her hands and bare arms were red and wet. There was a dab of blood on one of her cheeks. Her eyes were clear, bright, and calm. Her small forehead was smooth, her mouth and chin firmly set.

She walked up to me, her untroubled gaze holding my probably troubled one, and said evenly, just as if she had expected to find me there, had come there to find me:

"Take it. It is evidence. I killed him."

I said: "Huh?"

Still looking straight into my eyes, she said:

"You are a detective. Take me to where they will hang me."

It was easier to move my hand than my tongue. I took the bloody dagger from her. It was a broad, thick-bladed weapon, double-edged, with a bronze hilt like a cross.

Eric Collinson pushed past me, babbling words that nobody could have made out, going for the girl with shaking outstretched hands. She shrank over against the wall, away from him, fear in her face.

"Don't let him touch me," she begged.

"Gabrielle," he cried, reaching for her.

"No, no," she panted.

I walked into his arms, my body between him and her, facing him, pressing him back with a hand against his chest, growling at him: "Be still, you."

He took my shoulders in his big brown hands and began pushing me out of the way. I got ready to rap him on the chin with the heavy bronze dagger hilt. But we didn't have to go that far: looking over me at the girl he forgot his intentions of forcing me out of his path, and his hands went loose on my shoulders. I leaned on the hand that I had on his chest, moving him back until he was against the wall; and then stepped away from him, a little to one side, so I could see both him and her facing each other from opposite walls.

"Be still till we see what's happened," I told him, and turned to the girl, pointing the dagger at her. "What's happened?"

She was calm again.

"Come," she said. "I'll show you. Don't let Eric come, please."

"He won't bother you," I promised.

She nodded at that, gravely, and led us back down the corridor, around the corner, and up to a small iron door that stood ajar. She went through first. I followed her. Collinson was at my heels. Fresh air hit us when we went through the door. I looked up and saw dim stars in a dark sky. I looked down again. In the light that came through the open door behind us I saw that we were walking on a floor of white marble, or pentagonal tiles that imitated white marble. The place was dark except for the light from behind us. I took my flashlight out.

Walking unhurriedly on bare feet that must have found the tiled floor chilly, she led us straight to a square grayish shape that loomed up ahead. When she halted close to it and said, "There," I clicked on my light.

The light glittered and glistened on a wide altar of brilliant white, crystal, and silver.

On the lowest of the three altar steps Doctor Riese lay dead on his back.

His face was composed, as if he were sleeping. His arms were straight down at his sides. His clothes were not rumpled, though his coat and vest were unbuttoned. His shirt was all blood. There were four holes in his shirt-front, all alike, all the size and shape that the weapon the girl had given me would have made. No blood was coming from his wounds now, but when I put a hand on his forehead I found it not quite cold. There was blood on the altar steps, and on the floor below, where his noseglasses, unbroken, on the end of their black ribbon, lay.

I straightened up and swung the beam of my light into the girl's face. She blinked and squinted, but her face showed nothing except that physical discomfort.

"You killed him?" I asked.

Young Collinson came out of his trance to bawl: "No."

"Shut up," I told him, stepping closer to the girl, so he couldn't wedge himself between us. "Did you?" I asked her again.

"Are you surprised?" she inquired quietly. "You were there when my step-mother told of the cursed Dain blood in me, and of what it had done and would do to me and those who touched me. Is this," she asked, pointing at the dead man, "anything you should not have expected?"

"Don't be silly," I said while I tried to figure out her calmness. I had seen her coked to the ears before, but this wasn't that. I didn't know what this was. "Why did you kill him?"

Collinson grabbed my arm and yanked me around to face him. He was all on fire.

"We can't stand here talking," he cried. "We've got to get her out of here, away from this. We've got to hide the body, or put it some place where they'll think somebody else did it. You know how those things are done. I'll take her home. You fix it."

"Yeah?" I asked. "What'll I do? Frame it on one of the Filipino boys, so they'll hang him instead of her?"

"Yes, that's it. You know how to –"

"Like hell that's it," I said. "You've got nice ideas."

His face got redder. He stammered: "I didn't – didn't mean so they'll hang anybody, really. I wouldn't want you to do that. But couldn't it be fixed for him to get away? I – I'd make it worth his while. He could –"

"Turn it off," I growled. "You're wasting our time."

"But you've got to," he insisted. "You came here to see that nothing happened to Gabrielle and you've got to go through with it."

"Yeah? You're a smart boy."

"I know it's a lot to ask, but I'll pay –"

"Stop it." I took my arm out of his hands and turned to the girl again, asking: "Who else was here when it happened?"

"No one."

I played my light around, on the corpse and altar, all over the floor, on the walls, and saw nothing I hadn't seen before. The walls were white, smooth, and unbroken except for the door we had come through and another, exactly like it, on the other side. These four straight whitewashed walls, undecorated, rose six stories to the sky.

I put the dagger beside Riese's body, snapped off the light, and told Collinson: "We'll take Miss Leggett up to her room."

"For God's sake let's get her out of here – out of this house – now, while there's time!"

I said she'd look swell running through the streets barefooted and with nothing on but a bloodstained nightie.

I turned on the light again when I heard him making noises. He was jerking his arms out of his overcoat. He said: "I've got the car at the corner, and I can carry her to it," and started towards her with the coat held out.

She ran around to the other side of me, moaning: "Oh, don't let him touch me."

I put out an arm to stop him. It wasn't strong enough. The girl got behind me. Collinson pursued her and she came around in front. I felt like the center of a merry-go-round, and didn't like the feel of it. When Collinson came in front of me, I drove my shoulder into his side, sending him staggering over against the side of the altar. Following him, I planted myself in front of the big sap and blew off steam: "Stop it. If you want to play with us you've got to stop cutting up, and do what you're told, and let her alone. Yes or no?"

He straightened his legs under him and began: "But, man, you can't –"

"Let her alone," I said. "Let me alone. The next break you make I'm going to sock your jaw with the flat of a gun. If you want it now, say so. Will you behave?"

He muttered: "All right."

I turned around to see the girl, a gray shadow, running towards the open door, her bare feet making little noise on the tiles. My shoes made an ungodly racket as I went after her. Just inside the door I caught her with an arm around her waist.

The next moment my arm was jerked away, and I was flung aside, smacking into the wall, slipping down on one knee. Collinson, looking eight feet tall in the darkness, stood close to me, storming down at me, but all I could pick out of his many words was a "damn you."

I was in a swell mood when I got up from my knee. Playing nursemaid to a crazy girl wasn't enough: I had to be chucked around by her boy friend. I put all the hypocrisy I had into my voice when I said casually, "You oughtn't to do that," to him and went over to where the girl was standing by the door.

"We'll go up to your room now," I told her.

"Not Eric," she protested.

"He won't bother you," I promised again, hoping there'd be more truth to it this time. "Go ahead."

She hesitated, then went through the doorway. Collinson, looking partly sheepish, partly savage, and altogether discontented, followed me through. I closed the door, asking the girl if she had the key. "No," she said, as if she hadn't known there was a key.

We rode up in the elevator, the girl keeping me always between her and her fiancé, if that's what he still was. He stared fixedly at nothing. I studied her face, still trying to dope her out, to decide whether she had been shocked back into sanity or farther away from it. Looking at her, the first guess seemed likely, but I had a hunch it wasn't. We saw nobody between the altar and her room. I switched on her lights and we went in. I closed the door and put my back against it. Collinson put his overcoat and hat on a chair and stood beside them, folding his arms, looking at Gabrielle. She sat on the edge of the bed and looked at my feet.

"Tell us the whole thing, quick," I commanded.

She looked up at my face and said: "I should like to go to sleep now."

That settled the question of her sanity, so far as I was concerned: she hadn't any. But now I had another thing to worry me. This room was not exactly as it had been before. Something had been changed in it since I had been there not many minutes ago. I shut my eyes, trying to shake up my memory for a picture of it then; I opened my eyes, looking at it now.

"Can't I?" she asked.

I let her question wait while I put my gaze around the room, checking it up item by item, as well as I could. The only change I could put my finger on was Collinson's coat and hat on the chair. There was no mystery to their presence; and the chair, I decided, was what had bothered me. It still did. I went to it and picked up his coat. There was nothing under it. That's what was wrong: a green dressing-gown, or something of the sort, had been there before, and was not there now. I didn't see it elsewhere in the room, and didn't have enough confidence in its being there to search for it. The green mules were under the bed.

I said to the girl:

"Not now. Go in the bathroom and wash the blood off, and then get dressed. Take your clothes in there with you. When you're dressed, give your nightgown to Collinson." I turned to him. "Put it in your pocket and keep it there. Don't go out of the room until I come back, and don't let anybody in. I won't be gone long. Got a gun?"

"No," he said, "but I –"

The girl got up from the bed, came over to stand close in front of me, and interrupted him.

"You can't leave me here with him," she said earnestly. "I won't have it. Isn't it enough that I've killed one man tonight? Don't make me kill another." She was earnest, but not excited, speaking as if her words were quite reasonable.

"I've got to go out for a while," I said. "And you can't stay alone. Do what I tell you."

"Do you know what you're doing?" she asked in a thin, tired voice. "You can't know, or you wouldn't do it." Her back was to Collinson. She lifted her face so that I saw rather than heard the nearly soundless words her lips formed: "Not Eric. Let him go."

She had me woozy: a little more of it and I would have been ready for the cell next to hers: I was actually tempted to let her have her way. I jerked a thumb at the bathroom and said: "You can stay in there till I come back, if you want, but he'll have to stay here."

She nodded hopelessly and went into the dressing-alcove. When she crossed from there to the bathroom, carrying clothes in her arms, a tear was shiny beneath each eye.

I gave my gun to Collinson. The hand in which he took it was tight and shaky. He was making a lot of noise with his breath. I said: "Now don't be a sap. Give me some help instead of trouble for once. Nobody in or out: if you have to shoot, shoot."

He tried to say something, couldn't, grabbed my nearest hand, and did his best to disable it. I took it away from him and went down to the scene of Doctor Riese's murder. I had some difficulty in getting there. The iron door through which we had passed a few minutes ago was now locked. The lock seemed simple enough. I went at it with the fancy attachments on my pocketknife, and presently had the door open.

I didn't find the green gown inside. I didn't find Riese's body on the altar steps. It was nowhere in sight. The dagger was gone. Every trace of blood, except where the pool on the white floor had left a faintly yellow stain, was gone. Somebody had been tidying up.

11 GOD

I WENT BACK to the lobby, to a recess where I had seen a telephone. The phone was there, but dead. I put it down and set out for Minnie Hershey's room on the sixth floor. I hadn't been able to do much with the mulatto so far, but she was apparently devoted to her mistress, and, with the telephone useless, I needed a messenger.

I opened the mulatto's door – lockless as the others – and went in, closing it behind me. Holding a hand over the lens of my flashlight, I snapped it on. Enough light leaked through my fingers to show me the brown girl in her bed, sleeping. The windows were closed, the atmosphere heavy, with a faint stuffiness that was familiar, the odor of a place where flowers had died.

I looked at the girl in bed. She was on her back, breathing through open mouth, her face more like an Indian's than ever with the heaviness of sleep on it. Looking at her, I felt drowsy myself. It seemed a shame to turn her out. Perhaps she was dreaming of – I shook my head, trying to clear it of the muddle settling there. Lilies of the valley, moonflowers – flowers that had died – was honeysuckle one of the flowers? The question seemed to be important. The flashlight was heavy in my hand, too heavy. Hell with it: I let it drop. It hit my foot, puzzling me: who had touched my foot? Gabrielle Leggett, asking to be saved from Eric Collinson? That didn't make sense, or did it? I tried to shake my head again, tried desperately. It weighed a ton, and would barely move from side to side. I felt myself swaying; put out a foot to steady myself. The foot and leg were weak, limber, doughy. I had to take another step or fall, took it, forced my head up and my eyes open, hunting for a place to fall, and saw the window six inches from my face.

I swayed forward till the sill caught my thighs, holding me up. My hands were on the sill. I tried to find the handles on the bottom of the window, wasn't sure that I had found them, but put everything I had into an upward heave. The window didn't budge. My hands seemed nailed down. I think I sobbed then; and, holding the sill with my right hand, I beat the glass from the center of the pane with my open left.

Air that stung like ammonia came through the opening. I put my face to it, hanging to the sill with both hands, sucking air in through mouth, nose, eyes, ears, and pores, laughing, with water from my stinging eyes trickling down into my mouth. I hung there drinking air until I was reasonably sure of my legs under me again, and of my eyesight, until I knew myself able to think and move again, though neither speedily nor surely. I couldn't afford to wait longer. I put a handkerchief over my mouth and nose and turned away from the window.

Not more than three feet away, there in the black room, a pale bright thing like a body, but not like flesh, stood writhing before me.

It was tall, yet not so tall as it seemed, because it didn't stand on the floor, but hovered with its feet a foot or more above the floor. Its feet – it had feet, but I don't know what their shape was. They had no shape, just as the thing's legs and torso, arms and hands, head and face, had no shape, no fixed form. They writhed, swelling and contracting, stretching and shrinking, not greatly, but without pause. An arm drifted into the body, was swallowed by the body, came out again as if poured out. The nose stretched down over the gaping shapeless mouth, shrank back up into the face till it was flush with the pulpy cheeks, grew out again. Eyes spread until they were one gigantic eye that blotted out the whole upper face, diminished until there was no eye, and opened in their places again.

The legs were now one leg like a twisting, living pedestal, and then three, and then two. No feature or member ever stopped twisting, quivering, writhing long enough for its average outline, its proper shape, to be seen. The thing was a thing like a man who floated above the floor, with a horrible grimacing greenish face and pale flesh that was not flesh, that was visible in the dark, and that was as fluid and as unresting and as transparent as tidal water.

I knew – then – that I was off-balance from breathing the dead-flower stuff, but I couldn't – though I tried to – tell myself that I did not see this thing. It was there. It was there within reach of my hand if I leaned forward, shivering, writhing, between me and the door. I didn't believe in the supernatural – but what of that? The thing was there. It was there and it was not, I knew, a trick of luminous paint, a man with a sheet over him. I gave it up. I stood there with my handkerchief jammed to my nose and mouth, not stirring, not breathing, possibly not even letting my blood run through me. I was there, and the thing was there, and I stayed where I was.

The thing spoke, though I could not say that I actually heard the words: it was as if I simply became, through my entire body, conscious of the words:

"Down, enemy of the Lord God; down on your knees."

I stirred then, to lick my lips with a tongue drier than they were.

"Down, accursed of the Lord God, before the blow falls."

An argument was something I understood. I moved my handkerchief sufficiently to say: "Go to hell." It had a silly sound, especially in the creaking voice I had used.

The thing's body twisted convulsively, swayed, and bent towards me.

I dropped my handkerchief and reached for the thing with both hands. I got hold of the thing, and I didn't. My hands were on it, *in* it to the wrists, into the center of it, and shut on it. And there was nothing in my hands but dampness without temperature, neither warm nor cold.

That same dampness came into my face when the thing's face floated into mine. I bit at its face – yes – and my teeth closed on nothing, though I could see and feel that my face was *in* its face. And in my hands, on my arms, against my body, the thing squirmed and writhed, shuddered and shivered, swirling wildly now, breaking apart, reuniting madly in the black air.

Through the thing's transparent flesh I could see my hands clenched in the center of its damp body. I opened them, struck up and down inside it with stiff crooked fingers, trying to gouge it open; and I could see it being torn apart, could see it flowing together after my clawing fingers had passed; but all I could feel was its dampness.

Now another feeling came to me, growing quickly once it had started – of an immense suffocating weight bearing me down. This thing that had no solidity had weight, weight that was pressing me down, smothering me. My knees were going soft. I spit its face out of my mouth, tore my right hand free from its body and struck up at its face, and felt nothing but its dampness brushing my fist.

I clawed at its insides again with my left hand, tearing at this substance that was so plainly seen, so faintly felt. And then on my left hand I saw something else – blood. Blood that was dark and thick and real covered my hand, dripped from it, running out between my fingers.

I laughed and got strength to straighten my back against the monstrous weight on me, wrenching at the thing's insides again, croaking: "I'll gut you plenty." More blood came through my fingers. I tried to laugh again, triumphantly, and couldn't, choking instead. The thing's weight on me was twice what it had been. I staggered back, sagging against the wall, flattening myself against it to keep from sliding down it.

Air from the broken window, cold, pure, bitter, came over my shoulder to sting my nostrils, to tell me – by its difference from the air I had been breathing – that not the thing's weight, but the poisonous flower-smelling stuff, had been bearing me down.

The thing's greenish pale dampness squirmed over my face and body. Coughing, I stumbled through the thing, to the door, got the door open, and sprawled out in the corridor that was now as dark as the room I had just left.

As I fell, somebody fell over me. But this was no indescribable thing. It was human. The knees that hit my back were human, sharp. The grunt that blew hot breath in my ear was human, surprised. The arm my fingers caught was human, thin. I thanked God for its thinness. The corridor air was doing me a lot of good, but I was in no shape to do battle with an athlete.

I put what strength I had into my grip on the thin arm, dragging it under me as I rolled over on as much of the rest of its owner as I could cover. My other hand, flung out across the man's thin body as I rolled, struck something that was hard and metallic on the floor. Bending my wrist, I got my fingers on it, and recognized its feel: it was the over-size dagger with which Riese had been killed. The man I was lolling on had, I guessed, stood beside the door of Minnie's room, waiting to carve me when I came out; and my fall had saved me, making him miss me with the blade, tripping him. Now he was kicking, jabbing, and butting up at me from his face-down position on the floor, with my hundred and ninety pounds anchoring him there.

Holding on to the dagger, I took my right hand from his arm and spread it over the back of his head, grinding his face into the carpet, taking it easy, waiting for more of the strength that was coming back into me with each breath. A minute or two more and I would be ready to pick him up and get words out of him.

But I wasn't allowed to wait that long. Something hard pounded my right shoulder, then my back, and then struck the carpet close to our heads. Somebody was swinging a club at me.

I rolled off the skinny man. The club-swinger's feet stopped my rolling. I looped my right arm above the feet, took another rap on the back, missed the legs with my circling arm, and felt skirts against my hand. Surprised, I pulled my hand back. Another chop of the club – on my side this time – reminded me that this was no place for gallantry. I made a fist of my hand and struck back at the skirt. It folded around my fist: a meaty shin stopped my fist. The shin's owner snarled above me and backed off before I could hit out again.

Scrambling up on hands and knees, I bumped my head into wood – a door. A hand on the knob helped me up. Somewhere inches away in the dark the club swished again. The knob turned in my hand. I went in with the door, into the room, and made as little noise as I could, practically none, shutting the door.

Behind me in the room a voice said, very softly, but also very earnestly:

"Go right out of here or I'll shoot you."

It was the plump blonde maid's voice, frightened. I turned, bending low in case she did shoot. Enough of the dull gray of approaching daylight came into this room to outline a shadow sitting up in bed, holding something small and dark in one outstretched hand.

"It's me," I whispered.

"Oh, you!" She didn't lower the thing in her hand.

"You in on the racket?" I asked, risking a slow step towards the bed.

"I do what I'm told and I keep my mouth shut, but I'm not going in for strong-arm work, not for the money they're paying me."

"Swell," I said, taking more and quicker steps towards the

bed. "Could I get down through this window to the floor below if I tied a couple of sheets together?"

"I don't know – Ouch! Stop!"

I had her gun – a .32 automatic – in my right hand, her wrist in my left, and was twisting them. "Let go," I ordered, and she did. Releasing her hand, I stepped back, picking up the dagger I had dropped on the foot of the bed.

I tiptoed to the door and listened. I couldn't hear anything. I opened the door slowly, and couldn't hear anything, couldn't see anything in the dim grayness that went through the door. Minnie Hershey's door was open, as I had left it when I tumbled out. The thing I had fought wasn't there. I went into Minnie's room, switching on the lights. She was lying as she had lain before, sleeping heavily. I pocketed my gun, pulling down the covers, picked Minnie up, and carried her over to the maid's room.

"See if you can bring her to life," I told the maid, dumping the mulatto on the bed beside her.

"She'll come around all right in a little while: they always do."

I said, "Yeah?" and went out, down to the fifth floor, to Gabrielle Leggett's room.

Gabrielle's room was empty. Collinson's hat and overcoat were gone; so were the clothes she had taken into the bathroom; and so was the bloody nightgown.

I cursed the pair of them, trying to show no favoritism, but probably concentrating most on Collinson; snapped off the lights; and ran down the front stairs, feeling as violent as I must have looked, battered and torn and bruised, with a red dagger in one hand, a gun in the other. For four flights of downgoing I heard nothing, but when I reached the second floor a noise like small thunder was audible below me. Dashing down the remaining flight, I identified it as somebody's knocking on the front door. I hoped the somebody wore a uniform. I went to the door, unlocked it, and pulled it open.

Eric Collinson was there, wild-eyed, white-faced, and frantic.

"Where's Gaby?" he gasped.

"God damn you," I said and hit him in the face with the gun.

He drooped, bending forward, stopped himself with hands on the vestibule's opposite walls, hung there a moment, and slowly pulled himself upright again. Blood leaked from a corner of his mouth.

"Where's Gaby?" he repeated doggedly.

"Where'd you leave her?"

"Here. I was taking her away. She asked me to. She sent me out first to see if anybody was in the street. Then the door closed."

"You're a smart boy," I grumbled. "She tricked you, still trying to save you from that lousy curse. Why in hell couldn't you do what I told you? But come on; we'll have to find her."

She wasn't in any of the reception rooms off the lobby. We left the lights on in them and hurried down the main corridor.

A small figure in white pajamas sprang out of a doorway and fastened itself on me, tangling itself in my legs, all but upsetting me. Unintelligible words came out of it. I pulled it loose from me and saw that it was the boy Manuel. Tears wet his panic-stricken face and crying ruined all the words he was trying to speak.

"Take it easy, son." I said. "I can't understand a word you're saying."

I understood, "Don't let him kill her."

"Who kill who?" I asked. "And take your time."

He didn't take his time, but I managed to hear "father" and "mama."

"Your father's trying to kill your mother?" I asked, since that seemed the most likely combination.

His head went up and down.

"Where?" I asked.

He fluttered a hand at the iron door ahead. I started towards it, and stopped.

"Listen, son," I bargained. "I'd like to help your mother, but I've got to know where Miss Leggett is first. Do you know where she is?"

"In there with them," he cried. "Oh, hurry, do hurry!"

"Right. Come on, Collinson," and we raced for the iron door.

The door was closed, but not locked. I yanked it open. The altar was glaring white, crystal, and silver in an immense beam of blue-white light that slanted down from an edge of the roof.

At one end of the altar Gabrielle crouched, her face turned up into the beam of light. Her face was ghastly white and expressionless in the harsh light. Aaronia Haldorn lay on the altar step where Riese had lain. There was a dark bruise on her forehead. Her hands and feet were tied with broad white bands of cloth, her arms tied to her body. Most of her clothes had been torn off.

Joseph, white-robed, stood in front of the altar, and of his wife. He stood with both arms held high and widespread, his back and neck bent so that his bearded face was lifted to the sky. In his right hand he held an ordinary hornhandled carving knife, with a long curved blade. He was talking to the sky, but his back was to us, and we couldn't hear his words. As we came through the door, he lowered his arms and bent over his wife. We were still a good thirty feet from him. I bellowed:

"Joseph!"

He straightened again, turning, and when the knife came into view I saw that it was still clean, shiny.

"Who calls Joseph, a name that is no more?" he asked, and I'd be a liar if I didn't admit that, standing there – for I had halted ten feet from him, with Collinson beside me – looking at him, listening to his voice, I didn't begin to feel that perhaps, after all, nothing very terrible had been about to happen.

"There is no Joseph," he went on, not waiting for an answer to his question. "You may now know, as the world shall soon know, that he who went among you as Joseph was not Joseph, but God Himself. Now that you know, go."

I should have said, "Bunk," and jumped him. To any other man, I would have. To this one I didn't. I said: "I'll have to take Miss Leggett and Mrs. Haldorn with me," and said it indecisively, almost apologetically.

He drew himself up taller, and his white-bearded face was stern.

"Go," he commanded; "go from me before your defiance leads to destruction."

Aaronia Haldorn spoke from where she lay tied on the step, spoke to me:

"Shoot. Shoot now – quick. Shoot."

I said to the man:

"I don't care what your right name is. You're going to the can. Now put your knife down."

"Blasphemer," he thundered, and took a step towards me. "Now you will die."

That should have been funny. It wasn't.

I yelled, "Stop," at him. He wouldn't stop. I was afraid. I fired. The bullet hit his cheek. I saw the hole it made. No muscle twitched in his face; not even his eyes blinked. He walked deliberately, not hurrying, towards me.

I worked the automatic's trigger, pumping six more bullets into his face and body. I saw them go in. And he came on steadily, showing in no way that he was conscious of them. His eyes and face were stern, but not angry. When he was close to me the knife in his hand went up high above his head. That's no way to fight with a knife; but he wasn't fighting: he was bringing retribution to me, and he paid as little attention to my attempts to stop him as a parent does to those of a small child he's punishing.

I was fighting. When the knife, shining over our heads,

started down I went in under it, bending my right forearm against his knife-arm, driving the dagger in my left hand at his throat. I drove the heavy blade into his throat, in till the hilt's cross stopped it. Then I was through.

I didn't know I had closed my eyes until I found myself opening them. The first thing I saw was Eric Collinson kneeling beside Gabrielle Leggett, turning her face from the glaring light-beam, trying to rouse her. Next I saw Aaronia Haldorn, apparently unconscious on the altar step, with the boy Manuel crying on her and pulling with too nervous hands at her bonds. Then I saw that I was standing with my legs apart, and that Joseph was lying between my feet, dead, with the dagger through his neck.

"Thank God he wasn't really God," I mumbled to myself.

A brown body in white brushed past me, and Minnie Hershey was throwing herself down in front of Gabrielle Leggett, crying:

"Oh, Miss Gabrielle, I thought that devil had come alive and was after you again."

I went over to the mulatto and took her by the shoulder, lifting her up, asking her: "How could he? Didn't you kill him dead?"

"Yes, sir, but –"

"But you thought he might have come back in another shape?"

"Y-yes, sir. I thought he was –" She stopped and worked her lips together.

"Me?" I asked.

She nodded, not looking at me.

OWEN FITZSTEPHAN and I ate another of Mrs. Schindler's good dinners that evening, though my eating was a matter of catching bites between words. His curiosity poked at me with questions, requests to have this or that point made clear, and orders to keep talking whenever I stopped for breath or food.

"You could have got me in on it," he had complained before our soup was in front of us. "I knew the Haldorns, you know, or, at least, had met them once or twice at Leggett's. You could have used that as an excuse for somehow letting me in on the affair, so that I'd now have first-hand knowledge of what happened, and why; instead of having to depend on what I can get out of you and what the newspapers imagine their readers would like to think had happened."

"I had," I said, "enough grief with the one guy I did let in on it – Eric Collinson."

"Whatever trouble you had with him was your own fault, for selecting the wrong assistant, when such a better one was available. But come, my boy, I'm listening. Let's have the story, and then I can tell you where you erred."

"Sure," I agreed, "you'll be able to do that. Well, the Haldorns were originally actors. Most of what I can tell you comes from her, so a lot of maybes will have to be hung on it in spots. Fink won't talk at all; and the other help – maids, Filipino boys, Chinese cook, and the like – don't seem to know anything that helps much. None of them seems to have been let in on the trick stuff.

"As actors, Aaronia Haldorn says, she and Joseph were just pretty good, not getting on as well as they wanted to. About a year ago she ran into an old acquaintance – a onetime trouper – who had chucked the stage for the pulpit, and had made a go of it, now riding in Packards instead of day-coaches. That gave her something to think about. Thinking in that direction meant, pretty soon, thinking about Aimee, Buchman, Jeddu what's-his-name, and the other headliners. And in the end her thinking came to, why not us? They – or she: Joseph was a lightweight – rigged up a cult that pretended to be the revival of an old Gaelic church, dating from King Arthur's time, or words to that effect."

"Yes," said Fitzstephan; "Arthur Machen's. But go on."

"They brought their cult to California because everybody does, and picked San Francisco because it held less competition than Los Angeles. With them they brought a little fellow named Tom Fink who had at one time or another been in charge of the mechanical end of most of the well-known stage magicians' and illusionists' acts; and Fink's wife, a big village-smith of a woman.

"They didn't want a mob of converts: they wanted them few but wealthy. The racket got away to a slow start – until they landed Mrs. Rodman. She fell plenty. They took her for one of her apartment buildings, and she also footed the remodeling bill. The stage mechanic Fink was in charge of the remodeling, and did a neat job. They didn't need the kitchens that were dotted, one to an apartment, through the building, and Fink knew how to use part of that scattered kitchen-space for concealed rooms and cabinets; and he knew how to adapt the gas and water pipes, and the electric wiring, to his hocus-pocus.

"I can't give you the mechanical details now; not till we've had time to take the joint apart. It's going to be interesting. I saw some of their work – mingled right in with it – a ghost made by an arrangement of lights thrown up on steam rising from a padded pipe that had been pushed into a dark room through a concealed opening in the wainscoting under a bed.

The part of the steam that wasn't lighted was invisible in the darkness, showing only a manshape that quivered and writhed, and that was damp and real to the touch, without any solidity. You can take my word for its being a weird stunt, especially when you've been filled up with the stuff they pumped into the room before they turned their spook loose on you. I don't know whether they used ether or chloroform or what: its odor was nicely disguised with some sort of flower perfume. This spook – I fought with it, on the level, and even thought I had it bleeding, not knowing I had cut my hand breaking a window to let air in. It was a beaut: it made a few minutes seem like a lot of hours to me.

"Till the very last, when Haldorn went wild, there wasn't anything crude about their work. They kept the services – the whole public end of the cult – as dignified and orderly and restrained as possible. The hocus-pocusing was all done in the privacy of the victim's bedroom. First the perfumed gas was pumped in. Then the illuminated steam spook was sicked on him, with a voice coming out of the same pipe – or maybe there was another arrangement for that – to give him his orders, or whatever was to be given. The gas kept him from being too sharp-eyed and suspicious, and also weakened his will, so he'd he more likely to do what he was told. It was slick enough; and I imagine they squeezed themselves out a lot of pennies that way.

"Happening in the victim's room, when he was alone, these visions had a lot of authority, and the Haldorns gave them more by the attitude they took towards them. Discussion of these visions was not absolutely prohibited, but was discouraged. They were supposed – these spook sessions – to be confidential between the victim and his God, to be too sacred to be bragged about. Mentioning them, even to Joseph, unless there was some special reason for having to mention them, was considered in bad taste, indelicate. See how nicely that would work out? The Haldorns seemed to be *not* trying to capitalize on these spook sessions, seemed not to know what took place in them, and therefore to have no interest in whether the victim carried out his spook-given instructions or not. Their stand was that that was simply and strictly a concern of the victim's and his God's."

"That's very good," Fitzstephan said, smiling delightedly, "a neat reversal of the usual cult's – the usual sect's, for that matter – insistence on confession, public testimony, or some other form of advertising the mysteries. Go on."

I tried to eat. He said:

"What of the members, the customers? How do they like their cult now? You've talked to some of them, haven't you?"

"Yeah," I said; "but what can you do with people like them? Half of them are still willing to string along with Aaronia Haldorn. I showed Mrs. Rodman one of the pipes that the spooks came out of. When she had gasped once and gulped twice she offered to take us to the cathedral and show us that the images there, including the one on the cross, were made out of even more solid and earthly materials than steam; and asked us if we would arrest the bishop on proof that no actual flesh and blood – whether divine or not – was in the monstrance. I thought O'Gar, who's a good Catholic, would blackjack her."

"The Colemans weren't there, were they? The Ralph Colemans?"

"No."

"Too bad," he said, grinning. "I must look Ralph up and question him. He'll be in hiding by now, of course, but he's worth hunting out. He always has the most consistently logical and creditable reasons for having done the most idiotic things. He is" – as if that explained it – "an advertising man." Fitzstephan frowned at the discovery that I was eating again, and said impatiently: "Talk, my boy, talk."

"You've met Haldorn," I said. "What did you think of him?"

"I saw him twice, I think. He was, undoubtedly, impressive."

"He was," I agreed. "He had what he needed. Ever talk to him?"

"No; that is, not except to exchange the polite equivalents of 'pleased to meet you.' "

"Well, he looked at you and spoke to you, and things happened inside you. I'm not the easiest guy in the world to dazzle, I hope; but he had me going. I came damned near to believing he was God toward the last. He was quite young – in his thirties: they'd had the coloring – the pigment – in his hair and beard killed to give him that Father Joseph front. His wife says she used to hypnotize him before he went into action, and that without being hypnotized he wasn't so effective on people. Later he got so that he could hypnotize himself without her help, and toward the last it became a permanent condition with him.

"She didn't know her husband had fallen for Gabrielle till after the girl had come to stay in the Temple. Until then she thought that Gabrielle was to him, as to her, just another customer – one whose recent troubles made her a very likely prospect. But Joseph had fallen for her, and wanted her. I don't know how far he had worked on her, nor even how he had worked on her, but I suppose he was sewing her up by using his hocus-pocus against her fear of the Dain curse. Anyway, Doctor Riese finally discovered that everything wasn't going well with her. Yesterday morning he told me he was coming back to see her that evening, and he did come back, but he didn't see her; and I didn't see him – not then.

"He went back to see Joseph before he came up to the girl's room, and managed to overhear Joseph giving instructions to the Finks. That should have been fine, but wasn't. Riese was foolish enough to let Joseph know he had overheard him. Joseph locked Riese up – a prisoner.

"They had cut loose on Minnie from the very beginning.

She was a mulatto, and therefore susceptible to that sort of game, and she was devoted to Gabrielle Leggett. They had chucked visions and voices at the poor girl until she was dizzy. Now they decided to make her kill Riese. They drugged him and put him on the altar. They ghosted her into thinking that he was Satan – this is serious: they did this – come up from hell to carry Gabrielle down and keep her from becoming a saint. Minnie was ripe for it – poor boogie – and when the spirit told her that she had been selected to save her mistress, that she'd find the anointed weapon on her table, she followed the instructions the spirit gave her. She got out of bed, picked up the dagger that had been put on her table, went down to the altar, and killed Riese.

"To play safe, they pumped some of the gas into my room, to keep me slumbering while Minnie was at work. But I had been nervous, jumpy, and was sleeping in a chair in the center of the room, instead of on the bed, close to the gas-pipe; so I came out of the dope before the night was far gone.

"By this time, Aaronia Haldorn had made a couple of discoveries: first, that her husband's interest in the girl wasn't altogether financial; and second, that he had gone off center, was a dangerous maniac. Going around hypnotized all the time, what brains he had – not a whole lot to start with, she says – had become completely scrambled. His success in flimflamming his followers had gone to his head. He thought he could do anything, get away with anything. He had dreams, she says, of the entire world deluded into belief in his divinity: he didn't see why that would be any – or much – more difficult than fooling the handful that he had fooled. She thinks he actually had insane notions of his own divinity. I don't go that far. I think he knew well enough that he wasn't divine, but thought he could kid the rest of the world. These details don't make much difference: the thing is that he was a nut who saw no limit to his power.

"Aaronia Haldorn had, she says, no knowledge of Riese's

murder until after it was done. Joseph, using the vision-and-voice trick, sent Gabrielle down to see the corpse on the altar step. That would fit in, you see, with his original scheme to tie her to him by playing his divinity against her curse. Apparently, he intended joining her there, and putting on an act of some sort for her. But Collinson and I interrupted that. Joseph and Gabrielle heard us talking at the door, so Joseph held back, not joining her at the altar, and she came to meet us. Joseph's plan was successful this far: the girl actually believed the curse had been responsible for Riese's death. She told us she had killed him and ought to be hanged for it.

"As soon as I saw Riese's body I knew she hadn't killed him. He was lying in an orderly position. It was plain he had been doped before being killed. Then the door leading to the altar, which I imagined was kept locked, was open, and she didn't know anything about the key. There was a chance that she had been in on the killing, but none that she had done it alone as she confessed.

"The place was scientifically equipped for eavesdropping: both of the Haldorns heard her confession. Aaronia got busy manufacturing evidence to fit the confession. She went up to Gabrielle's room and got her dressing-gown; got the bloody dagger from where I had dropped it beside the body after taking it from the girl; wrapped the dagger in the dressing-gown, and stuck them in a corner where the police could find them easy enough. Meanwhile, Joseph is working in another direction. He doesn't – as his wife does – want Gabrielle carried off to jail or the booby-hatch. He wants her. He wants her belief in her guilt and responsibility to tie her to him, not take her away. He removes Riese's remains – tucking them in one of the concealed cabinets – and has the Finks clean up the mess. He's overheard Collinson trying to persuade me to hush up the doings, and so he knows he can count on the boy – the only other exactly sane witness – to keep quiet if I'm taken care of.

"Kill yourself into a hole, and the chances are a time comes when you have to kill yourself out. To this nut Joseph now, 'taking care of' me is simply a matter of another murder. He and the Finks – though I don't think we're going to prove their part – went to work on Minnie with the spooks again. She had killed Riese docilely enough: why not me? You see, they were handicapped by not being equipped for this wholesale murdering into which they had all of a sudden plunged. For instance, except for my gun and one of the maids' – which they didn't know anything about – there wasn't a firearm in the place; and the dagger was the only other weapon – until they got to dragging in carving sets and plumber's helpers. Then, too, I suppose, there were the sleeping customers to consider – Mrs. Rodman's probable dislike for being roused by the noise of her spiritual guides ganging up on a roughneck sleuth. Anyway, the idea was that Minnie could be induced to walk up to me and stick the dagger into me in a quiet way.

"They had found the dagger again, in the dressing-gown, where Aaronia had stuck it; and Joseph began suspecting that his wife was double-crossing him. When he caught her in the act of turning on the dead-flower stuff so strong in Minnie's room that it knocked her completely out – put her so soundly asleep that a dozen ghosts couldn't have stirred her into action – he was sure of her treachery; and, up to his neck now, decided to kill *her*."

"His wife?" Fitzstephan asked.

"Yeah, but what difference does that make? It might as well have been anybody else for all the sense it makes. I hope you're not trying to keep this nonsense straight in your mind. You know damned well all this didn't happen."

"Then what," he asked, looking puzzled, "did happen?"

"I don't know. I don't think anybody knows. I'm telling you what I saw plus the part of what Aaronia Haldorn told me which fits in with what I saw. To fit in with what I saw, most of it must have happened very nearly as I've told you.

If you want to believe that it did, all right. I don't. I'd rather believe I saw things that weren't there."

"Not now," he pleaded. "Later, after you've finished the story, you can attach your ifs and buts to it, distorting and twisting it, making it as cloudy and confusing and generally hopeless as you like. But first please finish it, so I'll see it at least once in its original state before you start improving it."

"You actually believe what I've told you so far?" I asked.

He nodded, grinning, and said that he not only believed it but liked it.

"What a childish mind you've got," I said. "Let me tell you the story about the wolf that went to the little girl's grandmother's house and –"

"I always liked that one, too; but finish this one now. Joseph had decided to kill his wife."

"All right. There's not much more. While Minnie was being worked on, I popped into her room, intending to rouse her and send her for help. Before I did any rousing, I was needing some myself: I had a couple of lungfuls of the gas. The Finks must have turned the ghost loose on me, because Joseph was probably on his way downstairs with his wife at that time. He had faith enough in his divinity-shield, or he was nutty enough, to take her down and tie her on the altar before he carved her. Or maybe he had a way of fitting that stunt into his scheme, or maybe he simply had a liking for bloody theatricals. Anyway, he probably took her down there while I was up in Minnie's room going around and around with the ghost.

"The ghost had me sweating ink, and when I finally left him and tottered out into the corridor, the Finks jumped me. I say they did, and know it; but it was too dark for me to see them. I beat them off, got a gun, and went downstairs. Collinson and Gabrielle were gone from where I had left them. I found Collinson: Gabrielle had put him outside and shut the door on him. The Haldorns' son – a kid of thirteen or so – came to us with the news that Papa was about to kill Mama, and that Gabrielle was with them. I killed Haldorn, but I almost didn't. I put seven bullets in him. Hard-coated .32's go in clean, without much of a thump, true enough; but I put seven of them in him – in his face and body – standing close and firing pointblank – and he didn't even know it. That's how completely he had himself hypnotized. I finally got him down by driving the dagger through his neck."

I stopped. Fitzstephan asked: "Well?"

"Well what?"

"What happened after that?"

"Nothing," I said. "That's the kind of a story it is. I warned you there was no sense to it."

"But what was Gabrielle doing there?"

"Crouching beside the altar, looking up at the pretty spotlight."

"But why was she there? What was her reason for being there? Had she been called there again? Or was she there of her own free will? How did she come to be there? What was she there for?"

"I don't know. She didn't know. I asked her. She didn't know she was there."

"But surely you could learn something from the others?"

"Yeah," I said; "what I've told you, chiefly from Aaronia Haldorn. She and her husband ran a cult, and he went crazy and began murdering people, and how could she help it? Fink won't talk. He's a mechanic, yes; and he put in his trick-machinery for the Haldorns and operated it; but he doesn't know what happened last night. He heard a lot of noises, but it was none of his business to go poking his nose out to see what it was: the first he knew anything was wrong was when some police came and started giving him hell. Mrs. Fink's gone. The other employees probably don't really know anything, though it's a gut they could make some good guesses.

Manuel, the little boy, is too frightened to talk – and will be sure to know nothing when he gets over his fright. What we're up against is this: if Joseph went crazy and committed some murders on his own hook, the others, even though they unknowingly helped him, are in the clear. The worst any of them can draw is a light sentence for taking part in the cult swindle. But if any of them admits knowing anything, then he lets himself in for trouble as an accomplice in the murder. Nobody's likely to do that."

"I see," Fitzstephan said slowly. "Joseph is dead, so Joseph did everything. How will you get around that?"

"I won't," I said; "though the police will at least try to. My end's done, so Madison Andrews told me a couple of hours ago."

"But if, as you say, you aren't satisfied that you've learned the whole truth of the affair, I should think you –"

"It's not me," I said. "There's a lot I'd like to do yet, but I was hired, this time, by Andrews, to guard her while she was in the Temple. She isn't there now, and Andrews doesn't think there's anything further to be learned about what happened there. And, as far as guarding her is necessary, her husband ought to be able to do that."

"Her what?"

"Husband."

Fitzstephan thumped his stein down on the table so that beer sloshed over the sides.

"Now there you are," he said accusingly. "You didn't tell me anything about that. God only knows how much else there is that you've not told me."

"Collinson took advantage of the confusion to carry her off to Reno, where they won't have to wait the Californian three days for their license. I didn't know they'd gone till Andrews jumped on my neck three or four hours later. He was kind of unpleasant about it, which is one of the ways we came to stop being client and operative."

"I didn't know he was opposed to Collinson as a husband for her."

"I don't know that he is, but he didn't think this the time, nor that the way, for their wedding."

"I can understand that," he said as we got up from the table. "Andrews likes to have his way in most things."

PART 3

QUESADA

13 THE CLIFF ROAD

ERIC COLLINSON wired me from Quesada:

> COME IMMEDIATELY STOP NEED YOU STOP TROUBLE DANGER STOP MEET ME AT SUNSET HOTEL STOP DO NOT COMMUNICATE STOP GABRIELLE MUST NOT KNOW STOP HURRY
>
> ERIC CARTER

The telegram came to the agency on Friday morning.

I wasn't in San Francisco that morning. I was up in Martinez dickering with a divorced wife of Phil Leach, alias a lot of names. We wanted him for spreading reams of orphan paper through the Northwest, and we wanted him badly. This ex-wife – a sweet-looking little blonde telephone operator – had a fairly recent photograph of Phil, and was willing to sell it.

"He never thought enough of me to risk passing any bum checks so I could have things," she complained. "I had to bring in my own share of the nut. So why shouldn't I make something out of him now, when I guess some tramp's getting plenty? Now how much will you give for it?"

She had an exaggerated idea of how much the photograph was worth to us, of course, but I finally made the deal with her. But it was after six when I returned to the city, too late for a train that would put me in Quesada that night. I packed a bag, got my car from the garage, and drove down.

Quesada was a one-hotel town pasted on the rocky side of a young mountain that sloped into the Pacific Ocean some eighty miles from San Francisco. Quesada's beach was too abrupt and hard and jagged for bathing, so Quesada had never got much summer-resort money. For a while it had been a hustling rum-running port, but that racket was dead now: bootleggers had learned there was more profit and less worry in handling domestic hooch than imported. Quesada had gone back to sleep.

I got there at eleven-something that night, garaged my car, and crossed the street to the Sunset Hotel. It was a low, sprawled-out, yellow building. The night clerk was alone in the lobby, a small effeminate man well past sixty who went to a lot of trouble to show me that his fingernails were rosy and shiny.

When he had read my name on the register he gave me a sealed envelope – hotel stationery – addressed to me in Eric Collinson's handwriting. I tore it open and read:

> Do not leave the hotel
> until I have seen you.
>
> E. C.

"How long has this been here?" I asked.

"Since about eight o'clock. Mr. Carter waited for you for more than an hour, until after the last stage came in from the railroad."

"He isn't staying here?"

"Oh, dear, no. He and his bride have got the Tooker place, down in the cove."

Collinson wasn't the sort of person to whose instructions I'd pay a whole lot of attention. I asked:

"How do you get there?"

"You'd never be able to find it at night," the clerk assured me, "unless you went all the way around by the East road, and not then, I'm sure, unless you knew the country."

"Yeah? How do you get there in the daytime?"

"You go down this street to the end, take the fork of the road on the ocean side, and follow that up along the cliff. It isn't really a road, more a path. It's about three miles to the house, a brown house, shingled all over, on a little hill. It's easily enough found in the daytime if you remember to keep to the right, to the ocean side, all the way down. But you'd never, never in the world, be able to find –"

"Thanks," I said, not wanting to hear the story all over again.

He led me up to a room, promised to call me at five, and I was asleep by midnight.

The morning was dull, ugly, foggy, and cold when I climbed out of bed to say, "All right, thanks," into the phone. It hadn't improved much by the time I had got dressed and gone downstairs. The clerk said there was not a chance in the world of getting anything to eat in Quesada before seven o'clock.

I went out of the hotel, down the street until it became a dirt road, kept to the dirt road until it forked, and turned into the branch that bent toward the ocean. This branch was never really a road from its beginning, and soon was nothing but a rocky path climbing along the side of a rocky ledge that kept pushing closer to the water's edge. The side of the ledge became steeper and steeper, until the path was simply an irregular shelf on the face of a cliff – a shelf eight or ten feet wide in places, no more than four or five in others. Above and behind the path, the cliff rose sixty or seventy feet; below and in front, it slanted down a hundred or more to ravel out in the ocean. A breeze from the general direction of China was pushing fog over the top of the cliff, making noisy lather of sea water at its bottom.

Rounding a corner where the cliff was steepest – was, in fact, for a hundred yards or so, straight up and down – I stopped to look at a small ragged hole in the path's outer rim. The hole was perhaps six inches across, with fresh loose earth piled in a little semicircular mound on one side, scattered on the other. It wasn't exciting to look at, but it said plainly to even such a city man as I was: here a bush was uprooted not so long ago.

There was no uprooted bush in sight. I chucked my cigarette away and got down on hands and knees, putting my head out over the path's rim, looking down. I saw the bush twenty feet below. It was perched on the top of a stunted tree that grew almost parallel to the cliff, fresh brown earth sticking to the bush's roots. The next thing that caught my eye was also brown – a soft hat lying upside down between two pointed gray rocks, half-way down to the water. I looked at the bottom of the cliff and saw the feet and legs.

They were a man's feet and legs, in black shoes and dark trousers. The feet lay on the top of a water-smoothed boulder, lay on their sides, six inches part, both pointing to the left. From the feet, dark-trousered legs slanted down into the water, disappearing beneath the surface a few inches above the knees. That was all I could see from the cliff road.

I went down the cliff, though not at that point. It was a lot too steep there to be tackled by a middle-aged fat man. A couple of hundred yards back, the path had crossed a crooked ravine that creased the cliff diagonally from top to bottom. I returned to the ravine and went down it, stumbling, sliding, sweating and swearing, but reaching the bottom all in one piece, with nothing more serious the matter with me than torn fingers, dirty clothes, and ruined shoes.

The fringe of rock that lay between cliff and ocean wasn't meant to be walked on, but I managed to travel over it most of the way, having to wade only once or twice, and then not up to my knees. But when I came to the spot where the feet and legs were I had to go waist-deep into the Pacific to lift the body, which rested on its back on the worn slanting side of a mostly submerged boulder, covered from thighs up by frothing water. I got my hands under the armpits, found solid ground for my feet, and lifted.

It was Eric Collinson's body. Bones showed through flesh and clothing on his shattered back. The back of his head – that half of it – was crushed. I dragged him out of the water and put him down on dry rocks. His dripping pockets contained a hundred and fifty-four dollars and eighty-two cents, a watch, a knife, a gold pen and pencil, papers, a couple of letters, and a memoranda book. I spread out the papers, letters, and book; and read them; and learned nothing except that what was written in them hadn't anything to do with his death. I couldn't find anything else – on him or near him – to tell me more about his death than the uprooted bush, the hat caught between rocks, and the position of his body had told me.

I left him there and went back to the ravine, panting and heaving myself up it to the cliff path, returning to where the bush had grown. I didn't find anything there in the way of significant marks, footprints, or the like. The path was chiefly hard rock. I went on along it. Presently the cliff began to bend away from the ocean, lowering the path along its side. After another half-mile there was no cliff at all, merely a bush-grown ridge at whose foot the path ran. There was no sun yet. My pants stuck disagreeably to my chilly legs. Water squelched in my torn shoes. I hadn't had any breakfast. My cigarettes had got wet. My left knee ached from a twist it had got sliding down the ravine. I cursed the detective business and slopped on along the path.

The path took me away from the sea for a while, across the neck of a wooded point that pushed the ocean back, down into a small valley, up the side of a low hill; and then I saw the house the night clerk had described.

It was a rather large two-story building, roof and walls brown-shingled, set on a hump in the ground close to where the ocean came in to take a quarter-mile u-shaped bite out of the coast. The house faced the water. I was behind it. There was nobody in sight. The ground-floor windows were closed, with drawn blinds. The second-story windows were open. Off to one side were some smaller farm buildings.

I went around to the front of the house. Wicker chairs and

a table were on the screened front porch. The screened porch-door was hooked on the inside. I rattled it noisily. I rattled it off and on for at least five minutes, and got no response. I went around to the rear again, and knocked on the back door. My knocking knuckles pushed the door open half a foot. Inside was a dark kitchen and silence. I opened the door wider, knocking on it again, loudly. More silence.

I called: "Mrs. Collinson."

When no answer came I went through the kitchen and a darker dining room, found a flight of stairs, climbed them, and began poking my head into rooms.

There was nobody in the house.

In one bedroom, a .38 automatic pistol lay in the center of the floor. There was an empty shell close to it, another under a chair across the room, and a faint odor of burnt gunpowder in the air. In one corner of the ceiling was a hole that a .38 bullet could have made, and, under it on the floor, a few crumbs of plaster. The bed-clothes were smooth and undisturbed. Clothes in the closet, things on and in table and bureau, told me this was Eric Collinson's bedroom.

Next to it, according to the same sort of evidence, was Gabrielle's bedroom. Her bed had not been slept in, or had been made since being slept in. On the floor of her closet I found a black satin dress, a once-white handkerchief, and a pair of black suede slippers, all wet and muddy – the handkerchief also wet with blood. In her bathroom – in the tub – were a bath-towel and a face-towel, both stained with mud and blood, and still damp. On her dressing-table was a small piece of thick white paper that had been folded. White powder clung to one crease. I touched it with the end of my tongue – morphine.

I went back to Quesada, changed my shoes and socks, got breakfast and a supply of dry cigarettes, and asked the clerk – a dapper boy, this one – who was responsible for law and order there.

"The marshal's Dick Cotton," he told me; "but he went up to the city last night. Ben Rolly's deputy sheriff. You can likely find him over at his old man's office."

"Where's that?"

"Next door to the garage."

I found it, a one-story red brick building with wide glass windows labeled *J. King Rolly, Real Estate, Mortgages, Loans, Stocks and Bonds, Insurance, Notes, Employment Agency, Notary Public, Moving and Storage*, and a lot more that I've forgotten.

Two men were inside, sitting with their feet on a battered desk behind a battered counter. One was a man of fifty-and, with hair, eyes, and skin of indefinite, washed-out tan shades – an amiable, aimless-looking man in shabby clothes. The other was twenty years younger and in twenty years would look just like him.

"I'm hunting," I said, "for the deputy sheriff."

"Me," the younger man said, easing his feet from desk to floor. He didn't get up. Instead, he put a foot out, hooked a chair by its rounds, pulled it from the wall, and returned his feet to the desk-top. "Set down. This is Pa," wiggling a thumb at the other man. "You don't have to mind him."

"Know Eric Carter?" I asked.

"The fellow honeymooning down to the Tooker place? I didn't know his front name was Eric."

"Eric Carter," the elder Rolly said; "that's the way I made out the rent receipt for him."

"He's dead," I told them. "He fell off the cliff road last night or this morning. It could have been an accident."

The father looked at the son with round tan eyes. The son looked at me with questioning tan eyes and said: "Tch, tch, tch."

I gave him a card. He read it carefully, turning it over to see that there was nothing on its back, and passed it to his father.

"Go down and take a look at him?" I suggested.

"I guess I ought to," the deputy sheriff agreed, getting up from his chair. He was a larger man than I had supposed – as big as the dead Collinson boy – and, in spite of his slouchiness, he had a nicely muscled body.

I followed him out to a dusty car in front of the office. Rolly senior didn't go with us.

"Somebody told you about it?" the deputy sheriff asked when we were riding.

"I stumbled on him. Know who the Carters are?"

"Somebody special?"

"You heard about the Riese murder in the San Francisco temple?"

"Uh-huh, I read the papers."

"Mrs. Carter was the Gabrielle Leggett mixed up in that, and Carter was the Eric Collinson."

"Tch, tch, tch," he said.

"And her father and step-mother were killed a couple of weeks before that."

"Tch, tch, tch," he said. "What's the matter with them?"

"A family curse."

"Sure enough?"

I didn't know how seriously he meant that question, though he seemed serious enough. I hadn't got him sized up yet. However, clown or not, he was the deputy sheriff stationed at Quesada, and this was his party. He was entitled to the facts. I gave them to him as we bounced over the lumpy road, gave him all I had, from Paris in 1913 to the cliff road a couple of hours ago.

"When they came back from being married in Reno, Collinson dropped in to see me. They had to stick around for the Haldorn bunch's trial, and he wanted a quiet place to take the girl: she was still in a daze. You know Owen Fitzstephan?"

"The writer fellow that was down here a while last year? Uh-huh."

"Well, he suggested this place."

"I know. The old man mentioned it. But what'd they take them aliases for?"

"To dodge publicity, and, partly, to try to dodge something like this."

He frowned vaguely and asked:

"You mean they expected something like this?"

"Well, it's easy to say, 'I told you so,' after things happen, but I've never thought we had the answer to either of the two mix-ups she's been in. And not having the answer – how could you tell what to expect? I didn't think so much of their going off into seclusion like this while whatever was hanging over her – if anything was – was still hanging over her, but Collinson was all for it. I made him promise to wire me if he saw anything funny. Well, he did."

Rolly nodded three or four times, then asked:

'What makes you think he didn't fall off the cliff?"

"He sent for me. Something was wrong. Outside of that, too many things have happened around his wife for me to believe in accidents."

"There's the curse, though," he said.

"Yeah," I agreed, studying his indefinite face, still trying to figure him out. "But thc troublc with it is it's worked out too well, too regularly. It's the first one I ever ran across that did."

He frowned over my opinion for a couple of minutes, and then stopped the car. "We'll have to get out here: the road ain't so good the rest of the way." None of it had been. "Still and all, you do hear of them working out. There's things that happen that makes a fellow think there's things in the world – in life – that he don't know much about." He frowned again as we set off afoot, and found a word he liked. "It's inscrutable," he wound up.

I let that go at that.

He went ahead up the cliff path, stopping of his own accord where the bush had been torn up, a detail I hadn't mentioned. I didn't say anything while he stared down at Collinson's body, looked searchingly up and down the face of the cliff, and then went up and down the path, bent far over, his tan eyes intent on the ground.

He wandered around for ten minutes or more, then straightened up and said: "There's nothing here that I can find. Let's go down."

I started back toward the ravine, but he said there was a better way ahead. There was. We went down it to the dead man.

Rolly looked from the corpse to the edge of the path high above us, and complained: "I don't hardly see how he could have landed just thataway."

"He didn't. I pulled him out of the water," I said, showing the deputy exactly where I had found the body.

"That would be more like it," he decided.

I sat on a rock and smoked a cigarette while he went around examining, touching, moving rocks, pebbles, and sand. He didn't seem to have any luck.

14 THE CRUMPLED CHRYSLER

WE CLIMBED TO the path again and went on to the Collinsons' house. I showed Rolly the stained towels, handkerchief, dress, and slippers; the paper that had held morphine; the gun on Collinson's floor, the hole in the ceiling, and the empty shells on the floor.

"That shell under the chair is where it was," I said; "but the other – the one in the corner – was here, close to the gun, when I saw it before."

"You mean it's been moved since you were here?"

"Yeah."

"But what good would that do anybody?" he objected.

"None that I know of, but it's been moved."

He had lost interest. He was looking at the ceiling. He said:

"Two shots and one hole. I wonder. Maybe the other went out the window."

He went back to Gabrielle Collinson's bedroom and examined the black velvet gown. There were some torn places in it – down near the bottom – but no bullet-holes. He put the dress down and picked up the morphine paper from the dressing-table.

"What do you suppose this is doing here?" he asked.

"She uses it. It's one of the things her step-mother taught her."

"Tch, tch, tch. Kind of looks like she might have done it."

"Yeah?"

"You know it does. She's a dope fiend, ain't she? They had had trouble, and he sent for you, and –" He broke off, pursed lips, then asked: "What time do you reckon he was killed?"

"I don't know. Maybe last night, on his way home from waiting for me."

"You were in the hotel all night?"

"From eleven-something till five this morning. Of course I could have sneaked out for long enough to pull a murder between those hours."

"I didn't mean nothing like that," he said. "I was just wondering. What kind of looking woman is this Mrs. Collinson-Carter? I never saw her."

"She's about twenty; five feet four or five; looks thinner than she really is; light brown hair, short and curly; big eyes that are sometimes brown and sometimes green; white skin; hardly any forehead; small mouth and teeth; pointed chin; no lobes on her ears, and they're pointed on top; been sick for a couple of months and looks it."

"Oughtn't be hard to pick her up," he said, and began poking into drawers, closets, trunks, and so on. I had poked into them on my first visit, and hadn't found anything interesting either.

"Don't look like she did any packing or took much of anything with her," he decided when he came back to where I was sitting by the dressing-table. He pointed a thick finger at the monogrammed silver toilet-set on the table. "What's the G. D. L. for?"

"Her name was Gabrielle Something Leggett before she was married."

"Oh, yes. She went away in the car, I reckon. Huh?"

"Did they have one down here?" I asked.

"He used to come to town in a Chrysler roadster when he didn't walk. She could only have took it out by the East road. We'll go out thataway and see."

Outside, I waited while he made circles around the house, finding nothing. In front of a shed where a car obviously had been kept he pointed at some tracks, and said, "Drove out this morning." I took his word for it.

We walked along a dirt road to a gravel one, and along that perhaps a mile to a gray house that stood in a group of red farm buildings. A small-boned, high-shouldered man who limped slightly was oiling a pump behind the house. Rolly called him Debro.

"Sure, Ben," he replied to Rolly's question. "She went by here about seven this morning, going like a bat out of hell. There wasn't anybody else in the car."

"How was she dressed?" I asked.

"She didn't have on any hat and a tan coat."

I asked him what he knew about the Carters: he was their nearest neighbor. He didn't know anything about them. He had talked to Carter two or three times, and thought him an agreeable enough young fellow. Once he had taken the missus over to call on Mrs. Carter, but Carter told them she was lying down, not feeling well. None of the Debros had ever seen her except at a distance, walking or riding with her husband.

"I don't guess there's anybody around here that's talked to her," he wound up, "except of course Mary Nunez."

"Mary working for them?" the deputy asked.

"Yes. What's the matter, Ben? Something the matter over there?"

"He fell off the cliff last night, and she's gone away without saying anything to anybody."

Debro whistled.

Rolly went into the house to use Debro's phone, reporting to the sheriff. I stayed outside with Debro, trying to get more – if only his opinions – out of him. All I got were expressions of amazement.

"We'll go over and see Mary," the deputy said when he came from the phone; and then, when we had left Debro, had crossed the road, and were walking through a field towards a cluster of trees: "Funny she wasn't there."

"Who is she?"

"A Mex. Lives down in the hollow with the rest of them.

Her man, Pedro Nunez, is doing a life-stretch in Folsom for killing a bootlegger named Dunne in a hijacking two–three years back."

"Local killing?"

"Uh-huh. It happened down in the cove in front of the Tooker place."

We went through the trees and down a slope to where half a dozen shacks – shaped, sized, and red-leaded to resemble boxcars – lined the side of a stream, with vegetable gardens spread out behind them. In front of one of the shacks a shapeless Mexican woman in a pink-checkered dress sat on an empty canned-soup box smoking a corncob pipe and nursing a brown baby. Ragged and dirty children played between the buildings, with ragged and dirty mongrels helping them make noise. In one of the gardens a brown man in overalls that had once been blue was barely moving a hoe.

The children stopped playing to watch Rolly and me cross the stream on conveniently placed stones. The dogs came yapping to meet us, snarling and snapping around us until one of the boys chased them. We stopped in front of the woman with the baby. The deputy grinned down at the baby and said:

"Well, well, ain't he getting to be a husky son-of-a-gun!"

The woman took the pipe from her mouth long enough to complain stolidly:

"Colic all the time."

"Tch, tch, tch. Where's Mary Nunez?"

The pipe-stem pointed at the next shack.

"I thought she was working for them people at the Tooker place," he said.

"Sometimes," the woman replied indifferently.

We went to the next shack. An old woman in a gray wrapper had come to the door, watching us while stirring something in a yellow bowl.

"Where's Mary?" the deputy asked.

She spoke over her shoulder into the shack's interior, and

moved aside to let another woman take her place in the doorway. This other woman was short and solidly built, somewhere in her early thirties, with intelligent dark eyes in a wide, flat face. She held a dark blanket together at her throat. The blanket hung to the floor all around her.

"Howdy, Mary," Rolly greeted her. "Why ain't you over to the Carters'?"

"I'm sick, Mr. Rolly." She spoke without accent. "Chills – so I just stayed home today."

"Tch, tch, tch. That's too bad. Have you had the doc?"

She said she hadn't. Rolly said she ought to. She said she didn't need him: she had chills often. Rolly said that might be so, but that was all the more reason for having him: it was best to play safe and have things like that looked after. She said yes but doctors took so much money, and it was bad enough being sick without having to pay for it. He said in the long run it was likely to cost folks more not having a doctor than having him. I had begun to think they were going to keep it up all day when Rolly finally brought the talk around to the Carters again, asking the woman about her work there.

She told us she had been hired two weeks ago, when they took the house. She went there each morning at nine – they never got up before ten – cooked their meals, did the housework, and left after washing the dinner dishes in the evening – usually somewhere around seven-thirty. She seemed surprised at the news that Collinson – Carter to her – had been killed and his wife had gone away. She told us that Collinson had gone out by himself, for a walk, he said, right after dinner the previous night. That was at about half-past six, dinner having been, for no special reason, a little early. When she left for home, at a few minutes past seven, Mrs. Carter had been reading a book in the front second-story room.

Mary Nunez couldn't, or wouldn't, tell us anything on which I could base a reasonable guess at Collinson's reason for sending for me. She knew, she insisted, nothing about them except that Mrs. Carter didn't seem happy – wasn't happy. She – Mary Nunez – had figured it all out to her own satisfaction: Mrs. Carter loved someone else, but her parents had made her marry Carter; and so, of course, Carter had been killed by the other man, with whom Mrs. Carter had now run away. I couldn't get her to say that she had any grounds for this belief other than her woman's intuition, so I asked her about the Carters' visitors.

She said she had never seen any.

Rolly asked her if the Carters ever quarreled. She started to say, "No," and then, rapidly, said they did, often, and were never on good terms. Mrs. Carter didn't like to have her husband near her, and several times had told him, in Mary's hearing, that if he didn't go away from her and stay away she would kill him. I tried to pin Mary down to details, asking what had led up to these threats, how they had been worded, but she wouldn't be pinned down. All she remembered positively, she told us, was that Mrs. Carter had threatened to kill Mr. Carter if he didn't go away from her.

"That pretty well settles that," Rolly said contentedly when we had crossed the stream again and were climbing the slope toward Debro's.

"What settles what?"

"That his wife killed him."

"Think she did?"

"So do you."

I said: "No."

Rolly stopped walking and looked at me with vague worried eyes.

"Now how can you say that?" he remonstrated. "Ain't she a dope fiend? And cracked in the bargain, according to your own way of telling it? Didn't she run away? Wasn't them things she left behind torn and dirty and bloody? Didn't she threaten to kill him so much that he got scared and sent for you?"

"Mary didn't hear threats," I said. "They were warnings – about the curse. Gabrielle Collinson really believed in it, and thought enough of him to try to save him from it. I've been through that before with her. That's why she wouldn't have married him if he hadn't carried her off while she was too rattled to know what she was doing. And she was afraid on that account afterwards."

"But who's going to believe – ?"

"I'm not asking anybody to believe anything," I growled, walking on again. "I'm telling you what I believe. And while I'm at it I'll tell you I believe Mary Nunez is lying when she says she didn't go to the house this morning. Maybe she didn't have anything to do with Collinson's death. Maybe she simply went there, found the Collinsons gone, saw the bloody things and the gun – kicking that shell across the floor without knowing it – and then beat it back to her shack, fixing up that chills story to keep herself out of it; having had enough of that sort of trouble when her husband was sent over. Maybe not. Anyway, that would be how nine out of ten women of her sort in her place would have played it; and I want more proof before I believe her chills just happened to hit her this morning."

"Well," the deputy sheriff asked; "if she didn't have nothing to do with it, what difference does all that make anyway?"

The answers I thought up to that were profane and insulting. I kept them to myself.

At Debro's again, we borrowed a loose-jointed touring car of at least three different makes, and drove down the East road, trying to trace the girl in the Chrysler. Our first stop was at the house of a man named Claude Baker. He was a lanky sallow person with an angular face three or four days behind the razor. His wife was probably younger than he, but looked older – a tired and faded thin woman who might have been pretty at one time. The oldest of their six children was a bow-legged, freckled girl of ten; the youngest was a fat and noisy infant in its first year. Some of the in-betweens were boys and some girls, but they all had colds in their heads. The whole Baker family came out on the porch to receive us. They hadn't seen her, they said: they were never up as early as seven o'clock. They knew the Carters by sight, but knew nothing about them. They asked more questions than Rolly and I did.

Shortly beyond the Baker house the road changed from gravel to asphalt. What we could see of the Chrysler's tracks seemed to show that it had been the last car over the road. Two miles from Baker's we stopped in front of a small bright green house surrounded by rose bushes. Rolly bawled:

"Harve! Hey, Harve!"

A big-boned man of thirty-five or so came to the door, said, "Hullo, Ben," and walked between the rose bushes to our car. His features, like his voice, were heavy, and he moved and spoke deliberately. His last name was Whidden. Rolly asked him if he had seen the Chrysler.

"Yes, Ben, I saw them," he said. "They went past around a quarter after seven this morning, hitting it up."

"They?" I asked, while Rolly asked: "Them?"

"There was a man and a woman – or a girl – in it. I didn't get a good look at them – just saw them whizz past. She was driving, a kind of small woman she looked like from here, with brown hair."

"What did the man look like?"

"Oh, he was maybe forty, and didn't look like he was very big either. A pinkish face, he had, and gray coat and hat."

"Ever see Mrs. Carter?" I asked.

"The bride living down the cove? No. I seen him, but not her. Was that her?"

I said we thought it was.

"The man wasn't him," he said. "He was somebody I never seen before."

"Know him again if you saw him?"

"I reckon I would – if I saw him going past like that."

Four miles beyond Whidden's we found the Chrysler. It was a foot or two off the road, on the left-hand side, standing on all fours with its radiator jammed into a eucalyptus tree. All its glass was shattered, and the front third of its metal was pretty well crumpled. It was empty. There was no blood in it. The deputy sheriff and I seemed to be the only people in the vicinity.

We ran around in circles, straining our eyes at the ground, and when we got through we knew what we had known at the beginning – the Chrysler had run into a eucalyptus tree. There were tire-marks on the road, and marks that could have been footprints on the ground by the car; but it was possible to find the same sort of marks in a hundred places along that, or any other, road. We got into our borrowed car again and drove on, asking questions wherever we found someone to question; and all the answers were: No, we didn't see her or them.

"What about this fellow Baker?" I asked Rolly as we turned around to go back. "Debro saw her alone. There was a man with her when she passed Whidden's. The Bakers saw nothing, and it was in their territory that the man must have joined her."

"Well," he said, argumentatively, "it could of happened that way, couldn't it?"

"Yeah, but it might be a good idea to do some more talking to them."

"If you want to," he consented without enthusiasm. "But don't go dragging me into any arguments with them. He's my wife's brother."

That made a difference. I asked:

"What sort of man is he?"

"Claude's kind of shiftless, all right. Like the old man says, he don't manage to raise nothing much but kids on that farm of his, but I never heard tell that he did anybody any harm."

"If you say he's all right, that's enough for me," I lied. "We won't bother him."

15 I'VE KILLED HIM

SHERIFF FEENEY, fat, florid, and with a lot of brown mustache, and district attorney Vernon, sharp-featured, aggressive, and hungry for fame, came over from the county seat. They listened to our stories, looked the ground over, and agreed with Rolly that Gabrielle Collinson had killed her husband. When Marshal Dick Cotton – a pompous, unintelligent man in his forties – returned from San Francisco, he added his vote to the others. The coroner and his jury came to the same opinion, though officially they limited themselves to the usual "person or persons unknown," with recommendations involving the girl.

The time of Collinson's death was placed between eight and nine o'clock Friday night. No marks not apparently caused by his fall had been found on him. The pistol found in his room had been identified as his. No fingerprints were on it. I had an idea that some of the county officials half suspected me of having seen to that, though nobody said anything of that sort. Mary Nunez stuck to her story of being kept home by chills. She had a flock of Mexican witnesses to back it up. I couldn't find any to knock holes in it. We found no further trace of the man Whidden had seen. I tried the Bakers again, by myself, with no luck. The marshal's wife, a frail youngish woman with a weak pretty face and nice shy manners, who worked in the telegraph office, said Collinson had sent off his wire to me early Friday morning. He was pale and shaky, she said, with dark-rimmed, bloodshot eyes. She had supposed he was drunk, though she hadn't smelled alcohol on his breath.

Collinson's father and brother came down from San Francisco. Hubert Collinson, the father, was a big calm man who looked capable of taking as many more millions out of Pacific Coast lumber as he wanted. Laurence Collinson was a year or two older than his dead brother, and much like him in appearance. Both Collinsons were careful to say nothing that could be interpreted as suggesting they thought Gabrielle had been responsible for Eric's death, but there was little doubt that they did think so.

Hubert Collinson said quietly to me, "Go ahead; get to the bottom of it;" and thus became the fourth client for whom the agency had been concerned with Gabrielle's affairs.

Madison Andrews came down from San Francisco. He and I talked in my hotel room. He sat on a chair by the window, cut a cube of tobacco from a yellowish plug, put it in his mouth, and decided that Collinson had committed suicide.

I sat on the side of the bed, set fire to a Fatima, and contradicted him:

"He wouldn't have torn up the bush if he'd gone over willingly."

"Then it was an accident. That was a dangerous road to be walked in the dark."

"I've stopped believing in accidents," I said. "And he had sent me an SOS. And there was the gun that had been fired in his room."

He leaned forward in his chair. His eyes were hard and watchful. He was a lawyer cross-examining a witness.

"You think Gabrielle was responsible?"

I wouldn't go that far. I said:

"He was murdered. He was murdered by – I told you two weeks ago that we weren't through with that damned curse, and that the only way to get through with it was to have the Temple business sifted to the bottom."

"Yes, I remember," he said without quite sneering. "You advanced the theory that there was some connecting link between her parents' deaths and the trouble she had at the Haldorns'; but, as I recall it, you had no idea what the link might be. Don't you think that deficiency has a tendency to make your theory a little – say – vaporous?"

"Does it? Her father, step-mother, physician, and husband have been killed, one after the other, in less than two months; and her maid jailed for murder. All the people closest to her. Doesn't that look like a program? And" – I grinned at him – "are you sure it's not going further? And if it does, aren't you the next closest person to her?"

"Preposterous!" He was very much annoyed now. "We know about her parents' deaths, and about Riese's, and that there was no link between them. We know that those responsible for Riese's murder are now either dead or in prison. There's no getting around that. It's simply preposterous to say there are links between one and another of these crimes when we know there's none."

"We don't know anything of the kind," I insisted. "All we know is that we haven't found the links. Who profits – or could hope to profit – by what has happened?"

"Not a single person so far as I know."

"Suppose she died? Who'd get the estate?"

"I don't know. There are distant relations in England or France, I dare say."

"That doesn't get us very far," I growled. "Anyway, nobody's tried to kill her. It's her friends who get the knock-off."

The lawyer reminded me sourly that we couldn't say that nobody had tried to kill her – or had succeeded – until we found her. I couldn't argue with him about that. Her trail still ended where the eucalyptus tree had stopped the Chrysler.

I gave him a piece of advice before he left:

"Whatever you believe, there's no sense in your taking unnecessary chances: remember that there might be a program, and you might be next on it. It won't hurt to be careful."

He didn't thank me. He suggested, unpleasantly, that doubtless I thought he should hire private detectives to guard him.

Madison Andrews had offered a thousand-dollar reward for information leading to discovery of the girl's whereabouts. Hubert Collinson had offered another thousand, with an additional twenty-five hundred for the arrest and conviction of his son's murderer. Half the population of the county had turned bloodhound. Anywhere you went you found men walking, or even crawling, around, searching fields, paths, hills, and valleys for clues, and in the woods you were likely to find more amateur gumshoes than trees.

Her photographs had been distributed and published widely. The newspapers, from San Diego to Vancouver, gave us a tremendous play, whooping it up in all the colored ink they had. All the San Francisco and Los Angeles Continental operatives who could be pulled off other jobs were checking Quesada's exits, hunting, questioning, finding nothing. Radio broadcasters helped. The police everywhere, all the agency's branches, were stirred up.

And by Monday all this hubbub had brought us exactly nothing.

Monday afternoon I went back to San Francisco and told all my troubles to the Old Man. He listened politely, as if to some moderately interesting story that didn't concern him personally, smiled his meaningless smile, and, instead of any assistance, gave me his pleasantly expressed opinion that I'd eventually succeed in working it all out to a satisfactory conclusion.

Then he told me that Fitzstephan had phoned, trying to get in touch with me. "It may be important. He would have gone down to Quesada to find you if I hadn't told him I expected you."

I called Fitzstephan's number.

"Come up," he said. "I've got something. I don't know

whether it's a fresh puzzle, or the key to a puzzle; but it's something."

I rode up Nob Hill on a cable car and was in his apartment within fifteen minutes.

"All right, spring it," I said as we sat down in his paper-, magazine-, and book-littered living room.

"Any trace of Gabrielle yet?" he asked.

"No. But spring the puzzle. Don't be literary with me, building up to climaxes and the like. I'm too crude for that – it'd only give me a bellyache. Just spread it out for me."

"You'll always be what you are," he said, trying to seem disappointed and disgusted, but not succeeding because he was – inwardly – too excited over something. "Somebody – a man – called me up early Saturday morning – half-past one – on the phone. He asked: 'Is this Fitzstephan?' I said: 'Yes;' and then the voice said: 'Well, I've killed him.' He said it just like that. I'm sure of those exact words, though they weren't very clear. There was a lot of noise on the line, and the voice seemed distant.

"I didn't know who it was – what he was talking about. I asked: 'Killed who? Who is this?' I couldn't understand any of his answer except the word 'money.' He said something about money, repeating it several times, but I could understand only that one word. There were some people here – the Marquards, Laura Joines with some man she'd brought, Ted and Sue Van Slack – and we had been in the middle of a literary free-for-all. I had a wisecrack on my tongue – something about Cabell being a romanticist in the same sense that the wooden horse was Trojan – and didn't want to be robbed of my opportunity to deliver it by this drunken joker, or whoever he was, on the phone. I couldn't make heads or tails of what he was saying, so I hung up and went back to my guests.

"It never occurred to me that the phone conversation could have had any meaning until yesterday morning, when I read about Collinson's death. I was at the Colemans', up in Ross.

I went up there Saturday morning, for the week-end, having finally run Ralph to earth." He grinned. "And I made him glad enough to see me leave this morning." He became serious again. "Even after hearing of Collinson's death, I wasn't convinced that my phone call was of any importance, had any meaning. It was such a silly sort of thing. But of course I meant to tell you about it. But look – this was in my mail when I got home this morning."

He took an envelope from his pocket and tossed it over to me. It was a cheap and shiny white envelope of the kind you can buy anywhere. Its corners were dark and curled, as if it had been carried in a pocket for some time. Fitzstephan's name and address had been printed on it, with a hard pencil, by someone who was a rotten printer, or who wanted to be thought so. It was postmarked San Francisco, nine o'clock Saturday morning. Inside was a soiled and crookedly torn piece of brown wrapping paper, with one sentence – as poorly printed with pencil as the address – on it:

ANY BODY THAT WANTS MRS. CARTER
CAN HAVE SAME BY PAYING $10000 –

There was no date, no salutation, no signature.

"She was seen driving away alone as late as seven Saturday morning," I said. "This was mailed here, eighty miles away, in time to be postmarked at nine – taken from the box in the first morning collection, say. That's one to get wrinkles over. But even that's not as funny as its coming to you instead of to Andrews, who's in charge of her affairs, or her father-in-law, who's got the most money."

"It is funny and it isn't," Fitzstephan replied. His lean face was eager. "There may be a point of light there. You know I recommended Quesada to Collinson, having spent a couple of months there last spring finishing *The Wall of Ashdod*, and gave him a card to a real estate dealer named Rolly – the deputy sheriff's father – there, introducing him as Eric Carter.

A native of Quesada might not know she was Gabrielle Collinson, née Leggett. In that case he wouldn't know how to reach her people except through me, who had sent her and her husband there. So the letter is sent to me, but starts off *Anybody that*, to be passed on to the interested persons."

"A native might have done that," I said slowly; "or a kidnapper who wanted us to think he was a native, didn't want us to think he knew the Collinsons."

"Exactly. And as far as I know none of the natives knew my address here."

"How about Rolly?"

"Not unless Collinson gave it to him. I simply scribbled the introduction on the back of a card."

"Said anything to anybody else about the phone call and this letter?" I asked.

"I mentioned the call to the people who were here Friday night – when I thought it was a joke or a mistake. I haven't shown this to anybody else. In fact," he said, "I was a little doubtful about showing it at all – and still am. Is it going to make trouble for me?"

"Yeah, it will. But you oughtn't mind that. I thought you liked first-hand views of trouble. Better give me the names and addresses of your guests. If they and Coleman account for your whereabouts Friday night and over the week-end, nothing serious will happen to you; though you'll have to go down to Quesada and let the county officials third-degree you."

"Shall we go now?"

"I'm going back tonight. Meet me at the Sunset Hotel there in the morning. That'll give me time to work on the officials – so they won't throw you in the dungeon on sight."

I went back to the agency and put in a Quesada call. I couldn't get hold of Vernon or the sheriff, but Cotton was reachable. I gave him the information I had got from Fitzstephan, promising to produce the novelist for questioning the next morning.

The marshal said the search for the girl was still going on without results. Reports had come in that she had been seen – practically simultaneously – in Los Angeles, Eureka, Carson City, Denver, Portland, Tijuana, Ogden, San Jose, Vancouver, Porterville, and Hawaii. All except the most ridiculous reports were being run out.

The telephone company could tell me that Owen Fitzstephan's Saturday-morning phone call had not been a long-distance call, and that nobody in Quesada had called a San Francisco number either Friday night or Saturday morning.

Before I left the agency I visited the Old Man again, asking him if he would try to persuade the district attorney to turn Aaronia Haldorn and Tom Fink loose on bail.

"They're not doing us any good in jail," I explained, "and, loose, they might lead us somewhere if we shadowed them. He oughtn't to mind: he knows he hasn't a chance in the world of hanging murder-raps on them as things now stack up."

The Old Man promised to do his best, and to put an operative behind each of our suspects if they were sprung.

I went over to Madison Andrews' office. When I had told him about Fitzstephan's messages, and had given him our explanation of them, the lawyer nodded his bony white-thatched head and said:

"And whether that's the true explanation or not, the county authorities will now have to give up their absurd theory that Gabrielle killed her husband."

I shook my head sidewise.

"What?" he asked explosively.

"They're going to think the messages were cooked up to clear her," I predicted.

"Is that what you think?" His jaws got lumpy in front of his ears, and his tangled eyebrows came down over his eyes.

"I hope they weren't," I said; "because if it's a trick it's a damned childish one."

"How could it be?" he demanded loudly. "Don't talk

nonsense. None of us knew anything then. The body hadn't been found when –"

"Yeah," I agreed; "and that's why, if it turns out to have been a stunt, it'll hang Gabrielle."

"I don't understand you," he said disagreeably. "One minute you're talking about somebody persecuting the girl, and the next minute you're talking as if you thought she was the murderer. Just what do you think?"

"Both can be true," I replied, no less disagreeably. "And what difference does it make what I think? It'll be up to the jury when she's found. The question now is: what are you going to do about the ten-thousand-dollar demand – if it's on the level?"

"What I'm going to do is increase the reward for her recovery, with an additional reward for the arrest of her abductor."

"That's the wrong play," I said. "Enough reward money has been posted. The only way to handle a kidnapping is to come across. I don't like it any more than you do, but it's the only way. Uncertainty, nervousness, fear, disappointment, can turn even a mild kidnapper into a maniac. Buy the girl free, and then do your fighting. Pay what's asked when it's asked."

He tugged at his ragged mustache, his jaw set obstinately, his eyes worried. But the jaw won out.

"I'm damned if I'll knuckle down," he said.

"That's your business." I got up and reached for my hat. "Mine's finding Collinson's murderer, and having her killed is more likely to help me than not."

He didn't say anything.

I went down to Hubert Collinson's office. He wasn't in, but I told Laurence Collinson my story, winding up:

"Will you urge your father to put up the money? And to have it ready to pass over as soon as the kidnapper's instructions come?"

"It won't be necessary to urge him," he said immediately. "Of course we shall pay whatever is required to ensure her safety."

16 THE NIGHT HUNT

I CAUGHT THE 5:25 train south. It put me in Poston, a dusty town twice Quesada's size, at 7:30; and a rattle-trap stage, in which I was the only passenger, got me to my destination half an hour later. Rain was beginning to fall as I was leaving the stage across the street from the hotel.

Jack Santos, a San Francisco reporter, came out of the telegraph office and said: "Hello. Anything new?"

"Maybe, but I'll have to give it to Vernon first."

"He's in his room in the hotel, or was ten minutes ago. You mean the ransom letter that somebody got?"

"Yeah. He's already given it out?"

"Cotton started to, but Vernon headed him off, told us to let it alone."

"Why?"

"No reason at all except that it was Cotton giving it to us." Santos pulled the corners of his thin lips down. "It's been turned into a contest between Vernon, Feeney, and Cotton to see which can get his name and picture printed most."

"They been doing anything except that?"

"How can they?" he asked disgustedly. "They spend ten hours a day trying to make the front page, ten more trying to keep the others from making it, and they've got to sleep some time."

In the hotel I gave "nothing new" to some more reporters, registered again, left my bag in my room, and went down the hall to 204. Vernon opened the door when I had knocked. He was alone, and apparently had been reading the newspapers that made a pink, green, and white pile on the bed. The room was blue-gray with cigar smoke.

This district attorney was a thirty-year-old dark-eyed man who carried his chin up and out so that it was more prominent than nature had intended, bared all his teeth when he talked, and was very conscious of being a go-getter. He shook my hand briskly and said:

"I'm glad you're back. Come in. Sit down. Are there any new developments?"

"Cotton pass you the dope I gave him?"

"Yes." Vernon posed in front of me, hands in pockets, feet far apart. "What importance do you attach to it?"

"I advised Andrews to get the money ready. He won't. The Collinsons will."

"They will," he said, as if confirming a guess I had made. "And?" He held his lips back so that his teeth remained exposed.

"Here's the letter." I gave it to him. "Fitzstephan will be down in the morning."

He nodded emphatically, carried the letter closer to the light, and examined it and its envelope minutely. When he had finished he tossed it contemptuously to the table.

"Obviously a fraud," he said. "Now what, exactly, is this Fitzstephan's – is that the name? – story?"

I told him, word for word. When that was done, he clicked his teeth together, turned to the telephone, and told someone to tell Feeney that he – Mr. Vernon, district attorney – wished to see him immediately. Ten minutes later the sheriff came in wiping rain off his big brown mustache.

Vernon jerked a thumb at me and ordered: "Tell him."

I repeated what Fitzstephan had told me. The sheriff listened with an attentiveness that turned his florid face purple and had him panting. As the last word left my mouth, the district attorney snapped his fingers and said:

"Very well. He claims there were people in his apartment when the phone call came. Make a note of their names. He claims to have been in Ross over the week-end, with the –

who were they? Ralph Coleman? Very well. Sheriff, see that those things are checked up. We'll learn how much truth there is to it."

I gave the sheriff the names and addresses Fitzstephan had given me. Feeney wrote them on the back of a laundry list and puffed out to get the county's crime-detecting machinery going on them.

Vernon hadn't anything to tell me. I left him to his newspapers and went downstairs. The effeminate night clerk beckoned me over to the desk and said:

"Mr. Santos asked me to tell you that services are being held in his room tonight."

I thanked the clerk and went up to Santos' room. He, three other newshounds, and a photographer were there. The game was stud. I was sixteen dollars ahead at twelve-thirty, when I was called to the phone to listen to the district attorney's aggressive voice:

"Will you come to my room immediately?"

"Yeah." I gathered up my hat and coat, telling Santos: "Cash me in. Important call. I always have one when I get a little ahead of the game."

"Vernon?" he asked as he counted my chips.

"Yeah."

"It can't be much," he sneered, "or he'd've sent for Red too," nodding at the photographer, "so tomorrow's readers could see him holding it in his hand."

Cotton, Feeney, and Rolly were with the district attorney. Cotton – a medium-sized man with a round dull face dimpled in the chin – was dressed in black rubber boots, slicker, and hat that were wet and muddy. He stood in the middle of the room, his round eyes looking quite proud of their owner. Feeney, straddling a chair, was playing with his mustache; and his florid face was sulky. Rolly, standing beside him, rolling a cigarette, looked vaguely amiable as usual.

Vernon closed the door behind me and said irritably:

"Cotton thinks he's discovered something. He thinks –"

Cotton came forward, chest first, interrupting:

"I don't think nothing. I know durned well –"

Vernon snapped his fingers between the marshal and me, saying, just as snappishly:

"Never mind that. We'll go out there and see."

I stopped at my room for raincoat, gun, and flashlight. We went downstairs and climbed into a muddy car. Cotton drove. Vernon sat beside him. The rest of us sat in back. Rain beat on top and curtains, trickling in through cracks.

"A hell of a night to be chasing pipe dreams," the sheriff grumbled, trying to dodge a leak.

"Dick'd do a sight better minding his own business," Rolly agreed. "What's he got to do with what don't happen in Quesada?"

"If he'd take more care of what does happen there, he wouldn't have to worry about what's down the shore," Feeney said, and he and his deputy sniggered together.

Whatever point there was to this conversation was over my head. I asked:

"What's he up to?"

"Nothing," the sheriff told me. "You'll see that it's nothing, and, by God! I'm going to give him a piece of my mind. I don't know what's the matter with Vernon, paying any attention to him at all."

That didn't mean anything to me. I peeped out between curtains. Rain and darkness shut out the scenery, but I had an idea that we were headed for some point on the East road. It was a rotten ride – wet, noisy, and bumpy. It ended in as dark, wet, and muddy a spot as any we had gone through.

Cotton switched off the lights and got out, the rest of us following, slipping and slopping in wet clay up to our ankles.

"This is too damned much," the sheriff complained.

Vernon started to say something, but the marshal was walking away, down the road. We plodded after him, keeping together more by the sound of our feet squashing in the mud than by sight. It was black.

Presently we left the road, struggled over a high wire fence, and went on with less mud under our feet, but slippery grass. We climbed a hill. Wind blew rain down it into our faces. The sheriff was panting. I was sweating. We reached the top of the hill and went down its other side, with the rustle of sea-water on rocks ahead of us. Boulders began crowding grass out of our path as the descent got steeper. Once Cotton slipped to his knees, tripping Vernon, who saved himself by grabbing me. The sheriff's panting sounded like groaning now. We turned to the left, going along in single file, the surf close beside us. We turned to the left again, climbed a slope, and halted under a low shed without walls – a wooden roof propped on a dozen posts. Ahead of us a larger building made a black blot against the almost black sky.

Cotton whispered: "Wait till I see if his car's here."

He went away. The sheriff blew out his breath and grunted: "Damn such a expedition!" Rolly sighed.

The marshal returned jubilant.

"It ain't there, so he ain't here," he said. "Come on, it'll get us out of the wet anyways."

We followed him up a muddy path between bushes to the black house, up on its back porch. We stood there while he got a window open, climbed through, and unlocked the door. Our flashlights, used for the first time now, showed us a small neat kitchen. We went in, muddying the floor.

Cotton was the only member of the party who showed any enthusiasm. His face, from hat-brim to dimpled chin, was the face of a master of ceremonies who is about to spring what he is sure will be a delightful surprise. Vernon regarded him skeptically, Feeney disgustedly, Rolly indifferently, and I – who didn't know what we were there for – no doubt curiously.

It developed that we were there to search the house. We

did it, or at least Cotton did it while the rest of us pretended to help him. It was a small house. There was only one room on the ground-floor besides the kitchen, and only one – an unfinished bedroom – above. A grocer's bill and a tax-receipt in a table-drawer told me whose house it was – Harvey Whidden's. He was the big-boned deliberate man who had seen the stranger in the Chrysler with Gabrielle Collinson.

We finished the ground-floor with a blank score, and went upstairs. There, after ten minutes of poking around, we found something. Rolly pulled it out from between bedslats and mattress. It was a small flat bundle wrapped in a white linen towel.

Cotton dropped the mattress, which he had been holding up for the deputy to look under, and joined us as we crowded around Rolly's package. Vernon took it from the deputy sheriff and unrolled it on the bed. Inside the towel were a package of hair-pins, a lace-edged white handkerchief, a silver hair-brush and comb engraved G. D. L., and a pair of black kid gloves, small and feminine.

I was more surprised than anyone else could have been.

"G. D. L.," I said, to be saying something, "could be Gabrielle Something Leggett – Mrs. Collinson's name before she was married."

Cotton said triumphantly: "You're durned right it could."

A heavy voice said from the doorway:

"Have you got a search-warrant? What the hell are you doing here if you haven't? It's burglary, and you know it."

Harvey Whidden was there. His big body, in a yellow slicker, filled the doorway. His heavy-featured face was dark and angry.

Vernon began: "Whidden I –"

The marshal screamed, "It's him!" and pulled a gun from under his coat.

I pushed his arm as he fired at the man in the doorway. The bullet hit the wall.

Whidden's face was now more astonished than angry. He jumped back through the doorway and ran downstairs. Cotton, upset by my push, straightened himself up, cursed me, and ran out after Whidden. Vernon, Feeney, and Rolly stood staring after them.

I said: "This is good clean sport, but it makes no sense to me. What's it all about?"

Nobody told me. I said: "This comb and brush were on Mrs. Collinson's table when we searched the house, Rolly."

The deputy sheriff nodded uncertainly, still staring at the door. No noise came through it now. I asked:

"Would there be any special reason for Cotton framing Whidden?"

The sheriff said: "They ain't good friends." (I had noticed that.) "What do you think, Vern?"

The district attorney took his gaze from the door, rolled the things in their towel again, and stuffed the bundle in his pocket. "Come on," he snapped, and strode downstairs.

The front door was open. We saw nothing, heard nothing, of Cotton and Whidden. A Ford – Whidden's – stood at the front gate soaking up rain. We got into it. Vernon took the wheel, and drove to the house in the cove. We hammered at its door until it was opened by an old man in gray underwear, put there as caretaker by the sheriff.

The old man told us that Cotton had been there at eight o'clock that night, just, he said, to look around again. He, the caretaker, didn't know no reason why the marshal had to be watched, so he hadn't bothered him, letting him do what he wanted, and, so far as he knew, the marshal hadn't taken any of the Collinsons' property though of course he might of.

Vernon and Feeney gave the old man hell, and we went back to Quesada.

Rolly was with me on the back seat. I asked him:

"Who is this Whidden? Why should Cotton pick on him?"

"Well, for one thing, Harve's got kind of a bad name, from being mixed up in the rum-running that used to go on here, and from being in trouble now and then."

"Yeah? And for another thing?"

The deputy sheriff frowned, hesitating, hunting for words; and before he had found them we were stopping in front of a vine-covered cottage on a dark street corner. The district attorney led the way to its front porch and rang the bell.

After a little while a woman's voice sounded overhead: "Who's there?"

We had to retreat to the steps to see her – Mrs. Cotton at a second-story window.

"Dick got home yet?" Vernon asked.

"No, Mr. Vernon, he hasn't. I was getting worried. Wait a minute; I'll come down."

"Don't bother," he said. "We won't wait. I'll see him in the morning."

"No. Wait," she said urgently and vanished from the window.

A moment later she opened the front door. Her blue eyes were dark and excited. She had on a rose bathrobe.

"You needn't have bothered," the district attorney said. "There was nothing special. We got separated from him a little while ago, and just wanted to know if he'd got back yet. He's all right."

"Was –?" Her hands worked folds of her bathrobe over her thin breasts. "Was he after – after Harvey – Harvey Whidden?"

Vernon didn't look at her when he said, "Yes;" and he said it without showing his teeth. Feeney and Rolly looked as uncomfortable as Vernon.

Mrs. Cotton's face turned pink. Her lower lip trembled, blurring her words.

"Don't believe him, Mr. Vernon. Don't believe a word he tells you. Harve didn't have anything to do with those

Collinsons, with neither one of them. Don't let Dick tell you he did. He didn't."

Vernon looked at his feet and didn't say anything. Rolly and Feeney were looking intently out through the open door – we were standing just inside it – at the rain. Nobody seemed to have any intention of speaking.

I asked, "No?" putting more doubt in my voice than I actually felt.

"No, he didn't," she cried, turning her face to me. "He couldn't. He couldn't have had anything to do with it." The pink went out of her face, leaving it white and desperate. "He – he was here that night – all night – from before seven until daylight."

"Where was your husband?"

"Up in the city, at his mother's."

"What's her address?"

She gave it to me, a Noe Street number.

"Did anybody – ?"

"Aw, come on," the sheriff protested, still staring at the rain. "Ain't that enough?"

Mrs. Cotton turned from me to the district attorney again, taking hold of one of his arms.

"Don't tell it on me, please, Mr. Vernon," she begged. "I don't know what I'd do if it came out. But I had to tell you. I couldn't let him put it on Harve. Please, you won't tell anybody else?"

The district attorney swore that under no circumstances would he, or any of us, repeat what she had told us to anybody; and the sheriff and his deputy agreed with vigorous red-faced nods.

But when we were in the Ford again, away from her, they forgot their embarrassment and became manhunters again. Within ten minutes they had decided that Cotton, instead of going to San Francisco to his mother's Friday night, had remained in Quesada, had killed Collinson, had gone to the city to phone Fitzstephan and mail the letter, and then had returned to Quesada in time to kidnap Mrs. Collinson; planning from the first to plant the evidence against Whidden, with whom he had long been on bad terms, having always suspected what everybody else knew – that Whidden was Mrs. Cotton's lover.

The sheriff – he whose chivalry had kept me from more thoroughly questioning the woman a few minutes ago – now laughed his belly up and down.

"That's rich," he gurgled. "Him out framing Harve, and Harve getting himself a alibi in *his* bed. Dick's face ought to be a picture for Puck when we spring that on him. Let's find him tonight."

"Better wait," I advised. "It won't hurt to check up his San Francisco trip before we put it to him. All we've got on him so far is that he tried to frame Whidden. If he's the murderer and kidnapper he seems to have gone to a lot of unnecessary foolishness."

Feeney scowled at me and defended their theory:

"Maybe he was more interested in framing Harve than anything else."

Feeney was against that. He wanted to grab the marshal *pronto*; but Vernon reluctantly backed me up. We dropped Rolly at his house and returned to the hotel.

In my room, I put in a phone call for the agency in San Francisco. While I was waiting for the connection knuckles tapped my door. I opened it and let in Jack Santos, pajamaed, bathrobed, and slippered.

"Have a nice ride?" he asked, yawning.

"Swell."

"Anything break?"

"Not for publication, but – under the hat – the new angle is that our marshal is trying to hang the job on his wife's boy friend – with homemade evidence. The other big officials think Cotton turned the trick himself."

"That ought to get them all on the front page." Santos sat on the foot of my bed and lit a cigarette. "Ever happen to hear that Feeney was Cotton's rival for the telegraphing hand of the present Mrs. Cotton, until she picked the marshal – the triumph of dimples over mustachios?"

"No," I admitted. "What of it?"

"How do I know? I just happened to pick it up. A fellow in the garage told me."

"How long ago?"

"That they were rival suitors? Less than a couple of years."

I got my San Francisco call, and told Field – the agency night-man – to have somebody check up the marshal's Noe Street visit. Santos yawned and went out while I was talking. I went to bed when I had finished.

17 BELOW DULL POINT

THE TELEPHONE bell brought me out of sleep a little before ten the following morning. Mickey Linehan, talking from San Francisco, told me Cotton had arrived at his mother's house at between seven and seven-thirty Saturday morning. The marshal had slept for five or six hours – telling his mother he had been up all night laying for a burglar – and had left for home at six that evening.

Cotton was coming in from the street when I reached the lobby. He was red-eyed and weary, but still determined.

"Catch Whidden?" I asked.

"No, durn him, but I will. Say, I'm glad you jiggled my arm, even if it did let him get away. I – well, sometimes a fellow's enthusiasm gets the best of his judgment."

"Yeah. We stopped at your house on our way back, to see how you'd made out."

"I ain't been home yet," he said. "I put in the whole durned night hunting for that fellow. Where's Vern and Feeney?"

"Pounding their ears. Better get some sleep yourself," I suggested. "I'll ring you up if anything happens."

He set off for home. I went into the café for breakfast. I was half through when Vernon joined me there. He had telegrams from the San Francisco police department and the Marin County sheriff's office, confirming Fitzstephan's alibis.

"I got my report on Cotton," I said. "He reached his mother's at seven or a little after Saturday morning, and left at six that evening."

"Seven or a little after?" Vernon didn't like that. If the marshal had been in San Francisco at that time he could hardly have been abducting the girl. "Are you sure?"

"No, but that's the best we've been able to do so far. There's Fitzstephan now." Looking through the café door, I had seen the novelist's lanky back at the hotel desk. "Excuse me a moment."

I went over and got Fitzstephan, bringing him back to the table with me, and introducing him to Vernon. The district attorney stood up to shake hands with him, but was too busy with thoughts of Cotton to bother now with anything else. Fitzstephan said he had had breakfast before leaving the city, and ordered a cup of coffee. Just then I was called to the phone.

Cotton's voice, but excited almost beyond recognition: "For God's sake get Vernon and Feeney and come up here."

"What's the matter?" I asked.

"Hurry! Something awful's happened. Hurry!" he cried and hung up.

I went back to the table and told Vernon about it. He jumped up, upsetting Fitzstephan's coffee. Fitzstephan got up too, but hesitated, looking at me.

"Come on," I invited him. "Maybe this'll be one of the things you like."

Fitzstephan's car was in front of the hotel. The marshal's house was only seven blocks away. Its front door was open. Vernon knocked on the frame as we went in, but we didn't wait for an answer.

Cotton met us in the hall. His eyes were round and bloodshot in a face as hard-white as marble. He tried to say something, but couldn't get the words past his tight-set teeth. He gestured towards the door behind him with a fist that was clenched on a piece of brown paper.

Through the doorway we saw Mrs. Cotton. She was lying on the blue-carpeted floor. She had on a pale blue dress. Her throat was covered with dark bruises. Her lips and tongue – the tongue, swollen, hung out – were darker than the bruises.

Her eyes were wide open, bulging, upturned, and dead. Her hand, when I touched it, was still warm.

Cotton, following us into the room, held out the brown paper in his hand. It was an irregularly torn piece of wrapping paper, covered on both sides with writing – nervously, unevenly, hastily scribbled in pencil. A softer pencil had been used than on Fitzstephan's message, and the paper was a darker brown.

I was closest to Cotton. I took the paper, and read it aloud hurriedly, skipping unnecessary words:

"Whidden came last night . . . said husband after him . . . frame him for Collinson trouble . . . I hid him in garret . . . he said only way to save him was to say he was here Friday night . . . said if I didn't they'd hang him . . . when Mr. Vernon came Harve said he'd kill me if I didn't . . . so I said it . . . but he wasn't here that night . . . I didn't know he was guilty then . . . told me afterwards . . . tried to kidnap her Thursday night . . . husband nearly caught him . . . came in office after Collinson sent telegram and saw it . . . followed him and killed him . . . went to San Francisco, drinking whiskey . . . decided to go through with kidnapping anyway . . . phoned man who knew her to try to learn who he could get money from . . . too drunk to talk good . . . wrote letter and came back . . . met her on road . . . took her to old bootleggers' hiding place somewhere below Dull Point . . . goes in boat . . . afraid he'll kill me . . . locked in garret . . . writing while he's down getting food . . . murderer . . . I won't help him . . . Daisy Cotton."

The sheriff and Rolly had arrived while I was reading it. Feeney's face was as white and set as Cotton's.

Vernon bared his teeth at the marshal, snarling:

"You wrote that."

Feeney grabbed it from my hands, looked at it, shook his head, and said hoarsely:

"No, that's her writing, all right."

Cotton was babbling:

"No, before God, I didn't. I planted that stuff on him, I'll admit that, but that was all. I come home and find her like this. I swear to God!"

"Where were you Friday night?" Vernon asked.

"Here, watching the house. I thought – I thought he might – But he wasn't here that night. I watched till daybreak and then went to the city. I didn't –"

The sheriff's bellow drowned the rest of Cotton's words. The sheriff was waving the dead woman's letter. He bellowed: "Below Dull Point! What are we waiting for?"

He plunged out of the house, the rest of us following. Cotton and Rolly rode to the waterfront in the deputy's car. Vernon, the sheriff, and I rode with Fitzstephan. The sheriff cried throughout the short trip, tears splashing on the automatic pistol he held in his lap.

At the waterfront we changed from the cars to a green and white motor boat run by a pink-cheeked, tow-headed youngster called Tim. Tim said he didn't know anything about any bootleggers' hiding places below Dull Point, but if there was one there he could find it. In his hands the boat produced a lot of speed, but not enough for Feeney and Cotton. They stood together in the bow, guns in their fists, dividing their time between straining forward and yelling back for more speed.

Half an hour from the dock, we rounded a blunt promontory that the others called Dull Point, and Tim cut down our speed, putting the boat in closer to the rocks that jumped up high and sharp at the water's edge. We were now all eyes – eyes that soon ached from staring under the noon sun but kept on staring. Twice we saw clefts in the rock-walled shore, pushed hopefully in to them, saw that they were blind, leading nowhere, opening into no hiding places.

The third cleft was even more hopeless-looking at first sight, but, now that Dull Point was some distance behind us, we couldn't pass up anything. We slid in to the cleft, got close enough to decide that it was another blind one, gave it up, and told Tim to go on. We were washed another couple of feet nearer before the tow-headed boy could bring the boat around.

Cotton, in the bow, bent forward from the waist and yelled: "Here it is."

He pointed his gun at one side of the cleft. Tim let the boat drift in another foot or so. Craning our necks, we could see that what we had taken for the shore-line on that side was actually a high, thin, saw-toothed ledge of rock, separated from the cliff at this end by twenty feet of water.

"Put her in," Feeney ordered.

Tim frowned at the water, hesitated, said: "She can't make it."

The boat backed him up by shuddering suddenly under our feet, with an unpleasant rasping noise.

"That be damned!" the sheriff bawled. "Put her in."

Tim took a look at the sheriff's wild face, and put her in.

The boat shuddered under our feet again, more violently, and now there was a tearing sound in with the rasping, but we went through the opening and turned down behind the saw-tooth ledge.

We were in a v-shaped pocket, twenty feet wide where we had come in, say eighty feet long, high-walled, inaccessible by land, accessible by sea only as we had come. The water that floated us – and was coming in rapidly to sink us – ran a third of the way down the pocket. White sand paved the other two thirds. A small boat was resting its nose on the edge of the sand. It was empty. Nobody was in sight. There didn't seem to be anywhere for anybody to hide. There were footprints, large and small, in the sand, empty tin cans, and the remains of a fire.

"Harve's," Rolly said, nodding at the boat.

Our boat grounded beside it. We jumped, splashed, ashore – Cotton ahead, the others spread out behind him.

As suddenly as if he had sprung out of the air, Harvey Whidden appeared in the far end of the v, standing in the sand, a rifle in his hands. Anger and utter astonishment were mixed in his heavy face, and in his voice when he yelled:

"You God-damned double-crossing –" The noise his rifle made blotted out the rest of his words.

Cotton had thrown himself down sideways. The rifle bullet missed him by inches, sang between Fitzstephan and me, nicking his hat-brim, and splattered on the rocks behind. Four of our guns went off together, some more than once.

Whidden went over backwards, his feet flying in the air. He was dead when we got to him – three bullets in his chest, one in his head.

We found Gabrielle Collinson cowering back in the corner of a narrow-mouthed hole in the rock wall – a long triangular cave whose mouth had been hidden from our view by the slant at which it was set. There were blankets in there, spread over a pile of dried seaweed, some canned goods, a lantern, and another rifle.

The girl's small face was flushed and feverish, and her voice was hoarse: she had a cold in her chest. She was too frightened at first to tell us anything coherent, and apparently recognized neither Fitzstephan nor me.

The boat we had come in was out of commission. Whidden's boat couldn't be trusted to carry more than three with safety through the surf. Tim and Rolly set off for Quesada in it, to get us a larger vessel. It was an hour-and-a-half's round trip. While they were gone we worked on the girl, soothing her, assuring her that she was among friends, that there was nothing to be afraid of now. Her eyes gradually became less scary, her breathing easier, and her nails less tightly pressed into her palms. At the end of an hour she was answering our questions.

She said she knew nothing of Whidden's attempt to kidnap her Thursday night, nothing of the telegram Eric had sent me. She sat up all Friday night waiting for him to return from his walk, and at daylight, frantic at his failure to return, had gone to look for him. She found him – as I had. Then she went back to the house and tried to commit suicide – to put an end to the curse by shooting herself.

"I tried twice," she whispered; "but I couldn't. I couldn't. I was too much of a coward. I couldn't keep the pistol pointing at myself while I did it. I tried the first time to shoot myself in the temple, and then in the breast; but I hadn't the courage. Each time I jerked it away just before I fired. And after the second time I couldn't even get courage to try again."

She changed her clothes then – evening clothes, now muddy and torn from her search – and drove away from the house. She didn't say where she had intended going. She didn't seem to know. Probably she hadn't had any destination – was simply going away from the place where the curse had settled on her husband.

She hadn't driven far when she had seen a machine coming towards her, driven by the man who had brought her here. He had turned his car across the road in front of her, blocking the road. Trying to avoid hitting his car, she had run into a tree – and hadn't known anything else until she had awakened in the cave. She had been here since then. The man had left her here alone most of the time. She had neither strength nor courage to escape by swimming, and there was no other way out.

The man had told her nothing, had asked her nothing, had addressed no words to her except to say, "Here's some food," or, "Till I bring you some water, you'll have to get along on canned tomatoes when you're thirsty," or other things of that sort. She never remembered having seen him before. She didn't know his name. He was the only man she had seen since her husband's death.

"What did he call you?" I asked. "Mrs. Carter? Or Mrs. Collinson?"

She frowned thoughtfully, then shook her head, saying:

"I don't think he ever called me by name. He never spoke unless he had to, and he wasn't here very much. I was usually alone."

"How long had he been here this time?"

"Since before daylight. The noise of his boat woke me up."

"Sure? This is important. Are you sure he's been here since daylight?"

"Yes."

I was sitting on my heels in front of her. Cotton was standing on my left, beside the sheriff. I looked up at the marshal and said:

"That puts it up to you, Cotton. Your wife was still warm when we saw her – after eleven."

He goggled at me, stammering: "Wh-what's that you say?"

On the other side of me I heard Vernon's teeth click together sharply.

I said:

"Your wife was afraid Whidden would kill her, and wrote that statement. But he didn't kill her. He's been here since daylight. You found the statement, learned from it that they *had* been too friendly. Well, what did you do then?"

"That's a lie," he cried. "There ain't a word of truth in it. She was dead there when I found her. I never –"

"You killed her," Vernon barked at him over my head. "You choked her, counting on that statement to throw suspicion on Whidden."

"That's a lie," the marshal cried again, and made the mistake of trying to get his gun out.

Feeney slugged him, dropping him, and had handcuffs on his wrists before he could get up again.

18 THE PINEAPPLE

"IT DOESN'T make sense," I said. "It's dizzy. When we grab our man – or woman – we're going to find it's a goof, and Napa will get it instead of the gallows."

"That," Owen Fitzstephan said, "is characteristic of you. You're stumped, bewildered, flabbergasted. Do you admit you've met your master, have run into a criminal too wily for you? Not you. He's outwitted you: therefore he's an idiot or a lunatic. Now really. Of course there's a certain unexpected modesty to that attitude."

"But he's got to be goofy," I insisted. "Look: Mayenne marries –"

"Are you," he asked disgustedly, "going to recite that catalogue again?"

"You've got a flighty mind. That's no good in this business. You don't catch murderers by amusing yourself with interesting thoughts. You've got to sit down to all the facts you can get and turn them over and over till they click."

"If that's your technic, you'll have to put up with it," he said: "but I'm damned if I see why I should suffer. You recited thc Mayenne–Leggett–Collinson history step by step last night at least half a dozen times. You've done nothing else since breakfast this morning. I'm getting enough of it. Nobody's mysteries ought to be as tiresome as you're making this one."

"Hell," I said; "I sat up half the night after you went to bed and recited it to myself. You got to turn them over and over, my boy, till they click."

"I like the Nick Carter school better. Aren't you even

threatened with any of the conclusions that this turning-them-over-and-over is supposed to lead to?"

"Yeah, I've got one. It's that Vernon and Feeney are wrong in thinking that Cotton was working with Whidden on the kidnapping, and double-crossed him. According to them, Cotton thought up the plan and persuaded Whidden to do the rough stuff while the marshal used his official position to cover him up. Collinson stumbled on the plan and was killed. Then Cotton made his wife write that statement – it's phony, right enough, was dictated to her – killed her, and led us to Whidden. Cotton was the first man ashore when we got to the hiding place – to make sure Whidden was killed resisting arrest before he could talk."

Fitzstephan ran long fingers through his sorrel hair and asked:

"Don't you think jealousy would have given Cotton motive enough?"

"Yeah. But where's Whidden's motive for putting himself in Cotton's hands? Besides, where does that layout fit in with the Temple racket?"

"Are you sure," Fitzstephan asked, "that you're right in thinking there must be a connection?"

"Yeah. Gabrielle's father, step-mother, physician, and husband have been slaughtered in less than a handful of weeks – all the people closest to her. That's enough to tie it all together for me. If you want more links, I can point them out to you. Upton and Ruppert were the apparent instigators of the first trouble, and got killed. Haldorn of the second, and got killed. Whidden of the third, and got killed. Mrs. Leggett killed her husband; Cotton apparently killed his wife; and Haldorn would have killed his if I hadn't blocked him. Gabrielle, as a child, was made to kill her mother; Gabrielle's maid was made to kill Riese, and nearly me. Leggett left behind him a statement explaining – not altogether satisfactorily – everything, and was killed. So did and was Mrs.

Cotton. Call any of these pairs coincidences. Call any couple of pairs coincidences. You'll still have enough left to point at somebody who's got a system he likes, and sticks to it."

Fitzstephan squinted thoughtfully at me, agreeing:

"There may be something in that. It does, as you put it, look like the work of one mind."

"And a goofy one."

"Be obstinate about it," he said. "But even your goof must have a motive."

"Why?"

"Damn your sort of mind," he said with good-natured impatience. "If he had no motive connected with Gabrielle, why should his crimes be connected with her?"

"We don't know that all of them are," I pointed out. "We only know of the ones that are."

He grinned and said:

"You'll go any distance to disagree, won't you?"

I said:

"Then again, maybe the goof's crimes are connected with Gabrielle because he is."

Fitzstephan let his gray eyes go sleepy over that, pursing his mouth, looking at the door closed between my room and Gabrielle's.

"All right," he said, looking at me again. "Who's your maniac close to Gabrielle?"

"The closest and goofiest person to Gabrielle is Gabrielle herself."

Fitzstephan got up and crossed the hotel room – I was sitting on the edge of the bed – to shake my hand with solemn enthusiasm.

"You're wonderful," he said. "You amaze me. Ever have night sweats? Put out your tongue and say, 'Ah.' "

"Suppose," I began, but was interrupted by a feeble tapping on the corridor door.

I went to the door and opened it. A thin man of my own

age and height in wrinkled black clothes stood in the corridor. He was breathing heavily through a red-veined nose, and his small brown eyes were timid.

"You know me," he said apologetically.

"Yeah. Come in." I introduced him to Fitzstephan: "This is the Tom Fink who was one of Haldorn's helpers in the Temple of the Holy Grail."

Fink looked reproachfully at me, then dragged his crumpled hat from his head and crossed the room to shake Fitzstephan's hand. That done, he returned to me and said, almost whispering:

"I come down to tell you something."

"Yeah?"

He fidgeted, turning his hat around and around in his hands. I winked at Fitzstephan and went out with Fink. In the corridor, I closed the door and stopped, saying: "Let's have it."

Fink rubbed his lips with his tongue and then with the back of one scrawny hand. He said, in his half-whisper:

"I come down to tell you something I thought you ought to know."

"Yeah?"

"It's about this fellow Whidden that was killed."

"Yeah?"

"He was –"

The door to my room split open. Floors, walls, and ceiling wriggled under, around, and over us. There was too much noise to be heard – a roar that was felt bodily. Tom Fink was carried away from me, backward. I had sense enough to throw myself down as I was blown in the opposite direction, and got nothing worse out of it than a bruised shoulder when I hit the wall. A doorframe stopped Fink, wickedly, its edge catching the back of his head. He came forward again, folding over to lie face-down on the floor, still except for blood running from his head.

I got up and made for my room. Fitzstephan was a mangled pile of flesh and clothing in the center of the floor. My bed was burning. There was neither glass nor wire netting left in the window. I saw these things mechanically as I staggered toward Gabrielle's room. The connecting door was open – perhaps blown open.

She was crouching on all fours in bed, facing the foot, her feet on the pillows. Her nightdress was torn at one shoulder. Her green-brown eyes – glittering under brown curls that had tumbled down to hide her forehead – were the eyes of an animal gone trap-crazy. Saliva glistened on her pointed chin. There was nobody else in the room.

"Where's the nurse?" My voice was choked.

The girl said nothing. Her eyes kept their crazy terror focused on me.

"Get under the covers," I ordered. "Want to get pneumonia?"

She didn't move. I walked around to the side of the bed, lifting an end of the covers with one hand, reaching out the other to help her, saying:

"Come on, get inside."

She made a queer noise deep in her chest, dropped her head, and put her sharp teeth into the back of my hand. It hurt. I put her under the covers, returned to my room, and was pushing my burning mattress through the window when people began to arrive.

"Get a doctor," I called to the first of them; "and stay out of here."

I had got rid of the mattress by the time Mickey Linehan pushed through the crowd that was now filling the corridor. Mickey blinked at what was left of Fitzstephan, at me, and asked:

"What the hell?"

His big loose mouth sagged at the ends, looking like a grin turned upside down.

I licked burnt fingers and asked unpleasantly:

"What the hell does it look like?"

"More trouble, sure." The grin turned right side up on his red face. "Sure – you're here."

Ben Rolly came in. "Tch, tch, tch," he said, looking around. "What do you suppose happened?"

"Pineapple," I said.

"Tch, tch, tch."

Doctor George came in and knelt beside the wreck of Fitzstephan. George had been Gabrielle's physician since her return from the cave the previous day. He was a short, chunky, middle-aged man with a lot of black hair everywhere except on his lips, cheeks, chin, and nose-bridge. His hairy hands moved over Fitzstephan.

"What's Fink been doing?" I asked Mickey.

"Hardly any. I got on his tail when they sprung him yesterday noon. He went from the hoosegow to a hotel on Kearny Street and got himself a room. He spent most of the afternoon in the Public Library, reading the newspaper files on the girl's troubles, from beginning to date. He ate after that, and went back to the hotel. He could have back-doored me. If he didn't, he camped in his room all night. It was dark at midnight when I knocked off so I could be on the job at six a.m. He showed at seven-something, got breakfast, and grabbed a rattler for Poston, changed to the stage for here, and came straight to the hotel, asking for you. That's the crop."

"Damn my soul!" the kneeling doctor exclaimed. "The man's not dead."

I didn't believe him. Fitzstephan's right arm was gone, and most of his right leg. His body was too twisted to see what was left of it, but there was only one side to his face. I said:

"There's another one out in the hall, with his head knocked in."

"Oh, he's all right," the doctor muttered without looking up. "But this one – well, damn my soul!"

He scrambled to his feet and began ordering this and that. He was excited. A couple of men came in from the corridor. The woman who had been nursing Gabrielle Collinson – a Mrs. Herman – joined them, and another man with a blanket. They took Fitzstephan away.

"That fellow out in the hall Fink?" Rolly asked.

"Yeah." I told him what Fink had told me, adding: "He hadn't finished when the blow-up came."

"Suppose the bomb was meant for him, meant to keep him from finishing?"

Mickey said: "Nobody followed him down from the city, except me."

"Maybe," I said. "Better see what they're doing with him, Mick."

Mickey went out.

"This window was closed," I told Rolly. "There was no noise as of something being thrown through the glass just before the explosion: and there's no broken windowglass inside the room. The screen was over it, too, so we can say the pineapple wasn't chucked in through the window."

Rolly nodded vaguely, looking at the door to Gabrielle's room.

"Fink and I were in the corridor talking," I went on. "I ran straight back through here to her room. Nobody could have got out of her room after the explosion without my seeing them – or hearing them. There wasn't finger-snapping time between my losing sight of her corridor-door from the outside, and seeing it again from the inside. The screen over her window is still OK."

"Mrs. Herman wasn't in there with her?" Rolly asked.

"She was supposed to be, but wasn't. We'll find out about that. There's no use thinking Mrs. Collinson chucked the bomb. She's been in bed since we brought her back from Dull Point yesterday. She couldn't have had the bomb planted there because she had no way of knowing that she was going to occupy the room. Nobody's been in there since except you, Feeney, Vernon, the doctor, the nurse, and me."

"I wasn't going to say she had anything to do with it," the deputy sheriff mumbled. "What does she say?"

"Nothing yet. We'll try her now, though I doubt if it'll get us much."

It didn't. Gabrielle lay in the middle of the bed, the covers gathered close to her chin as if she was prepared to duck down under them at the first alarm, and shook her head No to everything we asked, whether the answer fit or didn't.

The nurse came in, a big-breasted, red-haired woman of forty-something with a face that seemed honest because it was homely, freckled, and blue-eyed. She swore on the Gideon Bible that she had been out of the room for less than five minutes, just going downstairs for some stationery, intending to write a letter to her nephew in Vallejo while her patient was sleeping; and that was the only time she had been out of the room all day. She had met nobody in the corridor, she said.

"You left the door unlocked?" I asked.

"Yes, so I wouldn't be as likely to wake her when I came back."

"Where's the stationery you got?"

"I didn't get it. I heard the explosion and ran back upstairs." Fear came into her face, turning the freckles to ghastly spots. "You don't think – !"

"Better look after Mrs. Collinson," I said gruffly.

19 THE DEGENERATE

ROLLY AND I went back to my room, closing the connecting door. He said:

"Tch, tch, tch. I'd of thought Mrs. Herman was the last person in the world to –"

"You ought to've," I grumbled. "You recommended her. Who is she?"

"She's Tod Herman's wife. He's got the garage. She used to be a trained nurse before she married Tod. I thought she was all right."

"She got a nephew in Vallejo?"

"Uh-huh; that would be the Schultz kid that works at Mare Island. How do you suppose she come to get mixed up in – ?"

"Probably didn't, or she would have had the writing paper she went after. Put somebody here to keep people out till we can borrow a San Francisco bomb-expert to look it over."

The deputy called one of the men in from the corridor, and we left him looking important in the room. Mickey Linehan was in the lobby when we got there.

"Fink's got a cracked skull. He's on his way to the county hospital with the other wreck."

"Fitzstephan dead yet?" I asked.

"Nope, and the doc thinks if they get him over where they got the right kind of implements they can keep him from dying. God knows what for – the shape he's in! But that's just the kind of stuff a croaker thinks is a lot of fun."

"Was Aaronia Haldorn sprung with Fink?" I asked.

"Yes. Al Mason's tailing her."

"Call up the Old Man and see if Al's reported anything on

her. Tell the Old Man what's happened here, and see if they've found Andrews."

"Andrews?" Rolly asked as Mickey headed for the phone. "What's the matter with him?"

"Nothing that I know of; only we haven't been able to find him to tell him Mrs. Collinson has been rescued. His office hasn't seen him since yesterday morning, and nobody will say they know where he is."

"Tch, tch, tch. Is there any special reason for wanting him?"

"I don't want her on my hands the rest of my life," I said. "He's in charge of her affairs, he's responsible for her, and I want to turn her over to him."

Rolly nodded vaguely.

We went outside and asked all the people we could find all the questions we could think of. None of the answers led anywhere, except to repeated assurance that the bomb hadn't been chucked through the window. We found six people who had been in sight of that side of the hotel immediately before, and at the time of, the explosion; and none of them had seen anything that could be twisted into bearing on the bomb-throwing.

Mickey came away from the phone with the information that Aaronia Haldorn, when released from the city prison, had gone to the home of a family named Jeffries in San Mateo, and had been there ever since; and that Dick Foley, hunting for Andrews, had hopes of locating him in Sausalito.

District attorney Vernon and Sheriff Feeney, with a horde of reporters and photographers close behind them, arrived from the county seat. They went through a lot of detecting motions that got them nowhere except on the front pages of all the San Francisco and Los Angeles papers – the place they liked best.

I had Gabrielle Collinson moved into another room in the hotel, and posted Mickey Linehan next door, with the connecting door unlocked. Gabrielle talked now, to Vernon, Feeney, Rolly, and me. What she said didn't help us much. She had been asleep, she said; had been awakened by a terrible noise and a terrible jarring of her bed; and then I had come in. That was all she knew.

Late in the afternoon McCracken, a San Francisco police department bomb-expert, arrived. After examining all the fragments of this and that which he could sweep up, he gave us a preliminary verdict that the bomb had been a small one, of aluminum, charged with a low-grade nitroglycerine, and exploded by a crude friction device.

"Amateur or professional job?" I asked.

McCracken spit out loose shreds of tobacco – he was one of the men who chew their cigarettes – and said:

"I'd say it was made by a guy that knew his stuff, but had to work with what he could get his hands on. I'll tell you more when I've worked this junk over in the lab."

"No timer on it?" I asked.

"No signs of one."

Doctor George returned from the county seat with the news that what was left of Fitzstephan still breathed. The doctor was tickled pink. I had to yell at him to make him hear my questions about Fink and Gabrielle. Then he told me Fink's life wasn't in danger, and the girl's cold was enough better that she might get out of bed if she wished. I asked about her nerves, but he was in too much of a hurry to get back to Fitzstephan to pay much attention to anything else.

"Hm-m-m, yes, certainly," he muttered, edging past me towards his car. "Quiet, rest, freedom from anxiety," and he was gone.

I ate dinner with Vernon and Feeney in the hotel café that evening. They didn't think I had told them all I knew about the bombing, and kept me on the witness stand throughout the meal, though neither of them accused me pointblank of holding out.

After dinner I went up to my new room. Mickey was sprawled on the bed reading a newspaper.

"Go feed yourself," I said. "How's our baby?"

"She's up. How do you figure her – only fifty cards to her deck?"

"Why?" I asked. "What's she been doing?"

"Nothing. I was just thinking."

"That's from having an empty stomach. Better go eat."

"Aye, aye, Mr. Continental," he said and went out.

The next room was quiet. I listened at the door and then tapped it. Mrs. Herman's voice said: "Come in."

She was sitting beside the bed making gaudy butterflies on a piece of yellowish cloth stretched on hoops. Gabrielle Collinson sat in a rocking chair on the other side of the room, frowning at hands clasped in her lap – clasped hard enough to whiten the knuckles and spread the finger-ends. She had on the tweed clothes in which she had been kidnapped. They were still rumpled, but had been brushed clean of mud. She didn't look up when I came in. The nurse did, pushing her freckles together in an uneasy smile.

"Good evening," I said, trying to make a cheerful entrance. "Looks like we're running out of invalids."

That brought no response from the girl, too much from the nurse.

"Yes, indeed," Mrs. Herman exclaimed with exaggerated enthusiasm. "We can't call Mrs. Collinson an invalid now – now that she's up and about – and I'm almost sorry that she is – he-he-he – because I certainly never did have such a nice patient in every way; but that's what we girls used to say at the hospital when we were in training: the nicer the patient was, the shorter the time we'd have him, while you take a disagreeable one and she'd live – I mean, be there – forever and a day, it seemed like. I remember once when –"

I made a face at her and wagged my head at the door. She let the rest of her words die inside her open mouth. Her face turned red, then white. She dropped her embroidery and got up, saying idiotically: "Yes, yes, that's the way it always is. Well, I've got to go see about those – you know – what do you call them. Pardon me for a few minutes, please." She went out quickly, sidewise, as if afraid I'd sneak up behind her and kick her.

When the door had closed, Gabrielle looked up from her hands and said:

"Owen is dead."

She didn't ask, she said it; but there was no way of treating it except as a question.

"No." I sat down in the nurse's chair and fished out cigarettes. "He's alive."

"Will he live?" Her voice was still husky from her cold.

"The doctors think so," I exaggerated.

"If he lives, will he – ?" She left the question unfinished, but her husky voice seemed impersonal enough.

"He'll be pretty badly maimed."

She spoke more to herself than to me:

"That should be even more satisfactory."

I grinned. If I was as good an actor as I thought, there was nothing in the grin but good-humored amusement.

"Laugh," she said gravely. "I wish you could laugh it away. But you can't. It's there. It will always be there." She looked down at her hands and whispered: "Cursed."

Spoken in any other tone, that last word would have been melodramatic, ridiculously stagey. But she said it automatically, without any feeling, as if saying it had become a habit. I could see her lying in bed in the dark, whispering it to herself hour after hour, whispering it to her body when she put on her clothes, to her face reflected in mirrors, day after day.

I squirmed in my chair and growled:

"Stop it. Just because a bad-tempered woman works off her hatred and rage in a ten-twenty-thirty speech about –"

"No, no; my step-mother merely put in words what I have

always known. I hadn't known it was in the Dain blood, but I knew it was in mine. How could I help knowing? Hadn't I the physical marks of degeneracy?" She crossed the room to stand in front of me, turning her head sidewise, holding back her curls with both hands. "Look at my ears – without lobes, pointed tops. People don't have ears like that. Animals do." She turned her face to me again, still holding back her hair. "Look at my forehead – its smallness, its shape – animal. My teeth." She bared them – white, small, pointed. "The shape of my face." Her hands left her hair and slid down her cheeks, coming together under her oddly pointed small chin.

"Is that all?" I asked. "Haven't you got cloven hoofs? All right. Say these things are as peculiar as you seem to think they are. What of it? Your step-mother was a Dain, and she was poison, but where were her physical marks of degeneracy? Wasn't she as normal, as wholesome-looking as any woman you're likely to find?"

"But that's no answer." She shook her head impatiently. "She didn't have the physical marks perhaps. I have, and the mental ones too. I –" She sat down on the side of the bed close to me, elbows on knees, tortured white face between hands. "I've not ever been able to think clearly, as other people do, even the simplest thoughts. Everything is always so confused in my mind. No matter what I try to think about, there's a fog that gets between me and it, and other thoughts get between us, so I barely catch a glimpse of the thought I want before I lose it again, and have to hunt through the fog, and at last find it, only to have the same thing happen again and again and again. Can you understand how horrible that can become: going through life like that – year after year – knowing you will always be like that – or worse?"

"I can't," I said. "It sounds normal as hell to me. Nobody thinks clearly, no matter what they pretend. Thinking's a dizzy business, a matter of catching as many of those foggy glimpses as you can and fitting them together the best you can. That's why people hang on so tight to their beliefs and opinions; because, compared to the haphazard way in which they're arrived at, even the goofiest opinion seems wonderfully clear, sane, and self-evident. And if you let it get away from you, then you've got to dive back into that foggy muddle to wangle yourself out another to take its place."

She took her face out of her hands and smiled shyly at me, saying:

"It's funny I didn't like you before." Her face became serious again. "But –"

"But nothing," I said. "You're old enough to know that everybody except very crazy people and very stupid people suspect themselves now and then – or whenever they happen to think about it – of not being exactly sane. Evidence of goofiness is easily found: the more you dig into yourself, the more you turn up. Nobody's mind could stand the sort of examination you've been giving yours. Going around trying to prove yourself cuckoo! It's a wonder you haven't driven yourself nuts."

"Perhaps I have."

"No. Take my word for it, you're sane. Or don't take my word for it. Look. You got a hell of a start in life. You got into bad hands at the very beginning. Your step-mother was plain poison, and did her best to ruin you, and in the end succeeded in convincing you that you were smeared with a very special family curse. In the past couple of months – the time I've known you – all the calamities known to man have been piled up on you, and your belief in your curse has made you hold yourself responsible for every item in the pile. All right. How's it affected you? You've been dazed a lot of the time, hysterical part of the time, and when your husband was killed you tried to kill yourself, but weren't unbalanced enough to face the shock of the bullet tearing through your flesh.

"Well, good God, sister! I'm only a hired man with only a hired man's interest in your troubles, and some of them have had me groggy. Didn't I try to bite a ghost back in that Temple? And I'm supposed to be old and toughened to crime. This morning – after all you'd been through – somebody touches off a package of nitroglycerine almost beside your bed. Here you are this evening, up and dressed, arguing with me about your sanity.

"If you aren't normal, it's because you're tougher, saner, cooler than normal. Stop thinking about your Dain blood and think about the Mayenne blood in you. Where do you suppose you got your toughness, except from him? It's the same toughness that carried him through Devil's Island, Central America, and Mexico, and kept him standing up till the end. You're more like him than like the one Dain I saw. Physically, you take after your father, and if you've got any physical marks of degeneracy – whatever that means – you got them from him."

She seemed to like that. Her eyes were almost happy. But I had talked myself out of words for the moment, and while I was hunting for more behind a cigarette the shine went out of her eyes.

"I'm glad – I'm grateful to you for what you've said, if you've meant it." Hopelessness was in her tone again, and her face was back between her hands. "But, whatever I am, she was right. You can't say she wasn't. You can't deny that my life has been cursed, blackened, and the lives of everyone who's touched me."

"I'm one answer to that," I said. "I've been around you a lot recently, and I've mixed into your affairs enough, and nothing's happened to me that a night's sleep wouldn't fix up."

"But in a different way," she protested slowly, wrinkling her forehead. "There's no personal relationship with you. It's professional with you – your work. That makes a difference."

I laughed and said:

"That won't do. There's Fitzstephan. He knew your family, of course, but he was here through me, on my account, and was actually, then, a step further removed from you than I. Why shouldn't I have gone down first? Maybe the bomb was meant for me? Maybe. But that brings us to a human mind behind it – one that can bungle – and not your infallible curse."

"You are mistaken," she said, staring at her knees. "Owen loved me."

I decided not to appear surprised. I asked:

"Had you – ?"

"No, please! Please don't ask me to talk about it. Not now – after what happened this morning." She jerked her shoulders up high and straight, said crisply: "You said something about an infallible curse. I don't know whether you misunderstand me, or are pretending to, to make me seem foolish. But I don't believe in an infallible curse, one coming from the devil or God, like Job's, say." She was earnest now, no longer talking to change the conversation. "But can't there be – aren't there people who are so thoroughly – fundamentally – evil that they poison – bring out the worst in – everybody they touch? And can't that – ?"

"There are people who can," I half-agreed, "when they want to."

"No, no! Whether they want to or not. When they desperately don't want to. It is so. It is. I loved Eric because he was clean and fine. You know he was. You knew him well enough, and you know men well enough, to know he was. I loved him that way, wanted him that way. And then, when we were married –"

She shuddered and gave me both of her hands. The palms were dry and hot, the ends of her fingers cold. I had to hold them tight to keep the nails out of my flesh. I asked:

"You were a virgin when you married him?"

"Yes, I was. I am. I –"

"It's nothing to get excited about," I said. "You are, and have the usual silly notions. And you use dope, don't you?"

She nodded. I went on:

"That would cut your own interest in sex to below normal, so that a perfectly natural interest in it on somebody else's part would seem abnormal. Eric was too young, too much in love with you, maybe too inexperienced, to keep from being clumsy. You can't make anything horrible out of that."

"But it wasn't only Eric," she explained. "Every man I've known. Don't think me conceited. I know I'm not beautiful. But I don't want to be evil. I don't. Why do men – ? Why have all the men I've – ?"

"Are you," I asked, "talking about me?"

"No – you know I'm not. Don't make fun of me, please."

"Then there are exceptions? Any others? Madison Andrews, for instance?"

"If you know him at all well, or have heard much about him, you don't have to ask that."

"No," I agreed. "But you can't blame the curse with him – it's habit. Was he very bad?"

"He was very funny," she said bitterly.

"How long ago was it?"

"Oh, possibly a year and a half. I didn't say anything to my father and step-mother. I was – I was ashamed that men were like that to me, and that –"

"How do you know," I grumbled, "that most men aren't like that to most women? What makes you think your case is so damned unique? If your ears were sharp enough, you could listen now and hear a thousand women in San Francisco making the same complaint, and – God knows – maybe half of them would be thinking themselves sincere."

She took her hands away from me and sat up straight on the bed. Some pink came into her face.

"Now you *have* made me feel silly," she said.

"Not much sillier than I do. I'm supposed to be a detective. Since this job began, I've been riding around on a merry-go-round, staying the same distance behind your curse, suspecting what it'd look like if I could get face to face with it, but never getting there. I will now. Can you stand another week or two?"

"You mean – ?"

"I'm going to show you that your curse is a lot of hooey, but it'll take a few days, maybe a couple of weeks."

She was round-eyed and trembling, wanting to believe me, afraid to. I said:

"That's settled. What are you going to do now?"

"I – I don't know. Do you mean what you've said? That this can be ended? That I'll have no more – ? That you can – ?"

"Yeah. Could you go back to the house in the cove for a while? It might help things along, and you'll be safe enough there. We could take Mrs. Herman with us, and maybe an op or two."

"I'll go," she said.

I looked at my watch and stood up saying:

"Better go back to bed. We'll move down tomorrow. Good night."

She chewed her lower lip, wanting to say something, not wanting to say it, finally blurting it out:

"I'll have to have morphine down there."

"Sure. What's your day's ration?"

"Five – ten grains."

"That's mild enough," I said, and then, casually: "Do you like using the stuff?"

"I'm afraid it's too late for my liking or not liking it to matter."

"You've been reading the Hearst papers," I said. "If you want to break off, and we've a few days to spare down there, we'll use them weaning you. It's not so tough."

She laughed shakily, with a queer twitching of her mouth.

"Go away," she cried. "Don't give me any more assurances, any more of your promises, please. I can't stand any more tonight. I'm drunk on them now. Please go away."

"All right. Night."

"Good night – and thanks."

I went into my room, closing the door. Mickey was unscrewing the top of a flask. His knees were dusty. He turned his half-wit's grin on me and said:

"What a swell dish you are. What are you trying to do? Win yourself a home?"

"Sh-h-h. Anything new?"

"The master minds have gone back to the county seat. The red-head nurse was getting a load at the keyhole when I came back from feeding. I chased her."

"And took her place?" I asked, nodding at his dusty knees.

You couldn't embarrass Mickey. He said:

"Hell, no. She was at the other door, in the hall."

20 THE HOUSE IN THE COVE

I GOT FITZSTEPHAN'S car from the garage and drove Gabrielle and Mrs. Herman down to the house in the cove late the following morning. The girl was in low spirits. She made a poor job of smiling when spoken to, and had nothing to say on her own account. I thought she might be depressed by the thought of returning to the house she had shared with Collinson, but when we got there she went in with no appearance of reluctance, and being there didn't seem to increase her depression.

After luncheon – Mrs. Herman turned out to be a good cook – Gabrielle decided she wanted to go outdoors, so she and I walked over to the Mexican settlement to see Mary Nunez. The Mexican woman promised to come back to work the next day. She seemed fond of Gabrielle, but not of me.

We returned home by way of the shore, picking a path between scattered rocks. We walked slowly. The girl's forehead was puckered between her eyebrows. Neither of us said anything until we were within a quarter of a mile of the house. Then Gabrielle sat down on the rounded top of a boulder that was warm in the sun.

"Can you remember what you told me last night?" she asked, running her words together in her hurry to get them out. She looked frightened.

"Yeah."

"Tell me again," she begged, moving over to one end of her boulder. "Sit down and tell me again – all of it."

I did. According to me, it was as foolish to try to read character from the shape of ears as from the position of stars, tea-leaves, or spit in the sand; anybody who started hunting for evidence of insanity in himself would certainly find plenty, because all but stupid minds were jumbled affairs; she was, as far as I could see, too much like her father to have much Dain blood in her, or to have been softened much by what she had, even if you wanted to believe that things like that could be handed down; there was nothing to show that her influence on people was any worse than anybody else's, it being doubtful that many people had a very good influence on those of the opposite sex, and, anyway, she was too young, inexperienced, and self-centered to judge how she varied from the normal in this respect; I would show her in a few days that there was for her difficulties a much more tangible, logical, and jailable answer than any curse; and she wouldn't have much trouble breaking away from morphine, since she was a fairly light user of the stuff and had a temperament favorable to a cure.

I spent three-quarters of an hour working these ideas over for her, and didn't make such a lousy job of it. The fear went out of her eyes as I talked. Toward the last she smiled to herself. When I had finished she jumped up, laughing, working her fingers together.

"Thank you. Thank you," she babbled. "Please don't let me ever stop believing you. Make me believe you even if – No. It *is* true. Make me believe you always. Come on. Let's walk some more."

She almost ran me the rest of the way to the house, chattering all the way. Mickey Linehan was on the porch. I stopped there with him while the girl went in.

"Tch, tch, tch, as Mr. Rolly says." He shook his grinning face at me. "I ought to tell her what happened to that poor girl up in Poisonville that got so she thought she could trust you."

"Bring any news down from the village with you?" I asked.

"Andrews has turned up. He was at the Jeffries' place in

San Mateo, where Aaronia Haldorn's staying. She's still there. Andrews was there from Tuesday afternoon till last night. Al was watching the place and saw him go in, but didn't peg him till he came out. The Jeffries are away – San Diego. Dick's tailing Andrews now. Al says the Haldorn broad hasn't been off the place. Rolly tells me Fink's awake, but don't know anything about the bomb. Fitzstephan's still hanging on to life."

"I think I'll run over and talk to Fink this afternoon," I said. "Stick around here. And – oh, yeah – you'll have to act respectful to me when Mrs. Collinson's around. It's important that she keep on thinking I'm hot stuff."

"Bring back some booze," Mickey said. "I can't do it sober."

Fink was propped up in bed when I got to him, looking out under bandages. He insisted that he knew nothing about the bomb, that all he had come down for was to tell me that Harvey Whidden was his step-son, the missing village-blacksmith's son by a former marriage.

"Well, what of it?" I asked.

"I don't know what of it, except that he was, and I thought you'd want to know about it."

"Why should I?"

"The papers said you said there was some kind of connection between what happened here and what happened up there, and that heavy-set detective said you said I knew more about it than I let on. And I don't want any more trouble, so I thought I'd just come down and tell you, so you couldn't say I hadn't told all I knew."

"Yeah? Then tell me what you know about Madison Andrews."

"I don't know anything about him. I don't know him. He's her guardian or something, ain't he? I read that in the newspapers. But I don't know him."

"Aaronia Haldorn does."

"Maybe she does, mister, but I don't. I just worked for the Haldorns. It wasn't anything to me but a job."

"What was it to your wife?"

"The same thing, a job."

"Where is she?"

"I don't know."

"Why'd she run away from the Temple?"

"I told you before, I don't know. Didn't want to get in trouble, I – Who wouldn't of run away if they got a chance?"

The nurse who had been fluttering around became a nuisance by this time, so I left the hospital for the district attorney's office in the court house. Vernon pushed aside a stack of papers with a the-world-can-wait gesture and said, "Glad to see you; sit down," nodding vigorously, showing me all his teeth.

I sat down and said:

"Been talking to Fink. I couldn't get anything out of him, but he's our meat. The bomb couldn't have got in there except by him."

Vernon frowned for a moment, then shook his chin at me, and snapped:

"What was his motive? And you were there. You say you were looking at him all the time he was in the room. You say you saw nothing."

"What of that?" I asked. "He could outsmart me there. He was a magician's mechanic. He'd know how to make a bomb, and how to put it down without my seeing it. That's his game. We don't know what Fitzstephan saw. They tell me he'll pull through. Let's hang on to Fink till he does."

Vernon clicked his teeth together and said: "Very well, we'll hold him."

I went down the corridor to the sheriff's office. Feeney wasn't in, but his chief deputy – a lanky, pockmarked man named Sweet – said he knew from the way Feeney had spoken of me that he – Feeney – would want me to be given all the help I asked for.

"That's fine," I said. "What I'm interested in now is picking up a couple of bottles of – well, gin, Scotch – whatever happens to be best in this part of the country."

Sweet scratched his Adam's apple and said:

"I wouldn't know about that. Maybe the elevator boy. I guess his gin would be safest. Say, Dick Cotton's crying his head off wanting to see you. Want to talk to him?"

"Yeah, though I don't know what for."

"Well, come back in a couple of minutes."

I went out and rang for the elevator. The boy – he had an age-bent back and a long yellow-gray mustache – was alone in it.

"Sweet said maybe you'd know where I could get a gallon of the white," I said.

"He's crazy," the boy grumbled, and then, when I kept quiet: "You'll be going out this way?"

"Yeah, in a little while."

He closed the door. I went back to Sweet. He took me down an inclosed walk that connected the court house with the prison behind, and left me alone with Cotton in a small boiler-plate cell. Two days in jail hadn't done the marshal of Quesada any good. He was gray-faced and jumpy, and the dimple in his chin kept squirming as he talked. He hadn't anything to tell me except that he was innocent.

All I could think of to say to him was: "Maybe, but you brought it on yourself. What evidence there is is against you. I don't know whether it's enough to convict you or not – depends on your lawyer."

"What did he want?" Sweet asked when I had gone back to him.

"To tell me that he's innocent."

The deputy scratched his Adam's apple again and asked:

"It's supposed to make any difference to you?"

"Yeah, it's been keeping me awake at night. See you later."

I went out to the elevator. The boy pushed a newspaper-wrapped gallon jug at me and said: "Ten bucks." I paid him, stowed the jug in Fitzstephan's car, found the local telephone office, and put in a call for Vic Dallas's drug-store in San Francisco's Mission district.

"I want," I told Vic, "fifty grains of M. and eight of those calomel-ipecac-atropine-strychnine-cascara shots. I'll have somebody from the agency pick up the package tonight or in the morning. Right?"

"If you say so, but if you kill anybody with it don't tell them where you got the stuff."

"Yeah," I said; "they'll die just because I haven't got a lousy pill-roller's diploma."

I put in another San Francisco call, for the agency, talking to the Old Man.

"Can you spare me another op?" I asked.

"MacMan is available, or he can relieve Drake. Whichever you prefer."

"MacMan'll do. Have him stop at Dallas's drug-store for a package on the way down. He knows where it is."

The Old Man said he had no new reports on Aaronia Haldorn and Andrews.

I drove back to the house in the cove. We had company. Three strange cars were standing empty in the driveway, and half a dozen newshounds were sitting and standing around Mickey on the porch. They turned their questions on me.

"Mrs. Collinson's here for a rest," I said. "No interviews, no posing for pictures. Let her alone. If anything breaks here I'll see that you get it, those of you who lay off her. The only thing I can tell you now is that Fink's being held for the bombing."

"What did Andrews come down for?" Jack Santos asked.

That wasn't a surprise to me: I had expected him to turn up now that he had come out of seclusion.

"Ask him," I suggested. "He's administering Mrs. Collinson's estate. You can't make a mystery out of his coming down to see her."

"Is it true that they're on bad terms?"

"No."

"Then why didn't he show up before this – yesterday, or the day before?"

"Ask him."

"Is it true that he's up to his tonsils in debt, or was before the Leggett estate got into his hands?"

"Ask him."

Santos smiled with thinned lips and said:

"We don't have to: we asked some of his creditors. Is there anything to the report that Mrs. Collinson and her husband had quarreled over her being too friendly with Whidden, a couple of days before her husband was killed?"

"Anything but the truth," I said. "Tough. You could do a lot with a story like that."

"Maybe we will," Santos said. "Is it true that she and her husband's family are on the outs, that old Hubert has said he's willing to spend all he's got to see that she pays for any part she had in his son's death?"

I didn't know. I said:

"Don't be a chump. We're working for Hubert now, taking care of her."

"Is it true that Mrs. Haldorn and Tom Fink were released because they had threatened to tell all they knew if they were held for trial?"

"Now you're kidding me, Jack," I said. "Is Andrews still here?"

"Yes."

I went indoors and called Mickey in, asking him: "Seen Dick?"

"He drove past a couple of minutes after Andrews came."

"Sneak away and find him. Tell him not to let the newspaper

gang make him, even if he has to risk losing Andrews for a while. They'd go crazy all over their front pages if they learned we were shadowing him, and I don't want them to go that crazy."

Mrs. Herman was coming down the stairs. I asked her where Andrews was.

"Up in the front room."

I went up there. Gabrielle, in a low-cut dark silk gown, was sitting stiff and straight on the edge of a leather rocker. Her face was white and sullen. She was looking at a handkerchief stretched between her hands. She looked up at me as if glad I had come in. Andrews stood with his back to the fireplace. His white hair, eyebrows, and mustache stood out every which way from his bony pink face. He shifted his scowl from the girl to me, and didn't seem glad I had come in.

I said, "Hullo," and found a table-corner to prop myself on.

He said: "I've come to take Mrs. Collinson back to San Francisco."

She didn't say anything. I said:

"Not to San Mateo?"

"What do you mean by that?" The white tangles of his brows came down to hide all but the bottom halves of his blue eyes.

"God knows. Maybe my mind's been corrupted by the questions the newspapers have been asking me."

He didn't quite wince. He said, slowly, deliberately:

"Mrs. Haldorn sent for me professionally. I went to see her to explain how impossible it would be, in the circumstances, for me to advise or represent her."

"That's all right with me," I said. "And if it took you thirty hours to explain that to her, it's nobody's business."

"Precisely."

"But – I'd be careful how I told the reporters waiting downstairs that. You know how suspicious they are – for no reason at all."

He turned to Gabrielle again, speaking quietly, but with some impatience:

"Well, Gabrielle, are you going with me?"

"Should I?" she asked me.

"Not unless you especially want to."

"I – I don't."

"Then that's settled," I said.

Andrews nodded and went forward to take her hand, saying: "I'm sorry, but I must get back to the city now, my dear. You should have a phone put in, so you can reach me in case you need to."

He declined her invitation to stay to dinner, said, "Good evening," not unpleasantly, to me, and went out. Through a window I could see him presently getting into his car, giving as little attention as possible to the newspaper men gathered around him.

Gabrielle was frowning at me when I turned away from the window.

"What did you mean by what you said about San Mateo?" she asked.

"How friendly are he and Aaronia Haldorn?" I asked.

"I haven't any idea. Why? Why did you talk to him as you did?"

"Detective business. For one thing, there's a rumor that getting control of the estate may have helped him keep his own head above water. Maybe there's nothing in it. But it won't hurt to give him a little scare, so he'll get busy straightening things out – if he has done any juggling – between now and clean-up day. No use of you losing money along with the rest of your troubles."

"Then he – ?" she began.

"He's got a week – several days at least – to unjuggle in. That ought to be enough."

"But –"

Mrs. Herman, calling us to dinner, ended the conversation.

Gabrielle ate very little. She and I had to do most of the talking until I got Mickey started telling about a job he had been on up in Eureka, where he posed as a foreigner who knew no English. Since English was the only language he did know, and Eureka normally held at least one specimen of every nationality there is, he'd had a hell of a time keeping people from finding out just what he was supposed to be. He made a long and laughable story of it. Maybe some of it was the truth: he always got a lot of fun out of acting like the other half of a half-wit.

After the meal he and I strolled around outside while the spring night darkened the grounds.

"MacMan will be down in the morning," I told him. "You and he will have to do the watchdog. Divide it between you anyway you want, but one will have to be on the job all the time."

"Don't give yourself any of the worst of it," he complained. "What's this supposed to be down here – a trap?"

"Maybe."

"Maybe. Uh-huh. You don't know what the hell you're doing. You're stalling around waiting for the horseshoe in your pocket to work."

"The outcome of successful planning always looks like luck to saps. Did Dick have any news?"

"No. He tailed Andrews straight here from his house."

The front door opened, throwing yellow light across the porch. Gabrielle, a dark cape on her shoulders, came into the yellow light, shut the door, and came down the gravel walk.

"Take a nap now if you want," I told Mickey. "I'll call you when I turn in. You'll have to stand guard till morning."

"You're a darb." He laughed in the dark. "By God, you're a darb."

"There's a gallon of gin in the car."

"Huh? Why didn't you say so instead of wasting my time

just talking?" The lawn grass swished against his shoes as he walked away.

I moved towards the gravel walk, meeting the girl.

"Isn't it a lovely night?" she said.

"Yeah. But you're not supposed to go roaming around alone in the dark, even if your troubles are practically over."

"I didn't intend to," she said, taking my arm. "And what does practically over mean?"

"That there are a few details to be taken care of – the morphine, for instance."

She shivered and said:

"I've only enough left for tonight. You promised to –"

"Fifty grains coming in the morning."

She kept quiet, as if waiting for me to say something else. I didn't say anything else. Her fingers wriggled on my sleeve.

"You said it wouldn't be hard to cure me." She spoke half-questioningly, as if expecting me to deny having said anything of the sort.

"It wouldn't."

"You said, perhaps . . ." letting the words fade off.

"We'd do it while we were here?"

"Yes."

"Want to?" I asked. "It's no go if you don't."

"Do I want to?" She stood still in the road, facing me. "I'd give –" A sob ended that sentence. Her voice came again, high-pitched, thin: "Are you being honest with me? Are you? Is what you've told me – all you told me last night and this afternoon – as true as you made it sound? Do I believe in you because you're sincere? Or because you've learned how – as a trick of your business – to make people believe in you?"

She might have been crazy, but she wasn't so stupid. I gave her the answer that seemed best at the time:

"Your belief in me is built on mine in you. If mine's unjustified, so is yours. So let me ask you a question first: were you lying when you said, 'I don't want to be evil'?"

"Oh, I don't. I don't."

"Well, then," I said with an air of finality, as if that settled it. "Now if you want to get off the junk, off we'll get you."

"How – how long will it take?"

"Say a week, to be safe. Maybe less."

"Do you mean that? No longer than that?"

"That's all for the part that counts. You'll have to take care of yourself for some time after, till your system's hitting on all eight again, but you'll be off the junk."

"Will I suffer – much?"

"A couple of bad days; but they won't be as bad as you'll think they are, and your father's toughness will carry you through them."

"If," she said slowly, "I should find out in the middle of it that I can't go through with it, can I –?"

"There'll be nothing you can do about it," I promised cheerfully. "You'll stay in till you come out the other end."

She shivered again and asked:

"When shall we start?"

"Day after tomorrow. Take your usual snort tomorrow, but don't try to stock up. And don't worry about it. It'll be tougher on me than on you: I'll have to put up with you."

"And you'll make allowances – you'll understand – if I'm not always nice while I'm going through it? Even if I'm nasty?"

"I don't know." I didn't want to encourage her to cut up on me. "I don't think so much of niceness that can be turned into nastiness by a little grief."

"Oh, but –" She stopped, wrinkled her forehead, said: "Can't we send Mrs. Herman away? I don't want to – I don't want her looking at me."

"I'll get rid of her in the morning."

"And if I'm – you won't let anybody else see me – if I'm not – if I'm too terrible?"

"No," I promised. "But look here: you're preparing to put on a show for me. Stop thinking about that end of it. You're going to behave. I don't want a lot of monkey-business out of you."

She laughed suddenly, asking:

"Will you beat me if I'm bad?"

I said she might still be young enough for a spanking to do her good.

21 AARONIA HALDORN

MARY NUNEZ arrived at half-past seven the next morning. Mickey Linehan drove Mrs. Herman to Quesada, leaving her there, returning with MacMan and a load of groceries.

MacMan was a square-built, stiff-backed ex-soldier. Ten years of the island had baked his tight-mouthed, solid-jawed, grim face a dark oak. He was the perfect soldier: he went where you sent him, stayed where you put him, and had no ideas of his own to keep him from doing exactly what you told him.

He gave me the druggist's package. I took ten grains of morphine up to Gabrielle. She was eating breakfast in bed. Her eyes were watery, her face damp and grayish. When she saw the bindles in my hand she pushed her tray aside and held her hands out eagerly, wriggling her shoulders.

"Come back in five minutes?" she asked.

"You can take your jolt in front of me. I won't blush."

"But I would," she said, and did.

I went out, shut the door, and leaned against it, hearing the crackle of paper and the clink of a spoon on the water-glass. Presently she called:

"All right."

I went in again. A crumpled ball of white papers in the tray was all that remained of one bindle. The others weren't in sight. She was leaning back against her pillows, eyes half closed, as comfortable as a cat full of goldfish. She smiled lazily at me and said:

"You're a dear. Know what I'd like to do today? Take some

lunch and go out on the water – spend the whole day floating in the sun."

"That ought to be good for you. Take either Linehan or MacMan with you. You're not to go out alone."

"What are you going to do?"

"Ride up to Quesada, over to the county seat, maybe as far as the city."

"Mayn't I go with you?"

I shook my head, saying: "I've got work to do, and you're supposed to be resting."

She said, "Oh," and reached for her coffee. I turned to the door. "The rest of the morphine." She spoke over the edge of her cup. "You've put it in a safe place, where nobody will find it?"

"Yeah," I said, grinning at her, patting my coat-pocket.

In Quesada I spent half an hour talking to Rolly and reading the San Francisco papers. They were beginning to poke at Andrews with hints and questions that stopped just short of libel. That was so much to the good. The deputy sheriff hadn't anything to tell me.

I went over to the county seat. Vernon was in court. Twenty minutes of the sheriff's conversation didn't add anything to my education. I called up the agency and talked to the Old Man. He said Hubert Collinson, our client, had expressed some surprise at our continuing the operation, having supposed that Whidden's death had cleared up the mystery of his son's murder.

"Tell him it didn't," I said. "Eric's murder was tied up with Gabrielle's troubles, and we can't get to the bottom of one except through the other. It'll probably take another week. Collinson's all right," I assured the Old Man. "He'll stand for it when it's explained to him."

The Old Man said, "I certainly hope so," rather coldly, not enthusiastic over having five operatives at work on a job that the supposed client might not want to pay for.

I drove up to San Francisco, had dinner at the St. Germain, stopped at my rooms to collect another suit and a bagful of clean shirts and the like, and got back to the house in the cove a little after midnight. MacMan came out of the darkness while I was tucking the car – we were still using Fitzstephan's – under the shed. He said nothing had happened in my absence. We went into the house together. Mickey was in the kitchen, yawning and mixing himself a drink before relieving MacMan on sentry duty.

"Mrs. Collinson gone to bed?" I asked.

"Her light's still on. She's been in her room all day."

MacMan and I had a drink with Mickey and then went upstairs. I knocked at the girl's door.

"Who is it?" she asked. I told her. She said: "Yes?"

"No breakfast in the morning."

"Really?" Then, as if it were something she had almost forgotten: "Oh, I've decided not to put you to all the trouble of curing me." She opened the door and stood in the opening, smiling too pleasantly at me, a finger holding her place in a book. "Did you have a nice ride?"

"All right," I said, taking the rest of the morphine from my pocket and holding it out to her. "There's no use of my carrying this around."

She didn't take it. She laughed in my face and said:

"You *are* a brute, aren't you?"

"Well, it's your cure, not mine." I put the stuff back in my pocket. "If you –" I broke off to listen. A board had creaked down the hall. Now there was a soft sound, as of a bare foot dragging across the floor.

"That's Mary watching over me," Gabrielle whispered gaily. "She made a bed in the attic and refused to go home. She doesn't think I'm safe with you and your friends. She warned me against you, said you were – what was it? – oh, yes – wolves. Are you?"

"Practically. Don't forget – no breakfast in the morning."

The following afternoon I gave her the first dose of Vic Dallas's mixture, and three more at two-hour intervals. She spent that day in her room. That was Saturday.

On Sunday she had ten grains of morphine and was in high spirits all day, considering herself as good as cured already.

On Monday she had the remainder of Vic's concoction, and the day was pretty much like Saturday. Mickey Linehan returned from the county seat with the news that Fitzstephan was conscious, but too weak and too bandaged to have talked if the doctors had let him; that Andrews had been to San Mateo to see Aaronia Haldorn again; and that she had been to the hospital to see Fink, but had been refused permission by the sheriff's office.

Tuesday was a more exciting day.

Gabrielle was up and dressed when I carried her orange-juice breakfast in. She was bright-eyed, restless, talkative, and laughed easily and often until I mentioned – off-hand – that she was to have no more morphine.

"Ever, you mean?" Her face and voice were panicky. "No, you don't mean that?"

"Yeah."

"But I'll die." Tears filled her eyes, ran down her small white face, and she wrung her hands. It was childishly pathetic. I had to remind myself that tears were one of the symptoms of morphine withdrawal. "You know that's not the way. I don't expect as much as usual. I know I'll get less and less each day. But you can't stop it like this. You're joking. That would kill me." She cried some more at the thought of being killed.

I made myself laugh as if I were sympathetic but amused.

"Nonsense," I said cheerfully. "The chief trouble you're going to have is in being too alive. A couple of days of that, and you'll be all set."

She bit her lips, finally managed a smile, holding out both hands to me.

"I'm going to believe you," she said. "I do believe you. I'm going to believe you no matter what you say."

Her hands were clammy. I squeezed them and said:

"That'll be swell. Now back to bed. I'll look in every now and then, and if you want anything in between, sing out."

"You're not going off today?"

"No," I promised.

She stood the gaff pretty well all afternoon. Of course, there wasn't much heartiness in the way she laughed at herself between attacks when the sneezing and yawning hit her, but the thing was that she tried to laugh.

Madison Andrews came between five and half-past. Having seen him drive in, I met him on the porch. The ruddiness of his face had been washed out to a weak orange.

"Good evening," he said politely. "I wish to see Mrs. Collinson."

"I'll deliver any message to her," I offered.

He pulled his white eyebrows down and some of his normal ruddiness came back.

"I wish to see her." It was a command.

"She doesn't wish to see you. Is there any message?"

All of his ruddiness was back now. His eyes were hot. I was standing between him and the door. He couldn't go in while I stood there. For a moment he seemed about to push me out of the way. That didn't worry me: he was carrying a handicap of twenty pounds and twenty years.

He pulled his jaw into his neck and spoke in the voice of authority:

"Mrs. Collinson must return to San Francisco with me. She cannot stay here. This is a preposterous arrangement."

"She's not going to San Francisco," I said. "If necessary, the district attorney can hold her here as a material witness. Try upsetting that with any of your court orders, and we'll give you something else to worry about. I'm telling you this so you'll know how we stand. We'll prove that she might be in danger from you. How do we know you haven't played marbles with the estate? How do we know you don't mean to take advantage of her present upset condition to shield yourself from trouble over the estate? Why, man, you might even be planning to send her to an insane-asylum so the estate will stay under your control."

He was sick behind his eyes, though the rest of him stood up well enough under this broadside. When he had got his breath and had swallowed, he demanded:

"Does Gabrielle believe this?" His face was magenta.

"Who said anybody believed it?" I was trying to be bland. "I'm just telling you what we'll go into court with. You're a lawyer. You know there's not necessarily any connection between what's true and what you go into court with – or into the newspapers."

The sickness spread from behind his eyes, pushing the color from his face, the stiffness from his bones; but he held himself tall and he found a level voice.

"You may tell Mrs. Collinson," he said, "that I shall return my letters testamentary to the court this week, with an accounting of the estate, and a request that I be relieved."

"That'll be swell," I said, but I felt sorry for the old boy shuffling down to his car, climbing slowly into it.

I didn't tell Gabrielle he had been there.

She was whining a little now between her yawning and sneezing, and her eyes were running water. Face, body, and hands were damp with sweat. She couldn't eat. I kept her full of orange juice. Noises and odors – no matter how faint, how pleasant – were becoming painful to her, and she twitched and jerked continually in her bed.

"Will it get much worse than this?" she asked.

"Not much. There'll be nothing you can't stand."

Mickey Linehan was waiting for me when I got downstairs.

"The spick's got herself a chive," he said pleasantly.

"Yeah?"

"Yeah. It's the one I've been using to shuck lemons to take the stink out of that bargain-counter gin you bought – or did you just borrow it, the owner knowing you'd return it because nobody could drink it? It's a paring knife – four or five inches of stainless steel blade – so you won't get rust-marks on your undershirt when she sticks it in your back. I couldn't find it, and asked her about it, and she didn't look at me like I was a well-poisoner when she said she didn't know anything about it, and that's the first time she never looked at me that way, so I knew she had it."

"Smart of you," I said. "Well, keep an eye on her. She don't like us much."

"I'm to do that?" Mickey grinned. "My idea would be for everybody to look out for himself, seeing that you're the lad she dog-eyes most, and it's most likely you that'll get whittled on. What'd you ever do to her? You haven't been dumb enough to fool with a Mex lady's affections, have you?"

I didn't think he was funny, though he may have been.

Aaronia Haldorn arrived just before dark, in a Lincoln limousine driven by a Negro who turned the siren loose when he brought the car into the drive. I was in Gabrielle's room when the thing howled. She all but jumped out of bed, utterly terrorized by what must have been an ungodly racket to her too sensitive ears.

"What was it? What was it?" she kept crying between rattling teeth, her body shaking the bed.

'Sh-h-h," I soothed her. I was acquiring a pretty fair bedside manner. "Just an automobile horn. Visitors. I'll go down and head them off."

"You won't let anybody see me?" she begged.

"No. Be a good girl till I get back."

Aaronia Haldorn was standing beside the limousine talking to MacMan when I came out. In the dim light, her face was a dusky oval mask between black hat and black fur coat – but her luminous eyes were real enough.

"How do you do?" she said, holding out a hand. Her voice was a thing to make warm waves run up your back. "I'm glad for Mrs. Collinson's sake that you're here. She and I have had excellent proof of your protective ability, both owing our lives to it."

That was all right, but it had been said before. I made a gesture that was supposed to indicate modest distaste for the subject, and beat her to the first tap with:

"I'm sorry she can't see you. She isn't well."

"Oh, but I should so like to see her, if only for a moment. Don't you think it might be good for her?"

I said I was sorry. She seemed to accept that as final, though she said: "I came all the way from the city to see her."

I tried that opening with:

"Didn't Mr. Andrews tell you . . . ?" letting it ravel out.

She didn't say whether he had. She turned and began walking slowly across the grass. There was nothing for me to do but walk along beside her. Full darkness was only a few minutes away. Presently, when we had gone thirty or forty feet from the car, she said:

"Mr. Andrews thinks you suspect him."

"He's right."

"Of what do you suspect him?"

"Juggling the estate. Mind, I don't know, but I do suspect him."

"Really?"

"Really," I said; "and not of anything else."

"Oh, I should suppose that was quite enough."

"It's enough for me. I didn't think it was enough for you."

"I beg your pardon?"

I didn't like the ground I was on with this woman. I was afraid of her. I piled up what facts I had, put some guesses on them, and took a jump from the top of the heap into space:

"When you got out of prison, you sent for Andrews,

pumped him for all he knew, and then, when you learned he was playing with the girl's pennies, you saw what looked to you like a chance to confuse things by throwing suspicion on him. The old boy's woman-crazy: he'd be duck-soup for a woman like you. I don't know what you're planning to do with him, but you've got him started, and have got the papers started after him. I take it you gave them the tip-off on his high financing? It's no good, Mrs. Haldorn. Chuck it. It won't work. You can stir him up, all right, and make him do something criminal, get him into a swell jam: he's desperate enough now that he's being poked at. But whatever he does now won't hide what somebody else did in the past. He's promised to get the estate in order and hand it over. Let him alone. It won't work."

She didn't say anything while we took another dozen steps. A path came under our feet. I said:

"This is the path that runs up the cliff, the one Eric Collinson was pushed from. Did you know him?"

She drew in her breath sharply, with almost a sob in her throat, but her voice was steady, quiet and musical, when she replied:

"You know I did. Why should you ask?"

"Detectives like questions they already know the answer to. Why did you come down here, Mrs. Haldorn?"

"Is that another whose answer you know?"

"I know you came for one or both of two reasons."

"Yes?"

"First, to learn how close we were to our riddle's answer. Right?"

"I've my share of curiosity, naturally," she confessed.

"I don't mind making that much of your trip a success. I know the answer."

She stopped in the path, facing me, her eyes phosphorescent in the deep twilight. She put a hand on my shoulder: she was taller than I. The other hand was in her coat-pocket.

She put her face nearer mine. She spoke very slowly, as if taking great pains to be understood:

"Tell me truthfully. Don't pretend. I don't want to do an unnecessary wrong. Wait, wait – think before you speak – and believe me when I say this isn't the time for pretending, for lying, for bluffing. Now tell me the truth: do you know the answer?"

"Yeah."

She smiled faintly, taking her hand from my shoulder, saying:

"Then there's no use of our fencing."

I jumped at her. If she had fired from her pocket she might have plugged me. But she tried to get the gun out. By then I had a hand on her wrist. The bullet went into the ground between our feet. The nails of her free hand put three red ribbons down the side of my face. I tucked my head under her chin, turned my hip to her before her knee came up, brought her body hard against mine with one arm around her, and bent her gun-hand behind her. She dropped the gun as we fell. I was on top. I stayed there until I had found the gun. I was getting up when MacMan arrived.

"Everything's eggs in the coffee," I told him, having trouble with my voice.

"Have to plug her?" he asked, looking at the woman lying still on the ground.

"No, she's all right. See that the chauffeur's behaving."

MacMan went away. The woman sat up, tucked her legs under her, and rubbed her wrist. I said:

"That's the second reason for your coming, though I thought you meant it for Mrs. Collinson."

She got up, not saying anything. I didn't help her up, not wanting her to know how shaky I was. I said:

"Since we've gone this far, it won't do any harm and it might do some good to talk."

"I don't think anything will do any good now." She set her

hat straight. "You say you know. Then lies are worthless, and only lies would help." She shrugged. "Well, what now?"

"Nothing now, if you'll promise to remember that the time for being desperate is past. This kind of thing splits up in three parts – being caught, being convicted, and being punished. Admit it's too late to do anything about the first, and – well, you know what California courts and prison boards are."

She looked curiously at me and asked: "Why do you tell me this?"

"Because being shot at's no treat to me, and because when a job's done I like to get it cleaned up and over with. I'm not interested in trying to convict you for your part in the racket, and it's a nuisance having you horning in now, trying to muddy things up. Go home and behave."

Neither of us said anything more until we had walked back to the limousine. Then she turned, put out her hand to me, and said:

"I think – I don't know yet – I think I owe you even more now than before."

I didn't say anything and I didn't take her hand. Perhaps it was because she was holding her hand out that she asked:

"May I have my pistol now?"

"No."

"Will you give my best wishes to Mrs. Collinson, and tell her I'm so sorry I couldn't see her?"

"Yeah."

She said, "Goodbye," and got into the car; I took off my hat and she rode away.

22 CONFESSIONAL

MICKEY LINEHAN opened the front door for me. He looked at my scratched face and laughed:

"You do have one hell of a time with your women. Why don't you ask them instead of trying to take it away from them? It'd save you a lot of skin." He poked a thumb at the ceiling. "Better go up and negotiate with that one. She's been raising hell."

I went up to Gabrielle's room. She was sitting in the middle of the wallowed-up bed. Her hands were in her hair, tugging at it. Her soggy face was thirty-five years old. She was making hurt-animal noises in her throat.

"It's a fight, huh?" I said from the door.

She took her hands out of her hair.

"I won't die?" The question was a whimper between edge-to-edge teeth.

"Not a chance."

She sobbed and lay down. I straightened the covers over her. She complained that there was a lump in her throat, that her jaws and the hollows behind her knees ached.

"Regular symptoms," I assured her. "They won't bother you much, and you'll miss the cramps."

Fingernails scratched the door. Gabrielle jumped up in bed, crying:

"Don't go away again."

"No farther than the door," I promised, and went to it.

MacMan was there.

"That Mexican Mary," he whispered, "was hiding in the bushes watching you and the woman. I spotted her when she came out, and tailed her across to the road below. She stopped the limousine and talked with the woman – five–ten minutes. I couldn't get near enough to hear any of it."

"Where is she now?"

"In the kitchen. She came back. The woman in the heap went on. Mickey says the Mex is packing a knife and is going to make grief for us. Reckon he's right?"

"He generally is," I said. "She's strong for Mrs. Collinson, and doesn't think we mean her any good. Why in hell can't she mind her own business? It adds up that she peeped and saw Mrs. Haldorn wasn't for us, figured she was for Mrs. Collinson, and braced her. I hope Mrs. Haldorn had sense enough to tell her to behave. Anyway, there's nothing we can do but watch her. No use giving her the gate: we've got to have a cook."

When MacMan had gone Gabrielle remembered we had had a visitor, and asked me about it, and about the shot she heard and my scratched face.

"It was Aaronia Haldorn," I told her; "and she lost her head. No harm done. She's gone now."

"She came here to kill me," the girl said, not excitedly, but as if she knew certainly.

"Maybe. She wouldn't admit anything. Why should she kill you?"

I didn't get an answer to that.

It was a long bad night. I spent most of it in the girl's room, in a leather rocker dragged in from the front room. She got perhaps an hour and a half of sleep, in three installments. Nightmares brought her screaming out of all three. I dozed when she let me. Off and on through the night I heard stealthy sounds in the hall – Mary Nunez watching over her mistress, I supposed.

Wednesday was a longer and worse day. By noon my jaws were as sore as Gabrielle's, from going around holding my back teeth together. She was getting the works now. Light was positive, active pain to her eyes, sound to her ears, odors of any sort to her nostrils. The weight of her silk nightgown, the touch of sheets over and under her, tortured her skin. Every nerve she had yanked every muscle she had, continually. Promises that she wasn't going to die were no good now: life wasn't nice enough.

"Stop fighting it, if you want," I said. "Let yourself go. I'll take care of you."

She took me at my word, and I had a maniac on my hands. Once her shrieks brought Mary Nunez to the door, snarling and spitting at me in Mex-Spanish. I was holding Gabrielle down in bed by the shoulders, sweating as much as she was.

"Get out of here," I snarled back at the Mexican woman.

She put a brown hand into the bosom of her dress and came a step into the room. Mickey Linehan came up behind her, pulled her back into the hall, and shut the door.

Between the high spots, Gabrielle lay on her back, panting, twitching, staring at the ceiling with hopeless suffering eyes. Sometimes her eyes closed, but the jerking of her body didn't stop.

Rolly came down from Quesada that afternoon with word that Fitzstephan had come sufficiently alive to be questioned by Vernon. Fitzstephan had told the district attorney that he had not seen the bomb, had seen nothing to show when, where, and how it came into the room; but that he had an indistinct memory of hearing a tinkling, as of broken glass falling, and a thud on the floor close to him just after Fink and I had left the room.

I told Rolly to tell Vernon I'd try to get over to see him the next day, and to hang on to Fink. The deputy sheriff promised to deliver the message, and left. Mickey and I were standing on the porch. We didn't have anything to say to each other, hadn't all day. I was lighting a cigarette when the girl's voice came from indoors. Mickey turned away, saying something with the name of God in it.

I scowled at him and asked angrily:

"Well, am I right or wrong?"

He glared back at me, said, "I'd a damned sight rather be wrong," and walked away.

I cursed him and went inside. Mary Nunez, starting up the front stairs, retreated towards the kitchen when she saw me, walking backwards, her eyes watching me crazily. I cursed her and went upstairs to where I had left MacMan at the girl's door. He wouldn't look at me, so I made it unanimous by cursing him.

Gabrielle spent the balance of the afternoon shrieking, begging, and crying for morphine. That evening she made a complete confession:

"I told you I didn't want to be evil," she said, wadding the bedclothes in feverish hands. "That was a lie. I did. I've always wanted to, always have been. I wanted to do to you what I did to the others; but now I don't want you: I want morphine. They won't hang me: I know that. And I don't care what else they do to me, if I get morphine."

She laughed viciously and went on:

"You were right when you said I brought out the worst in men because I wanted to. I did want to; and I did – except, I failed with Doctor Riese, and with Eric. I don't know what was the matter with them. But I failed with both of them, and in failing let them learn too much about me. And that's why they were killed. Joseph drugged Doctor Riese, and I killed him myself, and then we made Minnie think she had. And I persuaded Joseph to kill Aaronia, and he would have done it – he would have done anything I asked – if you hadn't interfered. I got Harvey to kill Eric for me. I was tied to Eric – legally – a good man who wanted to make a good woman of me."

She laughed again, licking her lips.

"Harvey and I had to have money, and I couldn't – I was too afraid of being suspected – get enough from Andrews; so we pretended I had been kidnapped, to get it that way. It was a shame you killed Harvey: he was a glorious beast. I had that bomb, had had it for months. I took it from father's laboratory, when he was making some experiments for a moving picture company. It wasn't very large, and I always carried it with me – just in case. I meant it for you in the hotel room. There was nothing between Owen and me – that was another lie – he didn't love me. I meant it for you, because you were – because I was afraid you were getting at the truth. I was feverish, and when I heard two men go out, leaving one in your room, I was sure the one was you. I didn't see that it was Owen till too late – till I had opened the door a little and thrown the bomb in. Now you've got what you want. Give me morphine. There's no reason for your playing with me any longer. Give me morphine. You've succeeded. Have what I've told you written out: I'll sign it. You can't pretend now I'm worth curing, worth saving. Give me morphine."

Now it was my turn to laugh, asking:

"And aren't you going to confess to kidnapping Charlie Ross and blowing up the *Maine*?"

We had some more hell – a solid hour of it – before she exhausted herself again. The night dragged through. She got a little more than two hours' sleep, a half-hour gain over the previous night. I dozed in the chair when I could.

Sometime before daylight I woke to the feel of a hand on my coat. Keeping my breathing regular, I pushed my eyelids far enough apart to squint through the lashes. We had a very dim light in the room, but I thought Gabrielle was in bed, though I couldn't see whether she was asleep or awake. My head was tilted back to rest on the back of the chair. I couldn't see the hand that was exploring my inside coat-pocket, nor the arm that came down over my shoulder; but they smelled of the kitchen, so I knew they were brown.

The Mexican woman was standing behind me. Mickey had told me she had a knife. Imagination told me she was holding it in her other hand. Good judgment told me to let her alone. I did that, closing my eyes again. Paper rustled between her fingers, and her hand left my pocket.

I moved my head sleepily then, and changed a foot's position. When I heard the door close quietly behind me, I sat up and looked around. Gabrielle was sleeping. I counted the bindles in my pocket and found that eight of them had been taken.

Presently Gabrielle opened her eyes. This was the first time since the cure started that she had awakened quietly. Her face was haggard, but not wild-eyed. She looked at the window and asked:

"Isn't day coming yet?"

"It's getting light." I gave her some orange juice. "We'll get some solid food in you today."

"I don't want food. I want morphine."

"Don't be silly. You'll get food. You won't get morphine. Today won't be like yesterday. You're over the hump, and the rest of it's down-hill going, though you may hit a couple of rough spots. It's silly to ask for morphine now. What do you want to do? Have nothing to show for the hell you've been through? You've got it licked now: stay with it."

"Have I – have I really got it licked?"

"Yeah. All you've got to buck now is nervousness, and the memory of how it felt to have a skinful of hop."

"I can do it," she said. "I can do it because you say I can."

She got along fine till late in the morning, when she blew up for an hour or two. But it wasn't so bad, and I got her straightened out again. When Mary brought up her luncheon I left them together and went downstairs for my own.

Mickey and MacMan were already at the dining-room table. Neither of them spoke a word – to one another or to me – during the meal. Since they kept quiet, I did.

When I went back upstairs, Gabrielle, in a green bathrobe, was sitting in the leather rocker that had been my bed for two nights. She had brushed her hair and powdered her face. Her eyes were mostly green, with a lift to the lower lids as if she was hiding a joke. She said with mock solemnity:

"Sit down. I want to talk seriously to you."

I sat down.

"Why did you go through all this with me – for me?" She was really serious now. "You didn't have to, and it couldn't have been pleasant. I was – I don't know how bad I was." She turned red from forehead to chest. "I know I was revolting, disgusting. I know how I must seem to you now. Why – why did you?"

I said:

"I'm twice your age, sister; an old man. I'm damned if I'll make a chump of myself by telling you why I did it, why it was neither revolting nor disgusting, why I'd do it again and be glad of the chance."

She jumped out of her chair, her eyes round and dark, her mouth trembling.

"You mean – ?"

"I don't mean anything that I'll admit," I said; "and if you're going to parade around with that robe hanging open you're going to get yourself some bronchitis. You ex-hopheads have to be careful about catching cold."

She sat down again, put her hands over her face, and began crying. I let her cry. Presently she giggled through her fingers and asked:

"Will you go out and let me be alone all afternoon?"

"Yeah, if you'll keep warm."

I drove over to the county seat, went to the county hospital, and argued with people until they let me into Fitzstephan's room.

He was ninety per cent bandages, with only an eye, an ear, and one side of his mouth peeping out. The eye and the half-mouth smiled through linen at me, and a voice came through:

"No more of your hotel rooms for me." It wasn't a clear

voice because it had to come out sidewise, and he couldn't move his jaws; but there was plenty of vitality in it. It was the voice of a man who meant to keep on living.

I smiled at him and said:

"No hotel rooms this time, unless you think San Quentin's a hotel. Strong enough to stand up under a third-degree, or shall we wait a day or two?"

"I ought to be at my best now," he said. "Facial expressions won't betray me."

"Good. Now here's the first point: Fink handed you that bomb when he shook hands with you. That's the only way it could have got in without my seeing it. His back was to me then. You didn't know what he was handing you, but you had to take it, just as you have to deny it now, or tip us off that you were tied up with the Holy Grail mob, and that Fink had reasons for killing you."

Fitzstephan said: "You say the most remarkable things. I'm glad he had reasons, though."

"You engineered Riese's murder. The others were your accomplices. When Joseph died the blame was put all on him, the supposed madman. That's enough to let the others out, or ought to be. But here you are killing Collinson and planning God knows what else. Fink knows that if you keep it up you're going to let the truth out about the Temple murder, and he'll swing with you. So, scared panicky, he tries to stop you."

Fitzstephan said: "Better and better. So I killed Collinson?"

"You had him killed – hired Whidden and then didn't pay him. He kidnapped the girl then, holding her for his money, knowing she was what you wanted. It was you his bullet came closest to when we cornered him."

Fitzstephan said: "I'm running out of exclamatory phrases. So I was after her? I wondered about my motive."

"You must have been pretty rotten with her. She'd had a bad time with Andrews, and even with Eric, but she didn't mind talking about them. But when I tried to learn the details of your wooing she shuddered and shut up. I suppose she slammed you down so hard you bounced, and you're the sort of egoist to be driven to anything by that."

Fitzstephan said: "I suppose. You know, I've had more than half an idea at times that you were secretly nursing some exceptionally idiotic theory."

"Well, why shouldn't I? You were standing beside Mrs. Leggett when she suddenly got that gun. Where'd she get it? Chasing her out of the laboratory and down the stairs wasn't in character – not for you. Your hand was on her gun when that bullet hit her neck. Was I supposed to be deaf, dumb, and blind? There was, as you agreed, one mind behind all Gabrielle's troubles. You're the one person who has that sort of mind, whose connection with each episode can be traced, and who has the necessary motive. The motive held me up: I couldn't be sure of it till I'd had my first fair chance to pump Gabrielle – after the explosion. And another thing that held me up was my not being able to tie you to the Temple crowd till Fink and Aaronia Haldorn did it for me."

Fitzstephan said: "Ah, Aaronia helped tie me? What has she been up to?" He said it absent-mindedly, and his one visible gray eye was small, as if he was busy with other thoughts behind it.

"She's done her best to cover you up by gumming the works, creating confusion, setting us after Andrews, even trying to shoot me. I mentioned Collinson just after she'd learned that the Andrews false-trail was no good. She gave me a half-concealed gasp and sob, just on the off-chance that it'd lead me astray, overlooking no bets. I like her: she's shifty."

"She's so headstrong," Fitzstephan said lightly, not having listened to half I had said, busy with his own thoughts. He turned his head on the pillow so that his eye looked at the ceiling, narrow and brooding.

I said: "And so ends the Great Dain Curse."

He laughed then, as well as he could with one eye and a fraction of a mouth, and said:

"Suppose, my boy, I were to tell you I'm a Dain?"

I said: "Huh?"

He said: "My mother and Gabrielle's maternal grandfather were brother and sister."

I said: "I'll be damned."

"You'll have to go away and let me think," he said. "I don't know yet what I shall do. Understand, at present I admit nothing. But the chances are I shall insist on the curse, shall use it to save my dear neck. In that event, my son, you're going to see a most remarkable defense, a circus that will send the nation's newspapers into happy convulsions. I shall be a Dain, with the cursed Dain blood in me, and the crimes of Cousin Alice and Cousin Lily and Second-cousin Gabrielle and the Lord knows how many other criminal Dains shall be evidence in my behalf. The number of my own crimes will be to my advantage, on the theory that nobody but a lunatic could have committed so many. And won't they be many? I'll produce crimes and crimes, dating from the cradle.

"Even literature shall help me. Didn't most reviewers agree that *The Pale Egyptian* was the work of a sub-Mongolian? And, as I remember, the consensus was that my *Eighteen Inches* bore all the better known indications of authorial degeneracy. Evidence, son, to save my sweet neck. And I shall wave my mangled body at them – an arm gone, a leg gone, parts of my torso and face – a ruin whose crimes and high Heaven have surely brought sufficient punishment upon him. And perhaps the bomb shocked me into sanity again, or, at least, out of criminal insanity. Perhaps I'll even have become religious. It'll be a splendid circus. It tempts me. But I must think before I commit myself."

He panted through the uncovered half of his mouth, exhausted by his speech, looking at me with a gray eye that held triumphant mirth.

"You'll probably make a go of it," I said as I prepared to leave. "And I'm satisfied if you do. You've taken enough of a licking. And, legally, you're entitled to beat the jump if ever anybody was."

"Legally entitled?" he repeated, the mirth going out of his eye. He looked away, and then at me again, uneasily. "Tell me the truth. Am I?"

I nodded.

"But, damn it, that spoils it," he complained, fighting to keep the uneasiness out of his eye, fighting to retain his usual lazily amused manner, and not making such a poor job of it. "It's no fun if I'm really cracked."

When I got back to the house in the cove, Mickey and MacMan were sitting on the front steps. MacMan said "Hello" and Mickey said: "Get any fresh woman-scars while you were away? Your little playmate's been asking for you." I supposed from this – from my being readmitted to the white race – that Gabrielle had had a good afternoon.

She was sitting up in bed with pillows behind her back, her face still – or again – powdered, her eyes shining happily.

"I didn't mean for you to go away forever," she scolded. "It was nasty of you. I've got a surprise for you and I've nearly burst waiting."

"Well, here I am. What is it?"

"Shut your eyes."

I shut them.

"Open your eyes."

I opened them. She was holding out to me the eight bindles that Mary Nunez had picked my pocket for.

"I've had them since noon," she said proudly; "and they've got finger-marks and tear-marks on them, but not one of them has been opened. It – honestly – it wasn't so hard not to."

"I knew it wouldn't be, for you," I said. "That's why I didn't take them away from Mary."

"You knew? You trusted me that much – to go away and leave me with them?"

Nobody but an idiot would have confessed that for two days the folded papers had held powdered sugar instead of the original morphine.

"You're the nicest man in the world." She caught one of my hands and rubbed her cheek into it, then dropped it quickly, frowned her face out of shape, and said: "Except! You sat there this noon and deliberately tried to make me think you were in love with me."

"Well?" I asked, trying to keep my face straight.

"You hypocrite. You deceiver of young girls. It would serve you right if I made you marry me – or sued you for breach of promise. I honestly believed you all afternoon – and it *did* help me. I believed you until you came in just now, and then I saw –" She stopped.

"Saw what?"

"A monster. A nice one, an especially nice one to have around when you're in trouble, but a monster just the same, without any human foolishness like love in him, and – What's the matter? Have I said something I shouldn't?"

"I don't think you should have," I said. "I'm not sure I wouldn't trade places with Fitzstephan now – if that big-eyed woman with the voice was part of the bargain."

"Oh, dear!" she said.

23 THE CIRCUS

OWEN FITZSTEPHAN never spoke to me again. He refused to see me, and when, as a prisoner, he couldn't help himself there, he shut his mouth and kept it shut. This sudden hatred of me – for it amounted to that – had grown, I supposed, out of his knowing I thought him insane. He wanted the rest of the world, or at least the dozen who would represent the world on his jury, to think he had been crazy – and did make them think so – but he didn't want me to agree with them. As a sane man who, by pretending to be a lunatic, had done as he pleased and escaped punishment, he had a joke – if you wanted to call it that – on the world. But if he was a lunatic who, ignorant of his craziness, thought he was pretending to be a lunatic, then the joke – if you wanted to call it that – was on him. And my having such a joke on him was more than his egotism could stomach, even though it's not likely he ever admitted to himself that he was, or might be, actually crazy. Whatever he thought, he never spoke to me after the hospital interview in which I had said he was legally entitled to escape hanging.

His trial, when he was well enough to appear in court some months later, was every bit of the circus he had promised, and the newspapers had their happy convulsions. He was tried in the county court house for Mrs. Cotton's murder. Two new witnesses had been found, who had seen him walking away from the rear of the Cotton house that morning, and a third who identified his car as the one that had been parked four blocks away all – or all the latter part of – the previous night. The city and county district attorneys agreed that this evidence made the Cotton case the strongest against him.

Fitzstephan's plea was *Not guilty by reason of insanity*, or whatever the legal wording was. Since Mrs. Cotton's murder had been the last of his crimes, his lawyers could, and did, introduce, as proof of his insanity, all that he had done in the others. They made a high, wide, and handsome job of it, carrying out his original idea that the best way to prove him crazy was to show he had committed more crimes than any sane man could have. Well, it was plain enough that he had.

He had known Alice Dain, his cousin, in New York when she and Gabrielle, then a child, were living there. Gabrielle couldn't corroborate this: we had only Fitzstephan's word for it; but it may have been so. He said they concealed his relationship from the others because they did not want the girl's father – for whom Alice was then searching – to know that she was bringing with her any links with the dangerous past. Fitzstephan said Alice had been his mistress in New York: that could have been true, but didn't matter.

After Alice and Gabrielle left New York for San Francisco, Fitzstephan and the woman exchanged letters occasionally, but with no definite purpose. Fitzstephan then met the Haldorns. The cult was his idea: he organized it, financed it, and brought it to San Francisco, though he kept his connection with it a secret, since everyone who knew him knew his skepticism; and his interest in it would have advertised it as the fake it was. To him, he said, the cult was a combination of toy and meal-ticket: he liked influencing people, especially in obscure ways, and people didn't seem to like buying his books.

Aaronia Haldorn was his mistress. Joseph was a puppet, in the family as in the Temple.

In San Francisco Fitzstephan and Alice arranged so that he became acquainted with her husband and Gabrielle through other friends of the family. Gabrielle was now a young woman. Her physical peculiarities, which he interpreted pretty much as she had, fascinated him; and he tried his luck with her. He didn't have any. That made him doubly determined to land her: he was that way. Alice was his ally. She knew him and she hated the girl – so she wanted him to have her. Alice had told Fitzstephan the family history. The girl's father did not know at this time that she had been taught to think him her mother's murderer. He knew she had a deep aversion to him, but did not know on what it was based. He thought that what he had gone through in prison and since had marked him with a hardness naturally enough repellant to a young girl who was, in spite of their relationship, actually only a recent acquaintance.

He learned the truth about it when, surprising Fitzstephan in further attempts to make Gabrielle – as Fitzstephan put it – listen to reason, he had got into a three-cornered row with the pair of them. Leggett now began to understand what sort of a woman he was married to. Fitzstephan was no longer invited to the Leggett house, but kept in touch with Alice and waited his time.

His time came when Upton arrived with his demand for blackmail. Alice went to Fitzstephan for advice. He gave it to her – poisonously. He urged her to handle Upton herself, concealing his demand – his knowledge of the Leggett past – from Leggett. He told her she should above all else continue to keep her knowledge of Leggett's Central American and Mexican history concealed from him – a valuable hold on him now that he hated her because of what she'd taught the girl. Giving Upton the diamonds, and faking the burglary evidence, were Fitzstephan's ideas. Poor Alice didn't mean anything to him: he didn't care what happened to her so long as he could ruin Leggett and get Gabrielle.

He succeeded in the first of those aims: guided by him, Alice completely demolished the Leggett household, thinking, until the very last, when he pursued her after giving her the pistol in the laboratory, that he had a clever plan by which they would be saved; that is, she and he would: her husband didn't count with her any more than she with Fitzstephan. Fitzstephan had had to kill her, of course, to keep her from exposing him when she found that his clever plan was a trap for her.

Fitzstephan said he killed Leggett himself. When Gabrielle left the house after seeing Ruppert's murder, she left a note saying she had gone for good. That broke up the arrangement as far as Leggett was concerned. He told Alice he was through, was going away, and offered of his own accord to write a statement assuming responsibility for what she had done. Fitzstephan tried to persuade Alice to kill him, but she wouldn't. He did. He wanted Gabrielle, and he didn't think a live Leggett, even though a fugitive from justice, would let him have her.

Fitzstephan's success in getting rid of Leggett, and in escaping detection by killing Alice, encouraged him. He went blithely on with his plan to get the girl. The Haldorns had been introduced to the Leggetts some months before, and already had her nibbling at their hook. She had gone to them when she ran away from home. Now they persuaded her to come to the Temple again. The Haldorns didn't know what Fitzstephan was up to, what he had done to the Leggetts: they thought that the girl was only another of the likely prospects he fed them. But Doctor Riese, hunting for Joseph in Joseph's part of the Temple the day I got there, opened a door that should have been locked, and saw Fitzstephan and the Haldorns in conference.

That was dangerous: Riese couldn't be kept quiet, and, once Fitzstephan's connection with the Temple was known, as likely as not the truth about his part in the Leggett riot would come out. He had two easily handled tools – Joseph and Minnie. He had Riese killed. But that woke Aaronia up to his true interest in Gabrielle. Aaronia, jealous, could and would either make him give up the girl or ruin him. He persuaded Joseph that none of them was safe from the gallows while Aaronia lived. When I saved Aaronia by killing her husband, I also saved Fitzstephan for the time: Aaronia and

Fink had to keep quiet about Riese's death if they wanted to save themselves from being charged with complicity in it.

By this time Fitzstephan had hit his stride. He looked on Gabrielle now as his property, bought with the deaths he had caused. Each death had increased her price, her value to him. When Eric carried her off and married her, Fitzstephan hadn't hesitated. Eric was to be killed.

Nearly a year before, Fitzstephan had wanted a quiet place where he could go to finish a novel. Mrs. Fink, my village-blacksmith, had recommended Quesada. She was a native of the village, and her son by a former marriage, Harvey Whidden, was living there. Fitzstephan went to Quesada for a couple of months, and became fairly well acquainted with Whidden. Now that there was another murder to be done, Fitzstephan remembered Whidden as a man who might do it, for a price.

When Fitzstephan heard that Collinson wanted a quiet place where his wife could rest and recuperate while they were waiting for the Haldorns' trial, he suggested Quesada. Well, it was a quiet place, probably the quietest in California. Then Fitzstephan went to Whidden with an offer of a thousand dollars for Eric's murder. Whidden refused at first, but he wasn't nimble-witted, and Fitzstephan could be persuasive enough, so the bargain had been made.

Whidden bungled a try at it Thursday night, frightening Collinson into wiring me, saw the wire in the telegraph office, and thought he had to go through with it then to save himself. So he fortified himself with whiskey, followed Collinson Friday night, and shoved him off the cliff. Then he took some more whiskey and came to San Francisco, considering himself by this time a hell of a desperate guy. He phoned his employer, saying: "Well, I killed him easy enough and dead enough. Now I want my money."

Fitzstephan's phone came through the house switchboard: he didn't know who might have heard Whidden talking. He decided to play safe. He pretended he didn't know who was talking nor what he was talking about. Thinking Fitzstephan was double-crossing him, knowing what the novelist wanted, Whidden decided to take the girl and hold her for, not his original thousand dollars, but ten thousand. He had enough drunken cunning to disguise his handwriting when he wrote his note to Fitzstephan, not to sign it, and to so word it that Fitzstephan couldn't tell the police who had sent it without explaining how he knew who had sent it.

Fitzstephan wasn't sitting any too pretty. When he got Whidden's note, he decided to play his hand boldly, pushing his thus-far-solid luck. He told me about the phone call and gave me the letter. That entitled him to show himself in Quesada with an excellent reason for being there. But he came down ahead of time, the night before he joined me, and went to the marshal's house to ask Mrs. Cotton – whose relation to Whidden he knew – where he could find the man. Whidden was there, hiding from the marshal. Whidden wasn't nimble-witted, and Fitzstephan was persuasive enough when he wanted to be: Fitzstephan explained how Whidden's recklessness had forced him to pretend to not understand the phone call. Fitzstephan had a scheme by which Whidden could now collect his ten thousand dollars in safety, or so he made Whidden think.

Whidden went back to his hiding-place. Fitzstephan remained with Mrs. Cotton. She, poor woman, now knew too much, and didn't like what she knew. She was doomed: killing people was the one sure and safe way of keeping them quiet: his whole recent experience proved it. His experience with Leggett told him that if he could get her to leave behind a statement in which various mysterious points were satisfactorily – and not too truthfully – explained, his situation would be still further improved. She suspected his intentions, and didn't want to help him carry them out. She finally wrote the statement he dictated, but not until late in the morning. His description of how he finally got it from her wasn't pleasant; but he got it, and then strangled her, barely finishing when her husband arrived home from his all-night hunt.

Fitzstephan escaped by the back door – the witnesses who had seen him go away from the house didn't come forward until his photograph in the papers jogged their memories – and joined Vernon and me at the hotel. He went with us to Whidden's hiding-place below Dull Point. He knew Whidden, knew the dull man's probable reaction to this second betrayal. He knew that neither Cotton nor Feeney would be sorry to have to shoot Whidden. Fitzstephan believed he could trust to his luck and what gamblers call the percentage of the situation. That failing, he meant to stumble when he stepped from the boat, accidentally shooting Whidden with the gun in his hand. (He remembered how neatly he had disposed of Mrs. Leggett.) He might have been blamed for that, might even have been suspected, but he could hardly have been convicted of anything.

Once again his luck held. Whidden, seeing Fitzstephan with us, had flared up and tried to shoot him, and we had killed Whidden.

That was the story with which this crazy man, thinking himself sane, tried to establish his insanity, and succeeded. The other charges against him were dropped. He was sent to the state asylum at Napa. A year later he was discharged. I don't suppose the asylum officials thought him cured: they thought he was too badly crippled ever to be dangerous again.

Aaronia Haldorn carried him off to an island in Puget Sound, I've heard.

She testified at his trial, as one of his witnesses, but was not herself tried for anything. The attempt of her husband and Fitzstephan to kill her had, for all practical purposes, removed her from among the guilty.

We never found Mrs. Fink.

Tom Fink drew a five-to-fifteen-years jolt in San Quentin

for what he had done to Fitzstephan. Neither of them seemed to blame the other now, and each tried to cover the other up on the witness stand. Fink's professed motive for the bombing was to avenge his step-son's death, but nobody swallowed that. He had tried to check Fitzstephan's activities before Fitzstephan brought the whole works down on their ears.

Released from prison, finding himself shadowed, Fink had seen both reason for fear and a means to safety in that shadow. He *had* back-doored Mickey that night, slipping out to get the material for his bomb, and then in again, working all night on the bomb. The news he had brought me was supposed to account for his presence in Quesada. The bomb wasn't large – its outer cover was an aluminum soap container wrapped in white paper – and neither he nor Fitzstephan had had any difficulty in concealing it from me when it passed between them during their handshaking. Fitzstephan had thought it something Aaronia was sending him, something important enough to justify the risk in sending it. He couldn't have refused to take it without attracting my attention, without giving away the connection between him and Fink. He had concealed it until we had left the room, and then had opened it – to wake up in the hospital. Tom Fink had thought himself safe, with Mickey to testify that he had shadowed him from the time he had left the prison, and me to account for his behavior on the scene of the bombing.

Fitzstephan said that he did not think Alice Leggett's account of the killing of her sister Lily was the truth, that he thought she – Alice – had done the killing herself and had lied to hurt Gabrielle. Everybody took it for granted that he was right – everybody, including Gabrielle – though he didn't have any evidence to support what was after all only his guess. I was tempted to have the agency's Paris correspondent see what he could dig up on that early affair, but decided not to. It was nobody's business except Gabrielle's, and she seemed happy enough with what had already been dug up.

She was in the Collinsons' hands now. They had come to Quesada for her as soon as the newspapers put out their first extra accusing Fitzstephan of Eric's murder. The Collinsons hadn't had to be crude about it – to admit that they'd ever suspected her of anything: when Andrews had surrendered his letters testamentary, and another administrator – Walter Fielding – had been appointed, the Collinsons had simply seemed to pick her up, as was their right as her closest relations, where Andrews had put her down.

Two months in the mountains topped off her cure, and she came back to the city looking like nothing that she had been. The difference was not only in appearance.

"I can't really make myself believe that all that actually happened to me," she told me one noon when she, Laurence Collinson, and I were lunching together between morning and afternoon court-sessions. "Is it, do you think, because there was so much of it that I became callous?"

"No. Remember you were going around coked up most of the time. That saved you from the sharp edge. Lucky for you you were. Stay away from the morphine now and it'll always be a hazy sort of dream. Any time you want to bring it back clear and vivid, take a jolt."

"I won't, I won't, ever," she said; "not even to give you the – the fun of bullying me through a cure again. He enjoyed himself awfully," she told Laurence Collinson. "He used to curse me, ridicule me, threaten me with the most terrible things, and then, at the last, I think he tried to seduce me. And if I'm uncouth at times, Laurence, you'll have to blame him: he positively hadn't a refining influence."

She seemed to have come back far enough.

Laurence Collinson laughed with us, but not from any farther down than his chin. I had an idea he thought I hadn't a refining influence.

THE GLASS KEY

To Nell Martin

THE BODY IN CHINA STREET

I

GREEN DICE rolled across the green table, struck the rim together, and bounced back. One stopped short holding six white spots in two equal rows uppermost. The other tumbled out to the center of the table and came to rest with a single spot on top.

Ned Beaumont grunted softly – "Uhn!" – and the winners cleared the table of money.

Harry Sloss picked up the dice and rattled them in a pale broad hairy hand. "Shoot two bits." He dropped a twenty-dollar bill and a five-dollar bill on the table.

Ned Beaumont stepped back saying: "Get on him, gamblers, I've got to refuel!" He crossed the billiard-room to the door. There he met Walter Ivans coming in. He said, "'Lo, Walt," and would have gone on, but Ivans caught his elbow as he passed and turned to face him.

"D-d-did you t-talk to P-p-paul?" When Ivans said "P-p-paul" a fine spray flew out between his lips.

"I'm going up to see him now." Ivans's china-blue eyes brightened in his round fair face until Ned Beaumont, narrow of eye, added: "Don't expect much. If you could wait awhile."

Ivans's chin twitched. "B-b-but she's going to have the b-b-baby next month."

A startled look came into Ned Beaumont's dark eyes. He took his arm out of the shorter man's hand and stepped back. Then a corner of his mouth twitched under his dark mustache and he said: "It's a bad time, Walt, and – well – you'll save yourself disappointment by not looking for much before November." His eyes were narrow again and watchful.

"B-b-but if you t-tell him –"

"I'll put it to him as hot as I can and you ought to know he'll go the limit, but he's in a tough spot right now." He moved his shoulders and his face became gloomy except for the watchful brightness of his eyes.

Ivans wet his lips and blinked his eyes many times. He drew in a long breath and patted Ned Beaumont's chest with both hands. "G-g-go up now," he said in an urgent pleading voice. "I-I'll wait here f-for you."

II

Ned Beaumont went upstairs lighting a thin green-dappled cigar. At the second-floor landing, where the Governor's portrait hung, he turned towards the front of the building and knocked on the broad oaken door that shut off the corridor at that end.

When he heard Paul Madvig's "All right" he opened the door and went in.

Paul Madvig was alone in the room, standing at the window, with his hands in his trousers-pockets, his back to the door, looking through the screen down into dark China Street.

He turned around slowly and said: "Oh, here you are." He was a man of forty-five, tall as Ned Beaumont, but forty pounds heavier without softness. His hair was light, parted in the middle, and brushed flat to his head. His face was handsome in a ruddy stout-featured way. His clothes were saved from flashiness by their quality and by his manner of wearing them.

Ned Beaumont shut the door and said: "Lend me some money."

From his inner coat-pocket Madvig took a large brown wallet. "What do you want?"

"Couple of hundred."

Madvig gave him a hundred-dollar bill and five twenties, asking: "Craps?"

"Thanks." Ned Beaumont pocketed the money. "Yes."

"It's a long time since you've done any winning, isn't it?" Madvig asked as he returned his hands to his trousers-pockets.

"Not so long – a month or six weeks."

Madvig smiled. "That's a long time to be losing."

"Not for me." There was a faint note of irritation in Ned Beaumont's voice.

Madvig rattled coins in his pocket. "Much of a game tonight?" He sat on a corner of the table and looked down at his glistening brown shoes.

Ned Beaumont looked curiously at the blond man, then shook his head and said: "Peewee." He walked to the window. Above the buildings on the opposite side of the street the sky was black and heavy. He went behind Madvig to the telephone and called a number. "Hello, Bernie. This is Ned. What's the price on Peggy O'Toole? Is that all? . . . Well, give me five hundred of each. . . . Sure. . . . I'm betting it's going to rain and if it does she'll beat Incinerator. . . . All right, give me a better price then. . . . Right." He put the receiver on its prong and came around in front of Madvig again.

Madvig asked: "Why don't you try laying off awhile when you hit one of these sour streaks?"

Ned Beaumont scowled. "That's no good, only spreads it out. I ought to've put that fifteen hundred on the nose instead of spreading it across the board. Might as well take your punishment and get it over with."

Madvig chuckled and raised his head to say: "If you can stand the gaff."

Ned Beaumont drew down the ends of his mouth, the ends of his mustache following them down. "I can stand anything I've got to stand," he said as he moved towards the door.

He had his hand on the door-knob when Madvig said, earnestly: "I guess you can, at that, Ned."

Ned Beaumont turned around and asked, "Can what?" fretfully.

Madvig transferred his gaze to the window. "Can stand anything," he said.

Ned Beaumont studied Madvig's averted face. The blond man stirred uncomfortably and moved coins in his pockets again. Ned Beaumont made his eyes blank and asked in an utterly puzzled tone: "Who?"

Madvig's face flushed. He rose from the table and took a step towards Ned Beaumont. "You go to hell," he said.

Ned Beaumont laughed.

Madvig grinned sheepishly and wiped his face with a green-bordered handkerchief. "Why haven't you been out to the house?" he asked. "Mom was saying last night she hadn't seen you for a month."

"Maybe I'll drop in some night this week."

"You ought to. You know how Mom likes you. Come for supper." Madvig put his handkerchief away.

Ned Beaumont moved towards the door again, slowly, watching the blond man from the ends of his eyes. With his hand on the knob he asked: "Was that what you wanted to see me about?"

Madvig frowned. "Yes, that is –" He cleared his throat. "Uh – oh – there's something else." Suddenly his diffidence was gone, leaving him apparently tranquil and self-possessed. "You know more about this stuff than I do. Miss Henry's birthday's Thursday. What do you think I ought to give her?"

Ned Beaumont took his hand from the door-knob. His eyes, by the time he was facing Madvig squarely again, had lost their shocked look. He blew cigar-smoke out and asked: "They're having some kind of birthday doings, aren't they?"

"Yes."

"You invited?"

Madvig shook his head. "But I'm going there to dinner tomorrow night."

Ned Beaumont looked down at his cigar, then up at Madvig's face again, and asked: "Are you going to back the Senator, Paul?"

"I think we will."

Ned Beaumont's smile was mild as his voice when he put his next question: "Why?"

Madvig smiled. "Because with us behind him he'll snow Roan under and with his help we can put over the whole ticket just like nobody was running against us."

Ned Beaumont put his cigar in his mouth. He asked, still mildly: "Without you" – he stressed the pronoun – "behind him could the Senator make the grade this time?"

Madvig was calmly positive. "Not a chance."

Ned Beaumont, after a little pause, asked: "Does he know that?"

"He ought to know it better than anybody else. And if he didn't know it – What the hell's the matter with you?"

Ned Beaumont's laugh was a sneer. "If he didn't know it," he suggested, "you wouldn't be going there to dinner tomorrow night?"

Madvig, frowning, asked again: "What the hell's the matter with you?"

Ned Beaumont took the cigar from his mouth. His teeth had bitten the end of it into shredded ruin. He said: "There's nothing the matter with me." He put thoughtfulness on his face: "You don't think the rest of the ticket needs his support?"

"Support's something no ticket can get too much of," Madvig replied carelessly, "but without his help we could manage to hold up our end all right."

"Have you promised him anything yet?"

Madvig pursed his lips. "It's pretty well settled."

Ned Beaumont lowered his head until he was looking up under his brows at the blond man. His face had become pale.

"Throw him down, Paul," he said in a low husky voice. "Sink him."

Madvig put his fists on his hips and exclaimed softly and incredulously: "Well, I'll be damned!"

Ned Beaumont walked past Madvig and with unsteady thin fingers mashed the burning end of his cigar in the hammered copper basin on the table.

Madvig stared at the younger man's back until he straightened and turned. Then the blond man grinned at him with affection and exasperation. "What gets into you, Ned?" he complained. "You go along fine for just so long and then for no reason at all you throw an ing-bing. I'll be a dirty so-and-so if I can make you out!"

Ned Beaumont made a grimace of distaste. He said, "All right, forget it," and immediately returned to the attack with a skeptical question: "Do you think he'll play ball with you after he's re-elected?"

Madvig was not worried. "I can handle him."

"Maybe, but don't forget he's never been licked at anything in his life."

Madvig nodded in complete agreement. "Sure, and that's one of the best reasons I know for throwing in with him."

"No, it isn't, Paul," Ned Beaumont said earnestly. "It's the very worst. Think that over even if it hurts your head. How far has this dizzy blond daughter of his got her hooks into you?"

Madvig said: "I'm going to marry Miss Henry."

Ned Beaumont made a whistling mouth, though he did not whistle. He made his eyes smaller and asked: "Is that part of the bargain?"

Madvig grinned boyishly. "Nobody knows it yet," he replied, "except you and me."

Spots of color appeared in Ned Beaumont's lean cheeks. He smiled his nicest smile and said: "You can trust me not to go around bragging about it and here's a piece of advice. If that's what you want, make them put it in writing and swear to it before a notary and post a cash bond, or, better still, insist on the wedding before election-day. Then you'll at least be sure of your pound of flesh, or she'll weigh around a hundred and ten, won't she?"

Madvig shifted his feet. He avoided Ned Beaumont's gaze while saying: "I don't know why you keep talking about the Senator like he was a yegg. He's a gentleman and –"

"Absolutely. Read about it in the *Post* – one of the few aristocrats left in American politics. And his daughter's an aristocrat. That's why I'm warning you to sew your shirt on when you go to see them, or you'll come away without it, because to them you're a lower form of animal life and none of the rules apply."

Madvig sighed and began: "Aw, Ned, don't be so damned –"

But Ned Beaumont had remembered something. His eyes were shiny with malice. He said: "And we oughtn't to forget that young Taylor Henry's an aristocrat too, which is probably why you made Opal stop playing around with him. How's that going to work out when you marry his sister and he's your daughter's uncle-in-law or something? Will that entitle him to begin playing around with her again?"

Madvig yawned. "You didn't understand me right, Ned," he said. "I didn't ask for all this. I just asked you what kind of present I ought to give Miss Henry."

Ned Beaumont's face lost its animation, became a slightly sullen mask. "How far have you got with her?" he asked in a voice that expressed nothing of what he might have been thinking.

"Nowhere. I've been there maybe half a dozen times to talk to the Senator. Sometimes I see her and sometimes I don't, but only to say 'How do you do' or something with other people around. You know, I haven't had a chance to say anything to her yet."

Amusement glinted for a moment in Ned Beaumont's eyes and vanished. He brushed back one side of his mustache with a thumb-nail and asked: "Tomorrow's your first dinner there?"

"Yes, though I don't expect it to be the last."

"And you didn't get a bid to the birthday party?"

"No." Madvig hesitated. "Not yet."

"Then the answer's one you won't like."

Madvig's face was impassive. "Such as?" he asked.

"Don't give her anything."

"Oh, hell, Ned!"

Ned Beaumont shrugged. "Do whatever you like. You asked me."

"But why?"

"You're not supposed to give people things unless you're sure they'd like to get them from you."

"But everybody likes to –"

"Maybe, but it goes deeper than that. When you give somebody something, you're saying out loud that you know they'd like to have you give –"

"I got you," Madvig said. He rubbed his chin with fingers of his right hand. He frowned and said: "I guess you're right." His face cleared. He said: "But I'll be damned if I'll pass up the chance."

Ned Beaumont said quickly: "Well, flowers then, or something like that, might be all right."

"Flowers? Jesus! I wanted –"

"Sure, you wanted to give her a roadster or a couple of yards of pearls. You'll get your chance at that later. Start little and grow."

Madvig made a wry face. "I guess you're right, Ned. You know more about this kind of stuff than I do. Flowers it is."

"And not too many of them." Then, in the same breath: "Walt Ivans's telling the world you ought to spring his brother."

Madvig pulled the bottom of his vest down. "The world can tell him Tim's going to stay indoors till after election."

"You're going to let him stand trial?"

"I am," Madvig replied, and added with more heat: "You know damned well I can't help it, Ned. With everybody up for re-election and the women's clubs on the warpath it would be jumping in the lake to have Tim's case squared now."

Ned Beaumont grinned crookedly at the blond man and made his voice drawl. "We didn't have to do much worrying about women's clubs before we joined the aristocracy."

"We do now." Madvig's eyes were opaque.

"Tim's wife's going to have a baby next month," Ned Beaumont said.

Madvig blew breath out in an impatient gust. "Anything to make it tougher," he complained. "Why don't they think of those things before they get in trouble? They've got no brains, none of them."

"They've got votes."

"That's the hell of it," Madvig growled. He glowered at the floor for a moment, then raised his head. "We'll take care of him as soon as the votes are counted, but nothing doing till then."

"That's not going over big with the boys," Ned Beaumont said, looking obliquely at the blond man. "Brains or no brains, they're used to being taken care of."

Madvig thrust his chin out a little. His eyes, round and opaquely blue, were fixed on Ned Beaumont's. In a soft voice he asked: "Well?"

Ned Beaumont smiled and kept his voice matter-of-fact. "You know it won't take a lot of this to start them saying it was different in the old days before you put in with the Senator."

"Yes?"

Ned Beaumont stood his ground with no change in voice

or smile. "You know how little of this can start them saying Shad O'Rory still takes care of his boys."

Madvig, who had listened with an air of complete attentiveness, now said in a very deliberately quiet voice: "I know you won't start them talking like that, Ned, and I know I can count on you to do your best to stop any of that kind of talk you happen to hear."

For a moment after that they stood silent, looking eye into eye, and there was no change in the face of either. Ned Beaumont ended the silence. He said: "It might help some if we took care of Tim's wife and the kid."

"That's the idea." Madvig drew his chin back and his eyes lost their opaqueness. "Look after it, will you? Give them everything."

III

Walter Ivans was waiting for Ned Beaumont at the foot of the stairs, bright-eyed and hopeful. "Wh-what did he s-say?"

"It's what I told you: no can do. After election Tim's to have anything he needs to get out, but nothing stirring till then."

Walter Ivans hung his head and made a low growling noise in his chest.

Ned Beaumont put a hand on the shorter man's shoulder and said: "It's a tough break and nobody knows it better than Paul, but he can't help himself. He wants you to tell her not to pay any bills. Send them to him – rent, grocer, doctor, and hospital."

Walter Ivans jerked his head up and caught Ned Beaumont's hand in both of his. "B-by G-god that's white of him!" The china-blue eyes were wet. "B-b-but I wish he could g-get Tim out."

Ned Beaumont said, "Well, there's always a chance that something will come up to let him," freed his hand, said,

"I'll be seeing you," and went around Ivans to the billiard-room door.

The billiard-room was deserted.

He got his hat and coat and went to the front door. Long oyster-colored lines of rain slanted down into China Street. He smiled and addressed the rain under his breath: "Come down, you little darlings, thirty-two hundred and fifty dollars' worth of you."

He went back and called a taxicab.

IV

Ned Beaumont took his hands away from the dead man and stood up. The dead man's head rolled a little to the left, away from the curb, so that his face lay fully in the light from the corner street-lamp. It was a young face and its expression of anger was increased by the dark ridge that ran diagonally across the forehead from the edge of the curly fair hair to an eyebrow.

Ned Beaumont looked up and down China Street. As far up the street as the eye could see no person was there. Two blocks down the street, in front of the Log Cabin Club, two men were getting out of an automobile. They left the automobile standing in front of the Club, facing Ned Beaumont, and went into the Club.

Ned Beaumont, after staring down at the automobile for several seconds, suddenly twisted his head around to look up the street again and then, with a swiftness that made both movements one continuous movement, whirled and sprang upon the sidewalk in the shadow of the nearest tree. He was breathing through his mouth and though tiny points of sweat had glistened on his hands in the light he shivered now and turned up the collar of his overcoat.

He remained in the tree's shadow with one hand on the tree for perhaps half a minute. Then he straightened abruptly and began to walk towards the Log Cabin Club. He walked with increasing swiftness, leaning forward, and was moving at something more than a half-trot when he spied a man coming up the other side of the street. He immediately slackened his pace and made himself walk erect. The man entered a house before he came opposite Ned Beaumont.

By the time Ned Beaumont reached the Club he had stopped breathing through his mouth. His lips were still somewhat faded. He looked at the empty automobile without pausing, climbed the Club's steps between the two lanterns, and went indoors.

Harry Sloss and another man were crossing the foyer from the cloak-room. They halted and said together: "Hello, Ned." Sloss added: "I hear you had Peggy O'Toole today."

"Yes."

"For much?"

"Thirty-two hundred."

Sloss ran his tongue over his lower lip. "That's nice. You ought to be set for a game tonight."

"Later, maybe. Paul in?"

"I don't know. We just got in. Don't make it too late: I promised the girl I'd be home early."

Ned Beaumont said, "Right," and went over to the cloak-room. "Paul in?" he asked the attendant.

"Yes, about ten minutes ago."

Ned Beaumont looked at his wrist-watch. It was half-past ten. He went up to the front second-story room. Madvig in dinner clothes was sitting at the table with a hand stretched out towards the telephone when Ned Beaumont came in.

Madvig withdrew his hand and said: "How are you, Ned?" His large handsome face was ruddy and placid.

Ned Beaumont said, "I've been worse," while shutting the door behind him. He sat on a chair not far from Madvig's. "How'd the Henry dinner go?"

The skin at the corners of Madvig's eyes crinkled. "I've been at worse," he said.

Ned Beaumont was clipping the end of a pale spotted cigar. The shakiness of his hands was incongruous with the steadiness of his voice asking: "Was Taylor there?" He looked up at Madvig without raising his head.

"Not for dinner. Why?"

Ned Beaumont stretched out crossed legs, leaned back in his chair, moved the hand holding his cigar in a careless arc, and said: "He's dead in a gutter up the street."

Madvig, unruffled, asked: "Is that so?"

Ned Beaumont leaned forward. Muscles tightened in his lean face. The wrapper of his cigar broke between his fingers with a thin crackling sound. He asked irritably: "Did you understood what I said?"

Madvig nodded slowly.

"Well?"

"Well what?"

"He was killed."

"All right," Madvig said. "Do you want me to get hysterical about it?"

Ned Beaumont sat up straight in his chair and asked: "Shall I call the police?"

Madvig raised his eyebrows a little. "Don't they know it?"

Ned Beaumont was looking steadily at the blond man. He replied: "There was nobody around when I saw him. I wanted to see you before I did anything. Is it all right for me to say I found him?"

Madvig's eyebrows came down. "Why not?" he asked blankly.

Ned Beaumont rose, took two steps towards the telephone, halted, and faced the blond man again. He spoke with slow emphasis: "His hat wasn't there."

"He won't need it now." Then Madvig scowled and said: "You're a God-damned fool, Ned."

Ned Beaumont said, "One of us is," and went to the telephone.

V

TAYLOR HENRY MURDERED

BODY OF SENATOR'S SON FOUND
IN CHINA STREET

Believed to have been the victim of a hold-up, Taylor Henry, 26, son of Senator Ralph Bancroft Henry, was found dead in China Street near the corner of Pamela Avenue at a few minutes after 10 o'clock last night.

Coroner William J. Hoops stated that young Henry's death was due to a fracture of the skull and concussion of the brain caused by hitting the back of his head against the edge of the curb after having been knocked down by a blow from a blackjack or other blunt instrument on his forehead.

The body is believed to have been first discovered by Ned Beaumont, 914 Randall Avenue, who went to the Log Cabin Club, two blocks away, to telephone the police; but before he had succeeded in getting Police Headquarters on the wire, the body had been found and reported by Patrolman Michael Smitt.

Chief of Police Frederick M. Rainey immediately ordered a wholesale round-up of all suspicious characters in the city and issued a statement to the effect that no stone will be left unturned in his effort to apprehend the murderer or murderers at once.

Members of Taylor Henry's family stated that he left his home on Charles Street at about half-past nine o'clock to . . .

Ned Beaumont put the newspaper aside, swallowed the coffee that remained in his cup, put cup and saucer on the table beside his bed, and leaned back against the pillows. His face was tired and sallow. He pulled the covers up to his neck, clasped his hands together behind his head, and stared with dissatisfied eyes at the etching that hung between his bedroom-windows.

For half an hour he lay there with only his eyelids moving. Then he picked up the newspaper and reread the story. As he read, dissatisfaction spread from his eyes to all his face. He put the paper aside again, got out of bed, slowly, wearily, wrapped his lean white-pajamaed body in a small-figured brown and black kimono, thrust his feet into brown slippers, and, coughing a little, went into his living-room.

It was a large room in the old manner, high of ceiling and wide of window, with a tremendous mirror over the fireplace and much red plush on the furnishings. He took a cigar from a box on the table and sat in a wide red chair. His feet rested in a parallelogram of late-morning sun and the smoke he blew out became suddenly full-bodied as it drifted into the sunlight. He frowned now and chewed a finger-nail when the cigar was not in his mouth.

Knocking sounded on his door. He sat up straight, keen of eye and alert. "Come in."

A white-jacketed waiter came in.

Ned Beaumont said, "Oh, all right," in a disappointed tone and relaxed again against the red plush of his chair.

The waiter passed through to the bedroom, came out with a tray of dishes, and went away. Ned Beaumont threw what was left of his cigar into the fireplace and went into his bathroom. By the time he had shaved, bathed, and dressed, his face had lost its sallowness, his carriage most of its weariness.

VI

It was not quite noon when Ned Beaumont left his rooms and walked eight blocks to a pale gray apartment-building in Link Street. He pressed a button in the vestibule, entered the building when the door-lock clicked, and rode to the sixth floor in a small automatic elevator.

He pressed the bell-button set in the frame of a door marked 611. The door was opened immediately by a diminutive girl who could have been only a few months out of her teens. Her eyes were dark and angry, her face white, except around her eyes, and angry. She said, "Oh, hello," and with a smile and a vaguely placatory motion of one hand apologized for her anger. Her voice had a metallic thinness. She wore a brown fur coat, but not a hat. Her short-cut hair – it was nearly black – lay smooth and shiny as enamel on her round head. The gold-set stones pendent from her ear-lobes were carnelian. She stepped back pulling the door back with her.

Ned Beaumont advanced through the doorway asking: "Bernie up yet?"

Anger burned in her face again. She said in a shrill voice: "The crummy bastard!"

Ned Beaumont shut the door behind him without turning around.

The girl came close to him, grasped his arms above the elbows, and tried to shake him. "You know what I did for that bum?" she demanded. "I left the best home any girl ever had and a mother and father that thought I was the original Miss Jesus. They told me he was no good. Everybody told me that and they were right and I was too dumb to know it. Well, I hope to tell you I know it now, the . . ." The rest was shrill obscenity.

Ned Beaumont, motionless, listened gravely. His eyes were not a well man's now. He asked, when breathlessness had stopped her words for the moment: "What's he done?"

"Done? He's taken a run-out on me, the . . ." The rest of that sentence was obscenity.

Ned Beaumont flinched. The smile into which he pushed his lips was watery. He asked: "I don't suppose he left anything for me?"

The girl clicked her teeth together and pushed her face nearer his. Her eyes widened. "Does he owe you anything?"

"I won –" He coughed. "I'm supposed to have won thirty-two hundred and fifty bucks on the fourth race yesterday."

She took her hands from his arms and laughed scornfully. "Try and get it. Look." She held out her hands. A carnelian ring was on the little finger of her left hand. She raised her hands and touched her carnelian ear-rings. "That's every stinking piece of my jewelry he left me and he wouldn't've left me that if I hadn't had them on."

Ned Beaumont asked, in a queer detached voice: "When did this happen?"

"Last night, though I didn't find it out till this morning, but don't think I'm not going to make Mr. Son-of-a-bitch wish to God he'd never seen me." She put a hand inside her dress and brought it out a fist. She held the fist up close to Ned Beaumont's face and opened it. Three small crumpled pieces of paper lay in her hand. When he reached for them she closed her fingers over them again, stepping back and snatching her hand away.

He moved the corners of his mouth impatiently and let his hand fall down at his side.

She said excitedly: "Did you see the paper this morning about Taylor Henry?"

Ned Beaumont's reply, "Yes," was calm enough, but his chest moved out and in with a quick breath.

"Do you know what these are?" She held the three crumpled bits of paper out in her open hand once more.

Ned Beaumont shook his head. His eyes were narrow, shiny.

"They're Taylor Henry's I O Us," she said triumphantly, "twelve hundred dollars' worth of them."

Ned Beaumont started to say something, checked himself, and when he spoke his voice was lifeless. "They're not worth a nickel now he's dead."

She thrust them inside her dress again and came close to Ned Beaumont. "Listen," she said: "they never were worth a nickel and that's why he's dead."

"Is that a guess?"

"It's any damned thing you want to call it," she told him. "But let me tell you something: Bernie called Taylor up last Friday and told him he'd give him just three days to come across."

Ned Beaumont brushed a side of his mustache with a thumb-nail. "You're not just being mad, are you?" he asked cautiously.

She made an angry face. "Of course I'm mad," she said "I'm just mad enough to take them to the police and that's what I'm going to do. But if you think it didn't happen you're just a plain damned fool."

He seemed still unconvinced. "Where'd you get them?"

"Out of the safe." She gestured with her sleek head towards the interior of the apartment.

He asked: "What time last night did he blow?"

"I don't know. I got home at half-past nine and sat around most of the night expecting him. It wasn't till morning that I began to suspect something and looked around and saw he'd cleaned house of every nickel in money and every piece of my jewelry that I wasn't wearing."

He brushed his mustache with his thumb-nail again and asked: "Where do you think he'd go?"

She stamped her foot and, shaking both fists up and down, began to curse the missing Bernie again in a shrill enraged voice.

Ned Beaumont said: "Stop it." He caught her wrists and held them still. He said: "If you're not going to do anything about it but yell, give me those markers and I'll do something about it."

She tore her wrists out of his hands, crying: "I'll give you nothing. I'll give them to the police and not to another damned soul."

"All right, then do it. Where do you think he'd go, Lee?"

Lee said bitterly that she didn't know where he would go, but she knew where she would like to have him go.

Ned Beaumont said wearily: "That's the stuff. Wise-cracking is going to do us a lot of good. Think he'd go back to New York?"

"How do I know?" Her eyes had suddenly become wary.

Annoyance brought spots of color into Ned Beaumont's cheeks. "What are you up to now?" he asked suspiciously.

Her face was an innocent mask. "Nothing. What do you mean?"

He leaned down towards her. He spoke with considerable earnestness, shaking his head slowly from side to side with his words. "Don't think you're not going to the police with them, Lee, because you are."

She said: "Of course I am."

VII

In the drug-store that occupied part of the ground-floor of the apartment-building Ned Beaumont used a telephone. He called the Police Department's number, asked for Lieutenant Doolan, and said: "Hello. Lieutenant Doolan? . . . I'm speaking for Miss Lee Wilshire. She's in Bernie Despain's apartment at 1666 Link Street. He seems to have suddenly disappeared last night, leaving some of Taylor Henry's I O Us behind him. . . . That's right, and she says she heard him threaten him a couple of days ago. . . . Yes, and she wants to see you as soon as possible. . . . No, you'd better come up or send and as soon as you can. . . . Yes. . . . That doesn't make any difference. You don't know me. I'm just speaking for her because she didn't want to phone from his apartment. . . ." He listened a moment longer, then, without having said anything else, put the receiver on its prong and went out of the drug-store.

VIII

Ned Beaumont went to a neat red-brick house in a row of neat red-brick houses in upper Thames Street. The door was opened to his ring by a young Negress who smiled with her whole brown face, said, "How do you do, Mr. Beaumont?" and made the opening of the door a hearty invitation.

Ned Beaumont said: " 'Lo, June. Anybody home?"

"Yes, sir, they still at the dinner-table."

He walked back to the dining-room where Paul Madvig and his mother sat facing one another across a red-and-white-clothed table. There was a third chair at the table, but it was not occupied and the plate and silver in front of it had not been used.

Paul Madvig's mother was a tall gaunt woman whose blondness had been faded not quite white by her seventy-some years. Her eyes were as blue and clear and young as her son's – younger than her son's when she looked up at Ned Beaumont entering the room. She deepened the lines in her forehead, however, and said: "So here you are at last. You're a worthless boy to neglect an old woman like this."

Ned Beaumont grinned impudently at her and said: "Aw Mom, I'm a big boy now and I've got my work to look after." He flirted a hand at Madvig. " 'Lo, Paul."

Madvig said: "Sit down and June'll scrape you up something to eat."

Ned Beaumont was bending to kiss the scrawny hand Mrs. Madvig had held out to him. She jerked it away and scolded him: "Wherever did you learn such tricks?"

"I told you I was getting to be a big boy now." He addressed Madvig: "Thanks, I'm only a few minutes past breakfast." He looked at the vacant chair. "Where's Opal?"

Mrs. Madvig replied: "She's laying down. She's not feeling good."

Ned Beaumont nodded, waited a moment, and asked politely: "Nothing serious?" He was looking at Madvig.

Madvig shook his head. "Headache or something. I think the kid dances too much."

Mrs. Madvig said: "You certainly are a fine father not to know when your daughter has headaches."

Skin crinkled around Madvig's eyes. "Now, Mom, don't be indecent," he said and turned to Ned Beaumont. "What's the good word?"

Ned Beaumont went around Mrs. Madvig to the vacant

chair. He sat down and said: "Bernie Despain blew town last night with my winnings on Peggy O'Toole."

The blond man opened his eyes.

Ned Beaumont said: "He left behind him twelve hundred dollars' worth of Taylor Henry's I O Us."

The blond man's eyes jerked narrow.

Ned Beaumont said: "Lee says he called Taylor Friday and gave him three days to make good."

Madvig touched his chin with the back of a hand. "Who's Lee?"

"Bernie's girl."

"Oh." Then, when Ned Beaumont said nothing, Madvig asked: "What'd he say he was going to do about it if Taylor didn't come across?"

"I didn't hear." Ned Beaumont put a forearm on the table and leaned over it towards the blond man. "Have me made a deputy sheriff or something, Paul."

"For Christ's sake!" Madvig exclaimed, blinking. "What do you want anything like that for?"

"It'll make it easier for me. I'm going after this guy and having a buzzer may keep me from getting in a jam."

Madvig looked through worried eyes at the younger man. "What's got you all steamed up?" he asked slowly.

"Thirty-two hundred and fifty dollars."

"That's all right," Madvig said, still speaking slowly, "but something was itching you last night before you knew you'd been welshed on."

Ned Beaumont moved an impatient arm. "Do you expect me to stumble over corpses without batting an eye?" he asked. "But forget that. That doesn't count now. This does. I've got to get this guy. I've got to." His face was pale, set hard, and his voice was desperately earnest. "Listen, Paul: it's not only the money, though thirty-two hundred is a lot, but it would be the same if it was five bucks. I go two months without winning a bet and that gets me down. What good am I if my luck's gone? Then I cop, or think I do, and I'm all right again. I can take my tail out from between my legs and feel that I'm a person again and not just something that's being kicked around. The money's important enough, but it's not the real thing. It's what losing and losing and losing does to me. Can you get that? It's getting me licked. And then, when I think I've worn out the jinx, this guy takes a Mickey Finn on me. I can't stand for it. If I stand for it I'm licked, my nerve's gone. I'm not going to stand for it. I'm going after him. I'm going regardless, but you can smooth the way a lot by fixing me up."

Madvig put out a big open hand and roughly pushed Ned Beaumont's drawn face. "Oh, hell, Ned!" he said, "sure I'll fix you up. The only thing is I don't like you getting mixed up in things, but – hell! – if it's like that – I guess the best shot would be to make you a special investigator in the District Attorney's office. That way you'll be under Farr and he won't be poking his nose in."

Mrs. Madvig stood up with a plate in each bony hand. "If I didn't make a rule of not ever meddling in men's affairs," she said severely, "I certainly would have something to say to the pair of you, running around with the good Lord only knows what kind of monkey-business afoot that's likely as not to get you into the Lord only knows what kind of trouble."

Ned Beaumont grinned until she had left the room with the plates. Then he stopped grinning and said: "Will you fix it up now so everything'll be ready this afternoon?"

"Sure," Madvig agreed, rising. "I'll phone Farr. And if there's anything else I can do, you know."

Ned Beaumont said, "Sure," and Madvig went out.

Brown June came in and began to clear the table.

"Is Miss Opal sleeping now, do you think?" Ned Beaumont asked.

"No, sir, I just now took her up some tea and toast."

"Run up and ask her if I can pop in for a minute?"

"Yes, sir, I sure will."

After the Negress had gone out, Ned Beaumont got up from the table and began to walk up and down the room. Spots of color made his lean cheeks warm just beneath his cheek-bones. He stopped walking when Madvig came in.

"Oke," Madvig said. "If Farr's not in see Barbero. He'll fix you up and you don't have to tell him anything."

Ned Beaumont said, "Thanks," and looked at the brown girl in the doorway.

She said: "She says to come right up."

IX

Opal Madvig's room was chiefly blue. She, in a blue and silver wrapper, was propped up on pillows in her bed when Ned Beaumont came in. She was blue-eyed as her father and grandmother, long-boned as they and firm-featured, with fair pink skin still childish in texture. Her eyes were reddened now.

She dropped a piece of toast on the tray in her lap, held her hand out to Ned Beaumont, showed him strong white teeth in a smile, and said: "Hello, Ned." Her voice was not steady.

He did not take her hand. He slapped the back of it lightly, said, "'Lo, snip," and sat on the foot of her bed. He crossed his long legs and took a cigar from his pocket. "Smoke hurt the head?"

"Oh, no," she said.

He nodded as if to himself, returned the cigar to his pocket, and dropped his careless air. He twisted himself around on the bed to look more directly at her. His eyes were humid with sympathy. His voice was husky. "I know, youngster, it's tough."

She stared baby-eyed at him. "No, really, most of the headache's gone and it wasn't so awfully wretched anyway." Her voice was no longer unsteady.

He smiled at her with thinned lips and asked: "So I'm an outsider now?"

She put a small frown between her brows. "I don't know what you mean, Ned."

Hard of mouth and eye, he replied: "I mean Taylor."

Though the tray moved a little on her knees, nothing in her face changed. She said: "Yes, but – you know – I hadn't seen him for months, since Dad made –"

Ned Beaumont stood up abruptly. He said: "All right," over his shoulder as he moved towards the door.

The girl in the bed did not say anything.

He went out of the room and down the stairs.

Paul Madvig, putting on his coat in the lower hall, said: "I've got to go down to the office to see about those sewer-contracts. I'll drop you at Farr's office if you want."

Ned Beaumont had said, "Fine," when Opal's voice came to them from upstairs. "Ned, oh, Ned!"

"Righto," he called back and then to Madvig: "Don't wait if you're in a hurry."

Madvig looked at his watch. "I ought to run along. See you at the Club tonight?"

Ned Beaumont said, "Uh-huh," and went upstairs again.

Opal had pushed the tray down to the foot of the bed. She said: "Close the door." When he had shut the door she moved over in bed to make a place for him to sit beside her. Then she asked: "What makes you act like that?"

"You oughtn't to lie to me," he said gravely as he sat down.

"But, Ned!" Her blue eyes tried to probe his brown ones.

He asked: "How long since you saw Taylor?"

"You mean to talk to?" Her face and voice were candid. "It's been weeks and –"

He stood up abruptly. He said, "All right," over his shoulder while waking towards the door.

She let him get within a step of the door before she called: "Oh, Ned, don't make it so hard for me."

He turned around slowly, his face blank.

"Aren't we friends?" she asked.

"Sure," he replied readily without eagerness, "but it's hard to remember it when we're lying to each other."

She turned sidewise in bed, laying her cheek against the topmost pillow, and began to cry. She made no sound. Her tears fell down on the pillow and made a grayish spot there.

He returned to the bed, sat down beside her again, and moved her head from the pillow to his shoulder.

She cried there silently for several minutes. Then muffled words came from where her mouth was pressed against his coat: "Did-did you know I had been meeting him?"

"Yes."

She sat up straight, alarmed. "Did Dad know it?"

"I don't think so. I don't know."

She lowered her head to his shoulder so that her next words were muffled. "Oh, Ned, I was with him only yesterday afternoon, all afternoon!"

He tightened his arm around her, but did not say anything.

After another pause she asked: "Who – who do you think could have done it to him?"

He winced.

She raised her head suddenly. There was no weakness in her now. "Do you know, Ned?"

He hesitated, wet his lips, mumbled: "I think I do."

"Who?" she asked fiercely.

He hesitated again, evading her eyes, then put a slow question to her: "Will you promise to keep it to yourself till the time comes?"

"Yes," she replied quickly, but when he would have spoken she stopped him by grabbing his nearer shoulder with both hands. "Wait. I won't promise unless you'll promise me that they won't get off, that they'll be caught and punished."

"I can't promise that. Nobody can."

She stared at him, biting her lip, then said: "All right, then, I'll promise anyway. Who?"

"Did he ever tell you that he owed a gambler named Bernie Despain more money than he could pay?"

"Did – did this Despain – ?"

"I think so, but did he ever say anything to you about owing – ?"

"I knew he was in trouble. He told me that, but he didn't say what it was except that he and his father had had a row about some money and that he was – 'desperate' is what he said."

"Didn't mention Despain?"

"No. What was it? Why do you think this Despain did it?"

"He had over a thousand dollars' worth of Taylor's I O Us and couldn't collect. He left town last night in a hurry. The police are looking for him now." He lowered his voice, looking a little sidewise at her. "Would you do something to help them catch and convict him?"

"Yes. What?"

"I mean something a bit off-color. You see, it's going to be hard to convict him, but, if he's guilty, would you do something that might be a little bit – well – off-color to make sure of nailing him?"

"Anything," she replied.

He sighed and rubbed his lips together.

"What is it you want done?" she asked eagerly.

"I want you to get me one of his hats."

"What?"

"I want one of Taylor's hats," Ned Beaumont said. His face had flushed. "Can you get me one?"

She was bewildered. "But what for, Ned?"

"To make sure of nailing Despain. That's all I can tell you now. Can you get it for me or can't you?"

"I – I think I can, but I wish you'd –"

"How soon?"

"This afternoon, I think," she said, "but I wish –"

He interrupted her again. "You don't want to know

anything about it. The fewer know about it the better, and the same thing goes for your getting the hat." He put his arm around her and drew her to him. "Did you really love him, snip, or was it just because your father –"

"I did really love him," she sobbed. "I'm pretty sure – I'm sure I did."

2 THE HAT TRICK

I

NED BEAUMONT, wearing a hat that did not quite fit him, followed the porter carrying his bags through Grand Central Terminal to a Forty-second Street exit, and thence to a maroon taxicab. He tipped the porter, climbed into the taxicab, gave its driver the name of a hotel off Broadway in the Forties, and settled back lighting a cigar. He chewed the cigar more than he smoked it as the taxicab crawled through theater-bound traffic towards Broadway.

At Madison Avenue a green taxicab, turning against the light, ran full tilt into Ned Beaumont's maroon one, driving it over against a car that was parked by the curb, hurling him into a corner in a shower of broken glass.

He pulled himself upright and climbed out into the gathering crowd. He was not hurt, he said. He answered a policeman's questions. He found the hat that did not quite fit him and put it on his head. He had his bags transferred to another taxicab, gave the hotel's name to the second driver, and huddled back in a corner, white-faced and shivering, while the ride lasted.

When he had registered at the hotel he asked for his mail and was given two telephone-memorandum-slips and two sealed envelopes without postage stamps.

He asked the bellboy who took him to his room to get him a pint of rye whisky. When the boy had gone he turned the key in the door and read the telephone-memoranda. Both slips were dated that day, one marked 4:50 p.m., the other 8:05 p.m. He looked at his wrist-watch. It was 8:45 p.m.

The earlier slip read: *At The Gargoyle.* The later read: *At Tom & Jerry's. Will phone later.* Both were signed: *Jack.*

He opened one of the envelopes. It contained two sheets of paper covered by bold masculine handwriting, dated the previous day.

> She is staying at the Matin, room 1211, registered as Eileen Dale, Chicago. She did some phoning from the depot and connected with a man and girl who live E. 30th. They went to a lot of places, mostly speakies, probably hunting him, but don't seem to have much luck. My room is 734. Man and girl named Brook.

The sheet of paper in the other envelope, covered by the same handwriting, was dated that day.

> I saw Deward this morning, but he says he did not know Bernie was in town. Will phone later.

Both of these messages were signed: *Jack.*

Ned Beaumont washed, put on fresh linen from his bags, and was lighting a cigar when the bellboy brought him his pint of whisky. He paid the boy, got a tumbler from the bathroom, and drew a chair up to the bedroom-window. He sat there smoking, drinking, and staring down at the other side of the street until his telephone-bell rang.

"Hello," he said into the telephone. "Yes, Jack. . . . Just now. . . . Where? . . . Sure. . . . Sure, on my way."

He took another drink of whisky, put on the hat that did not quite fit him, picked up the overcoat he had dropped across a chair-back, put it on, patted one of its pockets, switched off the lights, and went out.

It was then ten minutes past nine o'clock.

II

Through double swinging glazed doors under an electric sign that said *Tom & Jerry's* down the front of a building within sight of Broadway, Ned Beaumont passed into a narrow corridor. A single swinging door in the corridor's left wall let him into a small restaurant.

A man at a corner-table stood up and raised a forefinger at him. The man was of medium height, young and dapper, with a sleek dark rather good-looking face.

Ned Beaumont went over to him. "'Lo, Jack," he said as they shook hands.

"They're upstairs, the girl and those Brook people," Jack told him. "You ought to be all right sitting here with your back to the stairs. I can spot them if they go out, or him coming in, and there's enough people in the way to keep him from making you."

Ned Beaumont sat down at Jack's table. "They waiting for him?"

Jack moved his shoulders. "I don't know, but they're doing some stalling about something. Want something to eat? You can't get anything to drink downstairs here."

Ned Beaumont said: "I want a drink. Can't we find a place upstairs where they won't see us?"

"It's not a very big joint," Jack protested. "There's a couple of booths up there where we might be hidden from them, but if he comes in he's likely to spot us."

"Let's risk it. I want a drink and I might as well talk to him right here if he does show up."

Jack looked curiously at Ned Beaumont, then turned his eyes away and said: "You're the boss. I'll see if one of the booths is empty." He hesitated, moved his shoulders again, and left the table.

Ned Beaumont twisted himself around in his chair to watch the dapper young man go back to the stairs and mount them. He watched the foot of the stairs until the young man came down again. From the second step Jack beckoned. He said, when Ned Beaumont had joined him there: "The best of them's empty and her back's this way, so you can get a slant at the Brooks as you go over."

They went upstairs. The booths – tables and benches set within breast-high wooden stalls – were to the right of the stair-head. They had to turn and look through a wide arch and down past the bar to see into the second-floor dining-room.

Ned Beaumont's eyes focused on the back of Lee Wilshire in sleeveless fawn gown and brown hat. Her brown fur coat was hanging over the back of her chair. He looked at her companions. At her left was a hawk-nosed long-chinned pale man, a predatory animal of forty or so. Facing her sat a softly fleshed red-haired girl with eyes set far apart. She was laughing.

Ned Beaumont followed Jack to their stall. They sat down with the table between them. Ned Beaumont sat with his back to the dining-room, close to the end of his bench to take full advantage of the wooden wing's shelter. He took off his hat, but not his overcoat.

A waiter came. Ned Beaumont said: "Rye." Jack said: "Rickey."

Jack opened a package of cigarettes, took one out, and, staring at it, said: "It's your game and I'm working for you, but this isn't a hell of a good spot to go up against him if he's got friends here."

"Has he?"

Jack put the cigarette in a corner of his mouth so it moved batonwise with his words. "If they're waiting here for him, it might be one of his hang-outs."

The waiter came with their drinks. Ned Beaumont drained his glass immediately and complained: "Cut to nothing."

"Yes, I guess it is," Jack said and took a sip from his glass. He set fire to the end of his cigarette and took another sip.

"Well," Ned Beaumont said, "I'm going up against him as soon as he shows."

"Fair enough," Jack's good-looking dark face was inscrutable. "What do I do?"

Ned Beaumont said, "Leave it to me," and caught their waiter's attention.

He ordered a double Scotch, Jack another rickey. Ned Beaumont emptied his glass as soon as it arrived. Jack let his first drink be carried away no more than half consumed and sipped at his second. Presently Ned Beaumont had another double Scotch and another while Jack had time to finish none of his drinks.

Then Bernie Despain came upstairs.

Jack, watching the head of the stairs, saw the gambler and put a foot on Ned Beaumont's under the table. Ned Beaumont, looking up from his empty glass, became suddenly hard and cold of eye. He put his hands flat on the table and stood up. He stepped out of the stall and faced Despain. He said: "I want my money, Bernie."

The man who had come upstairs behind Despain now walked around him and struck Ned Beaumont very hard in the body with his left fist. He was not a tall man, but his shoulders were heavy and his fists were large globes.

Ned Beaumont was knocked back against a stall-partition. He bent forward and his knees gave, but he did not fall. He hung there for a moment. His eyes were glassy and his skin had taken on a greenish tinge. He said something nobody could have understood and went to the head of the stairs.

He went down the stairs, loose-jointed, pallid, and bareheaded. He went through the downstairs dining-room to the street and out to the curb, where he vomited. When he had vomited, he went to a taxicab that stood a dozen feet away, climbed into it, and gave the driver an address in Greenwich Village.

III

Ned Beaumont left the taxicab in front of a house whose open basement-door, under brown stone steps, let noise and light out into a dark street. He went through the basement-doorway into a narrow room where two white-coated bartenders served a dozen men and women at a twenty-foot bar and two waiters moved among tables at which other people sat.

The balder bar-tender said, "For Christ's sake, Ned!" put down the pink mixture he was shaking in a tall glass, and stuck a wet hand out across the bar.

Ned Beaumont said, " 'Lo, Mack," and shook the wet hand.

One of the waiters came up to shake Ned Beaumont's hand and then a round and florid Italian whom Ned Beaumont called Tony. When these greetings were over Ned Beaumont said he would buy a drink.

"Like hell you will," Tony said. He turned to the bar and rapped on it with an empty cocktail-glass. "This guy can't buy so much as a glass of water tonight," he said when he had the bar-tenders' attention. "What he wants is on the house."

Ned Beaumont said: "That's all right for me, so I get it. Double Scotch."

Two girls at a table in the other end of the room stood up and called together: "Yoo-hoo, Ned!"

He told Tony, "Be back in a minute," and went to the girls' table. They embraced him, asked him questions, introduced him to the men with them, and made a place for him at their table.

He sat down and replied to their questions that he was back in New York only for a short visit and not to stay and that his was double Scotch.

At a little before three o'clock they rose from their table, left Tony's establishment, and went to another almost exactly like it three blocks away, where they sat at a table that could hardly have been told from the first and drank the same sort of liquor they had been drinking.

One of the men went away at half-past three. He did not say good-by to the others, nor they to him. Ten minutes later Ned Beaumont, the other man, and the two girls left. They got into a taxicab at the corner and went to a hotel near

Washington Square, where the other man and one of the girls got out.

The remaining girl took Ned Beaumont, who called her Fedink, to an apartment on Seventy-third Street. The apartment was very warm. When she opened the door warm air came out to meet them. When she was three steps inside the living-room she sighed and fell down on the floor.

Ned Beaumont shut the door and tried to awaken her, but she would not wake. He carried and dragged her difficultly into the next room and put her on a chintz-covered day-bed. He took off part of her clothing, found some blankets to spread over her, and opened a window. Then he went into the bathroom and was sick. After that he returned to the living-room, lay down on the sofa in all his clothes, and went to sleep.

IV

A telephone-bell, ringing close to Ned Beaumont's head, awakened him. He opened his eyes, put his feet down on the floor, turned on his side, and looked around the room. When he saw the telephone he shut his eyes and relaxed.

The bell continued to ring. He groaned, opened his eyes again, and squirmed until he had freed his left arm from beneath his body. He put his wrist close to his eyes and looked at his watch, squinting. The watch's crystal was gone and its hands had stopped at twelve minutes to twelve.

Ned Beaumont squirmed again on the sofa until he was leaning on his left elbow, holding his head up on his left hand. The telephone-bell was still ringing. He looked around the room with miserably dull eyes. The lights were burning. Through an open doorway he could see Fedink's blanket-covered feet on an end of the day-bed.

He groaned again and sat up, running fingers through his tousled dark hair, squeezing his temples between the heels of his palms. His lips were dry and brownly encrusted. He ran his tongue over them and made a distasteful face. Then he rose, coughing a little, took off his gloves and overcoat, dropped them on the sofa, and went into the bathroom.

When he came out he went to the day-bed and looked down at Fedink. She was sleeping heavily, face down, one blue-sleeved arm crooked above her head. The telephone-bell had stopped ringing. He pulled his tie straight and returned to the living-room.

Three Murad cigarettes were in an open box on the table between two chairs. He picked up one of the cigarettes, muttered, "Nonchalant," without humor, found a paper of matches, lit the cigarette, and went into the kitchen. He squeezed the juice of four oranges into a tall glass and drank it. He made and drank two cups of coffee.

As he came out of the kitchen Fedink asked in a woefully flat voice: "Where's Ted?" Her one visible eye was partially open.

Ned Beaumont went over to her. "Who's Ted?" he asked.

"That fellow I was with."

"Were you with somebody? How do I know?"

She opened her mouth and made an unpleasant clucking sound shutting it. "What time is it?"

"I don't know that either. Somewhere around daylight."

She rubbed her face into the chintz cushion under it and said: "A swell guy I turned out to be, promising to marry him yesterday and then leaving him to take the first tramp I run into home with me." She opened and shut the hand that was above her head. "Or am I home?"

"You had a key to the place, anyway," Ned Beaumont told her. "Want some orange-juice and coffee?"

"I don't want a damned thing except to die. Will you go away, Ned, and not ever come back?"

"It's going to be hard on me," he said ill-naturedly, "but I'll try."

He put on his overcoat and gloves, took a dark wrinkled

cap from one overcoat-pocket, put the cap on, and left the house.

V

Half an hour later Ned Beaumont was knocking on the door of room 734 at his hotel. Presently Jack's voice, drowsy, came through the door: "Who's that?"

"Beaumont."

"Oh," without enthusiasm, "all right."

Jack opened the door and turned on the lights. He was in green-spotted pajamas. His feet were bare. His eyes were dull, his face flushed, with sleepiness. He yawned, nodded, and went back to bed, where he stretched himself out on his back and stared at the ceiling. Then he asked, with not much interest: "How are you this morning?"

Ned Beaumont had shut the door. He stood between door and bed looking sullenly at the man in the bed. He asked: "What happened after I left?"

"Nothing happened." Jack yawned again. "Or do you mean what did I do?" He did not wait for a reply. "I went out and took a plant across the street till they came out. Despain and the girl and the guy that slugged you came out. They went to the Buckman, Forty-eighth Street. That's where Despain's holing up – apartment 938 – name of Barton Dewey. I hung around there till after three and then knocked off. They were all still in there unless they were fooling me." He jerked his head slightly in the direction of a corner of the room. "Your hat's on the chair there. I thought I might as well save it for you."

Ned Beaumont went over to the chair and picked up the hat that did not quite fit him. He stuffed the wrinkled dark cap in his overcoat-pocket and put the hat on his head.

Jack said: "There's some gin on the table if you want a shot."

Ned Beaumont said: "No, thanks. Have you got a gun?"

Jack stopped staring at the ceiling. He sat up in bed, stretched his arms out wide, yawned for the third time, and asked: "What are you figuring on doing?" His voice held nothing beyond polite curiosity.

"I'm going to see Despain."

Jack had drawn his knees up, had clasped his hands around them, and was sitting hunched forward a little staring at the foot of the bed. He said slowly: "I don't think you ought to, not right now."

"I've got to, right now," Ned Beaumont said.

His voice made Jack look at him. Ned Beaumont's face was an unhealthy yellowish gray. His eyes were muddy, red-rimmed, not sufficiently open to show any of the whites. His lips were dry and somewhat thicker than usual.

"Been up all night?" Jack asked.

"I got some sleep."

"Unkdray?"

"Yes, but how about the gun?"

Jack swung his legs out from beneath the covers and down over the side of the bed. "Why don't you get some sleep first? Then we can go after them. You're in no shape now."

Ned Beaumont said: "I'm going now."

Jack said: "All right, but you're wrong. You know they're no babies to go up against shaky. They mean it."

"Where's the gun?" Ned Beaumont asked.

Jack stood up and began to unbutton his pajama-coat.

Ned Beaumont said: "Give me the gun and get back in bed. I'm going."

Jack fastened the button he had just unfastened and got into bed. "The gun's in the top bureau-drawer," he said. "There are extra cartridges in there too if you want them." He turned over on his side and shut his eyes.

Ned Beaumont found the pistol, put it in a hip-pocket, said, "See you later," switched off the lights, and went out.

VI

The Buckman was a square-built yellow apartment-building that filled most of the block it stood in. Inside, Ned Beaumont said he wanted to see Mr. Dewey. When asked for his name he said: "Ned Beaumont."

Five minutes later he was walking away from an elevator down a long corridor towards an open door where Bernie Despain stood.

Despain was a small man, short and stringy, with a head too large for his body. The size of his head was exaggerated until it seemed a deformity by long thick fluffy waved hair. His face was swarthy, large-featured except for the eyes, and strongly lined across the forehead and down from nostrils past the mouth. He had a faintly reddish scar on one cheek. His blue suit was carefully pressed and he wore no jewelry.

He stood in the doorway, smiling sardonically, and said: "Good morning, Ned."

Ned Beaumont said: "I want to talk to you, Bernie."

"I guessed you did. As soon as they phoned your name up I said to myself: 'I bet you he wants to talk to me.' "

Ned Beaumont said nothing. His yellow face was tight-lipped.

Despain's smile became looser. He said: "Well, my boy, you don't have to stand here. Come on in." He stepped aside.

The door opened into a small vestibule. Through an opposite door that stood open Lee Wilshire and the man who had struck Ned Beaumont could be seen. They had stopped packing two traveling-bags to look at Ned Beaumont.

He went into the vestibule.

Despain followed him in, shut the corridor-door, and said: "The Kid's kind of hasty and when you come up to me like that he thought maybe you were looking for trouble, see? I give him hell about it and maybe if you ask him he'll apologize."

The Kid said something in an undertone to Lee Wilshire, who was glaring at Ned Beaumont. She laughed a vicious little laugh and replied: "Yes, a sportsman to the last."

Bernie Despain said: "Go right in, Mr. Beaumont. You've already met the folks, haven't you?"

Ned Beaumont advanced into the room where Lee and the Kid were.

The Kid asked: "How's the belly?"

Ned Beaumont did not say anything.

Bernie Despain exclaimed: "Jesus! For a guy that says he came up here to talk you've done less of it than anybody I ever heard of."

"I want to talk to you," Ned Beaumont said. "Do we have to have all these people around?"

"I do," Despain replied. "You don't. You can get away from them just by walking out and going about your own business."

"I've got business here."

"That's right, there was something about money." Despain grinned at the Kid. "Wasn't there something about money, Kid?"

The Kid had moved to stand in the doorway through which Ned Beaumont had come into the room. "Something," he said in a rasping voice, "but I forget what."

Ned Beaumont took off his overcoat and hung it on the back of a brown easy-chair. He sat down in the chair and put his hat behind him. He said: "That's not my business this time. I'm – let's see." He took a paper from his inner coat-pocket, unfolded it, glanced at it, and said: "I'm here as special investigator for the District Attorney's office."

For a small fraction of a second the twinkle in Despain's eyes was blurred, but he said immediately: "Ain't you getting up in the world! The last time I saw you you were just punking around for Paul."

Ned Beaumont refolded the paper and returned it to his pocket.

Despain said: "Well, go ahead, investigate something for us – anything – just to show us how it's done." He sat down facing Ned Beaumont, wagging his too-large head. "You ain't going to tell me you came all the way to New York to ask me about killing Taylor Henry?"

"Yes."

"That's too bad. I could've saved you the trip." He flourished a hand at the traveling-bags on the floor. "As soon as Lee told me what it was all about I started packing up to go back and laugh at your frame-up."

Ned Beaumont lounged back comfortably in his chair. One of his hands was behind him. He said: "If it's a frame-up it's Lee's. The police got their dope from her."

"Yes," she said angrily, "when I had to because you sent them there, you bastard."

Despain said: "Uh-huh, Lee's a dumb cluck, all right, but those markers don't mean anything. They –"

"I'm a dumb cluck, am I?" Lee cried indignantly. "Didn't I come all the way here to warn you after you'd run off with every stinking piece of –"

"Yes," Despain agreed pleasantly, "and coming here shows just what a dumb cluck you are, because you led this guy right to me."

"If that's the way you feel about it I'm damned glad I did give the police those I O Us, and what do you think of that?"

Despain said: "I'll tell you just exactly what I think of it after our company's gone." He turned to Ned Beaumont. "So honest Paul Madvig's letting you drop the shuck on me, huh?"

Ned Beaumont smiled. "You're not being framed, Bernie, and you know it. Lee gave us the lead-in and the rest that we got clicked with it."

"There's some more besides what she gave you?"

"Plenty."

"What?"

Ned Beaumont smiled again. "There are lots of things I could say to you, Bernie, that I wouldn't want to say in front of a crowd."

Despain said: "Nuts!"

The Kid spoke from the doorway to Despain in his rasping voice: "Let's chuck this sap out on his can and get going."

"Wait," Despain said. Then he frowned and put a question to Ned Beaumont: "Is there a warrant out for me?"

"Well, I don't –"

"Yes or no?" Despain's bantering humor was gone.

Ned Beaumont said slowly: "Not that I know of."

Despain stood up and pushed his chair back. "Then get the hell out of here and make it quick, or I'll let the Kid take another poke at you."

Ned Beaumont stood up. He picked up his overcoat. He took his cap out of his overcoat-pocket and, holding it in one hand, his overcoat over the other arm, said seriously: "You'll be sorry." Then he walked out in a dignified manner. The Kid's rasping laughter and Lee's shriller hooting followed him out.

VII

Outside the Buckman Ned Beaumont started briskly down the street. His eyes were glowing in his tired face and his dark mustache twitched above a flickering smile.

At the first corner he came face to face with Jack. He asked: "What are you doing here?"

Jack said: "I'm still working for you, far as I know, so I came along to see if I could find anything to do."

"Swell. Find us a taxi quick. They're sliding out."

Jack said, "Ay, ay," and went down the street.

Ned Beaumont remained on the corner. The front and side entrances of the Buckman could be seen from there.

In a little while Jack returned in a taxicab. Ned Beaumont got into it and they told the driver where to park it.

"What did you do to them?" Jack asked when they were sitting still.

"Things."

"Oh."

Ten minutes passed and Jack, saying, "Look," was pointing a forefinger at a taxicab drawing up to the Buckman's side door.

The Kid, carrying two traveling-bags, left the building first, then, when he was in the taxicab, Despain and the girl ran out to join him. The taxicab ran away.

Jack leaned forward and told his driver what to do. They ran along in the other cab's wake. They wound through streets that were bright with morning sunlight, going by a devious route finally to a battered brownstone house on West Forty-ninth Street.

Despain's cab stopped in front of the house and, once more, the Kid was the first of the trio out on the sidewalk. He looked up and down the street. He went up to the front door of the house and unlocked it. Then he returned to the taxicab. Despain and the girl jumped out and went indoors hurriedly. The Kid followed with the bags.

"Stick here with the cab," Ned Beaumont told Jack.

"What are you going to do?"

"Try my luck."

Jack shook his head. "This is another wrong neighborhood to look for trouble in," he said.

Ned Beaumont said: "If I come out with Despain, you beat it. Get another taxi and go back to watch the Buckman. If I don't come out, use your own judgment."

He opened the cab-door and stepped out. He was shivering. His eyes were shiny. He ignored something that Jack leaned out to say and hurried across the street to the house into which the two men and the girl had gone.

He went straight up the front steps and put a hand on the door-knob. The knob turned in his hand. The door was not locked. He pushed it open and, after peering into the dim hallway, went in.

The door slammed shut behind him and one of the Kid's fists struck his head a glancing blow that carried his cap away and sent him crashing into the wall. He sank down a little, giddily, almost to one knee, and the Kid's other fist struck the wall over his head.

He pulled his lips back over his teeth and drove a fist into the Kid's groin, a short sharp blow that brought a snarl from the Kid and made him fall back so that Ned Beaumont could pull himself up straight before the Kid was upon him again.

Up the hallway a little, Bernie Despain was leaning against the wall, his mouth stretched wide and thin, his eyes narrowed to dark points, saying over and over in a low voice: "Sock him, Kid, sock him. . . ." Lee Wilshire was not in sight.

The Kid's next two blows landed on Ned Beaumont's chest, mashing him against the wall, making him cough. The third, aimed at his face, he avoided. Then he pushed the Kid away from him with a forearm against his throat and kicked the Kid in the belly. The Kid roared angrily and came in with both fists going, but forearm and foot had carried him away from Ned Beaumont and had given Ned Beaumont time to get his right hand to his hip-pocket and to get Jack's revolver out of his pocket. He had no time to level the revolver, but, holding it at a downward angle, he pulled the trigger and managed to shoot the Kid in the right thigh. The Kid yelped and fell down on the hallway floor. He lay there looking up at Ned Beaumont with frightened bloodshot eyes.

Ned Beaumont stepped back from him, put his left hand in his trousers-pocket, and addressed Bernie Despain: "Come on out with me. I want to talk to you." His face was sullenly determined.

Footsteps ran overhead, somewhere back in the building a door opened, and down the hallway excited voices were audible, but nobody came into sight.

Despain stared for a long moment at Ned Beaumont as if horribly fascinated. Then, without a word, he stepped over the man on the floor and went out of the building ahead of Ned Beaumont. Ned Beaumont put the revolver in his jacket-pocket before he went down the street-steps, but he kept his hand on it.

"Up to that taxi," he told Despain, indicating the car out of which Jack was getting. When they reached the taxicab he told the chauffeur to drive them anywhere, "just around till I tell you where to go."

They were in motion when Despain found his voice. He said: "This is a hold-up. I'll give you anything you want because I don't want to be killed, but it's just a hold-up."

Ned Beaumont laughed disagreeably and shook his head. "Don't forget I've risen in the world to be something or other in the District Attorney's office."

"But there's no charge against me. I'm not wanted. You said –"

"I was spoofing you, Bernie, for reasons. You're wanted."

"For what?"

"Killing Taylor Henry."

"That? Hell, I'll go back and face that. What've you got against me? I had some of his markers, sure. And I left the night he was killed, sure. And I gave him hell because he wouldn't make them good, sure. What kind of a case is that for a first-class lawyer to beat? Jesus, if I left the markers behind in my safe at some time before nine-thirty – to go by Lee's story – don't that show I wasn't trying to collect that night?"

"No, and that isn't all the stuff we've got on you."

"That's all there could be," Despain said earnestly.

Ned Beaumont sneered. "Wrong, Bernie. Remember I had a hat on when I came to see you this morning?"

"Maybe. I think you did."

"Remember I took a cap out of my coat-pocket and put it on when I left?"

Bewilderment, fear, began to come into the swarthy man's small eyes. "By Jesus! Well? What are you getting at?"

"I'm getting at the evidence. Do you remember the hat didn't fit me very well?"

Bernie Despain's voice was hoarse: "I don't know, Ned. For Christ's sake, what do you mean?"

"I mean it didn't fit me because it wasn't my hat. Do you remember that the hat Taylor was wearing when he was murdered wasn't found?"

"I don't know. I don't know anything about him."

"Well, I'm trying to tell you the hat I had this morning was Taylor's hat and it's now planted down between the cushion-seat and the back of that brown easy-chair in the apartment you had at the Buckman. Do you think that, with the rest, would be enough to sit you on the hot seat?"

Despain would have screamed in terror if Ned Beaumont had not clapped a hand over his mouth and growled, "Shut up," in his ear.

Sweat ran down the swarthy face. Despain fell over on Ned Beaumont, seizing the lapels of his coat with both hands, babbling: "Listen, don't you do that to me, Ned. You can have every cent I owe you, every cent with interest, if you won't do that. I never meant to rob you, Ned, honest to God. It was just that I was caught short and thought I'd treat it like a loan. Honest to God, Ned. I ain't got much now, but I'm fixed to get the money for Lee's rocks that I'm selling today and I'll give you your dough, every nickel of it, out of that. How much was it, Ned? I'll give you all of it right away, this morning."

Ned Beaumont pushed the swarthy man over to his own side of the taxicab and said: "It was thirty-two hundred and fifty dollars."

"Thirty-two hundred and fifty dollars. You'll get it, every cent of it, this morning, right away." Despain looked at his watch. "Yes, sir, right this minute as soon as we can get there.

Old Stein will be at his place before this. Only say you'll let me go, Ned, for old times' sake."

Ned Beaumont rubbed his hands together thoughtfully. "I can't exactly let you go. Not right now, I mean. I've got to remember the District Attorney connection and that you're wanted for questioning. So all we can dicker about is the hat. Here's the proposition: give me my money and I'll see that I'm alone when I turn up the hat and nobody else will ever know about it. Otherwise I'll see that half the New York police are with me and – There you are. Take it or leave it."

"Oh, God!" Bernie Despain groaned. "Tell him to drive us to old Stein's place. It's on . . ."

3 THE CYCLONE SHOT

I

NED BEAUMONT leaving the train that had brought him back from New York was a clear-eyed erect tall man. Only the flatness of his chest hinted at any constitutional weakness. In color and line his face was hale. His stride was long and elastic. He went nimbly up the concrete stairs that connected train-shed with street-level, crossed the waiting-room, waved a hand at an acquaintance behind the information counter, and passed out of the station through one of the street-doors.

While waiting on the sidewalk for the porter with his bags to come he bought a newspaper. He opened it when he was in a taxicab riding towards Randall Avenue with his luggage. He read a half-column on the front page:

SECOND BROTHER KILLED

FRANCIS F. WEST MURDERED

CLOSE TO SPOT WHERE

BROTHER MET DEATH

For the second time within two weeks tragedy came to the West family of 1342 N. Achland Avenue last night when Francis W. West, 31, was shot to death in the street less than a block from the corner where he had seen his brother Norman run down and killed by an alleged bootleg car last month.

Francis West, who was employed as waiter at the Rockaway Café, was returning from work at a little after midnight, when, according to those who witnessed the tragedy, he was overtaken by a black touring car that came down Achland Avenue at high speed. The car swung in to the curb as it reached West, and more than a score of shots are said to have been fired from it. West fell with eight bullets in his body, dying before anybody could reach him. The death car, which is said not to have stopped, immediately picked up speed again and vanished around the corner of Bowman Street. The police are hampered in their attempt to find the car by conflicting descriptions given by witnesses, none of whom claims to have seen any of the men in the automobile.

Boyd West, the surviving brother, who also witnessed Norman's death last month, could ascribe no reason for Francis's murder. He said he knew of no enemies his brother had made. Miss Marie Shepperd, 1917 Baker Avenue, to whom Francis West was to have been married next week, was likewise unable to name anyone who might have desired her fiancé's death.

Timothy Ivans, alleged driver of the car that accidentally ran down and killed Norman West last month, refused to talk to reporters in his cell at the City Prison, where he is held without bail, awaiting trial for manslaughter.

Ned Beaumont folded the newspaper with careful slowness and put it in one of his overcoat-pockets. His lips were drawn a little together and his eyes were bright with thinking. Otherwise his face was composed. He leaned back in a corner of the taxicab and played with an unlighted cigar.

In his rooms he went, without pausing to remove hat or coat, to the telephone and called four numbers, asking each time whether Paul Madvig was there and whether it was known where he could be found. After the fourth call he gave up trying to find Madvig.

He put the telephone down, picked his cigar up from where he had laid it on the table, lighted the cigar, laid it on the edge of the table again, picked up the telephone, and called the City Hall's number. He asked for the District Attorney's office. While he waited he dragged a chair, by means of a foot hooked under one of its rounds, over to the telephone, sat down, and put the cigar in his mouth.

Then he said into the telephone: "Hello. Is Mr. Farr in.... Ned Beaumont.... Yes, thanks." He inhaled and exhaled smoke slowly. "Hello, Farr? . . . Just got in a couple of minutes ago. . . . Yes. Can I see you now? . . . That's right. Has Paul said anything to you about the West killing?. . . Don't know where he is, do you? Well, there's an angle I'd like to talk to you about. . . . Yes, say half an hour. . . . Right."

He put the telephone aside and went across the room to look at the mail on a table by the door. There were some magazines and nine letters. He looked rapidly at the envelopes, dropped them on the table again without having opened any, and went into his bedroom to undress, then into his bathroom to shave and bathe.

II

District Attorney Michael Joseph Farr was a stout man of forty. His hair was a florid stubble above a florid pugnacious face. His walnut desk-top was empty except for a telephone and a large desk-set of green onyx whereon a nude metal figure holding aloft an airplane stood on one foot between two black and white fountain-pens that slanted off to either side at rakish angles.

He shook Ned Beaumont's hand in both of his and pressed him down into a leather-covered chair before returning to his own seat. He rocked back in his chair and asked: "Have a nice trip?" Inquisitiveness gleamed through the friendliness in his eyes.

"It was all right," Ned Beaumont replied. "About this Francis West: with him out of the way how does the case against Tim Ivans stand?"

Farr started, then made that startled motion part of a deliberate squirming into a more comfortable position in his chair.

"Well, it won't make such a lot of difference there," he said, "that is, not a whole lot, since there's still the other brother to testify against Ivans." He very noticeably did not watch Ned Beaumont's face, but looked at a corner of the walnut desk. "Why? What'd you have on your mind?"

Ned Beaumont was looking gravely at the man who was not looking at him. "I was just wondering. I suppose it's all right, though, if the other brother can and will identify Tim."

Farr, still not looking up, said: "Sure." He rocked his chair back and forth gently, an inch or two each way half a dozen times. His fleshy cheeks moved in little ripples where they covered his jaw-muscles. He cleared his throat and stood up. He looked at Ned Beaumont now with friendly eyes. "Wait a minute," he said. "I've got to go see about something. They forget everything if I don't keep right on their tails. Don't go. I want to talk to you about Despain."

Ned Beaumont murmured, "Don't hurry," as the District Attorney left the office, and sat and smoked placidly all the fifteen minutes he was gone.

Farr returned frowning. "Sorry to leave you like that," he said as he sat down, "but we're fairly smothered under work. If it keeps up like this –" He completed the sentence by making a gesture of hopelessness with his hands.

"That's all right. Anything new on the Taylor Henry killing?"

"Nothing here. That's what I wanted to ask you about – Despain." Again Farr was definitely not watching Ned Beaumont's face.

A thin mocking smile that the other man could not see twitched for an instant the corners of Ned Beaumont's mouth. He said: "There's not much of a case against him when you come to look at it closely."

Farr nodded slowly at the corner of his desk. "Maybe, but his blowing town that same night don't look so damned good."

"He had another reason for that," Ned Beaumont said, "a pretty good one." The shadowy smile came and went.

Farr nodded again in the manner of one willing to be convinced. "You don't think there's a chance that he really killed him?"

Ned Beaumont's reply was given carelessly: "I don't think he did it, but there's always a chance and you've got plenty to hold him awhile on if you want to."

The District Attorney raised his head and looked at Ned Beaumont. He smiled with a mixture of diffidence and good-fellowship and said: "Tell me to go to hell if it's none of my business, but why in the name of God did Paul send you to New York after Bernie Despain?"

Ned Beaumont withheld his reply for a thoughtful moment. Then he moved his shoulders a little and said: "He didn't send me. He let me go."

Farr did not say anything.

Ned Beaumont filled his lungs with cigar-smoke, emptied them, and said: "Bernie welshed on a bet with me. That's why he took the run-out. It just happened that Taylor Henry was killed the night of the day Peggy O'Toole came in in front with fifteen hundred of my dollars on her."

The District Attorney said hastily: "That's all right, Ned. It's none of my business what you and Paul do. I'm – you see, it's just that I'm not so damned sure that maybe Despain didn't happen to run into young Henry on the street by luck and take a crack at him. I think maybe I'll hold him awhile to be safe." His blunt undershot mouth curved in a smile that was somewhat ingratiating. "Don't think I'm pushing my snoot into Paul's affairs or yours, but –" His florid face was turgid and shiny. He suddenly bent over and yanked a desk-drawer open. Paper rattled under his fingers. His hand came out of the drawer and went across the desk towards Ned Beaumont. In his hand was a small white envelope with a slit edge. "Here." His voice was thick. "Look at this and see what you think of it, or is it only damned foolishness?"

Ned Beaumont took the envelope, but did not immediately look at it. He kept his eyes, now cold and bright, focused on the District Attorney's red face.

Farr's face became a darker red under the other man's stare and he raised a beefy hand in a placatory gesture. His voice was placatory: "I don't attach any importance to it, Ned, but – I mean we always get a lot of junk like that on every case that comes up and – well, read it and see."

After another considerable moment Ned Beaumont shifted his gaze from Farr to the envelope. The address was typewritten:

M. J. Farr, Esq.
District Attorney
City Hall
City
Personal

The postmark was dated the previous Saturday. Inside was a single sheet of white paper on which three sentences with neither salutation nor signature were typewritten:

Why did Paul Madvig steal one of Taylor Henry's hats after he was murdered?

What became of the hat that Taylor Henry was wearing when he was murdered?

Why was the man who claimed to have first found Taylor Henry's body made a member of your staff?

Ned Beaumont folded this communication, returned it to its envelope, dropped it down on the desk, and brushed his mustache with a thumb-nail from center to left and from center to right, looking at the District Attorney with level eyes, addressing him in a level tone: "Well?"

Farr's cheeks rippled again where they covered his jaw-muscles. He frowned over pleading eyes. "For God's sake, Ned," he said earnestly, "don't think I'm taking that seriously. We get bales of that kind of crap every time anything happens. I only wanted to show it to you."

Ned Beaumont said: "That's all right as long as you keep

on feeling that way about it." He was still level of eye and voice. "Have you said anything to Paul about it?"

"About the letter? No. I haven't seen him since it came this morning."

Ned Beaumont picked the envelope up from the desk and put it in his inner coat-pocket. The District Attorney, watching the letter go into the pocket, seemed uncomfortable, but he did not say anything.

Ned Beaumont said, when he had stowed the letter away and had brought a thin dappled cigar out of another pocket: "I don't think I'd say anything to him about it if I were you. He's got enough on his mind."

Farr was saying, "Sure, whatever you say, Ned," before Ned Beaumont had finished his speech.

After that neither of them said anything for a while during which Farr resumed his staring at the desk-corner and Ned Beaumont stared thoughtfully at Farr. This period of silence was ended by a soft buzzing that came from under the District Attorney's desk.

Farr picked up his telephone and said: "Yes. . . . Yes." His undershot lip crept out over the edge of the upper lip and his florid face became mottled. "The hell he's not!" he snarled. "Bring the bastard in and put him up against him and then if he don't we'll do some work on him. . . . Yes. . . . Do it." He slammed the receiver on its prong and glared at Ned Beaumont.

Ned Beaumont had paused in the act of lighting his cigar. It was in one hand. His lighter, alight, was in the other. His face was thrust forward a little between them. His eyes glittered. He put the tip of his tongue between his lips, withdrew it, and moved his lips in a smile that had nothing to do with pleasure. "News?" he asked in a low persuasive voice.

The District Attorney's voice was savage: "Boyd West, the other brother that identified Ivans. I got to thinking about it when we were talking and sent out to see if he could still identify him. He says he's not sure, the bastard."

Ned Beaumont nodded as if this news was not unexpected. "How'll that fix things?"

"He can't get away with it," Farr snarled. "He identified him once and he'll stick to it when he gets in front of a jury. I'm having him brought in now and by the time I get through with him he'll be a good boy."

Ned Beaumont said: "Yes? And suppose he doesn't?"

The District Attorney's desk trembled under a blow from the District Attorney's fist. "He will."

Apparently Ned Beaumont was unimpressed. He lighted his cigar, extinguished and pocketed his lighter, blew smoke out, and asked in a mildly amused tone: "Sure he will, but suppose he doesn't? Suppose he looks at Tim and says: 'I'm not sure that's him'?"

Farr smote his desk again. "He won't – not when I'm through with him – he won't do anything but get up in front of the jury and say: 'That's him.' "

Amusement went out of Ned Beaumont's face and he spoke a bit wearily: "He's going to back down on the identification and you know he is. Well, what can you do about it? There's nothing you can do about it, is there? It means your case against Tim Ivans goes blooey. You found the carload of booze where he left it, but the only proof you've got that he was driving it when it ran down Norman West was the eyewitness testimony of his two brothers. Well, if Francis is dead and Boyd's afraid to talk you've got no case and you know it."

In a loud enraged voice Farr began: "If you think I'm going to sit on my –"

But with an impatient motion of the hand holding his cigar Ned Beaumont interrupted him. "Sitting, standing, or riding a bicycle," he said, "you're licked and you know it."

"Do I? I'm District Attorney of this city and county and

I –" Abruptly Farr stopped blustering. He cleared his throat and swallowed. Belligerence went out of his eyes, to be replaced first by confusion and then by something akin to fear. He leaned across the desk, too worried to keep worry from showing in his florid face. He said: "Of course you know if you – if Paul – I mean if there's any reason why I shouldn't – you know – we can let it go at that."

The smile that had nothing to do with pleasure was lifting the ends of Ned Beaumont's lips again and his eyes glittered through cigar-smoke. He shook his head slowly and spoke slowly in an unpleasantly sweet tone: "No, Farr, there isn't any reason, or none of that kind. Paul promised to spring Ivans after election, but, believe it or not, Paul never had anybody killed and, even if he did, Ivans wasn't important enough to have anybody killed for. No, Farr, there isn't any reason and I wouldn't like to think you were going around thinking there was."

"For God's sake, Ned, get me right," Farr protested. "You know damned well there's nobody in the city any stronger for Paul and for you than me. You ought to know that. I didn't mean anything by what I said except that – well, that you can always count on me."

Ned Beaumont said, "That's fine," without much enthusiasm and stood up.

Farr rose and came around the desk with a red hand out. "What's your hurry?" he said. "Why don't you stick around and see how this West acts when they bring him in? Or" – he looked at his watch – "what are you doing tonight? How about going to dinner with me?"

"Sorry, I can't," Ned Beaumont replied. "I've got to run along."

He let Farr pump his hand up and down, murmured a "Yes, I will" in response to the District Attorney's insistence that he drop in often and that they get together some night, and went out.

III

Walter Ivans was standing beside one of a row of men operating nailing-machines in the box-factory where he was employed as foreman, when Ned Beaumont came in. He saw Ned Beaumont at once and, hailing him with an uplifted hand, came down the center aisle, but in Ivans's china-blue eyes and round fair face there was somewhat less pleasure than he seemed to be trying to put there.

Ned Beaumont said, " 'Lo, Walt," and by turning slightly towards the door escaped the necessity of either taking or pointedly ignoring the shorter man's proffered hand. "Let's get out of this racket."

Ivans said something that was blurred by the din of metal driving metal into wood and they went to the open door by which Ned Beaumont had entered. Outside was a wide platform of solid timber. A flight of wooden steps ran down twenty feet to the ground.

They stood on the wooden platform and Ned Beaumont asked: "You know one of the witnesses against your brother was knocked off last night?"

"Y-yes, I saw it in the p-p-paper."

Ned Beaumont asked: "You know the other one's not sure now he can identify Tim?"

"N-no, I didn't know that, N-ned."

Ned Beaumont said: "You know if he doesn't Tim'll get off."

"Y-yes."

Ned Beaumont said: "You don't look as happy about it as you ought to."

Ivans wiped his forehead with his shirt-sleeve. "B-b-but I am, N-ned, b-by God I am!"

"Did you know West? The one that was killed."

"N-no, except that I went to s-see him once, t-to ask him to g-go kind of easy on T-tim."

"What'd he say?"

"He wouldn't."

"When was that?"

Ivans shifted his feet and wiped his face with his sleeve again. "T-t-two or three d-days ago."

Ned Beaumont asked softly: "Any idea who could have killed him, Walt?"

Ivans shook his head violently from side to side.

"Any idea who could've had him killed, Walt?"

Ivans shook his head.

For a moment Ned Beaumont stared reflectively over Ivans's shoulder. The clatter of the nailing-machines came through the door ten feet away and from another story came the whirr of saws. Ivans drew in and expelled a long breath.

Ned Beaumont's mien had become sympathetic when he transferred his gaze to the shorter man's china-blue eyes again. He leaned down a little and asked: "Are you all right, Walt? I mean there are going to be people who'll think maybe you might have shot West to save your brother. Have you got – ?"

"I-I-I was at the C-club all last night, from eight o'clock t-t-till after t-two this morning," Walter Ivans replied as rapidly as the impediment in his speech permitted. "Harry Sloss and B-ben Ferriss and Brager c-c-can tell you."

Ned Beaumont laughed. "That's a lucky break for you, Walt," he said gaily.

He turned his back on Walter Ivans and went down the wooden steps to the street. He paid no attention to Walter Ivans's very friendly "Good-by, Ned."

IV

From the box-factory Ned Beaumont walked four blocks to a restaurant and used a telephone. He called the four numbers he had called earlier in the day, asking again for Paul Madvig and, not getting him on the wire, left instructions for Madvig to call him. Then he got a taxicab and went home.

Additional pieces of mail had been put with those already on the table by the door. He hung up his hat and overcoat, lighted a cigar, and sat down with his mail in the largest of the red-plush chairs. The fourth envelope he opened was similar to the one the District Attorney had shown him. It contained a single sheet of paper bearing three typewritten sentences without salutation or signature:

> Did you find Taylor Henry's body after he was dead or were you present when he was murdered?
>
> Why did you not report his death until after the police had found the body?
>
> Do you think you can save the guilty by manufacturing evidence against the innocent?

Ned Beaumont screwed up his eyes and wrinkled his forehead over this message and drew much smoke from his cigar. He compared it with the one the District Attorney had received. Paper and typing were alike, as were the manner in which each paper's three sentences were arranged and the time of the postmarks.

Scowling, he returned each to its envelope and put them in his pocket, only to take them out again immediately to reread and re-examine them. Too rapid smoking made his cigar burn irregularly down one side. He put the cigar on the edge of the table beside him with a grimace of distaste and picked at his mustache with nervous fingers. He put the messages away once more and leaned back in his chair, staring at the ceiling and biting a finger-nail. He ran fingers through his hair. He put the end of a finger between his collar and his neck. He sat up and took the envelopes out of his pocket again, but put them back without having looked at them. He chewed his lower lip. Finally he shook himself impatiently and began to read the rest of his mail. He was reading it when the telephone-bell rang.

He went to the telephone. "Hello. . . . Oh, 'lo, Paul, where are you?. . . How long will you be there? . . . Yes, fine, drop in on your way. . . . Right, I'll be here."

He returned to his mail.

V

Paul Madvig arrived at Ned Beaumont's rooms as the bells in the gray church across the street were ringing the Angelus. He came in saying heartily: "Howdy, Ned. When'd you get back?" His big body was clothed in gray tweeds.

"Late this morning," Ned Beaumont replied as they shook hands.

"Make out all right?"

Ned Beaumont showed the edges of his teeth in a contented smile. "I got what I went after – all of it."

"That's great." Madvig threw his hat on a chair and sat on another beside the fireplace.

Ned Beaumont returned to his chair. "Anything happen while I was gone?" he asked as he picked up the half-filled cocktail-glass standing beside the silver shaker on the table at his elbow.

"We got the muddle on the sewer-contract straightened out."

Ned Beaumont sipped his cocktail and asked: "Have to make much of a cut?"

"Too much. There won't be anything like the profit there ought to be, but that's better than taking a chance on stirring things up this close to election. We'll make it up on the street-work next year when the Salem and Chestnut extensions go through."

Ned Beaumont nodded. He was looking at the blond man's outstretched crossed ankles. He said: "You oughtn't to wear silk socks with tweeds."

Madvig raised a leg straight out to look at the ankle. "No? I like the feel of silk."

"Then lay off tweeds. Taylor Henry buried?"

"Friday."

"Go to the funeral?"

"Yes," Madvig replied and added a little self-consciously: "The Senator suggested it."

Ned Beaumont put his glass on the table and touched his lips with a white handkerchief taken from the outer breast-pocket of his coat. "How is the Senator?" He looked obliquely at the blond man and did not conceal the amusement in his eyes.

Madvig replied, still somewhat self-consciously: "He's all right. I spent most of this afternoon up there with him."

"At his house?"

"Uh-huh."

"Was the blond menace there?"

Madvig did not quite frown. He said: "Janet was there."

Ned Beaumont, putting his handkerchief away, made a choked gurgling sound in his throat and said: "M-m-m. It's Janet now. Getting anywhere with her?"

Composure came back to Madvig. He said evenly: "I still think I'm going to marry her."

"Does she know yet that – that your intentions are honorable?"

"For Christ's sake, Ned!" Madvig protested. "How long are you going to keep me on the witness-stand?"

Ned Beaumont laughed, picked up the silver shaker, shook it, and poured himself another drink. "How do you like the Francis West killing?" he asked when he was sitting back with the glass in his hand.

Madvig seemed puzzled for a moment. Then his face cleared and he said: "Oh, that's the fellow that got shot on Achland Avenue last night."

"That's the fellow."

A fainter shade of puzzlement returned to Madvig's blue eyes. He said: "Well, I didn't know him."

Ned Beaumont said: "He was one of the witnesses against

Walter Ivans's brother. Now the other witness, Boyd West, is afraid to testify, so the rap falls through."

"That's swell," Madvig said, but by the time the last word had issued from his mouth a doubtful look had come into his eyes. He drew his legs in and leaned forward. "Afraid?" he asked.

"Yes, unless you like scared better."

Madvig's face hardened into attentiveness and his eyes became stony blue disks. "What are you getting at, Ned?" he asked in a crisp voice.

Ned Beaumont emptied his glass and set it on the table. "After you told Walt Ivans you couldn't spring Tim till election was out of the way he took his troubles to Shad O'Rory," he said in a deliberate monotone, as if reciting a lesson. "Shad sent some of his gorillas around to scare the two Wests out of appearing against Tim. One of them wouldn't scare and they bumped him off."

Madvig, scowling, objected: "What the hell does Shad care about Tim Ivans's troubles?"

Ned Beaumont, reaching for the cocktail-shaker, said irritably: "All right, I'm just guessing. Forget it."

"Cut it out, Ned. You know your guesses are good enough for me. If you've got anything on your mind, spill it."

Ned Beaumont set the shaker down without having poured a drink and said: "It might be just a guess, at that, Paul, but this is the way it looks to me. Everybody knows Walt Ivans's been working for you down in the Third Ward and is a member of the Club and everything and that you'd do anything you could to get his brother out of a jam if he asked you. Well, everybody, or a lot of them, is going to start wondering whether you didn't have the witnesses against his brother shot and frightened into silence. That goes for the outsiders, the women's clubs you're getting so afraid of these days, and the respectable citizens. The insiders – the ones that mostly wouldn't care if you had done that – are going to get something like the real news. They're going to know that one of your boys had to go to Shad to get fixed up and that Shad fixed him up. Well, that's the hole Shad's put you in – or don't you think he'd go that far to put you in a hole?"

Madvig growled through his teeth: "I know damned well he would, the louse." He was lowering down at a green leaf worked in the rug at his feet.

Ned Beaumont, after looking intently at the blond man, went on: "And there's another angle to look for. Maybe it won't happen, but you're open to it if Shad wants to work it."

Madvig looked up to ask: "What?"

"Walt Ivans was at the Club all last night, till two this morning. That's about three hours later than he ever stayed there before except on election- or banquet-nights. Understand? He was making himself an alibi – in our Club. Suppose" – Ned Beaumont's voice sank to a lower key and his dark eyes were round and grave – "Shad jobs Walt by planting evidence that he killed West? Your women's clubs and all the people who like to squawk about things like that are going to think that Walt's alibi is phony – that we fixed it up to shield him."

Madvig said: "The louse." He stood up and thrust his hands into his trousers-pockets. "I wish to Christ the election was either over or further away."

"None of this would've happened then."

Madvig took two steps into the center of the room. He muttered, "God damn him," and stood frowning at the telephone on the stand beside the bedroom-door. His huge chest moved with his breathing. He said from the side of his mouth, without looking at Ned Beaumont: "Figure out a way of blocking that angle." He took a step towards the telephone and halted. "Never mind," he said and turned to face Ned Beaumont. "I think I'll knock Shad loose from our little city. I'm tired of having him around. I think I'll knock him loose right away, starting tonight."

Ned Beaumont asked: "For instance?"

Madvig grinned. "For instance," he replied, "I think I'll have Rainey close up the Dog House and Paradise Gardens and every dive that we know Shad or any of his friends are interested in. I think I'll have Rainey smack them over in one long row, one after the other, this very same night."

Ned Beaumont spoke hesitantly: "You're putting Rainey in a tough spot. Our coppers aren't used to bothering with Prohibition-enforcement. They're not going to like it very much."

"They can do it once for me," Madvig said, "without feeling that they've paid all their debts."

"Maybe." Ned Beaumont's face and voice were dubious still. "But this wholesale stuff is too much like using a cyclone shot to blow off a safe-door when you could get it off without any fuss by using a come-along."

"Have you got something up your sleeve, Ned?"

Ned Beaumont shook his head. "Nothing I'm sure of, but it wouldn't hurt to wait a couple of days till –"

Now Madvig shook his head. "No," he said. "I want action. I don't know a damned thing about opening safes, Ned, but I do know fighting – my kind – going in with both hands working. I never could learn to box and the only times I ever tried I got licked. We'll give Mr. O'Rory the cyclone shot."

VI

The stringy man in horn-rimmed spectacles said: "So you don't have to worry none about that." He sat complacently back in his chair.

The man on his left – a raw-boned man with a bushy brown mustache and not much hair on his head – said to the man on his left: "It don't sound so God-damned swell to me."

"No?" The stringy man turned to glare through his spectacles at the raw-boned man. "Well, Paul don't never have to come down to my ward hisself to –"

The raw-boned man said: "Aw, nurts!"

Madvig addressed the raw-boned man: "Did you see Parker, Breen?"

Breen said: "Yes, I saw him and he says five, but I think we can get a couple more out of him."

The bespectacled man said contemptuously: "My God, I'd think so!"

Breen sneered sidewise at him. "Yes? And who'd you ever get that much out of?"

Three knocks sounded on the broad oaken door.

Ned Beaumont rose from the chair he was straddling and went to the door. He opened it less than a foot.

The man who had knocked was a small-browed dark man in blue clothes that needed pressing. He did not try to enter the room and he tried to speak in an undertone, but excitement made his words audible to everyone in the room. "Shad O'Rory's downstairs. He wants to see Paul."

Ned Beaumont shut the door and turned with his back against it to look at Paul Madvig. Only those two of the ten men in the room seemed undisturbed by the small-browed man's announcement. All the others did not show their excitement frankly – in some it could be seen in their suddenly acquired stoniness – but there was none whose respiration was exactly as it had been before.

Ned Beaumont, pretending he did not know repetition was unnecessary, said, in a tone that expressed suitable interest in his words: "O'Rory wants to see you. He's downstairs."

Madvig looked at his watch. "Tell him I'm tied up right now, but if he'll wait a little while I'll see him."

Ned Beaumont nodded and opened the door. "Tell him Paul's busy now," he instructed the man who had knocked, "but if he'll stick around awhile Paul'll see him." He shut the door.

Madvig was questioning a square-faced yellowish man about their chances of getting more votes on the other side of Chestnut Street. The square-faced man replied that he thought they would get more than last time "by a hell of a sight," but still not enough to make much of a dent in the opposition. While he talked his eyes kept crawling sidewise to the door.

Ned Beaumont sat astride his chair by the window again smoking a cigar.

Madvig addressed to another man a question having to do with the size of the campaign-contribution to be expected from a man named Hartwick. This other man kept his eyes from the door, but his reply lacked coherence.

Neither Madvig's and Ned Beaumont's calmness of mien nor their business-like concentration on campaign-problems could check the growth of tension in the room.

After fifteen minutes Madvig rose and said: "Well, we're not on Easy Street yet, but she's shaping up. Keep hard at it and we'll make the grade." He went to the door and shook each man's hand as they went out. They went out somewhat hurriedly.

Ned Beaumont, who had not left his chair, asked, when he and Madvig were the only ones in the room: "Do I stick around or beat it?"

"Stick around." Madvig crossed to the window and looked down into the sunny China Street.

"Both hands working?" Ned Beaumont asked after a little pause.

Madvig turned from the window nodding. "I don't know anything else" – he grinned boyishly at the man straddling the chair – "except maybe the feet too."

Ned Beaumont started to say something, but was interrupted by the noise the turning door-knob made.

A man opened the door and came in. He was a man of little more than medium height, trimly built with a trimness that gave him a deceptively frail appearance. Though his hair was a sheer sleek white he was probably not much past his thirty-fifth year. His eyes were a notable clear gray-blue set in a rather long and narrow, but very finely sculptured, face. He wore a dark blue overcoat over a dark blue suit and carried a black derby hat in a black-gloved hand.

The man who came in behind him was a bow-legged ruffian of the same height, a swarthy man with something apish in the slope of his big shoulders, the length of his thick arms, and the flatness of his face. This one's hat – a gray fedora – was on his head. He shut the door and leaned against it, putting his hands in the pockets of his plaid overcoat.

The first man, having advanced by then some four or five steps into the room, put his hat on a chair and began to take off his gloves.

Madvig, hands in trousers-pockets, smiled amiably and said: "How are you, Shad?"

The white-haired man said: "Fine, Paul. How's yourself?" His voice was a strong musical baritone. The faintest of brogues colored his words.

Madvig indicated with a small jerk of his head the man on the chair and asked: "You know Beaumont?"

O'Rory said: "Yes."

Ned Beaumont said: "Yes."

Neither nodded to the other and Ned Beaumont did not get up from his chair.

Shad O'Rory had finished taking off his gloves. He put them in an overcoat-pocket and said: "Politics is politics and business is business. I've been paying my way and I'm willing to go on paying my way, but I want what I'm paying for." His modulated voice was no more than pleasantly earnest.

"What do you mean by that?" Madvig asked as if he did not greatly care.

"I mean that half the coppers in town are buying their cakes and ale with dough they're getting from me and some of my friends."

Madvig sat down by the table. "Well?" he asked, carelessly as before.

"I want what I'm paying for. I'm paying to be let alone. I want to be let alone."

Madvig chuckled. "You don't mean, Shad, that you're complaining to me because your coppers won't stay bought?"

"I mean that Doolan told me last night that the orders to shut up my places came straight from you."

Madvig chuckled again and turned his head to address Ned Beaumont: "What do you think of that, Ned?"

Ned Beaumont smiled thinly, but said nothing.

Madvig said: "You know what I think of it? I think Captain Doolan's been working too hard. I think somebody ought to give Captain Doolan a nice long leave of absence. Don't let me forget it."

O'Rory said: "I bought protection, Paul, and I want it. Business is business and politics is politics. Let's keep them apart."

Madvig said: "No."

Shad O'Rory's blue eyes looked dreamily at some distant thing. He smiled a little sadly and there was a note of sadness in his musical slightly Irish voice when he spoke. He said: "It's going to mean killing."

Madvig's blue eyes were opaque and his voice was as difficultly read as his eyes. He said: "If you make it mean killing."

The white-haired man nodded. "It'll have to mean killing," he said, still sadly. "I'm too big to take the boot from you now."

Madvig leaned back in his chair and crossed his legs. His tone attached little importance to his words. He said: "Maybe you're too big to take it laying down, but you'll take it." He pursed his lips and added as an afterthought: "You are taking it."

Dreaminess and sadness went swiftly out of Shad O'Rory's eyes. He put his black hat on his head. He adjusted his coat-collar to his neck. He pointed a long white finger at Madvig and said: "I'm opening the Dog House again tonight. I don't want to be bothered. Bother me and I'll bother you."

Madvig uncrossed his legs and reached for the telephone on the table. He called the Police Department's number, asked for the Chief, and said to him: "Hello, Rainey. . . . Yes, fine. How are the folks? . . . That's good. Say, Rainey, I hear Shad's thinking of opening up again tonight. . . . Yes . . . Yes, slam it down so hard it bounces. . . . Right. . . . Sure. Good-by." He pushed the telephone back and addressed O'Rory: "Now do you understand how you stand? You're through, Shad. You're through here for good."

O'Rory said softly, "I understand," turned, opened the door, and went out.

The bow-legged ruffian paused to spit – deliberately – on the rug in front of him and to stare with bold challenging eyes at Madvig and Ned Beaumont. Then he went out.

Ned Beaumont wiped the palms of his hands with a handkerchief. He said nothing to Madvig, who was looking at him with questioning eyes. Ned Beaumont's eyes were gloomy.

After a moment Madvig asked: "Well?"

Ned Beaumont said: "Wrong, Paul."

Madvig rose and went to the window. "Jesus Christ!" he complained over his shoulder, "don't anything ever suit you?"

Ned Beaumont got up from his chair and walked towards the door.

Madvig, turning from the window, asked angrily: "Some more of your God-damned foolishness?"

Ned Beaumont said, "Yes," and went out of the room. He went downstairs, got his hat, and left the Log Cabin Club. He walked seven blocks to the railroad station, bought a ticket for New York, and made reservations on a night train. Then he took a taxicab to his rooms.

VII

A stout shapeless woman in gray clothes and a chubby half-grown boy were packing Ned Beaumont's trunk and three leather bags under his supervision when the door-bell rang.

The woman rose grunting from her knees and went to the door. She opened it wide. "My goodness, Mr. Madvig," she said. "Come right on in."

Madvig came in saying: "How are you, Mrs. Duveen? You get younger-looking every day." His gaze passed over the trunk and bags to the boy. "Hello, Charley. Ready for the job running the cement-mixer yet?"

The boy grinned bashfully and said: "How do you do, Mr. Madvig?"

Madvig's smile came around to Ned Beaumont "Going places?"

Ned Beaumont smiled politely. "Yes," he said.

The blond man looked around the room, at the bags and trunk again, at the clothes piled on chairs and the drawers standing open. The woman and the boy went back to their work. Ned Beaumont found two somewhat faded shirts in a pile on a chair and put them aside.

Madvig asked: "Got half an hour to spare, Ned?"

"I've got plenty of time."

Madvig said: "Get your hat."

Ned Beaumont got his hat and overcoat. "Get as much of it in as you can," he told the woman as he and Madvig moved towards the door, "and what's left over can be sent on with the other stuff."

He and Madvig went downstairs to the street. They walked south a block. Then Madvig asked: "Where're you going, Ned?"

"New York."

They turned into an alley.

Madvig asked: "For good?"

Ned Beaumont shrugged. "I'm leaving here for good."

They opened a green wooden door set in the red-brick rear wall of a building and went down a passageway and through another door into a bar-room where half a dozen men were drinking. They exchanged greetings with the bar-tender and three of the drinkers as they passed through to a small room where there were four tables. Nobody else was there. They sat at one of the tables.

The bar-tender put his head in and asked: "Beer as per usual, gents?"

Madvig said, "Yes," and then, when the bar-tender had drawn: "Why?"

Ned Beaumont said: "I'm tired of hick-town stuff."

"Meaning me?"

Ned Beaumont did not say anything.

Madvig did not say anything for a while. Then he sighed and said: "This is a hell of a time to be throwing me down."

The bar-tender came in with two seidels of pale beer and a bowl of pretzels. When he had gone out again, shutting the door behind him, Madvig exclaimed: "Christ, you're hard to get along with, Ned!"

Ned Beaumont moved his shoulders. "I never said I wasn't." He lifted his seidel and drank.

Madvig was breaking a pretzel into small bits. "Do you really want to go, Ned?" he asked.

"I'm going."

Madvig dropped the fragments of pretzel on the table and took a check-book from his pocket. He tore out a check, took a fountain-pen from another pocket, and filled in the check. Then he fanned it dry and dropped it on the table in front of Ned Beaumont.

Ned Beaumont, looking down at the check, shook his head and said: "I don't need money and you don't owe me anything."

"I do. I owe you more than that, Ned. I wish you'd take it."

Ned Beaumont said, "All right, thanks," and put the check in his pocket.

Madvig drank beer, ate a pretzel, started to drink again, set his seidel down on the table, and asked: "Was there anything on your mind – any kick – besides that back in the Club this afternoon?"

Ned Beaumont shook his head. "You don't talk to me like that. Nobody does."

"Hell, Ned, I didn't say anything."

Ned Beaumont did not say anything.

Madvig drank again. "Mind telling me why you think I handled O'Rory wrong?"

"It wouldn't do any good."

"Try."

Ned Beaumont said: "All right, but it won't do any good." He tilted his chair back, holding his seidel in one hand, some pretzels in the other. "Shad'll fight. He's got to. You've got him in a corner. You've told him he's through here for good. There's nothing he can do now but play the long shot. If he can upset you this election he'll be fixed to square anything he has to do to win. If you win the election he's got to drift anyhow. You're using the police on him. He'll have to fight back at the police and he will. That means you're going to have something that can be made to look like a crime-wave. You're trying to re-elect the whole city administration. Well, giving them a crime-wave and one it's an even bet they're not going to be able to handle – just before election – isn't going to make them look any too efficient. They –"

"You think I ought to've laid down to him?" Madvig demanded scowling.

"I don't think that. I think you should have left him an out, a line of retreat. You shouldn't have got him with his back to the wall."

Madvig's scowl deepened. "I don't know anything about your kind of fighting. He started it. All I know is when you got somebody cornered you go in and finish them. That system's worked all right for me so far." He blushed a little. "I don't mean I think I'm Napoleon or something, Ned, but I came up from running errands for Packy Flood in the old Fifth to where I'm sitting kind of pretty today."

Ned Beaumont emptied his seidel and let the front legs of his chair come down on the floor. "I told you it wouldn't do any good," he said. "Have it your own way. Keep on thinking that what was good enough for the old Fifth is good enough anywhere."

In Madvig's voice there was something of resentment and something of humility when he asked: "You don't think much of me as a big-time politician, do you, Ned?"

Now Ned Beaumont's face flushed. He said: "I didn't say that, Paul."

"But that's what it amounts to, isn't it?" Madvig insisted.

"No, but I do think you've let yourself be outsmarted this time. First you let the Henrys wheedle you into backing the Senator. There was your chance to go in and finish an enemy who was cornered, but that enemy happened to have a daughter and social position and what not, so you –"

"Cut it out, Ned," Madvig grumbled.

Ned Beaumont's face became empty of expression. He stood up saying, "Well, I must be running along," and turned to the door.

Madvig was up behind him immediately, with a hand on his shoulder, saying: "Wait, Ned."

Ned Beaumont said: "Take your hand off me." He did not look around.

Madvig put his other hand on Ned Beaumont's arm and turned him around. "Look here, Ned," he began.

Ned Beaumont said: "Let go." His lips were pale and stiff.

Madvig shook him. He said: "Don't be a God-damned fool. You and I –"

Ned Beaumont struck Madvig's mouth with his left fist.

Madvig took his hands away from Ned Beaumont and fell back two steps. While his pulse had time to beat perhaps three times his mouth hung open and astonishment was in his face. Then his face darkened with anger and he shut his mouth tight, so his jaw was hard and lumpy. He made fists of his hands, hunched his shoulders, and swayed forward.

Ned Beaumont's hand swept out to the side to grasp one of the heavy glass seidels on the table, though he did not lift it from the table. His body leaned a little to that side as he had leaned to get the seidel. Otherwise he stood squarely confronting the blond man. His face was drawn thin and rigid, with white lines of strain around the mouth. His dark eyes glared fiercely into Madvig's blue ones.

They stood thus, less than a yard apart – one blond, tall and powerfully built, leaning far forward, big shoulders hunched, big fists ready; the other dark of hair and eye, tall and lean, body bent a little to one side with an arm slanting down from that side to hold a heavy glass seidel by its handle – and except for their breathing there was no sound in the room. No sound came in from the bar-room on the other side of the thin door, the rattling of glasses nor the hum of talk nor the splash of water.

When quite two minutes had passed Ned Beaumont took his hand away from the seidel and turned his back to Madvig. Nothing changed in Ned Beaumont's face except that his eyes, when no longer focused on Madvig's, became hard and cold instead of angrily glaring. He took an unhurried step towards the door.

Madvig spoke hoarsely from deep down in him. "Ned."

Ned Beaumont halted. His face became paler. He did not turn around.

Madvig said: "You crazy son of a bitch."

Then Ned Beaumont turned around, slowly.

Madvig put out an open hand and pushed Ned Beaumont's face sidewise, shoving him off balance so he had to put a foot out quickly to that side and put a hand on one of the chairs at the table.

Madvig said: "I ought to knock hell out of you."

Ned Beaumont grinned sheepishly and sat down on the chair he had staggered against. Madvig sat down facing him and knocked on the top of the table with his seidel.

The bar-tender opened the door and put his head in.

"More beer," Madvig said.

From the bar-room, through the open door, came the sound of men talking and the sound of glasses rattling against glasses and against wood.

4 THE DOG HOUSE

I

NED BEAUMONT, at breakfast in bed, called, "Come in," and then, when the outer door had opened and closed: "Yes?"

A low-pitched rasping voice in the living-room asked: "Where are you, Ned?" Before Ned Beaumont could reply the rasping voice's owner had come to the bedroom-door and was saying: "Pretty soft for you." He was a sturdy young man with a square-cut sallow face, a wide thick-lipped mouth, from a corner of which a cigarette dangled, and merry dark squinting eyes.

" 'Lo, Whisky," Ned Beaumont said to him. "Treat yourself to a chair."

Whisky looked around the room. "Pretty good dump you've got here," he said. He removed the cigarette from his lips and, without turning his head, used the cigarette to point over his shoulder at the living-room behind him. "What's all the keysters for? Moving out?"

Ned Beaumont thoroughly chewed and swallowed the scrambled eggs in his mouth before replying: "Thinking of it."

Whisky said, "Yes?" while moving towards a chair that faced the bed. He sat down. "Where to?"

"New York maybe."

"What do you mean maybe?"

Ned Beaumont said: "Well, I've got a ducat that reads to there, anyway."

Whisky knocked cigarette-ash on the floor and returned the cigarette to the left side of his mouth. He snuffled. "How long you going to be gone?"

Ned Beaumont held a coffee-cup half-way between the tray and his mouth. He looked thoughtfully over it at the sallow young man. Finally he said, "It's a one-way ticket," and drank.

Whisky squinted at Ned Beaumont now until one of his dark eyes was entirely shut and the other was no more than a thin black gleam. He took the cigarette from his mouth and knocked more ash on the floor. His rasping voice held a persuasive note. "Why don't you see Shad before you go?" he suggested.

Ned Beaumont put his cup down and smiled. He said: "Shad and I aren't good enough friends that his feelings'll be hurt if I go away without saying good-by."

Whisky said: "That ain't the point."

Ned Beaumont moved the tray from his lap to the bedside-table. He turned on his side, propping himself up on an elbow on the pillows. He pulled the bed-clothes higher up over his chest. Then he asked: "What is the point?"

"The point is you and Shad ought to be able to do business together."

Ned Beaumont shook his head. "I don't think so."

"Can't you be wrong?" Whisky demanded.

"Sure," the man in bed confessed. "Once back in 1912 I was. I forget what it was about."

Whisky rose to mash his cigarette in one of the dishes on the tray. Standing beside the bed, close to the table, he said: "Why don't you try it, Ned?"

Ned Beaumont frowned. "Looks like a waste of time, Whisky. I don't think Shad and I could get along together."

Whisky sucked a tooth noisily. The downward curve of his thick lips gave the noise a scornful cast. "Shad thinks you could," he said.

Ned Beaumont opened his eyes. "Yes?" he asked. "He sent you here?"

"Hell, yes," Whisky said. "You don't think I'd be here talking like this if he hadn't."

Ned Beaumont narrowed his eyes again and asked: "Why?"

"Because he thought him and you could do business together."

"I mean," Ned Beaumont explained, "why did he think I'd want to do business with him?"

Whisky made a disgusted face. "Are you trying to kid me, Ned?" he asked.

"No."

"Well, for the love of Christ, don't you think everybody in town knows about you and Paul having it out at Pip Carson's yesterday?"

Ned Beaumont nodded. "So that's it," he said softly, as if to himself.

"That's it," the man with the rasping voice assured him, and "Shad happens to know you fell out over thinking Paul hadn't ought to've had Shad's joints smeared. So you're sitting pretty with Shad now if you use your head."

Ned Beaumont said thoughtfully: "I don't know. I'd like to get out of here, get back to the big city."

"Use your head," Whisky rasped. "The big city'll still be there after election. Stick around. You know Shad's dough-heavy and's putting it out in chunks to beat Madvig. Stick around and get yourself a slice of it."

"Well," Ned Beaumont said slowly, "it wouldn't hurt to talk it over with him."

"You're damned right it wouldn't," Whisky said heartily. "Pin your diapers on and we'll go now."

Ned Beaumont said, "Right," and got out of bed.

II

Shad O'Rory rose and bowed. "Glad to see you, Beaumont," he said. "Drop your hat and coat anywhere." He did not offer to shake hands.

Ned Beaumont said, "Good morning," and began to take off his overcoat.

Whisky, in the doorway, said: "Well, I'll be seeing you guys later."

O'Rory said, "Yes, do," and Whisky, drawing the door shut as he backed out, left them.

Ned Beaumont dropped his overcoat on the arm of a sofa, put his hat on the overcoat, and sat down beside them. He looked without curiosity at O'Rory.

O'Rory had returned to his chair, a deeply padded squat affair of dull wine and gold. He crossed his knees and put his hands together – tips of fingers and thumbs touching – atop his uppermost knee. He let his finely sculptured head sink down towards his chest so that his gray-blue eyes looked upward under his brows at Ned Beaumont. He said, in his pleasantly modulated Irish voice: "I owe you something for trying to talk Paul out of –"

"You don't," Ned Beaumont said.

O'Rory asked: "I don't?"

"No. I was with him then. What I told him was for his own good. I thought he was making a bad play."

O'Rory smiled gently. "And he'll know it before he's through," he said.

Silence was between them awhile then. O' Rory sat half-buried in his chair smiling at Ned Beaumont. Ned Beaumont sat on the sofa looking, with eyes that gave no indication of what he thought, at O'Rory.

The silence was broken by O'Rory asking: "How much did Whisky tell you?"

"Nothing. He said you wanted to see me."

"He was right enough as far as he went," O'Rory said. He took his finger-tips apart and patted the back of one slender hand with the palm of the other. "Is it so that you and Paul have broken for good and all?"

"I thought you knew it," Ned Beaumont replied. "I thought that's why you sent for me."

"I heard it," O'Rory said, "but that's not always the same thing. What were you thinking you might do now?"

"There's a ticket for New York in my pocket and my clothes are packed."

O'Rory raised a hand and smoothed his sleek white hair. "You came here from New York, didn't you?"

"I never told anybody where I came from."

O'Rory took his hand from his hair and made a small gesture of protestation. "You don't think I'm one to give a damn where any man comes from, do you?" he asked.

Ned Beaumont did not say anything.

The white-haired man said: "But I do care about where you go and if I have my way as much as I'd like you won't be going off to New York yet awhile. Did you never happen to think that maybe you could still do yourself a lot of good right here?"

"No," Ned Beaumont said, "that is, not till Whisky came."

"And what do you think now?"

"I don't know anything about it. I'm waiting to hear what you've got to say."

O'Rory put his hand to his hair again. His blue-gray eyes were friendly and shrewd. He asked: "How long have you been here?"

"Fifteen months."

"And you and Paul have been close as a couple of fingers how long?"

"Year."

O'Rory nodded. "And you ought to know a lot of things about him," he said.

"I do."

O'Rory said: "You ought to know a lot of things I could use."

Ned Beaumont said evenly: "Make your proposition."

O'Rory got up from the depths of his chair and went to a

door opposite the one through which Ned Beaumont had come. When he opened the door a huge English bulldog waddled in. O'Rory went back to his chair. The dog lay on the rug in front of the wine and gold chair staring with morose eyes up at its master.

O'Rory said: "One thing I can offer you is a chance to pay Paul back plenty."

Ned Beaumont said: "That's nothing to me."

"It is not?"

"Far as I'm concerned we're quits."

O'Rory raised his head. He asked softly: "And you wouldn't want to do anything to hurt him?"

"I didn't say that," Ned Beaumont replied a bit irritably. "I don't mind hurting him, but I can do it any time I want to on my own account and I don't want you to think you're giving me anything when you give me a chance to."

O'Rory wagged his head up and down, pleasantly. "Suits me," he said, "so he's hurt. Why did he bump off young Henry?"

Ned Beaumont laughed. "Take it easy," he said. "You haven't made your proposition yet. That's a nice pooch. How old is he?"

"Just about the limit, seven." O'Rory put out a foot and rubbed the dog's nose with the tip of it. The dog moved its tail sluggishly. "How does this hit you? After election I'll stake you to the finest gambling-house this state's ever seen and let you run it to suit yourself with all the protection you ever heard of."

"That's an *if* offer," Ned Beaumont said in a somewhat bored manner, "*if* you win. Anyhow, I'm not sure I want to stay here after election, or even that long."

O'Rory stopped rubbing the dog's nose with his shoe-tip. He looked up at Ned Beaumont again, smiled dreamily, and asked: "Don't you think we're going to win the election?"

Ned Beaumont smiled. "You won't bet even money on it."

O'Rory, still smiling dreamily, asked another question: "You're not so God-damned hot for putting in with me, are you, Beaumont?"

"No." Ned Beaumont rose and picked up his hat. "It wasn't any idea of mine." His voice was casual, his face politely expressionless. "I told Whisky it'd just be wasting time." He reached for his overcoat.

The white-haired man said: "Sit down. We can still talk, can't we? And maybe we'll get somewhere before we're through."

Ned Beaumont hesitated, moved his shoulders slightly, took off his hat, put it and his overcoat on the sofa, and sat down beside them.

O'Rory said: "I'll give you ten grand in cash right now if you'll come in and ten more election-night if we beat Paul and I'll keep that house-offer open for you to take or leave."

Ned Beaumont pursed his lips and stared gloomily at O'Rory under brows drawn together. "You want me to rat on him, of course," he said.

"I want you to go into the *Observer* with the lowdown on everything you know about him being mixed up in – the sewer-contracts, the how and why of killing Taylor Henry, that Shoemaker junk last winter, the dirt on how he's running the city."

"There's nothing in the sewer-business now," Ned Beaumont said, speaking as if his mind was more fully occupied with other thoughts. "He let his profits go to keep from raising a stink."

"All right," O'Rory conceded, blandly confident, "but there is something in the Taylor Henry business."

"Yes, we'd have him there," Ned Beaumont said, frowning, "but I don't know whether we could use the Shoemaker stuff" – he hesitated – "without making trouble for me."

"Hell, we don't want that," O'Rory said quickly. "That's out. What else have we got?"

"Maybe we can do something with the street-car-franchise extension and with that trouble last year in the County Clerk's office. We'll have to do some digging first, though."

"It'll be worth it for both of us," O'Rory said. "I'll have Hinkle – he's the *Observer* guy – put the stuff in shape. You just give him the dope and let him write it. We can start off with the Taylor Henry thing. That's something that's right on tap."

Ned Beaumont brushed his mustache with a thumb-nail and murmured: "Maybe."

Shad O'Rory laughed. "You mean we ought to start off first with the ten thousand dollars?" he asked. "There's something in that." He got up and crossed the room to the door he had opened for the dog. He opened it and went out, shutting it behind him. The dog did not get up from in front of the wine and gold chair.

Ned Beaumont lit a cigar. The dog turned his head and watched him.

O'Rory came back with a thick sheaf of green hundred-dollar bills held together by a band of brown paper on which was written in blue ink: *$10,000*. He thumped the sheaf down on the hand not holding it and said: "Hinkle's out there now. I told him to come in."

Ned Beaumont frowned. "I ought to have a little time to straighten it out in my mind."

"Give it to Hinkle any way it comes to you. He'll put it in shape."

Ned Beaumont nodded. He blew cigar-smoke out and said: "Yes, I can do that."

O'Rory held out the sheaf of paper money.

Saying, "Thanks," Ned Beaumont took it and put it in his inside coat-pocket. It made a bulge there in the breast of his coat over his flat chest.

Shad O'Rory said, "The thanks go both ways," and went back to his chair.

Ned Beaumont took the cigar out of his mouth. "Here's something I want to tell you while I think of it," he said. "Framing Walt Ivans for the West killing won't bother Paul as much as leaving it as is."

O'Rory looked curiously at Ned Beaumont for a moment before asking: "Why?"

"Paul's not going to let him have the Club alibi."

"You mean he's going to give the boys orders to forget Ivans was there?"

"Yes."

O'Rory made a clucking noise with his tongue, asked: "How'd he get the idea I was going to play tricks on Ivans?"

"Oh, we figured it out."

O'Rory smiled. "You mean you did," he said. "Paul's not that shifty."

Ned Beaumont made a modest grimace and asked: "What kind of job did you put up on him?"

O'Rory chuckled. "We sent the clown over to Braywood to buy the guns that were used." His gray-blue eyes suddenly became hard and sharp. Then amusement came back into them and he said: "Oh, well, none of that's big stuff now, now that Paul's hell-bent on making a row of it. But that's what started him picking on me, isn't it?"

"Yes," Ned Beaumont told him, "though it was likely to come sooner or later anyhow. Paul thinks he gave you your start here and you ought to stay under his wing and not grow big enough to buck him."

O'Rory smiled gently. "And I'm the boy that'll make him sorry he ever gave me that start," he promised. "He can –"

A door opened and a man came in. He was a young man in baggy gray clothes. His ears and nose were very large. His indefinitely brown hair needed trimming and his rather grimy face was too deeply lined for his years.

"Come in, Hinkle," O'Rory said. "This is Beaumont.

He'll give you the dope. Let me see it when you've shaped it up and we'll get the first shot in tomorrow's paper."

Hinkle smiled with bad teeth and muttered something unintelligibly polite to Ned Beaumont.

Ned Beaumont stood up saying: "Fine. We'll go over to my place now and get to work on it."

O'Rory shook his head. "It'll be better here," he said.

Ned Beaumont, picking up hat and overcoat, smiled and said: "Sorry, but I'm expecting some phone-calls and things. Get your hat, Hinkle."

Hinkle, looking frightened, stood still and dumb.

O'Rory said: "You'll have to stay here, Beaumont. We can't afford to have anything happen to you. Here you'll have plenty of protection."

Ned Beaumont smiled his nicest smile. "If it's the money you're worried about" – he put his hand inside his coat and brought it out holding the money – "you can hang on to it till I've turned in the stuff."

"I'm not worried about anything," O'Rory said calmly. "But you're in a tough spot if Paul gets the news you've come over to me and I don't want to take any chances on having you knocked off."

"You'll have to take them," Ned Beaumont said. "I'm going."

O'Rory said: "No."

Ned Beaumont said: "Yes."

Hinkle turned quickly and went out of the room.

Ned Beaumont turned around and started for the other door, the one through which he had come into the room, walking erectly without haste.

O'Rory spoke to the bulldog at his feet. The dog got up in cumbersome haste and waddled around Ned Beaumont to the door. He stood on wide-spread legs in front of the door and stared morosely at Ned Beaumont.

Ned Beaumont smiled with tight lips and turned to face

O'Rory again. The package of hundred-dollar bills was in Ned Beaumont's hand. He raised the hand, said, "You know where you can stick it," and threw the package of bills at O'Rory.

As Ned Beaumont's arm came down the bulldog, leaping clumsily, came up to meet it. His jaws shut over Ned Beaumont's wrist. Ned Beaumont was spun to the left by the impact and he sank on one knee with his arm down close to the floor to take the dog's weight off his arm.

Shad O'Rory rose from his chair and went to the door through which Hinkle had retreated. He opened it and said: "Come in a minute." Then he approached Ned Beaumont who, still down on one knee, was trying to let his arm yield to the strain of the dog's pulling. The dog was almost flat on the floor, all four feet braced, holding the arm.

Whisky and two other men came into the room. One of the others was the apish bow-legged man who had accompanied Shad O'Rory to the Log Cabin Club. One was a sandy-haired boy of nineteen or twenty, stocky, rosy-cheeked, and sullen. The sullen boy went around behind Ned Beaumont, between him and the door. The bow-legged ruffian put his right hand on Ned Beaumont's left arm, the arm the dog was not holding. Whisky halted half-way between Ned Beaumont and the other door.

Then O'Rory said, "Patty," to the dog.

The dog released Ned Beaumont's wrist and waddled over to its master.

Ned Beaumont stood up. His face was pallid and damp with sweat. He looked at his torn coat-sleeve and wrist and at the blood running down his hand. His hand was trembling.

O'Rory said in his musical Irish voice: "You would have it."

Ned Beaumont looked up from his wrist at the white-haired man. "Yes," he said, "and it'll take some more of it to keep me from going out of here."

III

Ned Beaumont opened his eyes and groaned.

The rosy-cheeked boy with sandy hair turned his head over his shoulder to growl: "Shut up, you bastard."

The apish dark man said: "Let him alone, Rusty. Maybe he'll try to get out again and we'll have some more fun." He grinned down at his swollen knuckles. "Deal the cards."

Ned Beaumont mumbled something about Fedink and sat up. He was in a narrow bed without sheets or bedclothes of any sort. The bare mattress was blood-stained. His face was swollen and bruised and blood-smeared. Dried blood glued his shirt-sleeve to the wrist the dog had bitten and that hand was caked with drying blood. He was in a small yellow and white bedroom furnished with two chairs, a table, a chest of drawers, a wall-mirror, and three white-framed French prints, besides the bed. Facing the foot of the bed was a door that stood open to show part of the interior of a white-tiled bathroom. There was another door, shut. There were no windows.

The apish dark man and the rosy-cheeked boy with sandy hair sat on the chairs playing cards on the table. There was about twenty dollars in paper and silver on the table.

Ned Beaumont looked, with brown eyes wherein hate was a dull glow that came from far beneath the surface, at the card-players and began to get out of bed. Getting out of bed was a difficult task for him. His right arm hung useless. He had to push his legs over the side of the bed one at a time with his left hand and twice he fell over on his side and had to push himself upright again in bed with his left arm.

Once the apish man leered up at him from his cards to ask humorously: "How're you making out, brother?" Otherwise the two at the table let him alone.

He stood finally, trembling, on his feet beside the bed. Steadying himself with his left hand on the bed he reached its end. There he drew himself erect and, staring fixedly at his goal, lurched towards the closed door. Near it he stumbled and went down on his knees, but his left hand, thrown desperately out, caught the knob and he pulled himself up on his feet again.

Then the apish man laid his cards carefully down on the table and said: "Now." His grin, showing remarkably beautiful white teeth, was wide enough to show that the teeth were not natural. He went over and stood beside Ned Beaumont.

Ned Beaumont was tugging at the door-knob.

The apish man said, "Now there, Houdini," and with all his weight behind the blow drove his right fist into Ned Beaumont's face.

Ned Beaumont was driven back against the wall. The back of his head struck the wall first, then his body crashed flat against the wall, and he slid down the wall to the floor.

Rosy-cheeked Rusty, still holding his cards at the table, said gloomily, but without emotion: "Jesus, Jeff, you'll croak him."

Jeff said: "Him?" he indicated the man at his feet by kicking him not especially hard on the thigh. "You can't croak him. He's tough. He's a tough baby. He likes this." He bent down, grasped one of the unconscious man's lapels in each hand, and dragged him to his knees. "Don't you like it, baby?" he asked and, holding Ned Beaumont up on his knees with one hand, struck his face with the other fist.

The door-knob was rattled from the outside.

Jeff called: "Who's that?"

Shad O'Rory's pleasant voice: "Me."

Jeff dragged Ned Beaumont far enough from the door to let it open, dropped him there, and unlocked the door with a key taken from his pocket.

O'Rory and Whisky came in. O'Rory looked at the man on the floor, then at Jeff, and finally at Rusty. His blue-gray eyes were clouded. When he spoke it was to ask Rusty: "Jeff been slapping him down for the fun of it?"

The rosy-cheeked boy shook his head. "This Beaumont is a son of a bitch," he said sullenly. "Every time he comes to he gets up and starts something."

"I don't want him killed, not yet," O'Rory said. He looked down at Ned Beaumont. "See if you can bring him around again. I want to talk to him."

Rusty got up from the table. "I don't know," he said. "He's pretty far gone."

Jeff was more optimistic. "Sure we can," he said. "I'll show you. Take his feet, Rusty." He put his hands under Ned Beaumont's armpits.

They carried the unconscious man into the bathroom and put him in the tub. Jeff put the stopper in and turned on cold water from both the faucet below and the shower above. "That'll have him up and singing in no time," he predicted.

Five minutes later, when they hauled him dripping from the tub and set him on his feet, Ned Beaumont could stand. They took him into the bedroom again. O'Rory was sitting on one of the chairs smoking a cigarette. Whisky had gone.

"Put him on the bed," O'Rory ordered.

Jeff and Rusty led their charge to the bed, turned him around, and pushed him down on it. When they took their hands away from him he fell straight back on the bed. They pulled him into a sitting position again and Jeff slapped his battered face with an open hand, saying: "Come on, Rip Van Winkle, come to life."

"A swell chance of him coming to life," the sullen Rusty grumbled.

"You think he won't?" Jeff asked cheerfully and slapped Ned Beaumont again.

Ned Beaumont opened the one eye not too swollen to be opened.

O'Rory said: "Beaumont."

Ned Beaumont raised his head and tried to look around

the room, but there was nothing to show he could see Shad O'Rory.

O'Rory got up from his chair and stood in front of Ned Beaumont, bending down until his face was a few inches from the other man's. He asked: "Can you hear me, Beaumont?"

Ned Beaumont's open eye looked dull hate into O'Rory's eyes.

O'Rory said: "This is O'Rory, Beaumont. Can you hear what I say?"

Moving his swollen lips with difficulty, Ned Beaumont uttered a thick "Yes."

O'Rory said: "Good. Now listen to what I tell you. You're going to give me the dope on Paul." He spoke very distinctly without raising his voice, without his voice losing any of its musical quality. "Maybe you think you won't, but you will. I'll have you worked on from now till you do. Do you understand me?"

Ned Beaumont smiled. The condition of his face made the smile horrible. He said: "I won't."

O'Rory stepped back and said: "Work on him."

While Rusty hesitated, the apish Jeff knocked aside Ned Beaumont's upraised hand and pushed him down on the bed. "I got something to try." He scooped up Ned Beaumont's legs and tumbled them on the bed. He leaned over Ned Beaumont, his hands busy on Ned Beaumont's body.

Ned Beaumont's body and arms and legs jerked convulsively and three times he groaned. After that he lay still.

Jeff straightened up and took his hands away from the man on the bed. He was breathing heavily through his ape's mouth. He growled, half in complaint, half in apology: "It ain't no good now. He's throwed another joe."

IV

When Ned Beaumont recovered consciousness he was alone in the room. The lights were on. As laboriously as before he got himself out of bed and across the room to the door. The door was locked. He was fumbling with the knob when the door was thrown open pushing him back against the wall.

Jeff in his underwear, barefoot, came in. "Ain't you a pip?" he said. "Always up to some kind of tricks. Don't you never get tired of being bounced off the floor?" He took Beaumont by the throat with his left hand and struck him in the face with his right fist, twice, but not so hard as he had hit him before. Then he pushed him backwards over to the bed and threw him on it. "And stay put awhile this time," he growled.

Ned Beaumont lay still with closed eyes.

Jeff went out, locking the door behind him.

Painfully Ned Beaumont climbed out of bed and made his way to the door. He tried it. Then he withdrew two steps and tried to hurl himself against it, succeeding only in lurching against it. He kept trying until the door was flung open again by Jeff.

Jeff said: "I never seen a guy that liked being hit so much or that I liked hitting so much." He leaned far over to one side and swung his fist up from below his knee.

Ned Beaumont stood blindly in the fist's path. It struck his cheek and knocked him the full length of the room. He lay still where he fell. He was lying there two hours later when Whisky came into the room.

Whisky awakened him with water from the bathroom and helped him to the bed. "Use your head," Whisky begged him. "These mugs'll kill you. They've got no sense."

Ned Beaumont looked dully at Whisky through a dull and bloody eye. "Let 'em," he managed to say.

He slept then until he was awakened by O'Rory, Jeff, and Rusty. He refused to tell O'Rory anything about Paul Madvig's affairs. He was dragged out of bed, beaten into unconsciousness, and flung into bed again.

This was repeated a few hours later. No food was brought to him.

Going on hands and knees into the bathroom when he had regained consciousness after the last of these beatings, he saw, on the floor behind the wash-stand's pedestal, a narrow safety-razor-blade red with the rust of months. Getting it out from behind the pedestal was a task that took him all of ten minutes and his nerveless fingers failed a dozen times before they succeeded in picking it up from the tile floor. He tried to cut his throat with it, but it fell out of his hand after he had no more than scratched his chin in three pieces. He lay down on the bathroom-floor and sobbed himself to sleep.

When he awakened again he could stand, and did. He doused his head in cold water and drank four glasses of water. The water made him sick and after that he began to shake with a chill. He went into the bedroom and lay down on the bare blood-stained mattress, but got up almost immediately to go stumbling and staggering in haste back to the bathroom, where he got down on hands and knees and searched the floor until he had found the rusty razor-blade. He sat on the floor and put the razor-blade into his vest-pocket. Putting it in, his fingers touched his lighter. He took the lighter out and looked at it. A cunning gleam came into his one open eye as he looked at the lighter. The gleam was not sane.

Shaking so that his teeth rattled together, he got up from the bathroom-floor and went into the bedroom again. He laughed harshly when he saw the newspaper under the table where the apish dark man and the sullen rosy-cheeked boy had played cards. Tearing and rumpling and wadding the paper in his hands, he carried it to the door and put it on the floor there. In each of the drawers in the chest of drawers he found a piece of wrapping-paper folded to cover the bottom. He rumpled them and put them with the newspaper against the door. With the razor-blade he made a long gash in the mattress, pulled out big handfuls of the coarse gray cotton with which the mattress was stuffed, and carried them to the door. He was not shaking now, nor stumbling, and he used both hands dexterously, but presently he tired of gutting the mattress and dragged what was left of it – tick and all – to the door.

He giggled then and, after the third attempt, got his lighter ignited. He set fire to the bottom of the heap against the door. At first he stood close to the heap, crouching over it, but as the smoke increased it drove him back step by step, reluctantly, coughing as he retreated. Presently he went into the bathroom, soaked a towel with water, and wrapped it around his head, covering eyes, nose, and mouth. He came stumbling back into the bedroom, a dim figure in the smoky room, fell against the bed, and sat down on the floor beside it.

Jeff found him there when he came in.

Jeff came in cursing and coughing through the rag he held against nose and mouth. In opening the door he had pushed most of the burning heap back a little. He kicked some more out of the way and stamped through the rest to reach Ned Beaumont. He took Ned Beaumont by the back of the collar and dragged him out of the room.

Outside, still holding Ned Beaumont by the back of the collar, Jeff kicked him to his feet and ran him down to the far end of the corridor. There he pushed him through an open doorway, bawled, "I'm going to eat one of your ears when I come back, you bastard," at him, kicked him again, stepped back into the corridor, slammed the door, and turned the key in its lock.

Ned Beaumont, kicked into the room, saved himself from a fall by catching hold of a table. He pushed himself up a little nearer straight and looked around. The towel had fallen down muffler-fashion around his neck and shoulders. The room had two windows. He went to the nearer window and tried to raise it. It was locked. He unfastened the lock and raised the window. Outside was night. He put a leg over the sill, then the other, turned so that he was lying belly-down across the sill, lowered himself until he was hanging by his hands, felt with his feet for some support, found none, and let himself drop.

5 THE HOSPITAL

I

A NURSE WAS doing something to Ned Beaumont's face.

"Where am I?" he asked.

"St. Luke's Hospital." She was a small nurse with very large bright hazel eyes, a breathless sort of hushed voice, and an odor of mimosa.

"What day?"

"It's Monday."

"What month and year?" he asked. When she frowned at him he said: "Oh, never mind. How long have I been here?"

"This is the third day."

"Where's the telephone?" He tried to sit up.

"Stop that," she said. "You can't use the telephone and you mustn't get yourself excited."

"You use it, then. Call Hartford six one one six and tell Mr. Madvig that I've got to see him right away."

"Mr. Madvig's here every afternoon," she said, "but I don't think Doctor Tait will let you talk to anybody yet. As a matter of fact you've done a whole lot more talking now than you ought to."

"What is it now? Morning or afternoon?"

"Morning."

"That's too long to wait," he said. "Call him now."

"Doctor Tait will be in in a little while."

"I don't want any Doctor Taits," he said irritably. "I want Paul Madvig."

"You'll do what you're told," she replied. "You'll lie there and be quiet till Doctor Tait comes."

He scowled at her. "What a swell nurse you are. Didn't anybody ever tell you it's not good for patients to be quarreled with?"

She ignored his question.

He said: "Besides, you're hurting my jaw."

She said: "If you'd keep it still it wouldn't get hurt."

He was quiet for a moment. Then he asked: "What's supposed to have happened to me? Or didn't you get far enough in your lessons to know?"

"Probably a drunken brawl," she told him, but she could not keep her face straight after that. She laughed and said: "But honestly you shouldn't talk so much and you can't see anybody till the doctor says so."

II

Paul Madvig arrived early in the afternoon. "Christ, I'm glad to see you alive again!" he said. He took the invalid's unbandaged left hand in both of his.

Ned Beaumont said: "I'm all right. But here's what we've got to do: grab Walt Ivans and have him taken over to Braywood and shown to the gun-dealers there. He –"

"You told me all that," Madvig said. "That's done."

Ned Beaumont frowned. "I told you?"

"Sure – the morning you were picked up. They took you to the Emergency Hospital and you wouldn't let them do anything to you till you'd seen me and I came down there and you told me about Ivans and Braywood and passed out cold."

"It's a blank to me," Ned Beaumont said. "Did you nail them?"

"We got the Ivanses, all right, and Walt Ivans talked after he was identified in Braywood and the Grand Jury indicted Jeff Gardner and two John Does, but we're not going to be able to nail Shad on it. Gardner's the man Ivans dickered with and anybody knows he wouldn't do anything without Shad's say-so, but proving it's another thing."

"Jeff's the monkey-looking guy, huh? Has he been picked up yet?"

"No. Shad took him into hiding with him after you got away, I guess. They had you, didn't they?"

"Uh-huh. In the Dog House, upstairs. I went there to lay a trap for the gent and he out-trapped me." He scowled. "I remember going there with Whisky Vassos and being bitten by the dog and knocked around by Jeff and a blond kid. Then there was something about a fire and – that's about all. Who found me? and where?"

"A copper found you crawling on all fours up the middle of Colman Street at three in the morning leaving a trail of blood behind you."

"I think of funny things to do," Ned Beaumont said.

III

The small nurse with large eyes opened the door cautiously and put her head in.

Ned Beaumont addressed her in a tired voice: "All right – peekaboo! But don't you think you're a little old for that?"

The nurse opened the door wider and stood on the sill holding the edge of the door with one hand. "No wonder people beat you up," she said. "I wanted to see if you were awake. Mr. Madvig and" – the breathless quality became more pronounced in her voice and her eyes became brighter – "a lady are here."

Ned Beaumont looked at her curiously and a bit mockingly. "What kind of lady?"

"It's Miss Janet Henry," she replied in the manner of one revealing some unexpected pleasant thing.

Ned Beaumont turned on his side, his face away from the nurse. He shut his eyes. A corner of his mouth twitched, but his voice was empty of expression: "Tell them I'm still asleep."

"You can't do that," she said. "They know you're not

asleep – even if they haven't heard you talking – or I'd've been back before this."

He groaned dramatically and propped himself up on his elbow. "She'll only come back again some other time," he grumbled. "I might as well get it over with."

The nurse, looking at him with contemptuous eyes, said sarcastically: "We've had to keep policemen in front of the hospital to fight off all the women that've been trying to see you."

"That's all right for you to say," he told her. "Maybe you're impressed by senators' daughters who are in the roto all the time, but you've never been hounded by them the way I have. I tell you they've made my life miserable, them and their brown roto-sections. Senators' daughters, always senators' daughters, never a representative's daughter or a cabinet minister's daughter or an alderman's daughter for the sake of variety – never anything but – Do you suppose senators are more prolific than –"

"You're not really funny," the nurse said. "It's the way you comb your hair. I'll bring them in." She left the room.

Ned Beaumont took a long breath. His eyes were shiny. He moistened his lips and then pressed them together in a tight secretive smile, but when Janet Henry came into the room his face was a mask of casual politeness.

She came straight to his bed and said: "Oh, Mr. Beaumont, I was so glad to hear that you were recovering so nicely that I simply had to come." She put a hand in his and smiled down at him. Though her eyes were not a dark brown her otherwise pure blondness made them seem dark. "So if you didn't want me to come you're not to blame Paul. I made him bring me."

Ned Beaumont smiled back at her and said: "I'm awfully glad you did. It's terribly kind of you."

Paul Madvig, following Janet Henry into the room, had gone around to the opposite side of the bed. He grinned affectionately from her to Ned Beaumont and said: "I knew you'd be, Ned. I told her so. How's it go today?"

"Nobly. Pull some chairs up."

"We can't stay," the blond man replied. "I've got to meet M'Laughlin at the Grandcourt."

"But I don't," Janet Henry said. She directed her smile at Ned Beaumont again. "Mayn't I stay – a little while?"

"I'd love that," Ned Beaumont assured her while Madvig, coming around the bed to place a chair for her, beamed delightedly upon each of them in turn and said: "That's fine." When the girl was sitting beside the bed and her black coat had been laid back over the back of the chair, Madvig looked at his watch and growled: "I've got to run." He shook Ned Beaumont's hand. "Anything I can get for you?"

"No, thanks, Paul."

"Well, be good." The blond man turned towards Janet Henry, stopped, and addressed Ned Beaumont again: "How far do you think I ought to go with M'Laughlin this first time?"

Ned Beaumont moved his shoulders a little. "As far as you want, so long as you don't put anything in plain words. They scare him. But you could hire him to commit murders if you put it to him in a long-winded way, like: 'If there was a man named Smith who lived in such and such a place and he got sick or something and didn't get well and you happened to drop in to see me some time and just by luck an envelope addressed to you had been sent there in care of me, how would I know it had five hundred dollars in it?' "

Madvig nodded. "I don't want any murders," he said, "but we do need that railroad vote." He frowned. "I wish you were up, Ned."

"I will be in a day or two. Did you see the *Observer* this morning?"

"No."

Ned Beaumont looked around the room. "Somebody's run off with it. The dirt was in an editorial in a box in the middle of the front page. *What are our city officials going to do about it?* A list of six weeks' crimes to show we're having a crime-wave. A lot smaller list of who's been caught to show the police aren't able to do much about it. Most of the squawking done about Taylor Henry's murder."

When her brother was named, Janet Henry winced and her lips parted in a little silent gasp. Madvig looked at her and then quickly at Ned Beaumont to move his head in a brief warning gesture.

Ned Beaumont, ignoring the effect of his words on the others, continued: "They were brutal about that. Accused the police of deliberately keeping their hands off the murder for a week so a gambler high in political circles could use it to square a grievance with another gambler – meaning my going after Despain to collect my money. Wondered what Senator Henry thought of his new political allies' use of his son's murder for this purpose."

Madvig, red of face, fumbling for his watch, said hastily: "I'll get a copy and read it. I've got to –"

"Also," Ned Beaumont went on serenely, "they accuse the police of raiding – after having protected them for years – those joints whose owners wouldn't come across with enormous campaign-contributions. That's what they make of your fight with Shad O'Rory. And they promise to print a list of the places that are still running because their owners did come across."

Madvig said, "Well, well," uncomfortably, said, "Good-by, have a nice visit," to Janet Henry, "See you later," to Ned Beaumont, and went out.

Janet Henry leaned forward in her chair. "Why don't you like me?" she asked Ned Beaumont.

"I think maybe I do," he said.

She shook her head. "You don't. I know it."

"You can't go by my manners," he told her. "They're always pretty bad."

"You don't like me," she insisted, not answering his smile, "and I want you to."

He was modest. "Why?"

"Because you are Paul's best friend," she replied.

"Paul," he said, looking obliquely at her, "has a lot of friends: he's a politician."

She moved her head impatiently. "You're his best friend." She paused, then added: "He thinks so."

"What do you think?" he asked with incomplete seriousness.

"I think you are," she said gravely, "or you would not be here now. You would not have gone through that for him."

His mouth twitched in a meager smile. He did not say anything.

When it became manifest that he was not going to speak she said earnestly: "I wish you would like me, if you can."

He repeated: "I think maybe I do."

She shook her head. "You don't."

He smiled at her. His smile was very young and engaging, his eyes shy, his voice youthfully diffident and confiding, as he said: "I'll tell you what makes you think that, Miss Henry. It's – you see, Paul picked me up out of the gutter, as you might say, just a year or so ago, and so I'm kind of awkward and clumsy when I'm around people like you who belong to another world altogether – society and roto-sections and all – and you mistake that – uh – *gaucherie* for enmity, which it isn't at all."

She rose and said, "You're ridiculing me," without resentment.

When she had gone Ned Beaumont lay back on his pillows and stared at the ceiling with glittering eyes until the nurse came in.

The nurse came in and asked: "What have you been up to now?"

Ned Beaumont raised his head to look sullenly at her, but he did not speak.

The nurse said: "She went out of here as near crying as anybody could without crying."

Ned Beaumont lowered his head to the pillow again. "I must be losing my grip," he said. "I usually make senators' daughters cry."

IV

A man of medium size, young and dapper, with a sleek, dark, rather good-looking face, came in.

Ned Beaumont sat up in bed and said: "'Lo, Jack."

Jack said, "You don't look as bad as I thought you would," and advanced to the side of the bed.

"I'm still all in one piece. Grab a chair."

Jack sat down and took out a package of cigarettes.

Ned Beaumont said: "I've got another job for you." He put a hand under his pillows and brought out an envelope.

Jack lit his cigarette before he took the envelope from Ned Beaumont's hand. It was a plain white envelope addressed to Ned Beaumont at St. Luke's Hospital and bore the local postmark dated two days before. Inside was a single typewritten sheet of paper which Jack took out and read.

> What do you know about Paul Madvig that Shad O'Rory was so anxious to learn?
>
> Has it anything to do with the murder of Taylor Henry?
>
> If not, why should you have gone to such lengths to keep it secret?

Jack refolded the sheet of paper and returned it to the envelope before he raised his head. Then he asked: "Does it make sense?"

"Not that I know of. I want you to find out who wrote it."

Jack nodded. "Do I keep it?"

"Yes."

Jack put the envelope in his pocket. "Any ideas about who might have done it?"

"None at all."

Jack studied the lighted end of his cigarette. "It's a job, you know," he said presently.

"I know it," Ned Beaumont agreed, "and all I can tell you is that there's been a lot of them – or several of them – in the past week. That's my third. I know Farr got at least one. I don't know who else has been getting them."

"Can I see some of the others?"

Ned Beaumont said: "That's the only one I kept. They're all pretty much alike, though – same paper, same typewriting, three questions in each, all on the same subject."

Jack regarded Ned Beaumont with inquisitive eyes. "But not exactly the same questions?" he asked.

"Not exactly, but all getting to the same point."

Jack nodded and smoked his cigarette.

Ned Beaumont said: "You understand this is to be strictly on the qt."

"Sure." Jack took the cigarette from his mouth. "The 'same point' you mentioned is Madvig's connection with the murder?"

"Yes," Ned Beaumont replied, looking with level eyes at the sleek dark young man, "and there isn't any connection."

Jack's dark face was inscrutable. "I don't see how there could be," he said as he stood up.

V

The nurse came in carrying a large basket of fruit. "Isn't it lovely?" she said as she set it down.

Ned Beaumont nodded cautiously.

The nurse took a small stiff envelope from the basket. "I bet you it's from her," she said, giving Ned Beaumont the envelope.

"What'll you bet?"

"Anything you want."

Ned Beaumont nodded as if some dark suspicion had been confirmed. "You looked," he said.

"Why, you –" Her words stopped when he laughed, but indignation remained in her mien.

He took Janet Henry's card from the envelope. One word was written on it: *Please!* Frowning at the card, he told the nurse, "You win," and tapped the card on a thumb-nail. "Help yourself to that gunk and take enough of it so it'll look as if I'd been eating it."

Later that afternoon he wrote:

My Dear Miss Henry –

You've quite overwhelmed me with your kindness – first your coming to see me, and then the fruit. I don't at all know how to thank you, but I hope I shall some day be able to more clearly show my gratitude.

Sincerely yours,
Ned Beaumont

When he had finished he read what he had written, tore it up, and rewrote it on another sheet of paper, using the same words, but rearranging them to make the ending of the second sentence read: "be able some day to show my gratitude more clearly."

VI

Ned Beaumont, in bathrobe and slippers this morning, was reading a copy of the *Observer* over his breakfast at a table by the window of his hospital-room when Opal Madvig came in. He folded the newspaper, put it face-down on the table beside his tray, and rose saying, "'Lo, snip," cordially. He was pale.

"Why didn't you call me up when you got back from New York?" she demanded in an accusing tone. She too was pale. Pallor accentuated the child-like texture of her skin, yet made her face seem less young. Her blue eyes were wide open and dark with emotion, but not to be read easily. She held herself tall without stiffness, in the manner of one more sure of his balance than of stability underfoot. Ignoring the chair he moved out from the wall for her, she repeated, imperatively as before: "Why didn't you?"

He laughed at her, softly, indulgently, and said: "I like you in that shade of brown."

"Oh, Ned, please –"

"That's better," he said. "I intended coming out to the house, but – well – there were lots of things happening when I got back and a lot of loose ends of things that had happened while I was gone, and by the time I finished with those I ran into Shad O'Rory and got sent here." He waved an arm to indicate the hospital.

Her gravity was not affected by the lightness of his tone.

"Are they going to hang this Despain?" she asked curtly.

He laughed again and said: "We're not going to get very far talking like this."

She frowned, but said, "Are they, Ned?" with less haughtiness.

"I don't think so," he told her, shaking his head a little. "The chances are he didn't kill Taylor after all."

She did not seem surprised. "Did you know that when you asked me to – to help you get – or fix up – evidence against him?"

He smiled reproachfully. "Of course not, snip. What do you think I am?"

"You did know it." Her voice was cold and scornful as her blue eyes. "You only wanted to get the money he owed you and you made me help you use Taylor's murder for that."

"Have it your own way," he replied indifferently.

She came a step closer to him. The faintest of quivers disturbed her chin for an instant, then her young face was firm and bold again. "Do you know who killed him?" she asked, her eyes probing his.

He shook his head slowly from side to side.

"Did Dad?"

He blinked. "You mean did Paul know who killed him?"

She stamped a foot. "I mean did Dad kill him?" she cried.

He put a hand over her mouth. His eyes had jerked into focus on the closed door. "Shut up," he muttered.

She stepped back from his hand as one of her hands pushed it away from her face. "Did he?" she insisted.

In a low angry voice he said: "If you must be a nitwit at least don't go around with a megaphone. Nobody cares what kind of idiotic notions you have as long as you keep them to yourself, but you've got to keep them to yourself."

Her eyes opened wide and dark. "Then he did kill him," she said in a small flat voice, but with utter certainty.

He thrust his face down towards hers. "No, my dear," he said in an enraged sugary voice, "he didn't kill him." He held his face near hers. A vicious smile distorted his features.

Firm of countenance and voice, not drawing back from him, she said: "If he didn't I can't understand what difference it makes what I say or how loud."

An end of his mouth twitched up in a sneer. "You'd be surprised how many things there are you can't understand," he said angrily, "and never will if you keep on like this." He stepped back from her, a long step, and put his fists in the pockets of his bathrobe. Both corners of his mouth were pulled down now and there were grooves in his forehead. His narrowed eyes stared at the floor in front of her feet. "Where'd you get this crazy idea?" he growled.

"It's not a crazy idea. You know it's not."

He moved his shoulders impatiently and demanded: "Where'd you get it?"

She too moved her shoulders. "I didn't get it anywhere. I – I suddenly saw it."

"Nonsense," he said sharply, looking up at her under his brows. "Did you see the *Observer* this morning?"

"No."

He stared at her with hard skeptical eyes.

Annoyance brought a little color into her face. "I did not," she said. "Why do you ask?"

"No?" he asked in a tone that said he did not believe her, but the skeptical gleam had gone out of his eyes. They were dull and thoughtful. Suddenly they brightened. He took his right hand from his bathrobe-pocket. He held it out towards her, palm up. "Let me see the letter," he said.

She stared at him with round eyes. "What?"

"The letter," he said, "the typewritten letter – three questions and no signature."

She lowered her eyes to avoid his and embarrassment disturbed, very slightly, her features. After a moment of hesitation she asked, "How did you know?" and opened her brown hand-bag.

"Everybody in town's had at least one," he said carelessly. "Is this your first?"

"Yes." She gave him a crumpled sheet of paper.

He straightened it out and read:

> Are you really too stupid to know that your father murdered your lover?
>
> If you do not know it, why did you help him and Ned Beaumont in their attempt to fasten the crime on an innocent man?
>
> Do you know that by helping your father escape justice you are making yourself an accomplice in his crime?

Ned Beaumont nodded and smiled lightly. "They're all pretty much alike," he said. He wadded the paper in a loose ball and tossed it at the waste-basket beside the table. "You'll probably get some more of them now you're on the mailing-list."

Opal Madvig drew her lower lip in between her teeth. Her blue eyes were bright without warmth. They studied Ned Beaumont's composed face.

He said: "O'Rory's trying to make campaign-material out of it. You know about my trouble with him. That was because he thought I'd broken with your father and could be paid to help frame him for the murder – enough at least to beat him at the polls – and I wouldn't."

Her eyes did not change. "What did you and Dad fight about?" she asked.

"That's nobody's business but ours, snip," he said gently, "if we did fight."

"You did," she said, "in Carson's speakeasy." She put her teeth together with a click and said boldly: "You quarreled when you found out that he really had – had killed Taylor."

He laughed and asked in a mocking tone: "Hadn't I known that all along?"

Her expression was not affected by his humor. "Why did you ask if I had seen the *Observer*?" she demanded. "What was in it?"

"Some more of the same sort of nonsense," he told her evenly. "It's there on the table if you want to see it. There'll be plenty of it before the campaign's over: this is going to be that kind. And you'll be giving your father a swell break by swallowing –" He broke off with an impatient gesture because she was no longer listening to him.

She had gone to the table and was picking up the newspaper he had put down when she came in.

He smiled pleasantly at her back and said: "It's on the front page, *An Open Letter to the Mayor.*"

As she read she began to tremble – her knees, her hands, her mouth – so that Ned Beaumont frowned anxiously at her, but when she had finished and had dropped the newspaper on the table and had turned to face him directly her tall body and fair face were statue-like in their immobility. She addressed him in a low voice between lips that barely moved to let the words out: "They wouldn't dare say such things if they were not true."

"That's nothing to what'll be said before they're through," he drawled lazily. He seemed amused, though there was a suggestion of anger difficultly restrained in the glitter of his eyes.

She looked at him for a long moment, then, saying nothing, turned towards the door.

He said: "Wait."

She halted and confronted him again. His smile was friendly now, ingratiating. Her face was a tinted statue's.

He said: "Politics is a tough game, snip, the way it's being played here this time. The *Observer* is on the other side of the fence and they're not worrying much about the truth of anything that'll hurt Paul. They –"

"I don't believe that," she said. "I know Mr. Mathews – his wife was only a few years ahead of me at school and we were friends – and I don't believe he'd say anything like that about Dad unless it was true, or unless he had good reason for thinking it true."

Ned Beaumont chuckled. "You know a lot about it. Mathews is up to his ears in debt. The State Central Trust Company holds both mortgages on his plant – one on his house too, for that matter. The State Central belongs to Bill Roan. Bill Roan is running for the Senate against Henry. Mathews does what he's told to do and prints what he's told to print."

Opal Madvig did not say anything. There was nothing to indicate that she had been at all convinced by Ned Beaumont's argument.

He went on, speaking in an amiable, persuasive tone: "This" – he flicked a finger at the paper on the table – "is nothing to what'll come later. They're going to rattle Taylor Henry's bones till they think up something worse and we're going to have this sort of stuff to read till election's over. We might just as well get used to it now and you, of all people, oughtn't to let yourself be bothered by it. Paul doesn't mind it much. He's a politician and –"

"He's a murderer," she said in a low distinct voice.

"And his daughter's a chump," he exclaimed irritably. "Will you stop that foolishness?"

"My father is a murderer," she said.

"You're crazy. Listen to me, snip. Your father had absolutely nothing to do with Taylor's murder. He –"

"I don't believe you," she said gravely. "I'll never believe you again."

He scowled at her.

She turned and went to the door.

"Wait," he said. "Let me –"

She went out and shut the door behind her.

VII

Ned Beaumont's face, after a grimace of rage at the closed door, became heavily thoughtful. Lines came into his forehead. His dark eyes grew narrow and introspective. His lips puckered up under his mustache. Presently he put a finger to his mouth and bit its nail. He breathed regularly, but with more depth than usual.

Footsteps sounded outside his door. He dropped his appearance of thoughtfulness and walked idly towards the window, humming *Little Lost Lady.* The footsteps went on past his door. He stopped humming and bent to pick up the sheet of paper holding the three questions that had been addressed to Opal Madvig. He did not smooth the paper, but thrust it, crumpled in a loose ball as it was, into one of his bathrobe-pockets.

He found and lit a cigar then and, with it between his teeth burning, stood by the table and squinted down through smoke at the front page of the *Observer* lying there.

AN OPEN LETTER TO THE MAYOR

SIR:

The *Observer* has come into possession of certain information which it believes to be of paramount importance in clearing up the mystery surrounding the recent murder of Taylor Henry.

This information is incorporated in several affidavits now in the *Observer*'s safety-deposit box. The substance of these affidavits is as follows:

1. That Paul Madvig quarreled with Taylor Henry some months ago over the young man's attentions to his daughter and forbade his daughter to see Henry again.
2. That Paul Madvig's daughter nevertheless continued to meet Taylor Henry in a furnished room he had rented for that purpose.
3. That they were together in this furnished room the afternoon of the very day on which he was killed.
4. That Paul Madvig went to Taylor Henry's home that evening, supposedly to remonstrate with the young man, or his father, again.
5. That Paul Madvig appeared angry when he left the Henry residence a few minutes before Taylor Henry was murdered.
6. That Paul Madvig and Taylor Henry were seen within half a block of each other, less than a block from the spot where the young man's body was found, not more than fifteen minutes before his body was found.
7. That the Police Department has not at present a single detective engaged in trying to find Taylor Henry's murderer.

The *Observer* believes that you should know these things and that the voters and taxpayers should know them. The *Observer* has no ax to grind, no motive except the desire to see justice done. The *Observer* will welcome an opportunity to hand these affidavits, as well as all other information it has, to you or to any qualified city or state official and, if such a course can be shown an aid to justice, to refrain from publishing any or all of the details of these affidavits.

But the *Observer* will not permit the information incorporated in these affidavits to be ignored. If the officials elected and appointed to enforce law and order in this city and state do not consider these affidavits of sufficient importance to be acted upon, the *Observer* will carry the matter to that higher tribunal, the People of this City, by publishing them in full.

H. K. MATHEWS, Publisher

Ned Beaumont grunted derisively and blew cigar-smoke down at this declaration, but his eyes remained somber.

VIII

Early that afternoon Paul Madvig's mother came to see Ned Beaumont.

He put his arms around her and kissed her on both cheeks until she pushed him away with a mock-severe "Do stop it. You're worse than the Airedale Paul used to have."

"I'm part Airedale," he said, "on my father's side," and went behind her to help her out of her sealskin coat.

Smoothing her black dress, she went to the bed and sat on it.

He hung the coat on the back of a chair and stood – legs apart, hands in bathrobe-pockets – before her.

She studied him critically. "You don't look so bad," she said presently, "nor yet so good. How do you feel?"

"Swell. I'm only hanging around here on account of the nurses."

"That wouldn't surprise me much, neither," she told him. "But don't stand there ogling me like a Cheshire cat. You make me nervous. Sit down." She patted the bed beside her.

He sat down beside her.

She said: "Paul seems to think you did something very grand and noble by doing whatever it was you did, but you can't tell me that if you had behaved yourself you would ever have got into whatever scrape you got into at all."

"Aw, Mom," he began.

She cut him off. The gaze of her blue eyes that were young as her son's bored into Ned Beaumont's brown ones. "Look here, Ned, Paul didn't kill that whipper-snapper, did he?"

Surprise opened Ned Beaumont's eyes and mouth. "No."

"I didn't think so," the old woman said. "He's always been a good boy, but I've heard that there's some nasty hints going around and the Lord only knows what goes on in this politics. I'm sure I haven't any idea."

Amazement tinged with humor was in the eyes with which Ned Beaumont looked at her bony face.

She said: "Well, goggle at me, but I haven't got any way of knowing what you men are up to, or what you do without thinking anything of it. It was a long while before ever you were born that I gave up trying to find out."

He patted her shoulder. "You're a humdinger, Mom," he said admiringly.

She drew away from his hand and fixed him with severe penetrant eyes again. "Would you tell me if he had killed him?" she demanded.

He shook his head no.

"Then how do I know he didn't?"

He laughed. "Because," he explained, "if he had I'd still say, 'No,' but then, if you asked me if I'd tell you the truth if he had, I'd say, 'Yes.' " Merriment went out of his eyes and voice. "He didn't do it, Mom." He smiled at her. He smiled with his lips only and they were thin against his teeth. "It would be nice if somebody in town besides me thought he didn't do it and it would be especially nice if that other one was his mother."

IX

An hour after Mrs. Madvig's departure Ned Beaumont received a package containing four books and Janet Henry's card. He was writing her a note of thanks when Jack arrived.

Jack, letting cigarette-smoke come out with his words, said: "I think I've got something, though I don't know how you're going to like it."

Ned Beaumont looked thoughtfully at the sleek young man and smoothed the left side of his mustache with a forefinger. "If it's what I hired you to get I'll like it well enough." His voice was matter-of-fact as Jack's. "Sit down and tell me about it."

Jack sat down carefully, crossed his legs, put his hat on the floor, and looked from his cigarette to Ned Beaumont. He said: "It looks like those things were written by Madvig's daughter."

Ned Beaumont's eyes widened a little, but only for a moment. His face lost some of its color and his breathing became irregular. There was no change in his voice. "What makes it look like that?"

From an inner pocket Jack brought two sheets of paper similar in size and make, folded alike. He gave them to Ned Beaumont who, when he had unfolded them, saw that on each were three typewritten questions, the same three questions on each sheet.

"One of them's the one you gave me yesterday," Jack said. "Could you tell which?"

Ned Beaumont shook his head slowly from side to side.

"There's no difference," Jack said. "I wrote the other one on Charter Street where Taylor Henry had a room that Madvig's daughter used to come to – with a Corona typewriter that was there and on paper that was there. So far as anybody seems to know there were only two keys to the place. He had one and she had one. She's been back there at least a couple of times since he was killed."

Ned Beaumont, scowling now at the sheets of paper in his hands, nodded without looking up.

Jack lit a fresh cigarette from the one he had been smoking, rose and went to the table to mash the old cigarette in the ashtray there, and returned to his seat. There was nothing in his face or manner to show that he had any interest in Ned Beaumont's reaction to their discovery.

After another minute of silence Ned Beaumont raised his head a little and asked: "How'd you get this?"

Jack put his cigarette in a corner of his mouth where it wagged with his words. "The *Observer* tip on the place this morning gave me the lead. That's where the police got theirs too, but they got there first. I got a pretty good break, though: the copper left in charge was a friend of mine – Fred Hurley – and for a ten-spot he let me do all the poking around I wanted."

Ned Beaumont rattled the papers in his hand. "Do the police know this?" he asked.

Jack shrugged. "I didn't tell them. I pumped Hurley, but he didn't know anything – just put there to watch things till they decide what they're going to do. Maybe they know, maybe they don't." He shook cigarette-ash on the floor. "I could find out."

"Never mind that. What else did you turn up?"

"I didn't look for anything else."

Ned Beaumont, after a quick glance at the dark young man's inscrutable face, looked down at the sheets of paper again. "What kind of dump is it?"

"Thirteen twenty-four. They had a room and bath under the name of French. The woman that runs the place claims she didn't know who they really were till the police came today. Maybe she didn't. It's the kind of joint where not much is asked. She says they used to be there a lot, mostly in the afternoons, and that the girl's been back a couple of times in the last week or so that she knows of, though she could pop in and out without being seen easily enough."

"Sure it's her?"

Jack made a noncommittal gesture with one hand. "The description's right." He paused, then added carelessly as he exhaled smoke: "She's the only one the woman saw since he was killed."

Ned Beaumont raised his head again. His eyes were hard. "Taylor had others coming there?" he asked.

Jack made the noncommittal gesture once more. "The woman wouldn't say so. She said she didn't know, but from the way she said it I'd say it was a safe bet she was lying."

"Couldn't tell by what's in the place?"

Jack shook his head. "No. There's not much woman stuff there – just a kimono and toilet things and pajamas and stuff like that."

"Much of his stuff there?"

"Oh, a suit and a pair of shoes and some underwear and pajamas and socks and so on."

"Any hats?"

Jack smiled. "No hats," he said.

Ned Beaumont got up and went to the window. Outside darkness was almost complete. A dozen raindrops clung to the glass and as many more struck it lightly while Ned Beaumont stood there. He turned to face Jack again. "Thanks a lot, Jack," he said slowly. His eyes were focused on Jack's face in a dully absent-minded stare. "I think maybe I'll have another job for you soon – maybe tonight. I'll give you a ring."

Jack said, "Right," and rose and went out.

Ned Beaumont went to the closet for his clothes, carried them into the bathroom, and put them on. When he came out a nurse was in his room, a tall full-bodied woman with a shiny pale face.

"Why, you're dressed!" she exclaimed.

"Yes, I've got to go out."

Alarm joined astonishment in her mien. "But you can't, Mr. Beaumont," she protested. "It's night and it's beginning to rain and Doctor Tait would –"

"I know, I know," he said impatiently, and went around her to the door.

6 THE OBSERVER

I

MRS. MADVIG opened her front door. "Ned!" she cried, "are you crazy? Running around on a night like this, and you just out of the hospital."

"The taxi didn't leak," he said, but his grin lacked virility. "Paul in?"

"He went out not more than half an hour ago, I think to the Club. But come in, come in."

"Opal home?" he asked as he shut the door and followed her down the hall.

"No. She's been off somewhere since morning."

Ned Beaumont halted in the living-room doorway. "I can't stay," he said. "I'll run on down to the Club and see Paul there." His voice was not quite steady.

The old woman turned quickly towards him. "You'll do no such thing," she said in a scolding voice. "Look at you, you're just about to have a chill. You'll sit right down there by the fire and let me get you something hot to drink."

"Can't, Mom," he told her. "I've got to go places."

Her blue eyes wherein age did not show became bright and keen. "When did you leave the hospital?" she demanded.

"Just now."

She put her lips together hard, then opened them a little to say accusingly: "You walked out." A shadow disturbed the clear blueness of her eyes. She came close to Ned Beaumont and held her face close to his: she was nearly as tall as he. Her voice was harsh now as if coming from a parched throat. "Is it something about Paul?" The shadow in her eyes became recognizable as fear. "And Opal?"

His voice was barely audible. "It's something I've got to see them about."

She touched one of his cheeks somewhat timidly with bony fingers. "You're a good boy, Ned," she said.

He put an arm around her. "Don't worry, Mom. None of it's bad as it could be. Only – if Opal comes home make her stay – if you can."

"Is it anything you can tell me, Ned?" she asked.

"Not now and – well – it might be just as well not to let either of them know you think anything's wrong."

II

Ned Beaumont walked five blocks through the rain to a drugstore. He used a telephone there first to order a taxicab and then to call two numbers and ask for Mr. Mathews. He did not get Mr. Mathews on the wire.

He called another number and asked for Mr. Rumsen. A moment later he was saying: " 'Lo, Jack, this is Ned Beaumont. Busy? . . . Fine. Here it is. I want to know if the girl we were talking about went to see Mathews of the *Observer* today and what she did afterwards, if she did. . . . That's right, Hal Mathews. I tried to get him by phone, there and home, but no luck. . . . Well, on the quiet if you can, but get it and get it quick. . . . No, I'm out of the hospital. I'll be home waiting. You know my number. . . . Yes, Jack. Fine, thanks, and ring me as often as you can. . . . 'By."

He went out to the waiting taxicab, got into it, and gave the driver his address, but after half a dozen blocks he tapped the front window with his fingers and gave the driver another address.

Presently the taxicab came to rest in front of a squat grayish house set in the center of a steeply sloping smooth lawn. "Wait," he told the driver as he got out.

The grayish house's front door was opened to his ring by a red-haired maid.

"Mr. Farr in?" he asked her.

"I'll see. Who shall I tell him?"

"Mr. Beaumont."

The District Attorney came into the reception-hall with both hands out. His florid pugnacious face was all smiling. "Well, well, Beaumont, this is a real pleasure," he said as he rushed up to his visitor. "Here, give me your coat and hat."

Ned Beaumont smiled and shook his head. "I can't stay," he said. "I just dropped in for a second on my way home from the hospital."

"All shipshape again? Splendid!"

"Feeling pretty good," Ned Beaumont said. "Anything new?"

"Nothing very important. The birds who manhandled you are still loose – in hiding somewhere – but we'll get them."

Ned Beaumont made a depreciatory mouth. "I didn't die and they weren't trying to kill me: you could only stick them with an assault-charge." He looked somewhat drowsily at Farr. "Had any more of those three-question epistles?"

The District Attorney cleared his throat. "Uh – yes, come to think of it, there were one or two more of them."

"How many?" Ned Beaumont asked. His voice was politely casual. The ends of his lips were raised a little in an idle smile. Amusement glinted in his eyes, but his eyes held Farr's.

The District Attorney cleared his throat. "Three," he said reluctantly. Then his eyes brightened. "Did you hear about the splendid meeting we had at – ?"

Ned Beaumont interrupted him. "All along the same line?" he asked.

"Uh – more or less." The District Attorney licked his lips and a pleading expression began to enter his eyes.

"How much more – or less?"

Farr's eyes slid their gaze down from Ned Beaumont's eyes to his necktie and sidewise to his left shoulder. He moved his lips vaguely, but did not utter a sound.

Ned Beaumont's smile was openly malicious now. "All saying Paul killed Taylor Henry?" he asked in a sugary voice.

Farr jumped, his face faded to a light orange, and in his excitement he let his startled eyes focus on Ned Beaumont's eyes again. "Christ, Ned!" he gasped.

Ned Beaumont laughed. "You're getting nerves, Farr," he said, still sugary of voice. "Better watch yourself or you'll be going to pieces." He made his face grave. "Has Paul said anything to you about it? About your nerves, I mean."

"N-no."

Ned Beaumont smiled again. "Maybe he hasn't noticed it – yet." He raised an arm, glanced at his wrist-watch, then at Farr. "Found out who wrote them yet?" he asked sharply.

The District Attorney stammered: "Look here, Ned, I don't – you know – it's not –" floundered and stopped.

Ned Beaumont asked: "Well?"

The District Attorney gulped and said desperately: "We've got something, Ned, but it's too soon to say. Maybe there's nothing to it. You know how these things are."

Ned Beaumont nodded. There was nothing but friendliness in his face now. His voice was level and cool without chilliness saying: "You've learned where they were written and you've found the machine they were written on, but that's all you've got so far. You haven't got enough to even guess who wrote them."

"That's right, Ned," Farr blurted out with a great air of relief.

Ned Beaumont took Farr's hand and shook it cordially. "That's the stuff," he said. "Well, I've got to run along. You can't go wrong taking things slowly, being sure you're right before you go ahead. You can take my word for that."

The District Attorney's face and voice were warm with emotion. "Thanks, Ned, thanks!"

III

At ten minutes past nine o'clock that evening the telephone-bell in Ned Beaumont's living-room rang. He went quickly to the telephone. "Hello. . . . Yes, Jack . . . Yes. . . . Yes. . . . Where? . . . Yes, that's fine. . . . That'll be all tonight. Thanks a lot."

When he rose from the telephone he was smiling with pale lips. His eyes were shiny and reckless. His hands shook a little.

The telephone-bell rang again before he had taken his third step. He hesitated, went back to the telephone. "Hello. . . . Oh, hello, Paul. . . . Yes, I got tired of playing invalid. . . . Nothing special – just thought I'd drop in and see you. . . . No, I'm afraid I can't. I'm not feeling as strong as I thought I was, so I think I'd better go to bed. . . . Yes, tomorrow, sure. . . . 'By."

He put on rain-coat and hat going downstairs. Wind drove rain in at him when he opened the street-door, drove it into his face as he walked half a block to the garage on the corner.

In the garage's glass-walled office a lanky, brown-haired man in once-white overalls was tilted back on a wooden chair, his feet on a shelf above an electric heater, reading a newspaper. He lowered the newspaper when Ned Beaumont said: "'Lo, Tommy."

The dirtiness of Tommy's face made his teeth seem whiter than they were. He showed many of them in a grin and said: "Kind of weatherish tonight."

"Yes. Got an iron I can have? One that'll carry me over country roads tonight?"

Tommy said: "Jesus! Lucky for you you could pick your night. You might've had to go on a bad one. Well, I got a Buick that I don't care what happens to."

"Will it get me there?"

"It's just as likely to as anything else," Tommy said, "tonight."

"All right. Fill it up for me. What's the best road up Lazy Creek way on a night like this?"

"How far up?"

Ned Beaumont looked thoughtfully at the garageman then said: "Along about where it runs into the river."

Tommy nodded. "The Mathews place?" he asked.

Ned Beaumont did not say anything.

Tommy said: "It makes a difference which place you're going to."

"Yes? The Mathews place." Ned Beaumont frowned. "This is under the hat, Tommy."

"Did you come to me because you thought I'd talk or because you knew I wouldn't?" Tommy demanded argumentatively.

Ned Beaumont said: "I'm in a hurry."

"Then you take the New River Road as far as Barton's, take the dirt road over the bridge there – if you can make it at all – and then the first cross-road back east. That'll bring you in behind Mathews's place along about the top of the hill. If you can't make the dirt road in this weather you'll have to go on up the New River Road to where it crosses and then cut back along the old one."

"Thanks."

When Ned Beaumont was getting into the Buick Tommy said to him in a markedly casual tone: "There's an extra gun in the side-pocket."

Ned Beaumont stared at the lanky man. "Extra?" he asked blankly.

"Pleasant trip," Tommy said.

Ned Beaumont shut the door and drove away.

IV

The clock in the dashboard said ten thirty-two. Ned Beaumont switched off the lights and got somewhat stiffly out of the Buick. Wind-driven rain hammered tree, bush, ground, man, car with incessant wet blows. Downhill, through rain and foliage, irregular small patches of yellow light glowed faintly. Ned Beaumont shivered, tried to draw his rain-coat closer around him, and began to stumble downhill through drenched underbrush towards the patches of light.

Wind and rain on his back pushed him downhill towards the patches. As he went downhill stiffness gradually left him so that, though he stumbled often and staggered, and was tripped by obstacles underfoot, he kept his feet under him and moved nimbly enough, if erratically, towards his goal.

Presently a path came under his feet. He turned into it, holding it partly by its sliminess under his feet, partly by the feel of the bushes whipping his face on either side, and not at all by sight. The path led him off to the left for a little distance, but then, swinging in a broad curve, brought him to the brink of a small gorge through which water rushed noisily and from there, in another curve, to the front door of the building where the yellow light glowed.

Ned Beaumont went straight up to the door and knocked.

The door was opened by a gray-haired bespectacled man. His face was mild and grayish and the eyes that peered anxiously through the pale-tortoise-shell-encircled lenses of his spectacles were gray. His brown suit was neat and of good quality, but not fashionably cut. One side of his rather high stiff white collar had been blistered in four places by drops of water. He stood aside holding the door open and said, "Come in, sir, come in out of the rain," in a friendly if not hearty voice. "A wretched night to be out in."

Ned Beaumont lowered his head no more than two inches in the beginning of a bow and stepped indoors. He was in a large room that occupied all the building's ground-floor. The sparseness and simplicity of the room's furnishings gave it a primitive air that was pleasantly devoid of ostentation. It was a kitchen, a dining-room, and a living-room.

Opal Madvig rose from the footstool on which she had

been sitting at one end of the fireplace and, holding herself tall and straight, stared with hostile bleak eyes at Ned Beaumont.

He took off his hat and began to unbutton his rain-coat. The others recognized him then.

The man who had opened the door said, "Why, it's Beaumont!" in an incredulous voice and looked wide-eyed at Shad O'Rory.

Shad O'Rory was sitting in a wooden chair in the center of the room facing the fireplace. He smiled dreamily at Ned Beaumont, saying, in his musical faintly Irish baritone, "And so it is," and, "How are you, Ned?"

Jeff Gardner's apish face broadened in a grin that showed his beautiful false teeth and almost completely hid his little red eyes. "By Jesus, Rusty!" he said to the sullen rosy-cheeked boy who lounged on the bench beside him, "little Rubber Ball has come back to us. I told you he liked the way we bounced him around."

Rusty lowered at Ned Beaumont and growled something that did not carry across the room.

The thin girl in red sitting not far from Opal Madvig looked at Ned Beaumont with bright interested dark eyes.

Ned Beaumont took off his coat. His lean face, still bearing the marks of Jeff's and Rusty's fists, was tranquil except for the recklessness aglitter in his eyes. He put his coat and hat on a long unpainted chest that was against one wall near the door. He smiled politely at the man who had admitted him and said: "My car broke down as I was passing. It's very kind of you to give me shelter, Mr. Mathews."

Mathews said, "Not at all – glad to," somewhat vaguely. Then his frightened eyes looked pleadingly at O'Rory again.

O'Rory stroked his smooth white hair with a slender pale hand and smiled pleasantly at Ned Beaumont, but did not say anything.

Ned Beaumont advanced to the fireplace. " 'Lo, snip," he said to Opal Madvig.

She did not respond to his greeting. She stood there and looked at him with hostile bleak eyes.

He directed his smile at the thin girl in red. "This is Mrs. Mathews, isn't it?"

She said, "It is," in a soft, almost cooing, voice and held out her hand.

"Opal told me you were a schoolmate of hers," he said as he took her hand. He turned from her to face Rusty and Jeff. " 'Lo, boys," he said carelessly. "I was hoping I'd see you some time soon."

Rusty said nothing.

Jeff's face became an ugly mask of grinning delight. "Me and you both," he said heartily, "now that my knuckles are all healed up again. What do you guess it is that makes me get such a hell of a big kick out of slugging you?"

Shad O'Rory gently addressed the apish man without turning to look at him: "You talk too much with your mouth, Jeff. Maybe if you didn't you'd still have your own teeth."

Mrs. Mathews spoke to Opal in an undertone. Opal shook her head and sat down on the stool by the fire again.

Mathews, indicating a wooden chair at the other end of the fireplace, said nervously: "Sit down, Mr. Beaumont, and dry your feet and – and get warm."

"Thanks." Ned Beaumont pulled the chair out more directly in the fire's glow and sat down.

Shad O'Rory was lighting a cigarette. When he had finished he took it from between his lips and asked: "How are you feeling, Ned?"

"Pretty good, Shad."

"That's fine." O'Rory turned his head a little to speak to the two men on the bench: "You boys can go back to town tomorrow." He turned back to Ned Beaumont, explaining blandly: "We were playing safe as long as we didn't know for sure you weren't going to die, but we don't mind standing an assault-rap."

Ned Beaumont nodded. "The chances are I won't go to the trouble of appearing against you, anyhow, on that, but don't forget our friend Jeff's wanted for West's murder." His voice was light, but into his eyes, fixed on the log burning in the fireplace, came a brief evil glint. There was nothing in his eyes but mockery when he moved them to the left to focus on Mathews. "Though of course I might so I could make trouble for Mathews for helping you hide out."

Mathews said hastily: "I didn't, Mr. Beaumont. I didn't even know they were here until we came up today and I was as surprised as –" He broke off, his face panicky, and addressed Shad O'Rory, whining: "You know you are welcome. You know that, but the point I'm trying to make" – his face was illuminated by a sudden glad smile – "is that by helping you without knowing it I didn't do anything I could be held legally responsible for."

O'Rory said softly: "Yes, you helped me without knowing it." His notable clear blue-gray eyes looked without interest at the newspaper-publisher.

Mathews's smile lost its gladness, flickered out entirely. He fidgeted with fingers at his necktie and presently evaded O'Rory's gaze.

Mrs. Mathews spoke to Ned Beaumont, sweetly: "Everybody's been so dull this evening. It was simply ghastly until you came."

He looked at her curiously. Her dark eyes were bright, soft, inviting. Under his appraising look she lowered her head a little and pursed her lips a little, coquettishly. Her lips were thin, too dark with rouge, but beautiful in form. He smiled at her and, rising, went over to her.

Opal Madvig stared at the floor before her. Mathews, O'Rory, and the two men on the bench watched Ned Beaumont and Mathews's wife.

He asked, "What makes them so dull?" and sat down on the floor in front of her, cross-legged, not facing her directly, his back to the fire, leaning on a hand on the floor behind him, his face turned up to one side towards her.

"I'm sure I don't know," she said, pouting. "I thought it was going to be fun when Hal asked me if I wanted to come up here with him and Opal. And then, when we got here, we found these –" she paused a moment – said, "friends of Hal's," with poorly concealed dubiety – and went on: "here and everybody's been sitting around hinting at some secret they've all got between them that I don't know anything about and it's been unbearably stupid. Opal's been as bad as the rest. She –"

Her husband said, "Now, Eloise," in an ineffectually authoritative tone and, when she raised her eyes to meet his, got more embarrassment than authority in his gaze.

"I don't care," she told him petulantly. "It's true and Opal is as bad as the rest of you. Why, you and she haven't even talked about whatever business it was you were coming up here to discuss in the first place. Don't think I'd've stayed here this long if it hadn't been for the storm. I wouldn't."

Opal Madvig's face had flushed, but she did not raise her eyes.

Eloise Mathews bent her head down towards Ned Beaumont again and the petulance in her face became playful. "That's what you've got to make up for," she assured him, "and that and not because you're beautiful is why I was so glad to see you."

He frowned at her in mock indignation.

She frowned at him. Her frown was genuine. "Did your car really break down?" she demanded, "or did you come here to see them on the same dull business that's making them so stupidly mysterious? You did. You're another one of them."

He laughed. He asked: "It wouldn't make any difference why I came if I changed my mind after seeing you, would it?"

"No – o – o" – she was suspicious – "but I'd have to be awfully sure you had changed it."

"And anyway," he promised lightly, "I won't be mysterious about anything. Haven't you really got an idea of what they're all eating their hearts out about?"

"Not the least," she replied spitefully, "except that I'm pretty sure it must be something very stupid and probably political."

He put his free hand up and patted one of hers. "Smart girl, right on both counts." He turned his head to look at O'Rory and Mathews. When his eyes came back to hers they were shiny with merriment. "Want me to tell you about it?"

"No."

"First," he said, "Opal thinks her father murdered Taylor Henry."

Opal Madvig made a horrible strangling noise in her throat and sprang up from the footstool. She put the back of one hand over her mouth. Her eyes were open so wide the whites showed all around the irises and they were glassy and dreadful.

Rusty lurched to his feet, his face florid with anger, but Jeff, leering, caught the boy's arm. "Let him alone," he rasped good-naturedly. "He's all right." The boy stood straining against the apish man's grip on his arm, but did not try to free himself.

Eloise Mathews sat frozen in her chair, staring without comprehension at Opal.

Mathews was trembling, a shrunken gray-faced sick man whose lower lip and lower eyelids sagged.

Shad O'Rory was sitting forward in his chair, finely modeled long face pale and hard, eyes like blue-gray ice, hands gripping chair-arms, feet flat on the floor.

"Second," Ned Beaumont said, his poise nowise disturbed by the agitation of the others, "she –"

"Ned, don't!" Opal Madvig cried.

He screwed himself around on the floor then to look up at her.

She had taken her hand from her mouth. Her hands were

knotted together against her chest. Her stricken eyes, her whole haggard face, begged mercy of him.

He studied her gravely awhile. Through window and wall came the sound of rain dashing against the building in wild gusts and between gusts the bustling of the near-by river. His eyes, studying her, were cool, deliberate. Presently he spoke to her in a voice kind enough but aloof: "Isn't that why you're here?"

"Please don't," she said hoarsely.

He moved his lips in a thin smile that his eyes had nothing to do with and asked: "Nobody's supposed to go around talking about it except you and your father's other enemies?"

She put her hands – fists – down at her sides, raised her face angrily, and said in a hard ringing voice: "He did murder Taylor."

Ned Beaumont leaned back against his hand again and looked up at Eloise Mathews. "That's what I was telling you," he drawled. "Thinking that, she went to your husband after she saw the junk he printed this morning. Of course he didn't think Paul had done any killing: he's just in a tough spot – with his mortgages held by the State Central, which is owned by Shad's candidate for the Senate – and he has to do what he's told. What she –"

Mathews interrupted him. The publisher's voice was thin and desperate. "Now you stop that, Beaumont. You –"

O'Rory interrupted Mathews. O'Rory's voice was quiet, musical. "Let him talk, Mathews," he said. "Let him say his say."

"Thanks, Shad," Ned Beaumont said carelessly, not looking around, and went on: "She went to your husband to have him confirm her suspicion, but he couldn't give her anything that would do that unless he lied to her. He doesn't know anything. He's simply throwing mud wherever Shad tells him to throw it. But here's what he can do and does. He can print in tomorrow's paper the story about her coming in and telling him she believes her father killed her lover. That'll be a lovely wallop. 'Opal Madvig Accuses Father of Murder; Boss's Daughter Says He Killed Senator's Son!' Can't you see that in black ink all across the front of the *Observer*?"

Eloise Mathews, her eyes large, her face white, was listening breathlessly, bending forward, her face above his. Wind-flung rain beat walls and windows. Rusty filled and emptied his lungs with a long sighing breath.

Ned Beaumont put the tip of his tongue between smiling lips, withdrew it, and said: "That's why he brought her up here, to keep her under cover till the story breaks. Maybe he knew Shad and the boys were here, maybe not. It doesn't make any difference. He's getting her off where nobody can find out what she's done till the papers are out. I don't mean that he'd've brought her here, or would hold her here, against her will – that wouldn't be very bright of him the way things stack up now – but none of that's necessary. She's willing to go to any lengths to ruin her father."

Opal Madvig said, in a whisper, but distinctly: "He did kill him."

Ned Beaumont sat up straight and looked at her. He looked solemnly at her for a moment, then smiled, shook his head in a gesture of amused resignation, and leaned back on his elbows.

Eloise Mathews was staring with dark eyes wherein wonder was predominant at her husband. He had sat down. His head was bowed. His hands hid his face.

Shad O'Rory recrossed his legs and took out a cigarette. "Through?" he asked mildly.

Ned Beaumont's back was to O'Rory. He did not turn to reply: "You'd hardly believe how through I am." His voice was level, but his face was suddenly tired, spent.

O'Rory lit his cigarette. "Well," he said when he had done that, "what the hell does it all amount to? It's our turn to hang a big one on you and we're doing it. The girl came in with the story on her own hook. She came here because she wanted to. So did you. She and you and anybody else can go wherever they want to go whenever they want to." He stood up. "Personally, I'm wanting to go to bed. Where do I sleep, Mathews?"

Eloise Mathews spoke, to her husband: "This is not true, Hal." It was not a question.

He was slow taking his hands from his face. He achieved dignity saying: "Darling, there is a dozen times enough evidence against Madvig to justify us in insisting that the police at least question him. That is all we have done."

"I did not mean that," his wife said.

"Well, darling, when Miss Madvig came –" He faltered, stopped, a gray-faced man who shivered before the look in his wife's eyes and put his hands over his face again.

V

Eloise Mathews and Ned Beaumont were alone in the large ground-floor room, sitting, in chairs a few feet apart, with the fireplace in front of them. She was bent forward, looking with tragic eyes at the last burning log. His legs were crossed. One of his arms was hooked over the back of his chair. He smoked a cigar and watched her surreptitiously.

The stairs creaked and her husband came half-way down them. He was fully clothed except that he had taken off his collar. His necktie, partially loosened, hung outside his vest. He said: "Darling, won't you come to bed? It's midnight."

She did not move.

He said: "Mr. Beaumont, will you – ?"

Ned Beaumont, when his name was spoken, turned his face towards the man on the stairs, a face cruelly placid. When Mathews's voice broke, Ned Beaumont returned his attention to his cigar and Mathews's wife.

After a little while Mathews went upstairs again.

Eloise Mathews spoke without taking her gaze from the fire. "There is some whisky in the chest. Will you get it?"

"Surely." He found the whisky and brought it to her, then found some glasses. "Straight?" he asked.

She nodded. Her round breasts were moving the red silk of her dress irregularly with her breathing.

He poured two large drinks.

She did not look up from the fire until he had put one glass in her hand. When she looked up she smiled, crookedly, twisting her heavily rouged exquisite thin lips sidewise. Her eyes, reflecting red light from the fire, were too bright.

He smiled down at her.

She lifted her glass and said, cooing: "To my husband!"

Ned Beaumont said, "No," casually and tossed the contents of his glass into the fireplace, where it sputtered and threw dancing flames up.

She laughed in delight and jumped to her feet. "Pour another," she ordered.

He picked the bottle up from the floor and refilled his glass.

She lifted hers high over her head. "To you!"

They drank. She shuddered.

"Better take something with it or after it," he suggested.

She shook her head. "I want it that way." She put a hand on his arm and turned her back to the fire, standing close beside him. "Let's bring that bench over here."

"That's an idea," he agreed.

They moved the chairs from in front of the fireplace and brought the bench there, he carrying one end, she the other. The bench was broad, low, backless.

"Now turn off the lights," she said.

He did so. When he returned to the bench she was sitting on it pouring whisky into their glasses.

"To you, this time," he said and they drank and she shuddered.

He sat beside her. They were rosy in the glow from the fireplace.

The stairs creaked and her husband came down them. He halted on the bottom step and said: "Please, darling!"

She whispered in Ned Beaumont's ear, savagely: "Throw something at him."

Ned Beaumont chuckled.

She picked up the whisky-bottle and said: "Where's your glass?"

While she was filling their glasses Mathews went upstairs.

She gave Ned Beaumont his glass and touched it with her own. Her eyes were wild in the red glow. A lock of dark hair had come loose and was down across her brow. She breathed through her mouth, panting softly. "To us!" she said.

They drank. She let her empty glass fall and came into his arms. Her mouth was to his when she shuddered. The fallen glass broke noisily on the wooden floor. Ned Beaumont's eyes were narrow, crafty. Hers were shut tight.

They had not moved when the stairs creaked. Ned Beaumont did not move then. She tightened her thin arms around him. He could not see the stairs. Both of them were breathing heavily now.

Then the stairs creaked again and, shortly afterwards, they drew their heads apart, though they kept their arms about one another. Ned Beaumont looked at the stairs. Nobody was there.

Eloise Mathews slid her hand up the back of his head, running her fingers through his hair, digging her nails into his scalp. Her eyes were not now altogether closed. They were laughing dark slits. "Life's like that," she said in a small bitter mocking voice, leaning back on the bench, drawing him with her, drawing his mouth to hers.

They were in that position when they heard the shot.

Ned Beaumont was out of her arms and on his feet immediately. "His room?" he asked sharply.

She blinked at him in dumb terror.

"His room?" he repeated.

She moved a feeble hand. "In front," she said thickly.

He ran to the stairs and went up in long leaps. At the head of the stairs he came face to face with the apish Jeff, dressed except for his shoes, blinking sleep out of his swollen eyes. Jeff put a hand to his hip, put the other hand out to stop Ned Beaumont, and growled: "Now what's all this?"

Ned avoided the outstretched hand, slid past it, and drove his left fist into the apish muzzle. Jeff staggered back snarling. Ned Beaumont sprang past him and ran towards the front of the building. O'Rory came out of another room and ran behind him.

From downstairs came Mrs. Mathews's scream.

Ned Beaumont flung a door open and stopped. Mathews lay on his back on the bedroom-floor under a lamp. His mouth was open and a little blood had trickled from it. One of his arms was thrown out across the floor. The other lay on his chest. Over against the wall, where the outstretched arm seemed to be pointing at it, was a dark revolver. On a table by the window was a bottle of ink – its stopper upside down beside it – a pen, and a sheet of paper. A chair stood close to the table, facing it.

Shad O'Rory pushed past Ned Beaumont and knelt beside the man on the floor. While he was there Ned Beaumont, behind him, swiftly glanced at the paper on the table, then thrust it into his pocket.

Jeff came in, followed by Rusty, naked.

O'Rory stood up and spread his hands apart in a little gesture of finality. "Shot himself through the roof of the mouth," he said. "Finis."

Ned Beaumont turned and went out of the room. In the hall he met Opal Madvig.

"What, Ned?" she asked in a frightened voice.

"Mathews has shot himself. I'll go down and stay with her till you get some clothes on. Don't go in there. There's nothing to see." He went downstairs.

Eloise Mathews was a dim shape lying on the floor beside the bench.

He took two quick steps towards her, halted, and looked around the room with shrewd cold eyes. Then he walked over to the woman, went down on one knee beside her, and felt her pulse. He looked at her as closely as he could in the dull light of the dying fire. She gave no sign of consciousness. He pulled the paper he had taken from her husband's table out of his pocket and moved on his knees to the fireplace, where, in the red embers' glow, he read:

> I, Howard Keith Mathews, being of sound mind and memory, declare this to be my last will and testament:
>
> I give and bequeath to my beloved wife, Eloise Braden Mathews, her heirs and assigns, all my real and personal property, of whatever nature or kind.
>
> I hereby appoint the State Central Trust Company the sole executor of this will.
>
> In witness whereof I have hereunto subscribed my name this. . .

Ned Beaumont, smiling grimly, stopped reading and tore the will three times across. He stood up, reached over the fire-screen, and dropped the torn pieces of paper into the glowing embers. The fragments blazed brightly a moment and were gone. With the wrought-iron shovel that stood beside the fire he mashed the paper-ash into the wood-coals.

Then he returned to Mrs. Mathews's side, poured a little whisky into the glass he had drunk from, raised her head, and forced some of the liquor between her lips. She was partly awake, coughing, when Opal Madvig came downstairs.

VI

Shad O'Rory came down the stairs. Jeff and Rusty were behind him. All of them were dressed. Ned Beaumont was standing by the door, in rain-coat and hat.

"Where are you going, Ned?" Shad asked.

"To find a phone."

O'Rory nodded. "That's a good enough idea," he said, "but there's something I want to ask you about." He came the rest of the way down the stairs, his followers close behind him.

Ned Beaumont said: "Yes?" He took his hand out of his pocket. The hand was visible to O'Rory and the men behind him, but Ned Beaumont's body concealed it from the bench where Opal sat with arms around Eloise Mathews. A square pistol was in the hand. "Just so there won't be any foolishness. I'm in a hurry."

O'Rory did not seem to see the pistol, though he came no nearer. He said, reflectively: "I was thinking that with an open ink-bottle and a pen on the table and a chair up to it it's kind of funny we didn't find any writing up there."

Ned Beaumont smiled in mock astonishment. "What, no writing?" He took a step backwards, towards the door. "That's a funny one, all right. I'll discuss it with you for hours when I come back from phoning."

"Now would be better," O'Rory said.

"Sorry." Ned Beaumont backed swiftly to the door, felt behind him for the knob, found it, and had the door open. "I won't be gone long." He jumped out and slammed the door.

The rain had stopped. He left the path and ran through tall grass around the other side of the house. From the house came the sound of another door slamming in the rear. The river was audible not far to Ned Beaumont's left. He worked his way through underbrush towards it.

A high-pitched sharp whistle, not loud, sounded somewhere behind him. He floundered through an area of soft mud to a clump of trees and turned away from the river among them. The whistle came again, on his right. Beyond the trees were shoulder-high bushes. He went among them, bending forward from the waist for concealment, though the night's blackness was all but complete.

His way was uphill, up a hill frequently slippery, always

uneven, through brush that tore his face and hands, caught his clothing. Three times he fell. He stumbled many times. The whistle did not come again. He did not find the Buick. He did not find the road along which he had come.

He dragged his feet now and stumbled where there were no obstructions and when presently he had topped the hill and was going down its other slope he began to fall more often. At the bottom of the hill he found a road and turned to the right on it. Its clay stuck to his feet in increasing bulk so that he had to stop time after time to scrape it off. He used his pistol to scrape it off.

When he heard a dog bark behind him he stopped and turned drunkenly to look back. Close to the road, fifty feet behind him, was the vague outline of a house he had passed. He retraced his steps and came to a tall gate. The dog – a shapeless monster in the night – hurled itself at the other side of the gate and barked terrifically.

Ned Beaumont fumbled along an end of the gate, found the catch, unfastened it, and staggered in. The dog backed away, circling, feinting attacks it never made, filling the night with clamor.

A window screeched up and a heavy voice called: "What the hell are you doing to that dog?"

Ned Beaumont laughed weakly. Then he shook himself and replied in not too thin a voice: "This is Beaumont of the District Attorney's office. I want to use your phone. There's a dead man down there."

The heavy voice roared: "I don't know what you're talking about. Shut up, Jeanie!" The dog barked three times with increased energy and became silent. "Now what is it?"

"I want to phone. District Attorney's office. There's a dead man down there."

The heavy voice exclaimed: "The hell you say!" The window screeched shut.

The dog began its barking and circling and feinting again.

Ned Beaumont threw his muddy pistol at it. It turned and ran out of sight behind the house.

The front door was opened by a red-faced barrel-bodied short man in a long blue night-shirt. "Holy Maria, you're a mess!" he gasped when Ned Beaumont came into the light from the doorway.

"Phone," Ned Beaumont said.

The red-faced man caught him as he swayed. "Here," he said gruffly, "tell me who to call and what to say. You can't do anything."

"Phone," Ned Beaumont said.

The red-faced man steadied him along a hallway, opened a door, said: "There she is and it's a damned good thing for you the old woman ain't home or you'd never get in with all that mud on you."

Ned Beaumont fell into the chair in front of the telephone, but he did not immediately reach for the telephone. He scowled at the man in the blue night-shirt and said thickly: "Go out and shut the door."

The red-faced man had not come into the room. He shut the door.

Ned Beaumont picked up the receiver, leaned forward so that he was propped against the table by his elbows on it, and called Paul Madvig's number. Half a dozen times while he waited his eyelids closed, but each time he forced them open again and when, at last, he spoke into the telephone it was clearly.

"'Lo, Paul – Ned. . . . Never mind that. Listen to me. Mathews's committed suicide at his place on the river and didn't leave a will. . . .Listen to me. This is important. With a lot of debts and no will naming an executor it'll be up to the courts to appoint somebody to administer the estate. Get that? . . . Yes. See that it comes up before the right judge – Phelps, say – and we can keep the *Observer* out of the fight – except on our side – till after election. Got that? . . . All right, all right, now listen. That's only part of it. This is what's got to be done now. The *Observer* is loaded with dynamite for the morning. You've got to stop it. I'd say get Phelps out of bed and get an injunction out of him – anything to stop it till you can show the *Observer*'s hired men where they stand now that the paper's going to be bossed for a month or so by our friends. . . . I can't tell you now, Paul, but it's dynamite and you've got to keep it from going on sale. Get Phelps out of bed and go down and look at it yourselves. You've got maybe three hours before it's out on the streets. . . . That's right . . . What? . . . Opal? Oh, she's all right. She's with me. . . . Yes, I'll bring her home. . . . And will you phone the county people about Mathews? I'm going back there now. Right."

He laid the receiver on the table and stood up, staggered to the door, got it open after the second attempt, and fell out into the hallway, where the wall kept him from tumbling down on the floor.

The red-faced man came hurrying to him. "Just lean on me, brother, and I'll make you comfortable. I got a blanket spread over the davenport so we won't have to worry about the mud and –"

Ned Beaumont said: "I want to borrow a car. I've got to go back to Mathews's."

"Is it him that's dead?"

"Yes."

The red-faced man raised his eyebrows and made a squeaky whistling sound.

"Will you lend me the car?" Ned Beaumont demanded.

"My God, brother, be reasonable! How could you drive a car?"

Ned Beaumont backed away from the other, unsteadily. "I'll walk," he said.

The red-faced man glared at him. "You won't neither. If you'll keep your hair on till I get my pants I'll drive you back, though likely enough you'll die on me on the way."

Opal Madvig and Eloise Mathews were together in the large ground-floor room when Ned Beaumont was carried rather than led into it by the red-faced man. The men had come in without knocking. The two girls were standing close together, wide-eyed, startled.

Ned Beaumont pulled himself out of his companion's arms and looked dully around the room. "Where's Shad?" he mumbled.

Opal answered him: "He's gone. All of them have gone."

"All right," he said, speaking difficultly. "I want to talk to you alone."

Eloise Mathews ran over to him. "You killed him!" she cried.

He giggled idiotically and tried to put his arms around her.

She screamed, struck him in the face with an open hand.

He fell straight back without bending. The red-faced man tried to catch him, but could not. He did not move at all after he struck the floor.

7 THE HENCHMEN

I

SENATOR HENRY put his napkin on the table and stood up. Rising, he seemed taller than he was and younger. His somewhat small head, under its thin covering of gray hair, was remarkably symmetrical. Aging muscles sagged in his patrician face, accentuating its vertical lines, but slackness had not yet reached his lips, nor was it apparent that the years had in any way touched his eyes: they were a greenish gray, deep-set, not large but brilliant, and their lids were firm. He spoke with studied grave courtesy: "You'll forgive me if I carry Paul off upstairs for a little while?"

His daughter replied: "Yes, if you'll leave me Mr. Beaumont and if you'll promise not to stay up there all evening."

Ned Beaumont smiled politely, inclining his head.

He and Janet Henry went into a white-walled room where coal burned sluggishly in a grate under a white mantelpiece and put somber red gleams on the mahogany furniture.

She turned on a lamp beside the piano and sat down there with her back to the keyboard, her head between Ned Beaumont and the lamp. Her blond hair caught lamplight and held it in a nimbus around her head. Her black gown was of some suede-like material that reflected no light and she wore no jewelry.

Ned Beaumont leaned over to knock ash from his cigar down on the burning coal. A dark pearl in his shirt-bosom, twinkling in the fire's glow as he moved, was like a red eye winking. When he straightened, he asked: "You'll play something?"

"Yes, if you wish – though I don't play exceptionally well – but later. I'd like to talk to you now while I've an opportunity." Her hands were together in her lap. Her arms, held straight, forced her shoulders up and in towards her neck.

Ned Beaumont nodded politely, but did not say anything. He left the fireplace and sat not far from her on a sofa with lyre ends. Though he was attentive, there was no curiosity in his mien.

Turning on the piano-bench to face him directly, she asked: "How is Opal?" Her voice was low, intimate.

His voice was casual: "Perfectly all right as far as I know, though I haven't seen her since last week." He lifted his cigar half a foot towards his mouth, lowered it, and as if the question had just come to his mind asked: "Why?"

She opened her brown eyes wide. "Isn't she in bed with a nervous break-down?"

"Oh, that!" he said carelessly, smiling. "Didn't Paul tell you?"

"Yes, he told me she was in bed with a nervous break-down." She stared at him, perplexed. "He told me that."

Ned Beaumont's smile became gentle. "I suppose he's sensitive about it," he said slowly, looking at his cigar. Then he looked up at her and moved his shoulders a little. "There's nothing the matter with her that way. It's simply that she got the foolish idea that he had killed your brother and – still more foolishly – was going around talking about it. Well, Paul couldn't have his daughter running around accusing him of murder, so he had to keep her home till she gets the notion out of her head."

"You mean she's –" she hesitated: her eyes were bright "– she's – well – a prisoner?"

"You make it sound melodramatic," he protested carelessly. "She's only a child. Isn't making children stay in their rooms one of the usual ways of disciplining them?"

Janet Henry replied hastily: "Oh, yes! Only –" She looked at her hands in her lap, up at his face again. "But why did she think that?"

Ned Beaumont's voice was tepid as his smile. "Who doesn't?" he asked.

She put her hands on the edge of the piano-bench beside her and leaned forward. Her white face was earnestly set. "That's what I wanted to ask you, Mr. Beaumont. Do people think that?"

He nodded. His face was placid.

Her knuckles were white over the bench-edge. Her voice was parched asking: "Why?"

He rose from the sofa and crossed to the fireplace to drop the remainder of his cigar into the fire. When he returned to his seat he crossed his long legs and leaned back at ease. "The other side thinks it's good politics to make people think that," he said. There was nothing in his voice, his face, his manner to show that he had any personal interest in what he was talking about.

She frowned. "But, Mr. Beaumont, why should people think it unless there's some sort of evidence, or something that can be made to look like evidence?"

He looked curiously and amusedly at her. "There is, of course," he said. "I thought you knew that." He combed a side of his mustache with a thumb-nail. "Didn't you get any of the anonymous letters that've been going around?"

She stood up quickly. Excitement distorted her face. "Yes, today!" she exclaimed. "I wanted to show it to you, to –"

He laughed softly and raised a hand, palm out in an arresting gesture. "Don't bother. They all seem to be pretty much alike and I've seen plenty of them."

She sat down again, slowly, reluctantly.

He said: "Well, those letters, the stuff the *Observer* was printing till we pulled it out of the fight, the talk the others have been circulating" – he shrugged his thin shoulders – "they've taken what facts there are and made a pretty swell case against Paul."

She took her lower lip from between her teeth to ask: "Is – is he actually in danger?"

Ned Beaumont nodded and spoke with calm certainty: "If he loses the election, loses his hold on the city and state government, they'll electrocute him."

She shivered and asked in a voice that shook: "But he's safe if he wins?"

Ned Beaumont nodded again. "Sure."

She caught her breath. Her lips trembled so that her words came out jerkily: "Will he win?"

"I think so."

"And it won't make any difference then no matter how much evidence there is against him, he'll –" her voice broke "– he'll not be in danger?"

"He won't be tried," Ned Beaumont told her. Abruptly he sat up straight. He shut his eyes tight, opened them, and stared at her tense pale face. A glad light came into his eyes, gladness spread over his face. He laughed – not loud but in complete delight – and stood up exclaiming: "Judith herself!"

Janet Henry sat breathlessly still, looking at him with uncomprehending brown eyes in a blank white face.

He began to walk around the room in an irregular route, talking happily – not to her – though now and then he turned his head over his shoulder to smile at her. "That's the game, of course," he said. "She could put up with Paul – be polite to him – for the sake of the political backing her father needed, but that would have its limits. Or that's all that would be necessary, Paul being so much in love with her. But when she decided Paul had killed her brother and was going to escape punishment unless she – That's splendid! Paul's daughter and his sweetheart both trying to steer him to the electric chair. He certainly has a lot of luck with women." He had a slender pale-green-spotted cigar in one hand now. He halted in front of Janet Henry, clipped the end of the cigar, and said, not accusingly, but as if sharing a discovery with her: "You sent those anonymous letters around. Certainly you did. They were written on the typewriter in the room where your brother and Opal used to meet. He had a key and she had a key. She didn't write them because she was stirred up by them. You did. You took his key when it was turned over to you and your father with the rest of his stuff by the police, sneaked into the room, and wrote them. That's fine." He began to walk again. He said: "Well, we'll have to make the Senator get in a squad of good able-bodied nurses and lock you in your room with a nervous break-down. It's getting to be epidemic among our politicians' daughters, but we've got to make sure of the election even if every house in town has to have its patient." He turned his head over his shoulder to smile amiably at her.

She put a hand to her throat. Otherwise she did not move. She did not speak.

He said: "The Senator won't give us much trouble, luckily. He doesn't care about anything – not you or his dead son – as much as he does about being re-elected and he knows he can't do that without Paul." He laughed. "That's what drove you into the Judith rôle, huh? You knew your father wouldn't split with Paul – even if he thought him guilty – till the election was won. Well, that's a comforting thing to know – for us."

When he stopped talking to light his cigar she spoke. She had taken her hand down from her throat. Her hands were in her lap. She sat erect without stiffness. Her voice was cool and composed. She said: "I am not good at lying. I know Paul killed Taylor. I wrote the letters."

Ned Beaumont took the burning cigar from his mouth, came back to the lyre-end sofa, and sat down facing her. His face was grave, but without hostility. He said: "You hate Paul, don't you? Even if I proved to you that he didn't kill Taylor you'd still hate him, wouldn't you?"

"Yes," she replied, her light brown eyes steady on his darker ones, "I think I should."

"That's it," he said. "You don't hate him because you think he killed your brother. You think he killed your brother because you hate him."

She moved her head slowly from side to side. "No," she said.

He smiled skeptically. Then he asked: "Have you talked it over with your father?"

She bit her lip and her face flushed a little.

Ned Beaumont smiled again. "And he told you it was ridiculous," he said.

Pink deepened in her cheeks. She started to say something, but did not.

He said: "If Paul killed your brother your father knows it."

She looked down at her hands in her lap and said dully, miserably: "My father should know it, but he will not believe it."

Ned Beaumont said: "He ought to know." His eyes became narrower. "Did Paul say anything at all to him that night about Taylor and Opal?"

She raised her head, astonished. "Don't you know what happened that night?" she asked.

"No."

"It hadn't anything to do with Taylor and Opal," she said, word tumbling over word in her eagerness to get them spoken. "It –" She jerked her face towards the door and shut her mouth with a click. Deep-chested rumbling laughter had come through the door, and the sound of approaching steps. She faced Ned Beaumont again, hastily, lifting her hands in an appealing gesture. "I've got to tell you," she whispered, desperately earnest. "Can I see you tomorrow?"

"Yes."

"Where?"

"My place?" he suggested.

She nodded quickly. He had time to mutter his address, she

to whisper, "After ten?" and he to nod before Senator Henry and Paul Madvig came into the room.

II

Paul Madvig and Ned Beaumont said good-night to the Henrys at half-past ten o'clock and got into a brown sedan which Madvig drove down Charles Street. When they had ridden a block and a half Madvig blew his breath out in a satisfied gust and said: "Jesus, Ned, you don't know how tickled I am that you and Janet are hitting it off so nice."

Ned Beaumont, looking obliquely at the blond man's profile, said: "I can get along with anybody."

Madvig chuckled. "Yes you can," he said indulgently, "like hell."

Ned Beaumont's lips curved in a thin secretive smile. He said: "I've got something I want to talk to you about tomorrow. Where'll you be, say, in the middle of the afternoon?"

Madvig turned the sedan into China Street. "At the office," he said. "It's the first of the month. Why don't you do your talking now? There's a lot of night left yet."

"I don't know it all now. How's Opal?"

"She's all right," Madvig said gloomily, then exclaimed: "Christ! I wish I could be sore at the kid. It'd make it a lot easier." They passed a street-light. He blurted out: "She's not pregnant."

Ned Beaumont did not say anything. His face was expressionless.

Madvig reduced the sedan's speed as they approached the Log Cabin Club. His face was red. He asked huskily: "What do you think, Ned? Was she" – he cleared his throat noisily – "his mistress? Or was it just boy and girl stuff?"

Ned Beaumont said: "I don't know. I don't care. Don't ask her, Paul."

Madvig stopped the sedan and sat for a moment at the wheel staring straight ahead. Then he cleared his throat again and spoke in a low hoarse voice: "You're not the worst guy in the world, Ned."

"Uh-uh," Ned Beaumont agreed as they got out of the sedan.

They entered the Club, separating casually under the Governor's portrait at the head of the stairs on the second floor.

Ned Beaumont went into a rather small room in the rear where five men were playing stud poker and three were watching them play. The players made a place for him at the table and by three o'clock, when the game broke up, he had won some four hundred dollars.

III

It was nearly noon when Janet Henry arrived at Ned Beaumont's rooms. He had been pacing the floor, alternately biting his finger-nails and puffing at cigars, for more than an hour. He went without haste to the door when she rang, opened it, and, smiling with an air of slight but pleasant surprise, said: "Good morning."

"I'm awfully sorry to be late," she began, "but –"

"But you're not," he assured her. "It was to have been any time after ten."

He ushered her into his living-room.

"I like this," she said, turning around slowly, examining the old-fashioned room, the height of its ceiling, the width of its windows, the tremendous mirror over the fireplace, the red plush of the furniture. "It's delightful." She turned her brown eyes towards a half-open door. "Is that your bedroom?"

"Yes. Would you like to see it?"

"I'd love to."

He showed her the bedroom, then the kitchen and bathroom.

"It's perfect," she said as they returned to the living-room. "I didn't know there could be any more of these left in a city as horribly up to date as ours has become."

He made a little bow to acknowledge her approval. "I think it's rather nice and, as you can see, there's no one here to eavesdrop on us unless they're stowed away in a closet, which isn't likely."

She drew herself up and looked straight into his eyes. "I did not think of that. We may not agree, may even become – or now be – enemies, but I know you're a gentleman, or I shouldn't be here."

He asked in an amused tone: "You mean I've learned not to wear tan shoes with blue suits? Things like that?"

"I don't mean things like that."

He smiled. "Then you're wrong. I'm a gambler and a politician's hanger-on."

"I'm not wrong." A pleading expression came into her eyes. "Please don't let us quarrel, at least not until we must."

"I'm sorry." His smile was apologetic now. "Won't you sit down?"

She sat down. He sat in another wide red chair facing her. He said: "Now you were going to tell me what happened at your house the night your brother was killed."

"Yes," issuing from her mouth, was barely audible. Her face became pink and she transferred her gaze to the floor. When she raised her eyes again they were shy. Embarrassment clogged her voice: "I wanted you to know. You are Paul's friend and that – that may make you my enemy, but – I think when you know what happened – when you know the truth – you'll not be – at least not be my enemy. I don't know. Perhaps you'll – But you ought to know. Then you can decide. And he hasn't told you." She looked intently at him so that shyness went out of her eyes. "Has he?"

"I don't know what happened at your house that night," he said. "He didn't tell me."

She leaned towards him quickly to ask: "Doesn't that show it's something he wants to conceal, something he has to conceal?"

He moved his shoulders. “Suppose it does?” His voice was unexcited, uneager.

She frowned. “But you must see – Never mind that now. I’ll tell you what happened and you can see it for yourself.” She continued to lean far forward, staring at his face with intent brown eyes. “He came to dinner, the first time we’d had him to dinner.”

“I knew that,” Ned Beaumont said, “and your brother wasn’t there.”

“Taylor wasn’t at the dinner-table,” she corrected him earnestly, “but he was up in his room. Only Father, Paul, and I were at the table. Taylor was going out to dinner. He – he wouldn’t eat with Paul because of the trouble they’d had about Opal.”

Ned Beaumont nodded attentively without warmth.

“After dinner Paul and I were alone for a little while in – in the room where you and I talked last night and he suddenly put his arms around me and kissed me.”

Ned Beaumont laughed, not loudly, but with abrupt irrepressible merriment.

Janet Henry looked at him in surprise.

He modified his laugh to a smile and said: “I’m sorry. Go on. I’ll tell you later why I laughed.” But when she would have gone on he said: “Wait. Did he say anything when he kissed you?”

“No. That is, he may have, but nothing I understood.” Perplexity was deepening in her face. “Why?”

Ned Beaumont laughed again. “He ought to’ve said something about his pound of flesh. It was probably my fault. I had been trying to persuade him not to support your father in the election, had told him that your father was using you as bait to catch his support, and had advised him that if he was willing to be bought that way he ought to be sure and collect his pound of flesh ahead of the election or he’d never get it.”

She opened her eyes wide and there was less perplexity in them.

He said: "That was that afternoon, though I didn't think I'd had much luck putting it over." He wrinkled his forehead. "What did you do to him? He was meaning to marry you and was chock-full of respect and what not for you and you must have rubbed him pretty thoroughly the wrong way to make him jump at you like that."

"I didn't do anything to him," she replied slowly, "though it had been a difficult evening. None of us was comfortable. I thought – I tried not to show that – well – that I resented having to entertain him. He wasn't at ease, I know, and I suppose that – his embarrassment – and perhaps a suspicion that you had been right made him –" She finished the sentence with a brief quick outward motion of both hands.

Ned Beaumont nodded. "What happened then?" he asked.

"I was furious, of course, and left him."

"Didn't you say anything to him?" Ned Beaumont's eyes twinkled with imperfectly hidden mirth.

"No, and he didn't say anything I could hear. I went upstairs and met Father coming down. While I was telling him what had happened – I was angry with Father as with Paul, because it was Father's fault that Paul was there – we heard Paul going out the front door. And then Taylor came down from his room." Her face became white and tense, her voice husky with emotion. "He had heard me talking to Father and he asked me what had happened, but I left him there with Father and went on to my room, too angry to talk any more about it. And I didn't see either of them again until Father came to my room and told me Taylor had – had been killed." She stopped talking and looked white-faced at Ned Beaumont, twisting her fingers together, awaiting his response to her story.

His response was a cool question: "Well, what of it?"

"What of it?" she repeated in amazement. "Don't you see?

How could I help knowing then that Taylor had run out after Paul and had caught up with him and had been killed by him? He was furious and –" Her face brightened. "You know his hat wasn't found. He was too much in a hurry – too angry – to stop for his hat. He –"

Ned Beaumont shook his head slowly from side to side and interrupted her. His voice held nothing but certainty. "No," he said. "That won't do. Paul wouldn't've had to kill Taylor and he wouldn't've done it. He could have managed him with one hand and he doesn't lose his head in a fight. I know that. I've seen Paul fight and I've fought with him. That won't do." He drew eyelids closer together around eyes that had become stony. "But suppose he did? I mean accidentally, though I can't believe even that. But could you make anything out of it except self-defense?"

She raised her head scornfully. "If it were self-defense, why should he hide it?"

Ned Beaumont seemed unimpressed. "He wants to marry you," he explained. "It wouldn't help him much to admit he'd killed your brother even –" He chuckled. "I'm getting as bad as you are. Paul didn't kill him, Miss Henry."

Her eyes were stony as his had been. She looked at him and did not speak.

His expression became thoughtful. He asked: "You've only" – he wriggled the fingers of one hand – "the two and two you think you've put together to tell you that your brother ran out after Paul that night?"

"That is enough," she insisted. "He did. He must've. Otherwise – why, otherwise what would he have been doing down there in China Street bare-headed?"

"Your father didn't see him go out?"

"No. He didn't know it either until we heard –"

He interrupted her. "Does he agree with you?"

"He must," she cried. "It's unmistakable. He must, no matter what he says, just as you must." Tears were in her eyes now. "You can't expect me to believe that you don't, Mr. Beaumont. I don't know what you knew before. You found Taylor dead. I don't know what else you found, but now you must know the truth."

Ned Beaumont's hands began to tremble. He slumped farther down in his chair so he could thrust his hands into his trousers-pockets. His face was tranquil except for hard lines of strain around his mouth. He said: "I found him dead. There was nobody else there. I didn't find anything else."

"You have now," she said.

His mouth twitched under his dark mustache. His eyes became hot with anger. He spoke in a low, harsh, deliberately bitter voice: "I know whoever killed your brother did the world a favor."

She shrank back in her chair with a hand thrown up to her throat, at first, but almost immediately the horror went out of her face and she sat upright and looked compassionately at him. She said softly: "I know. You're Paul's friend. It hurts."

He lowered his head a little and muttered: "It was a rotten thing to say. It was silly." He smiled wryly. "You see I was right about not being a gentleman." He stopped smiling and shame went out of his eyes leaving them clear and steady. He said in a quiet voice: "You're right about my being Paul's friend. I'm that no matter who he killed."

After a long moment of earnest staring at him she spoke in a small flat voice: "Then this is useless? I thought if I could show you the truth –" She broke off with a hopeless gesture in which hands, shoulders, and head took part.

He moved his head slowly from side to side.

She sighed and stood up holding out her hand. "I'm sorry and disappointed, but we needn't be enemies, need we?"

He rose facing her, but did not take her hand. He said: "The part of you that's tricked Paul and is trying to trick him is my enemy."

She held her hand there while asking: "And the other part of me, the part that hasn't anything to do with that?"

He took her hand and bowed over it.

IV

When Janet Henry had gone Ned Beaumont went to his telephone, called a number, and said: "Hello, this is Mr. Beaumont. Has Mr. Madvig come in yet? . . . When he comes will you tell him I called and will be in to see him? . . . Yes, thanks."

He looked at his wrist-watch. It was a little after one o'clock. He lit a cigar and sat down at a window, smoking and staring at the gray church across the street. Out-blown cigar-smoke recoiled from the window-panes in gray clouds over his head. His teeth crushed the end of his cigar. He sat there for ten minutes, until his telephone-bell rang.

He went to the telephone. "Hello. . . . Yes, Harry. . . . Sure. Where are you? . . . I'm coming downtown. Wait there for me. . . . Half an hour. . . . Right."

He threw his cigar into the fireplace, put on his hat and overcoat, and went out. He walked six blocks to a restaurant, ate a salad and rolls, drank a cup of coffee, walked four blocks to a small hotel named Majestic, and rode to the fourth floor in an elevator operated by an undersized youth who called him Ned and asked what he thought of the third race.

Ned Beaumont thought and said: "Lord Byron ought to do it."

The elevator-operator said: "I hope you're wrong. I got Pipe-organ."

Ned Beaumont shrugged. "Maybe, but he's carrying a lot of weight." He went to room 417 and knocked on the door.

Harry Sloss, in his shirt-sleeves, opened the door. He was a thickset pale man of thirty-five, broad-faced and partially bald. He said: "On the dot. Come on in."

When Sloss had shut the door Ned Beaumont asked: "What's the diffugalty?"

The thickset man went over to the bed and sat down. He scowled anxiously at Ned Beaumont. "It don't look so damned good to me, Ned."

"What don't?"

"This thing of Ben going to the Hall with it."

Ned Beaumont said irritably: "All right. Any time you're ready to tell me what you're talking about's soon enough for me."

Sloss raised a pale broad hand. "Wait, Ned, I'll tell you what it's about. Just listen." He felt in his pocket for cigarettes, bringing out a package mashed limp. "You remember the night the Henry kid was pooped?"

Ned Beaumont's "Uh-huh" was carelessly uttered.

"Remember me and Ben had just come in when you got there, at the Club?"

"Yes."

"Well, listen: we saw Paul and the kid arguing up there under the trees."

Ned Beaumont brushed a side of his mustache with a thumb-nail, once, and spoke slowly, looking puzzled: "But I saw you get out of the car in front of the Club – that was just after I found him – and you came up the other way." He moved a forefinger. "And Paul was already in the Club ahead of you."

Sloss nodded his broad head vigorously. "That's all right," he said, "but we'd drove on down China Street to Pinky Klein's place and he wasn't there and we turned around and drove back to the Club."

Ned Beaumont nodded. "Just what did you see?"

"We saw Paul and the kid standing there under the trees arguing."

"You could see that as you rode past?"

Sloss nodded vigorously again.

"It was a dark spot," Ned Beaumont reminded him. "I don't see how you could've made out their faces riding past like that, unless you slowed up or stopped."

"No, we didn't, but I'd know Paul anywhere," Sloss insisted.

"Maybe, but how'd you know it was the kid with him?"

"It was. Sure, it was. We could see enough of him to know that."

"And you could see they were arguing? What do you mean by that? Fighting?"

"No, but standing like they were having an argument. You know how you can tell when people are arguing sometimes by the way they stand."

Ned Beaumont smiled mirthlessly. "Yes, if one of them's standing on the other's face." His smile vanished. "And that's what Ben went to the Hall with?"

"Yes. I don't know whether he went in with it on his own account or whether Farr got hold of it somehow and sent for him, but anyhow he spilled it to Farr. That was yesterday."

"How'd you hear about it, Harry?"

"Farr's hunting for me," Sloss said. "That's the way I heard about it. Ben'd told him I was with him and Farr sent word for me to drop in and see him, but I don't want any part of it."

"I hope you don't, Harry," Ned Beaumont said. "What are you going to say if Farr catches you?"

"I'm not going to let him catch me if I can help it. That's what I wanted to see you about." He cleared his throat and moistened his lips. "I thought maybe I ought to get out of town for a week or two, till it kind of blows over, and that'd take a little money."

Ned Beaumont smiled and shook his head. "That's not the thing to do," he told the thickset man. "If you want to help Paul go tell Farr you couldn't recognize the two men under the trees and that you don't think anybody in your car could."

"All right, that's what I'll do," Sloss said readily, "but, listen, Ned, I ought to get something out of it. I'm taking a chance and – well – you know how it is."

Ned Beaumont nodded. "We'll pick you out a soft job

after election, one you'll have to show up on maybe an hour a day."

"That'll be –" Sloss stood up. His green-flecked palish eyes were urgent. "I'll tell you, Ned, I'm broke as hell. Couldn't you make it a little dough now instead? It'd come in damned handy."

"Maybe. I'll talk it over with Paul."

"Do that, Ned, and give me a ring."

"Sure. So long."

V

From the Majestic Hotel Ned Beaumont went to the City Hall, to the District Attorney's office, and said he wanted to see Mr. Farr.

The round-faced youth to whom he said it left the outer office, returning a minute later apologetic of mien. "I'm sorry, Mr. Beaumont, but Mr. Farr is not in."

"When will he be back?"

"I don't know. His secretary says he didn't leave word."

"I'll take a chance. I'll wait awhile in his office."

The round-faced youth stood in his way. "Oh, you can't do –"

Ned Beaumont smiled his nicest smile at the youth and asked softly: "Don't you like this job, son?"

The youth hesitated, fidgeted, and stepped out of Ned Beaumont's way. Ned Beaumont walked down the inner corridor to the District Attorney's door and opened it.

Farr looked up from his desk, sprang to his feet. "Was that you?" he cried. "Damn that boy! He never gets anything right. A Mr. Bauman, he said."

"No harm done," Ned Beaumont said mildly. "I got in."

He let the District Attorney shake his hand up and down and lead him to a chair. When they were seated he asked idly: "Anything new?"

"Nothing." Farr rocked back in his chair, thumbs hooked

in lower vest-pockets. "Just the same old grind, though God knows there's enough of that."

"How's the electioneering going?"

"It could be better" – a shadow passed over the District Attorney's pugnacious red face – "but I guess we'll manage all right."

Ned Beaumont kept idleness in his voice. "What's the matter?"

"This and that. Things always come up. That's politics, I guess."

"Anything I can do – or Paul – to help?" Ned Beaumont asked and then, when Farr had shaken his red-stubble-covered head: "This talk that Paul's got something to do with the Henry killing the worst thing you're up against?"

A frightened gleam came into Farr's eyes, disappeared as he blinked. He sat up straight in his chair. "Well," he said cautiously, "there's a lot of feeling that we ought to've cleared the murder up before this. That is one of the things – maybe one of the biggest."

"Made any progress since I saw you last? Turned up anything new on it?"

Farr shook his head. His eyes were wary.

Ned Beaumont smiled without warmth. "Still taking it slow on some of the angles?"

The District Attorney squirmed in his chair. "Well, yes, of course, Ned."

Ned Beaumont nodded approvingly. His eyes were shiny with malice. His voice was a taunt: "Is the Ben Ferriss angle one of them that you're taking it slow on?"

Farr's blunt undershot mouth opened and shut. He rubbed his lips together. His eyes, after their first startled widening, became devoid of expression. He said: "I don't know whether there's anything at all in Ferriss's story or not, Ned. I don't guess there is. I didn't even think enough of it to tell you about it."

Ned Beaumont laughed derisively.

Farr said: "You know I wouldn't hold out anything on you and Paul, anything that was important. You know me well enough for that."

"We knew you before you got nerves," Ned Beaumont replied. "But that's all right. If you want the fellow that was in the car with Ferriss you can pick him up right now in room 417 at the Majestic."

Farr was staring at his green desk-set, at the dancing nude figure holding an airplane aloft between two slanting pens. His face was lumpy. He said nothing.

Ned Beaumont rose from his chair smiling with thin lips. He said: "Paul's always glad to help the boys out of holes. Do you think it would help if he'd let himself be arrested and tried for the Henry murder?"

Farr did not move his eyes from the green desk-set. He said doggedly: "It's not for me to tell Paul what to do."

"There's a thought!" Ned Beaumont exclaimed. He leaned over the side of the desk until his face was near the District Attorney's ear and lowered his voice to a confidential key. "And here's another one that goes with it. It's not for you to do much Paul wouldn't tell you to do."

He went out grinning, but stopped grinning when he was outside.

8 THE KISS-OFF

I

NED BEAUMONT opened a door marked *East State Construction & Contracting Company* and exchanged good-afternoons with the two young ladies at desks inside, then he passed through a larger room in which there were half a dozen men to whom he spoke and opened a door marked *Private.* He went into a square room where Paul Madvig sat at a battered desk looking at papers placed in front of him by a small man who hovered respectfully over his shoulder.

Madvig raised his head and said: "Hello, Ned." He pushed the papers aside and told the small man: "Bring this junk back after awhile."

The small man gathered up his papers and, saying, "Certainly, sir," and, "How do you do, Mr. Beaumont?" left the room.

Madvig said: "You look like you'd had a tough night, Ned. What'd you do? Sit down."

Ned Beaumont had taken off his overcoat. He put it on a chair, put his hat on it, and took out a cigar. "No, I'm all right. What's new in your life?" He sat on a corner of the battered desk.

"I wish you'd go see M'Laughlin," the blond man said. "You can handle him if anybody can."

"All right. What's the matter with him?"

Madvig grimaced. "Christ knows! I thought I had him lined up, but he's going shifty on us."

A somber gleam came into Ned Beaumont's dark eyes. He looked down at the blond man and said: "Him too, huh?"

Madvig asked slowly, after a moment's deliberation. "What do you mean by that, Ned?"

Ned Beaumont's reply was another question: "Is everything going along to suit you?"

Madvig moved his big shoulders impatiently, but his eyes did not lose their surveying stare. "Nor so damned bad either," he said. "We can get along without M'Laughlin's batch of votes if we have to."

"Maybe," Ned Beaumont's lips had become thin, "but we can't keep on losing them and come out all right." He put his cigar in a corner of his mouth and said around it: "You know we're not as well off as we were two weeks ago."

Madvig grinned indulgently at the man on his desk. "Jesus, you like to sing them, Ned! Don't anything ever look right to you?" He did not wait for a reply, but went on placidly: "I've never been through a campaign yet that didn't look like it was going to hell at some time or other. They don't, though."

Ned Beaumont was lighting his cigar. He blew smoke out and said: "That doesn't mean they never will." He pointed the cigar at Madvig's chest. "If Taylor Henry's killing isn't cleared up pronto you won't have to worry about the campaign. You'll be sunk whoever wins."

Madvig's blue eyes became opaque. There was no other change in his face. His voice was unchanged. "Just what do you mean by that, Ned?"

"Everybody in town thinks you killed him."

"Yes?" Madvig put a hand up to his chin, rubbed it thoughtfully. "Don't let that worry you. I've had things said about me before."

Ned Beaumont smiled tepidly and asked with mock admiration: "Is there anything you haven't been through before? Ever been given the electric cure?"

The blond man laughed. "And don't think I ever will," he said.

"You're not very far from it right now, Paul," Ned Beaumont said softly.

Madvig laughed again. "Jesus Christ!" he scoffed.

Ned Beaumont shrugged. "You're not busy?" he asked. "I'm not taking up your time with my nonsense?"

"I'm listening to you," Madvig told him quietly. "I never lost anything listening to you."

"Thank you, sir. Why do you suppose M'Laughlin's wiggling out from under?"

Madvig shook his head.

"He figures you're licked," Ned Beaumont said. "Everybody knows the police haven't tried to find Taylor's murderer and everybody thinks it's because you killed him. M'Laughlin figures that's enough to lick you at the polls this time."

"Yes? He figures they'd rather have Shad running the city than me? He figures being suspected of one murder makes my rep worse than Shad's?"

Ned Beaumont scowled at the blond man. "You're either kidding yourself or trying to kid me. What's Shad's reputation got to do with it? He's not out in the open behind his candidates. You are and it's your candidates who're responsible for nothing being done about the murder."

Madvig put his hand to his chin again and leaned his elbow on the desk. His handsome ruddy face was unlined. He said: "We've been talking a lot about what other people figure, Ned. Let's talk about what you figure. Figure I'm licked?"

"You probably are," Ned Beaumont said in a low sure voice. "It's a cinch you are if you sit still." He smiled. "But your candidates ought to come out all right."

"That," Madvig said phlegmatically, "ought to be explained."

Ned Beaumont leaned over and carefully knocked cigar-ash into the brass spittoon beside the desk. Then he said, unemotionally: "They're going to cross you up."

"Yes?"

"Why not? You've let Shad take most of the riffraff from behind you. You're counting on the respectable people, the better element, to carry the election. They're getting leery. Well, your candidates make a grandstand-play, arrest you for murder, and the respectable citizens – delighted with these noble officials who are brave enough to jail their own acknowledged boss when he breaks the law – trample each other to death in their hurry to get to the polls and elect the heroes to four more years of city-administering. You can't blame the boys much. They know they're sitting pretty if they do it and out of work if they don't."

Madvig took his hand from his chin to ask: "You don't count much on their loyalty, do you, Ned?"

Ned Beaumont smiled. "Just as much as you do," he replied. His smile went away. "I'm not guessing, Paul. I went in to see Farr this afternoon. I had to walk in, crash the gate – he tried to dodge me. He pretended he hadn't been digging into the killing. He tried to stall me on what he'd found out. In the end he dummied up on me." He made a disdainful mouth. "Farr, the guy I could always make jump through hoops."

"Well, that's only Farr," Madvig began.

Ned Beaumont cut him short. "Only Farr, and that's the tip-off. Rutlege or Brody or even Rainey might clip you on their own, but if Farr's doing anything it's a pipe he knows the others are with him." He frowned at the blond man's stolid face. "You can stop believing me any time you want to, Paul."

Madvig made a careless gesture with the hand he had held to his chin. "I'll let you know when I stop," he said. "How'd you happen to drop in on Farr?"

"Harry Sloss called me up today. It seems he and Ben Ferriss saw you arguing with Taylor in China Street the night of the murder, or claim they did." Ned Beaumont was looking with eyes that held no particular expression at the blond man and his voice was matter-of-fact. "Ben had gone to Farr with it. Harry wanted to be paid for not going. There's a couple of your Club-members reading the signs. I've been watching Farr lose his nerve for some time, so I went in to check him up."

Madvig nodded. "And you're sure he's knifing me?"

"Yes."

Madvig got up from his chair and went to the window. He stood there, hands in trousers-pockets, looking through the glass for perhaps three minutes while Ned Beaumont, sitting on the desk, smoked and looked at the blond man's wide back. Then, not turning his head, Madvig asked: "What'd you say to Harry?"

"Stalled him."

Madvig left the window and came back to the desk, but he did not sit down. His ruddiness had deepened. Otherwise no change had come into his face. His voice was level. "What do you think we ought to do?"

"About Sloss? Nothing. The other monkey's already gone to Farr. It doesn't make much difference what Sloss does."

"I didn't mean that. I meant about the whole thing."

Ned Beaumont dropped his cigar into the spittoon. "I've told you. If Taylor Henry's murder isn't cleared up pronto you're sunk. That's the whole thing. That's the only thing worth doing anything about."

Madvig stopped looking at Ned Beaumont. He looked at a wide vacant space on the wall. He pressed his full lips together. Moisture appeared on his temples. He said from deep in his chest: "That won't do. Think up something else."

Ned Beaumont's nostrils moved with his breathing and the brown of his eyes seemed dark as the pupils. He said: "There isn't anything else, Paul. Any other way plays into the hands of either Shad or Farr and his crew and either of them will ruin you."

Madvig said somewhat hoarsely: "There must be an out, Ned. Think."

Ned Beaumont left the desk and stood close in front of the blond man. "There isn't. That's the only way. You're going to take it whether you like it or not, or I'm going to take it for you."

Madvig shook his head violently. "No. Lay off."

Ned Beaumont said: "That's one thing I won't do for you, Paul."

Then Madvig looked Ned Beaumont in the eyes and said in a harsh whisper: "I killed him, Ned."

Ned Beaumont drew a breath in and let it out in a long sigh.

Madvig put his hands on Ned Beaumont's shoulders and his words came out thick and blurred. "It was an accident, Ned. He ran down the street after me when I left, with a cane he'd picked up on the way out. We'd had – there'd been some trouble there and he caught up with me and tried to hit me with the stick. I don't know how it happened, but pulling it away from him I hit him on the head with it – not hard – it couldn't've been very hard – but he fell back and smashed his head on the curb."

Ned Beaumont nodded. His face had suddenly become empty of all expression except hard concentration on Madvig's words. He asked in a crisp voice that matched his face: "What happened to the cane?"

"I took it away under my overcoat and burned it. After I knew he was dead I found it in my hand, when I was walking down to the Club, so I put it under my overcoat and then burned it."

"What kind of cane was it?"

"A rough brown one, heavy."

"And his hat?"

"I don't know, Ned. I guess it was knocked off and somebody picked it up."

"He had one on?"

"Yes, sure."

Ned Beaumont brushed a side of his mustache with a

thumb-nail. "You remember Sloss's and Ferriss's car passing you?"

Madvig shook his head. "No, though they may have."

Ned Beaumont frowned at the blond man. "You gummed things up plenty by running off with the stick and burning it and keeping quiet all this time," he grumbled. "You had a clear self-defense plea."

"I know, but I didn't want that, Ned," Madvig said hoarsely. "I want Janet Henry more than I ever wanted anything in my life and what chance would I have then, even if it was an accident?"

Ned Beaumont laughed in Madvig's face. It was a low laugh and bitter. He said: "You'd have more chance than you've got now."

Madvig, staring at him, said nothing.

Ned Beaumont said: "She's always thought you killed her brother. She hates you. She's been trying to play you into the electric chair. She's responsible for first throwing suspicion on you with anonymous letters sent around to everybody that might be interested. She's the one that turned Opal against you. She was in my rooms this morning telling me this, trying to turn me. She –"

Madvig said: "That's enough." He stood erect, a big blond man whose eyes were cold blue disks. "What is it, Ned? Do you want her yourself or is it –" He broke off contemptuously. "It doesn't make any difference." He jerked a thumb carelessly at the door. "Get out, you heel, this is the kiss-off."

Ned Beaumont said: "I'll get out when I've finished talking."

Madvig said: "You'll get out when you're told to. You can't say anything I'll believe. You haven't said anything I believe. You never will now."

Ned Beaumont said: "Oke." He picked up his hat and overcoat and went out.

II

Ned Beaumont went home. His face was pale and sullen. He slouched down in one of the big red chairs with a bottle of Bourbon whisky and a glass on the table beside him, but he did not drink. He stared gloomily at his black-shod feet and bit a finger-nail. His telephone-bell rang. He did not answer it. Twilight began to displace day in the room. The room was dusky when he rose and went to the telephone.

He called a number. Then: "Hello, I'd like to speak to Miss Henry, please." After a pause that he spent whistling tunelessly under his breath, he said: "Hello, Miss Henry? . . . Yes I've just come from telling Paul all about it, about you. . . . Yes, and you were right. He did what you counted on his doing. . . ." He laughed. "You did. You knew he'd call me a liar, refuse to listen to me, and throw me out, and he did all of it. . . . No, no, that's all right. It had to happen. . . . No, really. . . . Oh, it's probably permanent enough. Things were said that can't easily be unsaid. . . . Yes, all evening, I think. . . . That'll be fine. . . . All right. 'By."

He poured out a glass of whisky then and drank it. After that he went into his darkening bedroom, set his alarm-clock for eight o'clock, and lay down fully clothed on his back on the bed. For a while he looked at the ceiling. Then he slept, breathing irregularly, until the alarm rang.

He got up sluggishly from his bed and, switching on lights, went into the bathroom, washed his face and hands, put on a fresh collar, and started a fire in the living-room fireplace. He read a newspaper until Janet Henry arrived.

She was excited. Though she at once began to assure Ned Beaumont that she had not foreseen the result of his telling Paul about her visit, had not counted on it, elation danced frankly in her eyes and she could not keep smiles from curving her lips while they shaped the apologetic words.

He said: "It doesn't matter. I'd've had to do it if I'd known how it was going to turn out. I suppose I did know down underneath. It's one of those things. And if you'd told me it would happen I'd only've taken that for a challenge and would've jumped to it."

She held her hands out to him. "I'm glad," she said. "I won't pretend I'm not."

"I'm sorry," he told her as he took her hands, "but I wouldn't have gonc a step out of my way to avoid it."

She said: "And now you know I'm right. He did kill Taylor." Her eyes were inquisitive.

He nodded. "He told me he did."

"And you'll help me now?" Her hands pressed his. She came closer to him.

He hesitated, frowning down at her eager face. "It was self-defense, or an accident," he said slowly. "I can't –"

"It was murder!" she cried. "Of course he'd say it was self-defense!" She shook her head impatiently. "And even if it was self-defense or an accident, shouldn't he be made to go into court and prove it like anybody else?"

"He's waited too long. This month he's kept quiet would be against him."

"Well, whose fault was that?" she demanded. "And do you think he would have kept quiet so long if it had been self-defense?"

He nodded with slow emphasis. "That was on your account. He's in love with you. He didn't want you to know he'd killed your brother."

"I do know it!" she cried fiercely. "And everybody's going to know it!"

He moved his shoulders a little. His face was gloomy.

"You won't help me?" she asked.

"No."

"Why? You've quarreled with him."

"I believe his story. I know it's too late for him to put it across in court. We're through, but I won't do that to him."

He moistened his lips. "Let him alone. It's likely they'll do it to him without your help or mine."

"I won't," she said. "I won't let him alone until he's been punished as he deserves." She caught her breath and her eyes darkened. "Do you believe him enough to risk finding proof that he lied to you?"

"What do you mean?" he asked cautiously.

"Will you help me find proof of the truth, whether he's lying or not? There must be positive proof somewhere, some proof that we can find. If you really believe him you won't be afraid to help me find it."

He studied her face awhile before asking: "If I do and we find your positive proof, will you promise to accept it whichever way it stacks up?"

"Yes," she said readily, "if you will too."

"And you'll keep what we find to yourself till we've finished the job – found our positive proof – won't use what we find against him till we've got it all?"

"Yes."

"It's a bargain," he said.

She sobbed happily and tears came to her eyes.

He said: "Sit down." His face was lean and hard, his voice curt. "We've got to get schemes rigged. Have you heard from him this afternoon or evening, since he and I had our row?"

"No."

"Then we can't be sure how you stand with him. There's a chance he may have decided later that I was right. That won't make any difference between him and me now – we're done – but we've got to find out as soon as we can." He scowled at her feet and brushed his mustache with a thumbnail. "You'll have to wait till he comes to you. You can't afford to call him up. If he's shaky about you that might decide him. How sure of him are you?"

She was sitting in the chair by the table. She said: "I'm as sure of him as a woman can be of a man." She uttered a little embarrassed laugh. "I know that sounds – But I am, Mr. Beaumont."

He nodded. "Then that's probably all right, but you ought to know definitely by tomorrow. Have you ever tried to pump him?"

"Not yet, not really. I was waiting –"

"Well, that's out for the time being. No matter how sure you are of him you'll have to be careful now. Have you picked up anything you haven't told me about?"

"No," she said, shaking her head. "I haven't known very well how to go about it. That's why I so wanted you to –"

He interrupted her again: "Didn't it occur to you to hire a private detective?"

"Yes, but I was afraid, afraid I'd go to one who'd tell Paul. I didn't know who to go to, who I could trust."

"I've got one we can use." He ran fingers through his dark hair. "Now there are two things I want you to find out, if you don't know them now. Are any of your brother's hats missing? Paul says he had a hat on. There was none there when I found him. See if you can find out how many he had and if they're all accounted for" – he smiled obliquely – "except the one I borrowed."

She paid no attention to his smile. She shook her head and raised her hands a little, dispiritedly. "I can't," she said. "We got rid of all his things some time ago and I doubt if anybody knew exactly what he had anyway."

Ned Beaumont shrugged. "I didn't think we'd get anywhere on that," he told her. "The other thing's a walking-stick, whether any of them – his or your father's – are missing, particularly a rough heavy brown one."

"It would be Father's," she said eagerly, "and I think it's there."

"Check it up." He bit his thumb-nail. "That'll be enough for you to do between now and tomorrow, that and maybe find out how you stand with Paul."

"What is it?" she asked. "I mean about the stick." She stood up, excited.

"Paul says your brother attacked him with it and was struck by it while Paul was taking it away from him. He says he carried the stick away and burned it."

"Oh, I'm sure Father's sticks are all there," she cried. Her face was white, her eyes wide.

"Didn't Taylor have any?"

"Only a silver-headed black one." She put a hand on his wrist. "If they're all there it will mean that –"

"It might mean something," he said and put a hand on her hand. "But no tricks," he warned her.

"I won't," she promised. "If you only knew how happy I am to have your help, how much I've wanted it, you'd know you could trust me."

"I hope so." He took his hand from hers.

III

Alone in his rooms Ned Beaumont walked the floor awhile, his face pinched, his eyes shiny. At twenty minutes to ten he looked at his wrist-watch. Then he put on his overcoat and went down to the Majestic Hotel, where he was told that Harry Sloss was not in. He left the hotel, found a taxicab, got into it, and said: "West Road Inn."

The West Road Inn was a square white building – gray in the night – set among trees back from the road some three miles beyond the city limits. Its ground-floor was brightly lighted and half a dozen automobiles stood in front of it. Others were in a long dark shed off to the left.

Ned Beaumont, nodding familiarly at the doorman, went into a large dining-room where a three-man orchestra was playing extravagantly and eight or ten people were dancing. He passed down an aisle between tables, skirted the dance-floor, and stopped in front of the bar that occupied one corner of the room. He was alone on the customers' side of the bar.

The bar-tender, a fat man with a spongy nose, said: "Evening, Ned. We ain't been seeing you much lately."

" 'Lo, Jimmy. Been behaving. Manhattan."

The bar-tender began to mix the cocktail. The orchestra finished its piece. A woman's voice rose thin and shrill: "I won't stay in the same place with that Beaumont bastard."

Ned Beaumont turned around, leaning back against the edge of the bar. The bar-tender became motionless with the cocktail-shaker in his hand.

Lee Wilshire was standing in the center of the dance-floor glaring at Ned Beaumont. One of her hands was on the forearm of a bulky youth in a blue suit a bit too tight for him. He too was looking at Ned Beaumont, rather stupidly. She said: "He's a no-good bastard and if you don't throw him out I'm going out."

Everyone else in the place was attentively silent.

The youth's face reddened. His attempt at a scowl increased his appearance of embarrassment.

The girl said: "I'll go over and slap him myself if you don't."

Ned Beaumont, smiling, said: " 'Lo, Lee. Seen Bernie since he got out?"

Lee cursed him and took an angry step forward.

The bulky youth put out a hand and stopped her. "I'll fix him," he said, "the bastard." He adjusted his coat-collar to his neck, pulled the front of his coat down, and stalked off the dance-floor to face Ned Beaumont. "What's the idea?" he demanded. "What's the idea of talking to the little lady like that?"

Ned Beaumont, staring soberly at the youth, stretched his right arm out to the side and laid his hand palm-up on the bar. "Give me something to tap him with, Jimmy," he said. "I don't feel like fist-fighting."

One of the bar-tender's hands was already out of sight beneath the bar. He brought it up holding a small bludgeon and put the bludgeon in Ned Beaumont's hand. Ned Beaumont let it lie there while he said: "She gets called a lot of things. The last guy I saw her with was calling her a dumb cluck."

The youth drew himself up straight, his eyes shifting from side to side. He said: "I won't forget you and some day me and you will meet when there's nobody around." He turned on his heel and addressed Lee Wilshire. "Come on, let's blow out of this dump."

"Go ahead and blow," she said spitefully. "I'll be God-damned if I'm going with you. I'm sick of you."

A thick-bodied man with nearly all gold teeth came up and said: "Yes you will, the both of you. Get."

Ned Beaumont laughed and said: "The – uh – little lady's with me, Corky."

Corky said, "Fair enough," and then to the youth: "Outside, bum."

The youth went out.

Lee Wilshire had returned to her table. She sat there with her cheeks between her fists, staring at the cloth.

Ned Beaumont sat down facing her. He said to the waiter: "Jimmy's got a Manhattan that belongs to me. And I want some food. Eaten yet, Lee?"

"Yes," she said without looking up. "I want a silver fizz."

Ned Beaumont said: "Fine. I want a minute steak with mushrooms, whatever vegetable Tony's got that didn't come out of a can, some lettuce and tomatoes with Roquefort dressing, and coffee."

When the waiter had gone Lee said bitterly: "Men are no good, none of them. That big false alarm!" She began to cry silently.

"Maybe you pick the wrong kind," Ned Beaumont suggested.

"You should tell me that," she said, looking up angrily at him, "after the lousy trick you played me."

"I didn't play you any lousy trick," he protested. "If Bernie had to hock your pretties to pay back the money he'd gypped me out of it wasn't my fault."

The orchestra began to play.

"Nothing's ever a man's fault," she complained. "Come on and dance."

"Oh, all right," he said reluctantly.

When they returned to the table his cocktail and her fizz were there.

"What's Bernie doing these days?" he asked as they drank.

"I don't know. I haven't seen him since he got out and I don't want to see him. Another swell guy! What breaks I've been getting this year! Him and Taylor and this bastard!"

"Taylor Henry?" he asked.

"Yes, but I didn't have much to do with him," she explained quickly, "because that's while I was living with Bernie."

Ned Beaumont finished his cocktail before he said: "You were just one of the girls who used to meet him in his Charter Street place now and then."

"Yes," she said, looking warily at him.

He said: "I think we ought to have a drink."

She powdered her face while he caught their waiter's attention and ordered their drinks.

IV

The door-bell awakened Ned Beaumont. He got drowsily out of bed, coughing a little, and put on kimono and slippers. It was a few minutes after nine by his alarm-clock. He went to the door.

Janet Henry came in apologizing. "I know it's horribly early, but I simply couldn't wait another minute. I tried and tried to get you on the phone last night and hardly slept a wink because I couldn't. All of Father's sticks are there. So, you see, he lied."

"Has he got a heavy rough brown one?"

"Yes, that's the one Major Sawbridge brought him from

Scotland. He never uses it, but it's there." She smiled triumphantly at Ned Beaumont.

He blinked sleepily and ran fingers through his tousled hair. "Then he lied, right enough," he said.

"And," she said gaily, "he was there when I got home last night."

"Paul?"

"Yes. And he asked me to marry him."

Sleepiness went out of Ned Beaumont's eyes. "Did he say anything about our battle?"

"Not a word."

"What did you say?"

"I said it was too soon after Taylor's death for me even to engage myself to him, but I didn't say I wouldn't a little later, so we've got what I believe is called an understanding."

He looked curiously at her.

Gaiety went out of her face. She put a hand on his arm. Her voice broke a little. "Please don't think I'm altogether heartless," she said, "but – oh! – I do so want to – to do what we set out to do that everything else seems – well – not important at all."

He moistened his lips and said in a grave gentle voice: "What a spot he'd be in if you loved him as much as you hate him."

She stamped her foot and cried: "Don't say that! Don't ever say that again!"

Irritable lines appeared in his forehead and his lips tightened together.

She said, "Please," contritely, "but I can't bear that."

"Sorry," he said. "Had breakfast yet?"

"No. I was too anxious to bring my news to you."

"Fine. You'll eat with me. What do you like?" He went to the telephone.

After he had ordered breakfast he went into the bathroom to wash his teeth, face, and hands and brush his hair. When he returned to the living-room she had removed her hat and coat and was standing by the fireplace smoking a cigarette. She started to say something, but stopped when the telephone-bell rang.

He went to the telephone. "Hello. . . . Yes, Harry, I stopped in, but you were out. . . . I wanted to ask you about – you know – the chap you saw with Paul that night. Did he have a hat? . . . He did? Sure? . . . And did he have a stick in his hand? . . . Oke. . . . No, I couldn't do anything with Paul on that, Harry. Better see him yourself. . . . Yes. . . . 'By."

Janet Henry's eyes questioned him as he got up from the telephone.

He said: "That was one of a couple of fellows who claim they saw Paul talking to your brother in the street that night. He says he saw the hat, but not the stick. It was dark, though, and this pair were riding past in a car. I wouldn't bet they saw anything very clearly."

"Why are you so interested in the hat? Is it so important?"

He shrugged. "I don't know. I'm only an amateur detective, but it looks like a thing that might have some meaning, one way or another."

"Have you learned anything else since yesterday?"

"No. I spent part of the evening buying drinks for a girl Taylor used to play around with, but there wasn't anything there."

"Anyone I know?" she asked.

He shook his head, then looked sharply at her and said: "It wasn't Opal, if that's what you're getting at."

"Don't you think we might be able to – to get some information from her?"

"Opal? No. She thinks her father killed Taylor, but she thinks it was on her account. It wasn't anything she knew that sent her off – not any inside stuff – it was your letters and the *Observer* and things like that."

Janet Henry nodded, but seemed unconvinced.

Their breakfast arrived.

The telephone-bell rang while they were eating. Ned Beaumont went to the telephone and said: "Hello. . . . Yes, Mom. . . . What?" He listened, frowning, for several seconds, then said: "There isn't much you can do about it except let them and I don't think it'll do any harm. . . . No, I don't know where he is. . . . I don't think I will. . . . Well, don't worry about it, Mom, it'll be all right. . . . Sure, that's right. . . . 'By." He returned to the table smiling. "Farr's got the same idea you had," he said as he sat down. "That was Paul's mother. A man from the District Attorney's office is there to question Opal." A bright gleam awakened in his eyes. "She can't help them any, but they're closing in on him."

"Why did she call you?" Janet Henry asked.

"Paul had gone out and she didn't know where to find him."

"Doesn't she know that you and Paul have quarreled?"

"Apparently not." He put down his fork. "Look here. Are you sure you want to go through with this thing?"

"I want to go through with it more than I ever wanted to do anything in my life," she told him.

Ned Beaumont laughed bitterly, said: "They're practically the same words Paul used telling me how much he wanted you."

She shuddered, her face hardened, and she looked coldly at him.

He said: "I don't know about you, I'm not sure of you. I had a dream I don't much like."

She smiled then. "Surely you don't believe in dreams?"

He did not smile. "I don't believe in anything, but I'm too much of a gambler not to be affected by a lot of things."

Her smile became less mocking. She asked: "What was this dream that makes you mistrust me?" She held up a finger, pretending seriousness. "And then I'll tell you one I had about you."

"I was fishing," he said, "and I caught an enormous fish – a rainbow trout, but enormous – and you said you wanted to look at it and you picked it up and threw it back in the water before I could stop you."

She laughed merrily. "What did you do?"

"That was the end of the dream."

"It was a lie," she said. "I won't throw your trout back. Now I'll tell you mine. I was –" Her eyes widened. "When was yours? The night you came to dinner?"

"No. Last night."

"Oh, that's too bad. It would be nicer in an impressive way if we'd done our dreaming on the same night and the same hour and the same minute. Mine was the night you were there. We were – this is in the dream – we were lost in a forest, you and I, tired and starving. We walked and walked till we came to a little house and we knocked on the door, but nobody answered. We tried the door. It was locked. Then we peeped through a window and inside we could see a great big table piled high with all imaginable kinds of food, but we couldn't get in through either of the windows because they had iron bars over them. So we went back to the door and knocked and knocked again and still nobody answered. Then we thought that sometimes people left their keys under door-mats and we looked and there it was. But when we opened the door we saw hundreds and hundreds of snakes on the floor where we hadn't been able to see them through the window and they all came sliding and slithering towards us. We slammed the door shut and locked it and stood there frightened to death listening to them hissing and knocking their heads against the inside of the door. Then you said that perhaps if we opened the door and hid from the snakes they'd come out and go away, so we did. You helped me climb up on the roof – it was low in this part of the dream: I don't remember what it was like before – and you climbed up after me and leaned down and unlocked the door, and all the snakes came slithering out. We lay holding our breath on the roof until the last of the hundreds and hundreds of them had slithered out of sight into the forest. Then we jumped down and ran inside and locked the door and ate and ate and ate and I woke sitting up in bed clapping my hands and laughing."

"I think you made that up," Ned Beaumont said after a little pause.

"Why?"

"It starts out to be a nightmare and winds up something else and all the dreams I ever had about food ended before I got a chance to do any actual eating."

Janet Henry laughed. "I didn't make all of it up," she said, "but you needn't ask which part is true. You've accused me of lying and I'll tell you nothing now."

"Oh, all right." He picked up his fork again, but did not eat. He asked, with an air of just having the thought: "Does your father know anything? Do you think we could get anything out of him if we went to him with what we know?"

"Yes," she said eagerly, "I do."

He scowled thoughtfully. "The only trouble is he might go up in the air and explode the works before we're ready. He's hot-headed, isn't he?"

Her answer was given reluctantly: "Yes, but" – her face brightened, pleadingly – "I'm sure if we showed him why it's important to wait until we've – But we are ready now, aren't we?"

He shook his head. "Not yet."

She pouted.

"Maybe tomorrow," he said.

"Really?"

"That's not a promise," he cautioned her, "but I think we will be."

She put a hand across the table to take one of his hands. "But you will promise to let me know the very minute we're ready, no matter what time of day or night it is?"

"Sure, I'll promise you that." He looked obliquely at her. "You're not very anxious to be in at the death, are you?"

His tone brought a flush to her face, but she did not lower her eyes. "I know you think I'm a monster," she said. "Perhaps I am."

He looked down at his plate and muttered: "I hope you like it when you get it."

9 THE HEELS

I

AFTER JANET HENRY had gone Ned Beaumont went to his telephone, called Jack Rumsen's number, and when he had that one on the wire said: "Can you drop in to see me, Jack?... Fine. 'By."

He was dressed by the time Jack arrived. They sat in facing chairs, each with a glass of Bourbon whisky and mineral water, Ned Beaumont smoking a cigar, Jack a cigarette.

Ned Beaumont asked: "Heard anything about the split between Paul and me?"

Jack said, "Yes," casually.

"What do you think of it?"

"Nothing. I remember the last time it was supposed to happen it turned out to be a trick on Shad O'Rory."

Ned Beaumont smiled as if he had expected that reply. "Is that what everybody thinks it is this time?"

The dapper young man said: "A lot of them do."

Ned Beaumont inhaled cigar-smoke slowly, asked: "Suppose I told you it was on the level this time?"

Jack said nothing. His face told nothing of his thoughts.

Ned Beaumont said: "It is." He drank from his glass "How much do I owe you?"

"Thirty bucks for that job on the Madvig girl. You settled for the rest."

Ned Beaumont took a roll of paper money from a trousers-pocket, separated three ten-dollar bills from the roll, and gave them to Jack.

Jack said: "Thanks."

Ned Beaumont said: "Now we're quits." He inhaled smoke and blew it out while saying: "I've got another job I want done. I'm after Paul's scalp on the Taylor Henry killing. He told me he did it, but I need a little more proof. Want to work on it for me?"

Jack said: "No."

"Why not?"

The dark young man rose to put his empty glass on the table. "Fred and I are building up a nice little private-detective business here," he said. "A couple of years more and we'll be sitting pretty. I like you, Beaumont, but not enough to monkey with the man that runs the city."

Ned Beaumont said evenly: "He's on the chutes. The whole crew's getting ready to ditch him. Farr and Rainey are –"

"Let them do it. I don't want in on that racket and I'll believe they can do it when it's done. Maybe they'll give him a bump or two, but making it stick's another thing. You know him better than I do. You know he's got more guts than all the rest of them put together."

"He has and that's what's licking him. Well, if you won't, you won't."

Jack said, "I won't," and picked up his hat. "Anything else I'll be glad to do, but –" He moved one hand in a brief gesture of finality.

Ned Beaumont stood up. There was no resentment in his manner, none in his voice when he said: "I thought you might feel that way about it." He brushed a side of his mustache with a thumb and stared thoughtfully past Jack. "Maybe you can tell me this: any idea where I can find Shad?"

Jack shook his head. "Since the third time they knocked his place over – when the two coppers were killed – he's been laying low, though they don't seem to have a hell of a lot on him personally." He took his cigarette from his mouth. "Know Whisky Vassos?"

"Yes."

"You might find out from him if you know him well enough. He's around town. You can usually find him some time during the night at Tim Walker's place on Smith Street."

"Thanks, Jack. I'll try that."

"That's all right," Jack said. He hesitated. "I'm sorry as hell you and Madvig split. I wish you –" He broke off and turned towards the door. "You know what you're doing."

II

Ned Beaumont went down to the District Attorney's office. This time there was no delay in ushering him into Farr's presence.

Farr did not get up from his desk, did not offer to shake hands. He said: "How do you do, Beaumont? Sit down." His voice was coldly polite. His pugnacious face was not so red as usual. His eyes were level and hard.

Ned Beaumont sat down, crossed his legs comfortably, and said: "I wanted to tell you about what happened when I went to see Paul after I left here yesterday."

Farr's "Yes?" was cold and polite.

"I told him how I'd found you – panicky." Ned Beaumont, smiling his nicest smile, went on in the manner of one telling a fairly amusing but unimportant anecdote: "I told him I thought you were trying to get up enough nerve to hang the Taylor Henry murder on him. He believed me at first, but when I told him the only way to save himself was by turning up the real murderer, he said that was no good. He said he was the real murderer, though he called it an accident or self-defense or something."

Farr's face had become paler and was stiff around the mouth, but he did not speak.

Ned Beaumont raised his eyebrows. "I'm not boring you, am I?" he asked.

"Go on, continue," the District Attorney said coldly.

Ned Beaumont tilted his chair back. His smile was mocking. "You think I'm kidding, don't you? You think it's a trick we're playing on you." He shook his head and murmured: "You're a timid soul, Farr."

Farr said: "I'm glad to listen to any information you can give me, but I'm very busy, so I'll have to ask you –"

Ned Beaumont laughed then and replied: "Oke. I thought maybe you'd like to have this information in an affidavit or something."

"Very well." Farr pressed one of the pearl buttons on his desk.

A gray-haired woman in green came in.

"Mr. Beaumont wants to dictate a statement," Farr told her.

She said, "Yes, sir," sat at the other side of Farr's desk, put her notebook on the desk, and, holding a silver pencil over the book, looked at Ned Beaumont with blank brown eyes.

He said: "Yesterday afternoon in his office in the Nebel Building, Paul Madvig told me that he had been to dinner at Senator Henry's house the night Taylor Henry was killed; that he and Taylor Henry had some sort of trouble there; that after he left the house Taylor Henry ran after him and caught up with him and tried to hit him with a rough heavy brown walking-stick; that in trying to take the stick from Taylor Henry he accidentally struck him on the forehead with it, knocking him down; and that he carried the stick away with him and burned it. He said his only reason for concealing his part in Taylor Henry's death was his desire to keep it from Janet Henry. That's all of it."

Farr addressed the stenographer: "Transcribe that right away."

She left the office.

Ned Beaumont said: "I thought I was bringing you news that would get you all excited." He sighed. "I thought you'd fairly tear your hair over it."

The District Attorney looked steadily at him.

Ned Beaumont, unabashed, said: "I thought at least you'd have Paul dragged in and confronted with this" – he waved a hand – " 'damaging disclosure' is a good phrase."

The District Attorney spoke in a restrained tone: "Please permit me to run my own office."

Ned Beaumont laughed again and relapsed into silence until the gray-haired stenographer returned with a typed copy of his statement. Then he asked: "Do I swear to it?"

"No," Farr said, "just sign it. That will be sufficient."

Ned Beaumont signed the paper. "This isn't nearly so much fun as I thought it was going to be," he complained cheerfully.

Farr's undershot jaw tightened. "No," he said with grim satisfaction, "I don't suppose it is."

"You're a timid soul, Farr," Ned Beaumont repeated. "Be careful about taxis when you cross streets." He bowed. "See you later."

Outside, he grimaced angrily.

III

That night Ned Beaumont rang the door-bell of a dark three-story house in Smith Street. A short man who had a small head and thick shoulders opened the door half a foot, said, "All right," and opened it the rest of the way.

Ned Beaumont, saying, " 'Lo," entered, walked twenty feet down a dim hallway past two closed doors on the right, opened a door on the left, and went down a wooden flight of steps into a basement where there was a bar and where a radio was playing softly.

Beyond the bar was a frosted glass door marked *Toilet*. This door opened and a man came out, a swarthy man with something apish in the slope of his big shoulders, the length of his thick arms, the flatness of his face, and the curve of his bowed legs – Jeff Gardner.

He saw Ned Beaumont and his reddish small eyes glistened.

"Well, blind Christ, if it ain't Sock-me-again Beaumont!" he roared, showing his beautiful teeth in a huge grin.

Ned Beaumont said, "'Lo, Jeff," while everyone in the place looked at them.

Jeff swaggered over to Ned Beaumont, threw his left arm roughly around his shoulders, seized Ned Beaumont's right hand with his right hand, and addressed the company jovially: "This is the swellest guy I ever skinned a knuckle on and I've skinned them on plenty." He dragged Ned Beaumont to the bar. "We're all going to have a little drink and then I'll show you how it's done. By Jesus, I will!" He leered into Ned Beaumont's face. "What do you say to that, my lad?"

Ned Beaumont, looking stolidly at the ugly dark face so close to, though lower than, his, said: "Scotch."

Jeff laughed delightedly and addressed the company again: "You see, he likes it. He's a –" he hesitated, frowning, wet his lips "– a God-damned massacrist, that's what he is." He leered at Ned Beaumont. "You know what a massacrist is?"

"Yes."

Jeff seemed disappointed. "Rye," he told the bar-tender. When their drinks were set before them he released Ned Beaumont's hand, though he kept his arm across his shoulders. They drank. Jeff set down his glass and put his hand on Ned Beaumont's wrist. "I got just the place for me and you upstairs," he said, "a room that's too little for you to fall down in. I can bounce you around off the walls. That way we won't be wasting a lot of time while you're getting up off the floor."

Ned Beaumont said: "I'll buy a drink."

"That ain't a dumb idea," Jeff agreed.

They drank again.

When Ned Beaumont had paid for the drinks Jeff turned him towards the stairs. "Excuse us, gents," he said to the others at the bar, "but we got to go up and rehearse our act." He patted Ned Beaumont's shoulder. "Me and my sweetheart."

They climbed two flights of steps and went into a small

room in which a sofa, two tables, and half a dozen chairs were crowded. There were some empty glasses and plates holding the remains of sandwiches on one table.

Jeff peered near-sightedly around the room and demanded: "Now where in hell did she go?" He released Ned Beaumont's wrist, took the arm from around his shoulders, and asked: "You don't see no broad here, do you?"

"No."

Jeff wagged his head up and down emphatically. "She's gone," he said. He took an uncertain step backwards and jabbed the bell-button beside the door with a dirty finger. Then, flourishing his hand, he made a grotesque bow and said: "Set down."

Ned Beaumont sat down at the less disorderly of the two tables.

"Set in any God-damned chair you want to set in," Jeff said with another large gesture. "If you don't like that one, take another. I want you to consider yourself my guest and the hell with you if you don't like it."

"It's a swell chair," Ned Beaumont said.

"It's a hell of a chair," Jeff said. "There ain't a chair in the dump that's worth a damn. Look." He picked up a chair and tore one of its front legs out. "You call that a swell chair? Listen, Beaumont, you don't know a damned thing about chairs." He put the chair down, tossed the leg on the sofa. "You can't fool me. I know what you're up to. You think I'm drunk, don't you?"

Ned Beaumont grinned. "No, you're not drunk."

"The hell I'm not drunk. I'm drunker than you are. I'm drunker than anybody in this dump. I'm drunk as hell and don't think I'm not, but –" He held up a thick unclean forefinger.

A waiter came in the doorway asking: "What is it gents?"

Jeff turned to confront him. "Where've you been? Sleeping? I rung for you one hour ago."

The waiter began to say something.

Jeff said: "I bring the best friend I got in the world up here for a drink and what the hell happens? We have to sit around a whole God-damned hour waiting for a lousy waiter. No wonder he's sore at me."

"What do you want?" the waiter asked indifferently.

"I want to know where in hell the girl that was in here went to."

"Oh, her? She's gone."

"Gone where?"

"I don't know."

Jeff scowled. "Well, you find out, and God-damned quick. What's the idea of not knowing where she went? If this ain't a swell joint where nobody – " A shrewd light came into his red eyes. "I'll tell you what to do. You go up to the ladies' toilet and see if she's there."

"She ain't there," the waiter said. "She went out."

"The dirty bastard!" Jeff said and turned to Ned Beaumont. "What'd you do to a dirty bastard like that? I bring you up here because I want you to meet her because I know you'll like her and she'll like you and she's too God-damned snooty to meet my friends and out she goes."

Ned Beaumont was lighting a cigar. He did not say anything.

Jeff scratched his head, growled, "Well, bring us something to drink, then," sat down across the table from Ned Beaumont, and said savagely: "Mine's rye."

Ned Beaumont said: "Scotch."

The waiter went away.

Jeff glared at Ned Beaumont. "Don't get the idea that I don't know what you're up to, either," he said angrily.

"I'm not up to anything," Ned Beaumont replied carelessly. "I'd like to see Shad and I thought maybe I'd find Whisky Vassos here and he'd send me to Shad."

"Don't you think I know where Shad is?"

"You ought to."

"Then why didn't you ask me?"

"All right. Where is he?"

Jeff slapped the table mightily with an open hand and bawled: "You're a liar. You don't give a God-damn where Shad is. It's me you're after."

Ned Beaumont smiled and shook his head.

"It is," the apish man insisted. "You know God-damned well that –"

A young-middle-aged man with plump red lips and round eyes came to the door. He said: "Cut it out, Jeff. You're making more noise than everybody else in the place."

Jeff screwed himself around in his chair. "It's this bastard," he told the man in the doorway, indicating Ned Beaumont with a jerk of his thumb. "He thinks I don't know what he's up to. I know what he's up to. He's a heel and that's what he is. And I'm going to beat hell out of him and that's what I'm going to do."

The man in the doorway said reasonably, "Well, you don't have to make so much noise about it," winked at Ned Beaumont, and went away.

Jeff said gloomily: "Tim's turning into a heel too." He spit on the floor.

The waiter came in with their drinks.

Ned Beaumont raised his glass, said, "Looking at you," and drank.

Jeff said: "I don't want to look at you. You're a heel." He stared somberly at Ned Beaumont.

"You're crazy."

"You're a liar. I'm drunk. But I ain't so drunk that I don't know what you're up to." He emptied his glass, wiped his mouth with the back of his hand. "And I say you're a heel."

Ned Beaumont, smiling amiably, said: "All right. Have it your way."

Jeff thrust his apish muzzle forward a little. "You think you're smart as hell, don't you?"

Ned Beaumont did not say anything.

"You think it's a damned smart trick coming in here and trying to get me plastered so you can turn me up."

"That's right," Ned Beaumont said carelessly, "there is a murder-charge against you for bumping off Francis West, isn't there?"

Jeff said: "Hell with Francis West."

Ned Beaumont shrugged. "I didn't know him."

Jeff said: "You're a heel."

Ned Beaumont said: "I'll buy you a drink."

The apish man nodded solemnly and tilted his chair back to reach the bell-button. With his finger on the button he said: "But you're still a heel." His chair swayed back under him, turning. He got his feet flat on the floor and brought the chair down on all fours before it could spill him. "The bastard!" he snarled, pulling it around to the table again. He put his elbows on the table and propped his chin up on one fist. "What the hell do I care who turns me up? You don't think they'd ever fry me, do you?"

"Why not?"

"Why not? Jesus! I wouldn't have to stand the rap till after election and then it's all Shad's."

"Maybe."

"Maybe hell!"

The waiter came in and they ordered their drinks.

"Maybe Shad would let you take the fall anyhow," Ned Beaumont said idly when they were alone again. "Things like that have happened."

"A swell chance," Jeff scoffed, "with all I've got on him."

Ned Beaumont exhaled cigar-smoke. "What've you got on him?"

The apish man laughed, boisterously, scornfully, and

pounded the table with an open hand. "Christ!" he roared, "he thinks I'm drunk enough to tell him."

From the doorway came a quiet voice, a musical slightly Irish baritone: "Go on, Jeff, tell him." Shad O'Rory stood in the doorway. His gray-blue eyes looked somewhat sadly at Jeff.

Jeff squinted his eyes merrily at the man in the doorway and said: "How are you, Shad? Come in and set down to a drink. Meet Mr. Beaumont. He's a heel."

O'Rory said softly: "I told you to stay under cover."

"But, Jesus, Shad, I was getting so's I was afraid I'd bite myself! And this joint's under cover, ain't it? It's a speakeasy."

O'Rory looked a moment longer at Jeff, then at Ned Beaumont. "Good evening, Beaumont."

" 'Lo, Shad."

O'Rory smiled gently and, indicating Jeff with a tiny nod, asked: "Get much out of him?"

"Not much I didn't already know," Ned Beaumont replied. "He makes a lot of noise, but all of it doesn't make sense."

Jeff said: "I think you're a pair of heels."

The waiter arrived with their drinks. O'Rory stopped him. "Never mind. They've had enough." The waiter carried their drinks away. Shad O'Rory came into the room and shut the door. He stood with his back against it. He said: "You talk too much, Jeff. I've told you that before."

Ned Beaumont deliberately winked at Jeff.

Jeff said angrily to him: "What the hell's the matter with you?"

Ned Beaumont laughed.

"I'm talking to you, Jeff," O'Rory said.

"Christ, don't I know it?"

O'Rory said: "We're coming to the place where I'm going to stop talking to you."

Jeff stood up. "Don't be a heel, Shad," he said. "What the

hell?" He came around the table. "Me and you've been pals a long time. You always were my pal and I'll always be yours." He put his arms out to embrace O'Rory, lurching towards him. "Sure, I'm smoked, but –"

O'Rory put a white hand on the apish man's chest and thrust him back. "Sit down." He did not raise his voice.

Jeff's left fist whipped out at O'Rory's face.

O'Rory's head moved to the right, barely enough to let the fist whip past his cheek. O'Rory's long finely sculptured face was gravely composed. His right hand dropped down behind his hip.

Ned Beaumont flung from his chair at O'Rory's right arm, caught it with both hands, going down on his knees.

Jeff, thrown against the wall by the impetus behind his left fist, now turned and took Shad O'Rory's throat in both hands. The apish face was yellow, distorted, hideous. There was no longer any drunkenness in it.

"Got the roscoe?" Jeff panted.

"Yes." Ned Beaumont stood up, stepped back holding a black pistol leveled at O'Rory.

O'Rory's eyes were glassy, protuberant, his face mottled, turgid. He did not struggle against the man holding his throat.

Jeff turned his head over his shoulder to grin at Ned Beaumont. The grin was wide, genuine, idiotically bestial. Jeff's little red eyes glinted merrily. He said in a hoarse good-natured voice: "Now you see what we got to do. We got to give him the works."

Ned Beaumont said: "I don't want anything to do with it." His voice was steady. His nostrils quivered.

"No?" Jeff leered at him. "I expect you think Shad's a guy that'll forget what we done." He ran his tongue over his lips. "He'll forget. I'll fix that."

Grinning from ear to ear at Ned Beaumont, not looking at the man whose throat he held in his hands, Jeff began to take in and let out long slow breaths. His coat became lumpy over his shoulders and back and along his arms. Sweat appeared on his ugly dark face.

Ned Beaumont was pale. He too was breathing heavily and moisture filmed his temples. He looked over Jeff's lumpy shoulder at O'Rory's face.

O'Rory's face was liver-colored. His eyes stood far out, blind. His tongue came out blue between bluish lips. His slender body writhed. One of his hands began to beat the wall behind him, mechanically, without force.

Grinning at Ned Beaumont, not looking at the man whose throat he held, Jeff spread his legs a little wider and arched his back. O'Rory's hand stopped beating the wall. There was a muffled crack, then, almost immediately, a sharper one. O'Rory did not writhe now. He sagged in Jeff's hands.

Jeff laughed in his throat. "That's keno," he said. He kicked a chair out of the way and dropped O'Rory's body on the sofa. O'Rory's body fell there face down, one hand and his feet hanging down to the floor. Jeff rubbed his hands on his hips and faced Ned Beaumont. "I'm just a big good-natured slob," he said. "Anybody can kick me around all they want to and I never do nothing about it."

Ned Beaumont said: "You were afraid of him."

Jeff laughed. "I hope to tell you I was. So was anybody that was in their right mind. I suppose you wasn't?" He laughed again, looked around the room, said: "Let's screw before anybody pops in." He held out his hand. "Give me the roscoe. I'll ditch it."

Ned Beaumont said: "No." He moved his hand sidewise until the pistol was pointed at Jeff's belly. "We can say this was self-defense. I'm with you. We can beat it at the inquest."

"Jesus, that's a bright idea!" Jeff exclaimed. "Me with a murder-rap hanging over me for that West guy!" His small red eyes kept shifting their focus from Ned Beaumont's face to the pistol in his hand.

Ned Beaumont smiled with thin pale lips. "That's what I was thinking about," he said softly.

"Don't be a God-damned sap," Jeff blustered, taking a step forward. "You –"

Ned Beaumont backed away, around one of the tables. "I don't mind plugging you, Jeff," he said. "Remember I owe you something."

Jeff stood still and scratched the back of his head. "What kind of a heel are you?" he asked perplexedly.

"Just a pal." Ned Beaumont moved the pistol forward suddenly. "Sit down."

Jeff, after a moment's glowering hesitation, sat down.

Ned Beaumont put out his left hand and pressed the bell-button.

Jeff stood up.

Ned Beaumont said: "Sit down."

Jeff sat down.

Ned Beaumont said: "Keep your hands on the table."

Jeff shook his head lugubriously. "What a half-smart bastard you turned out to be," he said. "You don't think they're going to let you drag me out of here, do you?"

Ned Beaumont went around the table again and sat on a chair facing Jeff and facing the door.

Jeff said: "The best thing for you to do is give me that gun and hope I'll forget you made the break. Jesus, Ned, this is one of my hang-outs! You ain't got a chance in the world of pulling a fast one here."

Ned Beaumont said: "Keep your hand away from the catchup-bottle."

The waiter opened the door, goggled at them.

"Tell Tim to come up," Ned Beaumont said, and then, to the apish man when he would have spoken: "Shut up."

The waiter shut the door and hurried away.

Jeff said: "Don't be a sap, Neddy. This can't get you anything but a rub-out. What good's it going to do you to try to turn me up? None." He wet his lips with his tongue. "I know you're kind of sore about the time we were rough with you, but – hell! – that wasn't my fault. I was just doing what Shad told me, and ain't I evened that up now by knocking him off for you?"

Ned Beaumont said: "If you don't keep your hand away from that catchup-bottle I'm going to shoot a hole in it."

Jeff said: "You're a heel."

The young-middle-aged man with plump lips and round eyes opened the door, came in quickly, and shut it behind him.

Ned Beaumont said: "Jeff's killed O'Rory. Phone the police. You'll have time to clear the place before they get here. Better get a doctor, too, in case he's not dead."

Jeff laughed scornfully. "If he ain't dead I'm the Pope." He stopped laughing and addressed the plump-mouthed man with careless familiarity: "What do you think of this guy thinking you're going to let him get away with that? Tell him what a fat chance he has of getting away with it, Tim."

Tim looked at the dead man on the sofa, at Jeff, and at Ned Beaumont. His round eyes were sober. He spoke to Ned Beaumont, slowly: "This is a tough break for the house. Can't we drag him out in the street and let him be found there?"

Ned Beaumont shook his head. "Get your place cleaned up before the coppers get here and you'll be all right. I'll do what I can for you."

While Tim hesitated Jeff said: "Listen, Tim, you know me. You know –"

Tim said without especial warmth: "For Christ's sake pipe down."

Ned Beaumont smiled. "Nobody knows you, Jeff, now Shad's dead."

"No?" The apish man sat back more comfortably in his chair and his face cleared. "Well, turn me up. Now I know what kind of sons of bitches you are I'd rather take the fall than ask a God-damned thing of either of you."

Tim, ignoring Jeff, asked: "Have to play it that way?"

Ned Beaumont nodded.

"I guess I can stand it," Tim said and put his hand on the door-knob.

"Mind seeing if Jeff's got a gun on him?" Ned Beaumont asked.

Tim shook his head. "It happened here, but I've got nothing to do with it and I'm going to have nothing to do with it," he said and went out.

Jeff, slouching back comfortably in his chair, his hands idle on the table before him, talked to Ned Beaumont until the police came. He talked cheerfully, calling Ned Beaumont numerous profane and obscene and merely insulting names, accusing him of a long and varied list of vices.

Ned Beaumont listened with polite interest.

A raw-boned white-haired man in a lieutenant's uniform was the first policeman to come in. Half a dozen police detectives were behind him.

Ned Beaumont said: "'Lo, Brett. I think he's got a gun on him."

"What's it all about?" Brett asked, looking at the body on the sofa while two detectives, squeezing past him, took hold of Jeff Gardner.

Ned Beaumont told Brett what had happened. His story was truthful except in giving the impression that O'Rory had been killed in the heat of their struggle and not after he had been disarmed.

While Ned Beaumont was talking a doctor came in, turned Shad O'Rory's body over on the sofa, examined him briefly, and stood up. The Lieutenant looked at the doctor. The doctor said, "Gone," and went out of the small crowded room.

Jeff was jovially cursing the two detectives who held him. Every time he cursed, one of the detectives struck him in the face with his fist. Jeff laughed and kept on cursing them. His false teeth had been knocked out. His mouth bled.

Ned Beaumont gave the dead man's pistol to Brett and stood up. "Want me to come along to headquarters now? Or will tomorrow do?"

"Better come along now," Brett replied.

IV

It was long past midnight when Ned Beaumont left police headquarters. He said good-night to the two reporters who had come out with him and got into a taxicab. The address he gave the driver was Paul Madvig's.

Lights were on in the ground-floor of Madvig's house and as Ned Beaumont climbed the front steps the door was opened by Mrs. Madvig. She was dressed in black and had a shawl over her shoulders.

He said: "'Lo, Mom. What are you doing up so late?"

She said, "I thought it was Paul," though she looked at him without disappointment.

"Isn't he home? I wanted to see him." He looked sharply at her. "What's the matter?"

The old woman stepped back, pulling the door back with her. "Come in, Ned."

He went in.

She shut the door and said: "Opal tried to commit suicide."

He lowered his eyes and mumbled: "What? What do you mean?"

"She had cut one of her wrists before the nurse could stop her. She didn't lose much blood, though, and she's all right if she doesn't try it again." There was as little of weakness in her voice as in her mien.

Ned Beaumont's voice was not steady. "Where's Paul?"

"I don't know. We haven't been able to find him. He ought to be home before this. I don't know where he is." She put a bony hand on Ned Beaumont's upper arm and now her voice shook a little. "Are you – are you and Paul – ?" She stopped, squeezing his arm.

He shook his head. "That's done for good."

"Oh, Ned, boy, isn't there anything you can do to patch it up? You and he –" Again she broke off.

He raised his head and looked at her. His eyes were wet. He said gently: "No, Mom, that's done for good. Did he tell you about it?"

"He only told me, when I said I'd phoned you about that man from the District Attorney's office being here, that I wasn't ever to do anything like that again, that you – that you were not friends now."

Ned Beaumont cleared his throat. "Listen, Mom, tell him I came to see him. Tell him I'm going home and will wait there for him, will be waiting all night." He cleared his throat again and added lamely: "Tell him that."

Mrs. Madvig put her bony hands on his shoulders. "You're a good boy, Ned. I don't want you and Paul to quarrel. You're the best friend he ever had, no matter what's come between you. What is it? Is it that Janet –"

"Ask Paul," he said in a low bitter voice. He moved his head impatiently. "I'm going to run along, Mom, unless there's something I can do for you or Opal. Is there?"

"Not unless you'd go up to see her. She's not sleeping yet and maybe it would do some good to talk to her. She used to listen to you."

He shook his head. "No," he said, "she wouldn't want to see me" – he swallowed – "either."

10 THE SHATTERED KEY

I

NED BEAUMONT went home. He drank coffee, smoked, read a newspaper, a magazine, and half a book. Now and then he stopped reading to walk, fidgeting, around his rooms. His door-bell did not ring. His telephone-bell did not ring.

At eight o'clock in the morning he bathed, shaved, and put on fresh clothes. Then he had breakfast sent in and ate it.

At nine o'clock he went to the telephone, called Janet Henry's number, asked for her, and said: "Good morning. . . . Yes, fine, thanks. . . . Well, we're ready for the fireworks. . . . Yes. . . . If your father's there suppose we let him in on the whole thing first. . . . Fine, but not a word till I get there. . . . As soon as I can make it. I'm leaving now. . . . Right. See you in minutes."

He got up from the telephone staring into space, clapped his hands together noisily, and rubbed their palms together. His mouth was a sullen line under his mustache, his eyes hot brown points. He went to the closet and briskly put on his overcoat and hat. He left his room whistling *Little Lost Lady* between his teeth and took long steps through the streets.

"Miss Henry's expecting me," he said to the maid who opened the Henrys' door.

She said, "Yes, sir," and guided him to a sunny bright-papered room where the Senator and his daughter were at breakfast.

Janet Henry jumped up immediately and came to him with both hands out, crying excitedly: "Good morning!"

The Senator rose in more leisurely manner, looking with

polite surprise at his daughter, then holding his hand out to Ned Beaumont, saying: "Good morning, Mr. Beaumont. I'm very glad to see you. Won't you – ?"

"Thanks, no, I've had breakfast."

Janet Henry was trembling. Excitement had drained her skin of color, had darkened her eyes, giving her the appearance of one drugged. "We have something to tell you, Father," she said in a strained uneven voice, "something that –" She turned abruptly to Ned Beaumont. "Tell him! Tell him!"

Ned Beaumont glanced obliquely at her, drawing his brows together, then looked directly at her father. The Senator had remained standing by his place at the table. Ned Beaumont said: "What we've got is pretty strong evidence – including a confession – that Paul Madvig killed your son."

The Senator's eyes became narrower and he put a hand flat on the table in front of him. "What is this pretty strong evidence?" he asked.

"Well, sir, the chief thing is the confession, of course. He says your son ran out after him that night and tried to hit him with a rough brown walking-stick and that in taking the stick away from your son he accidentally struck him with it. He says he took the stick away and burned it, but your daughter" – he made a little bow at Janet Henry – "says it's still here."

"It is," she said. "It's the one Major Sawbridge brought you."

The Senator's face was pale as marble and as firm. "Proceed," he said.

Ned Beaumont made a small gesture with one hand. "Well, sir, that would blow up his story about its being an accident or self-defense – your son's not having the stick." He moved his shoulders a little. "I told Farr this yesterday. He's apparently afraid to take many chances – you know what he is – but I don't see how he can keep from picking Paul up today."

Janet Henry frowned at Ned Beaumont, obviously perplexed by something, started to speak, but pressed her lips together instead.

Senator Henry touched his lips with the napkin he held in his left hand, dropped the napkin on the table, and asked: "Is there – ah – any other evidence?"

Ned Beaumont's reply was another question carelessly uttered: "Isn't that enough?"

"But there is still more, isn't there?" Janet demanded.

"Stuff to back this up," Ned Beaumont said depreciatively. He addressed the Senator: "I can give you more details, but you've got the main story now. That's enough, isn't it?"

"Quite enough," the Senator said. He put a hand to his forehead. "I cannot believe it, yet it is so. If you'll excuse me for a moment and" – to his daughter – "you too, my dear, I should like to be alone, to think, to adjust myself to – No, no, stay here. I should like to go to my room." He bowed gracefully. "Please remain, Mr. Beaumont. I shall not be long – merely a moment to – to adjust myself to the knowledge that this man with whom I've worked shoulder to shoulder is my son's murderer."

He bowed again and went out, carrying himself rigidly erect.

Ned Beaumont put a hand on Janet Henry's wrist and asked in a low tense voice: "Look here, is he likely to fly off the handle?"

She looked at him, startled.

"Is he likely to go dashing off hunting for Paul?" he explained. "We don't want that. There's no telling what would happen."

"I don't know," she said.

He grimaced impatiently. "We can't let him do it. Can't we go somewhere near the front door so we can stop him if he tries it?"

"Yes." She was frightened.

She led him to the front of the house, into a small room that was dim behind heavily curtained windows. Its door was within a few feet of the street-door. They stood close together in the dim room, close to the door that stood some six inches ajar. Both of them were trembling. Janet Henry tried to whisper to Ned Beaumont, but he sh-h-hed her into silence.

They were not there long before soft footfalls sounded on the hall-carpet and Senator Henry, wearing hat and overcoat, hurried towards the street-door.

Ned Beaumont stepped out and said: "Wait, Senator Henry."

The Senator turned. His face was hard and cold, his eyes imperious. "You will please excuse me," he said. "I must go out."

"That's no good." Ned Beaumont said. He went up close to the Senator. "Just more trouble."

Janet Henry went to her father's side. "Don't go, Father," she begged. "Listen to Mr. Beaumont."

"I have listened to Mr. Beaumont," the Senator said. "I'm perfectly willing to listen to him again if he has any more information to give me. Otherwise I must ask you to excuse me." He smiled at Ned Beaumont. "It is on what you told me that I'm acting now."

Ned Beaumont regarded him with level eyes. "I don't think you ought to go to see him," he said.

The Senator looked haughtily at Ned Beaumont.

Janet said, "But, Father," before the look in his eyes stopped her.

Ned Beaumont cleared his throat. Spots of color were in his cheeks. He put his left hand out quickly and touched Senator Henry's right-hand overcoat-pocket.

Senator Henry stepped back indignantly.

Ned Beaumont nodded as if to himself. "That's no good at all," he said earnestly. He looked at Janet Henry. "He's got a gun in his pocket."

"Father!" she cried and put a hand to her mouth.

Ned Beaumont pursed his lips. "Well," he told the Senator, "it's a cinch we can't let you go out of here with a gun in your pocket."

Janet Henry said: "Don't let him, Ned."

The Senator's eyes burned scornfully at them. "I think both of you have quite forgotten yourselves," he said. "Janet, you will please go to your room."

She took two reluctant steps away, then halted and cried: "I won't! I won't let you do it. Don't let him, Ned."

Ned Beaumont moistened his lips. "I won't," he promised.

The Senator, staring coldly at him, put his right hand on the street-door's knob.

Ned Beaumont leaned forward and put a hand over the Senator's. "Look here, sir," he said respectfully, "I can't let you do this. I'm not just interfering." He took his hand off the Senator's, felt in the inside pocket of his coat, and brought out a torn, creased, and soiled piece of folded paper. "Here's my appointment as special investigator for the District Attorney's office last month." He held it out to the Senator. "It's never been canceled as far as I know, so" – he shrugged – "I can't let you go off to shoot somebody."

The Senator did not look at the paper. He said contemptuously: "You are trying to save your murderous friend's life."

"You know that isn't so."

The Senator drew himself up. "Enough of this," he said and turned the door-knob.

Ned Beaumont said: "Step on the sidewalk with that gun in your pocket and I'll arrest you."

Janet Henry wailed: "Oh, Father!"

The Senator and Ned Beaumont stood staring into each other's eyes, both breathing audibly.

The Senator was the first to speak. He addressed his daughter: "Will you leave us for a few minutes, my dear? There are things I should like to say to Mr. Beaumont."

She looked questioningly at Ned Beaumont. He nodded. "Yes," she told her father, "if you won't go out before I've seen you again."

He smiled and said: "You shall see me."

The two men watched her walk away down the hall, turn to the left with a glance thrown back at them, and vanish through a doorway.

The Senator said ruefully: "I'm afraid you've not had so good an influence on my daughter as you should. She isn't usually so – ah – headstrong."

Ned Beaumont smiled apologetically, but did not speak.

The Senator asked: "How long has this been going on?"

"You mean our digging into the murder? Only a day or two for me. Your daughter's been at it from the beginning. She's always thought Paul did it."

"What?" The Senator's mouth remained open.

"She's always thought he did it. Didn't you know? She hates him like poison – always has."

"Hates him?" the Senator gasped. "My God, no!"

Ned Beaumont nodded and smiled curiously at the man against the door. "Didn't you know that?"

The Senator blew his breath out sharply. "Come in here," he said and led the way into the dim room where Ned Beaumont and Janet Henry had hidden. The Senator switched on the lights while Ned Beaumont was shutting the door. Then they faced one another, both standing.

"I want to talk to you as man to man, Mr. Beaumont," the Senator began. "We can forget your" – he smiled – "official connections, can't we?"

Ned Beaumont nodded. "Yes. Farr's probably forgotten them too."

"Exactly. Now, Mr. Beaumont, I am not a blood-thirsty man, but I'm damned if I can bear the thought of my son's murderer walking around free and unpunished when –"

"I told you they'll have to pick him up. They can't get out of it. The evidence is too strong and everybody knows it."

The Senator smiled again, icily. "You are surely not trying to tell me, as one practicing politician to another, that Paul Madvig is in any danger of being punished for anything he might do in this city?"

"I am. Paul's sunk. They're double-crossing him. The only thing that's holding them up is that they're used to jumping when he cracks the whip and they need a little time to gather courage."

Senator Henry smiled and shook his head. "You'll allow me to disagree with you? And to point out the fact that I've been in politics more years than you've lived?"

"Sure."

"Then I can assure you that they never will get the necessary amount of courage, no matter how much time they're given. Paul is their boss and, despite possible temporary rebellions, he will remain their boss."

"It doesn't look like we'll agree on that," Ned Beaumont said. "Paul's sunk." He frowned. "Now about this gun business. That's no good. You'd better give it to me." He held out his hand.

The Senator put his right hand in his overcoat-pocket.

Ned Beaumont stepped close to the Senator and put his left hand on the Senator's wrist. "Give me it."

The Senator glared angrily at him.

"All right," Ned Beaumont said, "if I've got to do that," and, after a brief struggle in which a chair was upset, took the weapon – an old-fashioned nickeled revolver – away from the Senator. He was thrusting the revolver into one of his hip-pockets when Janet Henry, wild of eye, white of face, came in.

"What is it?" she cried.

"He won't listen to reason," Ned Beaumont grumbled. "I had to take the gun away from him."

The Senator's face was twitching and he panted hoarsely. He took a step towards Ned Beaumont. "Get out of my house," he ordered.

"I won't," Ned Beaumont said. The ends of his lips jerked. Anger began to burn in his eyes. He put a hand out and touched Janet Henry's arm roughly. "Sit down and listen to this. You asked for it and you're going to get it." He spoke to the Senator: "I've got a lot to say, so maybe you'd better sit down too."

Neither Janet Henry nor her father sat down. She looked at Ned Beaumont with wide panic-stricken eyes, he with hard wary ones. Their faces were similarly white.

Ned Beaumont said to the Senator: "You killed your son."

Nothing changed in the Senator's face. He did not move.

For a long moment Janet Henry was still as her father. Then a look of utter horror came into her face and she sat down slowly on the floor. She did not fall. She slowly bent her knees and sank down on the floor in a sitting position, leaning to the right, her right hand on the floor for support, her horrified face turned up to her father and Ned Beaumont.

Neither of the men looked at her.

Ned Beaumont said to the Senator: "You want to kill Paul now so he can't say you killed your son. You know you can kill him and get away with it – dashing gentleman of the old school stuff – if you can put over on the world the attitude you tried to put over on us." He stopped.

The Senator said nothing.

Ned Beaumont went on: "You know he's going to stop covering you up if he's arrested, because he's not going to have Janet thinking he killed her brother if he can help it." He laughed bitterly. "And what a swell joke on him that is!" He ran fingers through his hair. "What happened is something like this: when Taylor heard about Paul kissing Janet he ran after him, taking the stick with him and wearing a hat, though that's not as important. When you thought of what might happen to your chances of being re-elected –"

The Senator interrupted him in a hoarse angry tone: "This is nonsense! I will not have my daughter subjected –"

Ned Beaumont laughed brutally. "Sure it's nonsense," he said. "And your bringing the stick you killed him with back home, and wearing his hat because you'd run out bare-headed after him, is nonsense too, but it's nonsense that'll nail you to the cross."

Senator Henry said in a low scornful voice: "And what of Paul's confession?"

Ned Beaumont grinned. "Plenty of it," he said. "I tell you what let's do. Janet, you phone him and ask him to come over right away. Then we'll tell him about your father starting after him with a gun and see what he says."

Janet stirred, but did not rise from the floor. Her face was blank.

Her father said: "That is ridiculous. We will do nothing of the sort."

Ned Beaumont said peremptorily: "Phone him, Janet."

She got up on her feet, still blank of face, and paying no attention to the Senator's sharp "Janet!" went to the door.

The Senator changed his tone then and said, "Wait, dear," to her and, "I should like to speak to you alone again," to Ned Beaumont.

"All right," Ned Beaumont said, turning to the girl hesitating in the doorway.

Before he could speak to her she was saying stubbornly: "I want to hear it. I've a right to hear it."

He nodded, looked at her father again, and said: "She has."

"Janet, dear," the Senator said, "I'm trying to spare you. I –"

"I don't want to be spared," she said in a small flat voice. "I want to know."

The Senator turned his palms out in a defeated gesture. "Then I shall say nothing."

Ned Beaumont said: "Phone Paul, Janet."

Before she could move the Senator spoke: "No. This is more difficult than it should be made for me, but –" He took out a handkerchief and wiped his hands. "I am going to tell you exactly what happened and then I am going to ask a favor of you, one I think you cannot refuse. However –" He broke off to look at his daughter. "Come in, my dear, and close the door, if you must hear it."

She shut the door and sat on a chair near it, leaning forward, her body stiff, her face tense.

The Senator put his hands behind him, the handkerchief still in them, and, looking without enmity at Ned Beaumont, said: "I ran out after Taylor that night because I did not care to lose Paul's friendship through my son's hot-headedness. I caught up with them in China Street. Paul had taken the stick from him. They were, or at least Taylor was, quarreling hotly. I asked Paul to leave us, to leave me to deal with my son, and he did so, giving me the stick. Taylor spoke to me as no son should speak to a father and tried to thrust me out of his way so he could pursue Paul again. I don't know exactly how it happened – the blow – but it happened and he fell and struck his head on the curb. Paul came back then – he hadn't gone far – and we found that Taylor had died instantly. Paul insisted that we leave him there and not admit our part in his death. He said no matter how unavoidable it was a nasty scandal could be made of it in the coming campaign and – well – I let him persuade me. It was he who picked up Taylor's hat and gave it to me to wear home – I had run out bareheaded. He assured me that the police investigation would be stopped if it threatened to come too near us. Later – last week, in fact – when I had become alarmed by the rumors that he had killed Taylor, I went to him and asked him if we hadn't better make a clean breast of it. He laughed at my fears and assured me he was quite able to take care of himself." He brought his hands from behind him, wiped his face with the handkerchief, and said: "That is what happened."

His daughter cried out in a choking voice: "You let him lie there, like that, in the street!"

He winced, but did not say anything.

Ned Beaumont, after a moment's frowning silence, said: "A campaign-speech – some truth gaudied up." He grimaced. "You had a favor to ask."

The Senator looked down at the floor, then up at Ned Beaumont again. "But that is for your ear alone."

Ned Beaumont said: "No."

"Forgive me, dear," the Senator said to his daughter, then to Ned Beaumont: "I have told you the truth, but I realize fully the position I have put myself in. The favor I ask is the return of my revolver and five minutes – a minute – alone in this room."

Ned Beaumont said: "No."

The Senator swayed with a hand to his breast, the handkerchief hanging down from his hand.

Ned Beaumont said: "You'll take what's coming to you."

II

Ned Beaumont went to the street-door with Farr, his gray-haired stenographer, two police-detectives, and the Senator.

"Not going along?" Farr asked.

"No, but I'll be seeing you."

Farr pumped his hand up and down with enthusiasm. "Make it sooner and oftener, Ned," he said. "You play tricks on me, but I don't hold that against you when I see what comes of them."

Ned Beaumont grinned at him, exchanged nods with the detectives, bowed to the stenographer, and shut the door. He walked upstairs to the white-walled room where the piano was. Janet Henry rose from the lyre-end sofa when he came in.

"They've gone," he said in a consciously matter-of-fact voice.

"Did – did they – ?"

"They got a pretty complete statement out of him – more details than he told us."

"Will you tell me the truth about it?"

"Yes," he promised.

"What –" She broke off. "What will they do to him, Ned?"

"Probably not a great deal. His age and prominence and so on will help him. The chances are they'll convict him of manslaughter and then set the sentence aside or suspend it."

"Do you think it was an accident?"

Ned Beaumont shook his head. His eyes were cold. He said bluntly: "I think he got mad at the thought of his son interfering with his chances of being re-elected and hit him."

She did not protest. She was twining her fingers together. When she asked her next question it was with difficulty. "Was – was he going to – to shoot Paul?"

"He was. He could get away with the grand-old-man-avenging-the-death-the-law-couldn't-avenge line. He knew Paul wasn't going to stay dummied up if he was arrested. Paul was doing it, just as he was supporting your father for re-election, because he wanted you. He couldn't get you by pretending he'd killed your brother. He didn't care what anybody else thought, but he didn't know you thought he had and he would have cleared himself in a second if he had."

She nodded miserably. "I hated him," she said, "and I wronged him and I still hate him." She sobbed. "Why is that, Ned?"

He made an impatient gesture with one hand. "Don't ask me riddles."

"And you," she said, "tricked me and made a fool of me and brought this on me and I don't hate you."

"More riddles," he said.

"How long, Ned," she asked, "how long have you known – known about Father?"

"I don't know. It's been in the back of my head for a long time. That was about the only thing that'd fit in with Paul's foolishness. If he'd killed Taylor he'd've let me know before this. There was no reason why he should hide that from me. There was a reason why he'd hide your father's crimes from me. He knew I didn't like your father. I'd made that plain enough. He didn't think he could trust me not to knife your father. He knew I wouldn't knife *him*. So, when I'd told him I was going to clear up the killing regardless of what he said, he gave me that phony confession to stop me."

She asked: "Why didn't you like Father?"

"Because," he said hotly, "I don't like pimps."

Her face became red, her eyes abashed. She asked in a dry constricted voice: "And you don't like me because – ?"

He did not say anything.

She bit her lip and cried: "Answer me!"

"You're all right," he said, "only you're not all right for Paul, not the way you've been playing him. Neither of you were anything but poison for him. I tried to tell him that. I tried to tell him you both considered him a lower form of animal life and fair game for any kind of treatment. I tried to tell him your father was a man all his life used to winning without much trouble and that in a hole he'd either lose his head or turn wolf. Well, he was in love with you, so –" He snapped his teeth together and walked over to the piano.

"You despise me," she said in a low hard voice. "You think I'm a whore."

"I don't despise you," he said irritably, not turning to face her. "Whatever you've done you've paid for and been paid for and that goes for all of us."

There was silence between them then until she said: "Now you and Paul will be friends again."

He turned from the piano with a movement as if he were about to shake himself and looked at the watch on his wrist. "I'll have to say good-by now."

A startled light came into her eyes. "You're not going away?"

He nodded. "I can catch the four-thirty."

"You're not going away for good?"

"If I can dodge being brought back for some of these trials and I don't think that'll be so hard."

She held her hands out impulsively. "Take me with you."

He blinked at her. "Do you really want to go or are you just being hysterical?" he asked. Her face was crimson by then. Before she could speak he said: "It doesn't make any difference. I'll take you if you want to go." He frowned. "But all this" – he waved a hand to indicate the house – "who'll take care of that?"

She said bitterly: "I don't care – our creditors."

"There's another thing you ought to think about," he said slowly. "Everybody's going to say you deserted your father as soon as he got in trouble."

"I am deserting him," she said, "and I want people to say that. I don't care what they say – if you'll take me away." She sobbed. "If – I wouldn't if only he hadn't gone away and left him lying there alone in that dark street."

Ned Beaumont said brusquely: "Never mind that now. If you're going get packed. Only what you can get in a couple of bags. We can send for the other stuff later, maybe."

She uttered a high-pitched unnatural laugh and ran out of the room. He lit a cigar, sat down at the piano, and played softly until she returned. She had put on a black hat and black coat and was carrying two traveling-bags.

III

They rode in a taxicab to his rooms. For most of the ride they were silent. Once she said suddenly: "In that dream – I didn't tell you – the key was glass and shattered in our hands just as we got the door open, because the lock was stiff and we had to force it."

He looked sidewise at her and asked: "Well?"

She shivered. "We couldn't lock the snakes in and they came out all over us and I woke up screaming."

"That was only a dream," he said. "Forget it." He smiled without merriment. "You threw my trout back – in the dream."

The taxicab stopped in front of his house. They went up to his rooms. She offered to help him pack, but he said: "No, I can do it. Sit down and rest. We've got an hour before the train leaves."

She sat in one of the red chairs. "Where are you – we going?" she asked timidly.

"New York, first anyhow."

He had one bag packed when the door-bell rang. "You'd better go into the bedroom," he told her and carried her bags in there. He shut the connecting door when he came out.

He went to the outer door and opened it.

Paul Madvig said: "I came to tell you you were right and I know it now."

"You didn't come last night."

"No, I didn't know it then. I got home right after you left."

Ned Beaumont nodded. "Come in," he said, stepping out of the doorway.

Madvig went into the living-room. He looked immediately at the bags, but let his glance roam around the room for a while before asking: "Going away?"

"Yes."

Madvig sat in the chair Janet Henry had occupied. His age showed in his face and he sat down wearily.

"How's Opal?" Ned Beaumont asked.

"She's all right, poor kid. She'll be all right now."

"You did it to her."

"I know, Ned. Jesus, I know it!" Madvig stretched his legs out and looked at his shoes. "I hope you don't think I'm feeling proud of myself." After a pause Madvig added: "I think – I know Opal'd like to see you before you go."

"You'll have to say good-by to her for me and to Mom too. I'm leaving on the four-thirty."

Madvig raised blue eyes clouded by anguish. "You're right, of course, Ned," he said huskily, "but – well – Christ knows you're right!" He looked down at his shoes again.

Ned Beaumont asked: "What are you going to do with your not quite faithful henchmen? Kick them back in line? Or have they kicked themselves back?"

"Farr and the rest of those rats?"

"Uh-huh."

"I'm going to teach them something." Madvig spoke with determination, but there was no enthusiasm in his voice and he did not look up from his shoes. "It'll cost me four years, but I can use those four years cleaning house and putting together an organization that will stay put."

Ned Beaumont raised his eyebrows. "Going to knife them at the polls?"

"Knife them, hell, dynamite them! Shad's dead. I'm going to let his crew run things for the next four years. There's none of them that can build anything solid enough for me to worry about. I'll get the city back next time and by then I'll have done my housecleaning."

"You could win now," Ned Beaumont said.

"Sure, but I don't want to win with those bastards."

Ned Beaumont nodded. "It takes patience and guts, but it's the best way to play it, I reckon."

"They're all I've got," Madvig said miserably. "I'll never have any brains." He shifted the focus of his eyes from his feet to the fireplace. "Have you got to go, Ned?" he asked almost inaudibly.

"Got to."

Madvig cleared his throat violently. "I don't want to be a God-damned fool," he said, "but I'd like to think that whether you went or stayed you weren't holding anything against me, Ned."

"I'm not holding anything against you, Paul."

Madvig raised his head quickly. "Shake hands with me?"

"Certainly."

Madvig jumped up. His hand caught Ned Beaumont's, crushed it. "Don't go, Ned. Stick it out with me. Christ knows I need you now. Even if I didn't – I'll do my damndest to make up for all that."

Ned Beaumont shook his head. "You haven't got anything to make up for with me."

"And you'll – ?"

Ned Beaumont shook his head again. "I can't. I've got to go."

Madvig released the other's hand and sat down again, morosely, saying: "Well, it serves me right."

Ned Beaumont made an impatient gesture. "That's got nothing to do with it." He stopped and bit his lip. Then he said bluntly: "Janet's here."

Madvig stared at him.

Janet Henry opened the bedroom-door and came into the living-room. Her face was pale and drawn, but she held it high. She went straight up to Paul Madvig and said: "I've done you a lot of harm, Paul. I've –"

His face had become pale as hers. Now blood rushed into it. "Don't, Janet," he said hoarsely. "Nothing you could do." The rest of his speech was unintelligibly mumbled.

She stepped back, flinching.

Ned Beaumont said: "Janet is going away with me."

Madvig's lips parted. He looked dumbly at Ned Beaumont and as he looked the blood went out of his face again. When his face was quite bloodless he mumbled something of which only the word "luck" could be understood, turned clumsily around, went to the door, opened it, and went out, leaving it open behind him.

Janet Henry looked at Ned Beaumont. He stared fixedly at the door.

ABOUT THE INTRODUCER

JAMES ELLROY is the author of *The Black Dahlia*, *My Dark Places*, and *L.A. Confidential*.

This book is set in BEMBO which was cut
by the punch-cutter Francesco Griffo
for the Venetian printer-publisher
Aldus Manutius in early 1495
and first used in a pamphlet
by a young scholar
named Pietro
Bembo.